WHITE NIGHT

Book 3 of the Sennenwolf Series

CAPES

White Night

Published by Capas LLC 2024
www.capescreates.com

Ebook ISBN: 979-8-9863167-5-8
Print ISBN: 979-8-9863167-6-5
Copyright © 2024 by Capes. All rights reserved.
www.capescreates.com

Cover design by Jelena Gajic
Check out her work on Instagram (@coverbookdesigns)

Illustration by Gega Dunatishvili
Check out his work on Instagram (@gegadatunashvili) or via Art Station

TOTW / INGC / TAB

PRAISE FOR SENNENWOLF SERIES

An INDIES Foreword finalist
Readers' Choice Book Awards finalist
Indies We Love selection from LoveReading

"A playful twist on the fantasy genre... Who knew witches liked to party?"
-*Kirkus*

"...A series worth committing to. Very highly recommend."
-*Readers' Favorite*

"Mutual interests give way to an unlikely alliance between a powerful wielder and the imminent Male Alpha of Velm in Capes's beautiful, romantic fantasy novel *West of Jaws*."
-*Foreword*

"A perfect read for fans of Witcher and similar fantasies."
-*IndieReader*

"A rich fantasy romance with characters you'll love and a twisting storyline that will keep you hooked."
-*LoveReading*

"I just want to say that I loved Helisent from the moment I first met her in West of Jaws, sprawled on the ground in the midst of a temper tantrum."
-Coralie Moss, author of *Calliope Jones* and *Sister Witches*

"The story is one of the most compelling I've ever read with such a fresh voice and unparalleled narrative."
-Erin K. Larson-Burnett, Author of *The Bear & The Rose*

THE SENNENWOLF SERIES

DEDICATION

For The Rat King (Part III)

HELLO, READERS...

I'd like to part the veil for a moment—it's tradition at this point.

I know we love Helisent-Samson scenes. They're the best, and putting these two in immediate proximity is my highest priority. But I'm also bound to respect the plot of this series so that their journey is fulfilling and meaningful. Just know that there is a (very near) future in which we all get exactly what we want.

Except for in Chapter One.

Enjoy!
-Capes

After months in Zarzynn, Helisent and her Tiny Army defeat the forces of Ezit to free hundreds of captive vampires and okeanids. But to secure their escape, Helisent is forced to shatter the mantle of her Landmark, effectively separating her magic from the limestone of Vex. She leaves Zarzynn with the only remnant of her Landmark: a red limestone wand.

In Cadmium, the Pletens, okeanids, and vampires are welcomed to Mieira with a multi-day festival. Clearbold and two members of Samson's pack are notably absent.

When the festivities die down, Helisent guides her warren, Zeu's den, and the Pletens west to Luz. On the way, a meddling ghost named Creepy Baby reappears, notifying the witch that her red magic seems to be claiming the caves of Tet.

Farther south, Samson decides that his wife, Brutatalika, and his grandmother, Sutnazzar, will travel to Mort rather than continue to Bellator. While the Kulapsifang was away in Zarzynn, it seems his claim to the throne has been challenged, and the only way to stabilize Velm is to defeat Clearbold once and for all.

White Night starts almost two months after our beloved crew returns from Zarzynn.

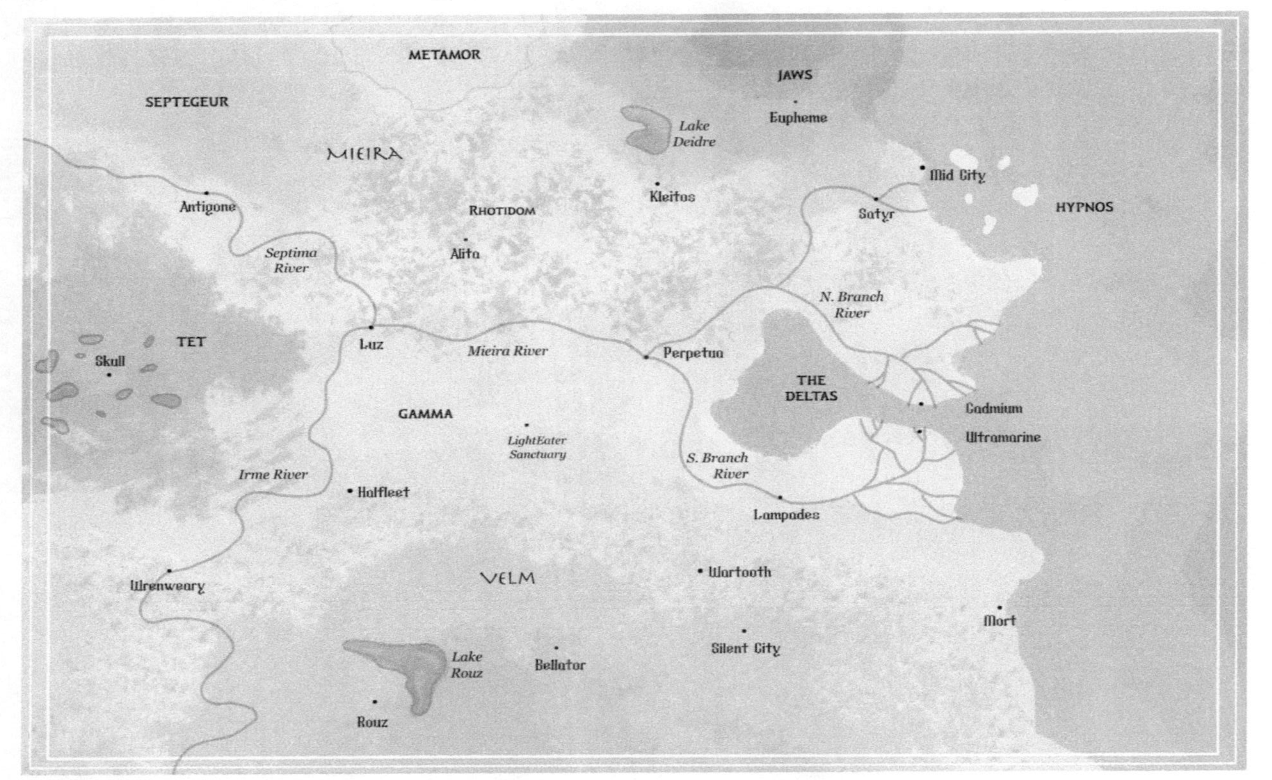

METAMOR
SEPTEGEUR
JAWS
MIEIRA
Lake Deidre
Eupheme
Antigone
Mid City
Kleitos
HYPNOS
Satyr
RHOTIDOM
Alita
Septima River
N. Branch River
TET
Luz
Mieira River
Perpetua
Skull
THE DELTAS
GAMMA
Cadmium
Ultramarine
LightEater Sanctuary
S. Branch River
Irme River
Halfleet
Lampades
VELM
Wartooth
Wrenweary
Mort
Lake Rouz
Bellator
Silent City
Rouz

CONTENTS

VIGNETTES

INTERLUDE I
(WHAT MUST BE DONE)

My nose twitches.

Adrenaline wakes me from a shallow sleep.

My mind latches onto the ala of a stranger.

Someone is here.

I sit up on my bed mat and pivot toward the scent.

A stranger crouches on the far side of our quiet camp, across the fire pit's dead coals.

Mist obscures his shadowy shape and the thin forest around us. Berevald sleeps to my left, Rex to my right; each snores lightly, still asleep.

I squint at the stranger, braced to find out if he's a friend or foe.

His eyes widen as we lock gazes, their whites stark. Dawn barely warms the sky or the chilly fog. But I can see the stranger, the whites of his eyes, and the white-wrapped bundle that sits near his feet.

I rip off my blanket and prepare to stand.

There must be an axe tucked inside the bundle. Maybe a vial of poison that's been masked with pungent oil.

We're nearing Bellator; tensions are rising.

The stranger doesn't shift, tracking my movements as I rise. I stare back, half awake and unsure how harshly to handle his intrusion.

I inhale deeply to study his ala. The stranger is in his sixties with a low generational count; less than 300, maybe less than 250. His musk is as potent as the muddy grass lining our camp.

Alone, he's not a threat.

I take a calming breath. "Who are you?" Then I inhale another, nostrils flaring as I search for more strangers within the mist.

The wolf keeps his hands in his lap, away from the bundle sitting in the dirt. A lock of blue-black hair slips past his ear, obscuring his narrow features. "They're offerings, Kulapsifang."

The bundle's lumps are soft, not rigid and tracing sharpened metal. In the next breath, I register the scent of red meat and sourdough bread.

The wolf explains in a low voice, "I trespassed because you've been avoiding the villages. I caught your scent two days ago. I've walked through the nights to offer you sustenance. Bellator knows you're near —the packs are sending word ahead of you. You shouldn't arrive unprepared, Kulapsifang."

I force the sleepiness from my mind.

Sending word ahead of us?

I could give a shit what Clearbold does.

I know too much to be swayed by fear. I know where Imperatriz is. I know that Clearbold worked with Anesot to strand her on Pit. I know that two Hosts in Ezit think my father is the Kulapsifang.

It won't matter soon.

I glance around our temporary camp just to be sure; nothing looks out of order, and the wolf's ala is musky but not heavy, hinting he hasn't lingered here long.

He isn't the first wolf to seek us out discreetly, far off the beaten path.

Last year, I would have treated this trespassing as a threat—even with a bundle of offerings. But this isn't the same Velm. Back then, he could have approached me in the daylight. He could have found me lounging in a village estate surrounded by gifts and pack leaders.

"I will leave now." He rises and his eyes lower, scanning me quickly. The man's frame is thinner than I'd originally thought.

The two-day trek must have taken a toll—especially considering how heavy the bundle is.

In my silence, he continues, "My village is two days west of Wartooth. We are only a few dozen wolves, but we hang the black banners of the Afadors. Every single home."

He bows his head and takes a step back. Mist shrouds half of him.

I come to my senses before he can disappear. "Wolf, what is your name?"

"Ebeneezer 231 Ronin."

I step past Rex, who is rising from a heavy sleep, and round the fire pit.

Ebeneezer takes a half-step back.

I stop in front of him. "Hello, Ebenezer. I'm happy to hear about the black banners hung in your village."

I haven't seen a black banner in weeks. When I left Velm for Zarzynn, they dangled from poles, from windowsills, from balconies.

But they've been replaced with the white flags of the Leofsige line, a foreign symbol scribbled at their ends.

"As you know, I've been gone for months. Your offerings are welcome, but my pack needs information, too. Whatever you know will help us, Ebeneezer."

I study the wolf's watery, blue-black eyes.

They reflect the pale mist like white clouds.

He tells me, "Spring was a time of great divide. High-ranking packs wandered into villages and handed out white flags. They told... they told many stories...

"That the 714th Kulapsifang did not kill the wooly.

"That the 713th Kulapsifang made deals with wielders who will threaten Velm.

"That the 712th Kulapsifang keeps a grave secret deep in the south.

"The pack leaders returned at midsummer leading the herbal caravans. And they only traded turmeric, feverfew, echinacea, and peppermint to those who had hung the white flags.

"My village has no stores for Night, my great Kulapsifang." His voice wavers. "We lost our healer and our hesperides to a violent exit. But we still wave the black flags, Kulapsifang."

Rage flickers through my body.

I've heard similar accounts from other wolves who have risked much to help me and my pack. Tales of exits in which non-wolves are forced out of villages, rumors about the failures of the Kulapsifangs, and troubling updates about the herbal caravans.

It's late summer, which means the caravans are making their way across my territory, depositing stores and providing small settlements with resources for the coming Night.

I meet Ebeneezer's eyes and nod.

Half of me wants to tell him—

I will walk into Bellator and challenge my father to a waricon. I will kill him, and take the throne. Then—stability, peace, hope.

But words mean little in times like these.

This wolf needs action.

I tell him, "Ebeneezer 231 Ronin. Return home with my blessing and the blessings of Hetnazzar. Your village's offering honors us both."

His lips tremble with a smile.

I tell him, "*De segen it tauma-kuro Kelnazzar.*"

Ebeneezer's jaw clenches with conviction. He straightens his back, rising to his full height to reply, "De segen it tauma-kuro Kelnazzar, Kulapsifang."

Bless the black Night.

I glance around for the nearest blade. Rex's throwing axe is within reaching distance from his bed mat. Wearily, my packmate watches me pick it up and turn back toward the stranger.

I lift the axe toward my neck and sheer away a few strands of hair. Since nearing Bellator, we've taken to avoiding the cold gaze of village leaders and their packmates, their meager offerings, and the possibility of a dangerous run-in. I've even taken to soaking my hair with cedar oil and other herbs, hoping to dim the spread of my ala.

I need to enter the city in good shape, as do Rex and Berevald.

Still, I'd like Ebeneezer to know my scent. To take it back to his village.

He looks from the axe to where I clutch the loose strands, then carefully takes them.

I tell him, "Flags don't lessen the cold of Night. Your village should do what it must to build your stores. I will pray that Hetnazzar leads healthy prey into your territory." I raise my eyebrows, hoping he understands. "Return home and sleep well. When you wake up, know this: I will do what must be done in Bellator, Ebeneezer. And I will try to end this before Night comes."

He staggers a step backward, sparing a cautious glance at Rex. "Thank you." He turns and hustles away, glancing back once before the mist swallows him whole. "Goodbye, Kulapsifang."

"De segen it tauma-kuro Kelnazzar," I whisper in his wake.

Bless the black Night.

I hiccup where I lay between my brothers.

I settle into my pillow and tug my blanket up to my chin.

Yves is sprawled across the living room floor to my left, Yngvi squished toward the wall to my right. The light from the kitchen window casts a gentle glow from the street. Outside, Luz has finally quieted, its residents waiting for dawn or fast asleep.

My brothers have stayed close in my orbit since we reunited in Cadmium and marched back to Luz.

Tomorrow, they'll leave to accompany Parsifal back to Antigone. Our papa is sleeping in the other room, his snoring echoing through the small apartment with gusto.

Then, theoretically, life will move on as usual, letting Zarzynn's memory fade like a distant nightmare. I'll settle into this quaint, two-bedroom apartment with my new warren: Esclamonde, Onesimos, and Butter. Downstairs are the Pletens—aside from Vulcan and Vega, who insisted on finding their own place.

It's a good setup.

So long as I don't wonder about Samson too much.

(I do.)

I hiccup again, then look around for my cup; it's out of reach near the window. "Yves, can you hand me—"

"Actually..." Yves sits up, rubbing his face sleepily. He twists to reach toward the pile of cushions—not to grab my drink, but the bottomless bag he shares with Yngvi. He drags it into his lap, shoves his hand inside, and starts looking for something. "We should probably do this now. There's going to be no waking you up once you fall asleep."

I yawn, eyeing his bag. "Well, hurry up. You're running out of time."

On my other side, Yngvi drags himself into a sitting position. With half-closed eyes, he watches Yves search the bottomless bag.

Yves finds what he's looking for. From what I can see in the dim light, it's a rectangular lump. Quickly, he lobs the soft-ish rectangle over me toward Yngvi. The bundle hits the side of his head with a gentle rustle.

Yngvi cries out dramatically.

I reach for the blockish item that landed near my shoulder. I squint, realizing it's a series of tightly tied letters jammed into a brick-like shape.

"We wrote them for you," Yves explains.

Yngvi has also switched his attention to the bundle. "Papa wrote you a lot of notes last year."

"We wrote some for you, too."

"You know, since we were the ones..." Yngvi glances at Yves. "In the first years of your life."

I look between them, too exhausted to read between their cryptic words. "What...?"

"Parsifal was barely there when we were growing up." Yves clears his throat, trying to sound sober. "I mean, he was physically there but mentally very far gone. We've never talked about that. We've never talked about a lot of things..."

"Oh, not this," I groan. "I'm way too fucked up for a heart-to-heart." I hiccup loudly, reeling where I lay. "See?" But they're both sitting up, looking from the other to me. The solemn mood is a shock at the end of a raucous, pleasant night—which has come at the tail end of a long and happy return to Luz. "Why are you two doing this?"

"Because you're turning into Parsifal," Yves says bluntly.

I gasp, causing Yngvi to quickly amend, "Not that that's bad."

"Parsifal is an admirable warlock," Yves confirms. "What I meant is that... you can turn into him, but don't stop there. Be... more, Helisent."

"You better hope he didn't wake up and hear that. These walls are thin."

"Pay attention," Yngvi says softly—too softly.

"Don't joke," Yves says equally quietly.

I cross my arms, pissed off that I'm too faded to figure out what's happening. "Whatever the fuck you two are trying to say, just say it."

The twins look at each other again.

"We talked to Absalom before he left for Antigone," Yves starts.

"We don't hate him anymore," Yngvi adds.

"He told us what happened in Ezit. The rampage. It was a *very* different tale from what we heard from papa. He doesn't talk about anything intense…"

Yngvi goes on, "But even if only *half* of what Absalom said is true…"

"Then the triplemoon in Ezit won't be the end," Yves concludes carefully. "We'll keep an eye on the Class in Antigone. And Absalom. But the rest of Mieira… the rest of Mieira needs you to watch over it."

My eyes flit from one to the other, little more than shadowy shapes in the salon.

I know that things are different now.

I know the festivities in Cadmium spread the false notion that we defeated Ezit.

I know that I was one of the primary destroyers of Zarzynn's capital city. That I will be the target of whatever retribution they seek.

I roll my eyes.

It's a weak defense mechanism against the near-silent, ever-roiling fear that Zarzynnian forces might find their way to Mieira—but it's all I have. "This is really nice of you two. Such a pleasant goodbye."

"If you're smart, you'll start looking soon," Yves goes on quietly.

"Be smart like mama was," Yngvi says. He sets the bundle of letters on my stomach. "Our advice is probably going to sound like shit on the first readthrough, but maybe not by the second."

Yves nods. "We wrote down the most important lessons Andromeda taught us. You should consider talking to—"

"Don't you dare bring up the necromancers." I'll cross that burning, sulfurous bridge when I'm ready. Maybe never. Butter has at least stopped prompting me to consider her mirror, and I've dubbed that a big win.

"Fine—don't do it for yourself." Yngvi taps the bundle emphatically. "But do it for the next generation. Think ahead, Helisent. Now is the time. We're safe now."

Yves nods again. "Papa at least did that. He didn't lift a finger to help himself, but he gave us everything he had." He twists, turning toward the window to pick up my cup. "Here."

I take the drink; it's not nearly as full as I'd like, but the lukewarm brandy is particularly potent. With a whine, I drain the wooden cup.

The next generation...

I know what they want: for me to start seriously looking for a life partner who is ready to raise my red witches.

Quietly, I admit, "If we're all being honest right now, then I think... I think I already fucked that part up."

I take a deep breath, trying to find the words to explain that every time I imagine selecting a warlock to father my red witches, I see only one man. He takes up my entire mind like a shadow, like a peaceful and silent thing that smells like leather and cedar and other things I never particularly liked.

With a yawn, Yngvi sinks back onto his bedding. "Are you sure you fucked it up?"

Yves settles in, too, mirroring his twin's yawn. "Because we don't think you did."

CHAPTER 1

THIS ISN'T THE END
(BUT I WISH IT WAS)

SAMSON

Suin,
For the record, Malasuntra was wrong when he said you don't have a voice.
But I'll let you figure out why.
-Suin

Overhead, the sister mountains of Baladhari and Meledhari welcome me back to Bellator.

Emerald vegetation clings to their purple-gray faces as they rise parallel into the sky.

Between them is a keyhole-like passage that leads from Velm's forested hills to its marble-plated capital. I stand in its center, breathing deeply.

Flecks of water spatter across my face as I stare up at the mountains. The droplets carry the sweet fragrance of summer, of moss and leaves soaked with sunlight.

Above, an archway of stark white marble connects Baladhari and Meledhari. Two brackets jut from it with a square white flag dangling between them.

When I last left Bellator, the flag was black. I have no idea how long that particular flag existed, but I know the Afadors have been represented by its color since Hetnazzar chose its first Kulapsifang.

The white flag undulates, its heavy fabric billowing loudly as cool wind whips through the landing. The breeze tussles my hair, still left down to my chest.

The landing between the sister mountains is empty aside from me and my packmates.

Rex shifts where he stands to my right, his shoulder brushing mine. "This isn't what I expected."

From my other side, Berevald asks, "And what were you expecting? For Pietrangelo and Riordon to throw us a welcome home party?"

Rex tsks. "Obviously not—but I figured those two would have left a messenger up here. Someone to alert them that we're back."

With a disgruntled sigh, I pull a cigarette from behind my ear. I bend between my packmates, shielding myself from the wind as I light it.

With a long drag, I stare to the north; we just crossed the vast plains and thick forests hugging the mountains that shelter Bellator. I turn to the south; there lies my capital, spilling into the valley, starting with a set of three hundred marble stairs.

Berevald takes the cigarette, eager for a drag. "What do you think, Samson?"

When he passes it back to me, I still don't have an answer.

For weeks, I've been focused on a simple plan: Waltz into the palace, find Clearbold, and challenge him to a waricon with a few cutting words. Since we sent my wife and grandmother east, I've been insistent on a direct path—but my packmates are eager to understand Velm's current state of affairs better.

We left Riordon and Pietrangelo behind last year to head to Mid City. Neither of them came to Cadmium to receive us on our return from Zarzynn; we've chosen to believe it's for good reason. That they've been busy uncovering Clearbold's plots in the meantime.

But I don't know that I need to understand Clearbold.

I just need to get rid of him.

I continue without a response, eager to see Bellator on the other side of the mountain pass.

My steps are quick, my packmates close at my sides as we head into the rocky passage. A brisk wind funnels through it, pushing against us.

On the other side, we fall still on the landing above the stairs.

Relief washes through me as I stare at my capital.

Bellator's streets sprawl across a shallow decline into a wide valley. At the height of summer, oaks, maples, and linden trees are in full bloom; their fluffy canopies peek above the marble-plated, two-story buildings and their steep rooftops. Narrow chimneys point toward the white-clouded sky. Livestock and small herds inch through the green parks dotting the city.

Unlike in Mierian cities, Velmic streets are broad and easy to navigate. The avenues divide the city into clean blocks labeled with numbers. From this vantage, I can trace the outline of Bellator's five primary neighborhoods, along with its industrial and economic districts. As far as the eye can see, the capital's tidy infrastructure pours into the great emerald valley with looming purple-gray mountains sheltering from every side.

I sigh deeply.

Aside from the white flags that hang from the windows and rooftops, the city looks the same.

I let my relief wash through me. Let it clear my mind for what comes next.

I turn to Rex. "Colsep wouldn't have left Bellator. Your father would have come to intercept us if the political situation were dangerous. The same for Pietrangelo and Riordon."

"That's an optimistic thought," Berevald says bluntly. "Am I the only one who smells danger?"

"Samson is right—my father would have come if Clearbold was planning to do anything stupid," Rex says. "I vote we go straight to the palace. We can't show weakness or hesitation. Not now."

I nod in agreement, scanning the city again and again. "We'll take a longer route to get there. That gives Pietrangelo and Riordon one last chance to join us." I pass the cigarette back to Berevald, who takes a drag before passing it to Rex. I look from one to the next. "Ready?"

Berevald rolls his neck. His long hair is tied back into a bun, his skin clean and scented of cedar. "As ready as I'll ever be."

Rex stamps out the butt. His tunic is a bit worn, but he looks well-rested despite our long journey. "Let's go."

I descend the stairs, the pair close behind me.

Instinct tells me not to waver or linger.

Halfway down, a few wolves notice our arrival. It sets off a quick chain of events: a few shouts to alert others, and then a great scramble. Wolves empty from buildings to watch us walk down the city's northernmost streets. Others crane from windows, necks strained.

I keep our pace slow; no fear, only intention.

The crowd quickly thickens. The muddled, musky mix of hundreds of alas dazes me. Some shout greetings; most whisper, their heads bent as they watch us pass.

Thanks to the added sunlight, most of my people have bronze-kissed cheeks. Their torcs glow brightly against their necks and upper arms. Some men are shirtless, their harem pants sitting low on their hips. The women wear camellia flowers behind their ears. Pups wander between the adults, shouting and full of energy.

The pups' eyes widen on us as we pass, watching half-hidden behind their elders.

My eyes leap from one face to another, eager to find Riordon or Pietrangelo.

Nothing.

By the time the palace's exterior plaza comes into view, hundreds trail us.

I bite back a relieved curse. Two figures wait in the center of the vast plaza; I know they're my packmates based on how they stand.

With each step, I make out more of Riordon's calm and sturdy features, more of Pietrangelo's dimpled cheeks and bright eyes.

I hope they've written down everything they've learned about Clearbold's plans for Velm.

I hope they're ready to hear everything we've uncovered in Zarzynn.

I can see Plan B unfolding already: I'll eat a meal and rest while they lay out the past months in Velm. With their insights, we'll craft an air-tight plan to dethrone Clearbold. And when I'm rested and prepared, I'll challenge my father. I'll tell him I know where my mother is. That I plan on bringing her home once his corpse is cold.

But as we near my packmates, Riordon shifts his gaze to the ground, hiding his face. Pietrangelo clutches his hands behind his back. His eyes jump from me to Rex to Berevald, then to the sky above.

Neither steps forward to smell my hair when we reach them.

Riordon stares at the ground, Pietrangelo at the sky.

I ignore the deepening pit in my stomach as I look from one to the other. "Hello, Riordon. Pietrangelo. You look healthy."

Riordon nods, jaw twitching.

Pietrangelo clears his throat. "Samson 714 Afador, you will enter Bellator Palace alone."

My packmates bristle at my side, growls in their throats.

The rut in my stomach deepens; I keep ignoring it.

The crowd watches silently.

They pack in around us at a respectful distance. Their whispers drop in volume as my pack reunites. I hear a few shushes, along with their boots scraping the marble ground.

Rex takes a half step in front of me. "That sounded like a command, Pietrangelo."

Berevald steps forward from my other side. "We're doing really well, by the way. Thanks for asking, Petey. Really fucking nice of you."

Riordon looks from Rex to Berevald. "You two will come with us."

He takes a step back and gestures toward a side street that curves around the palace. It leads to its lowest levels, carved deep into the earth centuries ago; a winding maze of record-keeping halls, fine art collections, and similarly quiet chambers.

"Samson will enter the palace alone," Riordon repeats. Dark smudges circle his eyes. His cheeks are gaunt, too.

I inhale deeply, studying the pair's alas. Cortisol is the primary note. Adrenaline, too.

Rex scoffs, turning toward me. Berevald does the same. They press their shoulders together, blocking my view of Riordon and Pietrangelo.

Neither says a thing, but their eyes search mine. Berevald's full features aren't cajoling; his animated eyes are narrowed and unconvinced. Rex's straight nose curls, his full lips twisted beneath.

We all smell danger now.

I look from Rex to Berevald. We'd planned on a cold reception from Clearbold and many in Bellator, but we hadn't planned on finding our packmates compromised. Though bound to Velm's greatest good and the current Male Alpha, both are loyal to me first as part of my council. Both are free to ignore a command from Clearbold in lieu of mine.

Unless, of course, their loyalties have shifted since I sailed to Zarzynn.

I keep my chin high.

I don't know what else to do.

I know what Rex's eyes tell me—to be separated is to be fatally weakened. I know what Berevald's eyes tell me—to take control now, to start commanding the pair as their rightful Alpha rather than acquiesce to Clearbold.

But before I start making power grabs, I need to get rid of Velm's current Alpha.

I need a pit full of sand and my father standing opposite me.

Rex and Berevald wait, eyes searching mine.

I tell them, "Go with your packmates. Get some rest. I'll see you tomorrow."

Neither moves.

I raise my eyebrows and hope they realize that I need to demonstrate some modicum of influence in front of the hundreds still watching us.

Berevald leans closer to me, lips parting like he's going to say something. He scoffs again at the last second, then wheels around. He runs into Pietrangelo's shoulder, knocking him back as he passes.

Rex lingers. He reaches out, wrapping his hand around my forearm. His eyes flash behind me, scanning the crowd that waits and watches our exchange.

He clears his throat. He shakes his head. "Samson."

He's saying, *This is a bad idea.*

I nod. "Rex."

I'm saying, *It's not your choice to make.*

But he doesn't move, fingers tightening. I grab my satchel's strap, lifting it to the right so he sees its outermost pocket.

Helisent's red paper star sits inside, only a few quick movements out of reach; Rex knows this.

I study the hue of his blue-black eyes, the familiar frame of his features. A deep sense of safety exudes from him and surrounds me.

He waits another long second before he turns away and follows Berevald. Riordon and Pietrangelo stalk close behind him, as though ready to propel him onward, away from me and toward the palace's underground passages.

I watch my four packmates reach the crowd, which parts to watch them go. Within a few steps, they disappear between the bodies. Rex glances back one more time before marching on, craning above the wolves surrounding him.

I glance at the plaza. I'm surrounded by hundreds who watch in rapt silence. But I'm alone, too.

I know this type of loneliness well. To my people, I'm more than a man; I'm the link between them and Hetnazzar.

I remember the first time I felt that responsibility with this much force.

I was twelve years old. Imperatriz had been missing for months, and there was no promising lead on her whereabouts. I was tugging a heavy sleigh made of wound saplings with all my might, driving it forward.

It felt like the wooly's head weighed three times more than me.

My limbs were frozen from the brutal winter, my lungs dry and burning. Snot and spit clung to my cheeks in icicles. My teeth and jaw ached after being gritted for hours.

My demigod had helped me drag the wooly's head to the edge of the city. Near its eastern entrance, Hetnazzar had crept away so I could drag it through the blustery night alone—through this plaza and into the palace.

Those who were awake at the late hour stirred their friends and family. Hundreds and then thousands of wolves lined the streets and craned from windows. In silence, they watched me drag the wooly's head step by step, street by street, up the incline toward Bellator Palace and the twin peaks nearby.

They searched me for a sign of weakness.

They search me for the same now as I beeline for the palace's open gate.

(If the Kulapsifang doesn't survive Night, how will they?)

My body trembles with anger and distress.

I'm suspicious of entering alone, but my temper won't let me deviate.

It lifts slightly when I leave the exterior plaza behind, striding into the palace's quainter interior courtyard. A towering colonnade of marble arches surrounds the open space. Tapestries hang from several, strung together with tiny, light threads that weigh hundreds of pounds.

I study my favorites. Hetnazzar creating a stone seat for itself in the city of Rouz; Hetnazzar growing lonely and creating us in its image from moonslight and snow; the great cow who fed Hetnazzar as the demigod worked to carve our world.

Halfway through the interior courtyard, a figure appears at its far end.

Otzo 503 Inma, Clearbold's most zealous packmate.

His features are blockish, devoid of emotion, as though carved from stone centuries ago. Only his eyes dance around, flashing from my hands to my eyes to my feet.

He puffs out his shoulders as though hoping to fill the broad archway that leads into the palace's sitting rooms.

I stop before Otzo.

His beady eyes flit over me again. "You missed the Fifty."

I study him, trying to hide my surprise. Of all the things I've thought of in the past months, Velm's political council has been the last.

Shit.

Velm is divided into twelve geographic regions, each of which is represented by a male and female pack leader. These twenty-four Representatives congregate in Bellator at least once a year to speak on behalf of their people as part of the Fifty.

Aside from Representatives, Bellator is also home to six orders. These oversee Velm's most important industries and institutions; each has four Members.

Together, Representatives and Members total forty-eight. Combined with the reigning Male and Female Alphas of Velm, that number is fifty.

The Fifty.

As the Kulapsifang, I've been permitted to sit with the Fifty during low-profile meetings. As a *married* Kulapsifang, it's my right to sit in on each—and to participate, too.

Before I can remind Otzo of that fact, he goes on, "Come. Clearbold is tired of waiting."

I follow five paces behind Otzo as he enters the palace. We pass through familiar rooms whose walls are taller than they are wide. Each is fitted with austere pieces of furniture, centuries old and gleaming like new. Along with the scent of cedar incense, my father's ala clogs the air. It's followed by Otzo's, by Malachai's, by Emerel's. Based on how faint their alas are, the latter pair must have left a short while ago.

Enemies.

I stare at Otzo's boots as we weave through the palace, listening to their soft thud against the marble, deep in thought.

In the ten minutes it takes to reach the throne room deep inside the palace, I start to wonder how I spent so many years in this place, with false Alphas like my father and Emerel lingering.

This is my territory—not Clearbold's.

Mine.

How have I lived with this indignity for so long?

When we near the throne room, Otzo gestures ahead of him.

Past the arched entrance sit two cubic thrones. They occupy the center of the room, each large enough to fit two wolves. Their armrests are wide, their backs low. The thrones are hard and geometric, crafted from whole pieces of marble and then shined into a blinding sheen. The room's walls are lined with the same gleaming marble. They stretch upward to a glass ceiling high above.

Here is where the Alphas sit and discuss.

Here is where they invite their most trusted advisors to sit in counsel with them.

(Here is where we hide the door that leads into the horn room.)

My eyes flit immediately to the metal door, painted white and barely visible at the far end of the room. The chamber is small and square; its walls climb even higher than the throne room.

And they're covered from floor to ceiling with sets of bloodred horns.

I can sense my father sitting on one of the thrones and staring at me.

But I can't pull my eyes from the door.

I can *feel* the horns in that room just like I could once feel Vex's magic in its pine barrens. Only now, it feels like the stirring and sudden potential of seedlings in springtime; explosive, waiting, fertile.

I know that magic is clinging to the sawed-off horns of Helisent's ancestors, and I know the wolves deserve to be punished for that sin, and I know I should have told her about the room's existence—

But I take strength in knowing her magic is near. It helps soothe and focus my rage.

I switch my gaze to Clearbold.

He wears the pure-black cape of Alphas. The fabric spreads around him like a blot of ink, contrary to the blinding white walls and the golden light of the midday sun. The sunlight reflects off the walls, casting a pale glow around the room.

My Alpha studies me, calm and unimpressed. "Atali." His voice is deep, a blunted and hoarse tone that grates on my mind.

Son.

I walk toward the dark cushion sitting before the thrones and sit down, folding my legs beneath me. I shrug my satchel off and set it at my side. Its opening remains casually ajar, its outer pocket slightly loosened. The former will give me access to Axerxa's gift, a red ax; the latter contains Helisent's red star, capable of summoning the witch quickly.

Just in case.

Behind me, footsteps drift out of earshot. Soon, Otzo's ala falls out of range, too.

Clearbold watches me, as though waiting; I stare back.

Without Riordon and Pietrangelo offering up any details about Velm's fate, it would be unwise to immediately challenge Clearbold to a waricon.

I want blood, certainly—but I need answers first.

Something. Anything.

So, I start things off lightly. "You've been busy in my absence, Clearbold."

I look at his face, so similar to mine. It's always bothered me to see my deep-set eyes when I look at him, my sturdy jaw and semi-flat, straight nose.

"Not nearly as busy as you, Samson." He reaches into his robe's pocket and pulls out a small letter. His eyes gutter, darkening like an animal's as they fix on mine. "I found this in your room in Rouz."

My gut clenches as Clearbold unfolds the paper.

I'd forgotten about the letter.

I wrote it with the help of Rex and Parsifal on the journey to

Zarzynn, eager to outline my father's meddling (in great detail) in the event we never returned.

Clearbold reads, "'*Even if I die again, this truth must survive...*'" He looks at me over the parchment and raises his eyebrows. "And who the fuck was this meant for? That loyal wife of yours or someone else?"

I meet my father's eyes; he wants to derail me. To make this about my failures.

So I pivot, "Imperatriz is healthy. I caught her scent recently."

He lowers the letter, fingers tightening on the paper.

His throat shifts as he swallows a deep breath.

He at least has the sense to fear my mother's life.

What she will do to him if she finds him alive.

He folds the letter and tucks it back into his robe. "You have misunderstood me greatly." As though agitated, he shakes his head. "Your mother was not who she said she was."

My jaw clenches as adrenaline leaps through my veins.

It's hard not to close the distance between us and take him by the throat.

Not who she said she was?

She needed no announcement as the Kulapsifang. No explanation.

"And even before your mother was born, your ancestors—well, Sutnazzar and Malasuntra also weren't who they pretended to be. And lies... lies from the Kulapsifangs..."

I sit back, eyes narrowing.

Is he talking about Malasuntra 711 Afador's bastard line?

And how the fuck would he know about that?

I only learned about my third cousin thanks to necromancy.

And, as far as I know, there are no necromancers in Mieira or Velm.

Clearbold raises his eyebrows again. "I killed twelve men to wed the Kulapsifang. And when I won, I thought I would be part of the Kulapsifang's world, near Hetnazzar. Instead, I realized my deepest-held beliefs were built on lies.

"Lies to uphold a power for others to wield.

"You were barely even mine. That's how little I mattered to the Afadors. I had to wait to meet you. Your mother and grandmother kept you for four days, Samson. They took you back here immediately after your birth on the triplemoon. Your grandmother slept on my side of the bed and your mother on the other. They kept you between them.

"I had to sneak in at night to meet you. I wanted to smell my heir. Wanted to hold you against my chest so you could hear *my* heartbeat, Samson. *My* drumbeat. I was nothing to my Kulapsifang, but you are half of me. I am half of you.

"And when I snuck into that room... and pulled you from the space between them, I found a red string around your ankle."

My eyes flash to the metal door waiting behind the thrones, then back to Clearbold.

A red string?

For months, my seething dreams have involved red strings—wrapped around me, the yew tree, my demigod.

I never once associated them with my mother, Clearbold, or Velm.

Don't lose focus, Samson.

"Speak clearly," I tell him. "You're rambling."

Clearbold leans forward, voice calm but angry when he says, "It was a spell from the red witch. From Andromeda North of Skull.

"She spent years terrorizing your mother until, one day, they were thick as thieves. I advised her often not to trust the witch, Samson.

"But they made a pact—Andromeda would aid the wolves who went north and Imperatriz would welcome all those who wanted to live in Velm. Your mother wanted to make the Northing real. Andromeda claimed to want the same."

Once again, I pause.

Why bring up Andromeda now? What's he getting at?

Clearbold goes on, "I waited for you. For my heir. I kept silent about your mother's plans for the Northing. But that changed when they kept you from me. When they tied that red string around your ankle...

"It wasn't a normal string. I ripped it off you. I couldn't burn it, so I buried it deep in the ground near a yew."

His words float into the air—

Andromeda, a red string, a yew tree—

For the first time, I wonder how long my life has been connected to Vexen magic.

But I have no answers—not even guesses—and it's not the right time to speculate.

My father barrels on, "When your mother woke, we argued, and she realized that her agreements were too radical. Even if she, as the Kulapsifang, could envision a future in which the Northing and Southing would unfold, Velm was far from ready."

Samsonfang canters closer to my conscious mind. I can feel my fangself circling this room, circling my thoughts; waiting, watching.

Keep the satchel close.

I slide my eyes toward where it sits inches away, its pocket slightly ajar.

Clearbold holds up my note again, features relaxing like he might smile. "And this letter—did you really think *I* trusted Anesot?" He chuckles, cold and humorless. "By the time I met the warlock, I knew not to trust magic. No matter its color. Anesot was a pawn. He needed *me*—not the other way around."

Clearbold speaks with slow clarity, "He needed shelter from a place called Zarzynn, Samson. From a city called Ezit and a House called Serac."

My heartbeat ratchets.

Those words on his lips—those words spoken in his voice—

Clearbold knows about Zarzynn.

About the mega-city of Ezit and the Houses that rule it.

I'd expected as much after hearing his name from the Hosts. Still, the reality of it is like a blow to the chest.

Anesot is the link between Clearbold and Ezit's Hosts?

I shake my head. *Wasn't he exiled from Ezit?*

Clearbold's eyes flit across me. "I've spent years wondering what Ezit looks like. Or what it *looked* like, I should say. From what I've heard, there's barely a city left."

The hairs across my body stand up.

And how the fuck does he know about the degree of damage?

In Cadmium, most beings swept the brutality of our raid under the rug. The news that would have trickled to Bellator since then would be minimal and tinged with hearsay.

Wrath and suspicion flicker through my mind and body. "What have you done? How deep does this go?"

My hand shifts on my thigh, inching toward the satchel.

Clearbold's voice rises to a gruff condemnation. "I did what was necessary. Once I knew Anesot was on the run and needed allies, I had him by the balls. First, he got rid of Imperatriz. Then he found Andromeda's daughters for me. He nearly had Helisent where I needed her—a single witch with all of her House's power. But he fucked that up when Helisent learned that he'd ordered Oko to kill Milisent, and I had to let it go.

"And why did I let it go, Samson? Where was my focus? It wasn't on the disappearing okeanids, or the necromancers they became. It wasn't on Anesot. Or the Class. Or even Helisent, necessarily."

I stare at his features, desperate to understand.

"Atali, did you learn nothing from me?" he goes on, voice low.

His words dredge up a long-lost instinct.

A drive to dominate, to manipulate, to control.

To use a wielder's deepest need as a bargaining chip.

Anesot wanted to be welcomed back to Ezit...

I shake my head again as the realization dawns. "You used Anesot to make a deal with Ezit's Hosts."

Finally, Clearbold smiles, small but true. "That warlock had many powerful enemies. And I allied with the strongest. Don't think so little of me—our people barely fought off the red line during the War Years. How the fuck do you think we'd fare against the five unified Houses of Ezit if they came to Velm—especially when your fucking mother was convinced that wielders could be trusted?

"Anesot was bait. Anesot was my path to a deal with the House of Serac first, and then the House of Argot."

Nausea, confusion, and desperation whirl within me.

A waricon against Clearbold won't fix this...

Think, Samson.

I stare at him, trying to overcome my loathing with logic. "You couldn't even trust Andromeda—what the *fuck* makes you think you're better off with wielders from Ezit?" I go still as another realization dawns. "Or is this not about wielders at all? Don't tell me, Clearbold— is this your plan to overthrow the Afadors? To use your allies across the sea to launch a fucking coup?" I almost don't recognize my voice— its pitch, its tone, its volume. "Do you think you're any better than a pawn to the Hosts of Serac and Argot? They will *destroy my people and my territory* the second they set foot in Velm."

I let my head hang forward. Dread and anguish sweep through me—

I have failed my people.

What was I doing while Clearbold was making these agreements?

How did I not notice?

We need survival first—and then comes justice.

I straighten, staring at him and trying to control myself—to focus solely on what must be done. "We still have time, Clearbold. We can... work together. We can try to understand—"

"Work with *you*? Imperatriz is gone, but you won't let her go. I see that, Samson. I see it clearly. No—this is what happens now. Malachai and I give Velm the future it deserves. At the top of the pecking order.

"My pacts with the Hosts of Serac and Argot have already yielded many gifts. A warlock named Suleiman gave me a stone that isn't indigenous to Mieira or Velm. A stone that can nullify magic and protect our people should another conflict begin."

I'd been right when I smelled Zeu's rosarium in Hella—

I knew that scent well.

I press my hands together, lowering my voice to a reasonable tone. "We would need *cities* built of rosarium to stand a chance against Ezit. Please trust me, Clearbold."

With each passing second, the idea of Velm facing Ezit's wrath sends a cold sweat across my body.

"Stand a chance *against* Ezit? Why would we fight our allies? Velm is safe, Samson. Thanks to my vision and my care." Clearbold sighs, watching me with some fragile type of intrigue. "Do you have any idea what you've done? What your little tantrum in Ezit almost cost my people?"

Sadness and regret pang within me, decidedly personal and sentimental.

I stare into his eyes. "I challenge you to a waricon, Clearbold 554 Leofsige. Tomorrow at dawn."

My father smiles. "Wonderful."

I turn when I hear footsteps in the hallway behind me.

I glance over my shoulder, doing a double-take.

An indigo warlock walks toward us. His large horns are shined, his cheek marred with a jagged scar that cuts from his left ear to the corner of his mouth. A black cape drags behind him as he steps into the throne room; it must have replaced the dainty, translucent veil he wore in Ezitlos. It shrouds his fitted pants and tunic.

His eyes fix on me, indigo and glowing.

I know this strong jaw, these small eyes, even before his ala hits me.

It can't be—it can't be—it can't be—

Halcyons' father.

The Male Host of Serac.

Suleiman.

Now.

I reach for my satchel, but my hand hits hard marble. My bag floats upward, drifting toward Suleiman's outstretched hand.

Run.

I shift onto my knees, eager to keep both men in front of me. But my calves lock in the next second, fixed against the cushion as though held by cold iron. My hands move behind my back in a second vice grip, compelled by Suleiman's magic. Like my calves, a hefty weight binds my wrists together—not to punish but to immobilize.

Panic bubbles in my stomach, in my mind, in my bones. I couldn't win a fight against his son; I'm no match for whatever comes next. Especially with my calves fixed to the ground.

Suleiman takes hold of the satchel.

I lock eyes with Halcyon's father as he squats before me to put us at eye level. I trace the jagged scar on his cheek; it's healed but fresh and pink.

Suleiman growls, "You killed my eldest. Then you took my youngest to Mieira. Tell me, is he still slinking around in Helisent's shadow? And where are my grandsons, Samson?"

He reaches forward and extends his pointer finger.

I clench my jaw as my tunic rips cleanly, following his fingertip as it moves down the center of my chest. I jerk away from him as he tugs the fabric aside and studies the scar over my heart.

It hasn't been red since I left Vex, but he leans closer, as though fascinated.

He presses his thumb against it, then his eyes flash to mine. "How very interesting that she lets you out of her sight."

With a sigh, Suleiman straightens to his full height and starts to fish through my satchel. Items clank as he tosses them to the floor: my notebook, spare leather, bricks of peat.

He finds the red axe and hands it to Clearbold with an appraising gaze. "The weapon is covered in Vexen magic."

With suspicious fascination, Clearbold turns the weapon over in his hands.

"Leave my fucking axe alone," I bark.

They ignore me as Suleiman rips through the rest of the bag, stopping with the outer pocket. He pulls the red star out and squints at it. "This paper—it's covered in magic, too." He glances at me, tucking the red star into one of his pockets. "The Vexen has given you many gifts, I see."

I watch it disappear, my heart thumping in my chest.

Get the fuck out of this. Find a way. Now.

I strain against the magical bindings on my calves and wrists, but meet cold, rigid resistance.

The warlock notices; a coy smile plays on his lips. He looks at my father next. "Well? I told you I wanted privacy."

Fuck, fuck, fuck.

I jerk against the magical bindings again, trying different angles before straining with all my might.

Clearbold stands. The golden sunlight reflecting off the walls hovers around his black robe, his dark hair. He studies the red ax, adjusting his grip on it. He takes one step from the throne, eyes set on me.

"Clearbold, there's still time," I tell him. "Don't do this to the wolves. Don't do this to Velm." My voice shakes with fear, with wrath, with disbelief. "Think about what you're doing."

Clearbold watches me evenly. After a long stretch of silence, he turns to the warlock. "You're certain they won't know?"

"Of course not," Suleiman purrs.

I try one last time, "Clearbold—"

"Then he's yours," my father tells the warlock.

I twist as Clearbold strides away from the throne room. "I challenged you to a waricon, you fucking *coward*."

No response.

I turn back to Suleiman, frozen, unbelieving, desperate. Clearbold's footsteps echo into silence within a few moments. The warlock watches me patiently.

I let my head hang and suck in a huge breath. Two breaths. One more.

I have no idea how Suleiman got here, but this is real.

I tell myself, *Here is the part where he tortures you.*

Helisent survived on that ship.

Your witch lived; you will, too.

Never surrender.

I raise my chin and stare up at Suleiman, trying not to look afraid.

I quantify this with cold logic; Clearbold has handed my people over to powerful sadists, and I'm first on the chopping block.

Just so long as Rex and Berevald are safe—just so long as Clearbold isn't leaving the palace to drag them into this room with me—

The warlock lifts a hand. His eyes are half-closed as he bares his fingers toward me.

"Everything I ever knew," he whispers, features twisting with conviction and cruelty. "Everything..."

He waits.

He wants me to beg.

"Nothing to say then, Samson? No apologies? No pleas?"

I think, *This is all my fault.*

I growl, "Fuck you."

Then I hear a high-pitched sound, like two glasses clanking together.

Heat explodes across me, wheedling into me from my toes to my ears.

Flames consume my body, sending my skin into gooey piles of wax, burning my hair and my scalp, curdling my fingernails.

Fire lashes inside my lungs, deep enough that the breath I scream out is thick with steam. My eyes boil in their sockets, bubbling like goo.

My body folds toward the ground, my hands bound behind me and my legs fixed to the floor.

Then, the world stops ending.

I gasp for breath, shouting and groaning and howling. I lift myself and straighten my back, desperate to gauge the damage.

I must be crazy—I must be dead already—

I see nothing out of place. My cut tunic dangles from my shoulders, its dark blue fabric clean and unsinged. My pale skin is unblemished, my eyes and nose and ears fully functional.

I blink as relief courses through me.

It's over.

We survived.

"Samson."

I let my head sag toward my chest again, let my lungs pull air in and out.

It was just a nightmare. Just a trick of the mind.

"Samson," Suleiman repeats my name, steady and calm.

I raise my head, jaw clenched. The pain is gone, but I can feel it waiting at a threshold; I know this pain and the thought of its return terrifies me.

I'm still bound by the ankles and wrists. Golden sunlight filters in from the roof above.

I could have survived five seconds or five hours of torture.

Please—

Please, no more—

I meet the warlock's glowing eyes. A smile tugs at his lips, skewing his scar. "I will punish every wolf for what you've done, Samson. I will save your father for last. Only then will he understand."

His smile broadens. He raises his hand again.

I hear the high-pitched clanking.

But if Clearbold has plans for me, then it means this isn't the end.

This isn't the end.

This isn't the end.

This isn't the end.

(But I wish it was.)

I wake up bound in a puddle in a dark room.

A coarse rope wraps around my wrists and ankles, looped around a wooden pole at my back. The pole is set in the center of a bowl-shaped hole carved into the ground and filled with ice-cold water.

I know the dungeon's setup well; I've put men who broke the law into similarly uncomfortable positions.

I've left them in places like this overnight while my war band debated on a course of action to take at dawn.

My body sags with exhaustion. My mind is just as overwhelmed.

I don't know how long I've been here.

I don't know how long I spent with Suleiman before losing consciousness.

All I know is that I'm tied up like a criminal. A small flame flickers in a sconce nearby. I flinch with each lash of the orange light, my body anticipating another bout of scorching pain.

My nose is clogged; I take deep and steadying breaths through my mouth. My limbs, tendons, and joints scream for relief. I can't tell which I need more of first: food, water, or rest. I drift in and out of consciousness.

I'm not alone. There's a man tied in the same position nearby, but he doesn't act like my packmates.

My dungeonmate pulls me back to reality with his shouting. He splashes and curses in his puddle. He screams a name. It sounds like *Telleheny*.

Eventually, someone cranks open the door.

Bright sunlight floods into the room. I reel back like the other bound wolf, hitting the wooden pole.

A man steps into the threshold. I blink for a long while to regain my vision. When I do, I recognize Otzo, along with the open-air corridor behind him; we must be in the single-room dungeon located near Bellator Palace's interior courtyard.

The wolf to my right strains against his bindings to spit at our captor.

Otzo moves, but he's too late to dodge the gob.

The prisoner cackles, low and off-kilter, as Otzo curses.

As the warm air wafts into the dungeon, my nose clears. I study my cellmate first, confirming he's not Rex or Berevald.

The wolf is covered in crusty, black dirt, obscuring his features. I realize he's wearing shorts—which is only common in the south.

Velm's *far* south.

I raise my chin, pulling in more of his scent.

Otzo stalks into the room and leers at the wolf. "Spit on me all you like, Afador. I'll be pissing on your corpse soon."

I blink as a wave of shock builds and breaks.

I study the stranger, both of us bent and bound. He stares back at me.

Hadadrimmon 324 Aithesson, fellow great-grandson of Malasuntra 711 Afador.

Otzo bends to tug my bindings loose. It occurs to me for the first time that I should be ashamed—of being tied in a cellar, covered in wet dirt, tired and hungry and cold.

But a lot has changed since I stepped into the throne room.

Part of me thinks I might be dead right now; I can't string a thought together, I can't smell properly, or keep the sounds I hear in the right order.

After a few rough yanks, the ropes around my wrists fall loose. Otzo moves on to Hadadrimmon.

Hadadrimmon, who smells a few years older than me, twists his neck to stare at his captor. He bears a hard expression, jaw clenched like he's ready to spit again.

Otzo backtracks toward the door. He throws a bundle of navy fabric to the ground, then slams a jug of water next to it. "You have five minutes."

Right—Clearbold had a plan for me.

I glance at the sconce on the wall.

And where is Suleiman? Where is the red star he stole?

Can Helisent sense that the red star has been compromised?

What about my packmates?

I comfort myself with the idea that Riordon and Pietrangelo must have already helped them escape the city. They must have known it would be too late for me, so they saved Rex and Berevald instead.

I can accept that.

Like me, Hadadrimmon focuses on freeing his hands from the rope. To free our legs, we flip onto our butts in the puddle, then twist back around. By the time we're free, we're newly soaked and filthy.

Hadadrimmon and I study the other as we stand.

Like most southerners, the wolf has a broad and tall stance. His neck is stout, his chest massive. His hair isn't fixed into a bun; it's partitioned with silver decals, most of which are now tangled and out of place. His body hair is thicker than mine, especially on his chest and arms.

I twist toward the light-soaked doorway that Otzo guards. I reach for the clean clothes and jug of water, dragging them into the dungeon's shadow.

I pull apart the layers and find two loincloths.

I hold up the navy blue fabric as the pieces fall into place.

I clear my throat. Though my voice is rough, I manage, "We're fighting a waricon, then?"

I study Hadadrimmon's posture. Though incredibly burly, he doesn't look trained to fight. That's how it goes with southerners. They don't have the discipline for organized bouts, instead built for raw power.

Which bodes well for me since it seems this is Clearbold's plan: shove me into a sanded pit with Hadadrimmon at its far end and hope I don't survive.

"Well, two waricons." The wolf plucks a loincloth from my hand. "I think you get papa first and then I get the little fucker."

I narrow my eyes, stomach dropping.

That would make more sense.

In my current state, I would beat Hadadrimmon. It wouldn't be pretty, but it would be better than facing Clearbold.

At his age, my father is in peak physical form—and he has survived multiple death-match waricons. Though I'm half Afador, I've spent two months on the road and at least one night at the mercy of a sadistic warlock.

In my current state...

I lean toward the dungeon's entrance, angling my head. Faintly, in the distance, I hear drumming and chanting.

"What?" Hadadrimmon laughs, low and humorless. "Aren't in your best form?"

Adrenaline sparks in my veins before succumbing to a numb nothing.

A waricon against Clearbold—just what I'd wanted when I walked into the palace.

I stare at the bright corridor outside.

You must fight, Samsonfang urges me.

Unlike me, Samsonfang hasn't lost his vigor and stubbornness and wrath. My fangself isn't entirely bound to this body. He doesn't realize I have no more strength.

No cunning, no determination, no energy.

Suleiman burned that away. Maybe for good.

You must fight, Samsonfang insists.

I look at the fabric in my hand and straighten as much as I can with the dungeon's low ceiling. "Do they know who you are?" I pull my pants off, then tie my loincloth into place.

Hadadrimmon studies me, looking amused. "Do *you* know who I am, Samson 714 Afador?"

"You are Hadadrimmon 342 Aithesson."

"And which lovely Leolite spilled the secret?"

"A Leolite?"

"A wolf who supports the Leofsige line. Are the rumors true, then? You've really been off in a foreign land all this time?" He reaches into the jug of water and attempts to clean a scratch near his ankle, rubbed raw from the ropes. "And how was your trip? Relaxing, I hope?"

"I was looking for Imperatriz."

"Right." He raises his eyebrows, expression lifting like he's about to laugh again. "And did you find her?"

Time isn't real in this dungeon. There is no reality, no Velm, no waricon, no red witch, no memory of her ala and laughter and jewelry.

It's very possible I'm already dead.

I tell him, "I did. She's marooned on an island called Pit."

Hadadrimmon smiles. Like his laugh, it's humorless, anchored in his dark eyes and their unfeeling hue. "I see. Not very helpful—but at least she's far from what's about to happen." He cranes his back, stretching as he approaches the entrance. "You do know what's about to happen, right?"

He looks at me, but I barely sense danger.

Even when he says, "Your father is going to kill you in front of Bellator to end the Afador line. Malachai is going to kill me after to make sure there are no survivors."

Before I can react, Hadadrimmon takes the jug of water and sloshes its contents onto Otzo's backside.

Otzo leaps away from the door with a loud curse, then we step out of the water-ridden dungeon.

End the Afador line?

I see a yew tree flicker in my mind's eye. The tree is strong where it juts from a mountainside, its branches vast and bowed.

I don't have the energy for sense anymore.

The yew tree flickers in my mind, an image that grows and grows with each passing minute.

I haven't seen the yew since I stood with Anesot in a rickety theatre in Alita.

I know what its image entails.

Doom spirals in my periphery like a shroud.

Outside the dungeon, drumming and chanting drift over the palace walls with more distinction. The familiar scents of evergreen needles and peat smoke fill the air.

Otzo guides us down the hallway that leads to the palace's gated entrance. Beyond it waits the expansive exterior plaza where Riordon and Pietrangelo awaited me yesterday.

Hadadrimmon follows at my side.

With each step, the chanting and drumming grow louder. The drumbeats are firm and powerful, landing in time with our steps. Thousands of alas clog the air; distinct, layered, and muddled with adrenaline and testosterone.

The gate comes into view; the guards see us and start tugging on long ropes. They throw their weight down to lift the wooden gate slat by slat.

We wait behind Otzo.

Hadadrimmon rolls his shoulders, then bends to reach for his toes. "Did you really kill the wooly when you were twelve?"

I stare ahead. Numbness settles over me like Night's endless white snow. "No."

Hadadrimmon stretches his arms next. "So, the rumors were true —Clearbold killed the wooly to spare you the shame?"

My entire body feels exhausted, unreal. "No."

Hadadrimmon grunts as he hikes his legs up, one after the other. "So, Sutnazzar? Grandmama Afador came to the rescue?"

"No." I tilt my head back and stare into the cloudless sky. Birds cross through it, screeching as they search for bugs.

It's a beautiful day.

"So, you didn't kill the wooly, and neither did Clearbold or Sutznazzar. Who did it, then, Samson?"

I barely hear my voice. "Hetnazzar."

He actually smiles this time, baring wide and healthy teeth. "I believe you."

That's when I start to think he's an asshole.

Surrounded by assholes.

Onward to my death.

Nothing makes sense.

The gate opens bit by bit.

Screaming and zealous wolves wait on its far side.

I wish Helisent were here.

She'd know how to make light of my tragic end.

I try to come up with a punch line on her behalf.

Big end for a boy-wolf, huh?

Not cruel enough.

This is what happens when you refuse to turn your powerful consort into a wife, my dear Afador.

Still not cruel enough.

Vieira dies with you, and then what will I do, Samson—you fucking big dumb wolf?

Ah, there it is.

I imagine she screams it at me topless.

And that's when it happens.

That's when the latent doom hanging in the air curdles into the acknowledgment of death—somewhere between the memory of pressing my cheek and my lips against the soft flesh of her breasts and her nipples perking between my tongue and teeth.

I'm not dead yet—soon, though.

And I'll never smell her again. Never hold her. Never see the red sheen of her form glow like Sennen.

My heart tries and fails to panic.

Not enough energy. Not enough sanity.

You must fight*, Samsonfang urges.

There's nothing left, I admit.

What I do next is try to die with dignity.

The gate hits the top of the archway.

The guards drop their arms, exhausted.

Otzo leads us onward through a fizzing crowd.

Wolves jeer and shout and clap, white flags clenched in their fists. Those surrounding the massive drums raise their arms, beating the rigid hide in unison.

Their words and questions overlap into a deluge my broken mind can't keep up with.

They curse my mother, her womb, my legacy, my name. They save their cruelest insults for Malasuntra and his bastard heir.

Otzo guides us along a narrow pathway that empties into a sprawling, sand-covered waricon arena.

We must not be the first to fight; the sand is already muddled with blood and sweat and ravines.

Otzo leaves Hadadrimmon and me alone at one side of the waricon arena. He heads toward where Clearbold and Malachai wait shirtless at its far end. They stand proudly; their packmates surround them, coating their hands with cedar oil and covering my father.

I realize Riordon and Pietrangelo are among my father's pack. Both are bent with exhaustion, heavy bruising across their bodies and faces. Riordon's neck bleeds, a deep bite carved just above his collarbone. The men stare into the distance, eyes half-closed as though they aren't sure where to look or what to do.

I wait for them to meet my eyes, for them to mouth some sort of explanation.

I glance around, searching for Rex and Berevald.

My nose twitches.

I smell Rex's sweat, his adrenaline, his blood. Berevald's hit me next. I search the waricon arena urgently; the largest pool of blood in the center of the square was Berevald's, the second-largest from Rex.

On the arena's northern edge, three women clothed in white bend over a body lying flat.

They block his face, his chest, and his feet.

I know him by the hand that lies slack in the sand. His skin is milky, tinted blue.

It can't be.

I stagger toward him, steps heavy in the sand.

"Not now." Hadadrimmon plants himself between me and the body. "Think about it later. Survive now. Think about that later. Let's go—wake the fuck up."

No.

No.

No.

I stare at Hadadrimmon's face. I study him, feature by feature, as he starts to coat my arms and chest and shoulders in cedar oil. He moves quickly, brusquely rubbing me down.

My body stops responding to my thoughts.

I look down at my hand, opening it and staring at my palm.

Rex...?

Berevald...?

"Samson—come back to earth. Think about that later. We'll find them later. We'll honor them later."

I hear my mother's voice growl, *Kill him.*

You must fight, Samsonfang urges.

I lose touch, awash in a state of terror and exhaustion and agony.

I stare at my hands.

I can feel the horns of Helisent's ancestors. I remember touching them, my fingertips tracing the husks hanging from the walls. I am a child. I do not understand that these horns signify the death of a people. I have no inkling that I will one day find the last of the red-horned beings, that she will take hold of my soul, and this is as far in life as I'll get.

Helisent's breasts—a piece of marble carved into the shape of a snowflake—my mother playing her kalimba—a dream of a yew tree—the red berries—a witchling in a red cloak in the canopy—the fuzzy emerald needles and their bright green ends—

The tree's shadows, feathered like its bundled needles—

Where it sits on a mountainside.

I see the yew tree.

"What are you saying?" Hadadrimmon grabs my cheeks. "Get it together."

"I see the yew tree. I'm going to—this is it—"

He takes my shoulders and guides me further into the waricon grounds. My feet shuffle and sink into the cool sand. The cedar oil on my body catches the wind's chill, pasting it to me.

At the other end of the square, Clearbold rolls his shoulders and sets his eyes on me.

Then my father walks to the center of the sanded pit.

To the right, the women grunt as they lift Rex's corpse.

The crowd parts so they can pass.

He only died because he knew I would, too.

He would not have died without me—

I know it. He swore.

I look back at my father.

I see nothing; a mirage of my own features, the smudges of evil shadows beneath his brow, a body that has killed twelve men with brute force.

Hadadrimmon shoves me toward the square. "Go. Be proud, Samson."

I keep looking from one jeering face to the next, from the white flags to the cloudless sky.

The drums stop suddenly. In their wake comes deafening silence.

From someplace out of sight, a speaker bellows to the crowd, "We now have a conclusion to eighteen years of uncertainty—a new future under the Leofsiges. One that won't be tainted by Mieira's ruthless, greedy wielders and its mindless nymphs. One that won't be tainted by a weak, flighty Kulapsifang and her lacking pup."

My father smiles a violent grin, first meeting my eyes and then staring into the tightly packed crowd around us. The wolves direct their proud gazes at him, their chins high and eyes bright. They hoot loudly with wordless proclamations of support.

The speaker shouts, "Let us bear witness to the rise of a new Kulapsifang. A new era for Velm, and a new hope for our future. One that is led by Clearbold 554 Leofsige and Velm's latest heir—Malachai 555 Leofsige."

Deafening cheers fill the silence.

Malachai raises his hands to clap, bearing a solemn and understated smile to all the wolves who shout and hoot and roar words of support.

Clearbold even turns back to clap in his direction.

When they quiet, the speaker raises his voice even louder, "Today, we witness the end of the Afadors. First, Samson 714 Afador. Second, the bastard Southie born from Malasuntra 711 Afador's secret affair. Today, we forsake the Kulapsifangs who have *forsaken us*."

I hear every word, but my mind is adrift.

I can't keep up as the speaker barrels on. I stare at the sand, disconnected and baffled by this moment.

I brought the wooly's head back. I left my wife with a braid of my mother's hair. I unearthed Clearbold's great deception and betrayal.

I was close...

I was close to finding her...

My body goes cold and clammy.

Eventually, I realize the crowd is silent again.

Hadadrimmon pushes my back with both hands. "*Go.*"

I walk unsteadily to meet my father in the arena's sanded center.

Clearbold lowers himself, and I mirror his form.

He tells me, voice low, "We cannot fear change, Samson."

Instinct alone spurs me on when he barrels into me and throws me onto my back.

Never surrender.

I escape the first pin, along with the second, and then the third. But the fourth hold comes shortly after the third, and my arms give out when I try to bear down and flip Clearbold. His hold on my neck tightens.

I clench my stomach and attempt to flip him again.

I try another angle, but my arms are useless.

And I'm losing oxygen.

I strain against my father's weight. Birds are still crisscrossing in the sky above.

Blue fades to gray. Gray fades to black.

Hold on, Samson.

I see the yew tree.

I see the wind caress its needles, shaking them and their bloodred berries where the trunk cranes from the mountainside.

Vieira dies with you, and then what will I do, Samson—you fucking big dumb wolf?

She laughs, and then Helisent lowers her voice to whisper gently, sweetly, beautifully, *You're scaring the witchling.*

I submerge into nothingness.

It feels like water. I can feel death in my lungs.

Something hits my chest, then something grabs my arm. It's not how I thought dying would feel. Death feels combative. It also feels quite hairy; fur brushes against my face and neck and back. The hold on my upper arm tightens. It strains, causing me to lean to the right.

My feet also seem to be moving.

Sand brushes my soles.

Someone is talking. "*Lekeli Kelnazzar*—I can't carry your dead weight. Wake up—wake up—wake up—"

A dense shadow covers me.

There's something furry to my left, something combative and noisy to my right.

I open my eyes and take in brief glimpses.

I'm staggering out of the waricon arena. My people back away from me with dumbstruck expressions. They scramble to make way, heads tilted back as they stare upward.

I'm covered in oil and blood and sand.

I'm walking toward the stairs that lead up to the marble archway between Baladhari and Meledhari.

Hadadrimmon supports my weight, one of my arms slung over his shoulders.

Hetnazzar walks above us, slowly enough to keep us sheltered beneath its front paws.

Maybe I'm not dead.

It's too soon to tell.

CHAPTER 2

CREEPY BABY, PART II
HELISENT

Honey Baby,
We spoke with Milisent in one of the necromancer's mirrors. She looks younger
than you now. She's really proud of that.
The Boys

I smooth the wide sleeves of my bloodred velvet robe.

My fingertips press into the soft fabric as I glance around the squat, subterranean room.

Luz's magical processor sits in its center, little more than a wooden table containing a grid of magical cylinders.

The cylinders sit upright in perfect order. Below the table, copper wires run from the bottoms of the cylinders toward fist-sized holes in the dirt wall.

The cylinders on the table glisten with golden dove; it fades and then brightens, as though the amorphous magic held inside were breathing calmly.

The hundreds of vials seem to hum a high note, too.

I know this pitch thanks to my time in Zarzynn; Talosen magic.

I glance at Ninigone, Head Witch of Luz, as she taps her long, clean nails against the table's ledge. Gilfoyle, the latest Head Warlock of Luz, stands at her side.

I raise my eyebrows, looking from one to the other as I try to figure out why I was summoned here. "So? Looks fine to me?"

Ninigone keeps tapping the wooden table. "We asked you to come because Absalom and Ethsevere want to run a copper line underground from Antigone to Luz. Copper conducts dove easily, so it should offer us a way to communicate more directly."

Every few seconds, light flickers in one of the cylinders. A metal tube responds, thrumming as it takes hold of the magic and ferries it into the city. Like the roots of a great kapok, the tubes run from the table and then spread throughout the room, wheedling into the dirt walls.

They emerge around the city, focused on the areas where magical dove is needed. Like to drain the laundry pools near the Irme River; to keep the sewer systems moving toward the constructed wetlands that purify the dark water; to organize documents for the city's record-keepers working in long halls.

"We use tracking and flying magic to send messages to other city councils," Gilfoyle explains, looking at me over his hooked nose. "But they're subject to delays. The monsoons in Rhotidom make it impossible to send word for days on end. The hottest days in Jaws, too."

Ninigone goes on, "If the line between Antigone and Luz works, we can extend it toward Perpetua, then the Deltas. It could unify Mieira in terms of reliable and quick communication."

I snort—that must be what I'm sensing in this dirt room. The fear-driven impulse to unify Mieira's cities just in case. "I see. And you want me to dig a trench from here to Antigone to lay the copper line?"

Ninigone clenches her jaw; she and Gilfoyle exchange a tense glance.

"Yes or no?" I push.

"Yes," Gilfoyle says.

At the same time, Ninigone says, "Of course not."

They share another terse glance.

Ninigone tries again. "Only if you think it's not a waste of time."

I'm different now: responsible, basically sober, and capable of analytical thinking. But I'm not that fucking different.

I blink at Ninigone, satisfaction clanging through me. "What *I* think?" I take a step toward Gilfoyle. "Before I start handing out valuable knowledge, I'd like to know what makes you think you're special enough to have earned my help. Hm, Gilfoyle? The warlock you replaced was very useful to me. Absalom is part of the Class now, thanks to that."

After he and Ethsevere returned to Antigone last month, the Class instated Absalom Metamor as its sixth official member—and, off the record, as my blessed little patsy.

I turn to Ninigone, too. "And what about you? *You* stuck me with a fucking mentee last year. Or did you think I'd forget?"

The witch tugs on her tawny cloak sleeves. "Esclamonde has proved very advantageous to you, has she not?"

"Only because I made her useful. She was *not* like that when you dropped her off." I raise my eyebrows to hammer home that point, then turn back to the table of golden-glowing cylinders.

The longer I study the processor, the more I wonder...

Magical processors are designed to store and redirect amorphous dove so that anyone—even a terrified wolf—can use their magic with a few simple commands. But neither glass cylinders nor metal wires can store and transport large sums of magic.

Only horns and tender flesh can do that.

Maybe other things, too, depending on which House magic comes from.

"Copper should work, but let's not forget that wielders take their magic from their respective Landmarks. Most wielders in Mieira are *golden*; their magic comes from waterfalls in the House of Talos. Copper might not be the best conduit. It might be better to use a material that's more familiar to the Landmark's natural state. So, think of it how a waterfall would think of it."

The Head Wielders of Luz snap their heads toward me.

"A waterfall?" Gilfoyle asks.

Ninigone shakes her head. "They don't think."

"Neither does the stone where my magic comes from, but that doesn't make it any less intelligent." I shrug. "Figure it out for yourselves, my dear Head Wielders."

Gilfoyle glances around the cramped room, eyes alight. "A waterfall... composed of air, earth, and water. A natural conduit..."

Ninigone throws him an exasperated look before turning to me. "I suppose we have much to ruminate on, then. I'll be in touch with questions. Your help would be... greatly appreciated."

I stare at the Head Witch, trying to get used to this new feeling.

Greatly appreciated? That's basically crazy talk coming from Ninigone.

"Okay. Let me know how that goes." I toss my hair over my shoulder, then cross the room toward the door. "In the meantime, I need to leave the city. Speak to Onesimos Eupheme Jaws if you need anything in my absence."

These two can hash out what to do with the copper line—

I need to focus on Tet's shale.

On a devil named Creepy Baby.

Ninigone shuffles behind me, following me to the door. "Where will you be?"

Light twinkles through the door's seams, beckoning. I open it and look back at the pair. Gilfoyle flinches from the sunlight, and Ninigone stares at me, a frown hanging from her lips.

"Ninigone, I'm not a lowly little drunkard on a trail of vengeance anymore, so you can't ask me things like that. I don't even think you were allowed to ask before."

I turn away and let the door swing shut in my wake.

I take the short set of stairs to the street; I'm on the edge of the market district, almost empty at this hour. I pull a flask of brandy from my warm velvet pocket, then pop open its top and take a long drink.

I sigh and stare around at the city.

In the swing of a boiling and sticky summer, the streets are slow-moving. Most shutters are closed, and the homes within quiet. Only a few merchants have opened their carts and stalls. Even the canaries have yet to wake; I hear a few shuffling wings in the canopy above. Only the swallows look undisturbed by the sunny and clear sky as they swoop between the two and three-story buildings, screeching.

I amble back toward home, enjoying the mostly empty streets.

A nymph does a double-take when she notices me from across the street. Chariovalda South Bend Gamma smiles, showing off her bright and straight teeth. "Helisent West of Jaws—just the witch I was looking for."

We meet in the middle of the street as she adjusts a heavy bag full of bright vegetables.

Like other hesperides, unpigmented skin covers parts of her body. In midsummer, the difference between her tan-brown skin, kissed by the sun, and milky skin is even more noticeable. The pale marks dot her hairline near her temple, while another larger series descends from her jaw to her neck.

"How are you?" I ask, returning her smile.

"Good. We've been seeing quite a bit of Zeu's den at Coil lately. Controversial opinion—vampires really aren't that spooky."

"Nothing will ever be creepier than a selkie."

Her features crumple. "They aren't that bad. Once you get used to the jelly, it's fine."

"Oh..."

"It's very fragrant." She tosses a hand out. "Anyway, I wanted to tell you that Gautselin hasn't been sleeping well the last two nights. He's been having nightmares. He asked me to tell you that he needs a week off. He has lots of client work to catch up on, too."

I blink at her, trying to keep my expression neutral.

As the proprietor of Luz's most expansive pleasure house, Coil, Gautselin has been happy to play stand-in for Samson. The unnumbered wolf brushes my hair and smokes cigarettes and lets me lie across his chest when I miss my Kulapsi-boy. As his partner in life and business, Chariovalda is aware of our arrangement; as a professional with a great need for dove, she's happy so long as Coil's cylinders stay full.

But none of us has brought up the dangerous possibility of a seething—the same curse that tied my mind to Samson's after he caught the scent of my sexual ala.

I've been careful to keep my pussy downwind from the wolf anytime we meet. And given all me and Gautselin do is cuddle while fully clothed, there's minimal risk.

But if he's having trouble sleeping now...

"Nightmares?" I squeeze my legs together. "What kind of nightmares?"

She raises her eyebrows. "Nothing in particular. I think it's the trouble in Velm. He's worried about his family. They live in Mort. He's waiting for a response to his last letter. It always takes longer than he'd like." She leans closer, licking her lips. "I think he's worried about Sandro, too. The local pack leaders here hung white flags. I don't know what that means, but Gautselin says it's bad."

Sandro...

I had this idea that the wolf's absence would hurt less if we didn't call him Samson.

I take another drink from my flask.

His absence wears on my mind—and there's no end to it in sight. "Well, he isn't the only one worried about Sandro."

I talk myself out of shadowing to the wolf once a day.

Part of me is relieved it's not a straight solution. Though I could shadow freely in Vex, I'm no longer residing in my House. And while I have a marble snowflake from Samson, which should be enough to track him, I'm hesitant to cross great distances via shadow to a place I've never been before.

It's a risk I'd have no problem taking—but only urgently.

A red star kind of urgently.

But Samson hasn't thrown the star; I trust he would if he needed to.

Chariovalda sets a warm hand on my wrist. "I know you have your warren... but they don't understand the wolves like I do. I'm always around. You know where to find me if you need someone."

I stare into her hazel eyes.

A lump gets stuck in my throat. "I don't need to understand the wolves. That doesn't matter to me. I just want mine back. Just for a little bit." I pat her hand. "Thank you, Chari. I'll leave Gautselin alone for a while. I'll be out of town, anyway."

I turn away before the lump in my throat goads a sniffle. Chariovalda squeezes my hand again before letting it go, then she turns in the opposite direction.

I return home quickly, eager to call on Esclamonde and Butter so we can escape the city.

We've been putting off a trip to Tet since we returned home from Cadmium. After months of drama, danger, and destruction, we needed a bit of downtime.

But Onesimos recently pointed out that Tet won't be nearly as nice when it isn't summertime.

I reach my new residence with a sigh, shouldering the heavy front door open. The city council thoughtfully allocated two apartments for me—one for my new warren and, one floor beneath, another for the Pletens. Like Zeu's den, they've acclimated wonderfully to life in Luz.

Mostly.

I pause on the floor below my apartment. The Pletens' door is almost fully open.

I hear Onesimos's gentle chiding echo from the long, well-lit hallway.

I follow the narrow passage where it empties into the kitchen.

Like nervous schoolchildren, Halcyon and his wives stand with their hands behind their backs near the kitchen table. The trio wears the long layers common to Plet, including floor-length pants and wrist-length shirts.

Ceyx and Cleo wear moonstone jewelry in their straight hair, along with droplets of moonstone in their ears. The languid sisters stand beside their husband with perfect postures. Now that I'm used to seeing the Pletens hiding their forms, it's obvious they're a few inches taller than Halcyon.

The warlock looks guilty, slightly hunched as he leans against the table.

Beside it, a ginkgo tree rustles its leaves against the large kitchen window. A few canaries have lined up along the sill, eyeing the table. Colorful produce and dollops of wrapped butter sit neatly atop packs of grains, rice, and sugar. Around them is a halo of shining utensils, plates, and cooking gadgets.

The Pletens look from the crowded table to the oread. They barely spare a glance in my direction.

On the other side of the kitchen, Onesimos taps his fingers against the wooden countertop. He sighs as he studies the food, his vermillion eyes dancing.

The *hoard* of food.

He turns when he sees me. "Good morning, Helisent. I was just going to give a little lesson on," he gestures to the cluttered table, "this mess."

"I'm going to bake pastries," Cleo cuts in, green eyes wide.

"People keep handing us gifts." Ceyx gestures into the adjoined salon. The room looks just as hopeless as the kitchen. Textiles, books, jewels and beads, paintings, pans, and dried herbs span the large room.

The sitting cushions are entirely covered, along with the low table. "We couldn't pay them with coins. So we need to—"

"No, no, no," Onesimos says, raising his thick eyebrows. "Helisent told me all about the coins. Forget they exist. Push them from your mind entirely. You don't need coins in Mieira—all you need to do is learn how to barter."

Ceyx, Cleo, and Halcyon look from him to me, as though desperate for help.

"But the coins..." Halcyon mumbles. "We saved for so long..."

"Saved them? For what? To build a house out of little metal circles? Actually, don't answer. Stupidity makes me cranky." The oread approaches the table, eyebrows tugged together. "I can appreciate that bartering is difficult—so let me make things painfully clear.

"Bartering creates a web, just like a spider's web. Every little barter is a strand of a sturdy yet flexible web.

"These webs unite Mieira's cities and its beings. They tie us together into a comfortable, livable shape.

"Say you find a naiad in Alita with a broken shoe, and you fix the shoe, and you enjoy a nice, long conversation with the naiad. The next time you see them, they will have something wonderful for you.

"Your giving is not forgotten; it isn't for nothing. The repaired shoe becomes much more than a shoe. It becomes a part of the web, *binding* you to the naiad, and then to the rest of the naiad's connections. See? Mieirans like to be bound, too."

Ceyx gives a little *hmph*, as though pleasantly surprised.

Cleo makes an optimistic, high-pitched noise. "I see."

Halcyon glances across the kitchen toward a drawer, as though distracted.

I lean against the wall, adding, "Hoarding—and this is quite the hoard, you three—bends the web. It puts pressure on one point of it. The web must be kept balanced. Which means all this shit has to go —before someone calls for a public beating."

Onesimos bares his palms toward the Pletens when they look affronted. "No one would beat the newcomers." He throws me a dirty look. "Maybe just a slap. I've been slapped a lot—it happens."

Ceyx and Cleo nod, focused intently on Onesimos.

Halcyon presses his lips into a thin line. He glances feverishly at a drawer on the far side of the kitchen.

I narrow my eyes, following his stare.

What's he hiding?

"We need sheets," Cleo says.

"How do we get them?" Ceyx asks.

A wide smile dimples Onesimos' cheeks. "Just go into the markets and start chatting, my beautiful and empowered green witches. You'll find what you need and more."

Cleo looks at Ceyx, and her sister returns her distraught glance.

"Why don't we cover a few examples?" I set a hand on Onesimos' shoulder; nymphs expect wielders to catch on quickly. Even I remember being slightly baffled by the freewheeling nature of bartering when I first left my homestead west of Jaws. "Simmy works at a school a few days a week. He teaches letters and spelling and songs. This is a *very* strategic choice since children are loving and show up almost every morning with little bounties. Muffins, drawings, shiny things. You name it. But the parents are more important. Parents love their children, and so they love the people who help their children. Right?"

More understanding blooms in Ceyx and Cleo's eyes.

"Yes," Cleo says, smiling at Onesimos.

With a sly smile, the oread explains, "I'm *excellent* with parents."

"Pen, a warlock who was part of our old warren," I go on, "works at a chicken coup. That's a lot of fucking eggs, my friends. And those eggs get him just about anything he wants. The better he cares for the chickens, the better the eggs, and the better the barters. The egg-web, we used to call it."

"And didn't Sene invite both of you to work with her?" Onesimos adds. "Your long layers have stirred quite a creative frenzy amongst the seamstresses. I've seen several women wearing outfits like yours. If you work with Sene, or any nymph like her, you benefit from her web, too."

Cleo looks at Ceyx, a smile on her lips. "I told you. Let's go later today." She looks at me and the oread. "Sene asked us about moon-stone decals."

Ceyx taps Halcyon on the shoulder. "You would do well at the school."

"Wonderful." Onesimos traces a circle in the air. "Remember—the bounty of the demigods provides for all in Mieira. One day soon, you will feel their desita. Then, you'll feel the web. You'll sense the interconnectedness of all life. For now, let's deal with this little hoard of yours..."

He heads to the sink and opens the cabinet below it, then takes out a large wooden bucket. With a sigh, he totes the empty bucket to the kitchen table.

Onesimos raises his eyebrows at the Pletens, shoving the bucket toward them. "Fill it, take it downstairs, and give out the goods. Repeat the process until this room is reasonably empty."

The Pletens look around, as though unsure where to start.

Onesimos picks up an orange and, with a chiding smile, shucks it into the bucket.

The others join him—slowly and gingerly deciding which pieces to part with.

"And is this the case with the wolves?" Halcyon asks as he places the wrapped butters into the bucket.

"Relations with the wolves are a little strained," Ceyx adds.

"We don't understand them," Cleo says pessimistically, shoveling the rest of the oranges into the bucket.

The oread explains, "Velm doesn't have any demigods doling out cornucopias. Wolves are concerned with survival. It makes their hearts smaller. Also, there seems to be a bit of a political crisis in Velm right now. Hopefully, we'll know more when Sam—sorry, Sandro—sends us a letter." Onesimos claps his hands clean. "Also, they don't like gossip. It makes them hard to read."

Cleo nods. "They don't speak at all."

Ceyx adds, "Especially not compared to the nymphs—the nymphs have so many questions. All the time."

Hidden down the hallway and out of sight, Memphis calls from his bedroom, "A naiad told me that the nymphs gossip because it lets them live many lives in one lifetime. You know, since they die young."

The Pletens look at Onesimos, their eyes wide.

Halcyon turns to the hall. "Memphis! Watch your mouth!"

Cleo wanders a few steps toward the bedroom. "My love, remember what we said about *gentle* statements?"

I crane for a view of the hall where Memphis pokes his head from his bedroom. His white hair is a short mess, his lips pulled into a tiny smile.

The warlockling says, "A naiad at the bathhouse told me nymphs only live until they're sixty. She didn't seem upset by it."

Onesimos cackles as he tosses a pomelo into the bucket. "The naiad bathhouse? Who sent you there?"

I also let out a laugh, surprised to hear that the youngest Pleten (and the shyest of the bunch) has found his way to the bathhouse. "Aren't you a little young for that?"

Memphis glances at me with a roguish blush. "A lot of things happen under the water."

Cleo rushes into his room. Halcyon is close behind, feet thudding against the floor as the warlockling's mother begins a hushed interrogation.

In their absence, Onesimos winks at Ceyx. "He was right. We like the gossip because it gives us life." Then he turns toward the drawer Halcyon has been eyeing. Like me, he noticed. "Helisent, let's see what the warlock was hiding."

I head to the drawer at the far end of the room and rip it open. Unpolished chunks of lapis lazuli clank as they shift, followed by pearls that catch the light like droplets of milk.

I tsk, eyes jumping from one precious piece to the next. There are enough to make me a fifty-strand necklace.

Ceyx pokes her head next to mine. She represses a giggle. "He heard Calypso likes lapis lazuli and pearls. He's smitten with her."

"Did you just notice?" He hasn't taken his eyes off her since Cadmium—it's a gaze I distinctly recognize from our time in Vex. Except in Zarzynn, when he was still watching me, I wasn't treated to covert drawers of delicate pearls and raw lapis lazuli.

Onesimos worms his head between ours, hair tickling my shoulder. He just brushed out his coiled vermillion hair, leaving his afro thick and pristine. "My fucking moons. Is he emptying the Deltas of pearls? Come on, ladies."

He reaches into the drawer to pull out a handful of precious pieces. I mimic him, squishing as many as I can into my palm; Ceyx does the same, taking almost half the pieces in her large hand.

We follow the oread across the room.

He empties his handful into the bucket, then Ceyx and I follow suit. The lapis lazuli and pearls scatter over the rest of the goods, falling toward the bottom of the bucket and disappearing.

Onesimos sets his hands on his hips, smiling happily at the Colyd witch. "Very good."

I almost roll my eyes.

The oread is laying it on thick. And I'm not close enough to Ceyx to know whether she's batting her lashes at him due to shy endearment or a more masterful sort of demure flirting.

Time to get the fuck out of here.

I dust my hands clean. "Right, well. I'll leave you to it. Esclamonde and Butter should be done packing upstairs." I glance at Ceyx. "We'll be gone for a few weeks. Me, Butter, and Esclamonde."

Now that his family is acclimated, Halcyon has started spending more and more time in the apartment we share above, tapping on Butter's windowpane or knocking lightly on the door or whispering her name through its seams. Simmy has been doing the same with Cleo and Ceyx; nobody seems to mind the back and forth. Not even Memphis.

And while I'll always have the oread to warm my bed, and I'm still invited into Butter and Halcyon's, I'm starting to loathe the love that's palpable in the air.

It's like a toxic fume.

"Best of luck on your journey." Ceyx nods.

Before I can thank her, the oread grabs my face with warm hands. He plants damp kisses across my cheeks and brow. "Be safe, my darling witch. Don't forget—"

"My favorite oread." I pull free from his hands, then catch them between mine. I squeeze them once. "I know."

Onesimos raises his eyebrows. "Good. Now get out of here before Halcyon tries to say goodbye to Butter again."

With a smile, I wave goodbye to the pair, then scamper down the hallway toward the front door. I shut it behind me, then jolt when I hear footsteps in the stairwell.

Butter and Esclamonde are halfway down the steps. Both women have bottomless bags slung across their bodies, their clothes and hair neatly arranged.

Esclamonde lights up with a smile. "We're ready, Helisent. I brought lots of parchment—I'll take notes the whole time. I also brought cinnamon. Mother says ghosts hate cinnamon."

Butter offers me a quick smile, then focuses on the door at my back.

I slide in front of her, blocking her view. "No more goodbyes, Butter. It's time to see what that creepy little ghost wants with my magic."

I sling my arm through hers, forcing the okeanid-witch-necromancer to follow me down the stairs. Like an obedient mentee, Esclamonde goes to her far side, penning Butter in.

We hold our formation until we reach the street. Butter breaks away then, tsking and smoothing her white curls and their turquoise ends.

"Did you bring the... your necromancy supplies?" I ask, glancing from her frown to her new, white bottomless bag.

"I always have the mirror with me." Butter glances over her shoulder, distracted. With a gasp and a wide smile, she raises a hand to wave.

Like me, Esclamonde twists to watch Halcyon crane from his apartment's window, waving goodbye amid the ginkgo tree's bright leaves.

I gag in jest.

That gets Butter's attention. She whips her head around to me. "Don't be like that. I'm leaving him to hunt down a ghost in a swamp-world with you. Or are you jealous?"

I roll my eyes. "It's not like that. My papa says that new love is like spring's bounty. As lovely as the flowers, as nauseating as their pollen."

As though on cue, Esclamonde's body buckles with a powerful sneeze, which partly lands on Butter's bright red sleeve.

"For fuck's sake," Butter hisses. "You did that on purpose."

"No, I didn't," Esclamonde grumbles. "How does someone even sneeze on purpose?"

"That's not my problem," Butter says. "If you sneeze on me again, I'll..."

I groan a long sigh.

My mind drifts to Sandro. Wherever he is, I'm sure he's happier than me.

I lick my lips and stare into Tet's abyss of beige-ish mist.

The fog reeks of mud and moss, sealing us into a dome of half-lit misery and stench.

We're not lost, I tell myself. *Samson and I spent two weeks wandering through Tet before finding our destination. This is totally normal.*

We've only spent five days in the mist so far.

Unfortunately, Butter and Esclamonde haven't acclimated to the sunless expanse or its sad quagmires, and I'm getting exhausted from pretending I have.

To my left, Esclamonde jolts and gasps every five minutes, reacting to splashes in the distance or ribbits from fat frogs. Her boots squelch in the mud, her bony hand clinging tight to me.

On my other side, Butter keeps her chin raised, baring a vexed but brave expression into the fog around us. She at least uses magic to drown out the sound of her boots in the mud. And her elderberry perfume hasn't fully faded from her robe's collar, offering a slight reprieve from Tet's unending rot.

"Everything I own is going to smell like mud," Butter groans. "And didn't you say that Creepy Baby *invited* us here? Where the fuck is this ghost of yours?"

The okeanid-witch-necromancer narrows her turquoise-gold eyes, straining forward to see through the dense mist. It hangs around us in a bubble, just as opaque as my first trip here.

"He didn't leave me a map, Butter," I tell her.

Another frog ribbits in the mist.

Esclamonde jolts into my side, throwing me and Butter off-balance. "Helisent, did you hear that?"

I ignore the mentee; I figure her outbursts are largely rhetorical at this point.

"Creepy Baby is a *proper* ghost, right?" Butter reaches out and runs a finger against the mist's edge. She looks at her finger afterward; like each time before, it's dry, not damp. "Not like these fucking junior ghosts, I hope?"

I'd forgotten about the junior ghosts—something Samson said I'd rather not know about last year.

I try to keep my tone light. "Yep. He's different from a junior ghost."

"I had no idea Tet would feel so..." Butter tsks, trailing off.

As Kierkeline's granddaughter, Butter is in a prime position to learn the art of GhostEating. As a necromancer, she seemingly has an even greater leg up.

But Butter has been too timid to reconnect with her grandmother —even though it's obvious we could use guidance and insight from a powerful GhostEater.

I can't blame her.

I still haven't faced Milisent or Andromeda.

Each time Butter unloads her mirror and pulls the fabric from its shining face, we find an excuse to keep counsel amongst ourselves. And though we haven't spoken about it, I know it's the same fear that drives us both away from the mirror.

I don't want to sit in front of Milisent or Andromeda and face the reality that both witches were greater than me. That maybe that's why they're gone—because they'd wasted their power and cunning on trying to help me.

They will look at me and think... *This is what I died for? Of all things —this?* And I will sit there with my stupid fucking face and smile like the world's most useless creature.

Instead of sitting in front of mirrors, Butter and I are barreling ahead. Into the future. Into mist.

With the mentee.

And while neither of us is nearly as jumpy or hysterical as Esclamonde, I hadn't realized how different waltzing into Tet would feel this time around.

First, I lack the companionship of an unfeeling and gruff Kulapsifang. Second, I lack the perpetual numbness brought on by brandy and dextro. Third, I'm also without the unrelenting drive to avenge my sister.

"You didn't know Tet would feel so... what?" I glance at Butter as I lead us forward.

"Full of death," Butter murmurs. "A truer death than what the deathlings know—but not *real* death. Not *all* the way. There are so many layers to death. Nobody realizes."

"What do you mean... *layers?*" I ask.

"Do we want to know?" Esclamonde squeaks.

"Well, necromancers know death as the Sea of Souls. We know of two types of death.

"There are the true dead; not even necromancers can find them with our mirrors. Then there are deathlings; they want to speak to those still living. They're willing to be called into our mirrors from the Sea of Souls.

"Then there's whatever the fuck is happening here. The death I sense right now... it's not the same forms that necromancers learn about.

"I can sense two more types of death—I'm guessing these are regular ghosts like Creepy Baby and then... junior ghosts. That's what Kierkeline called them. And I don't know anything about them except that they're everywhere and they're fucking weird and I fucking hate this."

For a long moment, I review her wayward monologue.

The thing about Butter is that I barely knew her in Ultramarine before joining her in Hypnos. Even then, we only had a few precious days of partying before we were kidnapped.

In other words, we're still in that phase of getting to know one another, beyond the bounds of trauma and parties.

I don't know whether to be frightened or comforted by her words.

"Why don't we worry about all that later?" I ask quietly. "Let's just find Creepy Baby for now. Maybe he'll have answers."

"Answers?" Esclamonde moans. "You said he tried to drown you."

I shake my arm slightly, hoping to loosen her death grip. Both women are taller than me, playing tug of war to guide us through the endless mist.

"We almost drowned in a magical sink—not out in the open like this," I tell the mentee. "It was a flash flood. And I think it had something to do with Skull, not the ghosts. That's what it seemed like. Butter—any idea what Skull might be? The ghosts made it seem like it wasn't a city at all."

"No idea," she says with a sigh. "I'll add it to the list."

Esclamonde jolts again. "Look, look, look!"

I yank my arm back to my side, preparing a smothering spell for the witchling.

I pause for the next second.

Thirty feet in the distance, obscured by mist, is an unmistakable green light.

A sink.

We fall still.

I squint toward the light; it has the same hue as the magical sink where Samson and I first met Creepy Baby. The ripe green color is like leaves covered in fresh dew.

From here, it looks like the exact same cave Samson and I entered.

I take off toward it, finally hopeful that we aren't on a doomed mission.

The arms looped through mine don't budge.

I pull free, then look back.

With a tsk, I study the frightened witches.

Butter's white curls are tangled, their cerulean-tinged ends caught inside her red cloak. Her jaw is tight, her full and magenta lips pressed into a thin line as she beholds the sink.

Esclamonde looks from Butter to me to the green light over my shoulder. She makes a low sound, taking half a step to stand slightly behind the okeanid-witch-necromancer. Her short, white hair is frayed and damp, her fitted pants skewed and stained with mud at the bottoms.

We're close to being a solid crew.

Which is great considering Onesimos is made for love, not leadership; considering my deal with Halcyon ended once we reached Luz; considering the King of Night and I still aren't on the best of terms; considering my dear, sweet Kulapsifang is traipsing through Velm with his wife.

I need brave allies.

I need these women to become those brave allies.

I straighten the sleeves of my velvet robe.

I give Butter a meaningful once-over, then study Esclamonde. "Ladies, ladies, ladies. Did you know they started calling us the Bloodies in Cadmium? You both dyed your robes red so they'd look like mine. And now they look like mine."

Butter made hers from shining silk; she has to undo the dozens of snags that nick the fabric at least once a week. "Calypso Butter Ultramarine, you are the only okeanid-witch-necromancer in Mieira. You're also going to inherit Kierkeline's role as a GhostEater someday. So, it's kind of crazy that you're this worked up about a magical sink and a manipulative ghost."

With a sigh, I move on to the next woman. Esclamonde's robe is made from cashmere, luxurious enough to wrap around herself like a blanket when she gets cold at after-hours parties. "Esclamonde Black Rock Antigone, you remain an enigma. I thought you would fail, but you didn't. I thought you would run, but you didn't. I also thought you'd be a bit more useful by this point, but you aren't. My blessed little mystery, get your shit together."

I finish smoothing my robe's sleeves, then straighten my jewelry. It's all damp and reeking from the mist.

When I look up, Butter is glaring at me with a curl to her nose. "Have you forgotten we're useless without magic? We should draw the ghost out of the sink."

Esclamonde shoves her hands into her sleeves, staring at the ground with a subdued pout.

"Fine. Let's see if he's home." I turn around before they can lose their nerve and beeline toward the green light. Each step is more like two—I take one, then wait for Butter to follow and drag Esclamonde with her.

Slowly, a crag of dark rocks comes into view. The jagged shale pebbles lead down an incline; the rocks grow in size and darken in color as they descend toward a blackened tunnel below. The cave's shadow is total, leaving little hint of what's within.

A pale green light hovers in the air around its entrance. The green hues whirl upward, rising into the sky in a cloudless tunnel.

Something jade flutters around the rocks below, half-real. Slowly, it forms a short and dense shape, and then approaches where we stand above.

As the faceless shape nears, its features become more distinct. Then the ghostling calls out in a low, gravelly voice, "I thought you'd bring the wolf."

I narrow my eyes on Creepy Baby as he clambers onto a slanted boulder ten feet away. He reaches its crest, then sets his hands on his hips. From a distance, I can't make out his wrinkles and stubble; his head looks particularly bulbous today.

The green-glowing ghost smiles as he watches us, belly protruding and tiny feet squarely set on the rock.

Butter makes a loud sound of disgust. Esclamonde shouts wordlessly, catching her leather boot in a divot and falling onto her butt.

I glare at him, a shiver on my spine. "There you are, tiny devil. We've been walking for days—could you not sense us?"

"Not immediately, red witch. How powerful do you think I am? And who have you brought me?" His round eyes narrow as he sets them on Butter. "I don't like this one. The junior ghosts don't like her, either. She smells like death and salt and hot sand." And then on to Esclamonde, who's busy dusting off her cloak. "What's with the littleling?"

"A *littleling*?" I raise my eyebrows. "That's rich. You look like you're five and five hundred at the same time."

"I'm closer to five hundred than five." With a sigh, Creepy Baby turns around. Like he once did in Alita, he leaps from the slanted rock onto the ground, bounding as though weightless. He glances back to where we stand, seemingly disappointed. "Come on, then."

He guides us further away from the cave of shadows and green light.

He looks back when we don't follow.

I set my hands on my hips as Butter and Esclamonde flank me. "Where are we going? I've been lenient with your vague plans, but I'd like some answers now, Creepy Baby. Why is my magic here? And what deal do you want to strike for helping me find it?"

His green-glowing eyes flicker over us one by one. "Because I want to be King of Tet and all its ghosts. That's the deal we'll strike. But first, to be a king, a place has to be alive."

I cross my arms. "I've heard drunkards in taverns at highmoons give a straighter answer."

"Witches trust nothing. I told you what I want; it's really that simple. I want to be the King of Tet. I want to be alive." The toddler's expression breaks. His eyebrows pull together, eyes doubling in size and wetness. "Isn't that enough—*the desire to live?*"

The more innocent the cover, the more sinister the trick.

"Tell me how you died and I'll believe you."

In a split second, Creepy Baby's façade of sadness lifts. He looks confused for a second, then annoyed. "I don't remember. You know, you were nicer last time."

With a quick pivot, Creepy Baby turns and walks on. Like it does with us, the mist lifts to form a sphere around him. He shifts his hands to clutch them behind his back.

I slide my eyes toward Butter as we follow. "Can you sense anything?" I whisper.

She shrugs, whispering back, "No red flags so far. But I know more about deathlings than ghosts. Keep your guard up."

From a few feet ahead of us, Creepy Baby starts to ramble, "The water took your essence throughout Tet, red witch. The flood took his, too. It... was a period of... waking."

I comb through his words, wondering what he means by *essence* and what the fuck that has to do with waking up.

I glance at Esclamonde. Normally, she'd be scribbling away on a piece of parchment. I elbow her, then gesture for her to start writing. She scrambles for her bottomless bag.

But the ghost quiets after that.

After an hour of marching, a cave comes into view—not amid the beige-and-gray mist, but on the ground. The muddy grass gives way to shale pebbles, dark in color and angular. These shift in hue—first a muted brown, then a rusted orange, then a rich red-orange, and finally a deep red. It's not nearly as vibrant as our cloaks, but I remember seeing similar shades in some of Vex's limestone caves.

I lean down to pick up a red shard.

I turn it over in my hands. It's not like the soft and pumice-like feel of limestone. The shale is dense and brittle, ripping through the soft mud in horizontal slabs.

I sense magic within the form; a lingering of bass, a thread of magical energy. It's not nearly as potent as the Hellastone, but it's reminiscent of the limestone hidden below Vex's pine barrens.

I rub the flat stone between my fingers as we continue toward the cave's entrance. This one looks similar to the first, only half its size. The tunnel looks just wide enough for me to pass through with Butter and Esclamonde at either side. The grotto that leads below is less manageable; it's steep and covered with loose rocks and pebbles.

Creepy Baby bounds ahead of us. He clambers onto a shale boulder, which puts him at eye level with me. "Inside, it's almost entirely red. I found another cave that's turning, too." He gestures west, into the mist. "Over that way. It's a smaller cave. I haven't found any more with your magic in them—just the two."

I narrow my eyes on the ghost, half talking to myself. "And... why Tet? There are caves throughout Mieira. Plenty of stone to pick from. Why come here?"

To this cesspool, specifically.

I have a few spare ideas, but I'd rather hear from one of Tet's long-time residents.

Creepy Baby blinks at me. "It's *your* magic. You tell me, witch."

"It's *your* realm, you little fuck." I roll my eyes and turn back. "Well, then. Let's have a look." I take hold of Esclamonde's narrow wrist. Butter takes my shoulder, then I float us below, avoiding the jagged shale. This far from the green sink, I have no trouble accessing my magic.

Creepy Baby waits at the cave's entrance as we approach.

Instead of waltzing inside, I set my hand on a jutting rock—

With a flick of my other hand, I send illuming magic through the cave. The spell runs along its tunnel-like ceiling, leaving pocks of flickering, peachy light throughout. Inside, the red stones are brighter in hue.

I flick my hand again. This time, sensing magic travels along the cave's walls, hugging them like ivy and cruising like the wind. Though a bit vague, sensing magic gives me an impression of the cave's size, shape, and constitution.

It forms an asymmetrical loop; if we entered and branched off to the left, we'd eventually rejoin the main tunnel and wind up at the same entrance. No other ways in or out.

With a hmph, I stand back on one foot, staring into the rough and unpromising cave. It's nothing like the refinement of Hella—not even a hint of decorative carvings or a rounded fountain.

And yet, I can sense Vex's magic clinging to the stones, driving deep into them. I can feel it soaking into the shale; it's similar to how I fill an empty cylinder with dove, except a bit more laborious.

A bit more lasting, too.

Creepy Baby wanders inside, glancing back. "So? What do you think?"

My palm runs along the coarse walls.

A shiver runs up my spine.

I sense something in these rocks besides my magic—and it brings a smile to my face.

I don't know what it is, but it's as potent as a demigod.

Not like a nymph demigod, though. Not like a wielders' Landmark, either.

It's gazing from the red shale; it knows I'm here.

I tilt my head, listening closely for the graze and bass of Vex's magic. Whatever powerful being is here, I can suddenly sense it lingering in the air, in the muddy fields surrounding us, in the damp mist looming all around. In the weak strands of grass and their soaked roots.

Whatever source of power I sense, it might be alive or long dead, or maybe still dying, or possibly in gestation.

I don't know.

All I know is that it's all around us—above, below, within, without.

"Oh..."

My fingers expand, fitting against the cold stone.

"Skull?" I whisper. "I think I... feel you."

Whatever the fuck Skull is, it's vaster than a city, much more tangible than a ghost.

Whatever Skull is, it doesn't seem to mind that Vex's magic is here, seeping into its core one shale pebble at a time.

CHAPTER 3

DAWN

SAMSON

Hetnazzar sits and stares northward.

The demigod has remained in the same position since dusk fell hours ago: facing the city with total focus. Warm city lights and cool moonslight trace its blue-black fur and its blue-black eyes.

From the low hilltop where we've been resting, Luz is clearly visible, as are the tops of the columns that line the temple district where the Septima and Irme Rivers join into the Mieira River.

Like my demigod, I face the city.

I'm little more than a ghost.

I can't feel my body or mind after weeks of marching back north.

Part of me is still worried I might be dead.

For over a month, I've trudged north in Hetnazzar's shadow with Hadadrimmon at my side.

The arrangement has been straightforward enough.

We set up camp at night; the demigod leaves and returns later with a fresh kill. By daylight, it leads us to fruit-bearing groves and unattended farmhouses. Hadadrimmon has been less hesitant to steal than me, slipping inside barns and storehouses before returning with bags full of grains and produce.

He and I have spoken little since the incident in Bellator.

Still, I like to think we're friendly.

He wakes me from the nightmares. He hands me rags to dry my sweat. He keeps our campfires small, having sensed quickly that the fire bothered me, and stamps them out as soon as our food is cooked. He packs our shared satchel (also stolen) when my mind goes blank. He rambles about nothing when my gaze locks on the horizon and refuses to move.

Now, he stands beside me, hands on his hips.

Like me and my demigod, he watches Luz's lights twinkle in the distance.

"You said you had allies in Luz, right?" The wolf brushes his tangled hair with his fingers. Like most southerners, he uses silver hair clips to part his hair into braids. Each is etched with unique designs; he's explained them multiple times, but I don't remember what they symbolize. "Hetnazzar must have taken us here for a reason."

I stare ahead, conflicted.

I imagine Helisent drinking in Soulless, jewelry twinkling in the candlelight and flecked with droplets of brandy.

I gaze up at my demigod.

The great wolf turns, staring over its nose at me.

Its blue-black eyes hum with peace, with the weight of Night, as they bore into mine.

I trust that Hetnazzar guided us here on purpose. I'm an extension of the demigod as my generation's Kulapsifang and Afador. Hetnazzar knows the red witch is the most powerful being in Mieira; he will have known her from my dreams, possibly from the Vexen magic that toils around my heart and keeps me alive.

Still...

I turn back toward Hadadrimmon. "We can't waltz into a city without a destination—or a place to hide. Remember Halfleet? A whole mob came running when they caught our scents. The only thing keeping them from stringing us up was Hetnazzar."

We'd sprinted back to camp to find Hetnazzar lounging near our shared satchel, sharp white fangs bared at our pursuers. Even then, the mob stuck around; a few wolves appealed to Hetnazzar to let them have us.

"The Afadors don't represent your interests anymore, my great demigod," the pack leader had said, kneeling near the demigod. "The Afadors disgrace your rule and realm."

Hetnazzar's only response was a low growl.

We didn't sleep that night, but we were still whole when dawn arrived, and then we walked northward once again.

That was three weeks ago.

The demigod turns its head back to Luz with a long sigh. I follow its gaze—

I'm too nervous to waltz into the city alone.

I can't confirm Helisent is actually close, and I don't have enough allies in Luz to chance wandering in.

At my side, Hadadrimmon struggles with his silver decals, pressing them into his half-tangled hair. "Hetnazzar could walk us a bit closer, no?" With only the half-full moons above and no fire between us, his features are obscured.

I glance at the demigod. "Sure, but it doesn't look like that's going to happen."

"Let's give him a minute."

"*Him?* Hetnazzar is neuter." I've spent most of our days wordless. Thankfully, Hadadrimmon has so many misguided ideas that they rile me to speech. Without his idiotic comments, I'd likely be non-verbal.

"Did you forget that I'm part Afador?" Hadadrimmon grunts. "Who's to say I'm wrong?"

"Me. You're wrong. Our demigod is neuter. If anything, it's female. Have you ever met a motherless wolf?"

"No. Never met a fatherless one, either."

"You know what I mean."

"No, I don't."

With a quick huff, Hetnazzar shifts its head toward a shadowy stretch of oaks. They cover the gradual decline that leads to Luz. Ribbons flutter from many branches, likely in celebration of the recent harvest. Though we left the first throes of autumn behind us in Velm, the cool and windy season hasn't quite begun in Mieira.

I squint toward the trees.

A shadow shifts within; something is coming.

I glance at the satchel that Hadadrimmon holds; it carries our only weapon, a rusted hammer. Without any other options, we've taken to standing close to Hetnazzar and baring frowns at the unknown. When we escaped Bellator, we had only our clothes and wits; since then, we haven't accrued much else.

I watch the shadows beneath the oaks for movement. I take in large, thorough breaths—

The being who approaches is a wolf.

I can't see them, but I recognize their ala on my second inhalation.

Relief flashes through me—

I know this wolf.

Gautselin Mort.

Or maybe it isn't relief. It's a remnant of relief.

(That's all I have anymore. Remnants of emotions.)

(The remnants of whoever Samson was before... before... before...)

"Whoever is coming, they have a low count," Hadadrimmon says.

"I know this wolf. He's a friend." The remnant of relief I felt flattens. *Is Gautselin a friend?* I can't quite remember. "I think."

A few minutes later, we catch sight of him beneath the oak trees. He rushes across the roots, snapping twigs and rustling the grass and talking to himself. When he finally catches sight of Hetnazzar, he staggers out of the shadows and sinks to his knees, eyes widening on our demigod; it doesn't look like he notices us standing near its haunch.

He breaks into a string of Velmic prayers and blessings; the words twist in my ears like curses.

De segen it tauma-kuro Kelnazzar. Bless the black Night.

De segen anata-no aiga, Hetnazzar. Welcome to my home, Hetnazzar.

The demigod stands and approaches the wolf, leaving me and Hadadrimmon exposed. Gautselin watches, mouth agape. When he finally notices me and Hadadrimmon, his eyes flit wildly from the demigod to where we stand. His open mouth wavers, like he can't find words.

His eyes flit back to my scalp—once, twice, thrice.

I keep forgetting they shaved my head.

I'd been too exhausted and shattered to notice when I woke in the dungeon in Bellator Palace that my scalp was shaved clean. I've been too distraught and spent since then to dwell on it—or the crescent scar near my collarbone.

A bite from Clearbold; the end of my dignity.

The same with my torcs; all gone.

"*Lekeli Kelnazzar.*" Gautselin sets his hands on his thighs as Hetnazzar retreats to its sitting position near us. Warily, it watches me and Hadadrimmon. "I've been having nightmares... and Hetnazzar... my demigod... and my Kulapsifang... oh, no."

My words lock in my throat, forming a lump.

This is the first friendly wolf we've encountered.

I haven't had to explain my bad fortune yet.

My absolute humiliation.

My utter shame. My scarred body.

My packlessness. Hairlessness. Torclessness.

"We need shelter and food," Hadadrimmon calls over in my silence. "Can you offer it without putting yourself at risk?"

Gautselin rambles from where he kneels in the grass, "I have all the shelter in the world. And plenty of food. Where I live, corridors lead to secret passages—and even those have unexpected turns. Come, I'll take you to Coil. Do they talk about Coil in Velm? Ah, look at your hair. I haven't seen silver clips like those in years. You're from the south, then. I guess no one has heard of Coil in the deep south."

Slowly, Gautselin stands. He bows to Hetnazzar, then gestures into the midden of oaks. "If we move fast enough, no one will be able to track your scents. Not before I mask them with dove at Coil. I didn't bring any dove with me... I've been absentminded lately... it's driving Chari up the walls... but the nightmares... I thought the nightmares were nothing. But our demigod travels by dreams, doesn't it?"

Gautselin spares one more bow for Hetnazzar. The demigod huffs, jerking its nose toward the city in the distance.

With that, Gautselin hustles downhill toward the grove. "Come on."

Hadadrimmon picks up our satchel, and we trail our guide. But I turn back before the shady woods cut us off.

Hetnazzar stares at me, as though expecting I might be hard to shake.

My feet root into the ground as Gautselin leads Hadadrimmon away.

You will be safe with her, Samsonfang whispers into my mind.

My fangself is the only part of me not destroyed by the incident in Bellator. The only part of me not reduced to remnants.

I stare into Hetnazzar's eyes, waiting for a stronger sign.

Go, Samsonfang repeats. ***Find her.***

I bow my head to Hetnazzar, tempted to promise to retake my realm soon. I bite back my words in the next second, wondering if the demigod wants that. After all, it's depositing me in Mieira—out of my territory and far from my capital.

I clear my throat. "I hope this isn't goodbye forever, great demigod."

Hetnazzar jerks its head toward the city again, a huff in its throat.

I turn away with a sigh, then hustle to catch up with the pair.

Gautselin staggers a few steps ahead of us, looking back to squint at us in the darkness. His eyes are wet and large, traced by the distant city lights that drift beneath the dark trees.

He reeks of dextro and myrrh and several sexual alas and ale.

Hadadrimmon leans closer to him, sniffing with all his might. "Coil is a brothel, then?"

"It's a *pleasure house*. I have two rooms made entirely of mirrors. I even have a selkie. He comes every other weekend. You just missed him. I'll get you both set up in the tower. It's the biggest room, lots of chairs, and not too many peepholes..."

Gautselin rambles on.

Hadadrimmon looks from the wolf to me often, as though expecting an explanation.

We keep walking.

The tower smells like dust and wood and bird nests.

Hadadrimmon and I wander inside as Gautselin holds open the door.

The pitched-black room is suitably large for two wolves, especially compared to the other small chambers we passed. Even better, it's a floor higher than the rest of Coil, which means it's spared from most of its scents—though its symphony of hedonism leeches up from the floorboards with gusto.

Gautselin runs into something as he fumbles with a match. Hadadrimmon and I shuffle around the room, feeling at its angles in hopes of finding a chair.

"Why are the matches always soaking fucking wet?" Gautselin throws the box to the ground with a curse. Then he leaves the room, the door hanging open behind him. His feet pound down the staircase nearby. "*I smell you!*"

After an hour of trailing the high wolf, his outbursts aren't nearly as distressing.

Using the subtle light from the hallway, I shuffle around to find a seat and then guide Hadadrimmon to one. The wooden chairs are dusty, but they're at least dry. Hadadrimmon sinks into his with a deep groan. Our shared satchel sits on the ground between his legs.

Gautselin rushes back into the room a moment later. I can't tell who he holds—just that he's got a squirming nymph caught between his hands.

"Hands off, Gotti!" the nymph grunts.

"Just get in here!"

"My *moons*, you're drunk—"

"Light the candles, oread!"

My nose twitches as the oread's familiar ala fills the room.

"Back off me! I'll tell Helisent—"

"Onesimos?" I ask.

The nymph shoves Gautselin, then snaps his fingers. The room's dozen candles flicker with light, outlining the room's cluttered mess of boxes. Gautselin turns to shut the door while Onesimos straightens his bloodred tunic and skirt. He looks from me to Hadadrimmon, then turns back to Gautselin.

"Throwing me into a dark room with three wolves?" Onesimos tsks. Like Gautselin, he smells suitably drunk and high for a night at Coil. A feather sticks out of his vermillion afro, and a streak of oil shimmers on his arm. "And what do you need to show me, aside from..."

We lock eyes.

He freezes, then wanders a bit closer.

I think I should be jealous of the oread—he's Helisent's longest-running lover. I've seen the witch light candles like him, and I know exactly how her magic learned that trick. Instead, I'm struck by how small his frame is, from his wrists to his neck. And how soft his warm brown skin looks.

He narrows his eyes. "That's... you, right? Samson 714 Afador?"

I clear my throat. "I'd like to see the witch."

Gautselin elbows Onesimos. "You have one of the stars, right?"

Onesimos gives me the once over, then turns to the unnumbered wolf. "Are you both stupid? Bring her dove. We'll clean him first. Then I'll throw the star." Onesimos turns his gaze toward Hadadrimmon. With each second, his features tighten with concern. "You should probably get out of here, my dear wolf."

"He's with me," I explain. "He's not going anywhere. Throw the star, Onesimos."

The oread shakes his head, then lowers his voice. "I'm sorry for whatever evil has befallen you, my dear Kulapsifang. But if I summon the witch and she sees you like this, she will shadow to Bellator, level the city, and then ask questions." He blinks at me; the moment seems very long and slow. "Or she might look to your left and see a wolf she doesn't know, and decide he's like all of those who have hurt you, and decide that he's going to be held accountable for this." He turns to where Gautselin waits by the door, "Get the dove, Gotti. She'll kill me if she thinks I didn't throw that star fast enough."

Gautselin nods, then he slips out of the room.

Hadadrimmon groans loudly as he stands from the chair. "I'll wait outside. Sounds very nice, whoever this witch is."

The wolf leaves; Gautselin takes his place a moment later. He hands a glass cylinder of bloodred dove to Onesimos, then backtracks to join Hadadrimmon outside.

The oread looks down at the light-filled glass cylinder; it sloshes like liquid within. Its light casts across his wide, soft features, infusing his vermillion hair and pupils with added brilliance.

Helisent's dove.

"I'll clean you," Onesimos goes on in his too-quiet voice. "It won't take long. Then she'll come, okay?"

I don't say anything. I'm unhappy with the idea of one of Helisent's lovers casting her dove on me; I'm also weary of how her dove ended up traded to Coil.

(Or, at least, partly.)

(I only have the remnants of unhappiness and weariness, after all.)

He holds the cylinder with one hand and reaches out to clasp mine with the other. "Did you know that she comes to Coil to barter with Gautselin? It's nothing sexual. She just likes to cuddle. I think it's all the chest hair." Magic grazes me as the cylinder trembles in Onesimos's hand. Bass tingles across my body; it's hard not to sigh with relief when it passes through me like a soothing melody. "And probably the barrel chest. I heard she even made him smoke cigarettes, but then Chari didn't like that, so he had to stop."

Onesimos releases my hand and takes a step back to study me. I don't feel any cleaner, but I haven't seen my reflection in over a month. I'm not sure it matters anymore. My face is probably another remnant.

The oread waits for some kind of response.

I manage, "Really?"

"Really." Truly and deeply, Onesimos smiles. "You should know, this is always when I meet people. Right when everything they ever knew... changes shape. It has to do with rocks and metal and heat. Nymph stuff. You get it."

He reaches into a belt lined with pockets and pulls out a familiar red star. I freeze; it brings to mind Suleiman and his indigo-tinted fingers and his world-ending fire for a second.

"I'm going to throw this and hopefully get in a few words before Helisent finds you. She's been in Tet, by the way. Her, Butter, and Esteban just got back a week ago. She's doing well. Okay. Look alive."

He reaches forward to fix my collar with a few tugs.

He takes a step back to study me, then approaches to smooth my left eyebrow.

I swat his hand away when he reaches for a third time.

He sets his hands on his hips. "You're very quiet."

Then he turns and waltzes from the room, shutting the door behind him.

The floor creaks as he steps into the hallway. Grunting and moaning and laughter trickle in from the lower floors. The candles burn around me, too small to incite a panic but large enough that I avoid their glow.

I stare at my palms while I wait.

I've been hyper-focused on finding the witch over the last weeks—especially once I realized Hetnazzar was guiding us toward Luz.

Now, suddenly, I'm afraid.

What if... what if the witch loved the Kulapsifang more than she loved Samson?

Then something barrels into one of the wooden walls outside. Helisent curses, then giggles. "Coil? My darling nymph—"

"It's a different type of surprise. Maybe take a deep breath. Are you well?"

Her cajoling is over, replaced with a lashing tone. "What happened?"

"It's Sandro," he says. Footsteps thud toward the door. "Wait—hold on—*Helisent*—"

The door rips open, and Helisent West of Jaws steps into the room.

She gasps as she locks eyes with me. She looks around the room as though checking for others. In the next second, red light leeches from her eyes. Her features tense, then her form unleashes; at first, her six horns are like tricks of the light, outlined in red radiance. In the next, their glowing shapes are filled with coarse and unpolished horns.

I try to stand, but the witch barrels into me. She knocks me back into the chair and the boxes it sits against. Her tiny feet perch on my thighs as she half-stands and half-floats over me.

Her warm hands hold my cheeks while her wild eyes, spewing red light, flutter across my features. Her hands sweep above my cheeks and run along the prickly hair lining my scalp.

"Who did this?" she whispers, fast and livid. "We'll go now—"

"No," barks the oread from the door.

She turns and, loud enough that I flinch, screeches, "*Get out!*"

As he shuts the door, Onesimos murmurs, "That's misdirected."

She whips her head back to me. "Tell me. Tell me who did this. Tell me where..."

She turns and looks again, studying the room for something she missed.

I recognize the movement.

She's looking for Rex and Berevald.

I still do it constantly. When I wake in the mornings, I expect them to be at my side. When I eat, I expect to split my haul with them. When I sleep at night, I strain for the sound of their breathing. When I get nervous, I expect to feel them standing beside me.

Helisent's hands take hold of my tunic, jerking it once. "I'll take care of it, Samson."

She curls forward with a growl that turns into a sniffle.

I wrap an arm around her, stroking her back while she sets her head on my shoulder.

I nuzzle her forehead horn, letting my lips cross over its fibrous husk. I pull her closer, eager to feel her weight press against my chest and belly and legs.

Once upon a time, Helisent in her form would have terrified me.

Now, I need that fierceness.

I need these jagged horns to protect me, their red hue to terrorize my enemies, their stored magic and its unfathomable infrasound to save my soul.

Her dreadful power is my shelter.

"Vex will do it," she says, her head set against my collar. "Anything, Samson. Tell me. Tell me what you want. We'll go now."

She sits up straight.

I study her features, taking comfort in their nearness, their sameness. So much has happened in the months since I last saw her in Cadmium, like the world has been born anew. Destroyed anew. But her features remain. The delicate white of her eyebrows and eyelashes, the cupid's bow curve of her lips, the soft and supple skin of her broad cheeks and high cheekbones, her dewy and bloodred skin. She wears more jewelry than when I left her, a blend of copper and bronze pieces piled with colorful thread and other decals. A small hint of brandy and perfume. The familiar caress of her velvet robe.

"I'm sorry, Samson. I'm sorry, I didn't know..." Tears fill her eyes, falling down her cheeks one after the other. She clamps down on her lower lip; it trembles anyway. "I thought I'd sense something..."

She sets her hand flat over my left peck and the bundle of scar tissue. "Tell me something. Tell me anything. Please."

Then she strokes the back of my head, my neck. Her eyes flit across my features desperately, waiting for a response.

The remnants of emotions float around me. Like moons orbiting a planet, I know it's all there and whole—just out of reach.

I try to tell her something.

I don't know where to start.

They separated me from my pack; I let it happen. Suleiman waltzed into the throne room; I let that happen, too. I let him take your red star out of my satchel. I woke in a dungeon, Helisent, and I was already half-dead. I know the scent of Rex's corpse. Of Berevald's, too. I didn't get to look at their bodies. I do not know where their remains are.

Then my father bit me in front of my people.

I could not stop him.

And...

Neither did they.

"It's okay," she whispers. "Can I hear your voice? Let me hear your voice. Please, sweet wolf."

She shifts to sit in my lap, folding her legs and perching atop my thighs. With each passing breath, I start to feel safer. Not saner, but safer. Hetnazzar took me here; Helisent has me now.

I clear my throat. "Hi."

She sniffles. "Hi." She clears her throat, too. "I love you."

My heart thuds in my chest. *Thank the fucking moons.* The remnants of love shiver throughout me, like the reviving breath of an almost dead animal. My hand finds hers, and I squeeze it.

More of my voice returns with that sense of safety and love. "Serac and Argot have a foothold in Velm. They're working with Clearbold. Suleiman..."

Her nose curls. "I see."

I squeeze her hand again. "I love you." I hope she realizes that nothing makes sense right now. Everything is out of order. But I'm trying. "The red star..."

She runs her hand down my cheek. "Yes, my love?"

"Don't follow them. One of them... Bellator isn't safe. Brutatalika is in Mort. Sutnazzar lives nearby. Hetnazzar took us north. It left us here. We can't go back. I lost... I lost..."

For a long time, we sit in silence.

She strokes my face and my scalp; red fingers, red horns, red eyes.

Safety.

Eventually, I realize Helisent is using magic to separate us from the rest of Coil; I can't hear or smell the debauchery from the floors below. By contrast, I can smell Helisent's ala better with every moment we spend in the stuffy room. Mine, too—even if it's less potent without a head of hair.

When I fail to offer any more coherent statements, Helisent uses her finger to tilt my chin. I look into her eyes and she tells me, "You are tired."

"Yes."

"Then I'll put you under so you can rest. So long as it isn't against your will, I can use magic on you. Or if it bothers you... Is it okay if I wield... if I do it so you can rest?"

She knows.

She knows what Suleiman did.

I have no idea how, but maybe it's similar to alas. They leave a palpable residue sometimes, one that others can smell for weeks afterward.

I sink back further into the chair.

Wave after wave of embarrassment washes over me.

This may be the first remnant that becomes whole again in the presence of Helisent's safety: humiliation.

She will know I screamed.

She will know I begged for him to let me go.

She will know I was too weak to stop him.

She will know.

"*Shhhhhh,*" the witch purrs like she may know already. She lays her hands on my chest. She watches me with calm, dead eyes. "Close your eyes. I will never leave. I will be here. Close your eyes, Samson. When you open them, I will be here. I will never leave."

Her dead expression doesn't shift.

I study her eyes for a long time.

"I'm sorry."

She tilts her head. Her white braids shift between her massive, glowing horns. "Don't be sorry. I told you to close your eyes. That's all you have to do."

"I'm sorry, Helisent."

It's all there is: sorrow, the lament of my failures, the utter gravity of losing something that existed for 714 generations.

"Be sorry when you wake up. For now, rest." The hands on my chest start to warm, then a golden peace pours through me. It starts in my chest and oozes outward with each breath until it fills my body, from my toenails to the tips of my ears.

My breaths come long and deep.

My head relaxes against the chair's back.

My eyes start to drift shut.

"I'll make sure you sleep through dawn, sweet wolf."

We might already be dreaming, climbing through the yew.

All I know is that I smell her ala, I feel her weight and warmth against me, I hear each pitch of her voice.

"It's always pain," she whispers.

CHAPTER 4

POLITICAL ANIMAL

HELISENT

Honey Baby,
How do both of us know how to swim, but you never learned? You could have
told us you didn't know. It's a pretty basic life skill. (What other important shit
don't you know?)
The Boys

I hold Samson's sleeping face between my hands.

My fingertips press into his cheeks as tears slip from my eyes. They trickle down my chin and fall onto his collar.

His lips are relaxed, his jaw loosening with each passing second. Only his deep-set eyes twitch, blue-black eyelashes flickering as though he's dreaming already. My fingertips trace his features as I remind myself he's safe now.

I run my hand across his spiky, short hair. He looks like a new man without his long, thick mane. Less patient, less kind, less loving.

My breath catches in my throat when I see the outline of a newly healed scar. It's on his collar, poking past his tunic. My finger traces it; I recognize the outline of a bite.

I take a deep breath.

He's safe now.

With me.

Aside from his shaved head and the scar, I can't find any direct sign of what he lived through. His body is leaner than it was in Cadmium months ago, his cheeks slightly gaunt. His hands are dirty—the line of brown beneath his short nails bothers me again and again and again.

They shaved his head; they left him unclean.

And it wasn't only wolves.

I can sense magic tangled around him.

First is my own; Simmy must have cleaned him before I arrived. The oread isn't very practiced at more complex spells like grooming. Even with a cylinder of dove, he's apt to miss dirt under the nails, wax in the ears, and other minute impurities.

The second source of magic is less certain, but I know it hums the same pitch as the House of Serac. I imagine it was Suleiman, Halcyon's father, who left his magic scattered around Samson's skull—but that's only because he mentioned the warlock by name. I'm not sure *what* the warlock did to him, and I have no idea how he got to Bellator.

Just that Samson's head is shaved and surrounded by a layer of Seracyd spell-work.

It feels like there's a sword plunged through my heart. I try to suck in a calming breath, but it's hard not to be taken back to Antigone seven years ago. I'd suffered a dual agony: losing my sister, and the betrayal of a lover. This almost feels the same. The loss of Samson's dignity, the fact that he was betrayed by his people.

The world has been cruel to me; I will not let it mistreat Samson, too.

Not how it did my sister.

The air hums around me with infrasound.

It shakes the planked walls of the tower room.

It silences the revelers on the floors below.

I slide off Samson, careful not to wake him.

I squeeze his hand so that he knows, even in sleep, I will never leave.

I turn for the door.

I open it and find three men standing in the hallway's heavy shadows: Gautselin, Onesimos, and a strange wolf. Circles dot their bodies with golden light; I forgot the tower room has so many peepholes.

I look at Gautselin first. He glances from my eyes to the walls, which are shaking violently with my magic. "Tell anyone he's here and I'll end you. I will go to Mort and find your—"

"No need to threaten me, Helisent West of Jaws," he says solemnly. If it weren't for the glaze of his eyes, I'd think he was sober based on his tone. "The Kulapsifang will have everything he needs."

His words do little to calm me. "Not even Chariovalda. Not until he's had time to rest. Do you understand?"

"I do."

"Go. I'll stay here and watch the door. He will need a large meal when he wakes up."

"Of course. Have mercy on the walls in the meantime, my dear witch." Gautselin beelines for the staircase at my back.

The second wolf, who is by far the largest specimen I've ever set my eyes on, takes a step in his direction, as though preparing to follow him. His long hair is tangled into braids, separated by silver clips. His eyes are deep-set like Samson's, but that's where the resemblance ends.

I raise my hand and bare my fingers at him.

He jolts, flattening his back against the wall with a thud. In the next second, he shifts forward, as though eager not to touch the shivering walls. His chest rises with heaving breaths as he looks from me to my hand.

Red light oozes from my eyes and trickles over the wolf's pale, tensed features. "We need to speak."

I look at Simmy next. He watches me with his chin lowered and a measured expression. "You can go. Don't tell anyone—"

"Or you'll threaten my family, too?" he shoots back, raising his eyebrows.

"Simmy—"

"You are misdirecting your anger." His lips almost smile, like he's delivering a punchline, but I know I've pushed him too far. He's never bothered by my words; only the volume with which I shout them. "And you're going to cause structural damage to Coil if you don't get ahold of yourself."

I know I yelled too loudly. I know my rage is frightening Coil's patrons.

But there's a sword plunged through my heart right now.

I swear to the fucking moons I hear crying echoing from the northwest again.

Quietly, I suggest, "*So then leave.*"

"*Gladly,*" he murmurs back, brushing past me to follow Gautselin down the stairs.

The nameless wolf watches him go with a stricken expression. I block the staircase in case he gets any ideas. Once Simmy has disappeared, I lower my hand.

"Where are Rex and Berevald?" I ask.

"*You* are Helisent West of Jaws?" His voice is deep, his words heavily accented. He must be from the far south.

"I could kill you one thousand times over, so let's not play games." With a forceful breath, I rein in my magic. With one last growl of bass, the walls fall still. I send halting magic toward the staircase in case anyone wanders up, then gesture the wolf toward the tower room. "Go inside and sit down."

He slides by me and disappears into the dimly lit room. I follow him and shut the door, then head to the shelves near the shuttered window. Half are lined with dusty bottles. With a huff, I uncork the first one I see, bring it to my lips, and throw my head back to guzzle.

Whatever liquor it is, it's strong and herbal.

I gulp until I feel like I'll heave, then lower the bottle.

The wolf sits in the empty chair next to Samson. He warily looks from me to my lover, whose snoring mounts with each breath. He focuses next on the half-empty bottle in my hand, then glances at my eyes.

I've reined in my magic, but not my form.

In an attempt at goodwill, I cross the room and hand the wolf the bottle. "I think it's schnapps. Tell me where Rex and Berevald are."

He glances at Samson once, then licks his lips. "Dead. Clearbold set up surprise waricons. He made his other packmates do it— someone named Pietrangelo, someone else named Riordon."

That will settle in later; maybe never.

Rex and Berevald are dead; Samson somehow escaped after facing an unknown period of torture. I shake my head, attempting to piece that together. A surprise waricon, a bite from Clearbold, a torture session from one of Ezit's Hosts...

How the fuck did Samson survive that?

It doesn't leave many possibilities. "I'm guessing Hetnazzar came for him?"

He gulps from the bottle, smacks his lips, then squints at the liquid sloshing inside. "Exactly. He threw us into a waricon first thing in the morning. Samson didn't have time to rest. He..." The wolf glances at Samson again, features stilling.

"How long did the warlock have him? The indigo warlock?"

The wolf stiffens. He takes a quick drink. "A long time."

"Like an hour or a month or—"

"A night. I never saw the warlock, but I smelled him. And I heard Samson. What he did to him. They brought him into the dungeon with me close to dawn. His head was shaved, but there wasn't a mark on him. No blood. No scars. Nothing. Then it was time for the waricon. He was losing. Clearbold bit him on the collar—the next bite would have been the neck, and he wouldn't have survived that."

The sword plunges deeper into my heart.

I feel at my neck, tracing the scar Pel left on my skin. In my form, it's easy to make out each fangmark.

I glance at Samson; I can see the pinkish mark on his collar from here.

My voice shakes. "And who the fuck are you?"

He finishes the liquor. "Hadadrimmon 342 Aithesson."

I rock back onto my heels; I hadn't expected that.

"I guess I need no introduction, then." His eyes narrow. "You know a lot about Velm, witch."

I stare at him for a long time. I don't know what to do with the fact that this is a semi-Afador. That Rex and Berevald are really gone. That this wolf is the only semblance of a pack Samson has left.

I take a deep breath and try to be nice. Or maybe just reasonable. "Would you like to sleep?"

"Yes." He slides his eyes toward Samson one last time. "I'd also love a large meal when I wake up. Maybe some tobacco, too. We've been out for weeks." He presses his back against the chair, eyes tracking me as I approach. "I thought witches only grew four horns."

To his credit, he doesn't flinch when I flatten my hand against his chest. Warmth tingles in my palm as healing magic thrums from my body into his.

I wait for his eyes to slip shut. "Who cares what you think?"

He laughs once, lips spreading into a smile, before his facial features slacken and he slumps in the chair. I keep my hand over his chest, letting my healing magic work through his body like it did with Samson's. I find a similar degree of exhaustion and malnutrition; nothing rest won't fix.

When he's knocked out, I backtrack to Samson.

I slide into his lap and lay my head against his shoulder. It's not comfortable with my horns in the way, but it's a bit more manageable after I use lifting magic to wrap his arms around me.

I keep thinking I'll relax and drop my form.

But I can't.

My body thrums with love.

With the urge to kill.

Samson speaks more the next day.

But he doesn't eat as much as he should.

I've seen the wolf put down a meal that would have lasted me a week after a long journey. Now, even after months of unending travel to and from Velm, he stares at his plate for thirty minutes before knocking his food around with a fork. I start to barter with him for tobacco; he gets a cigarette for every satisfactory meal he finishes. It works until Hadadrimmon starts sharing his stash of loose tobacco and rolling papers.

On the second day, I carve little holes in the vaulted ceiling so their smoke doesn't clog the room. I bring in soft fabrics and pillows so they can make beds on the hardwood.

I even barter with a local band to practice in the room below so the wolves won't get bored. I bring them cards, books, and plenty of sweets.

With Gautselin and Onesimos sworn to secrecy, the Kulapsifang and his cohort are safe.

For now.

By the third day, the pair is eager to stretch their legs. They stare out the window when I'm not there to entertain them. Gautselin denies that two wolves are being kept in his tower room, but word spreads like a virus in the market district. Soon, rumors circulate that he's training the pair in the art of pleasure.

By the fifth day, the pair are rested and cognizant enough to craft a plan—which is good, because Gautselin isn't sure how long he can keep the nymphs from investigating.

"Are you sure about this?" Samson asks when he's finished explaining. "If you're uncomfortable with shadowing magic, I don't want to push you. We can start by sending a letter to Mort."

Though I'm not sure I can deliver on their request to shadow us to the coastal Velmic city, I'd anticipated a request like this. His wife is in Mort, after all.

I even brought the wand, which weighs heavily in my bottomless bag.

I tap against the bag's wooden clip as I look from Samson to Hadadrimmon. "I can't guarantee we'll make it to Mort in a single go —especially not if we're bringing your sidekick.

"Back in Vex, I could shadow easily because we were in my House and close to my Landmark. Mieira and Velm aren't steeped in my magic. I know Coil well enough to shadow here... but Mort? That's different. Very different."

Hadadrimmon huffs as he sits on his bedding, watching me and Samson while he brushes and braids his hair. Since the pair arrived, he's claimed half the tower room for himself. "Just leave me here. I don't think anyone downstairs would notice an extra body."

"It's not safe to stay here alone. Gautselin is unnumbered. The local pack leaders don't respect him even when he's not harboring an enemy." Samson looks from the wolf to my bottomless bag. "Did you bring the... did you bring it?"

I cross my arms rather than call up the wand. "Yes, I have the wand. But... I need to think about how to do this."

I glance at Hadadrimmon; the fewer beings who know about the wand, the better. Since I returned from Zarzynn, I've kept it hidden away in my bottomless bag. Only Parsifal has touched the piece—and I'd like to keep it that way.

Vex is much greater than a simple wand, but this limestone rod is the core of my demigod.

A stray wolf really shouldn't be near it.

"Like I said," I go on, "I've never been to Mort—or any part of Velm. I also don't have any items from the city. Memories or keepsakes would simplify shadowing quite a bit, but since that's not possible, *you* are my only connection to the city."

I raise my eyebrows, studying Samson.

He still isn't speaking often or eating enough, but he's regained the color in his cheeks these last few days. The sterling twinkle in his deep-set eyes and the stubborn, annoying way he stands with his arms crossed.

(I'd once confused his timidity for brooding; if I didn't know him better, I'd confuse his desperation for conviction.)

Hadadrimmon snorts. "Samson is your only connection to Mort? Well, it seems like you two are *plenty* close, so—"

He lurches forward, clutching his neck.

I don't look away from Samson as I maintain the smothering spell on the wolf's throat.

"Are you positive he needs to come with us?" I ask. "The Southie is a liability."

Samson paces a few steps. He glances at Hadadrimmon, who's still squirming and gripping his throat. "Can we talk privately? Also, you shouldn't say Southie. It's derogatory."

I release Hadadrimmon from the smothering spell. Then I cast a larger one around Samson and me, sealing in our conversation—and sealing out Hadadrimmon's passionate cursing.

"Yes, my dear Kulapsifang?"

Samson wanders closer to me, chin lowered. "Are you sure you're comfortable doing this?"

Since he arrived at Coil in the dead of night and I shadowed to meet him, we've hardly had any privacy. Not with Samson staying hidden away in the tower room, not with Hadadrimmon lounging a few feet away. Certainly not with Samson's trauma still so fresh. Even if we'd had privacy during these days, I doubt I would have heard more out of him.

He's wounded.

I know what this is like.

I shrug; *does he not understand?* "I already told you I'd never leave."

"I don't know what will happen once we get to Velm."

He's mentioned that a few times, but I'm still unclear what he means. *Maybe the Leolites have already taken Mort? Maybe Brutatalika will leave him because of what happened in Bellator? Maybe Sutnazzar is already leading a rebellion?*

I take a breath and stare into his eyes, speaking slowly, "You got on that ship in Hypnos to find me even though you had no idea where it was going. Do you think that means nothing to me? Do you think you aren't worth saving, too, Samson?"

"In case you're a little unfamiliar with how this part goes—you're lost, you're broken, you don't know which way is up, and you have a long journey ahead of you. But if I could find my way out of the darkness, so can you. Here's a hint, my sweet wolf..." I lean toward him and bat my lashes. "Follow the glowing horns."

His tense expression loosens.

I offer a quick smile. "Like I said, you're my only connection to Mort. Lucky for us, Vex is plenty aware of your existence. I don't think it's a stretch for you to guide us through the shadow. Or, at least, I don't think it's dangerous to try. If anything, we'll end up someplace familiar to me."

Samson nods. "Okay. Let's try."

I reach into my bottomless bag and pull out the smooth wand. With a sigh, I lift the sealing spell around Samson and me. Hadadrimmon glares from his bedding while I focus on the shadow banking the room's eastern wall.

The darkness is hefty, but just to be sure, I fling a hand toward the room's single window. Its shutters close with a loud clack, leaving us in a deep shadow.

Samson takes his place at my shoulder.

Hadadrimmon stands and joins us. "I didn't like that, witch. How would you like—"

A low comment in Velmic from Samson cuts him off.

"Also, how does shadowing work?" Hadadrimmon asks in the next second, ignoring Samson. "We don't hear about advanced spells like this in the far south."

"We use the shadow like a portal, and my magic takes us wherever we want." I roll my shoulders. "Ideally."

I stare at the shadow, clutching the wand. Though the limestone is warm under my touch, it's not thrumming with unfathomable power like it did on the triplemoon in Ezit.

It feels like an ordinary stone as I raise it and point it at the shadow.

I adjust my grip and say, "Vex, we need to go to Mort. Mort is a coastal city in Velm. Samson knows it well. Listen to the sound of his voice. He will guide us." I glance over my shoulder. "Tell us where to go, Samson. Describe one of the estate's rooms. Be specific. Very specific."

Samson begins, "Vex, I ask for passage into Mort's Estate. I have lived in this estate throughout my life. My ala has filled its walls and drifted to its ceilings. I ask for your magic to portal us through this shadow and into the shadow of the western lounge."

The wand begins to thrum in my hand.

Vex's bass emanates from the stone and lightly shakes the boxes around us, the window's shutters, the shelves lined with bottles.

I stare ahead at the shadow, acutely aware that Vex is responding to Samson's command.

I glance at him from the corner of my eye. He looks calm and focused.

Unaware that he's guiding my magic.

That my magic is listening.

(Interesting. *Very* interesting.)

He goes on steadily, "There is a fireplace on its southern wall. In its center is a thick rug and many sitting cushions. A golden bowl sits near the fireplace, full of cedar incense. Vex, I ask that you take us into this room."

The shadow in the room's corner gurgles, almost like boiling water. Like a magnet pulled to its opposite, the wand guides me toward it.

"Now," I say with my first stride.

Samson sets his hand on my shoulder, Hadadrimmon behind him. The latter curses as we pierce the darkness. I'm relieved to sense the familiar croon of Vex's bass—but I keep moving, propelling us into its infrasound and, hopefully, toward Samson's destination.

The shadow surrounds us for a second.

Then the blinding hue of sunlight on shined white marble breaks through.

I follow it out of the shadow and onto a thick rug. But my feet tangle, like I'm falling downhill. I double-step just in time to catch myself from falling onto my belly.

Samson barrels into my shoulders and head in the next second, throwing my body downward.

I slam onto the carpet, yelping once and tensing as I prepare to be crushed by two adult wolves. A second battering force rams into Samson, knocking the air from his lungs. His hands hit the rug on either side of me. He raises himself in the nick of time to block the oncoming impact of Hadadrimmon's body.

After a curse from both wolves, Hadadrimmon slides off Samson's back onto the rug beside me. He curls downward, body buckling as he groans a few words in Velmic.

Samson rises onto his knees, hovering above me, and looks around. "Are you okay? This is it. We're here."

I nod, half-stunned. *Holy shit, I can't believe it worked.*

Samson wraps his hand around my arm, hauling me upward with him. I straighten my robe and dust myself off as Hadadrimmon rolls on the carpet, clutching his balls and moaning.

I pat him on the shoulder. "Sometimes my infrasound bothers the boys."

Then I look around eagerly.

I've never been to Velm before.

The lounge is cozier than I'd expected. Like all Velmic estates, the ceiling is at least twice as tall as the room is wide, creating a sense of cold grandeur. The fireplace is empty, but the golden bowl of cedar incense chugs away, filling the room with a strong and earthy scent. Sitting cushions are scattered around a white fur rug. A few ornate tapestries hang from the walls, sagging toward the ground heavily. A narrow doorway is closed off with a navy curtain. Another wall is entirely windowed; there, a second curtained door leads out onto a terrace. The marble veranda outside is at least twice the size of the lounge.

Samson ambles toward the curtain, then wanders outside into a fresh and gentle morning.

My mouth falls open as I approach the windowed wall; I hadn't expected a view like this.

Past the veranda's banister, Mort stretches out before us, cubic and pale and ending in a dark seam of ocean. Three-story and two-story buildings line the streets in tidy arrangements. Near the dark-sand beach, the structures seem to flatten to single stories.

I duck past the curtain and step onto the terrace.

I recoil with a gasp as the biting cold grazes my bare skin. I shiver when it fills my lungs and drives into my velvet robe. The summer hasn't ended in Mieira, but it's clearly autumn here. Possibly Night.

With another tremble, I pull my layers tight over my shoulders and trail Samson toward the banister. From here, the city reminds me of Luz's vast and clean temple district.

It's incredibly beautiful.

Pristine might be the right word.

Everything... matches.

The broad avenues that lead to the estate are particularly neat and uniform. They look like they were taken from a picture book.

Lumber pokes from the rooftops in perfect lines. Most edifices are decorated with slabs of shiny marble. The white marble is differentiated by its streaking; some have brown marks, others gray or black or pink or reddish. Even the trees and shrubs seem perfectly arranged, trimmed into rounded shapes, and sat in gridded plots along the sidewalks. Golden accents catch the light like pools of sunset, carved into decals along the storefronts, lampposts, fountains, and sculptures.

This early, Mort is asleep. Only a few shepherds are up, driving their flocks through the streets close to the ocean.

Samson sighs as he stares across the city, as though exhausted. I can't believe he doesn't seem affected by the chill; his arms are bare.

He turns to me, a glint in his eye and a tired smile on his lips. "Welcome to Velm, Helisent West of Jaws."

So many sentiments pass through my mind, but all I manage is a similarly tired smile.

He goes on, "I need to go inside—can you wait in the lounge with Hadadrimmon?"

I nod, then follow him back inside.

He walks around Hadadrimmon, who's now sitting up and looking around, then continues into the hallway. The curtain swings shut in his wake.

I make it to the rug before a wave of fatigue passes over me. Pain ratchets through my head next. I sink onto one of the cushions near Hadadrimmon.

When my mouth fills with saliva, I slump onto my hands. "I need a drink of water. That was... a *big* spell."

He huffs in response, then glances at the curtain that leads into the hallway. In the distance, I hear battering footsteps and quick words. These are followed by further commotion: shouting, a few gasps, more shouting.

I can't understand Velmic, but I listen all the same. It's clear Samson doesn't have any enemies in the estate; their surprise is delighted.

I listen to the racket as I battle my nausea.

I'm pleased that our attempt to shadow worked so well—but I'm not surprised it's taking its toll. The journey from Luz to Mort on foot would have taken more than two months.

Eventually, a female wolf wanders in. She exclaims something in Velmic when she sees us, then chats with Hadadrimmon. I barely notice their exchange. I'm still clinging to the cushions and trying not to throw up on the spotless fur rug.

Eventually, Hadadrimmon hands me a glass of water. It helps soothe my stomach, as does the mint tea the female attendant brings us after. Next is a large lunch consisting of a few meat and bread plat-ters. It doesn't take me nearly as long to regain my appetite as I would have thought.

While we munch, Hadadrimmon explains, "The attendant said there's a meeting happening between the Alphas and the local pack. They'll come back for us in the morning."

I glance at the doorway. The heavy curtain has been pulled across it for hours. At least the balcony offers us a view and fresh air, but... "We're not staying the night here."

Hadadrimmon tosses the rest of a meat pie into his mouth. "You sat there for an hour and a half holding your head. You'd pass out if you tried to shadow us back. And who says I want to go with you? Samson might be making a case for me to stay in Mort. If that's true, I will happily *never* shadow again and stay the rest of my days in this palace."

"It's not a palace, it's an estate. And what about your family?"

He swallows his bite with a dry laugh, then plucks a few dark grapes from their stem. "What do you think they did with the rest of my family? Blew them kisses after they dragged me to Bellator? Malachai was going to kill me, the *last* Afador, after Clearbold got rid of Samson."

I still can't get over the fact that I didn't sense anything. Considering Vexen magic keeps Samson alive, I figured it would have alerted me if he were near death.

Not even a nightmare. Not even a stray thought.

That wasn't the case for Samson. When he sailed to Zarzynn, he could sense my distress.

"Then why stay here?" I ask Hadadrimmon. "Make a family in Luz. That's what I did after my sister died. You met Gautselin. Unnumbered wolves are relatively safe in Luz. There's a warlock, Itzifone, who also looks out for them. You wouldn't be alone."

He gives me a vicious once-over. "What makes you think I'm unnumbered?"

I shrug, feeling suddenly timid. "I had just figured... since your torcs were taken..."

He makes a low, unimpressed sound. He avoids the topic, explaining, "I'd already been considering a move to Luz. It's not a terrible idea. Or, it wasn't until you shadowed me here."

I narrow my eyes, munching on a mouthful of grapes. "I don't get it."

"You don't have testicles."

I cackle. "I told you—you'll get used to it. Samson did. So did... You know... Rex and Berevald."

A long stretch of silence.

Hadadrimmon suggests, "Let's get me drunk next time just in case."

"What if we get drunk right now, too? Just in preparation." I study the spread of drinks and ornate dishes between us. "Did the lady-wolf not bring any booze? My fucking moons, you'd think I'd be offered a little dessert wine, at least."

Hadadrimmon grabs a large pitcher. I'd assumed the close-topped, silver piece was full of steaming tea. When the wolf lifts its lid and sets it between us, the scent of hard liquor wafts out and slaps me straight in the nostrils.

Hadadrimmon raises his eyebrows and wiggles them. "Moonshine. *Velmic* moonshine."

I cackle again. "Excellent. You didn't check for dextro, did you?"

"Dextro?" He huffs a laugh. "No. I would have smelled it."

I toss my hair over my shoulder and reach for an empty glass. "That's fine. I'm off it, anyways."

Hadadrimmon pours me a dribble of moonshine. Before I can correct him to fill the fucking glass, he lifts his cup. We clink them together, then throw our heads back to shoot the liquor.

I shout as flaming air spews from my eyes and nose and mouth.

I cough to clear my throat. "Oh, sweet death."

Hadadrimmon claps his hands as hard as he can, then barks something in Velmic. He clears his throat and shivers violently. "I've missed *masina*."

Then, like me, he reaches for the silver pitcher again.

"Maybe tap her shoulder," Samson suggests, voice low and sleepy.

"With what?" a woman whispers back.

"Your hand should be fine."

"*Should* be fine." The woman makes an uncertain sound. "Maybe I'll use a poker from the—"

"She wouldn't like that," Samson says.

I move my fingers first—just a tiny bit.

The voices stop.

I adjust slightly again. My head feels like it weighs a thousand pounds, and my mouth feels full of cotton. I almost open my eyes— but I can sense bright light filling the room.

I part my dry lips; it seems to take a great effort.

It feels like someone ran me over with a cart.

The woman says, "I think she's awake."

Something blocks out the light.

Samson says, "Good morning, Helisent."

I rally the courage to open one of my eyes. Backlit by bright light, it takes me a moment to realize Brutatalika is next to me. Her blue-black hair clings to her scalp, shimmering with fresh gel. Her eyes are like little burning coals, set deeply and designed to observe. Her lips are shapely and pink, tinted like the rouge in her pale cheeks.

Samson hovers over her shoulder with his lips pressed together, eyes jumping from his wife to me. Compared to her, he looks like a brute; he hasn't shaved his scruff, while his short hair makes him look untested and adolescent. At least he has his torcs back. They shimmer around his upper arms and neck.

The pair blink at me, features stricken.

Reality filters past my hangover, settling into place.

Right.

I'm in the Mortyd Estate, passed out on the fluffy rug.

Hadadrimmon must still be asleep; his peaceful snoring echoes from the other side of the room.

I close my eyes and relax back onto the rug. I try to figure out what to say. They could have at least let me wake up on my own.

After a few seconds, I manage, "Did you use the poker, Brutatalika?"

She huffs tensely. "*No—*"

"Kidding." I push my lips into a smile; even that hurts.

Then I force my eyes open again. Samson shifts out of place behind Brutatalika, leaving the light from the window to blind me. I recoil with a groan, trying to remember how much moonshine I drank last night compared to how much of my dinner I made it through.

Brutatalika shifts from her haunches onto her knees at my side. She sets her hands on her thighs, eyes dancing over me like she's not sure what to say or where to look.

I manage to haul myself up onto my elbows. "I know you'll probably push back on this, but if I could just have *one more little drink—*"

"No," Samson says from the other side of the room.

Brutatalika leans toward me, eyebrows bunched. The morning light catches on her golden torcs and earrings; they flash, threatening to blind me again. "Do you remember last night? When we came here after our meeting, you and Hadadrimmon were causing a ruckus on the terrace. Many in the city spotted you. We tried to bring you back inside to eat dinner, but you challenged Hadadrimmon to a waricon. That's very taboo, Helisent. Then you fell over where you were sitting. Hadadrimmon... well, Hadadrimmon didn't go down so easily."

Bits and pieces of the night float back into my mind.

One of the last things I remember is Hadadrimmon teaching me how to perform a chokehold, only to realize his huge neck was too big for my arm to hook around properly; I kept trying anyway. I recall nothing of a waricon challenge.

I rub the sleep from my eyes. "I think that wolf has a drinking problem."

Brutatalika rocks back, clearing her throat and glancing at the wall. "Yes..."

She glances over her shoulder next, as though desperate for help. On the other side of the room, Hadadrimmon lies on his back, limbs spread. Samson stands above him, feet planted at either side of the prone wolf's hips. The Kulapsifang slaps his cheek with one hand and splashes cold water with the other, dipping his fingers into a pitcher and flicking them at the wolf's face. He addresses him in Velmic between every other slap.

The Female Alpha turns back to me. "Why don't we leave the men?"

"What?" I squeak.

I don't have the wits to fight back if she attacks me now. I'll either kill her by accident, overdoing things in a state of hungover panic, or I'll be too indecisive, leaving her a perfect window to take hold of my neck and rip through my jugular.

"Breakfast is waiting for us in the other room. We'll wait for my packmates there." She straightens, raising her chin and looking suddenly authoritative. "I'd like you to join our meeting, Helisent West of Jaws. Is there some remedy that you take to cure your hangovers?"

"So, you want... join you? Breakfast?" I push myself into a sitting position, using floating magic since I'm half-tangled in my robe. I glance at Samson, desperate for him to step in and prevent his wife from isolating me in some distant room; he's still slapping a snoring Hadadrimmon. "Water is usually a solid start. For the hangover."

"Your banishment has been lifted, by the way. I should have started with that." She turns to grab a cup of water, then hands it to me."Velm needs your help. Desperately, it seems."

I take a sip and raise my eyebrows. "That's a striking proposition first thing in the morning. Usually, one would offer a witch a gift or glory or some other attractive bribe." I take another sip, desperate for a clear thought. "But I think we might be too knee-dip in shit for you to be handing out jewels just yet—or rubies, specifically, Brutatalika. *Rubies.*" One more sip, just slightly closer to sanity now. "And what about the waricon with Hadadrimmon? Someone needs to teach me how to wrestle if he's going to hold me to that."

"Please don't bring up the waricon." Brutatalika glances over her shoulder once more. Though Hadadrimmon has finally stirred, Samson keeps splashing him with water. "Women and men don't fight. Also... you aren't a wolf. That makes it even more inappropriate."

I gulp down the rest of the water, then flick my hand. It sets off my morning spell-work; hair-brushing, teeth-cleaning, face-washing, jewelry-tidying, and scent-freshening.

"Yes, but what if I'm exceedingly inappropriate?" Like I once did with Samson, I'd rather push my boundaries right here with her—in the daylight. And in front of Samson, who would presumably step in to mediate. "What, then? Do I still help you save Velm?"

"You would be making it much harder to save Velm since my husband would be obliged to fight on your behalf."

I blink at her.

My husband.

Oh?

Vomit stirs in my gut.

So she doesn't know I'm thinking about love or vomit, I smile wide and fake. "Does that mean if I challenge a female wolf, *you'd* be obliged to fight on my behalf?"

One of her lips twitches. "In theory, yes."

I huff. "Good to know. Well, then... first, you may feed me. Then, you may bribe me."

With a groan, I haul myself to my feet. I lean back to stretch, cracking my back and using magic to gather my robe. I let my stomach settle, full of water and masina and doubt. I ignore the men near the fireplace, the cedar incense the married Alphas must have lit.

With a heavy sigh, I trudge toward the door with the curtain tugged tight across it.

Brutatalika passes me, and I follow as she heads into the hallway.

I slow almost to a stop, my head tilting back as I study the massive estate around me.

Given that Brutatalika is almost as tall as Samson, her long legs put her strides ahead of me. She cruises through a vast hallway into another sitting lounge, passing room after room after room.

Ornate tapestries, heavy enough to bury me alive, hang from

almost every wall. The accents and furniture are similar to the Luzian and Cadmium Estates in terms of design and architecture. Many pieces are made of dark wood, others carved from marble. There are plenty of pale and brown furs, and even more golden accents and stitching.

I keep straining my neck to look up at the cavernous ceilings—I'm not sure how the wolves managed to build such a thing without magic. I'm also not sure why they'd bother. I could fit all three floors of my Luzian apartment building in one of the larger halls we pass through.

I chalk it up to a display of power.

Finally, Brutatalika leads us into a plain dining room. The low wooden table could seat at least twenty, but it's set for two.

It sits atop another fur rug with short and scratchy hair. A grand set of dark shelves covers one wall. The next is made entirely of glass, showcasing another view of a gray-skied Mort.

I follow Brutatalika to the table, happy with the simple meal. She wolfs down her food, then leaves the table to sit by the window with her back straight. It's almost a mirror of how Samson used to meditate in the mornings during our journey across Mieira.

I eat slowly, filling my stomach and letting my appetite build.

While I do, Brutatalika sits at the window in silence.

I try to figure out if I fucked things up with the Female Alpha this morning. I can't tell if she's ignoring me or simply focused on the day before her.

Hoping to make up for any oversteps, I offer, "Sorry for challenging Hadadrimmon to a waricon. I doubt he took it seriously."

She doesn't turn back to reply, "I have never seen such disorder inside an estate before."

"So... are we not getting off on the right foot? You're making it hard to tell."

"*Me?*" This time, she glances over her shoulder. Her eyebrows are tugged together, her coal eyes burning. "You're the one who threatened to bite a guest in my estate. You're the one who insinuated you'd start a conflict with a female wolf to see me fight a waricon for your honor."

She stares at me, waiting.

Fine, then.

"The list of deeds I've done for you is infinitely longer than the two little things you're bringing up. I thought you came into this room to bribe me." I take a deep breath, trying to figure out how to end this uncertain start. "Maybe we would benefit from some grimoire..."

Quickly, Brutatalika rises and takes her seat at the table. She reaches into a pocket in her harem pants and pulls out a small tin. She tips it over onto the clean marble between our plates, then gets to work separating two lines.

That's when it occurs to me for the first time—

That she is the last person to have slept with Samson.

I haven't touched him since our ships docked in Cadmium.

I sigh again.

I don't think I'm jealous, even if her beauty hurts me. I don't think it's wrong to share lovers.

Still, I'd prefer that Brutatalika be spared a secret affair. For her sake, for my sake, for Samson's. I keep secrets because they're useful and guarantee me things like safety, not because I particularly enjoy fooling others.

She leans down to snort her portion. She straightens with a long groan, holding her nostrils delicately. I move my half-empty plate out of the way, then clear my line.

Brutatalika gulps down her tea with another groan.

I do the same with my water, eager to kick the tangy drip on the back of my tongue. It's making me crave dextro.

"My name is Helisent West of—" Brutatalika pivots to the side and sneezes into the crease in her elbow.

With a sniffle, she straightens and looks at me.

"My name is Brutatalika 567—" I shift just in time, focusing the force of my sneeze on the empty cushion next to me.

Then I stare at Brutatalika and wait for her to ask me a series of highly inappropriate questions—just like Samson once did in a tavern east of Tet.

Instead, she starts speaking quickly, shoulders rising, "I had no idea what happened in Bellator. Word never reached Mort—which is surprising. It's been almost two months since Samson was attacked. Practiced messengers can cross the road between Mort and Bellator in a few weeks in this weather.

"If word hasn't spread, Clearbold wants to keep his coup a secret.

He must not have imagined that Hetnazzar would show up and help Samson. That makes sense. Clearbold is dumb how light is bright—everywhere, immediately, all at once."

Brutatalika's features twitch as she speaks. Like Samson, she's mastered the art of stony and unreadable expressions—but her features deviate at certain intervals. Her lips pinch and twist at 'word hasn't spread', while her eyebrows jump at 'come to help Samson'.

She goes on, "When Hetnazzar stepped into that waricon arena and saved Samson, it signaled three important things to those in Bellator. First, Hetnazzar supports the Afadors—he even saved Hadadrimmon, a distant relative from Malasuntra's bastard line.

"Second, Hetnazzar will not interfere directly in civil conflicts. Though our demigod saved Samson, it didn't take vengeance on the Leolites who sought to harm him. There have been similar precedents set in the past. The Leofsiges aren't the first wolves to attempt a coup —though they've gotten farther than any others.

"Third, if the Leolites win this conflict, it will not be based on spiritual superiority, which is what Clearbold wanted. That's why he had Samson's packmates kill Rex and Berevald. To display his influence and power. To show that Samson's pack was loyal to him first, and his son second.

"He wants to assume the position of the Afadors—but the Afadors weren't chosen by the people. The Afadors are like the nymph monarchs. Selected by a demigod. And when Clearbold tried to kill the Afadors, Hetnazzar *ignored* the Leolites to save Samson and Hadadrimmon. He will have no spiritual claim to this realm because of that.

"Instead, his power, should he take it, will come from brute force. And what is taken with brute force can always be retaken by more force. That's why it's so important for Velm to have the Afadors—to prevent fighting at the top of the food chain. Obviously."

Obviously?

I've gone over Velm's intricacies with Samson a few times, and he never spelled it out so clearly.

Oh, no.

She's smart. Real smart.

Brutatalika hangs her head and rubs her temples with a long sigh. A strand of blue-black hair slips from her bun as she does, caressing her chin. "It seems that Samson is uninterested in vengeance. He doesn't want a war against the Leolites, and it might not be necessary. Samson... with your help... could retake Bellator. Easily. He doesn't want bloodshed. He wants a clear path toward—"

"But you'd kill?" I raise my eyebrows, hoping to wheedle an opinion out of Brutatalika. "It sounds like you'd have no problem handling this with a decisive hand."

She meets my eyes. For a moment, she almost looks confused. "If we trusted each other, and if Samson weren't so against it, I would ask you to shadow us into Bellator like you shadowed him and Hadadrimmon into this estate. There, I would find Emerel. I wouldn't bother with a waricon. I'd bite her neck and watch her bleed, and then I'd find her worthless heir, and—"

"Okay. Just checking." I'm torn between the realization that Velm will sorely need Brutatalika's violent conviction and the trepidation that I might also face her wrath one day. "Good to know."

She nods. "But the role of the Kulapsifang's partner is to listen and support. For now, Samson's focus is on understanding Velm's predicament. When he sailed away from Hypnos, it sparked discontent across Velm—but the seeds of unrest had already been planted. Long ago, and extensively, it seems.

"In Velm, the Kulapsifangs mediate and lead political and spiritual affairs. But we're also ruled by what is known as the Fifty. Have you heard of it?"

"Briefly." To my surprise, I realize I've heard Gautselin mention the Fifty—not Samson, Rex, or Berevald. "There are two groups, if I recall. Members and Representatives."

"Exactly. Representatives act as ambassadors for Velm's twelve regions. They're local leaders, similar to the city councils in Mieira. The Orders are a bit different. Members of Velm's Orders work together in Bellator to create laws, decrees, and other types of legislation. It's a lot tougher to be selected as a Member of an Order than as a Representative. But any position in the Fifty is highly coveted.

"Since Imperatriz disappeared, both assemblies in the Fifty have been focused on Clearbold. They watch his decision-making, tally how he votes—and how his allies vote. Though he's managed to gain influence and respect within the Order and amongst the Representatives, most highly ranked remain loyal to Imperatriz. Most have been waiting for Samson to assume control.

"During this time, unfortunately, nobody was watching Malachai."

I huff pessimistically, then turn my attention to my nails when Brutatalika's eyes flash to mine.

To my surprise, she also scoffs. "Yes. Malachai is a particularly idiotic nuisance to me." After a long sigh, she goes on, "For now, that's all I know. That whatever Clearbold has been planning, Malachai is the fulcrum on which it works as his heir. In other words, I'm of the opinion we're better off keeping an eye on Malachai from here on out."

"Believe it or not, I had the chance to kill Malachi last year." I chew on my lip. "Probably should've taken it."

She looks down and straightens her napkin; I guess she didn't get the joke. She toys with her utensils next, lips twitching.

Based on our limited interactions, I find her complex, stony, and unreadable.

After a beat, she looks at me again, "Like I said, Samson wants a bloodless solution before a civil war. But the only way we see that happening is with Imperatriz here. Without her... the path ahead is long and violent.

"You managed to get to Pit once, Helisent. I need you to find your way there again. Use magic, use your horns, use our axes. Do whatever you need to do to find Imperatriz. Then bring back the Kulapsifang. I beg you."

My papa says that life is like a tapestry.

I've never thought much about tapestries.

He says that they take shape behind a veil. We weave them with our own hands, which gives us the illusion of control. But the only way anyone sees the true tapestry of destiny is when they die.

It's clear now that Brutatalika will be part of mine.

I can feel our threads tangling in a tapestry.

Tangling with Samson's into some unfathomable design.

"I will do what I can to help your people and your realm." I drum my fingertips against the table, unsure of where to look or what sort of expression to make. "You have my word."

"He can't stay in Velm—he and Hadadrimmon will be better off in Luz for now. There are too many Leolites in the city; they'll spread the word." Brutatalika's throat bobs; she looks at my hands, blinking. "I'll hold out in Mort for as long as I can. But he says that... if Clearbold comes, he wants me to betray him. He wants me to join the Leolites and survive until he can retake Velm. They haven't targeted me or my court. They aren't concerned with the women, it seems. Just the men."

She looks at me with a piercing gaze. "I pray to Hetnazzar you are half as powerful as the world thinks you are, Helisent West of Jaws."

I raise my eyebrows.

She still hasn't bribed me—not with a precious gem or even a whisper of luxurious fabrics.

She also hasn't acknowledged my demigod despite mentioning Hetnazzar.

She hasn't even attempted to gauge what I'd be willing to do for Velm.

Before I can remind her that witches prefer to solidify goodwill with *gifts* and *bribes*, footsteps echo from the doorway. I sigh with relief; Samson will remind her that I need to be assuaged with great care.

Brutatalika heads gracefully to the door. My gut clenches when I see three female wolves lined up, craning their necks to peek at where I sit at the table. Their eyes dart from the mess of grimoire powder to my hands. I stare back at them as Brutatalika whispers a few quick words in Velmic.

The women file in behind her and take the free cushions near my seat.

They barely move their eyes from me as they do so, finding a cushion, sinking onto their butts, and scooting closer to the low table. Like Rex and Berevald did with Samson, they glance at Brutatalika now and then, waiting for her to speak.

"Helisent West of Jaws, let me introduce you to Exultet 514 Cecil." Brutatalika gestures to the wolf at her side. "I consider her my right hand."

The wolf has broad shoulders and a sturdy abdomen. Her bulky arms rest on the table, crossed. Her cropped hair and layered bangs hang around her temples and ears. Her flat nose twitches as she focuses on me.

"I hear you're a friend of the unnumbered wolves," Exultet says in a mismatched, high-pitched voice. "That's my work here in Velm. I've been documenting the exits. There have been dozens since the wedding, mostly in the villages in Gamma."

"Exultet on the exits. Sounds easy enough." I raise my eyebrows. "And exits are...?"

"It's when a village decides it doesn't have the resources to support nymphs and wielders." Exultet pauses, as though choosing her words carefully. "Most villages force them out—some take more colorful routes to do that than others."

I slide my eyes toward Brutatalika. I'm not sure why she thinks this matters to me. "Sounds nice."

The Female Alpha gestures to the wolf sitting on my other side. "And this is Verita 454 Melfrey. She's a Representative of Wrot, Velm's westernmost province."

Verita bows her head; the movement reminds me of Ninigone's formal gestures. Unlike Brutatalika and Exultet, Verita has the narrow frame of a scholar. The same cold eyes, too.

They dart across me as she explains, "We've met before, Helisent West of Jaws. Briefly. In Antigone. I traveled there for a conference with two members of the Class, Ethsevere and Cosisent."

According to Absalom, Ethsevere and Cosisent are the only long-standing members of the Class worth trusting.

My head tilts as I meet Verita's gaze. "Interesting."

"Leda and I," she gestures to the fourth wolf at the table, "have been looking into other forms of unrest. My primary concern is the new wave of educators entering the schools in Wrenweary, the capital of Wrot. They were appointed by the Order of Education, which means they should be some of Velm's most innovative and forward-thinkers.

"Unfortunately, most seem to have an agenda, especially related to history. I've heard more than a few worrisome new accounts of the War Years and Velm's claim to Tet—"

"Tet?" I snort, looking from one wolf to the next. "No, no. Velm will not have Tet."

Verita's eyes narrow. "Of course not. No one will have Tet. Tet is Tet. No demigods. No beings. Only Skull."

Aware I have a nose full of grimoire, my answer is a long and low sound. It fools no one.

"And what are you doing in Tet, my dear witch?" Exultet asks.

In my silence, Brutatalika offers, "We should be allied during this difficult time."

Then where the fuck is my bribe, wolf?

Instead, I go with, "Velm is falling apart. Let's worry about that first. After that, we can discuss who will have Tet and why." The women lean forward, prepared to interject, but I hold up my hand. "I think this is going relatively well, but now you all have that look like you're about to say some uneducated shit—I know the expression well. Before we get nasty, I'd like to make one thing clear…"

I take a deep breath, drumming my fingers against the table and thinking.

I've been planning on allying with Brutatalika—only for Velm's sake, which is based on my love for Samson, and a begrudging acknowledgment that Velm's destiny is tied to my well-being. At least partly.

Since entering the Mortyd Estate, I've backtracked on that, doubting my patience and wherewithal to be allied with Brutatalika and Velm in general.

And now…

Well, I guess love makes people do viciously honorable things.

"You *actually* want to be allied with me, my dear wolves?"

Brutatalika clenches her jaw. "Yes."

I hold her eyes as I slowly let my form overtake me. My nails thicken as they drum against the table's cold marble; they lengthen and phase into a bloodred hue. I look out the window before I frighten the women, worried that direct eye contact would be taken as a threat now that my horns are out, my eyes are leeching the color of blood, and my tail is flicking behind my back.

I've gotten a lot more comfortable with my tail recently.

I lay its spade end in my hand and run my fingers along the flat bone that juts from its center. My seventh horn.

After a moment, I look up and meet Brutatalika's eyes. Her face is unreadable aside from a twitch of her right eye.

I tell her, "Wielders aren't demigodless, my dear Alpha. You've asked for my help, and I'm willing to give it, but you haven't once recognized Vex. Not even when we first met and you thanked me for saving Samson's life in Alita. Did you know, Brutatalika, that I wasn't the one who cast that life-saving spell?

"It was my demigod. Vex healed him because I called upon it—and because my demigod had been endeared to Samson. He had saved my life before. Vex understood this."

The wolves haven't moved a centimeter since I shifted into my form—not even to glance at one another. I can't tell if they're outright shocked, if they're terrified, if they're curious. But I can feel a palpable tension in the air.

"So, I hope everyone at this table can separate the witch who gets drunk on masina from the demigod whose magic runs through my horns. Because I see Vex as no less worthy than Hetnazzar. And I see myself as no less important than a Kulapsifang." I take a large breath, exhaling slowly before I go on, "And, let's be honest—the only reason I'm here is thanks to Samson and his meddling."

I reach for my water and then gulp down the rest of it.

I look at Brutatalika and fucking pray I'm not lying about this next part. "But maybe, by the time Velm is put back together, that won't be the only reason I am here."

The women glance at one another; no one speaks, no one allows their features to bend into any discernible expression.

I can't tell if Brutatalika is angry or at a loss for words.

Exultet shifts to square up to me and asks in her too-high voice, "Well, aren't you a political animal?"

I tilt my head with fake confusion. "An animal? Because of the horns?"

The women jolt in perfect tandem, eyes widening and hands reaching out to reassure me—but I keel backward with a long cackle before anyone gets a word out.

"Relax," I chuckle. "I was kidding."

I dry my eyes, reveling in their discomfort.

I think this might work after all.

CHAPTER 5

I REMIND MYSELF QUIETLY

SAMSON

Suin,
You always said that I was teasing you. It's true. I was. And it worked every
fucking time, you soft boy.
-Suin

I try to ignore Helisent's ala.

For three days, she hides away in the lounge with Hadadrimmon.

It's enough time for her ala to drift around the Mortyd Estate.

To leech into the bedroom I share with Brutatalika.

Now, as I pack my satchel, it's like she's standing beside my wife and our bed, her ala shaped into her ghost.

Brutatalika sighs as she rubs bintsuke oil onto her hands. Dawn has just grazed the sky; she's still waking from sleep, like me.

With calm concentration, she spreads it through my hair. Though I prefer cedar oil, I don't mind the bintsuke; its citrusy, musky scent reminds me of Brutatalika. And how she touches me reminds me of my packmates; thorough and efficient, more than lingering or gentle.

"I can't believe how much your hair has grown back." She massages her fingers behind my ears, evenly spreading the oil. I close my eyes, relaxed. "We're lucky they didn't cut mine. You'd be waiting a year for mine to grow this much."

Since I arrived, I haven't spoken much.

I've taken to jotting down notes during our formal meetings, worried I might forget something.

The proximity between Helisent and my wife hasn't helped. Though they seem to be getting along, I feel the witch's presence constantly; I swear she could see me through the walls when I bathed with Brutatalika, when my wife washed my short hair and held me in our bed, when she woke me with soft kisses.

I couldn't help but...

Pretend.

That my wife doesn't make me at least partly uneasy like every other wolf.

I open my eyes and study her features. Despite the rabid uncertainty, she looks determined and well-rested. Just as delicately fierce and lovely, too. "You would never get yourself into the mess I did."

She snorts, lifting her hands from my scalp. "Maybe not quite as quickly, but it's not like Clearbold gave you a choice." With a long sigh, her blue-black eyes flit across my face. "Try to hurry."

I take her hands; she tries to pull them away, saying they're covered in oil, but I hold on. I pull her closer, and she follows, setting her head against my collar so I can wrap my arms around her.

I close my eyes and press my lips against her thick hair. "I meant what I said, Tali. Play the role you must if they come to Mort."

It makes my heart thud just thinking about it—

A small army of wolves waving white flags, their eyes focused on Mort in the distance and the hilltop where its grand estate sits.

She exhales, long and warm against my collar. "I'd prefer not to be in that position." She pulls back, and I lift my arms. Her face is near when she says, "So *hurry*."

I think I love her. I think that remnant remains in me.

Last night, she ran her fingers over the crescent-shaped scar on my collar, then looked into my eyes. She didn't say anything; she has two similar scars from brutal waricons. But she didn't ignore it either, staring deeply at me before moving on.

I think, one day, she will be the first wolf to stop making me uneasy.

"I will."

She leans forward, and I meet her halfway, pressing my lips against hers.

I also like to think I'm getting better at making space in my heart for two people—but I hate that Helisent's ala has reached this room. I hate that I can't find a balance between them internally; I keep swinging from being pleasantly focused on this kiss to wondering where Helisent is to wishing I didn't think of her while close to Brutatalika.

Instinct drives me to both for separate reasons, and I judge myself for that. I've been raised to believe in the sanctity of monogamy; two partners, one love. Simple. Straightforward.

"Brutatalika?"

She opens her eyes and studies mine. "Samson?"

"Thank you."

Her eyebrows bunch again. "For what?"

"For winning the waricon series."

Her head tilts, but her expression remains stern and ruffled. "I didn't do it for you." She leans forward to kiss me again, then pulls back with a smile. "But I'm happy, too." Then she glances pointedly at the doorway behind me. "And I'll be even happier when you're back in Velm with Imperatriz by your side."

"I know." I take a step back, pausing for any more goodbyes. "Me, too."

Her expression hardens as she tells me, "You will succeed, Samson 714 Afador, just as you always have—against the odds. I believe this with my mind, my heart, and my soul."

Her words are steady and firm; not pleas or hopes, but prophecies.

I nod, honored by her confidence and filled with courage. "Yes, Brutatalika. I will."

She nods, too. "Then go quickly and don't look back, my Kulapsifang."

I take a deep breath, staring into her eyes.

Then I turn away and leave with heavy footsteps. The curtain swings shut as I head toward the eastern lounge.

I have to remind myself not to hang my head as I go; my wife trusts me, my witch trusts me, and I might even have a packmate.

Still, it's hard to remember how I walked before.

How I saw the world.

In the lounge, Helisent and Hadadrimmon are finishing off a cup of masina.

The witch smiles when she sees me, then gestures to the gulf of shadows near the terrace. At dawn, darkness clings to the room's walls.

I focus on the witch's smile, relieved it's survived our time here. And the meetings she sat through with Brutatalika and our Afadoric allies.

Even Hadadrimmon seems to be in relatively good spirits despite facing another long journey by shadow.

The pair stands at the ready on the white fur rug. Hadadrimmon casually holds a near-full pitcher of masina, as though prepared to bring it to Luz with him.

Helisent pulls the wand from her bottomless bag and points it toward a shadowy wall. "I should be able to take us back without your guidance, Samson. I know Luz like the back of my hand. Just try not to tackle me to the ground this time, boys."

I look at Hadadrimmon—he nearly killed us both last time. But he's glaring at Helisent. "Tell your magic to leave my nuts alone. How about that?"

The shadow starts boiling, and the wand starts glowing before he's finished ribbing.

Rather than respond, she takes off toward the shadow with a confident stride. I set my hand on her shoulder and take Hadadrimmon's arm with my free hand, dragging him with us. He double-steps to keep up with me while clinging to the silver pitcher.

As we step into Helisent's blackened portal, my momentum starts to slide forward, as if on a downhill decline. I catch myself again, trapped amid darkness and bass that vibrates throughout my body. In the next second, Hadadrimmon curses and rams into my back.

Light flickers in the darkness; a destination.

But my feet are tangled, and Hadadrimmon's full weight is on my back, and the fucking masina is spilling down my butt and legs, and the witch isn't moving fast enough to get out of our way—

I only have a split second to recalibrate—

Helisent scurries into what looks like a tiny hallway.

I throw my body to the left so I won't tackle her to the ground again.

I run into a shut door before Hadadrimmon catches up. Then he barrels into my back and throws my shoulder into the door, causing it to buckle open with a crack. We fall toward the ground face-first; the wolf lands atop me with a grunt.

I rise off my belly and throw my shoulder back, knocking Hadadrimmon to the side.

He slides onto the ground again, clutching his groin.

Helisent rushes over to slap his arm; once, twice, thrice. "You spilled the moonshine!" She grabs my arm next, gently guiding me upward. "Samson, are you okay?"

I slowly haul myself onto my feet. "I'm okay. Just a little wet."

Helisent's tiny hands flutter around to tidy my layers. She tsks when she finds the wet spot on my behind. After a graze of magic, it dries.

I glance around; we're in a small, messy room littered with items that smell like Esclamonde. I recognize her pointed boots near the door, now hanging from its hinges, along with her tiny pieces of jewelry and a thin scarf.

Commotion sounds from the apartment's other rooms.

An oread steps into view in the narrow hallway and leans against the dented door.

Onesimos crosses his arms and sighs, looking from me to Helisent to Hadadrimmon. "I have guests, you know." He turns and ambles back down the hallway.

A second later, two Colyd witches wander over. I squint, surprised to see Cleo and Ceyx inside what seems to be Helisent's apartment. The sisters watch us with their mouths agape. Cleo holds a wooden spoon covered in pale batter. Ceyx holds a half-filled glass of what smells like wine. Their eyes leap to each of us quickly, then they backtrack like the oread.

I glance at Helisent.

She doesn't look surprised to see the witches. She slips to the ground near Hadadrimmon. Beads of sweat line her forehead and upper lip; her ala cools as her blood pressure drops.

I squat at her side, setting a hand on her back. "Are you okay?"

"The nausea caught up to me faster this time." She fans her face with her hands, then turns to call into the hallway, "Simmy, I know we're fighting, but will you make me tea? Mint tea? Please?"

"We have some chamomile tea freshly made," Cleo calls back.

"I'll pour you a cup now," Ceyx chimes in.

I narrow my eyes, wondering about the arrangement of lovers.

Helisent said that Halcyon is with Butter now, right?

But I guess his wives have been endeared to the oread?

And... how does Helisent fit into this equation?

The most pressing question—*do I want to know?*

Helisent shifts to rest her head against my shoulder, taking long and slow breaths. Hadadrimmon appears to be doing the same, still draped across the floor and the mentee's belongings.

From the kitchen, the oread calls over, "Welcome back to Luz, Samson. Unfortunately, my dear Kulapsifang, word has spread about what happened in Bellator. Everyone knows you're on the run. Luz's pack leaders have been handing out flyers asking for your return. Apparently, the first wolf to find you and hand you over to the pack leaders *alive* gets a place amongst the local pack."

He wanders back into the room with a mug of steaming tea, which he sets beside Helisent. Then he squats onto his haunches near us. I go still at his nearness; Helisent is still resting her head on my shoulder, and I think this is her primary lover, and I'd rather not be seated between them when they seem to be in a disagreement.

But the oread doesn't seem to notice. He looks up at me, afro perfectly tended and eyes shining like fiery amber. "I guess the wolves combed through Coil looking for you. Roughed Gautselin up quite a bit. Don't worry—a healer already went to him."

Looking for me at Coil? I barely arrived in Luz a week ago. And I only spent five days at Coil before heading to Mort.

I'd expected word to spread more slowly.

But if there are wielders in Bellator, Clearbold can use their magic to communicate with his packmates and allies throughout the realm.

Throughout Mieira, too.

The hunt is on, then.

I look around in a panic. "Did they come here looking for me?" The small apartment is tidy, if a bit empty. Aside from a few cushions, shelves, and pillows, there isn't much in the bedroom or hallway. Nothing out of place or otherwise ransacked.

Helisent and Onesimos snort at the same time.

"Everyone knows where I live now," Helisent says, as though it explains everything.

From the kitchen, Cleo calls, "Onesimos, the batter is ready. Can you light the burners?"

Ceyx follows with, "Or should we come back later?"

Helisent raises her head. She glares at Onesimos before shouting into the hallway, "Bring your useless husband here! We need to talk to the three of you. It's about Pit."

"Halcyon's with Butter," Ceyx calls back. "He took her to a lake."

Helisent rolls her eyes. "There aren't any lakes around here."

"A river, then. He said they'd be back by tomorrow night."

"*Tomorrow night*. I see." The witch exchanges a long and meaningful look with Onesimos.

I guess the warren is growing, then.

See, Samson? Polyamory is normal in many parts of the world. You are not bad for having space in your heart for two women.

But we are Velmic, and you know this.

I turn to help Hadadrimmon. It seems like the oread and the witch might need a moment alone.

The wolf has barely shifted into a sitting position. Between gritted teeth, he asks, "She does it on purpose, doesn't she?"

To be fair, I'm not certain why shadowing hasn't similarly affected me. Once upon a time, and relatively recently, even a graze of Helisent's magic was enough to send me buckling and holding my balls.

"Maybe. Let's get you off the floor, bud." Slowly, he rises to his feet and follows me from the bedroom, slightly hunched.

The hallway empties into a kitchen and an adjoined salon. The kitchen is narrow, its walls covered in cabinets. A wood-burning stove sits beside a broad sink and a low window.

Ingredients are strewn over the kitchen table and countertops: rye flour, crumbled almonds, sugar, and other confectionery. Plus, an assortment of wrapped dairy products: goat's cheese, sheep's cheese, and creamy cow's cheese. Several bowls of sweet batter sit on the counter nearby.

I head into the salon. Pillows and cushions are strewn on a threadbare rug. There's a low table with a few dirty cups; on the walls are a few shelves with trinkets. A ginkgo tree hovers against the windows that dot both rooms, its fluttering green leaves drenched with pale light. Pleasant chatter from the street below emanates from one of the open windows.

It doesn't look like Hadadrimmon notices the Colyd witches. He holds his stomach and waddles into the salon before collapsing onto the rug.

Cleo winces a smile at me. "Hello, Samson. We didn't think we'd see you again so soon."

"Welcome to Luz." Ceyx eyes Hadadrimmon uncertainly. "Both of you."

"What do you need to know about Pit?" Cleo asks, turning back to stir the contents of a large bowl. "Vulcan probably knows more than Halcyon."

Ceyx turns to me, quickly explaining, "My son was a bit of an... optimist once. He worked with rebel groups in Plet who wanted to gain an advantage over Ezit by finding Pit and Silt. He got out of that circle quickly—but maybe he learned something helpful about the islands before that. Should I send for Vulcan? He and Vega live down the street, near Zeu's den."

I nod, eager to start the search for Pit. "Please—just so long as he doesn't bring the vampire."

(I'm not in the mood for Zeu's antics and posturing, and if I lose my temper now, there will be no calming me until blood has been drawn.)

Ceyx reaches for a necklace that's tucked into her shirt. She brings her long nail to the copper charm that dangles from a woven string, tapping it three times, then four more times in a different pattern. With a whir of high-pitched ultrasound, the charm shivers and then falls still.

Ceyx tucks it back into her green shirt. "Ideally, he'll be here within the hour. Realistically, I hope you're not in a rush."

Cleo bumps into her sister with her hip, then says something in Zarzyd. The women go back and forth, laughing without humor and ribbing each other.

Onesimos waltzes into the room a moment later. He squeezes himself between the sisters to study the progress of their baking. Both are almost a full head taller than the oread. "Ceyx, too much stirring. Look at all the bubbles. It will over-prove. And Cleo—where is the orange peel? You burnt the last batch of syrup."

Helisent walks in next. Her head swivels as she enters the salon, fixed on the oread as he happily instructs the sisters on extracting orange essence. Her features soften when she turns to me and Hadadrimmon.

With a long sigh, she takes the cushion next to me, setting down her tea and stretching out her short legs. She folds her arms behind her head, wheedling her fingers into her messy white hair. Her red robe is skewed, its sleeves collected at her elbows. Beneath the velvet, a new strapless dress hugs her chest, her belly, her hips. Her beaded necklaces, earrings, and armbands catch the light and twinkle.

I can tell by the set of her lips that she's grumpy and sleepy. But I can tell by the twinkle in her eye that she's plotting.

A smile pulls at my lips.

We're in the middle of a city, surrounded by beings deeply involved in their own private worlds.

But there's a red thread that runs from her to me.

It's invisible to everyone but us.

"What are you thinking?" I ask her quietly.

Her fingers tangle in her hair as she sighs again, this time relaxed. "I was thinking about Velm. It smelled like you."

I try not to shift too much on the cushions.

Every time my foot or hand knocks into the soft fabric, the alas of Onesimos, Esclamonde, Butter, Halcyon, and the Colyd sisters drift out. It's like sitting in a haze of semi-strangers; they're almost present in the room with us.

Still, in the darkness of the deep night, I'm mostly happy and content.

Probably the happiest and most content I've been since—

That Thing in Bellator.

That's how I think about it for now.

Nothing more, nothing less.

Just a thing that happened in Bellator that I'm going to confront and dismantle and reverse.

For now, I'm relaxed. Shouting from pups drifts in from the window, filling the salon with the sounds of a happy youth. My belly is full of baked goods and warm tea, my side warmed by Helisent.

Despite being surrounded by many alas, hers is prominent and familiar and scented heavily of safety.

She yawns deeply, her body shivering. "So? What do you think about what Vulcan said? I get his point about following a phoenix—all we'd have to do is wait for one to fly back to Zarzynn. But... let's be realistic, my sweet wolf."

Since the young warlock left the apartment with his mother and Cleo an hour ago, Helisent and I have tried to formulate a plan to find Pit. Preferably before the rest of the warren returns from their night out.

It's at least a familiar scenario—plotting our way through an impossible mission.

"I know it isn't ideal to find and follow a phoenix back toward Zarzynn," I counter, "but it may be the most reliable way to find the island. A phoenix is a better bet than a wielder or vampire helping us —that's for sure."

"Vulcan said the phoenixes *sometimes* fly over the islands." Helisent shifts, propping her head in her hand on an adjacent cushion. With almost no light filtering in from the windows, all I see are two glazed eyes and a flush of white hair. "And we can't hang out in Gamma and wait for one to take off—it's too close to Velm. We could be waiting for months. The wolves would put it together."

"Plus, you keep saying we can follow the phoenix—my dear wolf, can you fly? You're barely comfortable with me floating you out of a tree's canopy. Now, you want a high-speed chase with a phoenix in the clouds."

I can't help but smile at the idea. "I hadn't thought of it like that."

I run my hand over her scalp, tangling her silky tresses. It's a casual, light touch. I crave her warmth and presence, but I'm not ready to initiate intimacy—not with all my shame, not with the memory of Brutatalika's anxiety, not with my unending doubt about Velm's future.

About my worth as a Kulapsifang.

I don't think I could get hard if my life depended on it.

"Let's hear your brilliant idea, then," I suggest.

"We go to Antigone," she says excitedly, leaning closer.

"Antigone? What's in Antigone?"

"A lot of things. Are you still afraid of the city?"

"As you pointed out, I can't float like you, little bird. It would be like me telling you we should swim to an underwater city."

I can't see her smile clearly, but I can hear it in her voice. "There are no underwater cities, Samson." She sighs, letting her head rest against my chest. "I lived with Anesot for a year or so in Antigone. After he killed Milisent, I left our apartment abandoned. According to my brothers, no one ever moved in. Not even the nymphs wanted to risk it. They thought I'd cursed the apartment or that my magic had otherwise... marked that space."

My gut clenches; *a curse?*

Though rare, they're feared deeply in Velm—and even by most nymphs. Not even monarchs can undo their wicked purpose.

Especially not a curse from a powerful witch like Helisent.

While curses from warlocks are formidable, only a witch's will follow down generational lines. It will linger in silence, in shadows, until it can enact its purpose. Like a blood feud made animate, given life and resolve.

"I've thought about going back for years," Helisent goes on. "Anesot left a ton of shit there because he wouldn't go back, either. I think he was more afraid of a tracking spell than a curse. The apartment is full of our things.

"I say we search them.

"Anesot said he took your mother to Pit—which means he must have known the way. Maybe we can find some kind of record or clue he left behind. He liked to take notes.

"And speaking of warlocks, it would be a good chance to visit Absalom. He was inducted into the Class recently. I'd love to catch up. And... I think he should know what's happening in Bellator. The north needs to know what Clearbold is attempting."

I run my hand down her back while I consider the possibility.

All I know about Antigone is that it's a city built mostly of metal. Wielders strung bronze, copper, and iron cables and footpaths between rocky pillars that jut into the sky. One account of the city I read said that the tallest pillar, named Espiga, has over thirteen different levels. A nymph or wolf forced to navigate Espiga without magical dove might spend four or five hours climbing winding staircases to pass from its lowest floor to its sunny upper levels.

They say wolves don't last more than a week in the city, given the stench of the metal and the dizzying heights.

Still, like Helisent's idea to bribe a ghost to drive Oko out of hiding, it's a solid start.

Especially if Anesot kept some record of his trip to Pit.

"What is this silence, my sweet wolf? Is it optimistic or full of witch-doubting?"

"Optimistic—so long as you swear not to let me out of your sight."

She snuggles closer, purring lightly. "Say no more."

"Also, we need to figure out what to do with Hadadrimmon."

She huffs, pulling back. "I'll have the Bloodies look after him. He can stay here or in the tower at Coil. The local pack probably won't storm in there for a second time."

"The Bloodies?"

"That's my court. We have a name now. It's cute."

I glance at the window. Outside, the pups from earlier challenge one another. Their voices crack as they shout and laugh and goad one another on.

When they quiet, I say, "That works for me. Hadadrimmon certainly seems comfortable in Luz. Your warren seemed to like him well enough earlier, too."

"He'll be fine. Gautselin is going to keep him if he's not careful."

"I can think of worse fates."

"We'll leave tomorrow morning, then?"

"That's fine with me—but are you rested enough to shadow us into the city?"

"What? Shadow us into Antigone? Definitely not. I haven't been back in years. And even if I did go more often, it'd still be risky. There's lots of air in Antigone. That's how locals describe it.

"I know we've had good luck with shadowing so far, but... let's not push it. We should be able to reach the city the old-fashioned way in two weeks if we get up early enough. And I'll feel comfortable shadowing us back to Luz when we're ready. We won't lose too much time."

"Helisent, it might be dangerous to travel on foot. The pack leaders want me alive. To say I have a target on my back might be an understatement."

"I can cloak your scent very easily." She clears her throat. "Or does that bother you?"

"Of course, it bothers me. And my ala is only one-half of the problem. My face is the other. Can you hide that? And... my torcs. I found new pieces in Mort, and I'd rather not take them off again."

I can't stand how I feel without the weight of the torcs. I can't stand the idea that another wolf would look at me and assume I have no pack, no loved ones, no territory.

"At the risk of sounding stupid... how do you feel about hats?" the witch asks.

"No."

"A *nice* hat?"

"No."

"Then I'm afraid our best option is you taking off your torcs and pretending to be unnumbered." She sighs, patting my chest. "Have no fear, my dear Kulapsifang. I will avenge all the indignities that have fallen upon you."

A pathetic groan is my only reply.

I trace my torcs. I'd felt a little weird not slipping them off for bed, but now I'm happy I didn't.

We lay still for a while. The adolescent pups outside continue their antics, ratcheting things up with each new challenge. After a loud thud and the sound of shattered glass, the street falls conspicuously silent.

The witch yawns again. "Samson...?"

I do the same, sinking deeper into the cushions. "Helisent?"

"Will you take your shirt off? Nothing sexual."

A smile tugs at my lips. "Your oread told me that you've been bartering with Gautselin for—"

"You know nymphs lie more than wielders, right?"

"So, you *don't* miss me?" I tsk lightly. "It had felt right. You know, considering I still dream of you almost every night."

"Really?" Hands seize my shirt collar. Helisent pulls herself toward me, almost knocking into my nose. Once again, all I can see are the shimmering orbs of her eyes and a few strands of bright white hair. "You still dream of me? I figured the seething dreams only affected you if we were physically together."

"Near or far, I dream of you, little bird." I still see Helisent clambering through the yew tree. Sometimes, I climb after her. Other times, I stand beside the trunk. The faceless witch is there half the time, too, turned away and cradling something in her arms.

Once again, I hear a smile in her voice. "I hope they're good dreams." She tugs on my collar. "Is that a no to taking your shirt off, then?"

"It was a yes." I shift away from her, then reach for my hem. "I thought you wanted to take it off."

With a devilish giggle, her hands take hold of my shirt. Together, we shimmy it over my arms and head. With a happy sigh, her arms wrap around my abdomen and she pastes herself against me. One of her hands reaches up to stroke my scalp, fingernails tickling my short hair. Like she promised, it's not a sexual embrace.

We lay in the darkness.

Calm, silent, resting.

Like stars in the night sky.

How I imagine they look in a place called Vieira.

The next morning, we wander through the city with a short to-do list.

We leave Hadadrimmon passed out in Helisent's apartment, barter with Gautselin to aid the wolf, and then leave a long and detailed note for Helisent's Bloodies.

Once we have supplies for the road, we follow the Septima River to the northwest.

Before midday, the witch casts a lasting spell that smothers my ala. My torcs are hidden away inside her bottomless bag, too.

I look away anytime a wolf or small group wanders toward us on the wide dirt road. If I'm smoking, I exhale plumes strategically, trying to block my features. Sometimes, Helisent turns to me and pretends to wipe something off my cheek or brow, fussing like a doting mother.

Thankfully, there aren't too many wolves in the northwest. Of all Mieira's regions, the forest of Septegeur is the least likely place to find a unified pack.

In the afternoon, Helisent pulls out a familiar white lilith with red stitching. Only half of the metallic ornaments remain dangling from its bottom—and none look like the copper barb that Oko used to impale me.

At first, I can't help but glance at them, but then the witch gets moving, and the sound of the ornaments clanking together is peaceful and familiar.

When I walk at her side and Helisent takes my forearm, it feels like we're striding into the past.

The only true difference is the color of the witch's robe—now bloodred instead of dawn-colored peach.

And my lack of hair and torcs.

Still, the walking does me good.

With each stride toward the forest of Septegeur and the nightmarish city of Antigone, my focus tightens.

Get to Pit.

There's no other option—

Get to Pit. Find Imperatriz. Save Velm.

By the time the sun sets, we've reached the edge of Septegeur's deciduous woodlands. Though not nearly as dense as Rhotidom's jungle, trees tower overhead, casting thick, cool shadows. Growth droops from their sturdy branches; vines of bright yellow flowers, ivy with triangular leaves, and clumps of pale lichen.

The number of mammals lessens, their scat and fur and urine hardly palpable on the grassy ground. But the number of birds increases. They watch us from the canopy, calling out to one another as though announcing our arrival. Each is stranger than the last. Some have bright-colored combs and crests of pointed feathers. Others have absurdly long and narrow beaks. Some scamper along the grass with dainty legs and darting eyes.

Helisent says they're called cockatoos and parakeets; the flamboyant cousins of canaries. The others are cranes and ibises. At one point, she snorts and says, "You should be on the lookout for the cassowaries. They're fucking evil, Samson."

That night, we cut off the main road and delve into a thick grove of sycamores. I build a small fire; Helisent either doesn't notice its size or doesn't mind that I stamp it out once our food is prepared. She sets out a few cylinders of dove, lighting them with the glow of her magic as we finish setting up our camp.

Later, Helisent points to the largest sycamore in sight.

I follow the witch to the tree. I stare at its speckled trunk, instinct driving me to mark our campsite. Afraid of attracting any wandering Leolites, I resist.

Once again, I'm not sure if Helisent notices. She leans against me as her birch twigs create a dense and broad nest overhead, then she takes my hands to float us above. Once we're settled, she sets her bottomless bag in her lap and pulls out item after item: bedding, a tray of snacks and beauty products, and a jug of water with cups.

Like the rest of the day, it's a blend of comfort and nostalgia, interspersed with notable, painful changes.

I brush her hair. Afterward, Helisent looks at the brush, then my head, and winces a large smile. "You look handsome with short hair. I feel like I should have said that before."

She scrubs my face with one of her fruity concoctions, thorough and gentle. I shift around as needed, listening to the witch chatter about what she wants to feed me in Antigone, which shops we should visit, and where we'll stay.

By the time we lie down, I'm exhausted, clean, and full.

Helisent slips my shirt off and snuggles against me.

When I fall asleep, I dream of a yew tree.

Rather than watch Helisent clamber through its canopy, I'm walking toward a yew far in the distance. This one is much younger, almost scraggly-looking. Its branches don't look fit to survive a windy Night, while its trunk splits into two distinct directions, as though halved with an axe.

I walk toward the yew where it sits atop a stout hill.

The closer I get, the more I wonder if it's a yew tree at all—

The dream blurs, then shifts. Suddenly, I'm not looking at a tree, but a shack made of dark wood. I'm struck with a sense of familiarity and apprehension, intrigued and repelled at the same time.

Then I wake up.

In a birch-twig nest in a sycamore tree with Helisent sprawled next to me.

She sleeps on her back, one arm lying over my chest and the other dangling over the nest's edge. Her head rests against my shoulder, hair tangled with my chin's stubble.

I wake slowly.

I can see the yew-turned-shack in my mind's eye.

It fades gradually, leaving me to stare at the sycamore's green-leafed canopy. The morning light is dim and warm. In the canopies of neighboring trees, birds awaken with noisy squawks and chirping. Leaves and branches shift with their movement.

I lay still for a long time, listening to the forest wake up.

My chest expands with a large breath.

It feels like the first time I've breathed deeply since Bellator—which surprises me, considering I've been safe with Helisent for over a week now. Maybe my mind has registered safety, but not my body.

I take another long breath, soothed by how deeply it calms me.

How normal I feel with the witch's head on my chest, her hair tangled near my nose.

Sunlight shimmers against the broad sycamore leaves, a blend of gold and green.

"I am Samson 714 Afador," I remind myself quietly. "I am the Kulapsifang of Velm; heir of Imperatriz 713 Afador, of Hetnazzar, of Night."

Like Helisent said, I'm lost, and I'm broken, and the road ahead is long.

But I'm farther ahead than my enemies think.

I have a red witch at my side, and she has a powerful wand.

With her help, I will avoid a bloody civil war in Velm.

I will find Imperatriz.

I will retake control of Bellator, then the rest of my realm.

For now, my conviction is enough.

Helisent adjusts with a sigh, curling toward me. I turn onto my side and set my head in my hand, facing her as she shifts.

I run my finger down her cheek, over her nose's tall and narrow ridge. Gently, I run my fingertip across her long white lashes. They're like little blades of snow.

I inhale her scent deeply; she doesn't wear her mounds of jewelry to bed, which means I can smell her ala with greater distinction.

The warmth of her unblemished brown skin leaves my fingertips tingling as I trace her upper arms and wrists. She twitches now and then in response; her lips pull into a brief smile, eyebrows lifting.

I set my hand flat on her stomach, spreading my fingers out.

My hand spans her tummy, from her breasts to her pelvis. I don't linger there long, painfully aware that this is where she will grow her littlelings, and they won't be mine.

With a heavy breath, the witch wakes.

I pull my hand away.

She looks at me, eyes half-closed. Her voice is heavy with sleep. "Hmph?"

"It's... You look healthy."

Her features crumple with confusion. She yawns, eyes slipping shut again.

She inches toward me, eyes closed. My hand shifts onto her hip as she angles herself toward me.

With each touch, my attention focuses on her body's signals: the slight flush of blood to her cheeks, the scent of her vulva emanating from her hiked dress, the warmth and feel of her bare skin.

Virility is no longer a remnant.

Still, I feel shy, almost awkward.

Helisent watches me indolently, eyes half-closed. She adjusts in response, leaning her body toward me and hiking her leg to wrap it around my hips.

I run my hand down her hip, shifting to caress her inner thigh's silky skin. A second later, she props herself on her elbows and looks at me with flushed cheeks and messy hair.

Her red eyes flit across me. "You're teasing me."

It's as sudden as a slap in the face, as a fall to the ground below—

'You're teasing me.'

Those were words I once spoke to Rex.

When I wasn't sure if he was cuddling at night for warmth or affection. When I wasn't sure if he wanted only one kiss, or many kisses, or certain types of kisses, Rex had always waited for me to say those three words.

'You're teasing me.'

Really, those words were a question. Something like, 'What would you like, Rex?'

A sob rises from my chest, a lump in my throat.

"Oh, shit." Helisent's eyes widen as she sits up. "It's okay, it's okay, it's okay."

I crumple, body folding downward as sobs wrack my body. The

pain of losing Rex is too sudden and powerful for me to feel ashamed. For me to wonder if this is hurting Helisent's feelings, turning her off, or frightening her.

Her warmth surrounds me as I cry into my hands. Hot tears pour from my eyes and, within a few minutes, my nose is clogged, too. I can't make out Helisent's cooing, but I feel her soothing touches and hear the tone of her calming words.

I lost Rex.

Rex is dead.

They murdered him.

My people.

Our people.

As soon as I get a grip, I remember Berevald, and the sobbing starts again. Helisent passes me tissues, dries my tears, and lets me cry at my own pace. Once the worst has passed, she scoots closer to clean my face.

I stare around the sycamore tree.

I've never wept like this—not even when Imperatriz disappeared.

It's so fiercely painful; to remember Rex and Berevald, to mourn their loss, to take strength in their memory.

"I'm sorry," I mumble eventually. "That came out of nowhere."

She strokes my knee. "Don't be sorry." With a little glance, she angles toward me, as though asking permission. I sniffle, sitting up so she can take her place on my lap. There, she sets her head on my shoulder. "I didn't cry for years. You're doing much better than me."

I clamp my eyes shut to fend off another bout of sobbing.

"It hurts too much," I admit quietly.

"I know."

"It's my fault."

"It isn't, but I know."

"I love you, little bird."

"I love you, too, sweet wolf. Here, have a cigarette. I rolled you one."

For two weeks, I walk westward with Helisent.

Still days away, I mistake the first pale, sandstone rock pillars for Antigone. The massive columns come into view from a misted distance, looming over the green canopy like ten-story buildings with flat tops. They shoot upward from the ground with no incline, as rigid and straight as arrows.

Emerald vegetation clings to the tallest portions, hanging from crevices and nooks. The broader pillars even have full-grown trees craning from their tops. The tallest ones are shrouded with heavy mist, which looms amid the towering forests like smoke from a wildfire.

They're spread out as though placed randomly, separated by increasingly narrow footpaths that weave through the forest.

Another five pillars seem to constantly loom on the horizon.

Eventually, the giant sycamores and maples give way to prehistorically large ferns. The birds also grow larger—but I can only tell by their feathers and scat. Though I can sense a mammoth, flightless bird (which I suspect is the cassowary), I no longer see them in the underbrush or hear their calls from the canopy.

One evening, Helisent drags me by the wrist to the center of a vast opening. A few benches and fire pits dot the area. It's empty, but I can smell food and alas lingering, as though it was recently used.

"Look!" Helisent points to the west where the golden sun melts into the horizon.

A cluster of at least a dozen hulking pillars juts into the sky. They're by far the largest sandstone structures we've seen so far.

From a distance, the pillars obscure the sky, huddled together. Halfway up the giants are... tangles. I'm not sure how else to describe what I see, just that rope-like slack connects the pillars, growing denser near their tops. The width of the pillars also increases near their forested summits. Sunlight pools along certain structures, collecting on what looks like windows.

"Antigone," the witch says with a flourish of her hand. "The tallest pillar has a name. It's Espiga."

I blink, stunned.

The city isn't as big as I thought it'd be.

But it's at least five times higher than I'd imagined—and there also seems to be a dangerous number of structures clinging to the pillars.

I have no idea which portions of the city are sandstone, which are metal, and what is wielder-made versus nature-made.

It twinkles in the light like a mirage of jewels, in defiance of gravity.

Helisent lifts her eyebrows when I look down at her. "Do you like cats?"

"What?"

"Actually, don't worry about it. You'll get used to them. Let's go."

CHAPTER 6

THE TALLEST ROOM
IN BELLATOR PALACE

HELISENT

Honey Baby,
Sometimes, we feel like we'll always be eleven years old because that's when
Mama died. Do you feel like an infant? Like a tiny baby who sees everything
and understands nothing? You can tell us if you do.
The Boys

Yngvi clutches two fat cats to his sides.

Growlies, the engorged tabby, bares his teeth at Samson. Pitter-patter, the knobby and half-blind elder, directs her feral hiss at a cabinet instead. Yngvi grapples with their weight as he backs out of the dining room and into the kitchen of his small apartment. He slips, one of his mismatched socks catching on a floorboard.

I freeze, trying to take in the scene before I react.

I can't tell if Samson is in a homicidal rage or just a normal one.

The Kulapsifang stands in the dining room before a messy table. Our breakfast is displaced; the idli toppled to the ground, the sambar covered in claw marks. Samson's mug of tea sits on its side, steaming contents poured across the table.

The wolf slides his eyes from the first cat to the second.

He looks at my brother next.

Like me, Yngvi stares at Samson with wide eyes.

Though Growlies and Pitter-patter failed to break the skin with their vicious maws, I can see the clear outline of their bite marks on the pale skin of Samson's forearms.

The cats launched a coordinated attack over breakfast, swift and unexpected.

Gently, Samson shifts his gaze to me. "The next time—"

"They're *babies*, Samson," Yngvi wails, backing against the kitchen counter. His large eyes are wide, his narrow frame tangled in his robe. "You wouldn't hurt *babies*, would you?"

I whip my head toward my brother. "Shut up, Yngvi! I told you to lock them in your bedroom when we got here last night!" I turn to offer Samson an appeasing smile. "If a cat's bite doesn't break the skin, we call it a kiss. And wolves don't get upset over kisses. Right?"

Samson's painfully neutral expression hasn't shifted. He blinks at me. "If the cats *kiss* me again, I'm going to—"

"Samson, *no!*" Yngvi brings the squirming cats higher, flattening them against his chest. Given Growlies is mostly gut, the cat slides out of his grip, oozing toward the ground. Amid the confusion and tension, Pitter-patter hisses at a vial of salt.

Happy with the distance between the wolf and the cats, I reach for the front door at my back. I hold it open for him, hoping he leaves.

Samson looks away from my brother, into the cool and misty morning. He strides toward the exit without another glance at our forgone breakfast.

Moons help us.

I follow Samson as he ducks slightly to clear Yngvi's entrance. I turn back to shout, "Tell Growlies to fuck off."

"*He's a ba—*"

I shut the door before Yngvi can finish, then run into Samson's back.

He hasn't stepped off my brother's doormat. I scoot around him onto the wooden walking path. I look back to find Samson pulling a cigarette from behind his ear.

I light it for him with a snap of my fingers.

Unhappily, he takes a drag and looks around. Given that we arrived in the dead of night, Antigone was visible under romantic, golden light.

Not anymore.

Samson leans away from the door, craning his neck to study the streetless city. Above and below, thick metal cables cross through the air, connecting the pillars. Horizontal footpaths with sturdy handrails are fixed to them, acting like bridges to intertwine Antigone's thirteen levels with its mammoth pillars.

Sunlight filters in from above, running along the metallic cables and wooden planks that stretch between the pillars like a spider's web.

Yngvi's apartment sits nestled on the seventh level, almost smack in the center of the city.

Like most of the city's residents, he lives inside a building crafted of finely worked wood with copper and bronze accents. The hexagonal structure is rooted in one of Antigone's pillars, surrounded by apartments of the same size. Apparently, the dryads and wielders who first built the city borrowed the idea from beehives.

Footpaths hug the hexagonal structures, layered with enough spellwork that it's a wonder it doesn't bother male wolves to walk through the city.

Samson takes a long drag as he presses his back against Yngvi's door. His thick, dark hair has started to grow back, hiding his pale scalp. I can't tell if it makes him look younger or older. Probably younger, given his pout.

"We're going to meet with Absalom first, right?" he asks.

"Yep. He said to come first thing in the morning." I offer him an encouraging smile. "Are you ready?"

"Does he have cats?"

"I never noticed any with him in Luz. Let's keep our fingers crossed."

His eyes dart from the footpaths to the tangled levels above us. "Do we go above or below?"

"Up." I point out two tiled rooftops below, explaining, "The lower levels are for industry and trading. That's where most people work." I point above. "The upper levels are more residential. The top level—the best, I should add—is where members of the Class live. Absalom lives near their headquarters. He said to look for a red door."

Samson steps off Yngvi's doormat to grip the braided cable banister that runs along the footpath.

One house down, a transporting platform slowly sinks toward Antigone's lower levels. It shifts slightly back and forth, navigating the taut cables. The Class appoints wielders to manage the platforms, which provide the fastest transportation around the city.

In the early morning, a dozen or so nymphs and wielders stand quietly on the platform.

The wielders and dryads pivot as they pass by, their gold and amber eyes glued to Samson. The witches and warlocks are dressed in tailored tops, pants, and skirts, fitted with metallic charms and bright thread. The dryads wear long, colorful pieces; most of their jewelry is tucked into their vibrant hair, laced into braids and updos and ponytails.

Samson smokes and watches them pass with a frown.

When they're gone, I use floating magic to rise onto the footpath's braided handrail. With my feet balanced, I extend a hand toward Samson.

He takes one last drag before taking my hand with a small groan.

I cast more floating magic to kick off into the open air. My hair rises weightlessly, along with my red robe. Even my earrings and necklaces, normally heavy, float skyward.

I tug on Samson's hand. He looks doubtfully above.

I remind him, "Without floating magic, it'll take us hours to find Absalom's apartment."

Samson glances at our hands, intertwined, and gulps. "Will you be offended if I close my eyes?"

A devilish smile curls onto my lips. "No."

He lifts his chin and clamps his eyes shut. His fingers pinch mine again; this time, I realize it's frightened clinging. "I trust you," he announces.

I cast floating magic to lift him off the footpath, above its metal banister, and into the air with me. A dozen passing wielders stop to watch us rise, but they soon lose interest; young wielders often choose to float freely throughout the city, and I'm not *that* old.

Level by level, I guide us through the web of gleaming metal cables, footpaths, and transport platforms.

It takes a bit longer than expected—

I don't remember the city that well.

The brightly painted houses are familiar, as are the metal sculptures and ornate fountains. Now, I can appreciate that the multi-story water fountains resemble waterfalls, and that they could be a callback to the House of Talos in Zarzynn.

But I can't remember where neighborhoods end and begin; Red Tier to Black Rock to Upper Anti.

Thankfully, it's easy enough to guide us toward the light that saturates Antigone's upper levels.

Near the thirteenth, the number of footpaths and platforms lessens. In their place comes vibrant green growth; the same trees and ferns that litter the forest floor below also thrive here. They cling to the rough tops of the sandstone pillars, roots jutting from the rock and searching for dew.

Soon, I catch sight of the Class's single-room chamber. It sits inside Espiga's hollowed and circular top. The chamber's grand, carved veranda provides a three-hundred-and-sixty-degree view of the sky.

I circumnavigate the headquarters in search of a red door. This high up, we're in a haven of clear skies, sat amid the forested tops of Antigone's pillars. Samson's grip on my hand grows incrementally firmer the longer we float, but he doesn't curse or grumble.

With a start, I make out a red door in the distance.

"Almost there," I chirp.

As soon as the wolf's boots hit the sandstone landing near the red door, he reaches out blindly. Pinching my lips to avoid smiling, I lead him toward the pillar's sturdy side. This far up, Absalom's residence isn't crafted from metal and wood; his home is carved straight into the sandstone, instead.

Samson maneuvers with his eyes closed, pressing his back against the pillar's flat side.

He opens his eyes to study our surroundings. "*Lekeli Kelnazzar.*" He looks at me, jaw clenched. "*Why?*"

I turn to look for what set him off. Sunlight twinkles in a near-empty sky, warming our faces and the sandstone and the leafy vegetation. This high up, and with a strong breeze whipping around, I can't smell metal. I also see no cats.

I glance below into the misty darkness. Sunrise won't reach the lower levels for another few hours. At the moment, it looks like we've ascended from the underworld.

I arch an eyebrow in question. "I didn't realize you were *this* afraid of heights."

He scans me once, features tense. "It's not the heights—it's the fall."

With another unhappy growl, he turns away from me and inches up the stairs toward the red door. He keeps one hand on the sandstone and another white-knuckle grip on the copper railing.

I follow him to the red door. "Maybe that's what the cats were doing—trying to scare you straight off the ledge."

He turns to me, eyes wide as a new threat dawns.

Before I can assure him I was joking, the red door creaks open.

A witch with broad cheekbones and an upturned nose makes it half a step before she notices Samson, then jolts back inside with a gasp. She slams the door shut, then the witch shouts for Absalom, exclaiming something about a huge brute and trouble.

I step in front of Samson just in time to meet Absalom as he rips the red door open.

We scan each other.

Absalom's shoulder-length hair hasn't changed, though his boyish features are finally starting to lose their plump innocence. Even his eyes look slightly smaller—but it might be thanks to him just waking up. Aside from a skewed white robe, all the warlock wears is a pair of thigh-revealing yellow shorts.

"Kick her out, we don't have time to waste," I bark. I crane past Absalom, searching for the witch. "Has she never seen a fucking wolf before? How many cats do you have? Are they kissers? My fucking *moons,* Abby, look at this place. They sure are treating you—"

"Good morning, Helisent." Absalom turns into his dim apartment, leaving the door open behind him. "Hello, Samson."

I follow him into a tidy salon where two broad couches face one another. Between them is a narrow table laden with candles and tightly rolled scripts. Past the salon is another refined sitting room, followed by a sunny kitchen.

I crane my neck, still looking for the witch. But I don't see any trace of her pink robe in the salon, sitting room, kitchen, or hallway.

Absalom sits on the couch and gestures to the empty one across from him.

After Samson and I take our seats, he leans forward to shout into the kitchen, "I'll be there at sundown. I promise."

The witch, still out of sight, doesn't respond. All I hear is a doubtful tsk, then a grunt, and another door creaking shut.

Samson glances at the red door behind the couch. He throws me a confused look.

I explain, "All apartments in Antigone have two doors." He raises his eyebrows, fascinated. I explain further, "Wielders like privacy."

Samson leans back against the couch, crossing his arms. "Two doors? Sounds stressful."

"Mine has *three* doors, thank you." Absalom tugs his robe shut, then crosses his legs. He looks from me to Samson with an unamused bend to his brow. He turns his gaze to me first. "Helisent—are you planning on helping with the copper line? I told Ninigone and Gilfoyle that I needed to know whether you'd be willing to help, and they said you told them to think of it how a waterfall would think of it. I hope you realize that riddle has kept them very busy. They've been useless for months."

He focuses on the wolf next. "Also, I wondered when you would show up. What happened in Bellator? Clearbold sent a letter to the Class a few weeks ago. It read, 'When found, Samson 714 Afador is to be returned to Bellator.' It's a little vague, especially considering the length of his other letters."

Samson glares at the warlock with a dead expression.

I do the same. The warlock is my patsy; I'm not sure if that makes him intrinsically trustworthy.

Absalom looks between us with flitting eyes. "And what about Rex and—"

"Don't ask." The lethal cold of Samson's voice leaks into the room.

Absalom watches him for a moment, then shifts his gaze to me. "Right. And the copper line?"

"Who cares?" I cross my arms, too. "Get out the grimoire. Like I said, we don't have time to waste, and I'm not going to leave this room questioning whether or not you're still on the right side of history, my dear warlock." I clap my hands together when he opens his mouth to argue. "Grimoire!"

With narrowed eyes, he says, "Fine."

The warlock stands and heads into the second sitting room, white cloak flaring at his heels. On his way back to the couch, he sets his grooming magic in motion, which untangles his hair and smooths his cloak. With a sigh, he sits down and leans forward to open the tin of grimoire and then splits the powder into three lines.

We silently snort our lines, then sniffle and smack our lips. In a round circle, we confirm the powder works.

After that, Absalom starts again, "Considering you two barged into my home and upset my favorite lover, I'm going to start with the questions. First, though—I have a personal issue to resolve.

"That witch you just saw leaving is named Ruca. For years, I have pined quietly and fervently for Ruca. And, for years, the witch has avoided me—not because she doesn't like me, I recently learned, but because she heard *several rumors that I'm lazy in bed.*"

Absalom raises a finger toward me angrily. "Helisent West of Jaws, you are going to swear that you will stop telling people I'm lazy in bed. I understand why you wanted to punish me—but it's time to let that go."

I snort as several distinct emotions flood my mind. None of them calms me. "Let that go? Even the men who have betrayed me made me cum first. It's really not that hard, Absalom."

Even Samson has proved up for it over the last week or so— despite spending the first week in Septegeur crying and the months before that on the run.

In fact, I think his great misfortune has made him an even more giving lover.

Absalom's voice rises slightly, laced with repressed anger. "I understand that it's easier to tell a lie than it is to tell the truth—"

"The truth?" I tilt my head, baffled by whatever maneuver he's attempting right now. "And what's that, my dear warlock?"

Absalom glances at Samson before focusing back on me. "That the night we met, I took you home, and then you threw up all over my bed and passed out. After knocking down a shelf of precious goods."

"Wait, what?" I pause, expecting Absalom to sneeze. I watch his narrow, slightly hooked nose in expectation.

Nothing.

I comb back through the catacombs of memory and try to remember that warm summer night when I first met Absalom at

Solace. I recall a lot of brandy, warlocks posturing to be useful to me, and waking up in a sheen of sweat and regret.

Nothing about an important shelf or throwing up in someone's bed.

Absalom's expression darkens. "We have never slept together, Helisent West of Jaws."

"Maybe not at first." I hold up a finger, insisting, "I remember you, though."

Samson cuts in, "Maybe I'll wait outside while you two—"

"Not ever, Helisent. Not once."

"That second time was you. I'm sure. I woke up and said, 'Hello, dear warlock, what's your name?', and you smiled and said, 'Absalom Metamor'."

Absalom throws out his hands. "It. Was. Itzifone."

I narrow my eyes, still confused. "And why would Itzifone pretend to be you?"

Absalom jumps up from the couch, shouting, "Because he's lazy in bed!" He sinks back into place, crossing his arms and looking at me with raised eyebrows. "You're the *worst*."

"Worse than Itzifone? Doubt it." I smooth my hair and decide to be amused by this rather than embarrassed. Everyone has thrown up in bed after compromising a bit of furniture. (*Right?*) "You got out-warlocked, Absalom. But I understand how that might be frustrating. I'll start spreading rumors about Itzifone from here on out."

Arrantly, Absalom flicks a piece of lint from the couch cushion. "Good." Then his eyes flit from me to Samson, his expression impudent and wounded. "And how long has this been going on, then? Between you two. Since before you lost your memories in Alita, right?"

I look at Samson, and he looks at me, face stricken.

The Bloodies know about me and Samson. So does Zeu. I imagine Cleo and Ceyx suspect, along with their sons—and possibly the nymphs who traveled to Zarzynn with us. My papa and brothers are also aware.

Aside from that, our secret is safe. Very safe, as far as I can tell.

Along with the fact that our personalities are polar, the idea of powerful witches and wolves shacking up together is still far-fetched—especially where the Kulapsifangs are concerned.

Still, it's Samson's secret more than it's mine. He's the one with a spouse. And a throne to cling to.

Luckily, he's had a lifetime to master zhuzhing. Without missing a beat, he shifts his gaze to the warlock and lowers his chin. "Don't be fucking stupid, Absalom."

For a while, the warlock returns his stare, as though hoping to carve the truth from the wolf—*stupid for asking or stupid for thinking it's possible?*

After a long moment, Absalom licks his lips. "Fine, then. To what do I owe the pleasure?"

"We need to get to Pit," I tell him.

He nods with understanding. "And you're thinking of using a portal to get there?"

"A portal?" I ask. "Like shadowing?"

"No. Like a portal. A permanent portal."

"Oh..." I chew my lip, glancing around the apartment. "I never really—"

"Had to bother with a permanent portal?" Absalom looks at Samson and explains, "Wielders are capable of traveling great distances through portals. Shadowing like Helisent does is one way to do it.

"Think about a portal as a doorway that has to be built. Shadowing, by comparison, is like busting a hole through a wall.

"A portal is a more carefully thought-out and permanent passageway. Creating them requires a balance of magical power and teamwork. I haven't personally created one—wielders are too independent for that. The only portals used in Mieira were set up during the War Years, but those are long gone. All we have of these portals now is their legacy. A reminder that such things are possible."

Samson looks at his hands. Starting with his brow, his features tense and contort. "A portal... I see. And how far could a portal take someone? Would it be possible to... create a portal that takes someone from Zarzynn to our world?"

Absalom's golden eyes switch to mine, fevered. "*Our* world?"

My gut clenches. I stare back at the warlock, hoping he won't register my shock.

I haven't pushed Samson on what happened in Bellator—but I know Suleiman was there.

'*Serac and Argot have a foothold in Velm,*' he'd said.

But I never asked what type of foothold, or how Suleiman got to Bellator, or what the fuck he wants from Samson's realm.

I slide my eyes to Samson, who sits frozen, gaze locked ahead.

Suleiman set up a portal?

Fuck.

I look at Absalom, pretending I'm not five steps behind, "Answer the question. Could wielders create a portal to allow passage to and from Zarzynn? Theoretically, at least."

"*Theoretically...*" Absalom huffs, rubbing his face as though suddenly tired. "We don't need to speak in theories. As you know, Ethsevere and Cosisent both pushed for my induction into the Class. When I joined a few months ago, they had quite a bit of information to share with me. I'm talking hundreds of pages of notes and theories on Anesot, on Oko, on the potential of foreign wielders infiltrating Antigone.

"I had my own notes to compare with theirs. The three of us now suspect that the Houses of Col and Talos are embedded in Antigone —though we aren't sure to what degree. Cosisent insists they're arriving via a portal."

Once again, Absalom's gaze flickers to Samson. He quickly explains, "The Class is made up of six wielders. Along with me, Cosisent and Ethsevere can be trusted. The witchling—Helisent's witchling, Esclamonde—she's Ethsevere's niece."

The warlock looks back at me. "They think the portal was created and opened by Anesot and Oko. But considering both wielders were exiled to Plet before they came to Mieira, I'm a bit doubtful. Those two had few resources at their disposal when they came here.

"And why help the Houses of Col or Talos? I don't think it's out of the question that the portal would have been a more longstanding project from the green and golden Houses."

I sit back on the couch with a huff.

My mind races—I'm not sure how to calm it.

I see the veiled Hosts spread across Mieira and Velm. They watch me from the top of Espiga, from the core of cold Bellator.

I haven't escaped, then.

None of us has.

"What makes Cosisent think there's a portal nearby?" Samson asks.

"Antigone's population is rising after almost two decades of steady decline. With the fall of Ezit, we're worried the portal might be a target for refugees looking for a way out of Zarzynn. There's no way the Houses are living comfortably in Ezit. Not after what happened."

I rub my temples. "That's why you want the copper line between Luz and Antigone. So you can keep us updated on what you find. Maybe we should consider creating a portal between our cities. Between my magic and yours, I don't think we'd need to involve eight other wielders. We could set one up in case of emergency."

Absalom scratches his arm, glancing toward the window. Sunlight dances across his white hair and plump brown skin. "I appreciate the offer, but I don't have the time or resources to guard a portal. Anyone who found it, even a nymph or a wolf, might be able to use it. First, I'd rather find one in the gulches below. Assuming Cosisent is right."

"Fine. That's fair."

Absalom shakes his head, confused. "And what's your plan to get to Pit, if not a portal? I'm still not sure why you're here." He raises his eyebrows, shifting his gaze to Samson. "Or what the fuck happened in Bellator."

I look at Samson, trying to gauge whether he wants to break the news himself. The wolf stares ahead; he looks exhausted, annoyed.

Absalom adds quietly, "I'm sorry to hear about Rex and Berevald. If what I'm assuming is true."

Samson studies him for a long moment. "And what are you assuming happened in Bellator? Say what you mean, my dear warlock."

Absalom's expression goes neutral. He almost looks emotionless, maybe uncomfortable, as he tediously explains, "First, your head was recently shaved; I've seen numbered wolves target the unnumbered ones often enough. When the beating is done, they shave their heads. Second, your father's note hinted at discord in Bellator. Third, I haven't seen you without your packmates since your wedding."

Samson stares at him, deadpan. "Aren't you observant?"

"And you're zhuzhing now, which makes me think I might be on the right track."

"Go on, then. I'm stuck at the edge of my seat."

Absalom watches him, calm and certain now. "My dear Kulapsifang, I spent four years as Head Warlock of Luz. Luz's central location makes it a prime meeting spot for the Alphas and their northern allies. I kept an eye on the Luzian Estate when Clearbold visited. I never trusted your father, Samson. Many in the north were wary of him after your mother's disappearance—mostly because of how quickly he found another partner and bore another heir.

"One night, very late, I saw Anesot slink past its gate.

"I knew enough of Anesot to know he couldn't be trusted. The same with Clearbold. That fact that those two had met... and so late at night...

"Nothing good would come of it.

"Your father, Samson, has had no qualms about letting his feelings toward wielders and nymphs be known. Maybe not to the general public, but certainly to the Class and the demigods' monarchs.

"The moment I saw Anesot step out of that estate, I knew the warlock had made a mistake. He didn't understand how deeply Velm's hatred for wielders runs. I tried to confront him, but that ended poorly for me. Very poorly.

"It was the first time that I had caught the pair in cahoots, but it wasn't the last. For years, I had only a basic theory—that the pair were entangled in some bitter mess of a pact. You can imagine how intrigued I was to learn *you two* had allied years later.

"We all know how this period ended. Anesot died in Alita—and that was enough for me.

"Clearbold's ally, distasteful as he was, was dead. Even better, Samson, you'd been involved in his demise." Absalom looks at the wolf, a bend to his brow. "I respected that.

"But in Zarzynn... we started to uncover new information. Anesot wasn't just Anesot—he was an exile from the House of Serac. The same with Oko and the House of Col. That complicated things.

"Samson, when you went to Ezitlos with Helisent, the Hosts of Serac and Argot were under the impression that Clearbold was the Kulapsifang—not you or your mother. It was a deliberate lie. One that meant that Clearbold had interacted with the Hosts, possibly Malachai. And *how* would that have happened? Aside from captive okeanids, we were the first Mieirans to go to Zarzynn."

Samson sits up, scooting to the edge of the couch. I'm still struggling to string together Absalom's grand idea—but the wolf looks closer to understanding.

"Go on," Samson says.

"Let's go back to my first thought. That Anesot couldn't comprehend how deeply Clearbold's mistrust and loathing of wielders go. It's easy to underestimate an opponent you don't respect. Anesot and Clearbold both underestimated the other.

"But Ezit's Hosts... Ezit's Hosts would not be nearly as idiotic as the Male Alpha or Anesot."

Absalom shrugs lightly.

My heart thumps in my chest, then starts racing.

'Serac and Argot have a foothold in Velm.'

Not a foothold, but a golden invitation, it sounds like.

In our weighty silence, the warlock concludes, "Here's my grand theory: Clearbold was working with Anesot to embed himself with the Houses of Serac and Argot. If this is true, then we didn't only attack Ezit last spring. We also attacked Clearbold's most powerful allies."

The room feels like an airless vacuum for a moment.

Samson stares at the warlock, features bent.

I tug on my robe and fix my jewelry, feeling stupid.

I hadn't pieced any of that together.

At least, not so succinctly.

In a raw voice, Samson whispers, "I agree with you about the portal. They must have set up a portal in the palace. Clearbold might be dumb enough to ally with Serac and Argot, but he wouldn't let them wander around Velm as they please."

Absalom keels forward, sucking in a huge breath. "I'd really been hoping you were going to disagree with me."

"Unfortunately not." Samson sighs unsteadily. "Clearbold is working with the Houses of Serac and Argot. He has been for years—just like you thought. From what he said to me, it sounded like he was reporting on Anesot.

"And now, he's using the Houses to overthrow the Afadors. The wolves won't accept it—I'm not sure what makes Clearbold think they will. And I'm not sure what the fuck Serac and Argot want from Velm."

Speaking slowly, as though thinking through this idea right now, Absalom posits, "If Cosisent's theories are correct, it seems that Col and Talos want to control Septegeur. Compared to the other regions in Mieira, there are few demigods here. Fewer nymphs. It's here for the taking, at least in a spiritual sense.

"The same could be said for Velm. It's a vast territory that's largely unpopulated.

"So why not just kill the wolves and take it? What could the Hosts possibly need from your people, Samson?"

Samson looks away from Absalom. He curses under his breath and stands up. He paces the salon near the window, hands on his hips.

The warlock trails his movements. "You have three allies in the Class," he reminds the wolf quietly.

Suspicion boils in my bones.

I know this feeling; I've felt it before. In a noisy dining hall in Alita.

Samson's incredible penchant for secrecy.

Holy shit, he's hiding something again.

I won't be so stupid this time. I cross my arms. "Say it, Samson."

He squats near the coffee table, gripping its edge. He shakes his head. "Before he handed me over to Suleiman, Clearbold spoke of the Northing. He had strongly disagreed with my mother's plans for the Northing and her partnership with Andromeda North of Skull. Some wolves feel that anyone with a common enemy is their ally..."

Absalom makes a low noise, scooting against the couch's back. "The War Years, then. Suleiman knows your people held their own against wielders."

Samson looks at his hands. "There is a room in Bellator Palace. The tallest room in the palace. And the ceiling... is made of glass... He would have taken Suleiman into that room. And I think that the Host of Serac would have been very convinced by what he saw."

Absalom clears his throat, avoiding my gaze. "Ah, yes. There are rumors about the tallest room in Bellator Palace..."

Samson nods, jaw clenched. He looks at me and, almost silently, says, "I'm sorry."

I glance between the men.

As soon as I open my mouth to ask him to clarify, it clicks.

Once, long ago, Samson had told me that there were horns kept in Velm—*out of view from the public*, as though that would make a difference.

The tallest room...

I sink against the couch and tilt my head back. I stare up at the wooden beams that cross Absalom's sandstone ceiling. I sigh, letting self-hatred and regular hatred and doubt whirl within me like a windstorm.

Vex?

Did you know this?

Axerxa gave this wolf a fucking axe.

I summon a deep breath and pinch the bridge of my nose. Red fills my mind. "I hope you realize that wolves are fucking *disgusting*. You took me to Mort, and your stupid fucking wife begged me to help you —and *you never said you kept a trophy hall of*— say it. Tell me." I sit up straight and look at Samson, seething with every molecule of my body. "Right now, to my face. Tell me that wolves are disgusting. Admit it."

"They're from the War Years."

"You are disgusting to me." My voice rises and shakes. "All of you."

"Helisent—"

I bare my hand at him. It's a baseless threat as a centerheart, but I like how Samson's features bend with nervousness. "You are dangerously close to making a powerful enemy right now, boy-wolf."

"Let's forget about the... room, for a moment." Absalom leans toward us from the other couch, but I don't look away from Samson, and he doesn't look away from me. "For now, all we need to know is that Col and Talos are meddling in Septegeur while Serac and Argot do the same in Velm."

Samson finally tears his gaze away from me. He tells the warlock, "And we need to get to Pit. My best bet at retaking Velm is finding Imperatriz. Otherwise, I'll be retaking Velm with armies. I don't want that."

"Fine. That's wise of you. It's not the time for a civil war." Absalom tightens his robe with a long sigh. "I'll hold the north with Ethsevere and Cosisent in the meantime. We'll do what we can to keep Col and Talos at bay. You find a way to reclaim the south, Samson. Then all we have to worry about is the east."

I stare around Absalom's salon and try not to let my rage control me.

It's hard.

The men chatter on in low and serious voices.

My thoughts run on a loop—first excusing Samson's omission of this very disgusting fact, then taking secret joy in all of his misfortune, then acknowledging he shouldn't be blamed for the actions of his ancestors, then wondering how far I'll go for this fucking wolf.

"Helisent? Did you hear me?" Absalom asks.

"Obviously not. I'm fucking stewing over here." I stare at a green ottoman in the adjacent sitting room. I want to set it alight and watch it burn, but I don't want to punish Absalom's furniture for the wolf's misdeeds. "What do you want?"

"To suggest that you go to Red Tier. To the... apartment. That's your best bet at finding a way to Pit. Maybe Anesot kept notes there." He clears his throat. "The apartment is still empty."

"I'm not stupid, Absalom. Do you think we came all this way for a little chat?"

"Right. Well." Absalom glances at his front door, eyebrows raised. "I still have a white star. I'll throw one if something dire comes up."

"Fine." I can feel Samson looming between the table and the window, blocking the light and pouting at full force. "Tell this stupid wolf to get out of here. I'd tell him we're fighting, but... we're fighting."

Absalom huffs. "This is not my problem."

"You're *my* patsy, so he's *our* problem. Is it a wolf thing to betray people? He does it seasonally. I'm starting to think he likes it."

The warlock levels his golden eyes at me. "I'm your *what*?"

The Samson-shaped shadow inches closer to me. "Can we talk about this in private, Helisent?"

Absalom leans forward, eyes widening. "For the love of Espiga, did you set me up in the Class *as a patsy*?"

"What did the wolf say, Absalom?" I shift slightly away from the Samson-shaped shadow. "It's making noise at me."

Absalom curses under his breath. "Samson, why don't you take the front door? Helisent, you can take the back door. Also—*I'm not your patsy.*"

The shadow keeps hedging closer. "Helisent, I really am sorry."

I lean forward and slap the table with my palms. Then I swallow the pain that shoots through my fingers and stand up with a dignified and displeased groan. I straighten my robe and raise my chin, avoiding looking at either man.

Without a word, I round the couch and head toward the red door. I crank it open and look back at them.

In a rush, Samson stands and hustles toward me. Absalom scratches his chin and glances down the hall, as though surprised nobody is using the second door in the kitchen.

I stomp away from his apartment with tears in my eyes. I stalk down the path toward the sandstone stairs. I keep my weeping at bay, but my mind is too frantic to calm down.

I can't tell if I hate Samson right now.

The blow keeps landing, then healing, then landing again.

My feet scurry along the narrow paths as I descend back into Antigone's tangled copper and iron web. Now and then, Samson calls out my name; I can't tell if he wants me to listen to another apology or if he's scared of the heights or if I'm moving too quickly for him to follow, especially now that the pathways are flooded with Antigonians.

I don't look back once, boots heavy on the platforms and staircases that lead me to Red Tier.

Still, I try to find the right words—either a curse or a poignant observation that would communicate what it feels like to be utterly alone in life, then find someone who finally eases that pain, and then realize he's contributed greatly to that suffering. That if our positions were switched, he'd probably try to kill me as part of a blood feud.

I can't find the right words.

Over an hour later, we reach Red Tier, the lowest neighborhood in Antigone's upper levels. The eclectic district's painted housing comes into focus first, then its shivering and colorful flags. The fluttering banners, around the size of my hand, are pasted to almost every cable and banister in the three-level district. Amid the constant breeze, it almost looks like the technicolor fur of a great beast being tickled by the wind.

Around midday, the craftsmen and artists living in Red Tier are still lounging. At the tail end of the hazy summer, they do little aside from lying in open bay windows and strumming on sleepy instruments. Some lean onto the cable-suspended pathways to offer jewelry, metallic ornaments, talismans, and potions.

Now and then, their chatter and lighthearted music gutter to a stop. As I pierce further into Red Tier's curved platforms, I notice more silence.

A symphony of halted breath. And Samson, somewhere far behind, cursing and excusing himself and calling for me to wait.

A few heads crane from open windows, their golden eyes trailing me.

I guess there's a silver lining. If I weren't so focused on Samson's stupid fucking palace and its tallest room, I'd be dwelling on how uncomfortable it is to be in Red Tier. The neighborhood is constantly dressed for a festival, but my stint here ended in blood and betrayal.

The last time I walked these platforms, I had Milisent and Anesot at my sides.

With a long sigh, I turn onto a curved platform that leads to a lone green door. Its paint is green like Absalom's ottoman, pasted with dirt. Debris sits nestled into the corners of the doorframe; it hasn't been opened in years. Even the fluttering flags are threadbare and faded.

I sigh again, this time more forcefully, willing clarity back into my body as footsteps approach from behind.

Just go inside and look for clues on Pit.

Don't think about it—any of it.

When I reach for the handle, warm fingers take my wrist. From behind me, Samson whispers, "Please. I thought of it at the end. I could feel them in the room."

I don't turn back.

Just go inside first.

Don't think about it.

With my free hand, I send opening magic toward the door. It swings back into the dark apartment with a vicious creak. With its few windows shuttered, only the milky light from the doorway traces the large salon. I glance at the threadbare pieces of furniture I'd bartered for: a few lounging chairs, a large table, and shelves of amateur artwork.

Past the scents of grime and rust, I swear there's a trace of the cinnamon candles we used to burn.

I pull my wrist free from Samson's grip and head into the center of the living room. To the right, there's a door that leads into the bedroom—

My steps are noisy in the small apartment.

I look around, studying each dark corner, each forgotten piece of art: a ceramic clown, a glittery troll, a multi-headed snake. Cobwebs hang from the rafters and shelves. They remind me of tears. Wistful, pale tears, piled into the corners.

I crane my neck to see into the bedroom I shared with Anesot. In the center of the arched ceiling is a fragile wooden hatch door, its white paint chipping.

My breath catches when I see it.

Now that I'm inside the apartment, it's hard not to remember.

The first week I spent in this apartment was the happiest of my life. I was an adult, my sister was also an adult, and she lived above me and my bad-boy lover. My father and brothers came to bless the apartment a month later; that was the first time they'd argued with Anesot. And here is the little white door that led to Milisent's room, where I went to cry and convince her they'd been wrong about the warlock.

For a long while, memories replay in my mind.

In the apartment.

It's like stepping into the distant past and finding out that the past isn't silent.

It's yearning; these memories are alive, these memories dwell in this place, these memories will always connect me to this pain.

Here is the shape of pain: a narrow salon and a square bedroom. Here is its scent: grime, rust, cinnamon candles. Here is the next lover; also a failure.

I turn back toward Samson. He stands in the doorway in a darkened blur, the light at his back again.

I point at the large chair near the kitchen table. "Sit there and tell me about the horns. That's where Anesot used to beg my forgiveness. It will feel very familiar to me. I thought the past was dead, but I don't think it is, Samson. Convince me I'm wrong. Convince me I'm not making another mistake with you."

Samson takes one step into the room, ducking past the low threshold. He ambles toward me, head angled toward the chair. "I don't want to sit where he sat." He reaches over and drags the nearest chair toward him. It was Milisent's. I remember based on the flattened, yellow cushion. The chair creaks when he sits down, like it might buckle. "Would you like to sit?"

I cross my arms. "I'd like to break that chair and beat you with its leg."

He glances at the chair beside his. "Will you let me explain first? Please."

He pulls the chair toward him, arranging it so they face one another.

I extend my leg to kick over the chair. "Explain, then."

His eyes flit to mine, dark like storm clouds. I watch his hands wring together in his lap. His eyebrows bunch while he stares at them, lips moving like he's rehearsing his words.

"I was supposed to be raised by the Kulapsifang of Velm—and I was. Imperatriz led me until I turned twelve. I remember a lot about those years, but things changed drastically when Clearbold became my sole guardian.

"He did things differently.

"It wasn't until I was older and had more interactions with my grandmother, Sutnazzar, that I realized... Clearbold was doing things his own way. I wasn't raised how Kulapsifangs should be. Not after Imperatriz disappeared.

"I saw Sutnazzar in Rouz one year. I don't remember what comment I made—something about wielders. Something unkind. She learned then that Clearbold had taken me into the horn room. That's what he called it. It's in the back of the throne room. A small doorway. Nobody passes through that door; few know of its existence.

"Sutnazzar forbade me from entering the room, but Clearbold took me inside once a year. He would meditate in the room. He wanted me to think about my future as the Kulapsifang. To consider... threats. Threats made against my realm.

"I didn't understand the room when I was younger. What it meant. The older I became, the more uncomfortable it made me. Especially when I went north and began to spend more time around wielders. Looking back, I think I understand what Clearbold wanted."

Samson rubs his hands together, taking a deep breath. "Clearbold told me that he didn't trust Andromeda. He didn't like that our mothers were friends. It threatened him—he's always feared the

Northing. That was what he wanted. To make me afraid of wielders, and the red line, specifically."

I raise my eyebrows. "And why didn't you tell me this before? I told you that I'd felt a wolf's hide. I opened the door so we could... talk about these things. Right off the bat. But you lied."

"Last year in the tavern, before we entered Tet, I couldn't believe you asked me whether any horns were kept in Velm. I still didn't know if I trusted you, but I knew my people would need you. At the least, as a passive ally. At best, as an active ally. I didn't tell you because I didn't want to compromise that.

"And afterward... after the seething started... and even when we met in Zarzynn and you remembered me... I was ashamed. I love you. I didn't want you to know that my ancestors had participated in hunting the Vexen. I know wielders don't engage in blood feuds... but I feared a curse. That you would punish me for what my ancestors did.

"I knew I had to tell you eventually—but I wanted to wait until after I was in a position to do something about the horns. After I'd created some kind of plan."

I tsk, then wipe the tears that fill my eyes.

That's always the issue with Samson and all the pain he causes me.

I never actually blame him.

He's been handed a heaping pile of shit to manage. (Velm.) And now, he's lost almost everything. (Classic.) And there's always something much larger on the horizon. (Ezit's revenge.)

"And at the end? You said you could feel them at the end? The end of what?"

"When I was dying. How they... felt to touch."

My eyes jump to his. They're bleak and watery, like mine. "You never told me you were dying. Or that Clearbold was using Anesot to make a pact with Serac. I found that out from Absalom."

He shakes his head. "Helisent... I'm barely here. I hope you don't think I'm keeping secrets. I'm just..." He clears his throat. "I was a little embarrassed. That was the first thing I felt when you found me in Coil. Just... humiliation. About losing my realm. About my pack-mates dying. About what happened with Suleiman. About almost dying myself. I'm sorry for omitting so much. I promise—aside from the horn room, I wasn't consciously keeping things from you."

I study his features. He stares at me, waiting for a response.

Despite my best efforts, I can sense my heart tilting toward forgiveness. "I hope you know better than to ask to touch or see my horns again."

He keels forward slightly, a groan in his throat. "I see."

I add, "And I'll deal with Suleiman," so he knows I'm being reasonable.

His eyes jump to mine, then flit away. "Okay."

"And how many are there? The *tallest* room in Bellator Palace must be very impressive."

He looks at his hands. "Hundreds."

My blood runs cold. I glance at the open door behind us, relieved not to see any eavesdroppers. I toss up a smothering spell just in case. "Give a better range."

"At least seven hundred."

I fold my hands over my face, scream the word fuck into them, and then part my fingers to glare at the wolf. "Statistically speaking, that makes you way worse than Anesot. He only killed one of us."

Samson watches me where he's sat in Milisent's chair. The color drains from his cheeks.

"Look, I know you haven't raised a hand to a red wielder... but I'd figured we were done with all the secrecy after Zarzynn. I already told you that forgiveness isn't in my nature. Stop asking me for forgiveness. I won't..." I gesture to the apartment, hoping the stench and cobwebs and shelves of forgotten art paint a solid picture. "I can't do this anymore. I'm a grown-ass witch. I love you, Samson—and that's already hard enough."

He nods, then drops his head as though suddenly sheepish again.

I set my hands on my hips. "Well? Out with it."

"I'm trying to think if I have any more secrets."

"Fine. Be thorough."

"I didn't kill the wooly. Hetnazzar did."

"I already knew that. I spied on you and Rex one time."

"What? Really?"

"More secrets. Quickly."

"Samsonfang... Samsonfang is... very obsessed with you."

"You already told me that in Rhotidom."

"Sure, but it's like the horns. I barely told you enough."

"Then what am I missing?"

"He thinks our alas will mix one day."

"That's not possible."

"Tell that to Samsonfang."

I snort. "Fine. The next time I see him, I will."

Samson sits in silence for a few more minutes.

When he doesn't come up with any more secrets, I refocus on the task at hand. "If that's all, let's get this over with."

I turn and prepare my magic.

The only thing worse than hearing Samson's explanation is lingering in this awful place.

With a gesture of my hand, the candles dotting the apartment flicker to light.

With another flick of my fingers, I cast searching magic; the spell will look for anything hidden in the apartment. The croon of my bass skates along the walls, the cabinets, the shelves. They rattle lightly as the search unfolds. The sheets on the bed rise, then fall, as though sighing. The glass windows shake in their frames, the pots and pans and other small pieces jingle and clank like off-tune instruments.

A moment later, thumping echoes from the bedroom.

I wander past its threshold, leaving Samson behind.

A dust-riddled bed sits in the corner. A few stained-glass charms dangle against the square window above the headboard. A circular mirror hangs from the boudoir's door, laden with flowery bronze decals and dust.

I squint as I look upward. The white door, upheld by a fragile latch, sits at the crest of the arched ceiling. The thumping grows more distinct, echoing from the other side of the ceiling.

Milisent's bedroom? Like my apartment, it was left abandoned by Antigonians for fear of a curse.

I take a deep breath and hover up to the door. My fingers fit around the metal latch.

Samson wanders into the bedroom's doorway. "There's another room up there?"

"Milisent stayed in the apartment above ours." I open the door, and it falls toward me. I shift backward, letting the dust fall below. "We built the door to stay close."

"And the thumping?"

"It means my searching magic found something." I angle my head to stare through the square passage. From below, all I can see of Milisent's bedroom is its arched ceiling.

I remember every detail of her bedroom.

Her bed sat in almost the same position as mine and Anesot's. She put her boudoir beside the bed, not pushed against the opposite wall. She kept her favorite jewelry on a shelf near her bed and her shoes lined up beneath it. Her many, many shoes.

Careful not to snag my robe, I float from my old bedroom into Milisent's.

I see the line of shoes first. A tall pair of white suede boots, several jewel-laden slippers, then a pair of flat satin shoes with straps that wound up her calves. I'd hated them seven years ago—now, they're the first thing I notice.

I wander closer and pick up the red satin flats, then cast cleaning magic to dust their long and soft ribbons. "I take back everything I said about these, Mint." I scan the rest of the shoes, then press the strappy flats to my chest. "Mine."

I tiptoe around the room, scanning and dusting each item: a sketchbook, a vial of perfume, and shelves of amateur artwork, just like in my apartment. I clean her sheets, then tidy the bed. I sit on the mattress and toy with a nub of white chalk we'd used to scribble notes to one another on the walls. I bring it to the wood, then pause.

Eventually, I go with, 'I'm better now. I don't make the same mistakes. I miss you always.'

After another bout of teary nostalgia and tidying, I search the bed and floorboards for the source of the thumping. It doesn't take long for one of the floorboards to pop loose like a wooden tooth.

I stare into the shadowy nook hidden at Milisent's bedside. "Mint... were you keeping fucking secrets, too?"

I kneel on the floor and plunge my hand inside. I splay my fingers until I find a slip of paper folded into a tight bundle.

I pull it out and open it, but her writing is too faded and hectic to make out.

I float into the strong light below, then pad back toward the front door.

Samson follows, craning over my shoulder to look at the paper. "What does it say?"

I hold it up to the light and squint. "Let's see..."

Slowly, I sound out the words. Samson opens his satchel and pulls out a piece of parchment and a quill. He transcribes for me until we're sure his note matches the original.

Oko / Green Col, wind / overthrowing a host. Goes to Tet, takes phoenix ash to Tet > what does she want with phoenix ash? And Tet? Wind, phoenix ash, Tet > the Sennenwolf? Skull?

Anesot / Violet Serac, ice / overthrowing a Host? Aided escape for Sigurdi. 'When is our magic the strongest?' 'Do we like Tet?'

I scan each word multiple times, then pass the note to Samson.

I'm too shocked to do anything else—

I thought the revelations today would come from Anesot, not my sister.

Samson shakes his head in disbelief. "She must have suspected something all along. She got further than we did last year... look at this, Helisent. She knew about Col and Serac and Landmarks before we went to Zarzynn. She even knew that Col's power comes from cliffs and wind. She wrote 'ice' next to Serac—House of Glaciers."

I slide into Milisent's old chair and pinch the bridge of my nose. "I hadn't realized she suspected them of anything. She was... she was fond of them. Unless she..."

Here it is: she knew I'd choose Anesot over her, so she didn't make me choose because then she wouldn't be able to stay close and keep tabs on them.

She wouldn't be able to stay close and protect me.

"Fuck, Samson, I need booze. I'm going to start screaming or throwing up or—"

"She also wrote about the Sennenwolf, Skull, and Tet," he says, hunched over the letter. "Do you still have the notes from Itzifone? Maybe we can piece something together between those notes and this one."

I pull the note from his hand and fold it. "Did you forget what we came here for? It doesn't mention Pit, Samson. The notes are useless.

She was writing about what she thought Oko and Anesot were plotting. And that won't help us get to Pit."

"You're right—but it might help us understand Oko and Anesot's plans. She wrote *Sennenwolf*, Helisent. We haven't tied the Sennenwolf to any of this. All we know about the Sennenwolf is what a selkie told us, and that was vague enough.

"The same goes for Skull and Tet. Neither factored into our opinion on Zarzynn—not last year when we were hunting Oko, and not even when we were in Zarzynn. But Milisent was tying all of that together."

I look around and remember where I am. The adrenaline of Samson's second betrayal has faded—and I'm quickly tilting toward unwellness. "We need to get the fuck out of here."

He kneels in front of the chair. He sets his hands on my knees, thumbs stroking. "Have you spoken to Milisent yet? Or Andromeda? If Butter is still a capable necromancer, you can speak with them as soon as we're back in Luz."

My *moons*, his sanity and logical mind are sinful.

"No more questions until I've had a mouthful of hard liquor. Thank you very much. Let's go. Yngvi will have booze waiting at home."

He inches closer to me, thick eyebrows tugging together over his solemn eyes. "Can we walk back together?"

"Can you stop fucking betraying me?"

"Yes." He nods. "I promise."

"You better mean that."

"I do." He leans forward slowly. Eyeing me for objections, he sets his head in my lap. Then he nuzzles against my thighs before setting his head on his cheek and staring out the front door. "It smells like cinnamon and stress in here."

Later, we sit around Yngvi's kitchen table.

Yves and Kiki Red Tier join us wearing matching topaz jewelry. Growlies yowls from the bedroom, adamant for freedom. Pitter-patter slinks around the room and runs into the furniture as we drink and cajole.

I don't mention the trip to my old apartment. The note I found near Milisent's bed. The fact that Samson knows where our ancestors rest. That we still don't have a path to Pit.

Instead, we talk about nothing. My brothers keep Samson's mug of ale full at all times. Kiki Red Tier gets braver with her questions throughout the night. Eventually, she offers her wrist to Samson and asks what she smells like. Yves pouts and says she smells like argon, her favorite oil, but almost leaps onto the table with joy when Samson capitulates that Kiki carries traces of Yves's ala.

"I've heard about that!" he shouts with a snap of his fingers. "It's called *mixing*. Kiki, what have I been telling you—*we're in love*."

That's when a throwing star sails through the opened window, rips the edge of Yves's cloak, and sinks into the wooden wall with a loud *thunk*.

We whip our heads toward the sound.

With a curse, my brother tugs on his pale cloak and studies the clean cut. "Holy fucking *moons*, Yngvi. Who did you piss off? Tell them they owe me a new garment."

I scramble toward the throwing star. I recognize the iron piece from Zarzynn, a favorite of the vampires. "I think it's for me."

I use magic to free the piece, then dump it onto the table between our drinks. The warlocks, witch, and wolf lean forward, inspecting the weapon. A folded note falls from the throwing star's central finger hole.

I unfold it.

The local pack leaders sacked Coil, looking for Samson again. Zeu was there; that didn't go well. Hadadrimmon needs shelter. Maybe Gautselin, too. Creepy Baby is here, too. He won't shut up about Tet. He's very vulgar. Please come back to Luz immediately. Bring Zeu's throwing star. I'm doing great, by the way.

I love you. -Esteban

I blink at the paper, unsure where to start.
What does she mean by 'that didn't go well'?
Creepy Baby is back?
And when the fuck did the mentee start loving me?
I set the note down and reach for the half-full bottle of brandy in the center of the table. I throw my head back and chug as much as I

can before Samson finishes reading the note and gently pulls the bottle from my hand.

"We're not going back right now, are we?" he asks.

I turn away and head for the spare room where Samson and I slept last night.

He calls after me, uncertain and high-pitched. "Helisent?"

CHAPTER 7

HOGTIED IN HIS DEN

SAMSON

Suin,
I remember the first time Clearbold bit you. Colsep went to him after. He
wasn't alone. I never told you because my father forbade me, but you should
know; many sought to protect you from his teeth.
-Suin

I lift myself off the wooden floor.

A curtain hangs over me, its cool rod tilting across my shoulder blades. I swat at the dark fabric, disoriented.

I'd hoped to be more graceful when shadowing from Yngvi's apartment to Helisent's in Luz.

Not even a little bit.

I struggle on the floor, tangled in fabric.

The witch's tiny hands grab my triceps and tug me upward. "Oopsie boopsie!"

I rise with a groan. The scent of her apartment hangs around me; I can't see from beneath the curtain, but it smells like the mentee's bedroom again.

"Get out of here!" shrieks Esclamonde from close by. "This is my space!"

Thought so.

A second pair of hands grabs my free arm, nails digging in.

"Don't pull him!" Helisent hisses.

Then both sets of hands lift, and the witches start scuffling. One of them rams into my shoulder, then into my hip. I hit the wall again, trying to get out of their way while I free myself from the curtain.

By the time I've pulled it off, the witches are squabbling in earnest, and two men are watching from the doorway.

"Welcome back, my friends." Onesimos flashes a smile at me. "Did you get the note Esclamonde sent? Nobody was stabbed by the throwing star, I hope? Zeu insisted we use it to send the message. He's very concerned with being taken seriously."

Hadadrimmon crosses his arms, leaning against the doorframe. "He has Ferol hogtied in his den. He says he wants you to come and handle it as soon as possible."

I scan the wolf, searching for signs of distress or injury. If he's met Zeu, I can't imagine he thinks highly of the vampire—though I'm happy it seems like he's managed to avoid a fight with the King of Night.

The wolf and the oread both look well-fed and smell clean. Now that he's been in the apartment for a few weeks, Hadadrimmon's ala drifts out to me, noticeably pungent.

I toss the curtain to the ground. "I need to eat something before we go anywhere." I hang back at the last second, checking that Helisent isn't on the verge of collapse.

She stands near the window beside Esclamonde, fixing her hair—not slumping with nausea or fatigue. Compared to shadowing to and from Mort, the trip back from Antigone must be child's play.

I squeeze by Onesimos to follow Hadadrimmon into the kitchen.

He goes on, "It was the third time Ferol's pack stormed Coil looking for you. Well, for us. They would have had me, too, if it weren't for Zeu."

I pause in front of the cupboards, hand primed against the handle. *Zeu... helped Hadadrimmon?*

"I guess Ferol's raids have interrupted the vampire before. The first time, Zeu said he stood aside and let them ransack the place. The second time, Zeu said he and Ferol came to an agreement. I was there the last time Ferol's pack came in—and whatever agreement they struck, I don't think it involved Ferol tugging on his braids mid-coitus."

That's fucking rich.

I grunt in response, rifling through the cupboards. "Since when are you and Zeu friends?" I pull out a loaf of rye bread, then three lonely honeycakes.

"Since we met at Coil. He introduced himself after you left for Antigone—he could smell that we're related. I didn't realize they had noses like wolves."

I spare a glance at Hadadrimmon as he sidles against the countertop. "And you... get along?"

"Sure, why not? You should have seen the fight." Hadadrimmon scoffs again, leaning closer. "I only heard the first half of the fight because I was also... a bit indisposed. But I saw the second half. Zeu *kicked* him. Mid-air. And then he... I don't know how to describe it. Lots of turning and flipping. Very quickly."

I smile around a mouthful of honeycake. "Ah, yes. The kicks."

I saw enough bouts between the vampires in Hella to know what Hadadrimmon is referring to. They fight strategically; rather than the brute force of a waricon, it's about physical strategy. Spinning, kicking, holding, flipping—it was almost an art form.

One I would think very hard about before taking on again.

I munch on the soft, sweet bread, exhaling through my nose. "If you've been spending a lot of time at Coil, watch out for seethings. Just with the witches. You've heard the legends, right?"

Hadadrimmon's blue-black eyes glitter as they study mine. "Gautselin says that's all bullshit."

I raise my eyebrows, jaw working.

Bullshit?

A reel of images from my seething dreams plays through my mind.

I see a red witch with a pup, then a witchling with an adult wolf, both pairs creeping through the canopy of an ancient and massive yew tree. I see a loose bundle of red thread tangling my body. I smell the yew's bark, needles, and dew; I smell the witchling's hair, her oversized velvet robe. I see the precise hue of bloody red in her eyes.

"Really?" I swallow the rest of the honeycake, then head for another.

There's no way seethings can be chalked up to myth.

The dreams keep evolving.

I see a faceless witch. I see my demigod. In Septegeur, I even saw a shack on a hilltop.

I'm convinced these dreams are meaningful.

That they're at least partly real.

Hadadrimmon crosses his arms. "Gautselin says he's slept with at least a hundred witches and hasn't noticed any change. Not even when he slept with four-horns. Think about it—how could he employ male wolves if that were the case? He says the stories of seethings were started to keep wolves and wielders apart. It's all legend."

I shove the last honeycake into my mouth rather than respond.

I'll figure out how to bring this up to Gautselin later. When it's appropriate. When Ferol isn't hogtied in the King of Night's fucking den.

Hadadrimmon's eyebrows bunch as I finish the last honeycake. He clears his throat. "Right, well. We'll leave once you've finished your... meal." He leans toward me and sniffs. "You smell like wet metal. And birds. Did you find anything about how to get to Pit?"

I shake my head as I polish off a cup of water. "Not yet."

Then Hadadrimmon leads me to the front door. On the way, we pass Esclamonde's room; the curtain and rod are neatly arranged above the narrow window. The witches and the oread sit piled on the bed, their necks bent and their voices low.

"We'll all go together, then," Helisent whispers.

"What about Butter?" Esclamonde asks. "Her and Halcyon are at another lake. She said they'd be back soon."

"She couldn't sense anything about the ghosts last time," Onesimos reasons. "I think we'll be okay without her. Helisent, do you feel comfortable shadowing to Tet? Once you're rested, of course."

I knock on the doorframe. The trio whips their heads toward me. "We're heading to the den. Helisent, do you mind blocking our scents?"

The witch lifts a hand toward us. I don't notice the graze of her magic, though Hadadrimmon stiffens for a second. "Be careful. You and Hadadrimmon both have new stars. Throw them if you need me."

"Right." I narrow my eyes, wondering what the trio is up to. "Thanks."

"Creepy Baby left—but not before saying a bunch of cryptic shit. We're trying to decide whether we need to go back to Tet sooner rather than later." Helisent's smile doubles in size, then she waves at us with a slack hand. It almost looks like shooing. "Best of luck!"

We take a roundabout path to the den with Hadadrimmon in the lead.

With a smothering smell from Helisent shrouding our alas, we should be safe, especially in the dead of night. He guides us down alleys, first passing a famous spa and then Soulless. I amble at his side and smoke a cigarette, trying to enjoy the city's pleasant hush while we make our way to the den.

Eventually, Hadadrimmon stops before a stone staircase.

It leads from the street into the basement of a three-story stone building. In the center of the arts district, the large edifice's cold cobbled surface sticks out; most neighboring structures are built of dark, fragrant wood. Above, the broad windows are lined with fluttering paper ornaments, well-kept plants, and canary nests.

I glance from the optimistic terraces above to the undecorated staircase.

It leads to a shadowy, stone slab ten feet below. The door-like boulder has no handle, no hinges—only a rounded bottom, as though made for rolling.

Hadadrimmon claps me on the shoulder. "He said he'd smell us. No idea how that works."

"Right." Like I once did in Hella, I start to stretch in case this meeting goes awry. "How many live in the den?"

"I think everyone who came over from Zarzynn. There are around fifteen. Maybe twenty vampires total. I haven't seen them all lined up. The only time I saw the whole den together was when they dragged Ferol down here last night. It reminded me of nymph justice. Or what I've heard of nymph justice."

I glance at him while we wait. "And what do they say about nymph justice in the deep south?"

"Mob rule. Swift and violent."

I raise my eyebrows, relieved that vampire justice might not be so foreign.

Below, the door grinds against the ground with stern protest.

Inch by inch, the slab shifts to the side to reveal a black seam of darkness.

Zeu steps out of the underground room. His hooded eyes focus on me, their reddish iridescence on full display beneath the golden streetlamps.

As when we first met, bands of muscle trace his limbs, lined with dark veins. His gold-red mane is separated into four neat braids, and his hairless skin is spotlessly clean and bitterly white. His braids dangle against his bare chest near the soft feathers hanging from his necklace. Below, he wears a short white skirt, its fabric just as pristine as the pelt he once preferred in Zarzynn.

His full lips twitch as he looks from me to Hadadrimmon. "What the fuck happened to your hair?" He glances past us, as though searching for spies. "I believe I have one of your constituents."

My stomach clenches.

Even as a confident Kulapsifang, this would be a difficult situation to navigate.

I don't fully understand the vampires, and I hate their leader. Also, Ferol isn't just a wolf—he's Luz's male pack leader, one who might have challenged me even during my reign.

Plus, there's the question—*is Ferol my constituent if he doesn't want to be?*

Until Clearbold ousted me from Bellator, I'd seen every wolf as my constituent. My responsibility. A far-flung piece of myself that had to be guided, assisted, and organized; a far-flung piece of our demigod, too. Balanced at the top of Velm's hierarchy, it had all been straight-forward to look down at every other wolf and determine their place.

Now, I wonder how much of that power was granted by the wolves.

"Something like that." I sigh, studying the shadow past Zeu's shoulders. I don't hear any sounds of distress. So far, all I smell is a pit of damp stone and the offsetting scent of vampires and the blood they drink.

Zeu eyes me with a frown. "I hope you have a plan that will satisfy me, Sam-Sam. Ferol has insulted me greatly. Many times. And now he leaves his stench in my den."

"Let me in and let's find out." I glance at the wolf at my side. "Hadadrimmon will—"

"He is welcome amongst my den." Zeu waves a hand, then turns and disappears into the darkness. "We are brothers in Coil."

Brothers in Coil?

I glance at Hadadrimmon before we enter the gulf of darkness. He looks back at me with a defiant, reserved expression.

(Someday, he'll have to answer whether he's been at peace here in Luz or just descended into a whirling pool of hedonism.)

We descend the stairs and follow Zeu through the darkness, turning toward the glow of candlelight. The ground and low ceiling are frigid and cobbled, along with the walls.

Another short staircase leads into a circular, vast hall. The ceiling below is vaulted with a hulking chandelier hanging from its center.

I flinch, eyes narrowing as the dozens of candle flames flicker through my periphery.

I push away the memories of that Thing in Bellator.

It's easier right now than it usually is.

Because there, surrounded by a circle of shimmering candlelight, is a naked wolf bound on his stomach.

The scent of Ferol's distress sweeps over me, leaving a cold chill across my body. I smell the faint edges of testosterone and adrenaline, now overlaid by fatigue and cortisol.

My stomach clenches as a memory floats through my head.

I'd just joined my first war band when I first saw a wolf hogtied on their back, their hands and feet bound together with taut, coarse rope. The man had been left in that position for hours while the village council and war band leaders decided on an appropriate punishment. He'd been reported for abusing his livestock; we'd found evidence of egregious beatings and maimings.

The leader of our war band had bent at the waist to stare us novice wolves in the eyes.

"You look upon a sadist," he'd said.

I'd clenched my jaw. I didn't want anyone to know that the criminal's distress bothered me; the scent of his sweat and cortisol, the reddening of his cheeks, the slight bulge of his fingers. It had felt like he would burst—either his tendons or the ropes.

The wolf at my side was also frightened. I couldn't smell his terror, but I could tell by the way he pressed his shoulder against mine; leaning, bearing weight, sharing warmth. I'd pushed back to support my fellow wolf. I knew I'd met him in Bellator before, but I couldn't remember his name, only his face and frame—a bit gangly, too-large lips he hadn't grown into, a homely ala.

I clear my throat in the den.

I look at the wolf at my side.

Haddadrimmon, not Rex.

Hadadrimmon reels back a step. He quickly looks at the ground, then his feverish eyes search mine. I'd wondered if he'd ever seen someone hogtied before. If he'd ever spent time in a war band.

His surprise tells me that he hasn't faced this before.

I turn to Ferol.

He tries to move his head to look at me, then grits in pain. Rather than lie on his back like the sadist long ago, he's been forced onto his belly. His arms and legs are bent behind him, tied together into what looks like a back-breaking position.

Hadadrimmon takes another step back.

I take a step forward, toward the wolf.

My uncertainty from before is gone.

Ferol is my constituent.

Even if I hate him, his fate is tied to mine.

Even if he hates me, too.

I squat onto my haunches near the bound wolf's head. I avoid facing him so that he can't look directly at me. I'd discovered during my time in a war band that eye contact could drive some wolves mad, and I can tell that Ferol has been kept in this position for hours on end. Likely without food or water.

Beads of sweat drip from his reddened cheeks and temples. His veins bulge, prominent beneath his skin.

"What is his crime?" I ask. "Hadadrimmon mentioned he interrupted you at Coil."

Zeu comes to squat before Ferol, facing the wolf directly from a hand's length. "For the third time, this wolf interrupted me while I lay with someone at Coil. As you are aware, it is bothersome... to be interrupted."

He stares at me, one eyebrow arching without amusement.

I look back pointedly. "So why not beat him and chalk it up to testosterone like a reasonable man?"

"*I am reasonable*—this wasn't the first time. It was the *third*. And he touched my braids. Excuse me, it was not a touch, it was a *grab*. And I didn't beat him because I was advised that the wolves are accountable to you. Or to Velm. So, is it you or Clearbold? Who punishes this wolf and makes sure he stays," Zeu leans down, baring his teeth an inch from Ferol's sweaty face, "away from me and my den. Forever."

I sigh through my nose.

Uncertain of what to say, I try to summarize things how Helisent would; she's rarely at a loss for words. "It's not a great time to ask about Velm. Clearbold and I aren't... seeing eye-to-eye on things."

Zeu slaps his thighs and laughs.

The sound echoes through the den, causing a few vampires hiding in the shadows to snort and wake up. Though I can't see Zeu's denmates beyond the golden light of the candles, I can smell a few lining the room, can smell their half-drank cups of blood coagulating where they dot the undecorated floor.

"Such a unique way to put your situation." Zeu watches me with a half-smile. "Very optimistic. Go on, then."

I stare at the vampire, full of loathing for him, for Ferol, for my mess of a life. "It's my right as the Kulapsifang to rule Velm. But I've... Now, it's...

"Look, I can tell you how wolves enact justice. As a leader of the Luzian pack, Ferol's impropriety would be discussed at a regional level. To avoid creating conflict within packs, war bands punish wrongdoings. The leaders in Perpetua, Lampades, and Alita would decide on a punishment for Ferol, then bring in a war band to do the dirty work.

"It would be a serious sentence because you're a leader. Vampires are new to Mieira, so it's important that wolves establish a positive connection with you as the King of Night and leader of the den."

Zeu makes a low sound as he considers my words. "So, I write to the pack leaders in Luz, Perpetua, and Alita. Then they punish Ferol."

"Given... Velm's current... outlook... Ferol likely wouldn't be punished."

The vampire rolls his eyes. "Then you do it."

I shake my head. "The Kulapsifang rarely doles out punishments. Our role is more spiritual. We—"

"*Fuck you, Afador,*" Ferol shouts, straining against the ropes. "You couldn't even kill the wooly! And now you think you have the right to *judge* me. Only *Clearbold* or *Hetnazzar* can judge me."

I ignore Zeu's distracted smirk and focus on Ferol.

I study the wolf, trying to remember what it was like to feel a sense of authority.

With a deep breath, I recognize my anger, hold it, and then let it go. In its place comes pity, sweeping in like a flood. I sit with that, too.

I listen closely to what each tells me; rage, then pity.

This is what I intuit: Ferol's ignorance is a symptom of a higher issue. And punishing ignorance won't do anything but perpetuate it.

I take a deep breath. I pretend Rex is leaning at my side, pressing his shoulder against mine. I imagine Berevald does the same on my other side.

What would they say?

I tap on Zeu's shoulder, then shuffle him out of position. I take his place squatting in front of Ferol so the bound wolf can see me clearly.

Red muddles the whites of his eyes, spittle flecked onto his dry lips and chin.

I tell him, "You're right. I didn't kill the wooly. I was twelve. No twelve-year-old falls a wooly.

"When the wooly backed me against the boulders, Hetnazzar came for me." I lean closer, searching Ferol's eyes for a modicum of understanding. They stew and swirl with candlelight. "Hetnazzar came again when Clearbold pushed me into that waricon arena two months ago—after leaving me to be tortured all night by a warlock from Zarzynn. Both times, my demigod came for me. I don't have Velm, but it's clear I have the Hetnazzar's favor."

I can tell by the sheen of Ferol's pupils that he hates me. By the rigid clench of his jaw that he won't forget or forgive this moment.

But like an avalanche, the truth keeps its momentum. It barrels through me. "I cannot help you right now, my dear wolf." I shake my head. "You created discord with the King of Night. You have made a powerful enemy—which isn't the business of pack leaders, in case you've forgotten your role.

"The King of Night and his den helped save the okeanids in Ezit. Before that, I became friends with the Queen of Night. The vampires are honorable. Though they smell of blood, they've sought peace. *You* are the one who confused their scent and noise for danger."

I'd know a thing or two about that.

How many wielders have I approached with the same suspicion? How many times in Zarzynn did I feel the cold impulse to dominate the vampires?

Shame warms my cheeks.

Why has it never seemed this simple before?

Immediately, viciously, clearly, I see the wolves as we are.

Maybe for the first time in my life.

"As wolves, we're prone to doing this—mistaking the virtue of others for evil because we don't understand it. Because it alarms our fangselves. And even for all the control we like to think we have, there is no acknowledgment that we make those around us uneasy."

I stare at him, waiting for him to speak. Maybe to scream again. Possibly spit on me.

"You have lost Velm," he sneers. "You will never lead the wolves. Your words will never be law to me."

Quietly, I remind him, "I will, Ferol. And when I do, I will show the wolves that we do a great disservice by judging the world according to our standards. The world is not Velm; Velm is only one small part of the world. Do you understand?"

He looks away from me, a growl in his throat.

I stand and dust my hands clean. Hadadrimmon waits in the center of the chamber; he stares at me solemnly. A few vampires have shifted into the light to lounge on the stone floor. Their white skirts are spotless, their mouths stained with blood. They relax side by side, yawning and whispering in Zarzyd.

Zeu stands and heads back toward the entrance.

He glances back once, looking from me to Ferol with a withdrawn pessimism. He ignores the vampires who glance at him. One even asks a question, but the King of Night guides us swiftly back toward the entrance.

I follow, leaving Ferol hogtied in a room of candlelight and fangs. Hadadrimmon's shoulder brushes mine as he walks by my side.

The stone slab entrance remains half-opened. We follow Zeu up the short flight of stairs and back onto the street.

After a moment, the vampire gives me the once-over. "You didn't kill me when we first met."

I inhale deeply, trying to digest that statement. Helisent had stopped me from biting the vampire. I wasn't sure whether I would bite him to kill or establish dominance; I'm glad we never got the chance to find out.

"I was tempted," I admit.

"And you didn't kill Ferol." Zeu's eyes narrow.

I shrug, confused by this interaction. Vampires speak indirectly, sometimes in outright riddles. "Not for this, no. And I'd ask you for the same. Let him go, Zeu. You've made your point." I shrug again. "Would you take the life of one of your vampires so easily?"

"They aren't mine. I am theirs. I was Chosen. One day, we might choose someone else." Zeu glances at the stone slab at our backs. "But you were never chosen."

"I was chosen by my demigod." Zeu scoffs, so I follow up with, "But you're right. It isn't the same as being Chosen amongst vampires."

He nods, agreeing. "You told Ferol you were tortured by a warlock."

I inhale deeply again. I have no idea what he wants to glean from that statement, but I don't feel particularly endeared to share my pain with the vampire.

Zeu watches me evenly. He asks, "Could you smell him?"

Again with the odd questions. I study his slit pupils, admitting, "I smelled him, yes. Why?"

"It was Suleiman? Halcyon's father?"

Hadadrimmon jolts, as though surprised by that revelation, but doesn't say anything.

I try not to let the pain show. I try to maintain an entirely neutral, empty expression. (It's hard, and I don't think I do a good job, and it immediately makes me angry.) "Yes. Suleiman."

Zeu nods again. "We will go to Soulless, then. This is good. I was worried we would have nothing in common. But there's a saying from Plet—it's in Zarzyd, and I don't know how to translate it, but it goes like this, 'love divides and evil unites'."

Then the vampire takes off, crossing the street with quick, heavy steps.

My stomach drops as I watch him go.

I don't want to have anything in common with Zeu, especially not this.

But I follow after him, Hadadrimmon at my shoulder.

Soulless will have plenty of booze, at least.

Hours later, deep in the night, Helisent sets her hands on her hips and stares at me.

I try to sit up straight in her kitchen chair, but it's hard not to slouch.

I don't think I've ever been this drunk in my adult life. Or high.

A gentle breeze floats in from the open window. It shakes the leaves of the ginkgo biloba tree, sweeping into the room and cooling me before ruffling the hem of Helisent's soft, tawny dress.

"Who are you and what have you done with Samson 714 Afador?" she asks.

I can't tell if she's angry or enthralled.

When she found me huddled in the back corner of Soulless with Hadadrimmon on one side and Zeu on the other, she screeched loudly. She screeched again when she realized we'd been sharing a portion of dextro and that my pupils were, in her words, 'the size of fucking saucers'.

I know her yowling to indicate one of three things: delight, wrath, or awe. But I wasn't able to pinpoint which it was before she dragged me away from them by the wrist, ordered us drinks to go, and then marched me home.

Since then, I've stayed quiet, hoping to glean her mood before responding.

She sets her hands on her hips like she's angry, but she keeps giving me the once-over like she's planning on dragging me into the bedroom and undressing me.

After all, by some miracle, we're home alone.

"It's me." I clear my throat to keep from slurring. "The boy-wolf. Your *favorite* Kulapsi-boy."

No smile from the witch. "How fucked up are you? Rate yourself on a scale of one to ten. One being Esclamonde and ten being me. Well, the old me." She whines, staring up at the ceiling. "Fuck, I miss the old me."

I lean back and forth on the chair, trying to gauge my senses. "I can still walk. But I don't think I could dance. Does that paint a picture?"

"Yeah." She gives me the once-over again. "I can work with that."

"Okay. Cool." I lean back to tug off my shirt. The fabric sticks to my damp skin; the arm holes also seem significantly smaller than when I put it on. "Just... give me a second..."

"Oh? Wow. That's forward. You can keep your clothes on for now, Samson."

I blink into the dark fabric that's caught around my jaw. "Who are you and what have you done with Helisent West of Jaws?"

With a brush of her infrasound and a gentle rip, the fabric falls loose around my head and arm. It slips into my lap in a warm heap.

In its wake, I see a witch with braided white hair, mounds of twinkling jewelry, and a vivid frown. "I'm sober Helisent." She moves her hands off her hips to cross her arms, bracelets jangling together. "I told you, she's the fucking *worst*. Now try to focus. I'm leaving for Tet first thing in the morning."

I shake my head in alarm. "Tet? What? Why?" This time, I give her the once over. "We need to talk about you going to Tet. If a sink doesn't get you, a flash flood will. Can you swim yet?"

She rolls her eyes. "That's not—"

"Who taught you how to swim? I thought I would."

"I'm not going to Tet to swim. It's something else. I haven't told you yet. Here's what happened—on the way back from Cadmium this summer, Creepy Baby showed up and—"

"*Creepy Baby*?" I sit up in the chair. "What? Is that why he came to Luz?"

"Something like that. I had offered him... Well, I made him an offer in exchange for finding Oko. That's how I found her in Alita last year. Creepy Baby told me where she was. So, he showed up recently and said that—"

"He can *talk*?"

"Yeah." She nods, arms still crossed. "Real foul mouth on that little boy."

"Well, that's no surprise."

"You should see how he terrorizes Esteban." She holds a palm out to me. "Now, stop interrupting. Creepy Baby said that he'd noticed my magic in Tet. I went with Butter and Esteban a while back, and it turns out that my magic is... delving. One of the caves is red. Very red. I'm not sure how to describe it."

I narrow my eyes, trying desperately to keep up. Onesimos had mentioned she was in Tet, but I didn't know why.

Now, the alcohol in my gut lulls me into a heavy slumber; the dextro ratchets through my chest in a frenzy. I can't tell if this is how I'm supposed to feel.

"Delving?" I manage.

"Yes, *delving*. I think Vex has been vaguely aware of Tet since we went there. Vex's ejima must have learned about Tet through my memories."

I lean back in the chair. "So, you went to Tet with Creepy Baby?" I try not to sound too stunned or suspicious. Sometimes, it seems like the witch willingly and with great gusto puts herself in dangerous positions.

"With Butter and Esteban. It was a disaster—we got lost. We eventually found the ghost and the cave. But I guess he's found a few more caves since we left—all full of my magic. That's why Creepy Baby came back to haunt Esteban when we were in Antigone."

"So, you're going back?" I try to ignore the panic and distress packed into that notion.

"Yeah, tomorrow. Onesimos is going to come with me and Esteban. I know it's not the best timing... Trust me, finding Pit is still a priority for me. But I can't abandon my demigod. Not now—especially not if it's actually laying claim to Tet. At the same time, you can't stay here in Luz. It's too dangerous."

She offers me a hopeful smile, then continues, "So, while I touch base in Tet, you're going to Alita. Butter and Halcyon will be back tomorrow afternoon—they're taking you to mighty King Hemlock. There are fewer wolves up north, and Hemlock will be more than willing to shelter you. Parsifal will be in Alita, too. As soon as you get there, I'll shadow to meet you. It won't take long."

My stomach drops more with each word.

I stare at her; my head shakes involuntarily. "We can't be separated."

I don't trust anyone.

I don't even know if I trust Hadadrimmon fully.

As far as I'm concerned, deep in my heart, I'm in a two-being pack with Helisent.

And the last time I was separated from my pack...

Helisent shakes her head, too. "I can't drag you to Tet. Not when you need to be looking for a way to Pit. Anesot and Oko used to go to Alita all the time—Hemlock probably knows where they stayed. Just because my old apartment was a bust, that doesn't mean those two didn't leave a paper trail somewhere else. We just need to stay focused. I'll meet you there in a few weeks, and we can hunt down any leads you find."

I chew my lip.

We don't need to stay focused; we need to stay *together*.

But when I look up to argue my point, the witch is gone.

A moment later, she pads back into the room from the hallway, clutching an orange-wrapped bundle.

I freeze when I smell what's inside.

It's the bitter and unending ala of her demigod, of the limestone caves of Vex and the dry pine barrens above. It spews from the fabric like cold air from a cavern deep in the earth.

The wand.

She offers the bundle to me. "You're taking this with you. For protection, amongst other things."

I accept the bundle, careful to avoid touching the wand. "Helisent?"

She pulls up a spare chair to sit beside me, leaning over as she gazes at the orange fabric. "Open it."

I study her features. They're set, serious. "Vulcan told me Axerxa's wives gave this to him so that he could battle Ezit. He said it's all that remains of Vex's Landmark... which makes it your demigod."

I can feel the wand's weight amid the light fabric. It's heavier than I thought it'd be—and it's palpably buzzing with infrasound, as though partly activated.

I take a deep breath, feeling wholly underqualified to be this close to her demigod.

"Well, it is... but..." Helisent shrugs, scooting closer. She sets her head against my shoulder and stares down at the wand. It glows gently, hidden within the orange fabric. "When we spent the night in New Hypnos last year, you and I saw the same thing in a dream. We saw Hetnazzar bite the Hellastone to free the wand from it. Without that, I may have never found it or even realized it existed.

"I know it was only a dream, but... once, I heard a wolf say that

Hetnazzar travels by Night and by dreams. Maybe your demigod did it on purpose. And if that's true, then you deserve its protection."

My stomach drops further.

I shift so that she lifts her head. When she does, I look into her eyes. "That's a big assumption. If you saw Hetnazzar, would you walk up to it and touch it?"

"Well, yeah. Maybe. If I wanted to." Her head tilts with confusion. "Or is your demigod... not a fan of... being touched?"

I'm not even sure how to answer that.

A wolf would never feel compelled to touch Hetnazzar—we aren't like nymphs or the wielders they've influenced. We don't touch the things that spark curiosity; we observe, we consider, we debate.

In my silence, Helisent insists, "Regardless of what Hetnazzar likes and dislikes, I am the only Vexen and this is my demigod. I'm handing it to you so you'll be better protected in my absence this time."

She reaches over to peel aside the orange fabric. The slender and narrow rod, only the girth of my pinky finger, comes into view. It's as red as Helisent's magic, aglow like Sennen—and still spewing a faint curdle of bass.

"If Vex learned about Tet through your memories," I reason, "then it knows about the horn room."

She reaches up to stroke my face. "I know. But when I shadowed us to Mort the first time, *you* were the one who told my magic where to take us. That means—I hope you're listening closely with those fucking huge pupils of yours—my magic might do the same for Pit."

My eyes widen.

Me guide her magic?

"Helisent—"

"We need a backup plan here. Oko and Anesot... maybe we'll find some clue they left behind about reaching Pit. But I've been thinking... why not use your mind or my mind to get there instead? We have Vex's ejima on our side, Samson. We're helpless right now, but not my magic.

"I'm the direct option because I've been to Pit before, but I was half-dead and on a boat the whole time. That makes you a better conduit. You have a psychic connection to Imperatriz. You're not only mother and son, but Kulapsifangs. And, if things went well back in New Hypnos when we sent her my dove, then Imperatriz should have access to a large store of my magic. And if my magic has been with her on Pit, then it's not just some random place. Vex could be aware of Pit in the same way it was made aware of Tet. Tangentially, through ejima. Does that make sense?"

I stare at the naked wand, its orange layers pulled aside.

Even if her argument doesn't settle the anxiety in my stomach, it's not hard to follow her logic. "When do you come up with all these ideas?"

"I'm a born plotter." She leans closer, stroking my face again. Casually, she slings a leg over mine. "I've been ten steps ahead of you for years, my sweet wolf."

Still, my fingers pause a few inches away from the red stone.

I'm torn between the acknowledgement that this isn't a time to start a dalliance with another demigod, considering the sore state of Velm. Simultaneously, there might not be another option if I want to retake my realm.

Helisent keeps sidling closer to me, leaning more weight onto the leg slung over mine, and gently heaving her breasts against my arm.

I look away from her, trying to concentrate on the wand, and whether I should say something to it, and how I should touch it.

"Samson," Helisent cranes to whisper in my ear, "I'm trying to initiate sex magic right now. It seems like you're a bit confused. Here's how this will go: I made a little necklace so you can wear the wand, and then you're going to get undressed."

It clicks. I almost knock into Helisent as I turn to face her. "While I... the wand? You want to... with me?"

She blinks, impatient and unamused. "Yes. And it doesn't have ears, so you can say whatever you like." She gives me the once-over. "Or did you take too much tonight? I would have come and gotten you quicker if I'd realized you three were railing lines like it was your last night on earth. I mean, when the *fuck* did you and Zeu become tavern buddies?"

With a tsk, she stands up and gets to work slipping her dress over her head.

She tosses it to the side, leaving her jewelry on. Bangles circle her wrists, ankles, and upper arms. Heavy necklaces droop from her collar, partly covering her chest. She even has a torc-like piece encircling her left thigh.

Her brown skin is dark in the dim kitchen, outlined with gold from the single light on the countertop. The light traces her supple and soft thighs, curves up her hip, and grazes the soft mound of her belly and the swell of her wide, full breasts. She steps forward and takes the half-wrapped wand in one hand.

Quickly, she pulls a cord from the kitchen table and works it around the narrow piece. Then she loops the cord around my neck; the wand dangles from the thin strand of cordage, settling near my solar plexus.

I look down as its cool surface tickles my warm skin.

And then Helisent slides into my lap, obscuring the wand. She rises to present me with her bare breasts, gently stroking my scalp with her fingertips.

Every little question and objection drifts away. They still matter, just less than this.

Whatever the witch wants when her breasts are out.

I nuzzle forward to let their weight fall against my cheeks and chin, then kiss their fullness.

I look down when I feel something hard against my chest; the wand. It whirrs with light and bass.

I stiffen, shifting away from the witch to focus solely on the cool, red rod.

Helisent grabs my chin with a tsk and directs me back toward her breasts. With pints of ale and nosefuls of dextro whirling in me, it's a deluge. But in the back of my mind, I have qualms about this moment.

First, we shouldn't be in a kitchen if we're making love with a demigod present. We should be in a palace. (*My* palace.)

Second, I shouldn't be this fucked up. I should be sober and capable.

Third, it should be near the triplemoon; my magic will be more powerful when Vicente, Abdecalas, and Sennen are reflecting the full force of the sun. The doublemoon waits over a week away; even that would be better than this.

But it slips from my mind quickly. In what feels like the span of three breaths, I'm also naked, and my witch's heavy jewelry is scratching my skin, and I'm grabbing handfuls of her legs, her ass, her hips.

She slides off my lap and saunters toward the salon. Her sexual ala wafts from her, leaving a streak in the air that takes hold of my mind and body. She turns to watch me, her irises and the whites of her eyes now spewing red light.

I stand and follow.

She points to the cushions piled on the floor.

I sit down on the largest. The wand hangs from my neck; it glows as brightly as her eyes. The scent of frigid limestone fills the air, overpowering Helisent's sexual ala. I swear the air vibrates, too, alight with Vexen infrasound.

That impulse I felt in Vex overcomes me again—

I want Helisent to make me beg.

I want Helisent to take control.

Yes.

I lean forward to tug on her hips, and she falls toward me with a sultry giggle. I shift to lie back on the piled cushions, guiding her down toward me so that her knees fall near my shoulders.

She starts hovering instead. "What are you doing? I won't cum if I'm worried about crushing you."

I tsk. "Crush me? Don't be stupid." I slide my hands behind her calves and pull gently again. But she hovers once more; I angle my neck to look past her belly and meet her eyes. "I'm trying to do sex magic. I don't know if you can tell."

I'm also thrilled it seems like she hasn't sat on too many faces.

She makes an uncertain noise as she sidles down toward me. Sheltered between her thighs and wet vulva, I'm in a shroud of happiness. Her scent reminds me of limestone, of pine barrens, of tarnished jewelry, of honey.

Of safety and possession.

I fit my hands around her thighs as she arranges herself closer to my mouth.

She squirms one last time. "Your stubble tickles."

Slowly, she relaxes, and I run my tongue along her, shifting for better access. I lick her wet center, grazing her lips before plunging lightly inside.

I tease her with my tongue, leaning onto my elbow now and then to stroke her with my fingers. I don't stop until I feel her tense up, enjoying her weight on my face and chest and shoulders, savoring her scent as it smears across my face. With each touch, my cock hardens, my body twitching as it zeroes in on her signals.

I see the wand glow red in my periphery now and then, a flash that catches my attention.

I'm distracted and obsessed at the same time. Untethered by the dextro and booze, pulled swiftly and totally into Helisent's orbit.

The witch's legs clamp around my head as she groans and convulses, then she shifts onto her hip on a cushion.

Her chest heaves with each breath as she watches me, her nipples perked. She licks her lips as I sit up, glancing from her glowing red eyes to the glowing red wand dangling against my chest.

"More," she says.

She shifts onto her belly, toppling a few cushions so that I'm presented with her full ass, the backs of her supple thighs, the dripping seam peaking between them.

Lo anata sevi-no, Samsonfang growls.

You are mine.

The words rush from my lips. "*Lo anata sevi-no.*"

I bend to lick her thighs and then graze my teeth along one of her thick, round ass cheeks. I sit up and lean onto my hands, shifting into place behind her.

With a groan, I ease into her, deeper and deeper into her wet warmth.

The wand grazes her upper back as it dangles from the cord.

She folds her arms and sets her head on them. Her eyebrows pull together, mouth ajar as she moans. "Keep talking to me in Velmic."

Samsonfang heaves against my mind, desperate for this experience.

And I'm too fucked up to separate us right now.

We blur into a single being; a fangself and a man, a wolf's instinct and logic forging into one.

I feel a slight tear in my soul.

It's jarring; it's a great relief.

From that slight tear, a deeply held wish takes shape.

Samsonfang rushes forth—he brings it into existence—he does not recognize the line between the possible and the impossible—

"*You are the Female Alpha, and I am your Male Alpha,*" I purr Samsonfang's words into her ear. *"When the cold autumn winds come, I will take you into our bed, and I will make love to you, and I will stay inside of you."*

She moans, body shivering as I slowly tease her. I press my chest and abdomen against her back, the wand disappearing between us.

"And you will hold my essence, and it will become one with yours, and I will shelter and feed you through Night. I will keep the fire strong, and you will grow until the warm sun returns."

With each word, I'm more desperate for our bodies to touch, for our alas to tangle. I pick up my pace, pleasure and urgency coursing through me.

She moves in time with me, arching her back to meet each of my strokes. "More," she gasps. "Keep talking."

"And when the sun returns and the snow melts, the women will take you to the willows, and I will sit with the men in the tavern. They will worry with me, and they will wait with me until you come back with a pup bundled in your arms."

I wrap my hands around hers as I plunge deeper. Our bodies clap together, her ass jiggling against me. Her body grows tense again; her fingers tighten on mine. Between our bodies is the glowing wand, tracing my pale hue and her rich brown skin.

Our breaths hit the same pace, as do our shameless moans. I feel a thrum at my solar plexus.

I've felt this same sensation before—a gentle and light-filled croon of bass. It lingers in my chest before spreading throughout my body.

"And then we live forever," Samsonfang swears.

My breath catches in my throat as an orgasm explodes through me.

Red starlight wheels through my body, through my vision. The warm buzz I felt in my chest shoots through my abdomen, then my limbs.

It lingers around my groin, most palpable where mine and Helisent's bodies are linked.

It almost feels like the adrenaline of a scare.

This time, I can feel the energy lingering.

Tossed in with Samsonfang's ongoing deluge of urges, it's overwhelming and disorienting.

I pull away from Helisent, panting and staring at the wand. I sink back onto my haunches as she peels herself off the cushions. She turns around, her chest rising and falling with each breath.

Arrantly, she watches the wand, then her matching red eyes fix on me.

She licks her lips. "More, Samson."

More, Samson.

The witch paws at me for hours.

I lose my mind for her. Samsonfang, too.

I follow her across the cushions until my back hurts and the air grows humid with our sweat. Until she stops demanding more.

When we fall asleep amid a pile of damp cushions and tangled blankets, I dream a seething dream.

The dream is red, every color overlaid with vermillion and crimson hues. I know the sky is blue; right now, in this dream, it looks cherry-stained.

I'm standing outside of a shack on a hill. On the way to Antigone, I'd confused this shack with a yew tree, staring from a distance. Now, I see it clearly. The dwelling is small and handmade, but its windblown planks hint that it's lasted many years. The stones lining the foundation are covered in lichen. The door shifts as a breeze hits it; the threadbare curtain covering the glassless window beside it undulates.

I know I need to go into the cottage.

But everything is red and I've never been here before.

I stare at the small dwelling.

At the little curtain that flutters in the breeze.

I jolt when I see movement from within. For a split second, I think it will be the faceless witch. The witch has haunted my seething dreams before, her head turned away where she sits below the yew tree.

Maybe now she'll face me—

I brace for it as someone passes by the curtain. I see their body angle, as though they're about to pull the door open and look out. It scares me; this place is unknown, I've never dreamed in red, and I never got a warm feeling from the faceless witch.

Adrenaline shoots through my body.

It wakes me immediately.

I come to in a pile of cushions and blankets; Hadadrimmon is snoring at my side, also covered in blankets. I sit up, surprised not to find Helisent splayed out in his place. Instead, I find an orange bundle, wrapped tightly in parchment near my left hand.

The note reads, 'Don't let the wand out of your sight. If anything happens, ask Vex for help. Trust Vex. See you soon.'

My back hurts.

The walk isn't helping.

Because Halcyon and Butter weren't ready to leave for Alita until the late afternoon, Hadadrimmon and I had some time to recover from the previous night's festivities.

But not enough.

On our first day trailing the lovers into the jungle, my packmate rushes off the road to hurl into the bushes and make the same joke about Luzian moonshine.

Halcyon waits for him with patience the first two times, but after the third trip, Butter casts a healing spell on him. From there, Hadadrimmon picks up his pace, while I hobble along with an aching back.

By the next morning, we're deep inside the Rhotidic jungle.

Above, below, all around is the hectic and unfathomable thrum of life. We weave below towering trees, snaking vines, actual snakes, small shrubs, and the layered canopies overhead. The rotten mud and noisy animals and mammal-sized insects once again seize my attention. The fetid stench of fertile soil is accented by fragrant blossoms and the oily fur and feathers of eagles, sables, saigas, and more.

It enraptures Hadadrimmon.

We fall behind the warlock and the okeanid-witch-necromancer once more, so he can crane his neck toward the busy canopy. He babbles endlessly about the scents. I can't name all the mammals and flowers we come across—but I remember the novelty of smelling so many alas when I traveled here for the first time.

As dusk approaches, Hadadrimmon elbows me. "What's going on? You've barely said a word since we left Luz."

I sigh; I've been debating whether or not to speak of the witch's conduct. "Do you want the truth?"

"I asked, didn't I?"

Halcyon and Butter are too far ahead of us to hear, but I lower my voice just in case. "I think Helisent tried to fuck her magic into me the other night."

Hadadrimmon glances at me, a half-smile on his lips. "I see. And are—"

"Don't talk to me about it. Never talk to me about it. I just needed someone to know."

I can see his stupid smile from my periphery. "Well? She didn't hurt you, did she? Should I have a word with her the next time I see her, or—"

"My fangself was... very much part of that interaction."

My fangself made a full and detailed appeal to Helisent about why he's the right partner for her. Thankfully, Samsonfang doesn't speak Mieiran. And even though the witch doesn't speak Velmic, I'm not sure that matters—especially where magic is involved.

'And then we live forever.'

'More.'

We crossed a line. That's not the problem, so long as it yields results—the problem is that I should be curbing my love for the witch instead of stoking it.

Hadadrimmon looks appropriately wary now. "Fangself? What? How? The doublemoon is two weeks away. That can't be normal— even for a Kulapsifang."

"Yeah, no shit." I gesture to nothing. "The witch and me... I don't think it's normal."

The wolf scoffs, his playful attitude returning. "To be fair, I don't know if that's unique to Helisent. Very little seems normal about you, Samson, my dear Afador. I've been thinking that since our demigod dropped us off in the care of a Luzian gigolo. *'This can't be normal—but just hang in there, Hadadrimmon.'*

"Things haven't really taken a turn since then.

"I mean, we're on our way to a Rhotidic King. I never thought I'd get this far north, let alone be placed into the care of a nymph monarch. Normalcy might be a pipe dream for you."

"That's oddly soothing." I keep walking, glancing at Hadadrimmon and wondering when he became so insightful. "What do I look like to you? If you were Imperatriz and you saw me after eighteen years, what would you think?"

His eyebrows shoot up. "You want an answer to that?"

I throw his words back at him, "I asked, didn't I?"

He purses his lips. "I'd say you looked like your father."

I'd figured as much—though I was hoping he'd say something else. "Is that all?"

Hadadrimmon studies me with narrowed eyes. "I'd probably ask about your hair. Just to make sure you didn't cut it like that thinking it looks good."

I run a hand along my scalp. Almost four months since my head was shaved in Bellator, my hair is a spiky, uncouth mess of blue-black strands. I can't tell if I hated it more shaved—this mid-length has not been kind to me.

"It's growing fast," Hadadrimmon adds.

"Really?"

"Well, it's—"

"Fuck off."

CHAPTER 8

DIAMONDS (SUNLIGHT)

HELISENT

Honey Baby,
Do you remember your gold-hoarding phase? The golden bounty is still at the
homestead. I can't believe you haven't come back for it yet.
The Boys

Firelight flickers along the cave's uneven, crimson walls, flashing like lightning.

I sigh, unhappy to be back in Tet.

I can sense my magic lingering in the stone, buzzing lightly enough to be heard and felt. I can feel Skull, too, which is differentiated by its tone of magic. Not by pitch, per se, but by *tone*.

I'm still not sure how to explain that.

When I shadowed from Luz with Onesimos and Esclamonde, my magic transported us straight here—to the same tunnel-cave that Creepy Baby led us to on our first trip.

It's nothing like Hella.

No city streets, no fountains, no rococo carvings of delightful and stubborn wielders.

No Samson, either.

Just mossy red tunnels prone to frigid drafts and echoes.

Since our return, the witchling, oread, and I have turned one of the rounded coves into a livable camp. I sculpted a few benches from the shale, which sit around a large fire pit. A few low shelves line one wall, our supplies stacked neatly atop.

On the adjacent wall is a chalked map of Tet's caves. Though rudimentary, our scribblings are a solid start.

Like Creepy Baby hinted, my magic seems to be extending its reach in Tet. We've spent the last days trailing the ghost from cave to cave to log them.

In my absence, Vex has claimed several more tunnel-shaped caves —but they're still vastly outnumbered by the sinks. For now, we're recording both to glean whether Vexen magic is delving into new caves or overtaking the sinks.

It's a deceptively exhausting mission that leaves us slumped over our dinners each evening.

I figured we'd come here, take note of the caves, and then head back to Luz or Alita. Instead, we keep finding more red shale; pebbles lead to boulders that lead to cavernous, underground chambers.

Tonight, after a long and confusing day of exploring a region to the south, we sit slumped around the fire. Its flames illume and warm the frigid walls of our cove. We munch on a humble dinner: okra, rutabaga, lentils, and rice.

Creepy Baby sits atop a jutted rock between our campfire and the cave's primary tunnel. He wears a tattered pair of shorts and a neck scarf, leaving his bulging tummy bare.

Esclamonde turns her frown toward the ogling ghost. She doesn't say anything, just stabs at her meal with a fork and glances at me to make sure I know she's not at ease with his presence.

Onesimos, on the other hand, can't stop eyeing the ghostling. "You don't have the slender eyes of a hesperide, nor the thick hair of a dryad. And you don't have the same features as an okeanid or an oread. So, you must be a naiad?"

Creepy Baby blinks at him and scratches his belly. "Sure. Naiad." He glances away, raising his eyebrows. "I am a naiad." He nods. "Sounds good."

Onesimos sets his fork down, turning his full attention to the ghostling. "But you don't remember your demigod? Every nymph knows their demigod. It's instinct."

Creepy Baby raises his eyebrows. "It's like I told the witches—I don't remember anything. Just that I'm old."

He hunkers down on his rock, folding his legs to his chest and locking his arms over them. Firelight glimmers across his green form; it reflects off his watery eyes, then passes through his semi-transparent body.

"Is the rice good?" he asks, eyes fixed on our plates. "The rutabaga and okra look old. The lentils look perfect."

"Esteban cooked," I explain, pushing my food around my plate.

Esclamonde looks at me, one of her cheeks stuffed with food. "*Hey*. I cooked the—"

"I think I remember the taste of lentils," Creepy Baby announces. "They were slightly sweet, very nutty and earthy. The texture was... grainy and soft. They paired well with many foods."

Now, my fork goes still in my hand. "Wait—so you remember *some* things, then?"

Creepy Baby lifts his chin. "Oh, yes. I'm on the cusp of remembering *many* things."

I stare at the green-hued ghost, hoping to pull something from his words. He stares back at me. The first time we met, I'd been convinced he wanted to mislead or harm me in one of these caves, which the flash flood had confirmed. But Creepy Baby later offered me help in Alita, which I desperately needed. Since then, all he's claimed to want is the chance to become Tet's next king.

A demigodless king, apparently.

(And maybe not. Once upon a time, I'd considered myself demigodless. For now, all I know is that Creepy Baby is at least partly implicated in Skull's immediate past.)

"I can sense Skull," I tell him. "It's not as strong now as the first time I came here with Esclamonde and Butter. But it's here. It has the same pitch as my magic, just a different... tone. Or style. It's quieter and more subtle than Vexen magic. I'm guessing you can sense it, too?"

Creepy Baby lifts his eyebrows. "Of course."

"But it's not a demigod?"

He sets his chin on his folded arms. "I don't remember."

"But you remember lentils."

He smiles. "I think so."

"It *feels* like a demigod," Onesimos comments.

I look at him as he takes a heaping bite. The firelight dances across his dark brown skin. Sat between the crimson cave walls and the golden-orange firelight, his vermillion hair and eyes look like living extensions of Tet.

My head tilts. "What do you mean? What can you feel?"

The oread's orange-red eyes fix on me before jumping around the cave. "Remember when I took you and Esteban to the tourmaline caves in Jaws? Helisent, you said you could feel something inside the cave. You were sensing an oread demigod. Most Jawsic demigods dwell in caves.

"Oreads and our demigods love rock formations. We're much better at sensing metal and elements like magnesium and iron. But stone is another special part of our power—sturdiness, stability, patience. Naiads and okeanids are more focused on water, while hesperides can sense and manipulate the winds. Don't ask me how that works—I can't even guess. The same with dryads. They can find anything in the forest, even though it's overrun with life.

"An oread's power isn't so fluid or airy or busy.

"Just like I know many types of metallic alloys, I also know many types of rocks; they fill my home with beauty. They're born in three ways. In Jaws, our rocks are igneous, which means they're born from heat. Once upon a time, the volcanic cones of Jaws were giants that spewed lava. These were our first demigods—the exploding volcanoes. But they slowly gave way to basalt deposits. To obsidian, lava stone, and granite."

He raises his hand toward the wall, his broad palm and short fingers splayed. "Right now, we're sitting inside a shale cave, which is a type of sedimentary rock. These aren't born from heat. Shale comes from organic forms—and so does the limestone of Vex and the sandstone of Antigone. Once-living things break down and compact over time into sedimentary forms. Maybe that's why your magic prefers Tet's shale.

"Because it's similar to the limestone in the House of Vex.

"That doesn't answer all my questions, though. I wonder... why would Vex choose Tet over the Gammaforms of the plains or the pillars of Septegeur? Both are sandstone, which is also made from organic forms." Onesimos shrugs, turning back to his plate. "But I don't understand wielder magic—it's not nearly as subtle or pervasive as nymph magic."

He crosses his legs before reaching over and grabbing a crispy okra from Esclamonde's plate.

I stare at him, eyes narrowing.

I'd rather find out sooner rather than later why Vex came here.

I don't have time to play hide-and-seek with my demigod; I have two Kulapsifangs to save.

"Well, Tet is empty," I theorize. "There are dryad demigods in Septegeur and hesperide demigods in Gamma. The sandstone in both areas is already occupied with magic. They belong to the nymph demigods. Here, there's... well, I guess there's just Skull."

Onesimos nods, preparing another bite. "Whatever Skull is."

Like me, Esclamonde and Onesimos raise their heads to study the map scrawled across the wall. It looks like the ravings of an octopus given eight pieces of chalk.

Lunacy. Abject lunacy.

I shift toward Onesimos, jaw clenched. "When I was in Antigone with Samson, we realized Milisent had been suspicious of Anesot and Oko. She was taking notes on them. It seems like she thought Oko was taking phoenix ash to Tet. When Samson and I bartered with a ghost here last time around, that's what he'd requested, too.

"That means we aren't the first to be here with a long list of questions. We aren't the first to have bartered with ghosts, either. Let's... reverse-engineer it or something."

Onesimos sets down his plate, pivoting toward me. "Oko and Anesot were interested in Tet?"

I nod. "None of this shit adds up, Simmy."

Esclamonde keeps staring at the chalked map, her short white hair tucked behind her ears.

"I have a slightly controversial idea." Onesimos glances from me to Esclamonde. "How do the Bloodies feel about Zeu? I was a little suspicious at first. He likes to posture and speak in riddles.

"But Queen Clover invited him to Gamma, and he came back calmer. He's thick as thieves with Itzifone and Gautselin. He's also gotten close to Hadadrimmon. Even Elvira Ultramarine likes him— that speaks for itself.

"What I'm getting at is... Zeu knows an incredible amount about Ezit's Houses and their magic. As a magicless being, he might be more attuned to what's happening in Tet. As witches, you're both prone to thinking about magic in a certain way. The same is true for me as a nymph. Zeu will be a neutral third party."

"Zeu?" Creepy Baby shifts on his rocky perch, features tense. "The vampire who tried to kill me?"

"Yes, that one," the oread calls over. "What do you think?"

Esclamonde stares at me with wide eyes. She even jerks her chin to the side, as though pleading no.

I sigh, stewing over my relationship with Zeu.

I haven't told any of the Bloodies about Tol's death on the triplemoon.

I still see flashes of her face; her near-white features flecked with dark debris, blue droplets of rain hitting her open eyes. Zeu crouched over her body, grimacing. Samsonfang growling and looming over me. Bleeding in a flooded street in a city shaped like a bowl.

(And close on the heels of Tol's death is Kierkeline's, the wretched sound of her body solidifying into stone; the agony of being impaled by some sharp object in a dark clock tower in Lahar; the numbing and slow death on the ship that preceded every other trauma.)

It's enough to leave my hands shaking and damp again.

It's been easy to justify avoiding Zeu.

When our caravan arrived in Luz, he and his den restarted their lives. I did the same with my new warren. We've had little reason to interact since then. And though we were friendly in Cadmium and on the way to Luz, he distanced himself from me the second we were safe in the city.

I know why. And I don't want to face it, either.

But Onesimos is right.

I look from one Bloody to the next. "I'm willing to ask, but I don't know if he'll agree. We haven't spoken much since..."

"Well, he doesn't need to stay long," Onesimos offers. "Sandro and company will reach Alita soon. Just ask Zeu to come for a few days in the meantime."

Esclamonde makes another uneasy sound, scooting toward me.

"Fuck." I exhale through my nose, already annoyed by what comes next. "Fine."

A few days later, there's a fourth place occupied around the fire.

Zeu sits cross-legged to my left, staring into the flames with a peaceful, withdrawn expression.

I lean down to snort a thick line of dextro from a clean plate. For the first time in my life, it's not for recreation. It's to give me the energy to stay up all night with the King of Night and explore Tet's caves.

On the fire's far side, Onesimos and Esclamonde lay amid a pile of bedding. The oread snores lightly, but the witchling shifts every ten minutes, poking her head above the blanket to glance from me to the vampire.

At least Creepy Baby has fled in fear of the King of Night; Esclamonde only has one foe to keep an eye on.

This time, when she looks at me, I wink. Hopefully, she'll take it as a sign that Zeu can be trusted. Or, at the least, that she has no reason to follow us into Tet's foggy, cool night.

I massage my nostrils, sniffing again. Then I stand and wander around the camp, packing a few essentials into my bottomless bag.

I glance at the map on the wall.

In the days I spent haranguing Zeu in Luz and convincing him to shadow to Tet with me, the oread, witchling, and ghost have added new branches to the map.

Based on their additions, it looks like the caves are arranged in groups; for now, Vex seems to be claiming Tet's southeasterly clusters.

It's a bit too close to Velm for my liking, but I'm not sure how to steer my demigod back north.

Zeu mirrors me, standing and preparing his cross-body bag.

Though I've already explained the map and described where we are in relation to its winding, snake-like tunnels, I point to the nearest branch marked with a green smudge. "We're heading here tonight. I need to know if you can sense anything about the sinks. None of us can figure out what they are and why magic doesn't work inside them. But they might hold some clue about what Skull is. Or was. And why Vex is here."

He nods, then glances toward the cave's shadowy entrance, far from the healthy fire.

He heads toward it without me, and I follow.

To my surprise, he doesn't wear a pelt around his hips anymore.

Instead, a soft, white cotton skirt dangles halfway down his sturdy, sculpted thighs.

He wears his hair in four thick braids, the strands dotted with gems and pieces common to Gamma, including a maize tassel and one of the yellow ribbons used to celebrate the harvest season. They must be gifts from the Gammic monarch, Queen Clover. I even smell aloeswood drifting off his clean skin and lavender from his hair.

No bloodstained mouth or lips.

No posturing or snide comments.

In fact, he's been overwhelmingly calm since he arrived.

At the cave's circular, misshapen entrance, he finally turns to me. This far from the fire, the distended light pools in his iridescent irises. At once, they're pitched black, then aglow with reddish-orange. They trace the total black of his slitted pupil.

It's hard to look away.

"It's cold here," he says, voice low.

He's had similarly incongruous things to say to me all night. Even in Luz, when I was bribing him to follow me here, Zeu avoided direct answers. I hadn't realized he was going to come with me until he showed up at the agreed time and place for shadowing, a full bag at his hip and clean braids falling down his back.

He goes on, "You should have told me Tet would be so much cooler than Luz. The dampness doesn't help. I would have brought more layers."

I scan him. Wearing only his white skirt and the same leather-corded necklace with a few feathers, I'm not surprised he's cold. "I forgot. Do you want a—"

"Your wolf came into my den. Did he tell you? I let his wolf go."

I raise my eyebrows. "He mentioned it. Does that mean you two have reconciled?"

He gives me the once over. I can't tell if his lips twitch with a laugh or a grimace. "No. Probably not. But he was tortured by Suleiman, and so was I. I could tell by how he looked at the candles. The wielders in Ezit do that on purpose. Make you fear resources. Things that make you safe. They destroy your relationship to those things."

Fire?

That's how he hurt Samson?

I take a deep breath—I have no idea why he's telling me this.

What he expects me to conclude. It's easy to accept that he wants to hurt me by talking about Samson's pain.

Zeu's eyes study mine, flitting. "You're helping, right? Not Sam-Sam, but Velm. I didn't come this far to be tortured by Suleiman again. Neither did my people."

I raise my chin. "I will be more helpful to everyone once I have a stable home for my demigod. Are you ready to explore the sinks?"

I take off before he can respond. Despite the depth of night and the heavy drifts of fog, Zeu will be more than capable of following me by either sight or scent. So I stomp ahead of him, using magic to help me navigate the rocks up to Tet's muddy grass.

His feet squelch in the mud as I guide us to the nearest magical sink.

Even with the doublemoon approaching, thick mist obscures the moonslight. The silver, pink, and greenish hues of Marama and Laline fill the fog with illusory light.

Rather than risk getting lost, I send sensing magic toward the north where the green caves sit. I can only be sure I've found one when my magic sputters out, like a candle being snuffed.

We walk in silence until I see a graze of green light beckoning. The cave's rounded entrance nears and the green-tinted mist whorls, as though kicked up by a night breeze.

I propel myself forward, ignoring Zeu's and the sink's proximity. But, as it once went with Samson, I'm painfully aware that Zeu has honed his body into a weapon. That he knows about pain, endurance, and the mysteries of physical might.

The vampire's steps fall silent.

I pause, twenty feet from the sink.

Little more than a phantasmagoric shadow in the fog, Zeu's cool fingers take my elbow as his attention fixes on the sink. "Is that where you're taking me?"

"Yeah. The greenish light—it's a magical sink. My magic won't work inside of it." I try to study his face, looking for any hint of malice. "It'll be dark."

He turns toward me, fingers tightening. "Slit pupils are made for the night. Unless it's not the darkness that scares you."

I raise my eyebrows. "You've kept mine and Samson's secret."

Mentally, I add, *In exchange for my trust, Zeu.*

"Secrets are easy to keep," he murmurs. I still can't see him clearly—can only sense him looming over me in the mist, a hand on my arm. "But trust takes time to build."

I pull my arm free. "Stop playing games. Is this about Tol?" He hisses when I say her name, taking a quick step back. I charge forward, tired of his attitude and my guilt and our uncertainty. "I know you blame me for her death."

"It's not a matter of whether I blame you," he says coldly. "You were trapped inside the clock tower in Lahar on the triplemoon. She went inside to save you. She died because of that. It's not a matter of blame. It's a matter of cause and effect."

"Fine, then." My voice rises and, to my chagrin, shakes. "You don't trust me because of it. Just admit it."

"I have never trusted a wielder before in my life," he snaps, "and that will never change."

I gulp as his cruel, swift words land like a sword's blade in the soft mud between us.

He goes on, "The exchange is for *you* to trust *me*. All I have to do is keep your secret—which I have, by the way."

"Oh, well, thanks for the honesty. If you want to be really honest, then let's level with one another. It was never about trust or secrets. The goal of that trade was to manipulate me into getting closer to you with the hope that you'd be the next man I lured into the forest with a bowl of honey."

To my surprise, his voice changes in tone, shifting from anger to cajoling. "And did you bring a bowl of honey with you?"

Fuck this guy.

I raise my hand and slap him blindly. He angles his body with an amused sound as I wallop his bare abdomen. I wind up again, slapping him someplace near the ribs.

This time, he understands I'm trying to hurt him and chuckles. "Is this what you think fighting is?"

Even if he wasn't laughing, deep and throaty, I'd be able to tell by his half-hearted shielding that he finds this funny. It only spurs my temper. Unfortunately, it feels like I'm wailing against a shale wall.

With a grunt, I shift tactics and kick his shins with the balls of my feet—Esclamonde taught me that one.

He hisses, backing up a step. "What a dumb thing to do."

He's right; my foot aches already.

Also, I've lost track of the vampire in the mist.

"You're the worst!" I shout into the muddled haze. "You talk about helping and protecting your people in one second, then you're back to manipulations and one-sided trades in the next. Pick a fucking side, Zeu! Stop punishing the world for the fact that you don't have what you want!"

Something pokes me in the solar plexus. "Me not having what I want? Or *you* not having what you want?"

I slap at his hand when I realize he's pushing me back with a single finger. It doesn't budge, even when I grab his hand and try to throw it off me. "Zeu! No! Hey!" My scream turns into a squeal as my heel catches on a rock and I fall onto my butt with a splat. "Fuck you!"

From ten feet away, still hidden in the mist, Zeu mimics me with a high-pitched voice. "'*Fuck you*'."

I use magic to rise onto my feet, then dry and clean myself. I cringe as the mud lifts from my skin, hair, and clothes. "*Asshole*." I stomp after him, squinting into the mist and wondering how far he could have made it in. Though I could hear his footsteps before, there's not a sound now. "Where are you?"

A pale hand shoots through the mist and takes my arm; I barely have time to scream again.

"Stop yelling. You'll wake the ghosts. Are you actually scared, or do you just like to make noise? Is that why they call wielders birds? I doubt that's fair to the birds."

"Oh, whatever. You don't know anything about birds." I stagger after him, lost and confused. "Wait, where'd the sink go?"

"Can you really not see anything? Sometimes, wielders are so unimpressive. We're almost there."

Then the green-hued break in the misted darkness comes back into focus. I narrow my eyes; it looks like we'd stepped behind a boulder, blocking our path to the sink.

Zeu stops at the edge of the descending grotto, piled with jagged shale. He lets go of my arm, but I stick close to his side; I can barely make out the cave below. Without magical cylinders or campfires, it looks like a swirl of deep ocean, flooded with greenish light.

Zeu makes a low sound. "This is... not what I was expecting."

I press closer to his side. "What were you expecting?"

"I can sense magic here, but not normal magic." He inhales deeply, then makes a low, unhappy sound. "And it smells like rosarium. I don't suppose you ever learned what rosarium is in Zarzynn? Formally, I mean?"

"No, it was all exceedingly informal." I roll my eyes, trying to keep those memories at bay. "Thank you."

"Rosarium comes from Landmarks. From calcified Landmarks. That's where we harvest the stones in Zarzynn—straight from the ruined cities the Houses occupied before they built Ezit.

"A Landmark can die, but it takes a long time. As it does, the scent of its magic changes, and so does its color. Fully formed rosarium is pink, like you saw. But it takes centuries to decay to that point. You can find it in many colors throughout different stages of decay."

He smells rosarium?

I shift, surprised by his words. "And what can you sense about the magic here? Can you feel Skull?"

"Skull? I have no idea what that is. All I can tell you is that this smells like a dead Landmark."

I blink into the night. "And what about the ghosts?"

He huffs. "We don't have ghosts in Zarzynn. You said you bartered with a ghost who looked like a hesperide once. So, that would involve nymph magic—not wielder magic. And what about the War Years? You told me this is where it was fought. Have you factored that into all your theories?"

"It's in the mix—that's how the ghosts got here." I chew on my lip. "Probably."

"Right, well—we won't find any answers out here." He wraps his hand around my arm again, then takes a step down—straight into a blackened gulf, it seems. "Let's look. There might be solidified rosarium inside. If we find any, I get half for my den."

I make a long and uncertain sound.

"We wouldn't use it—it would be just in case," he clarifies.

I shake my head. "You can have the rosarium, Zeu. I don't care."

He waits a moment. Then, "You can trust me." He even squeezes my arm for emphasis.

"But I don't," I say with a loud scoff. "We're being honest with each other now, remember?"

"Then let's pretend. That's what Queen Clover taught me. When I went to Gamma, she told me we were going to pretend to be long-lost friends. She hugged me and said, 'Zeu, I haven't seen you in so many years. How have you been?'

"It felt... surprisingly normal. I spent two weeks there and, when it was time to leave, I felt like I'd known her for years."

I snort again. "That's called desita, Zeu."

He ignores me. "Let's pretend I trust you, and you pretend you trust me." His voice is low and near. "One day, we'll realize we aren't pretending anymore."

He squeezes my arm again, fingers gently goading me.

With a sigh, I relent, "That's probably our best option."

"Come on, then. Down into the sink."

"Fine." I lunge one step down, aiming for the rock next to him.

My boot slips on the uneven, wet surface. Zeu catches me with his free hand, which slides around my waist. He hugs me to him, steadying me.

I make another unhappy sound. "Can you swim? Like well enough to save us both in the event of a flash flood?"

"I'm good at everything, Helisent."

I can hear the smile in his voice.

His fingers press through my layers, their chill seeping into my skin. It reminds me of the metallic ornaments in Antigone. They're known for their beauty; how they twist in the slightest breeze and sing, how they catch the light and shimmer, how they give ideas to those who watch them closely.

They aren't really for touching.

But they come to mind when Zeu holds me. The coolness of his skin reminds me of how it felt to graze the bronze and copper ornaments in the early winter mornings.

We don't find rosarium in the green sink.

Or in any of the others we explore over the next week.

Still, mine and Zeu's work helps us refine the map on the wall. We detail the caves with more accuracy in terms of placement, shape, and scale. Green sinks still outnumber the Vexen caves, but we now have a more reliable map to log future changes.

I sleep through the days beside the light-tight chamber I create for the King of Night. I wake at dusk to eat breakfast from the dinner platters left out by the oread and the witchling.

During those hours before the heavy night, our time spent around the campfire becomes more comfortable.

It reminds me of the weeks I spent in Hella last spring. By the time the triplemoon arrived, the dens had outnumbered the Mieirans significantly—and it had felt natural.

But I'll return to Alita soon, and Zeu's den needs him. Just as soon as he arrived, he repacks his cross-body bag. Even Esclamonde stands to say goodbye, poking her head over Onesimos's shoulder as she watches the vampire stow away his items; a few throwing stars, a whetting stone, and empty glass cylinders—used for storing and carrying blood rather than dove.

The vampire stands and glances around the campsite. "Tell the green fucker I say goodbye. And that I need to speak with him next time I'm here. I bet he knows more than he's letting on."

"Good idea," Onesimos says over a yawn. "Say hello to Ceyx and Cleo for me. We'll be back soon."

The witchling watches him, eyes glittering. "Zeu, if you say hi to Ceyx and Cleo, will you go upstairs and make sure Memphis isn't sleeping in my room? He uses it when I'm gone, and then my pillow smells weird. His hair is too pungent."

Zeu raises his eyebrows, as though unpleasantly surprised by the mundane requests. "What do I do if he's in the bed?"

Esclamonde glances at me from the corner of her eye.

I stare back, waiting to see what she says.

"Tell him I sent you." She bunches her eyebrows and lowers her chin, baring an impressive glower at Zeu. "Make this face when you do."

I roll my eyes, but the King of Night smiles wide at the witchling. "Memphis Plet hasn't been scared of me for years, but I'll do my best." He steps forward to set a hand against Onesimos's shoulder, patting heartily. "Goodbye, oread."

Onesimos smiles, patting his hand. "Thanks again, Zeu."

The vampire turns and follows me from camp. I raise my arms and stretch, leaning back. I'm already imagining a full night's rest. Though Zeu has been a great help, I've outgrown nocturnal living.

In silence, we tread toward the cave's entrance. After two sloped curves, it comes into view, banked with gray mist and golden light from a cylinder. Beside it waits a cove that's perfect for shadowing.

Thanks to the omnipresence of my magic, the shadow stays 'fuzzy', so to speak.

I turn toward Zeu. Over the last week, our nitpicking and temperamental banter has evolved into a comfortable silence. Rather than let words get in the way of our budding friendship, we've taken a wordless approach.

I set my hands on my hips and offer the vampire a hopeful smile. "I think this went well."

He raises his eyebrows, nodding. "I think I respect you."

My stomach lurches. One step forward, two steps back. "Lovely."

"My respect is hard to come by," he reminds me.

I snort. "Oh, okay. Good to know."

I try to brush off his comment.

The Bloodies need allies; Zeu mostly acts like one.

(And I've gotten used to the scents of lavender and aloeswood; the way Zeu's slitted pupils make him look all-knowing and immortal; the soft pink of his lips, and the bushy and thick texture of his hair. I've even gotten used to pretending to trust the vampire.)

Quietly, Zeu comments, "Something is happening, isn't it? In Mieira? In Velm? Everywhere."

I close my eyes, chagrined at how quickly my heart races.

Two Houses in Septegeur, two more in Velm...

"You're nervous," Zeu comments. He studies me from head to toe, features pinched with confusion. "Your heartbeat sounds like a finch. Finches are such nervous birds."

He watches me expectantly.

Just keep pretending you trust him.

Like Queen Clover did.

I have no idea what Zeu understands about Velm, about Samson being deposed by his father, about our mission to find Imperatriz. The pair only spent a few hours in Solace before I dragged the wolf away—and I doubt Samson would have been very forthcoming during their conversations.

The vampire goes on, "I told you already, witch. My den didn't come all this way to be threatened again."

I stare at him, clenching my jaw.

I don't know what information is mine to share, but I refuse to let Zeu learn the hard way that Mieira and Velm aren't as safe as we once thought.

That his warmongers might be called to fight again.

Just keep pretending, Helisent.

"Suleiman is working with Clearbold on behalf of Serac." I force the words out before I can second-guess this decision. "Argot is also allied with Velm. Well, *Clearbold's* Velm. And Absalom thinks the Houses of Col and Talos may have set up a portal in Septegeur. He's the warlock from the Class. He was in Vex with us."

Zeu stares at the ground while he digests my revelation. A moment later, he looks up at me, then wanders closer. His eyes narrow, as though he's still deep in thought.

He concludes, "You aren't ready for that."

I clench my stomach as he inches closer to my face, eyes jumping over my features with lethal focus.

I can feel my finch heart start again.

My hand twitches toward the thick scar on my lower abdomen.

I see raindrops hitting Tol's open eyes. I see a warlock with six bright orange horns; his glowing eyes fix on me in a clocktower in the House of Lahar.

Nausea boils in my gut.

Fuck.

Zeu shifts backward, giving me space. "It was never a question of whether Ezit would seek retribution against Mieira—and Velm. It was only a question of *when*, Helisent. I have to say... I thought we'd have more time."

Like he's annoyed by the prospect, he sighs. "Fine, then. I'll come back to help you investigate the magical sinks. And I'll train you so that when you don't follow the plan during the next battle, you can take care of yourself." He sighs again, still annoyed. "You're well-equipped for large-scale spells—which is plenty of an advantage. But the Hosts and their mercenaries know this now. They will separate you from your allies. They will draw you into tight spaces. They will force you to wield smaller spells and wound you in a way that maximizes pain. It will distract you. You will fall quickly.

"I know exactly how I'd kill you.

"That's not a good thing, tiny witch."

Zeu looms closer, gaze fixed on me in a different sense now.

I stare back defiantly as a flush of warmth washes through me.

He keeps watching me; I can't tell if he's noticed how flushed I am.

I watch his lips move when he says, "I will teach your body to be strong. Right now, it's meant for lovemaking and drinking and sleeping and eating—"

"Oh, *okay*, well—"

"—which is fine. But it doesn't bode well for survival. To hold your own against your enemies—of which you now have *many*—you will need discipline, at least a little muscle, and a keen knowledge of the body's weak points."

No insult comes to mind, but I can feel my facial features pull into a frown. The warm flush is gone; in its place is rage. (Well, mostly. Even rage has that effervescent sheen of horniness.)

In my silence, Zeu goes on, "I pushed you over with a finger the first night I got here. One finger, Helisent. You *lost* against a *finger*."

I swing my arm toward him with a growl, aiming to land another slap.

Zeu catches my wrist and wraps his fingers around me in a vice grip. He drags me to him, and I gasp, boots slipping on the rock as my face nears his again. His fingers are cool and sturdy, spreading across my forearm.

Before I can bite him or yowl, his free hand presents me with a twinkling gem the size of a fingernail.

My eyes lock on the colorless jewel. I forget about his hold on my arm as the golden light from the cylinder refracts through the gem, doubling in hue and radiance as it shines across my cheek and neck.

Zeu's eyes flicker across mine, his voice low, "It's a diamond. I know you like jewels. This is my favorite. This is how I imagine sunlight looks—like light and diamonds. This is as close as I'll ever get to knowing. Don't tell me if I'm wrong. *Never* tell me the truth."

My breath catches in my throat.

In a flash of intuition, I understand Zeu better than I have before. *'Never tell me the truth.'*

To Pletens, trust revolves around being bound. To being equal.

To a once-degi vampire like Zeu, trust is about visibility.

Having spent a lifetime in the underground tunnels of Ezit and at the service of its most powerful and heartless wielders, something like a thought, a feeling, a sentiment must take on greater meaning. It must be all he had during those years; the ability to seal himself into an untouchable fortress.

'Never tell me the truth.'

It's a risk to share such a profound thought, just like it was a risk for me to waltz into a magical sink with him.

Because Zeu doesn't fear death; it's life that terrifies him.

I smile. "You trust me."

"You trusted me first," he snaps. Then he smiles, eyes glittering as they fix on the diamond. "They're forever, you know."

Zeu releases me so I can take the diamond. I let the sharp, twinkling piece fall into my palm.

Feeling victorious, I clear my throat and announce, "I have one request."

He stares at me, deadpan. "No, you have one diamond."

I bear a wide smile at him. "Do it for Esclamonde, too. Train her. She's my mentee, and it's the most annoying thing in the world. But..."

I shrug. He leads a den; I'm sure he gets it.

Instead, Zeu blinks at me. I swear I see multiple rebuttals shift through his slitted pupils. His only response is a low hiss that whistles through his teeth.

I still feel hopeful.

Even when he ignores me and turns toward the sheltered nook where a fuzzy shadow waits, pausing once to let me catch up.

I bound a few steps after him, the diamond clutched in my palm. "Please."

He makes another angry sound as I take his hand, then guide us into the fuzzy darkness, my mind focused on my apartment in Luz.

CHAPTER 9

A SECOND BODY

SAMSON

Suin,

You went from my bed to a witch's. On a personal level, that's extremely devastating. In a broader sense, I understand why some wolves might consider it healing to know a Kulapsifang is capable of that. I don't. I never will. But I understand how others could.

-Suin

A threadbare shack sits atop a hill.

Wind shakes the tallgrass and the thatched roof's tattered ends. The curtain hanging across the window shivers.

The cloudless sky is muddled red. The dark wood of the cottage is deep crimson. The fluttering tips of the grass are pale garnet. The ocean that spans from the nearby cliff is a few shades darker, littered with droplets of pure light from the bloodred sun.

Each night, the red seething dreams lead me to the same place.

A windblown shack.

Though it made me nervous at first, I've grown more familiar with this dreamscape on the way to Alita.

This time, I wander closer.

The cool wind drives into my tunic and pants. The starchy grass crunches beneath my bare feet. I roll my shoulders as I near the door.

I'll start with a gentle knock. If no one is home, I'll poke my head inside.

Before I reach the door, the wind dies suddenly.

In its place comes a thrumming bass. Infrasound oozes into the air around me, raising the air pressure. The same force mounts in my head, in my eyes, in my hands, in my throat.

I can't stand how it feels, but I push ahead, through the heavy infrasound.

The shack's narrow door drifts inward slowly, flooding the cramped, dark room with light.

In its corner, a woman sleeps on a low palette, facing the wall.

I fall still, my stomach clenched.

I've found her at last; the faceless witch.

You're ready, Samsonfang whispers.

With a deep breath, I take another step. The air parts around me, like I'm wading through solid currents of infrasound. I grit my teeth, moving forward.

I stop in the doorway.

I study the sleeping woman.

To my surprise, I realize she isn't the faceless witch from other dreams.

This woman has a long mane of dark gray hair bundled atop her pillow near her crown—not white tresses. Her fingers are interlaced, held gently near her mouth. Her neck is slender but sturdy, her jawline strong as it leads to parted lips. She wears a long cloak of thick fibers, ragged and uneven.

She's holding something...

My breath catches in my throat.

I step into the dwelling, no longer apprehensive but desperately curious. I angle my head to see what she holds between her interlocked fingers.

It's aglow with red light, vibrant like a magical cylinder of dove. It's hard to make sense of it; the entire dream is cast in red hues.

My eyes narrow as I inch closer.

It *is* a cylinder of dove.

Helisent's dove.

And the woman isn't a witch.

She's a wolf.

Sleeping alone in a shack high atop the hill.

Mama, Samsonfang insists.

My heart rushes to my throat—

I brace myself against the doorframe.

Everything reels for a long moment.

I remind myself that this is a dream.

This is just a figment of my mind.

These dreams are only dreams—*these dreams are only dreams—I should not hope for this—*

The woman stirs and wakes.

She shifts to look over her shoulder, eyes narrowing like she can sense my trespassing. Her cloak slips from one of her shoulders as she sits up and faces me. Her hair falls around her messily.

She is much older than I remember; she also looks younger than I thought she would. Her lips are still full, her cheekbones high, and the ends of her eyes are traced with delicate lines.

Her features contort as she watches me. "*Atali?*"

Son?

Mama.

My heart thuds in my chest.

She rises, and I step forward to meet her—

Then the dream erupts in a surge of infrasound and emotion.

I wake up reeling on my side, arms shooting outward as though still reaching.

I heave in a few breaths as the dream dissolves in my mind.

My heart keeps thumping in my chest.

I sit up and glance around our camp, silent and hazy amid the dawn. Though it's too early for Rhotidom's legion of birds to start singing, the insects have begun their daily croon.

Across the cold fire pit, Hadadrimmon snores lightly. From this angle, his hair bunches over his face, silver decals half-buried. Overhead, Halcyon and Butter sleep in the witch's broad mimosa nest. Fragrant and fuzzy pink-and-yellow flowers jut from the circular nest at odd angles, collecting the soft morning light. It's comically large for the tree's canopy; unlike Helisent, Butter doesn't waste time finding a sturdy tree for her nest.

I sit up with a groan and peel off my shirt.

The wand dangles from a thin leather cord. The red piece rests at my solar plexus, the exact shade as the scar above my heart.

Like Helisent requested, I've kept the wand on me at all times.

Since I left her apartment two weeks ago, the red dreams have incrementally intensified.

This is the first moment I realize Helisent's idea about the wand wasn't necessarily a lost cause—

My mind connects me to Imperariz. And if these dreams are real, they confirm Imperatriz has the witch's hefty offering of dove. In an asymmetrical circle, we're all tied together: me, Vex, Imperatriz.

I watch the red color slowly fade from my scar.

As it does, I sense the haze of what I've started calling my second body.

It's most palpable in the mornings when I wake from red dreams, like a ghost clinging to me.

It starts with a gentle migraine that lifts from my skull over ten minutes. The discomfort moves to my chest, abdomen, and legs; it fizzles, as though each portion of my body has fallen asleep. Then it gutters gently from my skin with infrasound that shakes the hairs across my body.

The only exception is my hands. They tremble with infrasound for longer, as though my second body struggles to extricate itself from my fingertips.

And then, for a split second, I can sense my second body hovering before me.

I swear it watches me. It might even be speaking.

Before it departs this morning, I whisper, "That's her. That's Imperatriz. That's who we need."

I repeat the words in my mind while I stare into the wild tangle of Rhoditom's green growth. Sturdy vines crawl along the massive trees; moss hangs from branches as they rise to the second canopy.

And yet I see nothing, focused on the image of my mother from the dream.

The way her voice sounded. How her hair fell around her shoulders. How she held the cylinder of dove.

I rub my face as doubt creeps in.

Was that really her?

Is the wand really this powerful?

And how the fuck do I get her home? To be this close without a way to save her is maddening—I don't know if I'll survive that letdown again.

I hold the red wand up and stare at it closely.

Just in case my second body is still here, I whisper, "Bring her to me—the woman in the shack on the hill. That's Imperatriz."

Someone stirs overhead.

I jolt, pulling on my shirt to hide the wand. Since the wielders discovered I was wearing it around my neck last week, they've been disgruntled—not necessarily with me.

Halcyon said he isn't thrilled with the idea of defending the wand in case of emergency. Butter said she figured Helisent wouldn't let it out of her sight—nonetheless encourage me to walk north with it strapped to my chest.

I look up to see Butter's half-asleep face tilted over the nest's ledge. Her blue-white hair dangles down toward me in a tangled braid. Her eyes are barely open, her lips and cheeks soft with sleep.

"Stop it with all the fussing at dawn," she calls down. "You keep waking me up."

Normally, I'd apologize and go back to sleep. But with Imperatriz's face in my mind, I'm less relaxed. "What can you sense? Do you know what's happening?"

She snorts, leaning further over the nest. "I'm not allowed to touch the wand, Samson. That's what Helisent says. So, how would I know what's happening down there?"

"You said it's waking you up."

"That's your mindless chatter," she snaps.

"I've barely said a word. I'm whispering."

Butter tsks. I think she also rolls her eyes, but I can't quite see. "Can't you feel the infrasound? I thought wolves were sensitive to it. You basically bathe in it every morning."

"I can feel it. It almost feels like... like... a second body." I'm too afraid to say 'magical twin' because I don't know what magic should feel like. "It's here every morning when I wake up, then it disappears. I don't know where it goes."

With a heavy sigh, Butter props her chin on her hand. "I wouldn't worry about it that much. Helisent *obviously* thought it through before handing you, a *wolf*, the last living remnant of her demigod. What could go wrong?"

I clear my throat. Over the last two weeks, I haven't managed to endear the okeanid-witch-necromancer—even though I'm now in solid standing with Halcyon, and Hadadrimmon hasn't delayed our journey with his hangovers anymore.

Unsure of how to win her approval, I go with, "This is kind of a bad time for sarcasm. For me, at least."

"It's kind of a bad time for everyone. You know, having to babysit you and ferry you around Mieira like a lost boy. You *and* your heathen sidekick. But here we are." Butter smiles widely from overhead. "Kind of in a bad time together."

I narrow my eyes.

Half of me wants to remind her (quickly and cruelly) that we ferried her out of Ezit at a very high price. Talk about a bad fucking time. The other half wants to know why she hates me. I'd thought, as one of Helisent's best friends, that Butter and I would be in good standing. I had also falsely assumed Helisent would never maroon me in the care of a friend who dislikes me so much.

I offer a quick smile to Butter. "Are you missing a big festival or something to be here helping us?"

She slaps her palms against the mimosa branches. "I'm missing my beauty sleep! Every morning! Waking up to infrasound and the ravings of a lost boy!"

With a yawn, Hadadrimmon stirs from the other side of the fire pit. "Don't forget his heathen sidekick."

With a frustrated growl, Butter turns back into the nest above, out of view.

Hadadrimmon offers me a half-smile from where he lies.

I smile back, then pull at my shirt's collar. I stare below; the wand is quiet, its color dimmed.

Later that day, Halcyon hangs back to walk with me as I bring up the group's rear.

This deep in the jungle, the pathways grow narrow. Some disappear altogether with the monsoons. One battered through the jungle surrounding Alita, causing mudslides and erasing dozens of trails. To guide wayward travelers, villages sent out their most experienced and talented singers.

The dryads sit high in trees along the recently destroyed trails. Rather than mark the path to Alita with ribbons, they mark it with booming ballads.

From high in the treetops, singers beat hand drums and belt out traditional songs and chants—about jacaranda trees, about ilama trees, about funnel spiders and glass frogs, about the electric eels that slither through the muddy creeks.

As soon as one voice fades into the distance, another echoes from the jungle's uppermost canopy.

When the warlock falls behind to walk beside me, I expect a question about orangutans or ilama trees. Unlike Hadadrimmon, Halcyon doesn't seem endeared by Rhotidom's wild growth; he's prone to staring into its depths before scurrying to catch up to Butter.

After he falls in line with me, he cranes his head to stare toward Butter. She sits on a golden-threaded lilith, inspecting her nails twenty feet ahead of us. Hadadrimmon walks at her side. With the roar of the insects at dusk, I can't hear a word of their conversation. Based on the wolf's smile and Butter's upheld chin, I'd bet he's teasing her.

Satisfied that they're occupied, Halcyon angles his head toward me, voice low. "I heard you this morning. A second body reminds me of how Helisent used to describe her magic—as a twin. A magical twin."

I nod. "I'm aware of the comparison."

"I'm guessing you're also aware of what the wand is." He raises his white eyebrows. His cropped white hair puffs up around his temple and ears, tangled with humidity.

I'm still not used to seeing the warlock with brown skin instead of his indigo-tinted tone. Without the added shading, his features look more chiseled. His eyes, too, seem to burst with color. For the first time since meeting him, I notice a small, deep scar near his left eye.

I nod again. "This isn't my first dalliance with the wand."

He blinks rapidly, as though unhappy to hear that. "I see. And when was the first... dalliance?"

I give him the once-over. "What's it to you, Halcyon? You and Butter have been pissed off since you realized I had it with me. Did Helisent not tell you when she—"

"Of course, she didn't." He glances ahead at Butter. "She sent a note asking us to take you to Hemlock in Alita, which we agreed to. I haven't been north, and I'd love to see Hemlock again. There was absolutely nothing that hinted this would involve the wand. She knows I would have said no if that were the case."

I tuck my hands behind my back, carefully considering his words.

"I don't understand. You were *overwhelmingly* at her disposal in Vex. What's changed since then?" I try to keep my voice light. "Or did you only help Helisent because you wanted something from her?"

And what the fuck was that, you little trash-man?

Halcyon lowers his voice again. "Don't talk to me about what Helisent wants." He glances at me from the corner of his eye. It's a fierce and bitter enough look that I forget what I was going to say. "Especially with her fucking demigod hanging from a string around your neck."

Quickly, I realize I've misinterpreted this situation.

Halcyon goes on, "Do *you* know what the witch wants?"

I try to keep up—try to figure out which of my words angered him.

"I imagine she wants her demigod to find safety in its new home," I reason.

Halcyon whips his head forward again. His jaw clenches and unclenches.

"Halcyon? If there's something you know that I don't, then it might be—"

"Nobody knows. That's the problem. You having... a *dalliance* with the wand is..." He scoffs but doesn't finish his sentence.

"All I did was tell it about Mort. It's a city in Velm—that's where Brutatalika lives with the rest of our allies. I asked Helisent to shadow us there, but she'd never been. So I told the wand what it looked like and where I wanted to go. There was no other way to get there quickly. We didn't have a choice, Halcyon."

"And it listened?" Now, he seems to be tilting back toward curiosity more than anger. "That first time?"

"Exactly. I didn't touch it back then, but it listened to my voice. It understood what I wanted."

We walk in silence. Like I do, I imagine Halcyon is chewing on his words.

I speak first. "Whatever it is you think I'm doing... my only goal with the wand revolves around saving Velm and finding Imperatriz.

I'm not doing this for glory. There's no ulterior motive except finding my mother and dethroning Clearbold before Serac and Argot can destroy my realm." With each word, rage in my gut kindles. "And it's really fucking rich of you to have such strong opinions about the wand and Velm, considering it's your father sitting and plotting in *my* fucking palace right now. Probably parsing out my fucking territory to his assistants."

"And whose father invited him there?" Halcyon shoots back.

Another stretch of loaded silence.

Eventually, he asks, "You haven't... told it to do anything, right? Not without Helisent's supervision?"

I still don't get it—whatever point he's trying to make.

'Bring her to me. The woman from the dream. From the cottage on the moor.'

I feel for the wand through my shirt, pinching it between my fingers. I clear my throat. "Not really. Nothing major."

"Nothing major." Halcyon sighs. "I see. But you're sensing a second body in the mornings?"

"Only for a few minutes. I'm having intense dreams. I think it's related to that."

He stops walking; he waits for me to pause. With a surprisingly reasonable expression, he explains, "Samson... please think about what you're doing. The wand is the most potent form of Vexen magic. It's likely where most of her House's ejima is stored.

"I understand that you are a Kulapsifang, and this makes you particularly linked to your own demigod, Hetnazzar. But you are far from a wielder, and you are out of your league with a magical demigod. It isn't Helisent—it isn't a witch. It's a demigod. It wants things, and you'd be the dumbest fucking being on this planet to assume you can fathom what a demigod wants. What it will ask from you in exchange for all you've taken."

The warlock stares at me, chin lowered.

My stomach drops.

But here's the truth—

"You don't remember your mother, Halcyon, so I think it only makes sense to use the examples of Ceyx or Cleo. Eighteen years... in a place like Pit..." I don't breathe life into that example, wary that these are the mothers of his sons. But I let my statement settle in.

"You never set foot inside your own House in Ezit, either, but if you had… and if the fate of the House of Serac was *your* responsibility, Halcyon…" I also don't extrapolate on that, either, letting the warlock's imagination run wild. "If that were the case, I think you would do a lot more than ask a demigod for a favor."

I start walking again.

For a while, the warlock doesn't say anything, just sighs heavily and drags his feet to follow.

Eager to improve the mood, I change the subject. "So, how do you like the jungle? I hope you're ready to see King Hemlock in all his glory. I heard birds sing to him every morning. They perch on his shoulders. They'll even brush his beard if they have time. Or maybe that's the sables. I can never remember."

Halcyon sighs again. Like me, he seems eager to leave the conversation behind.

"Well, we didn't have mosquitoes in Plet or Zarzynn. I'm not sure if you noticed while you were there." He looks at me, unimpressed. "There are a *lot* of mosquitoes here. They're like tiny, tiny vampires. It's the fucking worst."

We travel for another week at a dwindling pace.

With few packs roaming Rhotidom, the wielders rarely cloak mine and Hadadrimmon's scents. It's been a relief not to fixate on my safety. To mark our campsites with Hadadrimmon and get back into some semblance of normalcy.

But we run into two more heavy downpours, which delay our journey. When we wake up and dry ourselves, the pathways are gone, no more than smears of mud below the towering canopy. We wait two more days for the dryad singers to set up their camps in the treetops to guide us onward. From there, the journey slows; following a song isn't nearly as direct as following a footpath.

I like to think it gives Helisent added time in Tet.

And it gives me a few more precious days to make a connection to the wand.

Each night, I let the lulling madness of the jungle pull me into sleep. Dreaming, I step through a reddened world to sit with my mother in the shack atop the hill.

In the next dreams, I find her asleep. Rather than wake her, I sit on the edge of the palette to watch her breathe deeply and calmly. A few days later, she opens the door to find me standing in the grass, as though she could sense me coming. But as soon as she speaks, the cadence and sound of her voice sends me reeling back toward my bed mat in Rhotidom.

It's too intense to remember her voice. I'm thankful there's no ala to study in the dream. It would make it impossible to wake up and not go mad.

It's already hard enough to be so near her in sleep, then wake up so far from Pit. I'm closer than ever before, and yet not at all.

With mounting desperation, I wake in the mornings and whisper to the wand and my second body, "Bring her to me. Bring her to where I am in Mieira."

I think of Halcyon every time I say the words.

I can appreciate the reality that I'm contending with the Vexen demigod through its magical wand. And I'll accept the consequences.

So long as Imperatriz is back, it won't matter what happens to me.

She will erase my failures.

Imperatriz will drive the Leofsiges from Velm.

Imperatriz will sit on the throne in Bellator.

And the wolves will forgive my weakness.

At last.

Only a day's journey from Alita, I dream of a shack again.

I step into the red dream with confidence.

The door swings open as I approach, as though gesturing me inside. As I near it, I realize Imperatriz is standing with her hand on its latch and a smile on her face.

I take a deep breath, trying to control my emotions. I'm more accustomed to seeing her now, but I still brace myself for the sound of her voice.

I can't keep waking up as soon as I hear it.

We need to speak so that I can explain what's happening.

That this dream might not be just a dream.

My mother raises her pointer finger to her lips. She makes a low *shh* sound.

She steps outside and meets me on the red grass. She looks to the left, then the right, as though ensuring we're alone; I also turn and spin. Around us span hilly, dry moors—if they were vaster, I'd wonder if we were near Mort. But the cliffs are too high, the ocean's horizon muddled with a thick fog that's foreign to Velm's coast.

When I turn, Imperatriz has stepped back into the shack.

I wait until she comes back outside with two items.

In her right hand, she holds a familiar bloodred axe. She adjusts her grip on it, keeping it slack at her side. In her left hand, she holds a cylinder of dove. It's just as full and dark as when I saw Helisent package it inside the rickety hovel in New Hypnos.

She glances at my right hand.

I look down and realize I'm holding a red ax, too.

Axerxa's gift.

I raise it, studying it closely. Its leather is slightly worn, its steel blade nicked in the same spot I'd tarnished it. I stare at the replica, stunned by its precision to the real ax—which must be safely tucked away inside one of Clearbold's satchels.

I squint at the axe my mother holds; it looks like another replica, from the pattern of the taut leather cords on its shaft to the shape of the sharpened steel blade.

Imperatriz smiles at me.

I smile back.

I take a deep breath. With my heart rate in check, I take a step toward her.

But something catches me by the neck. It's forceful enough that I reach up with my free hand, expecting to feel my shirt's collar. There's nothing there, my fingers roving over my skin. Each breath is a struggle as precious oxygen fails to pass into my lungs.

I shake my head, hoping the feeling will fade. The axe falls from my hand.

I almost feel fingers gripping me, a forceful weight bearing down against my jugular.

I bend, realizing I desperately need air—

Imperatriz rushes toward me, dropping the cylinder and axe.

Before she reaches me, the dreamscape fades to black.

It expands into a painful gulf that I fall into, away from the shack and my mother, something dragging me back to reality by the neck.

My body twitches as I wake and open my eyes.

Red light filters over my vision, as though my mind is half asleep.

Adrenaline roars through me, mindless and scattered—

Dawn hasn't fully arrived yet—

And there's a mature male wolf straddling my chest, his face contorted. He grips my jugular with both hands, bearing down his weight and pinning me to the ground.

Oh, shit.

I hear commotion around the camp, grunting and cursing and shouting. Nearby, it sounds like Hadadrimmon is also struggling for breath. A gust of ultrasound echoes from nearby—not the mimosa nest overhead, but in the distance, as though Halcyon and Butter are now fighting elsewhere.

An ambush.

I shift under my attacker's weight, desperate to rip free and take a breath. Then I feel another heavy body bearing down over my legs.

The meager blush of dawn offers little light. Shadows hang heavy from the trees, pooling around the ground.

I clench my right hand; there's no axe in it.

With a wave of adrenaline, I rip my body to the right, then send a fist toward my attacker's inner elbow. He buckles downward, and I surge upward to ram my forehead into his nose. It cracks under the force, blood gushing downward. Droplets fall on my tongue and teeth as I gasp for breath, our heads locked close. I'm not sure what happens to the wolf pinning my legs—only that I have a moment of relief.

The shift from dream to waking nightmare is sudden, total.

Think, Samson.

I can feel my second body clinging to my limbs and head as I stand and stagger away from the attackers.

I look around, desperate to find my satchel and Helisent's star— but it's across the camp, half-hidden under a bush.

That's as far as I get before the wolf who pinned my legs rushes forward into my stomach. He knocks me onto my back near the fire pit, forcing the breath from my lungs again.

On my back, I realize the mimosa nest is in shambles, torn branch by branch from the sturdy ilama tree where Butter wove it last night.

I hear more ultrasound in the distance; wherever Butter and Halcyon are, they're engaged in a separate fight.

I grapple with the wolf in the middle of the fire pit, ash and charcoal streaking across our hands and arms. We run into two more bodies as Hadadrimmon manages to disengage his own attackers. Still gasping for breath, I can't gauge whether I've met these wolves before —just that four male adults are leading an assault, along with unknown wielders in the distance.

They came at dawn.

To launch an attack while we slept.

Like fucking Leolite cowards.

Free from his own scuffle, Hadadrimmon grabs my opponent by his shoulder, then bears his weight down to strike the back of his head. With a gargled grunt, the man slips to the ground, unconscious.

I make eye contact with Hadadrimmon; he looks at me, equally shocked and wrathful. One of his eyes is swollen shut, his upper lip torn and bloody. "Where the fuck are the wielders?"

All I get out is, "I don't know."

With one wolf knocked out and another tending a shattered nose, we each have a single opponent to focus on.

I roll my shoulders, squaring up to the nearest stranger. All I need to do is outlast this wolf and hope that Hadadrimmon can hold his own until help arrives.

We rush forward, meeting the other with brute strength.

After a short bout, I manage to pin my opponent—

Then his packmate with the broken nose returns.

I can't tell what he's doing until he lunges behind me and I feel a cord catch around my neck. I let go of the other wolf, desperate to get my fingers between the cord and my skin before it pulls taut.

I'm too late.

With a single pull, the wolf rips the cord backward, and my body follows. I gargle, attempting to breathe; it feels like my eyes will burst from my head.

I grit my teeth.

Fuck, fuck, fuck.

Things go slowly after that. They almost fall still.

I don't fight the wolves, focused instead on the tightening noose. And they don't fight me; the one with the broken nose sinks back onto his haunches, panting as he holds the cord tight. The other stands over me, hands ready, should I somehow break loose.

I can't hear Hadadrimmon struggling.

No flares of ultrasound in the distance.

Only a roaring in my ears as blood pools in my head.

And the phantom-like presence of my second body.

It doesn't pull away from me this morning. It lingers—in the top of my skull, my fingertips, my feet. The wand, tucked inside my shirt, thrums against my skin.

In quick succession, it's buzzing doubles and triples and quadruples.

This is all I have: a roar of blood, the sensation of a second body, the wand's infrasound.

Hold on.

I stare into the shadow of the ilama tree as I focus on the noose and my neck and oxygen.

The shadow twists and moves. It almost reminds me of the aurora borealis that's visible from deep within Velm—

Flares of red, which form contours.

The contours in the shadows expand. They form comprehensive shapes. I make out a thatched roof. I see a narrow door beside a square window with a swaying curtain.

A little shack.

Yes—it sits atop a hill.

Far from where I'm dying in Rhotidom.

The shack's red edges fill the shadow. With each second, they come into starker focus. I could count the thatched sticks of the roof, the planks used for the walls, the bundles of dry grass shooting up near the doorframe.

I strain my entire body, desperate for breath. For oxygen. For sanity. With each passing second, my body shakes.

Never surrender.

A woman walks out of the cottage.

She is holding a red axe in one hand.

She is watching me.

She comes closer; her features contort with rage.

It's hard to put it all together. I don't have enough oxygen or sense. My eyes are going to burst from my head.

Never surrender.

With each second, the vision becomes clearer; its red hue lessens. The sky is blue, the grass is more brown than green. The wooden structure is dark, the fluttering curtain a pale green.

The Kulapsifang is holding a bloodred axe.

It's stark compared to her dark gray hair, which drifts to her hips, thick and straight. She rushes toward me from the vision, quick enough that her colorless cloak trails her.

"*Samson,*" she says, features bent with alarm.

The sound reverberates around my head.

I can't tell if it's real—

I'm dying again.

I can feel my second body clinging to me. I can feel Imperatriz watching from a shadow that's full of color.

It's just as visceral and clear as the sensation of being choked, of the cord tightening around my neck as enemies flank me, waiting.

Fight, Samson.

Adrenaline courses through me as my second body lingers. Rather than detach and dissipate, it seems to settle in—drifting slowly into place while my body shakes with the urge to inhale.

Infrasound courses through my body, then into the air.

It spreads everywhere all at once. It knocks the wolves off their feet, shakes the ilama tree and its leaves. Mimosa flowers and broken twigs fall like rain from above.

I shift onto my side, coughing and gasping for breath.

I kick my legs to put some distance between myself and the wolves.

The infrasound fizzles out.

The wolves watch from a few feet away, wary. Too exhausted and disoriented to run or fight, I huff down oxygen desperately. My best bet for outlasting them is endurance. But for that to pay off, I need to do more damage than a broken nose.

I look from one to the next as my senses realign, desperate to find a weakness—a thick scar I can reopen, a weak knee that's prone to dislocating. Anything.

The pair wanders closer, eyeing me uneasily.

I glance at the shadow below the ilama—from where I sit now, it's obscured.

I can't tell if the vision of my mother is out of sight from this angle or if it has disappeared. If it was real at all.

But with each second I survive and fill my lungs with oxygen, I can feel my second body with greater distinction.

It pools in my core, vibrating a deep bass. It sparks, shooting toward my fingertips. Desperate, I address my second body in a low and broken voice, "Bring her to me here in Mieira. Now."

The wolves grunt laughter.

The one with the cord raises his eyebrows. "Talking to the red witch's magic?"

The other spits on my shoulder. "We heard you were a witch-fucker."

"It's the thing he's got on him. The rod. I told you I could feel it before."

"It won't do anything." The wolf sniffs, eyes locked on my chest. "Just feels weird. Like a magical healing."

In unison, they lunge forward, one targeting my legs and the other my upper half. I manage to knee the former in the jaw, sending him staggering to the side. But he quickly rejoins his packmate as we grapple. Within a few swift movements, the noose is once again wrapped around my throat.

They drag me to the ground again.

The ilama shadow is still out of sight.

The cord sinks into the same impression the first left. I can feel my face redden, my eyes bulging and my chest rising in search of oxygen.

I lose my breath quicker this time.

Never surrender.

The shadowy forest fades to gray.

Black splotches fill my vision, expanding into others like blots of ink. Soon, all I feel is the ground beneath me, the force of gravity pasting me to this earth.

This is it.

Before I lose touch with reality altogether, I grit out one word.

It's an apology more than anything else.

"Mama."

As soon as the word leaves my lips, my second body rattles to life beneath my skin. Then it soars through the jungle with a reverberating bass that's ten times stronger than the last pulse.

I hear the trees shudder, leaves flapping in their wake. I feel the earth shake, the pebbles and twigs and dry leaves shifting along the ground. Birds squawk loudly as they rush into the sky.

The cord and wolves slide off me. I gasp for breath, throat opening as I lie on the ground with my vision still black.

Then comes a pervasive, calming silence, thickened by the infrasound's heavy aftermath.

I pant desperately, waiting for some conclusion.

Instead, someone trips over my legs with a gasp.

I force my eyes open, clenching my jaw to control my wild breathing.

Between black splotches, I see one of the wolves topple to the ground near my head. Another faces me, sunken onto his knees and his eyes wide with terror.

I blink, confused by the sudden turn.

A pale hand clutches the wolf's hair, dragging his head backward and exposing his neck.

There is a female wolf behind him.

She looks very familiar.

She raises a red axe and cuts his jugular.

Red pours from his throat, staining his skin like black cherry juice.

She drops the wolf.

She steps around the fallen body, eyes fixed on another who scrambles behind me.

I don't see what she does with him.

My body is heavy against the dirt and leaves.

Halfway into a blackout slumber, the woman's ala fills my mind.

A smile forms on my lips before oblivion falls.

This ala.

Home, victory, dominion, courage, shelter.

The woman comes close. Her warm, sturdy hands cradle my head. She shifts, lifting my head into her lap.

"*You*," she says with a quiet sob.

I smile.

I lean into her warmth as my body succumbs to an endless exhaustion.

"Mama."

I drift in and out of sleep.

Cool wind seeps between teak and rosewood walls. The breeze paints a foul picture; I must be in a fertile and busy place. Incense melds with compost, with flowers and stinky dyes. The scents of fresh silk and the filthy worms it comes from. Trees and leaves covered in a sticky, recent rain.

A sable must have been living in this room; I can smell its nest someplace overhead.

And outside are the saigas. So many saigas, and all their shit.

I notice the noisy clatter next. Merchants argue with one another loudly, shouting across great distances. Groups wander by, chatting nonsense that can only be fueled by dextro and freshly broken hearts.

I remember this nightmarish city—

I've been here before.

Alita.

Memories crash through my mind—

The campsite. The ambush. The noose. The red-filled shadow. The second body.

Imperatriz.

I jolt upward as my eyes open.

I'm in a small bedroom. A window lines the bed to my left, while a wolf in a chair sits close to my right.

Imperatriz flinches from my sudden movement. She reaches out in the next second, setting a calming hand on my arm.

My throat locks as our eyes meet. She looks exactly how she did in the red dreams: her cheeks are full, her jaw is strong, and her full lips are set. She's aging around her eyes, which are just as deep-set and piercing as ever. I have no idea how much time has passed since I lost consciousness, but she looks well-rested and focused.

She smiles.

I must have forgotten that smile.

It reaches her eyes, it fills them with sparkles.

"Atali." Her voice is calm and pleased. "Samson 714 Afador. My Kulapsifang."

I don't think I smile back. I must be staring at her, a lump in my throat. I don't know what to say.

I look like Clearbold. He must be the last person you want to see right now. I'm sorry.

But I don't want to talk about him quite yet.

Are you okay?

What a stupid and basic question—so unfit for unpacking eighteen years of hardship.

Please tell me you're not angry with me. Tell me someone already broke the news about my failures in Velm.

Selfish and childish.

I clear my throat. "Hello, Imperatriz 713 Afador."

She scoots closer to my narrow bed, hand tightening on my arm. "Did you rest?" She straightens my tunic with her free hand. "I know you must be upset with me. But it will be better now. I'm back. Okay?"

I don't know why, but fear prickles my spine.

Maybe I'm afraid of getting everything I've wanted for so long.

The vast and unending set of possibilities that this reality opens up—

Imperatriz is back. And she will save Velm.

I set my hand over hers. I let its warmth seep into mine.

She's here, Samson, I assure myself. *She's alive.*

"I'm sorry it took me so long to find you," I say around the lump in my throat. "I know I look like Clearbold. Also... Velm..." With a start, I remember the wand. My hand shoots to my chest, feeling for the narrow piece. "I had—"

"A warlock named Halcyon took the piece from you earlier. He said that he'd hold onto it for now. He was very adamant about not touching it." My mother's head tilts, a vague smile on her lips. "And I prayed to Hetnazzar that you would grow in Clearbold's image. I figured he'd be too vain to kill someone who looked like him. Tell me he's alive—I beg you."

"He's alive."

Her smile grows. She reaches up to stroke my cheek. "Very good."

She stares at me, content. I stare back, uncertain how to bridge everything that's happened over the last two decades. Now that I've remembered the wand, I imagine Imperatriz has a few pressing questions about her return to Rhotidom.

(So do I.)

But, for whatever stupid reason, I start with, "I have a half-brother."

My mother's features bend into a grimace. "Emerel, then?"

I nod, relieved she's not too surprised. "His name is Malachai."

"Well, then. I'll take care of Clearbold if you'll take care of the pup." She strokes my cheek again, a quick smile on her lips.

"We have a long way to go before that's an option, Imperatriz. I've... failed."

She rolls her eyes. "Atali. Am I not your mother anymore? Or do you only call me mama when you're dying on a forest floor?" She scoots from her stool onto the edge of my bed. She turns to me, running a large and warm hand through my short hair.

I can't remember if she used to touch me like this when I was a child. It feels foreign and familiar, at the same time. At first, my instinct is to melt under her touch. Then I remember she's a wolf, and she's been gone for eighteen years, and I'm not even sure I knew her well before she disappeared.

Maybe I still don't know her now.

Imperatriz's eyes search mine, her features falling. "If anyone has failed, it's me. You're not the Alpha yet, Samson. You're a Kulapsifang in training. I'm here now. These problems are not yours. Everything is okay now."

I set my head against her shoulder, angling my nose into her hair. We sigh, emptying our lungs. She shifts her head past my shoulder to do the same; I wish she could smell me with the force and clarity that I can smell her, but my lack of hair has weakened my ala.

I let my body relax with a few long breaths.

Imperatriz pulls away, tears in her eyes. She wipes them from her cheeks, then settles back into her stool. But she doesn't release my arm, her thumb stroking me.

She clears her throat, then says, "We need to talk about something else."

I nod, leaning toward her so she doesn't lift her hand away.

I'd been hoping she'd know where to start the hefty conversation that comes next.

"In the jungle... how I returned to Mieira... it was magic." She looks down, her eyebrows pulled together. "A very powerful magic. I imagine it was very startling."

I shake my head. "I can explain. It's..."

She shakes hers, too, raising her chin to look at me urgently. "Let me speak first—please. It's important to me. I'm not sure if you've met a witch named Milisent West of Jaws. I was in good standing with her mother, Andromeda North of Skull. She died in childbirth a few years before you were born. Milisent is likely the last red wielder in Mieira. I..." Imperatriz licks her lips with another shake of her head. "I met her second daughter earlier this year. The youngest. Helisent. I did what I could, but I don't know if she survived. She was in a very bad way—and I don't know where they took her. I was given a cylinder of powerful red dove, which I believe was in exchange for helping her. It must have been either Milisent who sent it or, if she did find a way to survive, then Helisent. Helisent West of Jaws."

I watch her lips when she says the witch's name.

"Helisent is alive and well, thanks to you." Her eyes flash to me, a small gasp in her throat. "The help you offered likely saved her life. She survived the journey to Ezit. The warlock who took the wand off me... he's from Plet. His name is Halcyon. He also helped save her."

I pause as Imperatriz's brow bends with disbelief. She shifts like she might interrupt me, but stays silent.

"Milisent died seven years ago." I decide to skip over the tale of Anesot. For now, at least. "Helisent is the last of the red line. As you're aware, she was taken from Hypnos last year along with a ship of okeanids. I went to Ezit—"

"You *what?*" Imperatriz says, flinching. She scans me in the next second. "You went to *Ezit?*"

"Yes. I sailed to Zarzynn with eight others. We were searching for you, along with Helisent and the lost okeanids. I knew you were on Pit, but we couldn't find a way there. That's why Helisent sent you the dove. It was an offering on her behalf and mine. After we located the witch, we gathered in the House of Vex—her House. We met with vampires, then raided Ezit on the triplemoon. We took home the okeanids... but I'm sorry that I couldn't find a way to Pit at that time. I'm sorry that I left you behind."

I shake my head—it would have made a world of difference.

Maybe Rex and Berevald would still be here. Both had pushed when it came to finding Pit. And I'd been the one who wanted to play things conservatively.

Instead, Imperatriz focuses elsewhere. "You went... into Ezit? The mega-city?"

"Yes, that one."

She snorts, angling her head to stare at me. "Samson, atali, I heard many tales on Pit. People don't just... go into Ezit."

"Well, we waited for a triplemoon. An okeanid demigod also helped us. It had followed us from Mieira—it's a long story. That was earlier this year. In spring.

"When I came back... Clearbold had made his move in my absence. I went to Bellator to try to take control of Velm, and that... didn't go well. That was at summer's end."

She sits back, her brow still bunched together. "I found you with another wolf, Hadadrimmon. He gave me a *very* brief update. Where is your pack, Samson? And... you would have gone to Silent City, right? Or did Velm fall before you had the chance to marry?"

"My pack is gone. Or half of it is. It's hard to say. My wife is safe in Mort. Her name is Brutatalika 567 Sigivald. Maybe you—"

"Brutatalika?" Imperatriz's expression softens, and her smile rekindles. "Well, didn't you get lucky? I remember her. I remember her well.

"And is this the part where we tell each other what happened? I would like to know you, Samson, and to hear what's happened over these eighteen years. You say it's a long story, but I've waited many years to hear it. I don't know how much longer I can wait. So long as you're rested and ready to speak, I'd like to start from the beginning."

This room reminds me of Helisent.

Of the only night we spent in Alita before we argued and parted ways.

I stare at Imperatriz; the longer I sit with her and converse, the more comfortable I feel. The more the remnant of trust and security reforms.

But I never actually thought about what to tell Imperatriz about my life.

Maybe I never actually believed I'd come face to face with her again.

Maybe now that I am, I'm unwilling to compromise my future or her future in Velm with a thing like the truth.

Because it all makes sense now with her sitting beside me. 'This is the story. This is how it happened, from Point A to Point B.'

It won't make sense if I tell the truth about the red witch. If I tell her that the wand brought her through the shadow of the ilama tree—not a cylinder of dove. If I tell her that I engaged in sex magic with the hopes of finding Pit—and maybe also just because I crave being bonded to the witch. If I tell her that I dream in red thanks to a seething—and that my demigod has appeared in some of these dreams.

No.

Not yet.

Maybe not ever.

"Well," I start, licking my lips. "I didn't look like Clearbold back when I was twelve. Not yet, at least. That first winter after you were taken, he sent me into the forest outside Bellator..."

CHAPTER 10

JINGLES

HELISENT

Honey Baby,
We know you lie about your birthday, but we won't forget. Happy thirty-sixth,
you old broad.
The Boys

Zeu straddles my hips, bearing his weight into his hands where they're locked around my wrists.

My back presses against the cold, hard shale as he pins me, waiting for me to fight my way out of the hold.

I avoid looking at Zeu as I thrash. I put every ounce of strength into my hips, trying to buck him off me.

I pant and grit my teeth as blood rushes to my face.

Zeu looks down at me patiently. "Stop panicking. Deep breaths. Look at my body. Look at what's happening."

"I *can't*!"

Once, my papa took me to northern Hypnos, where massive lizards sit in the tributaries near the sea and wait for their prey. We watched one greenish beast clamp its triangular and fang-lined maw onto a saiga. It had twisted and rolled to drag the horned saiga into the muddy water, and all we ever saw again were small waves and frantic bubbles popping along the surface.

Desperate to get the vampire off me, I buck and twist and roll like the green lizard beast.

"What are you doing?" Zeu asks. "What is this? I didn't teach you this."

The vampire's braids fall toward me as he holds my wrists, slipping over his shoulder and tickling my stomach. I swear I can feel his balls where they're resting near my belly button.

I open my mouth and shriek as loudly as I can.

"My *ears*," he hisses. "What did I tell you—"

"Jingles, jingles, jingles!" I bellow.

Zeu slides off me immediately and stands. He crosses his arms as he fixes an unimpressed look on me. "You *have* to stop with the screaming. It echoes in the cave."

I ignore him, trying to get ahold of myself. I've never felt my mind *pant* before, but I can sense it keenly now.

I stare around the red shale cave, disheartened.

Since Zeu returned a few days ago, I've been patiently waiting for word that Samson, Hadadrimmon, and the Bloodies reached Alita. Rainstorms threw the group off-track—which means I've been stuck in Tet training with the King of Night.

I blame the monsoons for my misfortune.

"Go get Esteban," Zeu goes on. "You're done for the night."

I lie flat on my back, spanning my arms as I suck in large breaths. "Is this going to make me skinny? I refuse to be skinny, Zeu."

He pokes my tummy. "Not like Esteban."

"How the *fuck* is she doing so well?"

So far, Zeu's plan to train me involves what he calls 'martial arts'. Apparently, that involves him chasing us around the cave to 'get our blood moving' and then making us sit against the walls with no chairs to 'develop muscle' and then forcing us to eat a bunch of protein to 'feed the muscle'. The only thing I hate more than what he calls jiu-jitsu is what he calls bökh. Thankfully, he says we're too light to engage in the latter.

Onesimos watched our first bout and insisted we come up with a safe word.

I have screeched the word 'jingles' often since then.

Esclamonde... not nearly as much as I would have thought.

"Esteban is incredibly disciplined," Zeu says. "I'm surprised you haven't noticed."

I tsk. "If this is supposed to help me, why do I feel so weak?"

"Because you need months of training, not a few days."

I gulp down a breath. It feels like my lungs are on fire. "It's only been a few days?"

"Four, to be exact."

"There has to be a spell for this."

"If there was a spell that conditioned the body, Ezit would have never bothered with vampires like me. Before they discovered necromancy, that's pretty much all we did. Fought on their behalf."

I sit up with a huff, fixing my eyes on him. "Then why the *fuck* am I doing this? I don't foresee a future that involves a lot of physical combat, Zeu."

"Nobody ever plans on fighting, Helisent." Zeu claps his hands clean, then he tends to the red dust covering his white skirt. "But it still comes in handy. Remember Pel? He didn't have rosfrost with him when he bit you."

With a series of heaving and groaning, I manage to pull myself onto my feet. I ignore his comment, stomping past the vampire and heading back toward our campsite.

"Send the witchling," Zeu calls after me.

I follow my nose through the winding cave. I can smell the savory trail of a large meal—and it was Onesimos's turn to cook tonight, not Esclamonde's.

I pick up my pace as the fire comes into view.

On its far side, Esclamonde stretches with her legs spread, reaching toward the ground between them. With a few huffs, she rocks lower. Though her frame is narrow, she's started to fill out her form—not with soft curves, but angular muscle. Even her face is more sculpted; her jaw stronger, her neck thicker.

Onesimos smiles as he sits at the fire, two plates balanced in his lap. "Excellent form!" He notices me and then holds up one of the plates. "I made you one, Honey. Come sit with me. Look at Esteban— look at her go! She'll be a contortionist in no time."

I frown as I sit beside the oread and accept the food.

When Esclamonde smiles at me, a proud glaze in her eyes, I nod toward the cove where I exited. "Master Zeu is waiting."

"Ready." She pops up onto the balls of her feet, then takes off toward the level spot where we train. Her long legs shift into an impressive stride, propelling her onward quickly.

I watch her go. Once she's out of view, I turn back to Onesimos. "I have this urge to make her the most powerful thing that ever existed and yet... I'll never take her seriously. Did you see her knobby little knees? They remind me of glass ornaments. Maybe a bird's skeleton. Yngvi brought a dead pigeon home once, and we took out all of its insides so we could see its bones. It had... *so* many. I didn't realize something so small could be so complex."

"Her knees are very knobby. That's true." Onesimos taps my plate. "Why don't you eat?"

I dig in without another word. Halfway through the meal, I realize Onesimos has barely touched his plate. Instead, he's staring pensively into the fire.

I study his fixed gaze, his thoughtful blinking. He's always been prone to long bouts of pensive silence—especially when there's a flame nearby. But the stretches of focused staring have become more common since we settled back into life in Luz.

And it's become even more pronounced in the caves of Tet, where we spend hours near the fire each night.

I elbow him. "Are you okay?"

He shifts quickly, as though snapping out of a trance. "Being inside this cave has made me think of home. A lot." He glances at my plate and then takes it out of my hands. "If you're done, I have something to show you." He sets my plate below his, then reaches into his pocket. He pulls out a tightly folded note and hands it to me. "Halcyon sent this. It arrived an hour ago. He says they made it to Alita—safe and sound."

I nearly rip the parchment, fragile and damp with rain, as I unfold it.

I scan the words twice. *'We arrived in Alita late last night. Everyone is safe and resting. Come immediately.'*

I stand up and race toward the supply shelves. I start scooping up the most important pieces—bottles of shampoo and body oil, my diamonds, the pair of strappy red shoes I stole from Milisent.

While I shove them into my bottomless bag, I look over my shoulder and tell Onesimos, "I'm leaving. I'll be back when—"

"I'm going with you," he says with a demure smile.

I pause, fingers wrapped around my favorite wooden cup. "Come with me? After we got back to Luz, you said you were done traveling. I barely got you to come here. Why the change of heart?"

He shrugs. "Alita is close to Jaws. I'd like to visit home."

I narrow my eyes.

My thoughts and emotions rattle between the excitement of reuniting with Samson and the oread's strange smile.

I'm not sure what that little smile is telling me right now. I've never had trouble translating the oread's expressions—

So, what's in this one? And why right now—whatever it is?

He can't be going *home* already. As in, permanently.

...Right?

I clear my throat. "You said you'd stay in Luz with me for two more years. Do you remember? When we got back from Cadmium, you said you were planning on going home soon, and I said I still needed you, and you said I had you for two more years."

He stands up and sets our plates near the water-filled basin we use for washing. "Don't be angry with me, Helisent." Like I do, he rounds the campsite, picking up his most important belongings and stashing them in his cross-body bag.

"I'm not angry." I slip on my robe and sling my bag into place. "But it hasn't been two years. It's been two months."

I hate every selfish word.

He stands on the other side of the fire, his cloak in one hand and his bag in the other. "It's been six months."

I nod, feeling like the world is spinning.

In fact, I lied; I'm angry.

Onesimos and I have spent the last seven years as best friends and lovers. Our bond transcends the scope of both; there's even a tiny part of him that feels like a brother to me.

Simmy is a reflection of my soul, tied to mine in every way.

And he's now forty years old.

Though I'm not far behind him, I'm only one-fourth into my lifespan.

Onesimos, should he be very lucky and aided by my healing magic, will see his sixty-fifth year. He is more than halfway there. And he's always told me he wanted to go home before his elder years took hold.

"I'm not angry," I insist. But there's a ball welling up in my throat, and tears in my eyes. All the joy of learning Samson made it to Alita fades to nothing—a hollow, empty nothing. I have the suspicious feeling that this is adulthood; swinging from one emotional high straight into a crater. "It's just... your home is in Luz. One of them, at least. I know nymphs have like ten homes. But I'd like it if you remembered your Luzian home."

He lowers his chin, golden flames dancing in his vermillion pupils. "I know. I'll never forget my favorite warren."

"Right. Your favorite warren."

The Onesimos offers me a hopeful, weak smile, and I do my best to smile back.

Is this really fucking happening right now—he's leaving Luz for a long time, if not for good?

In silence, we spend the next few minutes writing a note for Esclamonde and Zeu on the wall in chalk, alerting them that we've been called to Alita but will return as soon as possible. In the meantime, we forbid Zeu from abandoning the witchling; we forbid the witchling from asking too many questions and writing down too many observations in her notebook.

I stare at the note and sigh.

Far in the distance, Zeu's instructive shouting echoes.

I drag my feet away from the fire, from the note on the wall, and head to the portal that waits in the nook near the cave's entrance. The short journey doesn't help calm my nerves. When we reach the dark corner, Onesimos takes my hand. I pretend I'm not crying, trying to hide my sniffles.

He brings my hand to his lips and kisses it. "Don't shadow us if you aren't ready, Honey. There's no rush. Halcyon said everyone was safe and sound."

I huff a long sigh. It takes a while for my thoughts to calm. And when they do, and I'm able to focus on Alita, my mind wanders to the first warren Onesimos and I started together. "Do you remember the warren in Afters?"

The oread laughs once, deep and true. "I could never forget it. Such a tiny little room."

"And the faded blue door."

"I think it's red now. They painted it red after we left."

"It was next to the laundry hall. It always smelled nice because of that. Remember when we met Pen that first night?"

"Yes," says Onesimos, a smile in his voice. "He forgot to dress up, so he walked around in his form for half an hour, trying to scare the nymphs and impress the witches."

"Of course. Good times."

The oread's warm hand squeezes mine. "I remember it clearly."

Without a fire nearby, all we have is the light from a magical cylinder, dimmed to protect the shadowing portal. It traces his full features.

I close the distance to peck him. I linger for a moment, pressing against his soft lips to savor their warmth, their familiarity.

I pull back when a lump forms in my throat again.

Like he can sense it, Onesimos squeezes my hand once more. "Let's go check on Sandro. Okay?"

I exhale shakily. "Yeah. Ready."

I guide us around the nook's slanted wall and into the thrumming shadow. I hold the warren in my mind; the blue door, the citrus-and-coconut scent of detergent, the jacaranda tree that grew outside.

Onesimos clings to my arm as we pass through a bass-filled darkness and exit into a rickety, wood-paneled hovel.

I look around, trying to remember if I've been in this room before. In the dead of night and surrounded by noisy beings, it's hard to get my bearings. Two dryads share a sleeping mat at one end of the cramped room. Narrow shelves run along two walls, littered with trash and half-empty cups. On the far side is a hesperide standing against the wall, one of her legs hiked up and resting on the low windowsill. An okeanid kneels between her legs, a hand supporting her thigh while they crane upwards to pleasure her.

Like me, Onsimos turns in a circle, looking around.

The hesperside grips the wall with all her might, body arching toward the heavens.

Onesimos elbows me, his eyes wide. "Holy shit. You did it. It's our old warren."

I huff, prepared to argue that we could have never been so lost or destitute to live in a place like this. The current residents are using a torn sheet as a curtain. Instead of citrusy laundry detergent, all I smell is clove cigarettes and mud.

The scent doesn't help my nausea as a vortex of fatigue consumes me.

I keel sideways as splotches overtake my vision. Onesimos grabs my arms with a curse as I topple onto my knees.

The hesperide and okeanid finally notice us. The last thing I hear is them screaming angrily, and Onesimos chortling wildly as he tries to explain.

I sit up in a rush, my head spinning.

I think of Onesimos first, his laughter still echoing in my ear.

And then I'm thinking of Samson—

Where is the wolf, and has he found a nothing-scented candle yet?

I glance around a dim cabin.

It's nighttime. There must be a party in full swing; beyond the song of the insects is the sound of happy shouting and Alita bells. Fireworks clang through the air, powerful enough to shake the thin glass in the window by my bedside.

I squint into the madness outside, trying to figure out why I'm alone in the dark room.

When I turn in the other direction, I see Butter. She sits at my bedside near a glowing cylinder; the light traces her turquoise-gold eyes and shapely lips. Her hair is tied back into tight braids, accented with jacaranda flowers.

"You passed out after you shadowed," she explains. "Alita is farther from Tet than you thought. We're near Hemlock's bungalow in the city center."

I flinch as another firework shoots into the air and explodes; it sounds like it's directly over the roof. "And the party?"

Butter blinks at me, her expression strange and still. "Imperatriz is back."

I flinch again, my mind racing.

I look at Butter, wide-eyed and desperate for an explanation. "What? How? *Imperatriz?* When?"

I can't fully read her apprehensive expression. "You gave him the wand," is all she says.

"And?" I pull my blanket off, looking out the window and searching for Samson. The tightly packed bodies block the light from the bonfires and fireworks and magical cylinders. A few tall and broad beings look like wolves, but I can't see any of their features. In the distance, I make out a stage—but that's also flooded with partygoers.

"And?" Butter asks, a humorless laugh in her throat. "And he fucking wielded a portal, and then his fucking mother walked through it."

I blink at Butter, waiting for the punchline.

"Samson can't wield. Even with the wand—that was never..." I huff down a few breaths. "I gave him the wand to protect him. I'd hoped that it would link him to Pit..."

I stare blankly at the dark wall ahead of me.

Butter sits back in her chair. When I finally look at her, it's easier to decipher her tense expression. The sheen in her eyes is a cold and hard stubbornness. A light that turns into shards; they break off and splinter into me.

A condemnation.

"Were you there when it happened?" I rub my face and take another calming breath. "He doesn't know *how* to wield. He's fucking scared of heights—and, and cats—he's not a fucking wielder Butter."

"I know what I felt," the okeanid-witch-necromancer snaps. She crosses her arms, chewing bitterly on her lip before she tells me, "We were ambushed at dawn two days ago. There were four wolves and an Argyd warlock. They got the drop on us—I couldn't even figure out which way was up. I woke up falling out of my nest. If it weren't for the protective spells Halcyon had put up at night, we would've both been dead. Without question. After that, things moved quickly.

"Halcyon and I were separated from Samson and Hadadrimmon— the wolves went straight for them. So, I wasn't there when he wielded. I didn't see it myself. All I know is that your magic... your magic was there. I felt it gain strength. I felt it... Well, I don't know what happened. It exploded. It was everywhere. *Everywhere*, Helisent.

"After the warlock was dead, we went back to our camp. Hadadrimmon and Samson were both out cold." Her voice shakes with shock and anger. "And there was another wolf there. A female wolf. Imperatriz 713 Afador—in the flesh. I didn't want to ask her what had happened. She was... You could tell it was a lot. She was focused on Samson."

My stomach coils.

Imperatriz is back, and they're celebrating her arrival in the streets right now—

So why does this feel so bad?

Panic thrums through me.

Butter goes on, "The next day, we reached Alita. After we had the chance to rest, I asked Samson what happened. He'd been talking about the wand, Helisent. He'd been dreaming of Imperatriz since we left Luz. He said he was waking up feeling like he had a second body."

Butter levels another condemning look at me.

This time, it feels like a punch to the stomach.

I don't know how to react to that statement.

A second body?

Since we left Luz?

That sounds like a magical twin...

But no part of me actively thought the wand would have such an immediate and lasting impact. I'd sent it primarily to protect Samson, and to hopefully begin building a link between his mind and my magic and his mother. I'd done sex magic with him to bridge any remaining gaps between my magic and the wolf.

Thank the fucking moons I didn't tell Butter about the sex magic.

"No thoughts on the second body, then? Interesting." Butter tsks. "When I asked him how Imperatriz got here, he said the wand did it. Like the dreams and the second body, he couldn't explain it. Just that he'd been close to death, and then his mother walked through a shadow."

I sit and stew, riled by each of her words.

None of this should have been possible.

At best, I still would have shadowed Imperatriz to us—or us to Pit.

I take long and deep breaths, trying to calm myself.

If Samson is wielding my magic...

No, don't think that.

Don't let yourself believe that.

I throw my hands up, frustrated with all of my oversights, with the fact that Butter hasn't broken any of this news to me softly. "So? What's your argument? Samson has a right to ask the wand for a boon. He's saved my life multiple times. And... the wand was *supposed* to protect him. If he needed help, he had every right to ask—especially if he thought there was a possibility of reuniting with Imperatriz. I don't know if you've noticed, my dear Calypso, but Velm is *fucked* right now."

For a long time, Butter doesn't respond.

She sucks on her teeth and looks past me, out the window.

As I prepare to tell her I'm leaving, she fixes her glazed eyes on me again.

"Maybe, Helisent. Maybe you're correct, and Samson has every right to use your demigod's power how he sees fit. He's saved your life, and now his life is in shambles, and it's time for you to return the favor. I can respect that.

"But the real issue here isn't the wand. It's why you gave it to him."

She shrugs her shoulders.

I narrow my eyes as I piece together her point.

"It's what you think will happen next." Butter raises her chin. "Tell me, my dear friend—what do you think happens next?"

My body starts to shake. I ignore it. Ignore every guilty thought and private fear that passes through me.

In a small voice, I reason, "He needed me. His demigod needed me. His Kulapsifang needed me."

Butter takes a deep breath, nostrils flaring. "And now she's back. Do you get it?"

I give her the once over, still ignoring my shaking voice. "Me and Samson—"

"I will not let you ruin yourself for a fucking wolf."

Oh, no.

A sticky, tar-like feeling overcomes me; I've felt this before.

Not again.

It's the urge to push away everyone I love and cling to my lover.

Because I love Samson, and I love the witch who Samson loves, and without Samson's love, I'm no longer that witch, and if I'm no longer that witch—

And if Simmy goes back home, too—

I clench my hands into fists. "That *fucking wolf* helped free you from Ezit."

"And I will always be thankful for that, but that's not what I'm talking about right now. I'm talking about the possibility that you handed him that wand thinking he might ever be more to you than a wolf." Butter leans closer. She lowers her voice—maybe in an attempt to soften the blow. "Velm will never hand you their Kulapsifang. You're fucking delusional if you think that's an option. I *need* you to see this coming. I *need* you to understand that this is where it ends. With Imperatriz."

I stare at her.

Her counsel is wise.

Yet, it feels like the world is ending. My body shivers with some kind of conclusion my mind and heart can't catch up with.

The truth...

I have never once planned on letting Samson go.

I have lived with the assumption that he will always partly be mine; Kulapsifangs are allowed to have private affairs, after all. Someday, I'll have to watch Brutatalika grow as round as a moon with their child, and that will hurt enough that I'll probably disappear for a while, but offspring can be fun, and at some point, I'll get used to that blue-black-haired stinker of a child. It will be half of Samson, after all.

And when I've processed the child's existence, things will be sexy again.

"Go on." Butter gestures toward the window where the bonfires blaze and the Alitians dance. "Go find him and Imperatriz. See what they say to you—I'll tell you now." She angles her head toward me to hiss, "They'll ask you to shadow them to Mort. Where Brutatalika is waiting for her husband."

I shift backward, gut clenching.

I hate that tears pool in my eyes.

Butter lifts her chin, declaring, "He doesn't choose you. He will never have that option. And every time you sacrifice something for him, you leave a scar on your heart that will never heal."

Something in me snaps.

I swing my legs off the bed.

I leave my robe and my bottomless bag behind.

I stagger to the door and open it.

I don't look back at Calypso.

I have no idea if she follows me.

I don't flick my fingers to cast my grooming magic. My hair is flat and oily, my face and clothes probably not much cleaner.

I disappear quickly into the crowd. I let the frantic bodies jostle me as I walk toward the stage in the distance. It sits near Alita's central plaza, where Velm's white marble column shoots into the sky. I pass a dryad who eats flames at the ends of sticks, then belches them out of her throat like a dying phoenix. Next to her, another dryad dances with a staff with colorful ribbons at either end. I watch the fabric wheel around in strange patterns.

It feels like Alita is celebrating the end of the world with me.

The end of all these private dreams I hadn't realized I was dreaming with Samson.

The end...

I don't know how much time passes before I reach the stage.

A band gathers atop the raised platform, spinning in a circle as they raise their Alita bells and blow the bronze horns skyward. A slew of drummers sit nearby with instruments of all shapes and sizes. A small group of revelers lead a chant just behind them; a sable wearing a vest stands proudly atop one of their shoulders.

Past the ever-shifting silhouette of the crowd, amid the city's first-floor rooftops, I notice the semi-aglow hue of a dryad demigod. The being is hunched down in the plaza, its bent legs and feet perfectly laid in the city streets, surrounded by reeling nymphs.

The dryad demigod's eyes are wide with intrigue and delight, its head tilted as it closely watches the dancing group.

A few cheers erupt, then a wave of desita washes through the crowd in a gentle wave.

It takes my breath away for a second; hopeful, engrossing, distracting.

But it's gone in the next.

I look away from the demigod, refocusing on the stage.

Two wolves sit on its ledge. They wear thick strands of lilac flowers looped around their heads. The buds almost glow against their hair. The female wolf is older, her hair dark gray. The crowd seems to shift around her, heads ticking in her direction. The wolf at her side is young and handsome, with a red line around his neck just above his golden torc. His short hair splays against the flower crown, catching against the fragile petals.

Another troop of staff dancers crisscrosses before me, blocking and then revealing the Kulapsifangs as they proudly sit before the raucous crowd.

Looking at the pair, I wouldn't think they'd spent the last eighteen years separated. That my magic pulled the elder Kulapsifang through a shadow that crossed hundreds, maybe thousands, of miles. That it was the younger Kulapsifang who commanded that feat.

I would know immediately they were mother and son.

I would know immediately that they aren't like the rest of us, more akin to the dryad demigod who watches the festivities keenly.

"Jingles," I whisper. "Jingles, jingles, jingles."

Hemlock East of Alita, Rhotidic King and lush, smiles when he sees me.

The dryad monarch stands before an ornately carved mahogany door. Depictions of trees and flowers, of long-beaked birds and round-eyed mammals are etched into the wood in great detail.

The door leads into the Alita Gardens, a neatly tended courtyard in the city's northern streets. It's hidden behind towering walls covered in lush greenery, a perfect extension of the jungle that surrounds the city.

Before I reach him, Hemlock turns to a passing elder dryad. He says, "You've heard correctly, my dear sister. The Kulapsifang of Velm, Imperatriz 713 Afador, is safely inside the courtyard. She will be meeting with Helisent West of Jaws—and speak of the devil."

Hemlock opens his arms to me, his smile widening.

I'm not in the mood to entertain either dryad. To pretend I'm not filled to the brim with last night's dextro and hatred.

The elder grins at me, her stunning silver jewelry catching the cloudy light.

I try to smile back; it feels more like baring my teeth. "Hello, my dear dryads." The woman smiles and waits like she expects me to go on. I shift toward Hemlock. "Shall we? I believe I'm late."

I took off into the crowd last night.

I cloaked my scent so nobody could find me.

When the brandy didn't help settle my mood, and the dextro also failed, and the unending reel of festivities started to feel like a play at my expense, I stretched out alone on a rooftop and stared into the cloudy sky. I drifted off at dawn, then woke up beneath the sun, covered in sticky sweat. I finished off the dextro for a bit of energy—

And here I am, thirty minutes later.

Trying to smile at Hemlock and the dryad.

The king must read through my fake smile. He quickly shoulders open the door, then gestures me inside while offering a parting blessing to the nymph. The door clicks shut behind us, then Hemlock guides me toward a stone basin of clear water.

I follow, mouth parting with wonder.

Despite spending years in Alita, I never visited the Gardens.

I never would have fathomed...

Bronze and wooden partitions rise from the ground, forming short walls that outline pathways and sitting areas. Most are covered with crawling ivy and vines of flowers. Lilies crane in a square patch to my right, surrounding an oval pond with lotus flowers and their flat pads. To my left is a sitting area surrounded by tangles of passionflower; I can smell them from here.

At the stone basin, Hemlock fills a wooden cup with water. With a more reserved smile, he offers me the drink. As he does, a songbird with purple and green feathers takes a seat on his shoulder, swooping in from the entry gate.

I study the king next. His copper-brown skin is smooth but aging with fine wrinkles, his turquoise hair neatly swept behind his ears. To my pleasure, his beard is just as thick and well-groomed as ever. Below is a large jacaranda-bead necklace. The beads shine like honeyed amber, jewel-like.

I drink the cool and refreshing water, then smack my lips. "It's flavored?"

"Starfruit." He gestures toward a tub nearby. A leafy tree cranes from it, no taller than my shoulders. Heavy marigold fruits hang from it. They look like oranges with slices cut from their sides. "Welcome to the Gardens. It's a pleasure to have you. How are you, Helisent? The last time I saw you in Cadmium, an okeanid was stuffing your bottomless bag with lapis lazuli."

I blink at the king, wishing I had rehearsed a few responses. "Oh, you know."

A sable scurries from one of the dirt paths before the king can respond. Its long and slender body wriggles as it hustles, brown fur gleaming healthily. Between its short and stubby ears is a lilac hat. A sash crosses from its shoulder to its belly, dotted with silver decals.

"I see." Hemlock tucks his hands behind his back as the sable stops beside his bare feet. "Pennyroyal will show you the way. Breakfast is waiting." Pennyroyal leans onto its haunches to crane up toward me, nose and whiskers twitching. "I'll eat with the others. Let's see if I have it straight—there's a small crowd here. Halcyon, Calypso, Parsifal, Samson, and a wolf named Hadadrimmon. You'll share a private meal with Imperatriz. She requested—"

"I'm eating *alone* with Imperatriz?" *Fuck—I should have done more dextro.* "When did Parsifal get here? And where's Onesimos? He's an oread. He should have received an invitation to the Gardens, as well. We shadowed here together yesterday."

Hemlock's bushy eyebrows shoot up. "Ah, yes, Onesimos. I met with him earlier. He asked me to give you this." The king reaches into his cloak and pulls out a note. "Such a gentleman. He's welcome to the Gardens any time. Also, your father has been in Alita for a week or so."

I take the note. Half of me wants to burn it rather than face whatever sentimental goodbye the oread penned.

I look around.

Like last night's festivities, this heaven is hell to me.

I shove the note into my bottomless bag. "Well, then. See you soon." I eye the well-dressed sable. "After you, Pennyroyal."

Hemlock bows his head as a second songbird perches beside the first on his shoulder. "Enjoy, my dear witch."

The sable darts from Hemlock's feet, racing down the left-hand path and disappearing around a corner.

With a sigh, I follow.

The creature races through the courtyard. We pass a palapa where grapes dangle toward the ground, dark and inviting; a narrow passage covered with carnivorous flowers shaped like bells; a few low kapoks with woven hammocks strung between them.

Pennyroyal skids to a stop before turning between two bronze pillars that lead into a nook.

I steel myself before following the mammal into the cove with ivy-covered walls. Just in case I'm even less prepared than I think, I cloak my scent and vitals so the Kulapsifang can't register my racing heart or stress.

Then I step into the nook.

Imperatriz faces away from me, a heavy black cloak draped over her broad shoulders. Rather than wear her gray hair in a tight bun at the nape of her neck, it flows down her back and collects on the cushion, straight and thick.

She sits before a low table that's piled with platters of dumplings, curries, rice dishes, and piles of colorful fruits. Incense burns, smoke curling around the square cove and pooling amid the mature ivy. My nose twitches; it doesn't smell like anything.

I take my seat.

I force my eyes to the Kulapsifang as I settle into place.

I'm struck immediately by how unfamiliar she looks. She has a few traces of Sutnazzar's features: a straight and flat nose, a strong jaw, and a wide mouth. She has the same piercing eyes as Samson. They twinkle with something otherworldly; it might be beauty or power. Or both.

Eyes aside, their strongest resemblance is their stature.

The type of weighty silence that seems to roll off of them.

I don't remember her face from Pit; it's a comfort.

After a glance, I start filling my plate; I don't know what else to do.

I'm sad, I'm relieved, I'm nervous, I'm...

Lonely, already.

"You look healthy," she says in a deep and steady voice.

I pause with my spoon poised above my plate. I take a deep breath to control the wave of painful emotions that comes with the sound of her voice.

I don't remember her face—but I remember her voice in great detail.

'Be still, daughter of Andromeda.'

I force myself to meet her eyes again. "Yes. Much better now."

Then I take a huge bite, so she leads the conversation. I'm too strung out and suspicious and brokenhearted. Too uncertain about how this relationship is going to go.

Right now; ten years into the future.

All of it.

I chew on my food and watch the incense curl around us.

The Kulapsifang seems ill at ease. She glances at me, then looks at her hands. Slowly, almost painstakingly, she explains, "I feel... that it's too late for an apology. Still, I want you to know that I recognize the gravity of my mistakes."

I glance at her, cheeks full of rice. I remind myself to keep chewing.

An apology?

Is that what's about to happen?

"Mistakes?" I ask around my mouthful.

Imperatriz nods. "Your mother and I had radical plans for Mieira and Velm. Though it took us many years to become proper allies, our bond was strong. Our vision was clear. I..." She clears her throat. She hasn't filled her plate yet, seemingly content to strangle a pair of chopsticks. "When Andromeda died, I was even more determined to prove our partnership could still bear fruit. Because of this, I didn't see the signs that I should have.

"I was blinded by my pursuit of glory, driven by what I wanted for the wolves instead of what Velm needed. And what Velm needed was more time to accept the Northing. Not just a vague plan to move north, but a more elaborate understanding of why Velm couldn't stay cloistered."

I pick at my plate, uninspired by her words.

I'm still not sure why the wolves consider the Northing so radical. Why it's so deeply offensive to imagine living amongst nymphs and wielders. Why Clearbold's Leolites decided to blame Samson for the possibility of such a reality.

Imperatriz sets down her chopsticks and straightens her utensils, her plate, her placemat. "I should have known the ruse to draw me to Hypnos was thanks to Anesot's plotting. But I didn't see that. And so I was led onto the boat... and..." She shakes her head with an angry sigh. "I take responsibility for not dealing with Anesot. I take responsibility for what he did to Milisent West of Jaws. Oko, too. Samson explained that he had a sidekick. When I was taken to Pit, I had only just learned her name."

She looks up at me, jaw clenched. "I take responsibility for what happened to my son. And for what happened to you, Helisent. I knew I had failed when I found you on that ship last spring. I thought—"

"I don't think about my time on the ship often." I raise my eyebrows, surprised to find my footing in this conversation. For how little I understand Imperatriz's conclusions about the Northing, her self-loathing is obvious.

"And Anesot has been dead for over a year," I go on, pointing to the general area of the Afters neighborhood. "I tortured him a few streets that way. Eyes and testicles. Oko, too. Just the hands for her. They suffered appropriately for their wrongdoings. And then they died in agony."

She tilts her head as she looks at me.

Her lips part, then shut again, as though she's surprised.

"I used to blame myself for the evil others find themselves capable of. Not anymore." I narrow my eyes. "It seems you still do, though."

"I am the Kulapsifang of Velm," she says, as though it explains everything.

"And I'm the last living Vexen, the only red wielder in this world. But I just go by Helisent."

A smile traces her lips. "I see." She reaches forward to start filling her plate. "You're different than your mother. *Very* different."

"I take after my father."

Her smile widens. "I'm happy to see that Parsifal is doing well. He was one of the first to come and find me when we reached the city."

"Yeah, I have the feeling he's going to outlive us all."

She huffs a laugh, as though agreeing.

For a few minutes, we eat in silence. Though I'm still depressed and suspicious—about the wand, about Samson's future, about mine— it's a comfortable enough meal.

Pennyroyal saunters in halfway through, leaving a wide berth between him and Imperatriz. He sidles up to my lap and bares his baleful brown eyes at me; I share a few scraps with him.

Imperatriz glances at the palmfuls of rice I offer Pennyroyal. Her nostrils flare as its whiskers tickle my wrist.

I bite back a smile. "Your son once threw a fit in this city because I pet a saiga."

She shakes her head once. "It's mealtime, Helisent."

I give the sable's forehead a scratch. "For my dear Pennyroyal, too."

After a healthy helping of my rice, the sable scampers off. I watch it go while the Kulapsifang watches me. "You are close to my son."

I reach for my drink and chug the rest of the water, giving myself time to find a neutral answer. "We've been allies for a while."

She nods. "He says you're friends, as well."

I study her eyes, hoping to glean the insinuation there.

We've been lucky in regard to our affair so far —but this isn't any wolf. It's Samson's mother, one of the few beings who can presumably interpret his reticent expressions and laconic statements. Who can see through his zhuzhing.

They've been separated for eighteen years, but my papa insists that people never change.

"Friends, yes." I set my spoon down, looking for the right words. "But I have to be honest, Imperatriz. I don't find the wolves or Velm that impressive. I understand little of your culture, despite being friends with Samson and a handful of other wolves—all unnumbered, I should add. I'm not trying to rile you up, but I hope you're able to offer the wolves more than Clearbold did once you're back in Bellator. His reign has been shit, to put it lightly."

Deadpan, she looks at me and raises her eyebrows. "Can you understand why I found the Northing so appealing, then?" She lets that sink in for a moment. "I ask forgiveness and leniency on behalf of the wolves, especially the younger generation that has grown up in Clearbold's hyper-conservative regime. Give my people time, Helisent."

"I like to think I'm becoming more patient. And I have plenty of problems to deal with myself. No final judgments being cast here." I scrape my plate clean, then sit back against the ivy-covered wall. "So, when are you going to ask me to shadow you to Mort? I figured that was the point of this meeting."

She straightens, as though shocked by my words. "That's not why I'm here."

I scrunch my nose. "Then what the fuck are we doing here? No offense."

"We're two of the most influential beings in Mieira. I wanted to establish a connection with you personally. And... I wanted to check on you. To make sure that you'd recovered from the ship. And to thank you for saving my Kulapsifang. He says it's happened a few times now." She swallows, eyes darting like she's feeling suddenly timid. "I'm glad you two had each other in my absence."

'*In my absence.*'

She reaches for her cup, which I realize is full of dark wine, and takes a few gulps. (That's interesting—Samson never drinks this early.) "I also need to thank you and your magic for paving the way for my return. I can't offer you enough for what you've done—I mean that literally. I have few resources at my disposal. But... when the day comes that I'm sitting on the throne in Bellator Palace, you will be the first honored. All of Velm will know your name."

I offer her a saccharine smile, anticipating a fantastic bribe further down the line. "Then let's get you back to Mort sooner rather than later, my dear Kulapsifang."

She bows her head with a wide smile. "I would very much like to go home."

She twists, reaching into a bag at her side. To my great surprise, she pulls out a large cylinder of my dove. Red magic sloshes inside, nearly full even though Imperatriz has had it for months.

Suddenly, I wonder—

Is this how Imperatriz thinks she got back to Mieira? With my dove?

I extend my hand to collect the cylinder, thoughts racing.

I need to talk to Samson—about the wand, about his second body, about what he told Imperatriz.

I clear my throat. "Thank you."

Imperatriz bows her head again. "Don't thank me. It's you who deserves thanks, Helisent. It meant a lot to wake up with that dove in my cottage. It gave me more hope than you can ever know." Once I've tucked the cylinder away, she offers me a genuine smile. I see Samson in that smile—but only when he's feeling goofy and a bit drunk. "Shall we? I know where the others are eating. I'm sure Parsifal would love to see you."

I stand with a sigh. "Of course."

With a full stomach, only a few hours of sleep, and a brain full of dextro, I'm halfway in a haze as I follow the Kulapsifang of Velm through the courtyard. Pennyroyal intercepts us after we take two turns, squeaking and rushing like it's offended we left without its guidance.

Imperatriz concedes, letting the sable lead the way.

We follow it into a sitting area between two shallow ponds. Leafy strands of grass hang over the water, a few with fuzzy, light-brown ends. The group sits between them in a semi-circle.

I notice Samson first; his eyes shift from his mother to me, his expression subdued but hopeful. I notice the mark around his neck again, half-hidden by his torc; it's deep and pink, almost like a scar. His hair is messy in the humidity, but he looks well-rested.

Hadadrimmon sits to one side of Samson, my papa on the other; the pair seems engaged in an argument, leaning over the wolf. My papa wears a brand new peridot cloak with a few jacaranda bead accents.

Hemlock, Halcyon, and Calypso sit nearby, also engrossed in conversation. The dryad king gesticulates with his hand, as though explaining something to the pair, who watch with widened eyes.

The group pauses when Pennroyal dashes into the cove.

"Pennyroyal!" my papa shouts, opening his arms as the creature rushes toward him. He gasps when he sees me, quickly dodging the sable. "*Honey Baby!*"

He crushes me into a hug. "Hi, Papa," I say, setting my head on his shoulder.

"And where have you been?" He pulls back and smooths my hair with a heavy hand. "I was looking for you all night."

"I was with Onesimos," I lie.

With a wide smile, he reaches over to squeeze Imperatriz's hand, which she returns. Based on the way the Kulapsifang looks around the circle, she isn't nearly as familiar with the others. She openly stares at Halcyon and Calypso, then glances at me, as though expecting an introduction.

I take a deep breath. "Right. Let me introduce you to part of my court. We call ourselves the Bloodies—from our robes, not a penchant for violence."

"The Bloodies," Imperatriz murmurs. "I see."

I point to Halcyon. "This is Halcyon Plet. He's one of my ambassadors. That's Calypso Ultramarine. She's also an... ambassador. I guess. She's a necromancer, too.

"There are three more who couldn't make it. Onesimos, an oread. Esclamonde Black Rock Antigone, my witchling apprentice. And Zeu, King of Night. He's a vampire. He's... a... I'm still figuring it out." I snap my fingers when the idea clicks. "He's a personal trainer." I flash a smile at Parsifal. "I'm getting buff, Papa."

"Buff?" Parsifal returns to his seat and picks at his plate again. "Why?"

Hemlock smiles up at me, a songbird sitting on his shoulder once more. This time, it's a tiny yellow finch that looks to be whispering secrets into his ear. "That's good to hear. I was wondering how Zeu was doing. Queen Clover of Gamma sent me a letter—she's been very impressed with his den."

"Yes, he's full of surprises." I force a fake smile onto my face, uncertain of what comes next.

I can sense Samson in my periphery, but I'm not sure if it's appropriate to ask for a moment alone with him. In fact, the longer I stand here, the less I want that. I know what that conversation entails; if not a formal goodbye, then at least the start of one.

He and I only had a month together before being separated again.

I mean, someday, we'll have privacy once more.

But it's not enough.

And right now, the Gardens feel loaded with the unfathomable willpower of Imperatriz 713 Afador and all she's plotting.

Eighteen years' worth of retribution brews in the air like a storm in the sky.

"Hemlock, my dear king, do you happen to have a shadow in this courtyard?" I keep smiling dumbly, keep staring at the yellow finch on Hemlock's shoulder. "A suspiciously large one?"

"A *fuzzy* shadow? I remember those from Zarzynn. Midday is close, so our options are limited." Rather than look around for a shadow, the king glances at Imperatriz, then Samson. "We don't need one *right away*, do we? Just one more little snack, Helisent. The Gardens were created by my demigod generations ago; the great being can sense us gathered here. It would be dishonorable to leave before we share its desita." Hemlock's smile doubles in size. "Oh! And we have grapefruit brandy, too. Jugs of it. Queen Otrera sent it."

I glance around, searching for a full pitcher. "Fine."

Parsifal pats the cushion at his side, and I head over, happy that he'll serve as a buffer between me and Samson.

Still, we share a split second of eye contact.

In that split second, I try to tell the wolf—
We need to talk. It's really important.
I swear he returns my glance with a tiny nod that says—
Agreed. Also, everything is different now, and it will always be.

CHAPTER 11

A FLIMSY THING
LIKE MARRIAGE

SAMSON

I barrel out of a shadow hugging the lounge's wall in Mort.

Helisent darts to the side, well aware that she needs to clear the clumsy wolves.

I catch myself on my second step, one hand wrapped around Imperatriz's arm.

She and I ram into the fireplace's mantle, sending a large candelabra to the ground. Hadadrimmon rushes in behind us; he slams into my shoulder and then the wall beside me, grunting as the air knocks out of him.

My mother pushes off the mantle, steadying herself as she looks around. At my side, Hadadrimmon slides to the ground with a groan.

Helisent stands to the side and straightens her velvet robe. She watches my mother; I do the same as she takes a few steps around the lounge.

Imperatriz wanders over to the glass windows that lead onto the veranda. Her head tilts as she studies the city of Mort, spanning neatly from the estate toward the dark and wild sea. The trees have dropped their leaves, while the conifers' emerald hues look deeper, almost colder.

Night is riding the tail end of the brief, blustery autumn.

There's no snow in the streets, but the sky has muddled into steel. The sun won't come back for months. We call it *lanu lago* in Velmic; gray sky maw, the first sign that Night is tightening its grip.

Even inside the estate, I can sense it in the air.

A preternatural stillness that isn't quite stillness.

Something that watches from the cold as we lock away Night's stores and guide our livestock into the barns.

A heavy sort of peace.

One that comes from having no other option.

Imperatriz pulls the heavy curtain aside and steps onto the veranda. It drifts shut in her wake, sealing Helisent and me into a loaded silence. With a jerk of her chin, the witch casts a smothering spell around Hadadrimmon, who remains curled on the ground.

Between his presence and my mother's nearness, we aren't nearly as alone as I'd like. And though Helisent is in reach, it feels like we're standing a thousand miles away.

I take a step toward her, inhaling her ala deeply, like my last breath before plunging into the water.

I've tried and failed to script a goodbye to her—and now that we have a modicum of privacy, she looks at me like she's tried and failed to do the same.

The witch looks smaller than ever before, her red sleeves pulled tight around her. Even her jewelry seems less bright, less fragrant. Her white hair is neat, pulled into braids and accented with tiny jewels that shine like melted snow.

She glances from me to Imperatriz. Outside, my mother wanders toward the edge of the terrace to stare across the city.

Helisent holds out her hand; in her palm are four black stars. "Throw them if you need me. Emergencies only. You know how it goes."

I take them from her hand, letting my fingers graze her skin. "Do you still have my snowflake? The marble piece?"

And did you know that Halcyon and Butter think we're idiots for involving the wand in our affair? And that it felt like I had a second body?

Helisent nods, raising her chin. "It's in my bottomless bag. Would you like it back?"

My gut clenches. I take another step toward her. "No. That wasn't what I meant. Do you want to... give it back?"

She shakes her head. She glances at Hadadrimmon sheepishly, then at the doorway that leads further into the estate. Softly, she says, "I don't know how this goes, Samson."

I stare at her hands, desperate to hold them. "Me, neither, little bird."

"Are you..." She glances at the terrace, making sure Imperatriz is out of earshot.

I crane my ears to listen for any chatter in the estate. I figure we have a few more minutes until our alas drift through the halls and alert others to our presence—and I really need that time, no matter how brief.

"Can you wield now?" Helisent asks, red eyes flitting over me worriedly. "Or was it a one-off with the wand?"

"A one-off, I think. Imperatriz had the cylinder of your dove. It was just like you said—my mind connected us. Vex did all the work. I just asked it to bring her to me. I was dying, too. Again. I think that helped. Kind of like... panic magic."

"Panic magic would have caused you to lose your memory, so that can't be it." She clears her throat. "Calypso told me you felt a... second body."

It takes me a second to catch up; I'm not sure when she started calling Butter by her real name. "I only felt it when I had the wand. And only in the mornings. Now that you have the wand again, every-thing is... back to normal."

"I see." She clears her throat, features falling. "Good."

Desperate for a few more seconds of normalcy with the witch, I ask, "How is everything in Tet?"

She sighs. "I marooned Zeu there with Esclamonde. They seem to get along well enough."

I nod, trying to swallow every negative thought about the King of Night. I want to say that Helisent must really trust him now if she left him alone with her apprentice. Especially in such a remote place. I want to know what the fuck 'personal trainer' means. I want to know if the two small bruises near her wrist are from his fingers, because once I got the thought into my head during our lunch in the Gardens that those bruises looked like fingertips, I realized those fingers were large, and I knew they weren't mine.

"How is everything with Imperatriz?" Helisent asks.

I keep nodding nervously. "Good. I want to find a way to thank you and thank Vex. Now isn't the right time for that, but I want you to know—"

"Don't talk to me like that. Like we're strangers or, worse, political allies." Helisent crosses her arms. "I just wanted to make sure Imperatriz isn't going to be..." She studies my eyes. "Don't make me say it. I'm sure you get it."

Like Clearbold?

I raise my eyebrows, relieved to believe the words when I speak them, "Absolutely not. All will be well."

In tandem, we shift to watch Imperatriz as she surveys the city. The wind catches her black cloak and her thick gray hair, twisting them. I can't remember if she kept it down when I was a child; I've never seen a numbered wolf wear their hair down for such a long stretch. Even when I was in Zarzynn with my pack and we lacked the oil to do our hair properly, we still tugged it back most days.

I chalk it up to pride.

Her ala will carry far thanks to her thick and healthy hair.

"That's good to hear." Helisent watches me, her jaw tense.

I take a step closer, hand flexing, desperate for one last touch.

"Helisent..." I clear my throat, uncertain of what to say.

How to let her go.

It keeps getting harder.

Her features twist, then she looks down. "I won't see you for a while, will I?"

My gut clenches. My words shiver. "Maybe not."

Helisent keeps looking at the ground, jaw taut. "That makes sense. I guess it can't be helped."

"Helisent..."

She looks up at me, her gaze withdrawn but her eyes bursting with emotion. "Samson." Then, with a groan, she sinks onto one of the cushions. "Could I have some water? Or, if you're still playing favorites at all, mint tea? Lots of honey, please. I'll rest in here like last time, then shadow back to Luz once I'm feeling well enough."

I kneel at her side when I realize her blood sugar is dropping. "Of course. Take some deep breaths."

I help her get comfortable, bringing over a pillow and then a blanket. The windows and doorways are designed to be drafty and keep the air moving in the dead of winter when homes are sealed tight.

With a sigh, the witch settles in, her snow hair poking above a shroud of blankets.

My heart squeezes.

I think of the promises that Samsonfang made her before we parted in Luz.

'I will hold you through Night, and feed you through Night, and keep the fire strong, and you will grow through Night until the warm sun returns.'

They echo through my mind, eyes locked on the witch. She slumps forward, eyes closing.

I turn as Imperatriz re-enters the room. She does a double-take when she sees Helisent. "What happened?" She looks at Hadadrimmon next. "Lekeli, he looks like he's going to vomit."

"Shadowing takes a toll." I stand up. "Helisent needs mint tea with honey. The spellwork is exhausting. Maybe Hadadrimmon, too. Shadowing makes him a little... uncomfortable."

"You go," Imperatriz tells me, quickly kneeling to take my spot at Helisent's side. She looks up at me, hair tangled over her shoulder. "Ask the kitchen for the mint tea. I'll stay with the witch."

I head to the door, looking back as my mother raises the blanket and fishes Helisent's hand from underneath. She places her fingers on her inner wrist, feeling for her pulse. The witch opens her eyes a sliver to watch her.

"Where is Brutatalika?" my mother asks. "Does she like to sleep in? I would like to see the Female Alpha sooner rather than later."

I stop in the doorway, hand on the curtain.

Helisent pouts openly, staring at Imperatriz before looking up at me. Her cheeks are wan like her lips. She clears her throat. "Goodbye, Samson."

I stand in the threshold, frozen in place.

I know I should go into the estate and find Brutatalika. Tell her the good news. Welcome my redemption. Watch my mother give my people hope.

Instead, I'm panicking.

Because I did it—I managed to get Imperatriz back from Pit and closer to her capital—

But I still feel a slight tear in my soul; it's the same rupture that opened in Luz. It widens ever so slightly.

The adoration of wolves, the marble thrones in Bellator, my political marriage...

They will never heal this rupture.

I come to when Imperatriz glances over her shoulder, as though wondering why I haven't left.

Quickly, I say, "Goodbye, Helisent," and then I turn away while I still have the strength to.

I haven't felt my second body since I wore the wand like a necklace in Rhotidom.

But I can't say I feel normal either.

Instead of a wolf with a second body, I walk around like a ghost. A ghost that's shuffled amid earth-shattering celebrations. A ghost that's living a miracle.

Shortly after I leave the lounge, the estate catches wind of our alas. It sets off a frantic series of whispers, which turn into blissful shouts. When Imperatriz ventures into the hallway, she's swarmed by dozens of wolves. She receives them calmly, turning and bowing her head to offer quick, humble smiles.

Eighteen years...

I slip back into the lounge to leave Helisent her tea. She's already asleep, crumpled beneath the blankets. Hadadrimmon is also in a deep slumber, half-hidden amidst the cushions in the corner.

With the curtain only half-pulled aside, I don't have the bull-headed courage to bend down and sniff Helisent's clean white braids. So I stare at her for a few minutes instead, ignoring the lump in my throat as the wolves cheer and weep and ask questions outside.

Then I drag my feet away again.

In the evening, I sit for a meal between my mother and Brutatalika.

Imperatriz smiles at my wife, happier than I've seen her since returning a few days ago. She offers Brutatalika warm touches; a hand on her wrist, a stroke of her cheeks, a long and warm embrace.

She avoids questions about Velm and the Fifty and that Thing in Bellator.

Instead, my mother asks about our marriage in Silent City, what sort of honeymoon we had, and whether we've thought about a symbol. Like the Afadors, every other lineage has a carved symbol—normally, married Alphas create a unified symbol together.

I wish she would speak dryly.

I wish she'd ask direct questions about our marriage.

Not... personal questions.

But I know that's not fair.

I should be thankful and relieved that my mother and wife seem compatible. I should feel honored that my mother avoids political questions to get to know us on a deeper level.

So, I turn into a ghost instead.

I am Samson's Ghost as I embrace my mother after the long and celebratory dinner in Mort's dining hall.

I am Samson's Ghost as I follow Brutatalika into our bedroom.

I am Samson's Ghost when she kisses me feverishly, smiling and setting her forehead against mine.

"We did it, Lapsi." She presses her lips to Samson's Ghost.

Samson's Ghost kisses her back while I think about the small and purplish marks near Helisent's wrists.

Brutatalika presses herself against me, relaxed and triumphant, and we lie on the bed. But Samson's Ghost isn't fully there.

He's adrift amid the slightly acidic scent of Velm's cedar incense as it burns in our bedroom's corner. When I slip off my torcs and they knock together, the sound brings to mind the jingling metal ornaments tied to the bottom of a floating lilith. I can't shake the memory of the metallic chimes.

Fragrant smoke, harmonious metal.

The taste of Brutatalika, like rosemary and winter fires, and the bitter and ancient scent of Vex's limestone, tepid and cold and unending. A flimsy thing like marriage held in the gentle hands of something far greater; a demigod of stone and magic and dreams.

I wake at dawn and can't remember where I am.

Brutatalika sleeps at my side, breathing deeply and peacefully. Her hair is braided and pooled on her pillow. One of her hands rests on my bare chest.

My ears twitch; I hear the shouting of hundreds.

Adrenaline shivers through my veins. I sit up and double-check that Brutatalika is safe at my side; she is, still fast asleep. I tilt my head to better hear the sounds from the doorway.

I sit up further—the tone and pitch of the crowd are elated, incredulous, almost zealous. It doesn't sound like they're demanding a bloody waricon.

Right.

I'm in Mort. Its residents must know Imperatriz is back.

I set my hand on Brutatalika's shoulder. "Tali, wake up." Like me, she comes to and focuses on the shouting, sitting up and bunching her brow. I smile, stroking her shoulder. "They're happy."

I shift to rise, but the hand that rests on my chest flattens, pushing me back down.

"Then let's enjoy it for a moment." My wife cuddles close with a heavy sigh; her eyes slip closed again.

I sink back onto the bed, taking her hand in mine.

I'm not in the mood to lie down and listen; I want to greet the wolves. I want to watch them offer my mother boons, gifts, and reassurance; I need to know they won't mistrust her like they mistrusted me.

I wait as long as I can, then squeeze her hand. "Ready?"

Brutatalika doesn't shift an inch, laughing quietly. "It's been two minutes." She rises with another sigh, her loosening hair splayed around her face. Her features are puffy with sleep, her lips and cheeks aglow. "I would like three more. Five is a perfect number, isn't it?"

"Three more minutes, then."

She sets her head back on my chest. I set my free hand on her head, stroking while I count down from one hundred and eighty.

After a quick breakfast, Brutatalika and I leave the estate's main entrance.

An arched colonnade leads onto a vast landing, which descends into the city with a stubby and wide set of stairs. It's a windy day, but the clouds have parted for a while, filling the marble walls and marble-plated floor with light.

We fall still, stunned by the sight.

As far as I can see, wolves clog Mort's streets, standing patiently as they inch toward the stairs near us. They hold black flags, waving them high from the ends of sturdy poles. Children sit on their parents' shoulders, craning their heads, shouting and smiling.

Eager for a glimpse of Imperatriz 713 Afador, where she stands at the top of the stairs.

Most wolves are dressed in their formal tunics and cloaks. Their hair is pulled back into buns and laden with golden jewelry, like their necks and wrists.

Brutatalika's shoulder brushes mine; she stares at the scene with a happy *hmph*.

I glance at her, full of pride.

Had Brutatalika not held Mort in my absence, Helisent might not have had a place to shadow me and my mother.

We watch from a distance as Imperatriz greets the crowd from the landing. Wolves climb the stairs so my mother can embrace them; the wolves take in her ala, then set an offering into her hands. Soon, the Alpha's ala will carry around the city via these bodies, and theirs will be pasted to my mother's hair and cloak.

A muddled group of scents that bonds all of Mort's wolves.

Attendants surround Imperatriz, ready to tote away the growing mound of gifts. A healthy pile of offerings sits nearby Imperatriz: fabric, figurines, herbs, and more.

As we watch, more wolves start to notice me and my wife.

I look from one face to the next, desperate for a sign of insurrection. But my people smile happily, studying me and Brutatalika with curiosity before whispering to their neighbors.

These seem like good whispers, unlike those that followed me into Bellator from the passage between Baladhari and Meledhari.

For a long time, I watch the scene unfold.

I let it reassure me.

(Let it distract me from Helisent's sudden, cleaving absence.)

After a while, the crowd goes silent. A cry sounds from the top of the stairs, causing the hairs on my arms and neck to rise. A wolf staggers toward my mother, hunched and weeping.

The crowd makes way as Imperatriz kneels and embraces the wolf.

I approach, worried that the shrouded figure might mean to do her harm.

Then I jolt—I know this stranger's ala.

Mysi 489 Gethsemane.

I can't see her face, shrouded beneath her dirty hands, but I'd know that ala anywhere.

I had figured she was dead, her body somewhere in or near Bellator like her son's.

I take off.

Toward all that remains of Rex 507 Kaneling.

Mysi must have traveled from Bellator to Mort—*and where is Rex's father, Colsep 506 Kaneling?*

Imperatriz squats onto her haunches to hug Mysi to her chest. She sets a hand on Mysi's back, another on her head.

Imperatriz does a double-take when she sees me, eyes stricken. She opens one hand toward me, beckoning—

I kneel beside them, ignoring the hush that's fallen over the crowd.

"Mysi," I say quietly, setting my hand on her shoulder.

The wolf raises her head and fixes her teary eyes on me. I brace myself for a curse or an insult, but she only shakes her head and wails.

Imperatriz helps Mysi rise with a hand on her elbow. I shift forward to take my mother's place, supporting her. Mysi's head falls against my chest for a moment, then she lets me guide her back toward the roofed colonnade where Brutatalika waits.

As we walk, I realize her boots are ripped and dirty. Her hair is as oily and unkempt. I'm relieved that her body doesn't feel too thin, wrapped in multiple layers.

She must have walked a long way alone.

I guide us toward a bench further into the estate. Once we're out of view from the crowd, I look back. Brutatalika stands in the doorway, hands wrung together. She glances from me to my mother, as though eager to keep an eye on us both.

Mysi slumps on the bench, head hung and tears damp on her cheeks. Now that we're farther from the group, I can smell the exhaustion in her ala. She reeks of progesterone and cortisol, of dehydration and malnutrition.

On the bench, I dry her tears with my tunic, then brush the short, unkempt hair from her face.

Rex took after her, from his lips to his jaw to his almond eyes.

My heart aches for him and his mother. Anger flickers next; Mysi needs protecting. I failed Rex—I won't fail his mother.

Uncertain of where to start, I go with, "How is Colsep? Is he resting? Should I go and bring him here?"

Mysi straightens, shaking her head and resting her back against the wall. She takes my hand between hers and squeezes it. She doesn't say anything, just shakes her head as more tears slip from her almond eyes.

Another wave of grief washes over me.

Colsep is gone, too.

Soon, tears fill my eyes, too.

I feel such a deep and sharp pain that it steals my voice. For a long time, we sit in silence, wordless and shocked and comforted.

"He knew," I whisper eventually. "And I didn't listen to him."

She nods, looking into my eyes. "Colsep did, too. He wanted to go to Cadmium when word spread that you three were home. He wanted to intercept you, Berevald, and Rex on the road. To warn you that things had changed in Bellator." She reaches up and strokes my cheek. "And I didn't listen to him, either."

Mysi's lips wobble, then she buckles into a fresh round of weeping. I scoot closer and hold her against my chest.

Mysi can understand the pain I feel.

And this is as close to Rex as I'll ever be again.

I rest my head on her shoulder. "I think about him all the time, Mysi. I never speak about him, though. I feel like I can't—not until I've set things right." I release a long breath. "You'll be safe here in Mort."

She pulls back, shaking her head. "I came to warn you, Samson. What's happening in Bellator..." She glances toward the entryway where Brutatalika patiently watches over. "There's magic in the city. I felt it a dozen times before I fled. It felt like little pulses. They passed through the city like... like drumbeats, but higher-pitched. I don't know where the spells came from."

I make a low noise. "Like two glasses clinking together? High-pitched in that way?"

Mysi nods, lips pinched together. "Like that. Like drumbeats of glass."

The Houses of Serac and Argot, then.

I nod, hoping it looks like I'm taking that realization in stride.

In reality, my gut is sinking; if the Hosts are casting magic in the city, it means Clearbold has lost his grip on them.

It means the buffer between my people and the cruelty of Ezit's Houses is shrinking quickly.

"We'll take care of it," I tell her. "Today, Imperatriz and I will meet with Brutatalika's pack. With their intel, we'll be able to make a plan. If it doesn't bother Imperatriz, I'd like you to speak to us about what's happening in Bellator. If you're willing."

She nods. "Of course. And... Imperatriz. How, Samson? And *when*? Nobody in the west knows that she's back. They need to know—the west... the west is falling."

My stomach drops again.

The west is falling? What does that mean?

I try to take that in stride, too. "It happened a few days ago. Helisent West of Jaws took us to Mort from Rhotidom. That's where she..." I pause, realizing I don't know what to say about the portal. About the wand. About the red witch's magic. About the truth. "She came back."

"How?"

"Magic."

Mysi frowns, brow bent. "Magic?"

I offer a commiserative smile, hoping it eases her tension. "The good kind. The kind that sounds deep like a heartbeat, not high-pitched. A real drum. Not one made of glass."

Mysi watches me doubtfully.

Brutatalika approaches. With a gentle smile, she takes Mysi's hand. "Come, Mysi. Let's get you washed up and fed before the meetings begin. You'll feel more articulate when you're clean and full."

Mysi looks up at my wife with a neutral expression. Though the women met briefly at our wedding, I hadn't thought to wonder if Rex's parents approved of our marriage.

With a sigh, Mysi stands. Brutatalika sets a hand on her back as she guides her into the estate.

Further down the hall, Brutatalika leans toward her and says, "I'm still getting used to the concept of magic myself. It helps to have Samson explain it. He knows a lot about the subject. He says we should think of our fangselves as magical. After all, it must be Hetnazzar's magic that turns our skin on the triplemoons. I think he's right. Don't you, Mysi?"

They turn toward the guest halls before I hear a reply.

When they're gone, I head back to the entryway to join my mother.

The crowd has crept onto the mezzanine past the stairs. I can barely make out Imperatriz as the wolves shift around her, craning over shoulders for a better look at their Kulapsifang. Attendants scramble around the pile of gifts, which has grown exponentially; chunks of marble fit for carving, fine furs with embroidered hems, and thick fibers dyed in bright colors.

Most items will be redistributed back into the city—but the process of gifting and receiving is important in Velm, similar to the nymph's bartering.

Imperatriz turns toward me with an understated grin.

She raises her hand to beckon me over once more. "Atali," she calls.

Another hush falls as I approach. This time, the entire crowd seems to notice my presence.

The last time I felt this many eyes on me, I was being marched into a waricon arena.

My heart thumps in my chest without my wife at my side.

The wolves make room around my mother. I pass them, expecting Imperatriz to gesture to the mounds of goods at her feet and ask me to help the attendants. I tally the pieces, figuring which are heaviest.

Instead, Imperatriz loops her arm through mine and makes space at her side.

She nods toward the piles of loot. "They're making offerings to both of us. I suppose we'll share with our Female Alpha, too." A few in the crowd chuckle at that, bearing their smiles at me. "Come. Stay by my side. Or have I missed the chance to rule with you?"

She squeezes my hand, waiting for an answer.

I squeeze hers back. "No. You haven't missed your chance."

Later, I sit in the tallest room in the Mortyd Estate.

Above, a cloudy night sky fills the glass-domed ceiling. It's the doublemoon; the lights of Vicente and Abdecalas pierce the thin clouds and fill the vast room with green, pink, and silver light.

We sit in a semi-circle with candelabras dotting the floor. Along with Mysi, Brutatalika's pack (Verita, Exultet, and Leda) has joined me and my mother.

We stare at a massive canvas map, seated on cushions in a semi-circle. It takes up most of the wall, offering a detailed look at Velm—not only our largest cities but also our rivers, mountain ranges, and prominent villages. Where Halfleet sits on the Irme River, where Wartooth sits a few hours northwest of Silent City.

Notes on population, industry, and politics dot the map. Rather than scribble directly onto the painted canvas, these details are written on wooden tiles and slotted into brackets near the cities. They're updated according to the censuses conducted each year.

The latest additions are miniature flags. These flags, either white, black, or yellow, hang from the brackets dotting the map.

White for the areas held by Leolites.

Black for those held by wolves loyal to the Afadors.

Yellow for everyone caught in between.

I look from one end of the map to the next.

A lot has happened in my two-month absence.

Most yellow markers are clumped in Velm's central-west portion, along with its northernmost border with Gamma. The west is almost entirely covered with white markers, just like Mysi hinted this morning.

Like Bellator, Rouz and Wrenweary belong to the Leolites.

Exultet stands before the map, prepared to present her findings next. She points out the yellow markers first. "The villages with red dots have launched exits. Some villages have two red dots—these signify places where wolves were forced from the villages alongside nymphs and wielders. Anyone who opposes the Leolites and their white flags is subject to violence, it seems."

Imperatriz sighs, long and frustrated. "I see."

My mother has said little since the meeting started an hour ago. It began with Mysi describing the tension in Bellator and the ongoing presence of magical pulses.

Imperatriz asks, "Is there any evidence that magic is being used to facilitate the exits? I imagine the Houses of Argot and Serac want to remove any wielders and nymphs who could challenge their power. Magically, at least."

Exultet clears her throat. "I don't have that information. My informants aren't able to directly involve themselves safely. They're following the exits and logging them. But I don't disagree. The fewer nymphs and wielders in Velm, the less magical opposition Ezit's Hosts will face."

Imperatriz narrows her eyes. "Indeed. Thank you, Exultet." My mother glances at the agenda I wrote for her, then she turns toward the wolf sitting beside Mysi. "Verita, you will speak next. It says here that you are a member of the Fifty and a Representative of Wrot. But you're a bit far from Wrot, aren't you?"

Exultet sits down. Despite her overbearing nature, she seems skittish in front of Imperatriz.

Verita, too, stands quickly like she's nervous. Before she heads to the map, she sets a bundle of letters before my mother.

Imperatriz barely spares the pile a glance, keeping her eyes focused on the map instead.

Verita's slender face and build remind me of wielders. Even her shawl is long, dragging near her feet like a cloak. "My Kulapsifang, these notes come directly from my informant and ally, Cartimandua 487 Ashurbanipol."

My mother's eyes shoot to Verita, and Verita bows her head, as though answering a question.

I rack my brain, trying to remember who Cartimandua is. I've heard the name mentioned in relation to the Fifty, but I don't recall anything more.

"She is well," Verita goes on. "She will be pleased to hear of your return. She resides in Bellator as a Member of the Order of Culture.

"As you noted, I represent Wrot. I left the region in the spring to join Brutatalika after she was wed to Samson 714 Afador. In that time, Leolites challenged my position. That being said, I still have my allies within the Order."

With a tick of her head and a nasty smile, Verita goes on, "May I state for the record: I find it disgusting that so many wolves in the Fifty hid their loyalty to you. If we had all—"

"I understand," Imperatriz interrupts. "But let's try to focus. The time for righteousness is usually much, much later than we like to think."

Verita takes a long and unsteady breath. "Of course, my Kulapsifang. Back to the letters. Since Samson was ousted from Bellator, Cartimandua has been covertly sending reports from the city. Her latest is quite troubling.

"Apparently, at the last gathering of the Fifty, Clearbold introduced Suleiman, the Male Host of Serac. There was a witch with him, Kessrys, the Female Host of Argot, with skin as white as Night's deadliest snow. According to Clearbold, their fellow Hosts didn't survive the invasion of Ezit in spring."

I sit back, adrenaline coursing through me.

Very quickly, my priorities change—

I'm less concerned about the reality that wielders are in my city. Now, I'm thinking back to my conversation with Absalom in Antigone—

What the fuck do Serac and Argot want with Velm?

What could we possibly have to offer?

Bellator's collection of Vexen horns would have given the parties involved a reason to ally, but I don't understand what would *keep* them in Velm.

Verita goes on, "When Clearbold presented the Hosts to the Fifty, he put forth an... interesting version of the invasion of Ezit. According to Clearbold, Suleiman, and Kessrys, the okeanids who resided in Ezit arrived voluntarily. They were described as willing participants in the art of necromancy.

"The Hosts described Samson, by contrast, as violent and bloodthirsty, united with the last living Vexen to destroy the peaceful city of Ezit.

"Shortly after their introduction to the Fifty, Suleiman and Kessrys restored Bellator's grand library. New marble plating was installed on the exterior. New shelves were put up inside. The Hosts hid their horns when they did this, according to Cartimandua. And they wore white capes. Clearbold and Malachai, too, have hung up their black capes for white ones."

Verita turns to the map, backtracking toward its western portion and pointing at Wrenweary. "I have another powerful ally in the west.

Demre 511 Lengleye, a member of the Order of Education. Four new guilds have opened in your absence, my great Kulapsifang. Your scholars are thriving.

"Demre has remained neutral since your disappearance. Despite this, I think he is trustworthy. He is a true scholar, unconcerned with politics."

"Scholarship is highly political," Imperatriz says with a scoff.

Verita lowers her chin, looking more shocked than embarrassed. "Pardon?"

"Someone has to write the books, don't they?" Imperatriz shrugs. "It's all opinion. Even the placement of the stars. Don't you think someone on the opposite side of the planet would have a different opinion about the stars?"

Verita stares at my mother. She blinks slowly, either distressed or confused. "No. I think they see the same stars as us, my great Kulapsifang."

Imperatriz says, "Well, then. On with it."

Verita glances at Brutatalika, as though eager for reassurance. A moment later, she goes on, pointing to Bellator's place on the map. "When Demre left Bellator to return to Wrenweary, he passed thousands of wolves moving east." She moves her hand across the map to indicate a wave-like front moving from the Irme River toward Mort, across the plains of Gamma, and the thick forests farther south. "Most were doing so under the cover of night. Some were heading north, he said. Others were pushing east in search of family or new packs.

"Like Mysi said, the west has fallen. And wolves are fleeing en masse." Verita tucks her hands behind her back, shifting on her feet. "Unfortunately, because of this, my correspondence with Cartimandua and Demre is being delayed more each month."

"Wonderful." Imperatriz studies the agenda without sparing a second glance at Verita. "Leda? You're next. I hope you have something nice to tell me."

Verita bows her head, then walks back to her cushion with heavy steps.

Leda 486 Kellybold takes her place. She's a head shorter than the rest of Brutatalika's pack and, like Absalom Metamor, looks far younger than her age. To balance out her youthful appearance, Leda has a penchant for making nasty remarks, and those nasty remarks have a strange way of endearing others to her.

Me included.

Unlike Exultet and Verita, she's not shy as she takes center stage.

With a proud sigh, she drops another stack of letters in front of my mother. "Nice? Well, I could tell you many nice things, but I think you deserve the truth instead, my great Kulapsifang." Leda backtracks to stand in front of the map. "Shortly after Brutatalika and Samson were wed last year, Brutatalika asked me to look into a large fire in central Velm. The fire destroyed a barn that was packed with elderberry, echinacea, and tulsi. These winter herbs were already packaged and ready to be sent in a caravan to dozens of locations further east.

"Let me cut ahead for a second—I believe that these caravans are being purposefully interrupted to destabilize villages that harbor wolves loyal to the Afadors. And potentially those who fought to protect their wielders and nymphs when the exits started.

"I know we need to focus on Bellator, but the caravans are a serious problem. Velm's wolves won't have the herbs they need for winter. All the basics have been compromised—elderberry for colds, echinacea for the elders, and tulsi for the children.

"But back to that first barn. When I arrived, I found the scent of a female ala near the barns. A few villagers had seen the place go up in flames—one had seen a young woman fleeing the area. The description matched the ala enough that I walked day and night to find her."

Leda narrows her eyes, staring at the notes set before Imperatriz. "Like I said, I don't have anything nice to share with you. When I found the wolf, I realized she was younger than I'd originally thought. Her ala had smelled mature, but she wasn't older than sixteen. And her generational count was very low. When I approached her camp, I recognized yet another scent—the ala of Malachai 555 Leofsige. It's a hard one to forget.

"I really didn't want to run into him, so I decided the fastest way to get information and get out safely was to lie like a witch."

Lie like a witch?

I glare at Leda.

A witch wouldn't have to lie. A witch could have used magic to dissect and take control of the situation.

"I shared my masina with the wolf and pretended to get drunk quickly," Leda says, raising her eyebrows. "It took one night for her to trust me. And when she was drunk for a second time, she told me that she was one of several women who were tasked with... well, she called them missions. Apparently, Malachai is hosting a sort of... competition to hand out places in his immediate pack. I guess he's adding men *and* women if she's involved. She said her mission was to destroy a large store of winter herbs meant for the east, then leave behind the turquoise hair of a dryad."

Imperatriz makes an angry, low sound.

Leda nods her head emphatically.

Eventually, my mother says, "Clearbold wants to tarnish Samson's reputation to alienate our people from the Afadors. The same for Helisent and Mieira's wielders. I see he didn't forget about doing wrong by the nymphs, either. Such a thorough man."

Leda keeps nodding. "I was able to do enough damage control to prevent an exit from this village, but the problem remains—the east has few herbs for Night. It wasn't the only barn burned."

"And what are all of these notes?" Imperatriz picks up one of the pages before setting it down absentmindedly. "Tales from your time with Malachai's packmate?"

"No. Well, sort of. We've kept in touch. I don't push her directly for information about Malachai and what sort of 'missions' he's having her complete. But, like I said, she was young and with little generational power." Leda clears her throat. "What I mean to say is—I doubt Malachai has any plans to grant her a place in his pack, and once he's cut her loose, I'd like for her to think of me. To feel comfortable communicating with me. Her name is Hypatia."

Imperatriz taps on the letters. "Hypatia sounds fatally naive. We will tread lightly with whatever information she provides. Thank you, Leda."

Imperatriz gestures to the open cushion, which Leda scurries toward.

We sit in silence after that.

We watch Imperatriz while she stares at the map from her seat, eyes darting back and forth.

Eventually, she says, "I'm surprised to see so many white markers in the west. The Leofsiges are from the southeast, not far from Mort.

Why take the west, then? Samson, you also mentioned that Mort was the first place where Leolite symbols were carved."

I chime in, "Even up until my wedding, most rumors about the Leofsiges and Malachai were focused around Mort. When I returned from Zarzynn, it had flipped—and that's a drastic change to make in only a few months. That means that Clearbold's pivot to the west coincides with our trip to Zarzynn and the arrival of the Hosts."

"I agree," Verita says, fixing her eyes on me and nodding. "The better question is... what do the Hosts want in the west?"

"Let's push Demre for his opinion. He's a scholar, after all." Imperatriz shifts toward me. "As for the west... the only connection I can make is to Helisent West of Jaws. She was in Tet before she shadowed to Alita, correct?"

"Exactly," I confirm, studying Tet's empty portion of the map. "She's been spending time there recently. But I have no idea why Clearbold or Malachai would interfere with her—or Tet. Clearbold has always been suspicious of it. I think most wolves are. It's still seen as a graveyard of the War Years."

"So, what is Helisent doing there?" Imperatriz asks. "I have a hard time understanding what a witch would want with a quagmire covered in fog and magical sinks."

I chew on my words for a moment, folding my arms—which the semicircle of wolves notices. I glance at them as I explain carefully, "It's... difficult for me to articulate. I'm allied with Helisent West of Jaws. I'm also friends with her. She's a witch, which means I rarely understand what she's telling me in confidence versus what she's sharing openly. And she hates talking politics, which doesn't help.

"But I will say this—Helisent is in Tet because she's interested in the caves. It has to do with her demigod and her magic. I haven't spoken to her about her plans in Tet directly."

Imperatiz makes a pensive sound. "I can appreciate it's a difficult balance. I remember feeling that I was walking a tightrope with her mother.

"For now, let's figure out why the west matters so much to Clearbold. And to his Seracyd and Argyd allies. But let's avoid drawing early conclusions.

"I don't want us overstepping until we're sure we know what Serac and Argot want from Velm.

"Samson—can you point out where we have other allies in Mieira? It's clear Hemlock East of Alita liked us well enough. I was thoroughly spoiled in Rhotidom."

I stand and head toward the map. I start with Tet. "Helisent West of Jaws splits her time between Tet and Luz. In Luz, we also have allies in the Bloodies, Helisent's court. Along with…" I consider naming Gautselin, but I'm not sure if he'd like to be name-dropped in a meeting like this. "Well, there's Zeu, King of Night. He's a powerful vampire from Zarzynn. He was once held as a degi by the Houses of Serac and Argot, so I think he'd be amenable to our cause. We aren't friends, but I like to think we aren't enemies, either. He lives in Luz with his den."

From there, I outline my friendship with a few monarchs throughout Mieira. King Hemlock in Rhotidom, Queen Otrera in Hypnos, and a few other pack leaders throughout the north. I end with Septegeur and my connections to the Class, including Absalom and, on behalf of Absalom, Ethsevere and Cosisent.

It ends with me outlining the possibility of the Houses of Talos and Col having a portal in Septegeur. It puts a damper on the mood, especially after the uplifting realization that I've made a slew of connections in Mieira.

(Largely thanks to a drunken red witch.)

When I've spoken my peace and returned to my cushion, Imperatriz stands.

She faces the map, leaving her back to us.

When she turns around, she looks more annoyed than discouraged or uncertain. "Truth has always been a simple solution. When facing lies and deceit, when facing insurmountable hardship, when facing oneself.

"But truth isn't a traditional weapon. In the face of violence and ignorance, it must be wielded very, very cleverly.

"I will not raise a hand to my own people—at least, not to common wolves like Hypatia. When I am sitting in Bellator again, I will take my time holding pack leaders, Representatives, and Members responsible for their wrongdoings. For their greed. I'm certain Clearbold has made many golden promises.

"Until then, I will lead us west from Mort.

"We will spread the news of my return, starting with Lampades,

Perpetua, and Luz." She turns to study the map again, outlining her plan with a finger. "If there's an exodus to the east, we'll run into thousands of desperate wolves on our journey. They will be the first to smell my ala and hear my words. Along the way, we will rally the loyal wolves. We will rally our nymph and wielder allies, too. From Luz, we'll go south to reclaim Bellator with whatever allies we've made along the way."

She oozes confidence, from her stance to her unimpressed gaze.

It's easy to forget already—

The truth behind Imperatriz's return to Mieira.

Imperatriz told the tale to eager wolves last night, but no one asked me for any details. Not even Brutatalika delved too deeply into how Imperatriz 713 Afador walked from a shack on Pit toward a wavering shadow and found herself in Rhotidom's humid jungle. When my mother explained that it was a great feat of magic owed to her by Helisent, Brutatalika's lips twitched once, and she said nothing.

She will ask again.

And so will others once the sheen of Imperatriz's return has faded.

CHAPTER 12

MY MORTAL WOUNDS

HELISENT

Honey Baby,
We remember when you were red all the time. Papa used to sing you the Red
Song so you'd stay in your form; Mint did, too. But you wouldn't have it. You
started hiding early. Too early.
The Boys

I sit alone at my kitchen table.

I keel toward the wood, a groan in my throat.

I set my hand over my heart.

Samson's absence feels like a mortal wound.

And I would fucking know; I've been mortally wounded before. By weapons, by men, by many things.

It's like having a golden sword plunged through my heart, my hand warm on its hilt.

I set my head against the wooden table and whimper.

Children play in the street below my apartment, sheltered by the ginkgo tree's canopy. The scent of baked goods wafts into my window from the kitchen below, where Ceyx and Cleo keep cooking Onesimos's favorite recipes.

What's worse than a mortal wound?

Two.

Life has skidded back to normal here in Luz. The Bloodies have all returned.

Aside from the oread.

Esclamonde also hasn't graced the apartment since she and Zeu returned from Tet yesterday. The vampire hasn't sent word bemoaning the fact that I abandoned him with Creepy Baby and the mentee—but it's not hard to imagine him stewing in his subterranean den.

Butter has also avoided the apartment. I hear her laughter and tsking echo up from the window below. She seems to have found her place amongst Halcyon's wives. Memphis calls her name like he's been doing it his whole life; Calypso, not Butter.

I exhale against the kitchen table.

After a particularly loud yelp from below, I rise to shove my head out the window, scream at the children to shut it, and then slam the pane shut.

With another whimper, I reach for the bottle of grapefruit brandy on the table. I raise my head to tilt its narrow opening to my mouth. It's the only medicine for my mortal wounds.

A few minutes later, a loud knock echoes from the front door.

I roll my eyes and wonder how the children got inside.

The door opens with a creak and, instead of a throng of irate preteens, I hear Esclamonde. "Helisent? Are you home?"

I pause, shocked to hear the mentee. "Maybe." I figure she's angry with me, but my mortal wounds are making me fussy, bordering on irate. I'm in no mood to apologize, no matter how warranted. "Who's asking?"

"It's us," Butter calls in. "Well, me and Esteban."

Though the door is obviously open, I don't hear them walking toward the kitchen.

"Aren't we fighting?" I take another gulp of brandy, then set my head flat on the table again.

"I'm not mad at you," Esclamonde hollers loudly.

"Why don't we talk for a minute?" Butter chimes in. "We know you have Queen Otrera's grapefruit brandy in there."

"The door isn't locked. As you've noticed."

I hear the women enter the apartment and beeline for the kitchen. They enter the room, awkwardly studying me as they stand in its center.

Esclamonde steps forward to pat my shoulder with a stiff hand.

Her thick robe is prim and clean, but I can tell by the smears under her eyes that she didn't sleep well last night.

Butter clears her throat and takes the open chair across the table from me, ruggedly scooting it in. Her white hair is smoothed back into tight braids, accentuated with pearls. They match the sets in her ears and her choker-style necklace. She's wearing a cerulean sweater—not her red silk robe.

What a bitch move.

The okeanid-witch-necromancer jerks her chin toward the cupboards. "Esteban—three glasses, please."

"Right." The mentee quickly collects the glasses and places them on the table.

I cross my arms and look out the window.

I don't know where to start. My voice shakes when I say, "It feels like I'm dying slowly of a self-inflicted wound. Not to be dramatic. Butter, remember death? Remember what that felt like? Well, that's how I feel right now."

I groan loudly, then glance at the women.

Esclamonde stares at me, eyebrows tugged together. Across the small table, Butter watches me with a look of concern—not bitter wrath or smugness.

Ah, they pity me.

I lean into that, raising my eyebrows at Butter. "You can say 'I told you so' now."

Butter finishes her portion of brandy with a massive gulp. "Actually, I feel kind of bad about what I said."

Esclamonde shrugs. "I was never mad at you. Zeu and I get along really well. When we got back to Luz, he invited me to stay in his den. I've been with the vampires in—"

"You been *what*?" I bark.

Her voice lowers uncertainly. "I stayed with Zeu's—"

"No, I heard you." I can't believe the witchling survived a night in a den of vampires—though I'm glad she came to distract me with this revelation. "Did they hurt you? Were you bitten? Did they show you their fangs? Where did you sleep?"

"What?" Esclamonde's golden eyes flutter from me to Butter. "Nobody hurt me or touched me. Well, someone braided my hair. It looked awful, so I took it out. And I slept next to Zeu. He shared his blanket with me. He made one of the vampires sing for me. I couldn't understand what she was saying. Her song echoed. It sounded like three women singing. You'd like it, Helisent."

I nod slowly. "Okay. Well, that's fine."

"Zeu *invited* me. I had the right to go there." Esclamonde shrugs again, looking a bit more stubborn now. "I figured you could use a few days alone with Onesimos. I didn't know he went home." She leans closer to me, eyes wide. "Why did he go home? Did he tell you what he's doing in Jaws? When is he coming back?"

I'd love to have an answer.

"He's visiting home," I tell her confidently. "Nymphs like to do that from time to time."

Samson's sword is golden, plunged into my heart; Onesimos's is made of smooth and shined obsidian, nudging the golden weapon with every breath I take.

Butter strokes Esclamonde's arm. "I'm sure he'll be back after winter. Jaws stays temperate all year. He'll be back with the spring rains. You'll see."

Esclamonde sits back in her chair. She finally picks up her brandy and takes a long sip. "He didn't leave anything for me? No letter?"

I twist to point into the salon; I left the oread's vague note on the low table. "No, he left one. It's for both of us. Go take a look, if you want."

Onesimos didn't say a thing about coming home. The note consists of three little lines—of which I feel I deserve more.

'I dreamed of a strange little creature in a volcanic vent. It's near Jaws's tourmaline caves. I think it's a snail—I'll be certain soon.'

Even for a nymph, it's vague.

Butter strokes the mentee's arm again. "See? He'll be..."

The witchling stands and races into the salon. She picks up the note and squats to read it, curled over herself like a question mark.

Butter stares after her. "Oh. Wow. Okay." With a snort, she turns to look at me, remembers we're fighting, and then glances out the window awkwardly.

We sip on our brandy.

Lucky for me, Butter starts. "Right, so. Like I said... I feel bad about what I said in Alita. Or not what I said, but how I said it. It's just...

"Helisent, you didn't ask me or Halcyon what we thought about you giving Samson the wand.

"I know Vex isn't my demigod. And I know we haven't known each other for a long time, but... I'm a fucking Bloody, aren't I? You and I have been through a lot of shit. Probably more bad shit than good shit. Halcyon, too. And *we're all Bloodies*. Equally. Together.

"I'm not your sidekick. We're all here as *equals*. Even Esteban. Well, theoretically."

As though on cue, Esclamonde storms back into the room. She slaps the letter onto the table with a scowl. "This means nothing. I've read it twenty times, and it means *nothing*. Why would Simmy send something so useless?"

I pat her empty stool. "I have no idea. Let's talk about the note later."

She sits down and crosses her arms, a vexed gaze on the letter.

Butter ignores the mentee, still focused on me. "I should have said things differently when we spoke in Alita. Your magic brought the Kulapsifang of Velm home. It's quite a feat. I didn't mean to erase that."

I turn to look out the window, relieved to understand Butter's perspective. Still, I stew, trying to sort through an internal quagmire of doubt and guilt and fear.

When I'm ready, I turn to Esclamonde first. "Sorry for abandoning you. Again. I think it's building character, but... I'll try to stop." I move on to Butter. "I'm an idiot. I'm always an idiot. It's really charming. Do you have sisters?"

She shakes her head, confused. "No. I'm an only child."

I gesture to the mentee. "And you?"

Esclamonde refills our cups. "Mother says only wild animals give birth more than once."

"Well, this is kind of what it feels like. You know, messing up and coming back together and slowly evolving. As one." I look pointedly at the other witches, implicating all of us. "I never wanted to feel this again, to be honest. Love is dangerous. And trust is what... what the weak cling to..."

I close my eyes. I take a deep breath. The quagmire of negativity inside me swells and bubbles.

I take another breath. "Butter, you're right. I'm sorry for not talking to you about the wand. I'm sorry you were attacked for harboring Samson, and that you woke up falling out of your nest in front of your lover. I'm sure that was undignified."

"You can't fathom the indignity, Helisent." Butter straightens her pearl jewelry with a dainty touch. "No one looks cute when they're falling to the ground thirty feet below. First thing in the morning."

Esclamonde looks at her brandy, pinching her lips like she's hiding a smile.

I pat Butter's hand. "I know. I'm sorry. We're all equals. No more secrets."

Butter sighs optimistically. Still, her eyes are steely when she says, "*Equals.*"

I nod emphatically. "Equals. Are we all good, then?"

Butter smiles. "Yeah. All good."

"Same." Esclamonde nods, scooting her chair in. "I think we should celebrate by bartering for rose quartz earrings. An oread just brought a whole cart from Jaws. Apparently, they heal the heart." She glances at my chest. "You know, for your *mortal wounds*. Also, can I stay here tonight? The den gets cold."

"You live here, Esteban. I didn't get rid of your bed." I try not to roll my eyes. "Good idea on the earrings, by the way. What color are they? I need something that matches the diamonds Zeu gave me."

Butter clears her throat conspicuously. "What if we do that tomorrow?"

She takes her bottomless bag and sets it on the table. She undoes the bunched tie that closes the bag, then reaches inside to pull out a rigid, flat plane. It's covered in pale fabric and weighs more than it should based on how Butter handles it. Like me, Esclamonde stares intently as she slowly unwraps and flips the object.

I jolt in my seat when I see a mirror's warped surface.

Butter sets it on the table with its pane facing the ceiling.

I avoid staring into it, terrified the okeanid-witch-necromancer might be summoning a deathling already.

I shake my head with blatant alarm.

"I know," Butter says. "I hate to surprise you, but I thought you'd run for the hills if I said it was time."

She looks at me, presumably waiting for an outburst. I make a low, unconvinced noise instead.

She goes on, "We have the apartment to ourselves—and we're on this women's empowerment vibe. I spoke with Kierkeline recently, and it really helped me. Maybe it will be healing for you, too." She clears her throat with a guilty smile. "Plus, your mother and sister know that we're friends. Meres sent them my way—I think she was sick of their haranguing. They harangue often, Helisent. And with incredible gusto."

A dozen excuses bubble into my mind.

I've been running out of them lately.

Butter reaches out and pats my hand. "I'm going to set the mirror up in the salon. Come in when you're ready. You don't have to pick between them—I'll let them decide who speaks first."

She stands and takes her mirror, doubling back for her cup of brandy. Esclamonde watches me from the stool, glancing toward the hallway as though prepared to stop me from fleeing. I face the window while Butter sets up the mirror in the salon; first comes a sound like glass scraping against glass, then of ice solidifying. Finally, a deep and peaceful exhalation.

Esclamonde fills my cup to the brim, then I toss my head back to drink. She nudges the bottom of the cup when I stop halfway through.

"Ready when you are," Butter calls over. "I set up a smothering spell, too. No eavesdropping. I promise."

I panic, setting my magic in motion to pull my hair into a pleasing series of braids, to shine and tidy my jewelry, to clean my skin and curl my eyelashes. I glance down; I'm still wearing the strappy sandals I stole from Milisent's room in Antigone.

The witchling hauls me upward by the shoulder.

"Chill out, I'm going."

But she follows me into the salon, pointy fingers digging into my back.

My eyes lock on Butter in the room's corner.

A mirror sits propped against the wall. The designs etched into its golden border remind me of the Deltas. Butter sits with one of her hands behind the mirror. She nods toward the pane, lips pinched with a small smile.

There's someone inside it, but I avoid gazing directly at them.

I step forward and sit down.

I clear my throat, preparing to see either Milisent or my mother.

But I stare at the ground for a long moment, pulling my robe into my lap and trying to look dignified.

"Holy fucking *moons*, you look like Parsifal," someone says with a loud cackle.

I look into the mirror and make a noise between a gasp and a shout. I blink, unable to quantify what I'm seeing.

Who I'm seeing.

It's a witch with a narrow face and an arched nose. Her eyes aren't overly large, and her eyebrows are angled and thin. Her white hair is cut into bangs that fall across her forehead in a straight line, and her ears and neck are layered with colorful, beaded necklaces. I can't tell if the beads are unrefined or artsy and elite.

Her irises are bloodred, jumping quickly across my features. Her lips pull into a crazed smile that's almost too large for her face. "A fucking exact copy of Parsifal. *Wow.*"

Andromeda North of Skull.

"You look like Yves," I murmur, too shocked to get out anything else. I keep blinking, thinking I'll see something other than a female version of my brother. "And Yngvi, but mostly Yves." I lean closer, my body alight with nervous energy. "Same nose, same eyebrows, same face shape."

"Your father would have made a beautiful woman." Andromeda rolls her eyes, like she can't believe no one ever believed her. "I always knew I was right."

"That's what I say about Yves! And Yngvi, but mostly Yves." I slap my thigh with a cackle. "*Beautiful* ladies."

Andromeda tilts her head. "You have his smile. Even his teeth. Moons, he must be flattered that one of you finally took after him. I was worried after the twins. They were as tall as him by the time they were eight or nine." She rolls her eyes again. "That sort of thing is never good for a man's ego. Parsifal always had a perfectly sized ego, so I never worried—not until his sons started to get taller than him. But you must have always been his favorite. It's for the best you never looked like me."

She keeps babbling, raising her finger and pressing it against the glass as she talks about my hair and jewelry; she likes it all, but she thinks I should create a diadem for the diamonds. "It should be the centerpiece. It looks like starlight. Where did you get it? I spent time in the gem markets from Septegeur to the Deltas and never saw anything so nice."

She doesn't bring up my birth, her death.

She doesn't bring up Milisent's death, either.

For hours, we chat about nothing.

Only small and useless things like jewelry and my apartment and what types of booze I like and which cities I've spent the most time in and what sorts of enemies I've made.

By the end of the afternoon, I'm not entirely motherless. And I haven't thought of my mortal wounds in hours.

Butter and Esclamonde sit together in the salon's corner, the okeanid-witch-necromancer's hand behind the mirror. They chatter and drink on the other side of the smothering spell. It surprises me—I thought Butter would need to concentrate throughout the visitation. But I'm thankful; their private conversation lets me fully immerse myself in my own.

Hours later, when I start my goodbye to Andromeda, she throws her hands up. "Sorry for keeping you—I'm not sure how time works anymore. It's all a fucking mess on this side. Honey—your sister says we call you that—will you come back soon? There's a lot we didn't get to. I have to teach you about politics, and curses, and—oh, fuck, we didn't even talk about Imperatriz 713 Afador. We should do that. In good time. Okay? Come back for me."

My cheeks hurt from smiling so much. "Politics and curses and Velm. Right. Sounds good." She could have said shit and demons and Velm, and I still would have agreed heartily.

Then Andromeda North of Skull waves at me, and I wave back, and she fades into the mirror gradually. I watch her go, inching closer to the mirror until I'm staring at a reflection of myself.

My eyes are glazed and crazed, my lips still pulled into a half-smile.

Butter leans toward me, breaking the smothering spell. "So? Looks like it went well?"

I press my lips together, trying not to smile. "It did. Could you bring up Milisent, too? Are you too tired?"

Butter slides her eyes toward Esclamonde; now, it looks like she's saying, 'I told you so.' Then she shrugs. "Sure." She taps on the back of her mirror for a moment; it almost reminds me of a hand drum.

Then she reinstates the smothering spell, and I stare into the pane, no longer shy about what it might be like to see Milisent, but desperate.

Butter was right; I can't believe I've put this off for so long.

I stare into the mirror hungrily. Like my mother's image faded gradually into the background, Milisent's slowly comes into focus.

Before her features are fully visible, as though behind a misted blur, she shouts a greeting. "What the fuck have you been doing, Honey? Ignoring me? Are we fucking fighting?" Fully visible now, she nears the mirror and squints at me. "Oh, no. Oh, fuck. You're old."

I stare back—she's right. Milisent looks like a younger version of me.

Seven years.

It's been seven years without her voice, her touch, her sense of humor.

Like it's been nothing—only a nightmare, only a filament of obstacles—we descend into a familiar routine of banter, teasing, and sharing. The sun sets, and I light a few magical cylinders to give me and Mint enough light to catch up at our leisure. I only notice the passage of time when my stomach starts to growl.

By then, Esclamonde is asleep, curled on the ground with her head resting on Butter's thigh. Butter is slumped against the wall with her eyes closed, one of her hands behind the mirror's pane.

I study the Bloodies, touched that they've stayed all this time. If I didn't think it would hurt Milisent, I'd tell her about today's revelation —that I have sisters again.

Instead, I say, "I have to go, Mint. I'll be back, though. For you and Andromeda."

She shakes her head. "Wait, wait, wait, Honey. I wanted to talk to you about something important. I'm guessing you already found the note by my bed. The notes I was taking on Anesot and Oko." She raises her eyebrows. "Please say yes."

I nod like it wasn't a very recent revelation.

I've been purposefully avoiding any mention of Antigone, Anesot, Oko, and our life there.

"Thank the moons. I know it wasn't much, but it was all I could piece together." She sighs with relief. "Well? Did you find it, then?"

I narrow my eyes. "Find what?"

The note mentioned Oko and Anesot taking phoenix ash to Tet, along with details about their Houses in Ezit.

"The Sennenwolf. Or Skull." She shakes her head. "I'm not sure which is more important, but they were definitely looking for one of those."

I sit back as the information sinks in. "I doubt they knew much about either. I mean, neither do I. All we have are legends from Antigone. Why look for either?"

All I know about the Sennenwolf is what Kierkeline told me long ago in Ultramarine.

She'd said it was a Velmic weapon used before the War Years—one that made Bloody Betty look like child's play. And only once it had been destroyed could the wielders fight Velm during the War Years.

Plus, whatever Skull is.

Whatever event led Tet to be filled with magical sinks.

Rather than rebut me, Milisent sighs. "I'd hoped you would have pieced it together by now. I never could. But you'll keep trying, right?"

I smile. "I spend a lot of time in Tet. I'll keep trying. Let's talk about it more next time."

She smiles. "Next time."

"Yeah."

"Cool. I miss you, Honey Baby."

"I miss you too, Mint Mili."

Two weeks later, I'm still without a lover.

But I'm better at handling the sharpened implements wedged into my heart; Samson's golden sword, Simmy's obsidian dagger.

With only me, Butter, and Esclamonde in the apartment, life starts to pick up a normal rhythm again.

Without Onesimos slipping downstairs to pester the Colyd witches, they wander upstairs more often. Halcyon, too. I've taken to sleeping in the salon; it gives the mentee and the lovers their own bedrooms, respectively.

I've even come home multiple times to find Memphis sprawled on Esclamonde's bed or in our salon.

"I like the lighting better here," says the warlockling-turned-muse. "The ginkgo looks nicer from this angle. And I can."

That's his favorite new term—

"I can."

The warlockling can walk alone through Luz. He can call on his brother and stay with him and Vega in the stone building where I once lived. He can spy through the windows at the naiad bathhouse, harangue Zeu and his den for answers to questions, and spend afternoons lounging in my salon with a bowl of figs set on his stomach. Plet had been too dangerous for such quaint adventures.

After a long afternoon of lounging with Memphis and eating figs, I head to Solace in search of a more adult adventure.

The tavern is half-full as dusk falls; most of its patrons are still hanging on from their morning drinking sessions. I wedge myself between them at the bar. To my great pleasure, Itzifone hustles behind it, refilling mugs and glasses and chattering away about a brawl that happened the other night.

Overhead, the bar's chandelier casts dim light. The magical cylinders are barely aglow, as though Itzifone is almost out of dove again.

I lean over the bar, damp with ale and liquor, to toss flecks of the broken bottle at the warlock. He flinches from the first with a tsk, makes me a drink, and then ignores me as I keep at it.

One eventually plops into the frothy ale he holds. With a curse, Itzifone whips his head toward me, "What the fuck can I help you with, Helisent?"

I shrug, setting my chin on my palm. "I'm flirting. Aren't we having fun?"

A line of ruffled patrons turns toward me: three naiads with rings under their eyes, an unnumbered wolf with a scar on his chin, a dryad with reddened eyes.

Then there's Itzifone, his spotless emerald robe in stark opposition to his exhausted bearing and messy hair, cropped at his shoulders. "We're *what*?" He turns away, focusing on a couple with empty mugs at the other end of the bar.

I sit back in my seat with a huff. I lower my head to sip on my perfectly chilled bitterroot brandy.

Ten minutes later, Itzifone slides into view and leans onto the bar. "Okay. I'm ready to be flirted with." He smiles, tilting his head with a leer.

I study his familiar features with a long sigh, no longer novel or inviting to me.

I used to flirt with the Kulapsifang of Velm.

Now, this.

My playful attitude wilts quickly. "How's sweet mother Draginine?"

His features crumple. "What? Why? She's in Hypnos." He leans forward to check on my drink. "You haven't drunk anything. What's wrong? You don't like brandy anymore?"

I shrug. "What the fuck is Draginine doing in Hypnos? She seemed too old for travel when I saw her last year. No offense."

Itzifone sets his hands on his hips, annoyed with the question. "The only healer in Mieira more qualified than her was Kierkeline. GhostEaters rely extensively on healing skills. Given that Draginine is now Mieira's *only* GhostEater, she went to Hypnos to help the necromancers who came back from Ezit. They're all fucked up after what happened.

"You know, sick in their minds and souls. It takes a special type of magic to heal those kinds of wounds. And she's interested in necromancy. It's a win-win." He waves a hand in the air. "Is this your idea of flirting? It's not my idea of flirting. Less mother talk."

"That's nice of her. Hey, she should come here and teach Butter all the GhostEater stuff. I figured she'd come back to Luz to extoll your many abilities and qualifications anyway."

"She brought it up a while ago, but I told her Luz was too dangerous. What with Ferol acting like a wild animal and Samson hiding out at Coil. And I wanted to see how everything would pan out with Zeu's den." Itzifone sets his elbows on the bar and bares another winning smile at me. "I'm sure she'll come back to remind you of how handsome, levelheaded, and ambitious I am. In no time."

Someone leans into view, nudging their way between me and the surly naiad at my side.

I jolt, prepared to tell them to fuck off. I gasp with surprise when I realize it's Absalom.

The red-cloaked warlock looks from me to Itzifone, nose curled with loathing.

Itzifone doesn't budge an inch from his place on the other side of the bar. His golden eyes leap over the uninvited guest. "Ew. I thought you moved to Antigone."

Absalom leans onto his elbow on the bar. "I'll have an ale, thank you."

Itzifone cackles deep and true. "No. Scram. We're flirting."

I smile apologetically at Itzifone. "Actually, my dear warlock, I was supposed to shame you for lying to me about being Absalom. Twice, if I recall correctly." I straighten my fingers and slam my palm onto the bar, baring a frown at Itzifone. The rest of the patrons jump at the sound. "Shame! Shame, shame, shame!"

With a sly and understated smile, Itzifone slides his eyes toward me, then to Absalom. "I see." His smile grows for a split second. "An ale, you said?"

When the warlock turns away, Absalom focuses on me. "Good evening."

I scan him; from his leather boots and their shining buckles to his cloak and its bronze decals, he looks... mature. Powerful. Like he's part of the Class thanks to his own ingenuity instead of being overly involved in my business.

"Is that why you came all the way to Luz?" I ask. "To make sure I shamed Itzifone?"

"No. Not quite. Ninigone and Gilfoyle finished the line between Antigone and Luz. I needed to make sure it worked. I thought we'd catch up while I was in town." He nods toward the staircase in the tavern's corner. It leads to a second-floor landing, which is starting to fill up quickly. "Shall we?"

We wait for Itzifone to make Absalom's ale; he pretends to forget twice, but when he eventually slides the pint down toward us, it's filled to the brim and slightly cool. Absalom takes a sip, then a gulp, and then asks me to check the ale for poison.

I roll my eyes. "A bartender's ale is their reputation. Don't be stupid. Let's go."

We head upstairs and find a table in the corner. The groups sitting around us are noisy and preoccupied, but that doesn't stop the warlock from casting a smothering spell. Intrigued by how quickly he's guzzling his ale and the sheen in his eyes, I stay quiet.

Despite the shielding spell, he leans toward me and keeps his voice low. "We found the portal."

My eyes widen. "Oh, *shit*. Cosistent was right?"

He nods. "It's half a day's journey from Antigone—farther than we thought. The only reason we found it was thanks to a dryad. He showed up in Antigone, saying he'd found his demigod guarding something strange. The demigod must have sensed the portal."

I take a sip of my drink, relieved to hear there's a demigod involved. "What's it doing, then?"

"Observing the portal, as far as we can tell." Absalom takes another gulp of his ale, then wipes his mouth. "Cosisent and I stayed with the demigod for four days. Two days in, a group of wielders stepped through the portal. All Talosens from Ezit. They looked horrible, Helisent. Cosisent and I had assumed it would be the upper classes of Ezit using the portal. But this was a family in shambles. I mean... they were in really bad shape."

"And what?" I push. "Isn't that better than Ezit's elite families using it?"

"In theory, yes. But one of the wielders... she was very young. Maybe thirteen or fourteen. She lost one of her arms during the invasion. It was blown off at the elbow. It was barely healed, Helisent. And it's been over half a year since the raid on Ezit."

I make a low noise. The aftermath of our invasion was inevitably cruel—maybe more so than the invasion itself. I've wondered often what that reality looks like; I can't say I've hoped for something optimistic.

Absalom goes on, "We took the wielders to Antigone and found them a place to stay. I wasn't sure if they recognized me—I don't think they did. They were skittish, so we left them alone with a dryad guide. I stayed to watch the apartment. Within a day or two, they had visitors. Dozens of kind guests, most of whom were wielders."

I raise my eyebrows. "Wielders?"

We certainly aren't aggressive toward newcomers, but no one in Antigone would posit that its wielders are overtly welcoming, either.

Absalom nods. "I was just as shocked. We think there's a network set up in Antigone for Zarzynnian refugees. I went back to speak with the family. I pushed as much as I felt comfortable, but all they would tell me was that Ezit had fallen.

"That the city is in shambles and its remaining wielders are making power grabs. The Landmarks are all gone, too. Stolen. I guess the gorgons and vampires are attempting to take control. Vex is their stronghold. Though much of the barrens were destroyed, some caves are still standing.

"Based on our brief interactions with the family, we've been able to identify other refugees. We have around thirty families on the list now. I imagine they're all Talosen wielders who survived the invasion and are desperate for safety."

I shake my head, both surprised and dismayed. I'm relieved there's a portal to save anyone who survived the mayhem in Ezit, but... "Abby, my darling, are we sure they're in Antigone for refuge? And not for revenge? Let's think about what's happening in Velm right now."

"No. We're not." He shrugs as though overwhelmed, almost crazed. "Welcome to my hell."

I nudge his ale toward him. "Okay, well, have some more of your medicine."

He takes a drink, then goes on, "We're forming a council to help integrate those who come to Mieira. I could use Cleo and Ceyx's help. Halcyon's, too. They would understand what types of concerns Zarzynnians have about life here. They've settled into Luz, right?"

I finish off my drink, then glance at the staircase leading below. "They're happy enough. But they're Pletens, not Zarzynnians. I'd also recommend you speak with Zeu. His people were deeply affected by Ezit's evil. And did you forget about our okeanids? They might feel similarly to the vampires. They will see you helping the enemies they only recently liberated themselves from."

Absalom leans toward me, insisting, "A witchling with a barely healed stump is not an enemy."

"Not yet, she isn't."

He stares at me, lips parting like he's surprised by my pessimism.

I stare back, just as stunned by his optimism.

With great care, he explains, "Septegeur is under the protection of three dryad demigods. The Class has no authority over them. And so long as a demigod is watching over the portal and letting its wielders pass, then we will follow its example. Just like the nymphs did when *we* arrived, Helisent. Our people were Antigone's first refugees. Those were *my* ancestors and *your* ancestors. The dryads didn't drive us out even though we were... well, according to legend, unruly and greedy.

But now you'd have us do the same? Close the gate now that we're comfortably inside?"

I make another low noise, unconvinced. "Well, when you put it like that..."

He leans toward me, beseeching, "I will not let Antigone turn into Ezit. Please understand me, Helisent—we invaded Ezit to free the okeanids and, if we could, the vampires who had been taken captive. Nothing more, nothing less. And that is *done now*. This is not a war."

I sit back, distressed and overwhelmed. "Then I'll take you to see the Pletens. They'll have a few words of advice, I'm sure. But you need to speak with Zeu. And Queen Otrera.

"When your ancestors and my ancestors arrived, we didn't carry a bloody legacy with us. We wanted peace, so it was easier to find. The vampires and okeanids have a right to decide whether those who committed grave violence against their people should be offered a second chance. Maybe the witchling deserves a good life—but that might not be true across the board."

Absalom nods, features smoothing with relief. "Good. Thank you." He leans back in his chair, reaching for his ale again. "I heard what happened in Alita, by the way."

I raise my eyebrows. "Word has spread quickly, then. That was only a few weeks ago."

"I figured you'd have a lot to share with me, but maybe I was wrong."

My eyebrows bunch. "What the fuck is that supposed to mean?"

"You clearly hadn't even talked to Itzifone—"

"Oh, I see. We're talking about your ego."

He rolls his eyes. "No, it's fine, let's skip ahead. So? You made a portal to Pit? I didn't think you'd figure that out so quickly. I'm not *surprised*, I'm just saying..."

Nobody needs to know about the wand. About Samson's second body.

(About the possibility that I've bitten off more than I can chew with the Kulapsifangs.)

"Well, thank Vex." I smile wide, tossing my hair over my shoulder.

"Imperatriz is well?"

"She is. I shadowed the Kulapsifangs back to Mort. I assume

they're making a plan to retake Velm, but who knows? Is Clearbold still writing to the Class asking for his son?"

"Not lately, no." Like he's been at it for years, Absalom finishes his pint of ale, then lifts the cup like he's ready for another.

"Power is changing you, Abby."

He nods as he meets my eyes. "Unfortunately, yes. For the better, too."

"Speaking of developing a conscience... I should tell you that I'm taking Tet. Not formally, just informally."

Absalom bows his head, then pinches the bridge of his nose. "Oh? Just informally, then?"

"I destroyed my Landmark on the triplemoon." With my delicate words, Absalom lifts his head and looks at me. "Based on one of the gorgon's prophecies, I knew destruction would be important to me. But the decision... the decision was made out of fear. I could feel my magic looking for a place to live without its limestone caves."

He crosses his arms. "What does that have to do with Tet?"

"Shale is like limestone. Tet's caves are compatible with my magic's original Landmark."

"But they're magical sinks, Helisent."

"Not all of them. Not anymore."

"And... Skull?" He quickly amends, "Not that I particularly believe in Skull."

"What? Why not? I swear, I can sense it in the caves. I can feel it... interacting with Vexen magic. It's not antagonistic. And it definitely doesn't seem like a city of ghosts. We haven't had too many run-ins with them—just Creepy Baby, but that's a long story."

"*We?* And who the *fuck* is Creepy Baby?"

"Me and the Bloodies. That's my court. Creepy Baby is a ghost—and possibly an ally. It's too soon to tell. When I went to Antigone to look for notes Anesot had on Pit, I found some papers from Milisent. My sister thought him and Oko were looking for the Sennenwolf."

Absalom's features bunch, baffled. "The Sennenwolf?"

"Yeah, the Sennenwolf. Have you heard of it? A selkie and a GhostEater have both brought it up to me. Separate occasions."

"Yes, I've heard of the Sennenwolf. My father told me about it when I was a child. Usually, to scare me into obeying him." The warlock presses his hands together. "I know where the good libraries are hidden in Antigone. I'll find you every text written about the Sennenwolf—but on one condition."

I gesture toward the stairs. "I already told Iztifone the truth. He's full of shame down there."

"Not that."

I roll my eyes preemptively. "I'm not taking Tet—my demigod is. Vex doesn't know right from wrong."

"Not that, either. The condition is that we stay focused on what matters most right now, okay? Tet, the Sennenwolf, Itzifone's honor... We'll get to everything at the right time. For now, stay available to Ninigone and Gilfoyle. They're monitoring the line for breaking news on the portal and the refugees. Me, Cosisent, and Ethsevere will send word about them. The line is the fastest way to communicate. That's our priority now—keeping Antigone safe." He pauses, then adds, "And helping the Kulapsifangs retake Velm."

"And asking the vampires and okeanids about what to do with the refugees. You need to do that, too."

"Yes. Of course."

"Fine. Can I have a kiss? If we're done talking business."

Absalom gives me the once-over, nose curled. "You can't be serious."

"I'm very lonely, Abby. And I hear you're not lazy in bed. Is that a no? Just one. Or—let's compromise." I scoot my chair toward him. "Come and sit on my lap. I need to feel a man's *weight*."

He snorts. "You would need three of me to get what you're looking for."

I pat my thighs. "Come on. I don't bite."

He stares at my lap with obvious disdain. "This is weird."

"Everything is weird. It's always been weird. Come here."

I grab his wrist, and he stands with a long sigh. Begrudgingly, he backs toward me butt-first to sit in my lap. He slings an arm around the back of my chair to brace himself, and I wrap my arms around him; one on his lower back, and one on his knees. He teeters from side to side for a moment, his lean frame poorly balanced atop my supple thighs.

I tsk. "Fuck, your ass is bony."

"This is what you wanted." He sounds amused now, almost happy.

I groan out a long sigh. "This is shit."

"Well, I tried." He slides off my lap, then reaches for his empty cup. Before I can ask him for a refill, he takes mine, too, and totes them downstairs.

I sit and wait for another round, picking at the table's warped grain and eavesdropping on the conversations around me. Makarios, one of my former warrenmates, is sitting with one of the raucous groups—but I don't feel like socializing tonight, so I hunker down in the corner to stay hidden.

Absalom doesn't reappear atop the stairs.

Instead, Zeu bounds up them with my cup in one hand. Its contents slosh over the side as he squeezes past the group to take Absalom's seat. I barely spare him a glance—I'd been happy enough drinking with the warlock.

"I'm not in the mood to argue," I tell the King of Night as he sits down. "I know you're probably mad that I abandoned you with the mentee, but—"

"What? The mentee?" Zeu scoots in his chair, giving me an aggressively confused look and sliding my drink toward me. "I can't believe you drink that. Nasty."

I take a long sip. "Esclamonde. Esteban. Whatever. I'm her mentor."

"I thought you left her in my care in Tet as a gesture of trust."

Now, it's my turn for confusion. "Oh." I take another drink. "I see."

Zeu falls still, blinking at me. "You didn't... do that on purpose?"

"I'm incredibly negligent. You'll get used to it. So, are we not fighting?" I give him the once-over. I would very much like to feel the weight of this man, but I sincerely doubt it would end as cleanly as my moment with Absalom. "Where's the warlock? I was having my way with him."

"He told me you needed to feel the weight of a man." Zeu scoots closer. "And I said, 'Absolutely, she does'."

Jaw clenched, he stares at me—focused, critical.

A blush actually warms my cheeks. "Oh?"

Me and Zeu?

I've thought about it often.

This time, when I consider what it would be like to be undressed and tangled with the King of Night, it hurts. Like there's something lodged in my heart again, slowly leeching the life out of me.

(I doubt Samson is happy with any of my lovers, but I don't know if he'd forgive me if I slept with Zeu, and I really don't know how to feel about the wolf's dominion over my loins and mind and heart.)

(He's not even *here*. And still... he's always here. That's how it feels.)

"You trained with me for a few days, then disappeared. You thought I wouldn't notice." Zeu shakes his head, lowering his voice, "But I am a warmonger. Did you forget? Your body matters to me now. I refuse to walk away from something I started and did not finish. And when I finish, you will be deadly."

I can't tell if he's trying to turn me on or not. I can't tell if it's working. "I'm staying in Luz for now. My patsy needs me here. No more training in Tet for now."

"We don't need Tet to train." Zeu points to the corner between the wall and the landing's banister. "There's enough space right here to do pushups. Do ten. Let's go."

I direct a feral gaze at him; he stares back, as though serious about that suggestion.

I hold his eyes while I reach over and tip his large jug of ale.

It falls to the side and sends golden ale spilling across the table and floor. He stands with a loud curse, hands and skirt sopping.

I gesture to the ground. "Well, now it's all wet. Go away."

CHAPTER 13

THE TRIPLEMOON, SAMSONFANG PART IV

SAMSON

Suin,

I've known the secret to the Northing for years. It's going north, Samson. It's really that simple. But you like to overthink, don't you?
-Suin

As we near Lampades, it almost looks like it's burning.

Though Lampades's muddy streets have dried with the first graze of winter, the incense piles are still burning. Their smoke rises into the cloudy, pale sky as though born from pyres.

Hidden amidst the city's streets is the wide, slow-moving South Branch River. Its stodgy waters run through the low moors and grasslands like a snake. Lampades expands along its shores from the north and south, as though clinging to the river's edge.

I step closer to Brutatalika, our shoulders brushing, as we approach.

Ten feet in front of us, Imperatriz leads the march. Behind us trail over two hundred wolves. The pack of ardent supporters left Mort with us one month ago, convicted, energized, and optimistic.

Brutatalika elbows me, a half-smile on her lips. Quietly, she says, "Remember the naiad demigod? I saw you here when it passed through Lampades last summer."

"I remember," I whisper back. "You had pollen smeared all over your face."

She turns to me with a huff. The muddled winter light fills her eyes with gray shapes. "Is that why you wouldn't eat dinner with me? I found that incredibly rude, you know."

Like the wolves walking behind us, her mood has transformed over the last month. On the way to Lampades, we've passed dozens of villages. In each, we've been treated to large meals, spiced drinks, and soft bedding.

Newlyweds have sought out my wife and I, eager for blessings.

Drinking spirits with the next generation of Alphas brings luck to young couples; crossing a small fire with the next generation of Alphas protects weathered homesteads; brushing our hair with combs belonging to the ill heals their ailments.

I've never been asked for so many boons.

In the past, I considered them a nuisance; now, they honor me.

With each new village, I've drifted closer to Hadadrimmon, too, forming an informal two-man pack with my long-lost cousin. Some nights, I set up my bed near his rather than Brutatalika's. Thankfully, her pack doesn't seem to mind his presence. Exultet, especially, seems intrigued by the idea of a 'modern' pack unsegregated by gender.

I bump Brutatalika's shoulder again. "I was playing hard to get."

"I see. I'd comforted myself by saying you were shy."

"That's true, too." I offer her a subtle smile. "I'm shy."

She rolls her eyes, though there's still a half-smile on her lips.

Before she can taunt me again, Leda starts chattering at a breakneck pace behind us. As we enter the city's outer streets, she talks about sweet delicacies, legends of a nothing-scented incense, and the vast concert grounds on the other side of the South Branch River.

Soon, a few nymphs spot us on Lampades's outskirts; hurried shouts and exclamations quickly follow. Naiads and hesperides clog the streets to watch us pass as went enter the city, shouting greetings and alerting their friends.

Wolves wander into the streets, their smiles and bright eyes fixed on my mother as she leads the group.

"We'll leave a fresh loaf of rosemary bread at the Lampadyc Estate," offers a young woman.

"Kulapsifang Draga, we have fresh myyrh," an elder chimes in. "Mounds and mounds."

"Great Kulapsifang, please offer us a blessing." A young man holds out a fussy infant, wrapped in navy fabric. "She's one week old."

Imperatriz slows her pace, allowing the crowd time to experience our presence. She's done the same in the small villages we've passed; a drawling pace and a display of confidence.

All the while, naiads and hesperides and okeanids whisper to one another and run down our ranks like they're counting us.

When we reach the cubic estate in the city center, the local pack leaders stand rigidly before its entrance. Leda's mother is easy to pick out; the women are nearly identical, with stout frames and full cheeks prone to smiling. The rest of the wolves, including the male pack leader, are vaguely familiar to me.

Imperatriz steps forward to greet the pack. They politely bend their necks to smell her thick hair, which she has yet to tie back.

Imperatriz follows them into the estate after the greeting. I stride after her, guiding the rest of my and Bruatalika's pack.

After a short walk, we're deposited into its central courtyard. A bare linden tree sits in one corner, a few scraggly bushes below it. A low and arched marble colonnade surrounds the square, open-air space. Compared to the wooden and shabby stone structures outside, the oasis of silence and scentlessness is a welcome reprieve.

I turn when I hear a trickle of laughter from the hallway.

It's followed by a wave of alas that catches me entirely off-guard—

Queen Otrera's healthy scent, tangled with Meres's, Aura's, and Eos's. Like in Zarzynn, Meres's ala is marked with death's cold and pungent fragrance.

The nymphs aren't alone.

I also smell the GhostEater from Alita.

I can't remember the ancient witch's name, only that she was buried in a lilac robe and silver jewelry. Though antagonistic, she'd been encouraging and helpful to me and Helisent—similar to Kierkeline.

The women round a corner into the courtyard.

Relief courses through me—the nymphs and witch are well, their clothes clean, and their moods energetic.

Otrera guides her group to meet ours. A cerulean cape neatly drapes over her shoulders. Pearls dot her black hair, which is arranged in a half-up, half-down hairdo.

Aura and Eos stand beside her with their arms looped together. The pair also wear prim, azure cloaks. Eos doesn't have locs anymore —instead, her hair is shaved low like Aura's. The women wear matching diadems, huge chunks of shined lapis lazuli fitted into their crests. They bring out the dark blue in their eyes, a unique shade that shifts like the ocean's currents.

Meres ambles behind the group, pulling up the rear with the GhostEater. To my great surprise, the necromancer doesn't wear the lapis lazuli common to okeanids. Instead, she's outfitted in a lilac cloak and silver jewelry, almost perfectly matching the GhostEater. Her black skin glows, soft and healthy compared to the witch's brown wrinkles.

I barely have time to smile before the nymphs rush toward me.

"Samson!" they shout.

Aura and Eos barrel into my stomach first. I bend forward to embrace the pair as they lock their arms around me and squeeze. Then comes Meres, fitting herself behind Aura and Eos. With a large smile, she reaches up to press her hand to my chest, patting lightly.

Queen Otrera adds to the pile last. She strokes my shoulder, baring a wide smile. "Hello, my dear Kulapsifang. You look a bit different."

The GhostEater stands a few feet away, squinting at me. "It's the hair. Men have never looked handsome with short hair. Hello, Samson. I didn't bring you a nothing-scented incense stick, so don't ask. I've already been harassed by several wolves begging for olfactory relief."

One by one, the okeanids extract themselves.

Meres takes my hand and turns toward the silent, watching wolves. Lampades' pack members maintain their rigid stances, their eyes slightly widened. Brutatalika watches with a bend to her brow that's mirrored by the rest of her pack. In fact, only Hadadrimmon looks unsurprised. The wolf studies the estate, as though more fascinated by the construction than my interaction with the nymphs.

Imperatriz eyes me and the group neutrally, waiting for an introduction.

Meres announces to the wolves, "I've been telling everyone in Mid

City that Samson 714 Afador carried me out of Ezit, but they don't believe me. I know you can't spare him quite yet, my dear wolves, but he must come to Hypnos. Everyone in Mid City thinks I'm zhuzhing the truth." Still holding my hand, Meres leans past me to study Brutatalika. "And this is your wife, Samson? She will come, too."

"You are most certainly invited, Brutatalika 567 Sigivald," Queen Otrera confirms. The okeanid turns to my mother next, tilting her head. "And you are welcome, my dear Kulapsifang. Did you know there's a panel in Mid City's tavern that reads 'Imperatriz was here'? Actually, several panels say this. It's hard to tell which are fakes and which are originals. The okeanid who used to run the tavern let anyone carve anything anywhere."

Imperatriz comes forward to greet the women, a laugh in her throat. "I probably carved most of them. Hello, my dear queen." She glances over our ranks quickly. "And welcome, my dear okeanids. My son didn't tell me he'd made so many friends."

"We're building him a statue in Mid City," Aura says.

Eos nods proudly. "A miniature, obviously. Berevald and Rex, too. Where are they?"

Meres squeezes my hand. Her eyes search mine, expression still.

I shake my head once.

Meres' expression doesn't shift. "Only one is waiting. I wasn't sure if we had lost them both."

Rex. I know.

I squeeze her hand. "Both."

Queen Otrera makes a low sound. "I'm sorry to hear that, Samson 714 Afador. We came here when we heard the news of Clearbold's coup."

Meres releases my hand to rejoin the group. The nymphs and GhostEater stand around Otrera as she eyes the pack leaders, a strange glint in her eyes. "We came to offer support to Samson 714 Afador, and to all the wolves who support his reign.

"For eighteen years, Clearbold has failed to inspire the admiration of the Hypnotic nymphs. But our opinion of wolves, and even Velm, has changed radically in the last months. Like Meres said, Samson was the first to rescue one of us from the city. He carried Meres through the night and delivered her safely to Hella."

The Queen pauses, looking from me to my mother. "For this, my demigod's bounty is yours. Food, supplies, feats of magic. I'm also willing to ask local naiad monarchs to make offerings to the wolves in the Deltas. You will tell me what your people need, and it will be done, Imperatriz. For you *and* for Samson."

"And for Rex and Berevald," Aura adds. At her side, Eos nods, her eyebrows tugged together.

Queen Otrera gestures to the necromancer and the witch, continuing, "I have also come to safely deliver Draginine West of Jaws and Meres Hypnos to you. The women are heading to Luz. The pack here told us about a caravan headed from Mort to Luz—I'm sure Draginine and Meres wouldn't mind sharing their resources with your people so long as you have space for them in your caravan."

Draginine hobbles forward next.

She offers a toothy, disingenuous smile to the pack leaders. It warms slightly when she turns toward me and Imperatriz. "Your son wandered into Bugs Alita last summer, following in the red witch's shadow. He hardly spoke a word—which intrigued me. You certainly never shut up any time we met, Imperatriz. Sutnazzar was similar. Spewing words like vomit. Both of you."

Imperatriz blinks patiently at the witch. "Such a lovely epitaph, my dear Draginine."

The old witch scoffs. "Sutnazzar had a thousand thoughts in the wrong order, and you had yours in the right order, but you never used the right words to speak with witches. And then there was Samson." Draginine turns her gaze to me, expression neutral as she fidgets with one of her silver brooches. "I have spent months considering your silence, young wolf. It intrigues me, as does your friendship with Helisent West of Jaws. It gives me hope for a better future. Mieira has desperately needed a Kulapsifang who spoke less and acted more."

She turns to my mother. "I imagine your people will need a capable healer in a time of such uncertainty. This is my offer in exchange for safe passage in your caravan: healings."

Surprised silence fills the courtyard.

I stare at the witch, a smile on my lips.

To the wolves, it must sound like a critique—but I remember similar tirades from Draginine last year. And from Kierkeline in Zarzynn. By now, I know to trust the icy witches instead of the cajoling ones.

It seems my mother has already learned this lesson.

Rather than balk, Imperatriz grins. "It seems you've given great thought to helping our realm. It's greatly appreciated, Draginine West of Jaws. The same to you, Queen Otrera."

The okeanids glance at one another.

Queen Otrera clears her throat lightly. "We aren't acting solely out of goodwill. The reality is that many nymphs and wielders fear the wolves. Clearbold's Velm has been particularly unkind. Clearbold's Velm does not believe in unity.

"We do. Our people have only recently defeated a great enemy in Ezit—the call for peace is strong. We need Velm to be whole for that peace to be realized. We need the Afadors back in Bellator." Queen Otrera watches me evenly. "Maybe not forever. But definitely for now."

From a distance, Perpetua almost looks normal.

Mismatched buildings layer the horizon, piled like an afterthought. From here, it looks like Luz—an incongruous combination of wooden buildings, stone dwellings, and single-floor marble homes.

Things have changed drastically since we left Lampades a few weeks ago.

The road to Perpetua unveils a new reality.

Hundreds of wolves camp out along the broad dirt lane. Hopeless, sick, destitute, lost, and traumatized wolves sit waiting for a glimpse of the Kulapsifang.

Unlike our arrival in the villages around Mort and Lampades, wolves don't step forward with offerings—or even requests. Most watch with haunted eyes from the roadside where they sit beside threadbare camps. The leafless, skeletal forest of the South Branch River is brown and dry as far as the eye can see; the wolves are camped beneath a graveyard of lindens, maples, and sycamores.

Leda and Exultet flank our caravan. The pair hand out flyers to those who step forward with questions.

Last week, Draginine helped us script and replicate a series of notes. Though brief, the leaflets outline the news of Imperatriz's disappearance, her time on Pit, and her return. The bags slung around Leda and Exultet are flat, nearly empty of leaflets.

I can see the GhostEater in my periphery as we near Perpetua's outer streets. She shares her ornate lilith, covered in silver ornaments and chimes, with Meres. Though the okeanids returned home after our meeting in Lampades, the necromancer and the GhostEater have stayed close. Since we left the smoky city, I haven't seen them separate once.

I shift closer to Brutatalika so that our arms brush.

Over six weeks into our journey, we're exhausted.

The trail of desolation doesn't lessen as we enter the city. Wolves line the sidewalks, huddled in small groups. Some have hesperides and naiads with them; they also watch us pass with a balance of wonder and numbness. Their numbers increase as we near the Perpetual Estate. Inside, we find the sickest wolves: elders, pups, and adults.

The pack leaders drag their feet to greet us with lackluster relief. They usher us into another courtyard, clean and tidy and clogged with sickly alas.

Draginine and Meres slip off their lilith to tend to the wounded. A few healers approach: one witch and two warlocks. They gesture Draginine onward to the most serious cases.

The pack leaders glance across our ranks.

The female leader explains, "The triplemoon is coming. We've been working day and night to help the newcomers find packs. We're trying to cobble together sympathetic groups. Tensions are high. Illnesses are passing through the camps, and the food stores are already running low. We're receiving hundreds of wolves every week. Even if we can clear the city of wolves on the triplemoon, and fan out far enough to avoid run-ins, I'm afraid fighting will be inevitable."

My mother and I have discussed the triplemoon ardently; unfortunately, the pack leader is right. Fangselves are difficult to control, even when life is easy for wolves.

The pack leaders are pleased to hear about the trail of resources headed for Perpetua. Though the caravans of food, herbs, and supplies won't arrive for at least another month, they will come in spades. From Hypnos, from the Deltas, from eastern Velm.

The male pack leader brings us boxes of dyed strips of fabric. He looks at me and Brutatalika, body stooped. "If you wouldn't mind,

Samson 714 Afador and Brutatalika 567 Sigivald. We need help arranging packs for the triplemoon. They'll find each other before phasing using these strips. Try to keep the packs small—five to six at most. We've been pairing up wolves from similar places, but I'll let you and our Female Alpha decide how to organize the loners."

I take the box, then Brutatalika and I guide our pack back to the city's outermost streets.

Like the pack leader said, the wolves camped outside the city are eager for help—and blessings. My wife and I jump over a few low fires; we shoot water like it's liquor to give luck; we brush our hair with every comb within reach.

One young woman even steps forward with a squirming baby. The little male is nearly a year old, loud and strong and unhappy. She shoves the heavy baby into my hands. I lift him with a hand on his butt, situating him so he can smell my short hair.

With a few huffs, the baby quiets. He falls against my chest, one of his hands slapping my shoulder. The other takes hold of the torc around my neck. A little more flailing, a little more sniffing, another exclamation; then silence.

"Is he sleeping?" his mother asks, angling around me to study his face. She rounds back to my front, eyes wide. "He is. He's out. He's barely slept in days."

I nod, waiting for her to take her son. He's definitely asleep now.

"It's not a problem," Brutatalika says, stepping toward the woman. She smiles, then strokes the baby's back before turning to Hadadrimmon. She nods toward the satchel of dyed fabric slung around my free arm. "Hadadrimmon will help Samson while your son rests. What's his name?"

The mother smiles with relief. "I'm waiting to find his father. He left on a hunt near Wartooth before the... before the conflict started. My village disbanded shortly after. I don't know where he is."

Wolves name their children together; this child may not have one for months.

I glance at Hadadrimmon as he carefully takes the satchel. He elbows me, guiding me onward to a new group. We leave Brutatalika to comfort the child's mother, her packmates orbiting them quietly.

I hobble around with a free hand for the rest of the day. Hadadrimmon helps me assign temporary packs for the triplemoon while keeping track of Brutatalika's pack. The baby barely moves; farting and huffing and sighing like a tiny king. I hadn't realized they could make such a consistent stench—but by the end of the day, I'm used to it, and that's also surprising.

By dusk, we've wandered through one-third of the masses. It's a solid start, even if my left arm hurts from carrying the sleeping child all afternoon.

That night, with the baby returned to his mother and our strips of fabric distributed, we gather in the packhouse. We listen to Verita read her latest intel: a letter penned by Clearbold. Apparently, it was intercepted outside Bellator on the road to Wrenweary.

It outlines a list of supplies needed in Wrenweary, including weapons like axes, daggers, and bows.

The letter also mentions timroot. Though difficult to harvest, timroot is an herbal sedative powerful enough to knock out even a powerful wielder. But, unlike rosarium, it isn't immediately effective—and it takes an experienced trickster to convince a wielder to ingest timroot. Today, it's mostly used as a sleep aid and to help settle difficult pregnancies for powerful witches.

Verita passes the letter around afterward. Imperatriz pauses long and hard, staring at the parchment in her hand.

With a knowing look, she passes it to me.

I skim it, then hand the letter back to Verita. "This isn't Clearbold's handwriting. Or his signature. Is it possible this is a forgery designed to mislead us?"

Verita shakes her head, alarmed. "Impossible. It was one of hundreds of letters headed from Bellator to Wrenweary. The rest were personal letters sent between family and friends. I reviewed them myself—they're far too mundane to be a hoax."

The male pack leader leans toward us. "There are others you can ask. We have almost two dozen Leolites held captive. We sent word asking a war band from Mort to deal with them, but I doubt they've received the letter. Now that you're here, Imperatriz 713 Afador, they're yours to judge and punish. Or interrogate, if you please."

Imperatriz raises her eyebrows. "I wish you had mentioned that earlier. What are their crimes?"

"Two were caught spreading disinformation about the Afadors. A few more attempted a coup against Perpetua's pack. The rest of the dissenters were part of specialized war bands seeking out Samson 714 Afador. We lost track of four more wolves. They were heading north. We also managed to capture a witch—a white witch, unlike anything we'd ever seen. The Head Witch and Warlock of Perpetua executed her."

An Argyd wielder? This far east?

An execution?

Even for the Class, it's a hefty sentence.

"Where are they?" Imperatriz asks.

The pack leader stands, gesturing back out into the street. Imperatriz follows without another look back.

I don't see her again that day.

At dawn, I wake, my gut tangled with anxiety.

I listen for the sounds of unrest but hear only hushed debates. It takes me a few minutes to recognize my mother's voice. Silently, I creep from the bed and pull on my clothes. I head into the hallway on the estate's second floor, then toward the terrace overlooking the courtyard.

To my surprise, the open-air space isn't packed with sickly wolves. I don't know where they've been moved, but in the place of sickly alas, I smell abject fear.

Below, two dozen bound wolves sit beneath the arched colonnade. Cortisol and adrenaline fill the air like clotted blood. Nearby, the male and female pack leaders stand resolutely, features expressionless.

In the center of the empty courtyard, my mother sharpens a curved sickle etched with gold traces. The metallic sound slices through the peaceful morning. Her gray hair hangs over her shoulder, neat and brushed.

I've seen this weapon in estates and packhouses across Velm and Mieira, though I've yet to wield it myself.

The executioner's sickle, meant to harvest life just like the golden grains of Gamma.

The bound wolves watch my mother's hand as she tugs a whetstone down the sickle's blade.

It glitters like a shard of sunlight.

My heart races in my chest—

I walk to the stairs, heading below. By the time I reach the mezzanine, the first wolf has been dragged into position in front of Imperatriz. He kneels in the center of the square courtyard, his hands and ankles tied.

The pale morning light refracts off the marble floor and walls. The air is almost aglow like the moons.

My mother rounds to the wolf's front.

A thick strand of fabric is taut between his lips, tied at the back of his head. His eyes widen on Imperatriz, but he doesn't cry out or beg.

His chest rises and falls with panic.

My mother extends her arm so the sickle grazes his neck, primed.

"Hevlov 438 Brindson," Imperatriz says, voice low and steady, "you hung the white flags and disgraced Hetnazzar."

Don't let her do this.

My body shivers, but no words come out of my mouth.

"I hand you back to our demigod," Imperatriz says, barely more than a whisper.

I can't fathom it—

How gently and easily she slides the sickle across his throat.

How his blood rushes forth and hits the ground with a loud splatter.

It pools and spreads against my mother's boots, her black cloak. She doesn't move.

The wolf splutters and curls forward. He slides onto his shoulder in the pool of blood.

Imperatriz's eyes flash toward the next wolf sitting bound beneath the colonnade.

The female pack leader steps forward to drag the dying wolf's body from the center of the courtyard. He jerks and writhes with his last breaths. The male pack leader hauls the next prisoner toward Imperatriz.

My shoulder rests against the marble column near the staircase.

I have never felt more alone in my life.

Even with Imperatriz, I'm silent.

She's making a grave mistake right now.

Violent retribution builds cities like Ezit.

I have seen enough violence.

Survived its frigid graze.

I have killed enough to last a lifetime.

And this I have learned:

Violence is an illness.

Killing the violent does not destroy that illness.

Because an illness cannot be destroyed or killed.

It must be cured.

My people need healing.

For now, I watch the courtyard fill with blood. I watch my mother stand amid the glistening tides that lap over the white marble; the red blood fills the shape of her shadow on the ground.

Its vivid sheen brings my witch to mind.

I keep my gaze locked on the glossy red blood, on the ripples that break through the puddles as my mother raises the executioner's sickle again and again.

The moons churn my mind as they grow in fullness.

We leave Perpetua and continue westward, following the Mieira River to Luz.

As we do, we find shanty villages overrun with wolves. They watch us pass; they read the leaflets Draginine continues to replicate; they keep hope for the incoming bounty of the demigods from the Deltas and Hypnos.

We venture off the path to Luz twice to meet with Gammic monarchs. Rather than beg them for help, we thank them.

A Gammic King and a Gammic Queen I recognize from Luz have been housing wolves and distributing food, clean water, and other aid for months. Not because anyone asked, but because they could. Their fields were rich in harvests when displaced wolves wandered into their villages.

We leave both monarchs with promises of recognition and thanks in the future.

Then we keep on the path to Luz.

The moons grow in fullness with each day we march westward, hidden in the sunlight above.

With each day spent walking below them, my mind refocuses.

Samsonfang takes hold thought by thought, instinct by instinct, dream by dream.

We made her many promises.

I clear my mind of his obsessive musing easily at first, but his impulses multiply in context and passion as the moons wax above.

She is mine, and I am hers, he tells me.

I will keep my promises, he insists.

Let me free, he begs.

I stare to the east, raising my chin.

The wind moves westward, shifting powerfully across the plains. The tallgrass around me and Hadadrimmon shivers like the ocean's wavering surface. The grass's soft ends tickle my hips and hands.

I close my eyes and inhale deeply through my nose as sunlight warms my face.

From a great distance, I smell a faint trace of my mother's ala. I pick up a few of Brutatalika's pheromones, half-imagined in the wind.

We parted ways with the women yesterday morning. Since then, Hadadrimmon and I have pushed west in search of solitude. The women will phase as a pack under the full moons, leaving Hadadrimmon and I to do the same in our own temporary territory.

We aren't alone. I can smell other wolves crossing the plains, out of eyesight but tangible.

With thousands of wolves spread across Gamma, there are bound to be run-ins and violent scuffles.

But I'm more worried about my fangself.

The witch is in Luz, he insists. **And with who?**

I set my hand on my hips, jaw clenched.

I tell my fangself, *We will be in Luz soon. Don't worry about the witch.*

I jolt when Hadadrimmon sets a heavy hand on my shoulder. "Let's keep moving. You can talk to yourself after we find cover. Look— there's a grove a mile or two to the north. I say we head for that."

I slide my eyes toward him, slightly chagrined.

I'd thought I was hiding Samsonfang's badgering well enough.

Hadadrimmon sets his hand on my other shoulder, pivoting me toward the north forcefully. Sure enough, I count two dark groves situated like splotches on a hill in the distance. I glance around, narrowing my eyes to study the grassy, meadow-like hills that stretch out in all directions.

I still can't see any wolves—hopefully, the grove is empty.

With a sigh, I take off.

I chew on my thoughts and roll a cigarette, conflicted about whether or not to warn Hadardrimmon about Samsonfang's focus on the witch.

For a while, we walk in silence, passing the cigarette back and forth.

Right before it burns out, I realize I'm not the only one who seems nervous.

Hadadrimmon keeps rubbing his scalp, fussing with his silver hair clips. He even clears his throat twice, as though eager to start a conversation.

As the groves come into focus and the sun tilts toward the horizon, he gestures to a dark patch of trees further to the northwest. The second patch is sparser, separated by a half-mile from the one we're approaching.

"Maybe I'll go there to phase. To the other grove. That way, you can..." Hadadrimmon narrows his eyes as he looks at me. "You know. Get used to my scent."

I arch an eyebrow. "What does that mean? I've smelled you day in and day out for months. I think I'm used to it."

"Not *my* scent. Hadadrimmonfang's." He directs another pointed look my way. "I can't tell if we're a pack, and the Kulapsifangs are... You know."

I shake my head, confused. "The Kulapsifangs are... what?"

Quietly, he says, "I can't imagine you're going to like smelling another Afador of similar age."

Realization dawns.

Siblings don't always get along as fangselves, especially when resources are spread thin.

I've never dreamed of phasing near Malachaifang; that wouldn't go well. (For him.) Even in my pale skin, it's been hard not to instigate fights with my half-brother.

Hadadrimmon goes on, "It's a stressful time for the wolves—for all of us, but especially you. I don't have the..." He clears his throat, looking away from me. "I used to play the soto, you know."

My feet go still. I study Hadadrimmon, from his bulky forearms and wrists to his scuffed boots.

Him? Playing Velm's most complex instrument?

I can't imagine his thick fingers plucking the soto's delicate strings, pulled tight across an ornate wooden board.

I try not to sound too surprised. "The soto? Why didn't you mention it before? I'm sure we've passed a few music houses since we left Mort. They would have let you practice."

He shrugs. "I'm not here as a musician."

I nod, still uncertain about where this conversation is going. Before, Hadadrimmon seemed to be hinting that I was a danger to him. Now, he's talking about his hobbies.

"I had to pick something early on. Some kind of talent or skill. It's easy to hate a wolf, but it's hard to be angry with art. So that was what I gave my people. Songs. Beautiful melodies. They liked it." He shakes his head, features pinching. "Malachai's little pack destroyed my soto after they found me. Just beat her against the rocks. I can still hear her cords snapping. All seventeen. Telleheny's last song."

Telleheny...

I heard him scream that name when we were locked in the dungeon at Bellator Palace.

Telleheny is an instrument?

I chew my lip, trying to string his monologue together. From fang-selves to art to Malachai's pack—

'It's easy to hate a wolf, but it's hard to be angry with art.'

Wolves don't fear artists. Wolves revere art like they do educational guilds and hearty meals.

I see.

"And what?" I ask, trying not to feel offended. "I'm not aggressive, Hadadrimmon. I don't harbor any negative or suspicious feelings towards you."

He nods, a strange expression on his face. "And Samsonfang?"

I scoff. "Are you afraid of me?" I'm not sure whether to be angered or saddened. Of all the raw emotions this wolf has seen from me, wrath isn't one of them. "Do I look too much like Clearbold for you to trust me? Or is it my scent?"

Bluntly, Hadadrimmon says, "Well, it doesn't help. But that's not my point. Samson, I am honest about who and what I am. And I am someone who shouldn't have existed. A bastardized... something that could have been a Kulapsifang, but never will be. It's easy to quantify with words, but all our fangselves have are instincts."

I almost flinch at his words.

For a split second, I'm jealous.

That he lives free of the Kulapsifang's burden.

That he plays instruments.

That no one will look to him for leadership.

He goes on, "You've been good to me since we escaped Bellator. You've kept me by your side even though I shouldn't have a place with the Alphas. The wolves respect you now more than ever. Many look at you like you're the Alpha already. And I'm still part of that equation. So?"

I shrug, still confused and increasingly distraught by this conversation.

He will leave me, too.

Quietly, I ask, "Hadadrimmon, do you not want to be here?"

"I would like to feel *welcome* here." With a scoff, he turns away. "I'm going to the other grove. You take this one. Only packmates phase together."

I trail him as he leaves me on the dimming plains. (I fucking knew it.) "What's gotten into you? Just say what you mean."

Hadadrimmon whips back around, his eyes wild and his jaw tense. "Oh, I'm sorry. Is that not how someone in the Kulapsifang's bastard cousin should act?" He bows, stooping near my feet to mock me. "Please, *have mercy*."

My features bunch as I watch his performance.

I study his expression; he's not angry or conniving, but... uncertain.

I huff, stunned by what I intuit. "Are you fussing because I haven't asked you to be in my pack formally? Look, I figured we were—"

"*Call me fussy again.*" Hadadrimmon's expressive eyes widen as he raises his finger to point at my chest. He takes a step toward me, features twisted.

I hold my ground, meeting his gaze. "I didn't say you were fussy. I said you were *fussing*. Like a pup."

"Oh, that's rich." Hadadrimmon reels back with a sarcastic laugh. "I'm fussing? *Me?* You're the one who likes to be coddled by a witch. I see how she treats you, like this helpless little—"

"*Watch your mouth.*" I raise my hand, too, pointing at his chest.

Not the witch.

Hadadrimmon tosses his thick, dark hair over his shoulder with a flourish. Then he bends his knees, lowering himself a few inches to impersonate me. *"Oh, look at me—the Kulapsi-baby and my big-titted—"*

Driven by Samsonfang's bristling, I lunge forward and seize the wolf's shirt. I drag him closer to me, preparing a violent curse.

Hadadrimmon barely shifts, raising his knee to my groin before I get out a syllable.

I buckle at the waist with a gargled cry. Then Hadadrimmon's palm is on my face, guiding me quickly and deftly to the ground. Not a slap, but not a caress, either.

The tallgrass envelopes me as I clutch my balls. Nauseating pain courses from my groin up to my throat.

"I don't play fair," Hadadrimmon says, lowering himself toward me. "If you actually knew me, you'd know that."

I stare up at him from my back, narrowing my eyes.

It's a lot to process.

The sun is setting, and the sky is boiling with golden light.

Hadadrimmon looks violently uncertain now. Almost childlike.

I take a deep breath to gauge his vitals; his pheromones don't hint at an aggressive rage.

His dark eyes stew as I study them.

I can understand Hadadrimmon's solitude. His insecurity. His feeling that he should not have been born.

I watch him from the ground and try to ignore the pain that radiates throughout my stomach. "Would you like to join my pack, Hadadrimmon?"

He turns away on his heels. "I'll have to think about it."

I sit up, watching him go. With a groan, I drag myself to my feet and trail him. "Are you going to fucking leave me here in the meantime?"

Ten feet away, he stops and wheels around. He watches me approach him, still visibly upset.

I'm not positive why this moment is so loaded for him, but I can appreciate that we're both a little slow to trust.

Wary about another knee to the crotch, I angle my body as I stop before him. "Hadadrimmon 342 Aithesson, it would be nonsense for us not to be in a pack together. Are you really going to refuse?"

He turns his back to me again, setting off toward the groves. "I said I'll have to think about it."

Despite the rebuttal, he waits for me to reach his side before taking off again. With another groan and a limp, I carry on.

Eventually, when it seems like his mood has calmed, I confide, "I'm sorry that your village didn't accept you. The wolves haven't been very nice to me, either. Not always."

Hadadrimmon makes a low noise. "Yeah, I figured that in Bellator. Sorry for talking about the witch's tits. I know they're special to you."

"Sorry for not asking you to be in my pack earlier." I pause, looking for the right words. "I just... Things didn't work out for my last packmates. I'm painfully aware of that."

"Don't worry—I'm hard to kill."

Though my heart aches at that thought, I smile. "That's good to hear. But I'd prefer it if you were impossible to kill."

"I can't promise that."

"I know."

We reach the grove of juniper trees, half of which are covered in ivy. Before we disappear into the coverage, we turn back. Hadadrimmon comes forward to embrace me, smelling my hair. I do the same, comforted by his powerful ala.

Then we watch the sun set from the cover of the juniper trees.

We separate when darkness settles upon the world.

I strip down and set my clothes in a neat pile. I kneel in the cold, dry leaves, hand braced against a trunk. I shiver as hormones race through my body; I reach into my mouth to pull out the thick foam that marks my transition.

For a split second, the pain of turning skin reminds me of Suleiman's torture—

But it passes quickly.

And then Samsonfang is free.

She's in the west.

I rush from the shelter of the junipers on the hilltop. Hadadrimmonfang enters the moonslight with me. He runs beside me and nudges my hind leg, then my abdomen.

I turn back and angle my snout toward his face. I smell his cheek, then his ear.

He is healthy. I am healthy.

This is good; we are a pack.

I bark to declare this; he barks to confirm it.

We turn toward the west.

That's where the rest of my pack is.

Helisent.

Pink, gray, and green moonslight pours over the plains that roll toward Luz. I can't see the city's light in the distance, but I know we're closing in on it.

My witch is there.

With a whine, I canter toward the Mieira River.

It's the most direct way to reach the city; follow the river.

What is she doing in Luz? Is she with other males? I made many promises to her. I can't keep them so far from her.

Why are we so far from her?

Is she alone?

Hadadrimmonfang follows. He stops to roll in the grass, to sniff for mammal trails.

Soon, we reach the Mieira River.

No—no—no—

You must return to the juniper trees at dawn.

I pick up my pace.

I am angry with Samson; I am angry with myself.

I was close to Helisent West of Jaws. I was in Samson's mind when we went to bed with Helisent and her wand.

And I swore to live forever with her. The only way to live forever is through a child. What starts with one pup will go on with another pup, down and down and down into a line of descendants that began from our flesh being made one.

For fuck's sake—we have a wife.

You have a wife, I tell Samson. *I have a witch.*

And she could be with other men in the city.

They will want to live forever with her, too.

I rush along the river's shore. A handful of wolves mill around the tallgrass lining the water. First a dozen, and then two dozen. Hadadrimmonfang stays close to me. He nips at some; I ignore the encroachers.

I go west as fast as I can.

The small pack follows.

It grows with each mile we put behind us.

Hadadrimmonfang keens nervously at their presence; he does not trust them.

Pups who yipe and play and roll. Elders who trail behind, their noses kept low to the ground. The young males who posture and growl and fight.

None comes too close.

Hadadrimmonfang stays at my shoulder. He nudges me now and then to remind me of his presence.

I nudge him back when I stop to mark my territory.

I claim the river; I claim its current. I might even smell my witch on it as the river flows from Luz.

The pack swells more and more as the night goes on.

A symphony of panting becomes as loud as the river.

It takes me back. It shows me the way.

Westward, westward, westward.

Toward the witch and her heavy robe.

I should bathe both in my scent.

You are so fucking dumb for this. Don't do this.

I howl to remind Samson that I am our voice tonight.

My witch is in that city.

And these legs were made for running.

I wake in the dry grass, my body aching.

I manage to sit up, blinded by the sun.

I look around.

Hadadrimmon is already awake, staring at me from where he sits twenty feet away. Like me, he's hidden by swaths of golden, dry grass. It's tall enough to cover him to his shoulders.

I look around, hopeful that I might see some semblance of the junipers where we disrobed. All I see are fields of wavering, dry grain and fallen husks.

Hadadrimmon yells over, "Where are we?"

I look around and try to gauge how far my fangself made it last night. I follow Hadadrimmon's gaze over my shoulder. My stomach sinks when I see the faint outline of Luz in the distance, perfectly lit with the first light of dawn.

Oh, shit.

We must be two or three days ahead of our caravan.

I turn back to Hadadrimmon; his expression changes from baffled to amused. He points a finger at the city. "We ran to fucking *Luz*? All the way to *Luz*?"

I stand up and start to clean myself. A blush spreads throughout my body. This isn't just a lapse in control over my fangself—this is a full-on loss of control.

Worse, I can smell dozens of wolves in the fields surrounding us. The impromptu pack that followed me last night will wake up here, and they won't be nearly as spirited as my packmate when they start wondering where we are.

And why.

Hadadrimmon cackles loudly, falling onto his back in the grass and out of sight. "You fucking soft boy."

"Not now," I shout.

I suck on my teeth, set my hands on my hips, and try to figure out how the fuck to play this off.

She's mine.

CHAPTER 14

EVERYONE ALREADY KNOWS WHAT YOU THINK

HELISENT

Honey Baby,
Warlocks used to come to the homestead when they knew Papa wasn't there. It
went the same every time. The men drank with Mama, and she laughed and
asked for refills while we quietly robbed them blind.
The Boys

Zeu says that blood is alive.

It is willpower swimming within our veins.

I like to think that, one day, his argument will make sense.

For now, I squint around Skull Hall, searching for movement out of the corner of my eye and listening for the sound of the vampire's feet against the shale.

A lot has changed in the last few months.

I've split my time between Tet and Luz with Zeu and Esclamonde.

What began with a snake-like map of Tet's red caves and green sinks has evolved into a detailed chart.

Half of the caves we've logged in Tet now belong to Vex. Its magic is overtaking sinks quicker than we can record them.

We've even found new branches of existing caves, starting in the tunnel-cave where I began my foray into Tet last autumn.

During one of his solo outings, Zeu followed a winding cavern to a secret passage behind a cluster of stalagmites. Layered with shadows, the corridor had been hidden in plain sight for months—but not even my magic had sensed its presence. Like me, Zeu suspects it could have been a sink until recently.

The passage led to a circular chamber as tall as Luz's three-story buildings. Arched colonnades encircle its center point on all sides. High above is a shadowy, domed ceiling.

Along with the colonnade and domed ceiling, someone carved round, asymmetrical basins into the shale floor in the cardinal directions. They're too shallow and small to be used for laundry, but too large to be an accident.

Grime and moss cling to the walls, filling the hall with a musky and stuffy stench. Zeu suspects there's a spring nearby, spewing humid air to feed the fuzzy green moss.

Since discovering the cave, we've noticed slender and dotted designs etched into the archways. Last week, we found three adjoining passages branching out from the chamber.

The passages have straight walls, with neatly sloped ceilings. Each ends at a sudden, flat wall—similar to the dead-end where Samson and I bartered with a ghost last year.

We call it Skull Hall.

Not only is it a confirmation that Tet hasn't always been a lifeless wasteland of ghosts, mist, battlefields, and magical sinks, but it's also laden with Skull's omnipresence.

With each week I spend in Tet, it's easier to distinguish its presence from Vexen magic.

Skull's energy is peaceful and heavy and pervasive. Something silent and lurking but not evil.

And while there's plenty of uncertainty surrounding my demigod's presence in Tet, and the caves have become miserably cold with the winter chill, I'm at least thankful for the distraction.

Time passes more slowly in Luz.

Here, far from the city, I'm safe from my loneliness.

Not totally safe—especially not with Zeu training me and the mentee—but safer.

Today, I inch through Skull Hall and try to sense where the vampire and Esclamonde are hiding. Zeu designed this exercise to 'develop my defensive senses' and 'be proactive rather than reactive'.

He says it wouldn't be training if I didn't hate it.

I raise my hands and flick my fingers—

My sensing magic grazes the chamber's curved walls. It moves slowly, first finding and grazing the red shale before moving outwards. At first, I sense nothing. No blood, no creeping vampire.

Just the domed ceiling overhead and the perfectly symmetrical colonnade beneath.

Empty, peaceful; full of Vexen magic and Skull's peaceful energy.

I go still, concentrating.

I sense a tiny flush of heat, almost like the speckled plumage of a starling. I can't see or smell or hear Zeu's blood, but my magic can sense his body where it toils with life.

I close my eyes, latching onto this strange sensation.

I've never sensed another's presence through their blood before.

Holy shit, Zeu wasn't lying.

Blood is alive.

I keep my hands up, shifting my fingers to cast more sensing magic.

There's something else near the vampire—

More blood, more frantic life.

Esclamonde?

I open my eyes and wander toward an archway where I sense the pair. It's an imprecise art; all I know is that they're somewhere to my right, not too far but not close enough to touch. Zeu keeps Skull Hall dark on purpose, eager for my senses to develop quickly.

A pebble skitters across the uneven ground.

With a gasp, I turn to my right—

I knew it.

Something bony barrels into my chest and head, then lanky limbs close around me. I fall to the ground, a body toppled over mine.

Within seconds, my back is on the cold shale, and Esclamonde is straddling my hips, pressing her upper half over my face and locking her arms around me.

Zeu is close by, hidden in the darkness. "Create a frame with your arms, Helisent." I can barely hear him around mine and Esclamonde's grunting. "Use your hips to make an angle—"

"I said no more sneak attacks!" I shout as I rock back and forth, trying to get Esclamonde's weight off my abdomen. "This was an *exercise*—"

"It's training!" the mentee grits out, pinning me.

"It's my fucking cave! You can't—not in *my own cave*—"

"Escape the side mount!" Zeu insists. In my periphery, I make out his pale limbs.

"*Kiiiiyaaaaa!*" the mentee shouts as she bears her weight down on me.

"Esteban! You rat of a witch! You made me scrape my elbow!"

"Grip your legs!" Zeu goes on. "Use those thighs!"

"Vex! Vex, help me!"

With an uncertain shout, Esclamonde loses her balance. I use the momentary relief to raise my knees and pit them between me and the panting, skinny witch. She yields, sliding off me.

With a flick of my fingers, I light the cylinders in Skull Hall. Zeu and Esclamonde reel as golden light beams down from overhead.

Now that I can see, I lunge upward and slap the witchling's cheek.

She gasps, then leans forward to return the favor—

Zeu grabs her wrist, holding her in place. He smiles down at me. "So? Could you sense us?"

I tsk, brushing my hair from my face. "Yes. I was just getting the hang of it when you did a sneak attack—which I remember specifically banning a few days ago."

"Every attack is a sneak attack. Remember how useless you were last autumn?" He tilts his head, a genuine smile on his lips. "Look at you now. You know—"

"*What the fuck are you three doing?*" a woman shouts.

We look toward the entrance to Skull Hall.

I'm still on my back on the ground, knees raised toward where Esclamonde sits. Zeu still holds her wrist, standing above us both.

Butter rushes toward us with a livid expression. Her red silk robe billows behind her, her white curls and their turquoise ends bouncing with each step. Her jewelry shifts angrily, too; the lapis lazuli of okeanids, pearls from Halcyon.

The warlock walks at her side, looking equally disappointed, hands tucked behind his back. His hair is neatly arranged, left longer on the top and then faded into a short buzz on the sides. He wears a red silk scarf tied neatly around his neck, accented with pearl studs.

Half of me wants to poke fun at the pair for matching; the rest of me is concerned by how frustrated they look.

"Oh, my fucking *moons*." Butter gestures toward Esclamonde. The witchling recently cut her hair into a pixie style; I'm also not used to it. "Look at this—Halcyon, do you see this?"

Halcyon sighs, looking from Esclamonde's head to Zeu. When he meets my eyes, he raises his eyebrows. "Helisent, the meeting started thirty minutes ago."

He might as well have slapped me in the face.

I jolt upwards, then use lifting magic to set myself on my feet; no time to waste. "What? No? That's impossible. It's a—it's a fucking waning Cap and waxing Marama. Not the right—"

"The meeting started thirty minutes ago," Halcyon repeats loudly.

Butter claps her hands together. "Hurry the fuck up. Imperatriz has been in Luz for three days. Monarchs and members of the Class are there to meet with her—but she insists on waiting for the Bloodies."

I start spewing curses as I rush out of Skull Hall and back toward our camp. Zeu and Esclamonde are close behind, fussing with their clothes and making excuses to Halcyon and Butter.

I can barely think straight.

Two months without Samson—

Every other week, updates on Imperatriz's march to Luz have trickled to places like Coil and Solace. Most tales are bleak, focused on the shanty villages that had popped up around Gamma. Without packs or territories, fears were heightened during the recent triplemoon.

Marooned in Tet, I haven't heard much else since.

Except for a letter that arrived last week, requesting my and the Bloodies presence at a formal meeting hosted by Imperatriz in Luz.

We haven't written once.

I don't know if he's still in love with me. And now, I don't have hours to spend before a looking glass to prepare a perfectly disinterested and deeply erotic gaze. No time to sample different arrangements of my jewelry, no time to scrub myself clean from head to toe in case we manage to find a moment of privacy, no time to look over all the talking points I've written down for us.

Back at camp, I rush to prepare for the trip.

Halcyon keeps his hands tucked behind his back, his indigo eyes trailing me. "Absalom Metamor is at the meeting. He's with a witch named Ranavalona Red Tier. Ceyx and Cleo have been working closely with Absalom regarding the refugees in Antigone—they're almost positive Ranavalona is Colyd."

Esclamonde gasps from the other side of the fire pit. "Ranavalona? Nobody told me Ranavalona would be there." Her lips press together, then her eyes jump to mine. "She poisoned my bird when I was little. Twice."

"The same bird? Twice?" Zeu asks, hurriedly brushing his hair with aloeswood oil.

"No." The witchling gulps. "Brothers."

"A family annihilator." Zeu makes a low sound as he moves on to braiding his long tresses. "Sounds like she's from Ezit, all right."

Butter claps as loudly as she can. "Let's gossip on the way there. *Imperatriz has been waiting for thirty minutes.*"

Thanks to my habitual shadowing, the portal in Tet leads us to my apartment in Luz. From there, we take off toward the temple district where Imperatriz is hosting her pan-Mieiran meeting.

When we make it to the vast plaza where the Septima River meets the Irme River, it's packed with bodies. Wolves, nymphs, and wielders gather in shifting groups.

I've never seen Luz so crowded before.

Almost unanimously, it looks like the nymphs and wielders are performing for the wolves. They sing, they script stories, they dance, they pull items from their pockets to entertain the puplings with sleights of hand.

Unlike those on the outskirts of the temple district, the wolves packed around its central point wear ragged layers. Some have unkempt hair, tangled to their chests rather than pulled into neat buns. Even those with traditional buns lack the oil needed for tight updos.

Some are gaunt, some are forlorn, some are distracted.

All look exhausted.

Dread kindles in my stomach.

I don't know what I expected—but seeing so many distraught wolves terrifies me.

They must have followed Imperatriz here, *and how much longer does the suffering continue?*

We round group after group, delaying our path to a massive tent with a pitched roof. Thick wooden poles support the canvas, jutting upward like they're going to poke through the fabric. On one end is a wide entrance, upheld by a few horizontal beams.

I rush ahead—

I straighten my hair and cloak as we enter the tent's dim threshold.

Diamonds dangle from the plain diadem wrapped around my crown; they're tied to the ends of red string, shimmering like droplets of ice. Esclamonde wears a similar diadem over her pixie cut. Hers is narrower, its diamonds smaller.

Still, she looks relatively regal. And adult.

Even Zeu made an effort. He traded his white skirt for a red silk layer; Butter has commented on the fabric multiple times. She says it matches her red silk robe and Halcyon's neck scarf. She insists he should have chosen velvet to match my robe or cashmere to match Esclamonde's.

I ignore their opinionated chatter as I waltz out of the tent's foyer.

The pale canvas hangs from a single pole in the center of the rounded meeting area, gracefully slackening toward its outer supports. Candelabras and stacks of burning incense dot the tent's outer rim. The space is divided into four sitting areas; three are already occupied.

I scan the groups—

First is the Class. Absalom Metamor wears a red cloak, matching the Bloodies. At his side, a pinch-faced witch watches us. Ranavalona Red Tier. A narrow bottle of wine sits before them, its contents parsed into two fragile-looking glasses.

Then the nymph monarchs. King Hemlock sits between two others, his bushy beard groomed with oil and his lilac layers creaseless and soft. Queen Clover sits to one side, silken yellow and orange ribbons tied into her braids to match her thick, flowing cloak. Her fair skin is dotted with unpigmented patches, as regal as the silver birches. They move up her collar, toward her neck and jaw.

On Hemlock's other side is a dryad king I've never seen before. Similar to Hemlock, he keeps his beard full and long. It dangles to his belly button in a twisted style, decorated with a few tiny, bright flowers. Unlike Hemlock, he wears an undyed beige cloak.

Last are the wolves. Imperatriz sits between Samson and Brutatalika, wearing her heavy black cloak. To my surprise, both Samson and Brutatalika wear similar variations of her black layer rather than navy blue. The trio is laden with gold. As though recently shined, their jewelry catches the candlelight, flashing brightly. Navy-tinted kohl lines their eyes.

I try to skim the trio quickly; I've never seen Samson so done up before. I've read about wolves applying kohl for formal events, but I hadn't realized this was one of those.

I hadn't realized that the wolf could be any more handsome to me.

His hair is long enough to be swept over now; a tress falls near his temple, black as night on the blue ocean. Like his wife, he wears gold studs in his ears. His torcs also seem to have etchings, too fine for me to make out.

There aren't rings under his eyes. His cheeks aren't gaunt.

There's a tangible shift in his presence—

I have many questions for my wolf.

Has he felt his second body anymore? Has Imperatriz started to ask hard questions about how she returned to Mieira? Does he have answers? Is Hadadrimmon a worthy packmate?

For a split second, his presence almost reminds me of Skull.

Weighty, silent, observant.

I force my eyes to the empty cushions nearby, guiding the Bloodies to our seats. I announce, "My apologies for the delay. I got the moon cycles mixed up. It's hard to see the sky in Tet."

I take the central cushion while the Bloodies claim the seats around me. I notice a short battle between Butter and Zeu to claim the cushion at my right hand. After a comment from Halcyon, the vampire relents. The men sit behind Esclamonde and Butter, shrouded amid our bright red layers.

Quickly, I introduce my court, then glance at the wielders to my left.

My eyes lock on Ranavalona; she returns my gaze with down-turned lips. "You must be Ranavalona Red Tier." I suck on my teeth, looking from her thin braids to her long nails with distaste. I don't remember her from my time in Antigone, but I've heard her name whispered before. "I think you owe my mentee some fucking birds."

I move on to the nymphs without another glance at the wielders.

Queen Clover leans to one side, peering past my shoulder to wink at Zeu. I realize Esclamonde and I aren't the only women with diamonds; the Gammic Queen wears a handful around her neck, a few more dangling from one of her yellow ribbons.

I focus on the beige-cloaked dryad king. "What's your name, my dear king? It seems we haven't met."

"Salem Septegeur, King of Septegeur." The dryad's cheeks wrinkle with a full smile. I glance between him and Hemlock; the pair have the same wide and happy features. Salem notices my observation, explaining, "Hemlock East of Alita is my second cousin."

With a matching grin, Hemlock corrects him, "First cousins, actually."

"First cousins?" Salem turns toward the king, tugging on the thin end of his beard. "I thought Sybil was your cousin."

"She's my sister. From another dryad, of course. I am my father's *only* nymph." Hemlock sits up a bit straighter, puffing out his chest.

"Oh, I see. That's no surprise. Sybil is sweet as a lychee."

"We've been saying that for years." Hemlock slaps his thigh happily, leaning toward his fellow king like he's planning to chat for a while.

(I take the distraction to slide my eyes toward Samson; he's not watching me, but Ranavalona.)

"Gentleman," Queen Clover cuts in, reaching over to pat Salem's arm. "Let's catch up later. The Kulapsifang has traveled a great distance and faced many obstacles to reach Luz. We're here to discuss Velm—although I hope you'll tell Sybil I said hello."

Queen Clover gestures to Imperatriz with a smile.

Imperatriz bows her head, then turns to face the Bloodies. Like Samson, she seems to have transformed over the last months. In Alita, she seemed direct and thoughtful. Now, she looks lethally focused and weathered. Physically, she appears fit—but in her eyes, there are still storms brewing. The storms have grown, too; I can feel their thunder from here.

"Hello, Helisent West of Jaws." Imperatriz glances at those seated around me. "It's a pleasure to see you again, Calypso Ultramarine and Halcyon Plet. And it's nice to meet you finally, Esclamonde Black Rock Antigone. The same to you, Zeu. I've wanted to put a name to your face for a very long time now."

Zeu scoffs loudly. From the corner of my eye, I see him turn a scowl toward Samson.

To my surprise, Samson glowers openly at the vampire—enough that it straightens my spine. The shift in mood is startling; the last time I saw him, he was drinking and snorting dextro with Zeu like long-lost friends. Or, at least, drinking buddies.

"I spent several years with Hyd on Pit," Imperatriz goes on, kohl-lined eyes fixed on the vampire. "She was one of my only friends. She spoke of two young leaders, Vic and Zeu. Samson tells me that Vic resides in Vex."

I sit back, shocked by the revelation.

Imperatriz wasn't alone on Pit? She shared her time with exiled vampires?

Judging by Zeu's weighty silence, he's also shocked by this.

"Hyd?" he asks quietly. "I have not thought of Hyd in many, many years. Is she well?"

"She was." Imperatriz's gaze doesn't waver. "She died quickly two years ago. I buried her with stones outlining her body. She will be safe in darkness forever now."

Another long pause. Zeu clears his throat before responding, "Thank you. Hyd deserved a good resting place. She was part of the team that helped me escape Ezit."

"So I heard. She sang your praises often. Welcome to Mieira." With a deep breath, Imperatriz reaches forward and fills her golden chalice. The circle sits in silence, watching the stream of dark wine fill the cup with a delectable sound. She takes a drink before beginning, "Thank you for coming to this meeting. On the journey from Mort to Luz, I've sat with stray wolves, monarchs, city councils, and everyone in between. I've heard many stories—and they demonstrate how feeble the rope of trust is between my people and the wielders and nymphs of Mieira.

"I have already apologized to Helisent for my failures as a Kulapsi-fang. Now, I extend this apology to each of you. My own caprice and bullheadedness led me to make unwise decisions. These decisions led to Clearbold taking charge of my realm."

The immediate, general apology throws me off guard.

She must have a big ask in mind.

I figured as much when I was invited to the meeting, but I can't help but slide my eyes toward the Class members and nymph monarchs. Only Ranavalona looks to be outwardly displeased with Imperatriz's words.

I glance one more time at Samson—

This time, I catch him watching me. For a split second, I stare into his dark eyes, desperate for some semblance of familiarity. But I can't tell what he feels for me in that minuscule span.

Imperatriz looks around the circle once more. "We've successfully stabilized Mort, Lampades, Perpetua, and now Luz. Problematic leaders like Ferol have been ousted and replaced during this time. But this is only a small step in navigating Velm's current state of conflict.

"Leolites and their Zarzynnian allies still have control of Bellator and Rouz, along with Wrenweary, our western capital. They control most villages and smaller cities across the plains, like Halfleet and Wartooth.

"As Queen Clover of Gamma is well aware, wolves in Velm are fleeing north and east en masse.

"We estimate around ten thousand now call the plains home. They live in squalor; the fortunate have tents to sleep under. Many have only what they carry in their satchels.

"My original plan was to ride out Night here in Luz, monitoring the displaced populations on the plains. Night has fallen; it significantly limits what is possible in Velm. But we've intercepted dozens of letters leaving the capital and have met with wolves who have escaped Bellator.

"According to our sources, the city is under magical influence.

"Unfortunately, last week, we received word that there are also degis in the capital." Pointedly, Imperatriz looks at Zeu. "A vampire, I have no problem with. A degivampire—well, I think we can agree they have no place in Bellator, Velm, or anywhere else in the world."

Zeu makes a low noise. "We can agree on that."

"Then I'll speak plainly—I believe the degivampires are being used to spread terror and bend the wolves to the Leolites' will. Bullheaded as they may be, I doubt Clearbold and Malachai want their Argyd and Seracyd allies wielding often in our capital. That leaves few options to control any wolves who refuse to fall in line.

"Biting, obviously, has significantly different connotations for wolves and vampires. A bite might sway a wolf more than a spell." She turns toward the Bloodies once more. "Again, I mean no offense to your people, Zeu. I speak from the experience of meeting and becoming friends with Hyd."

"A wolf named Elvira Ultramarine has worked with my den to explain the implications of biting," he responds neutrally. "I understand your concern. Though I want to clarify that vampires bite to eat—just like every other creature born in this world."

Imperatriz nods. "I appreciate your understanding. Vampires have been gravely mistreated by Ezit's Houses. I like to think our causes here are sympathetic."

My body fizzles with excitement—I wish she'd get to the point already.

She's doling out compliments and heavy eye contact like I do at taverns at closing time.

Imperatriz moves on, glancing at me, then Hemlock, then Absalom. "I cannot leave Bellator at the mercy of the Leolites, Hosts, and their degis until the snow melts in spring. It gives Clearbold too much time to continue his plotting, and my people too much time to suffer from his cruelty.

"But the journey to Bellator this time of year lasts two months on foot—it's grueling even when Night's coldest stretch isn't on the horizon. There are thousands of wolves camped around Luz who would love to retake the capital, but I can't lead my people to Bellator without the appropriate supplies.

"Even with the mighty bounty of the nymph demigods, there is no supply chain long enough to feed and shelter thousands of wolves on the march. In winter, nonetheless. These wolves have already endured enough. First, my people must survive. Then I will give them justice."

My eyes jump to Samson.

She's going to ask the Bloodies to go south with her.

Did he plan this?

He watches me with a painfully neutral expression, blinking his kohl-lined eyes while they study me.

"Helisent West of Jaws," Imperatriz says, causing me to jolt, "I ask that you and the Bloodies accompany me. With your help, we can reclaim Bellator with minimal violence and hardship."

I go still, a sigh in my throat. Though I'd anticipated a request similar to this, it isn't an easy choice.

Every sentiment is contradictory. I want Velm to thrive; I also want little to do with it. I want Samson to succeed on the throne; I'd rather have him for myself, though. I want to punish Suleiman for hurting Samson; I'm also not excited about the prospect of round two with Ezit's Hosts.

Imperatriz pivots before I have time to process and respond. She turns her attention toward the Class's representatives. "Absalom, you are more than welcome to join us in our march, though I understand if you're unable to spare the time or energy as part of the Class. Ranavalona, if you enter Velm, I will personally cut you down. "

Then on to the nymph monarchs. "I ask that your demigods continue to spare whatever you can for my people. The wolves desperately need resources—those from Gamma, Septegeur, Rhotidom, and even Metamor. Whatever can be spared will be treasured."

When Imperatriz finishes, the silence doesn't last long.

Hemlock is the first to speak, directing his optimistic gaze toward Samson. "Like I told you in Alita, my dear Afadors... my demigod will have plenty to spare for your people. Night doesn't touch Rhotidom. Taro and fig and orange trees produce through winter in my realm. I hope your people like fruit."

Queen Clover smiles, seated at his side. "As you already know, Imperatriz, I am happy to continue providing for the wolves. My demigod, too."

Salem is last. He tugs on his beard, amber eyes studying the wolves apologetically. "I don't know that I will have as much to spare. I've heard rumors of a portal in Velm. I'm sure you've heard of another in Septegeur. Just like your wolves have faced displacement, so have the residents of a destroyed Ezit. My demigod is monitoring their arrival closely. I must stay and attend the arrival of these refugees, as well."

Zeu tsks loudly. "Maybe the okeanid's demigod should come and keep watch instead. The Hypnotic Demigod would know better than to keep the portal open for Ezit's wielders. Just wait—"

"We talked about this," Absalom cuts in, leveling a neutral but firm gaze at the vampire. "I laid out all of your concerns to the Class and Antigone's monarchs. We *agreed* that not all wielders would be punished for the actions—"

"Not until my den goes to Antigone," Zeu snaps. "Then we'll see who's punished and for what."

"Oh, goodness," King Salem murmurs, tugging more forcefully on his beard's end. "You've insulted my demigod, my dear King of Night. And threatened my realm with violence."

I do a double-take when King Salem stands suddenly—

His eyes widen, their whites fully visible from the other side of the tent. Though he's short, he's stocky and well-built. His feet widen into a powerful stance, his hands clenched into fists at his sides.

The change in mood is total, unforgiving, panic-inducing.

The king's beige robe undulates with nymph magic, and a stubby snake descends from its hem near his calf. The creature's forked tongue flicks in the air as it raises its head to look around the tent.

The folviper.

Mieira's most venomous and aggressive snake.

With it comes a deluge of demigod power, which shivers through the tent.

It reminds me of the fizzling energy felt in Ezit when the okeanid demigod took its vengeance—a force the opposite of desita. A sort of vacuous gulf of potential violence that sets the senses on high alert.

Hemlock's face drains of color as the viper emerges. Clover watches its head rise and shift toward where I sit with the Bloodies, her jaw tense.

Though twenty feet away, a folviper can cover that distance swiftly. And I'd hate to find out what else King Salem has hidden in his cloak. Folviper aside, even some flowers in Septegeur are poisonous enough to kill.

Especially those imbued with a demigod's power.

I scramble to my feet, baring my palms at the king. "Now, now." I turn to Zeu, who also stands. In Zarzyd, I explain to the vampire, "A folviper's venom will kill you faster than I can cast healing magic, you stupid motherfucker. Now sit down and shut up." I direct a forced smile at King Salem next. "My dear king, I don't think Zeu is any less deserving of our grace than the wielders your great demigod is allowing into Septegeur. Both are victims of Ezit."

King Salem doesn't lift his gaze from Zeu when he gently tells me, "We do not measure peace by the number of wrongdoings righted. We measure peace by each individual's willingness to change for the better. Without individual sacrifice, the great bounty of our world cannot be attained and shared.

"Do you understand, my dear witch? Not whether something is *right* or *wrong*, but simply whether it has a greater *purpose*."

I throw up my hands. "But you didn't know him last year. Trust me —he's come a long way. Ask Queen Clover." I tsk, glancing at Ranavalona. "Also, I sincerely doubt wielders like Ranavalona have individually sacrificed a *thing* for Septegeur's greater good."

"Though you once called Antigone home, you know little of Septegeur's greater good. Please do not forget that." King Salem raises his eyebrows, as though finished with his argument.

After one last hard glance at Zeu, he returns to his cushion. Me and the vampire do the same, eyes glued to the nymph.

The viper disappears within the folds of his cloaks, but I keep staring at his wide sleeves and hem, wondering where it's hiding.

King Salem directs his attention to Imperatriz. He takes a long, slow breath, then continues, "My apologies, my dear Kulapsifang. As I was saying—Colyd and Talosen wielders are making their way into Septegeur via a portal. My demigod and the other two dryad demigods in Septegeur have welcomed them. But their arrival has put a strain on the forest's food chain. The trophic cascade, as we call it, needs time to evolve.

"But I hope to make myself clear—me and my demigod wish you all the best in Velm. I do not doubt that the wolves will thrive under your leadership, Imperatriz."

Absalom pitches in next, throwing a strange glance at Zeu. "For this reason, I also cannot leave my post in Antigone. However, I do have an offering for your people. Hundreds of wielders in Antigone have contributed dove for your needs. It will be meager compared to an offering from Helisent, but I'm sure every spell matters. Mundane and great alike."

Imperatriz bows her head, then sets her eyes on me.

I know my answer, but she pleaded for help from all the Bloodies. Not just me.

I raise a finger. "Just a moment. I need to confer..."

I turn around and cast a smothering spell around our cushions. Despite the privacy, we press our shoulders together, forming a tight circle.

I look at each Bloody, holding out a fist to declare, "*We must march*—"

"Everyone already knows what you think," Butter cuts in, holding a palm in my direction. "We need to hear from the rest of the group. Let's start with Halcyon. Halcyon, what do you think?"

"Now that my family is safe in Luz, I'd like to fight." The warlock licks his lips. "And if there are Seracyd wielders in Bellator, then I should be there to fight them. Especially Suleiman. Vulcan will also be interested in joining. Possibly Vega."

Butter stares at him, jaw clenched with surprise.

Mine falls open.

I never thought I'd see the father of two volunteer to engage in violence—in Ezit, in Mieira, anywhere. Now that I know him better, I think it's a miracle he took on Pel and Jen to rescue me in the first place.

Zeu speaks next. "I agree. Imperatriz gave Hyd a good resting place. That alone makes me care about Bellator's fate. Many in my den will be eager for another fight—and to explore Velm. But I'll only lead them south if my den is permitted passage into Velm now *and* in the future. The last I heard, all vampires were banned from Velm."

Esclamonde's wide eyes jump from me to Zeu. "I can go, right? With all of you?"

I shrug, glancing at Zeu. He shrugs back, then says, "You're ten times better than Helisent at grappling. I don't see why not."

The witchling smiles toothily, looking around the circle.

Butter looks at me. "Do you really want to spend two months traveling south with Samson and—"

"*Shh*," I hiss.

Butter rolls her eyes. "I can feel the smothering spell you cast around us. And we already know your secret. Don't avoid the question." She presses her palms together like she's summoning great patience. "*Please*. See? I'm asking nicely. Two months. Also, snow. You've heard of it, right? You want us to walk into Velm in the dead of Night?"

I look away as though deep in thought.

When an appropriate amount of time has passed, I go with, "I understand your concerns, Butter, but I'm not going to say no. Even if it wasn't for Samson, I would go. You heard Imperatriz—the Leolites took Wrenweary. It's close to Tet. And Tet is mine. Sorry—*ours*."

I glance around the circle.

Only Esclamonde watches me with unbridled confidence. Zeu keeps glancing over his shoulder, as though checking that King Salem's folviper hasn't reappeared; Halcyon glances at Butter, as though worried he pissed her off; and Butter stares at me, visibly unconvinced by my reasoning.

"Any objections?" I ask.

"I think this is unwise," Butter says. "I just need more time to figure out why, specifically."

She crosses her arms with a pout, sliding her eyes toward the wolves.

Good enough.

I lift the smothering spell as the Bloodies shift back into place on our cushions.

I straighten my back, hoping to look regal as I offer a measured smile to Imperatriz. "Sure, you will have the Bloodies' help—but there are two conditions. First, Zeu will bring along any denmates who want to join. They will march to Bellator with the understanding that Velm's resources will someday be shared with them. When the time is right, of course. Do you agree?"

Imperatriz doesn't look phased. "I do."

"Lovely. The second condition is that I will follow you with the Bloodies, but they are not your subjects. I am also not your subject. We will make our own decisions, even in your territory—with deference to your guidance and wisdom, of course."

Imperatriz slides her eyes away from me. She stares down at the goblet of wine set before her.

Silence hangs in the air as she thinks through my second condition.

"With deference to my guidance and wisdom," she emphasizes, lowering her chin to study me. "Correct?"

I return her gaze, batting my lashes. "*So* much deference, Imperatriz."

Another stretch of silence. Then, "And if I am not there to provide my guidance and wisdom, do you agree to defer to Samson's guidance and wisdom as the 714th Kulapsifang born in Velm?"

I only have a split second to talk myself out of the dozen or so retorts that pop into my head—

Guidance, wisdom, my tender flesh—all will be deferred to Samson 714 Afador.

Maybe something like, *I was born to be guided by your son's very large wisdom.*

I blink once.

I glance at the wolf where he sits like a kohl-eyed, golden-flecked demigod.

Don't be a fucking pervert for once in your life.

"For sure." I clear my throat, hoping to sound casual. "No worries. When do we leave?"

Two hours later, I'm swaying to a tropical orchestra.

Despite the hordes of sad and sickly wolves, Luzians manage to cobble together a city-wide block party. A few bands even play from raised platforms that dot the city center.

In search of space and fresh air, the Bloodies and I manage to claim an abandoned platform. From there, we shout conversations over the music and play drinking games between the musical acts.

Slowly, as the night goes on, the wolves start to relax; I even see a few smiles and hear a few booming laughs.

I pivot at each wolf's voice and steal glances at the dark-haired, pale-skinned beings who pass.

Wolf after wolf after wolf passes by, enrapt by the party.

Since the meeting ended hours ago, I've consoled myself with the idea that I might spot Samson in the crowd. I have no idea what the Kulsapsifangs are doing; they may still be entrenched in diplomatic meetings in the tent. When we took off, Imperatriz had asked for a private audience with Zeu. After ensuring King Salem wasn't also hanging back, the Bloodies and I scurried toward the sound of music and fireworks.

I dance and try to ignore my proximity to the wolf.

How we're so near after months, and still leagues apart.

Butter moves in perfect rhythm to my right. Esclamonde does her best to my left. The fabrics of our red robes collect between us, a blend of velvet and cashmere and silk. After spending months in Luz, both witches know the city's popular anthems and songs.

We're almost like a warren, but better.

At our feet sit Halcyon, Vulcan, and Memphis. The Pletens sway and chat with one another, with Memphis squished between the grown warlocks. Though he's still narrow-framed, he's started to shoot up in height as he nears his fifteenth birthday. From this angle, the only indication that the warlock is ten years younger than his brother is the size of the bowl-like goblets of ale that Vulcan and Halcyon balance on their thighs. By comparison, Memphis's cup is tiny, cradled between his hands.

I keep my chalice full of brandy.

I dance between Butter and Esclamonde with my eyes half-closed.

Like always, the brandy runs out quickly.

In the dead of night and surrounded by hundreds of revelers, I descend the platform with an empty pitcher. Butter shouts over the crowd to point out the nearest liquor merchant around the corner, but Vulcan leans toward us to disagree. He points to a squat okeanid half-visible between two hesperides and insists he's pulling around a vat of shandy—we just can't see it.

I wave the pair off when they start arguing.

I descend into the jostling bodies.

I give up on finding the okeanid within a few minutes, then turn for the corner Butter indicated. It's a familiar sort of madness that I treasure—especially considering how isolated I've been in Tet.

I double back on that when a warlockling hurls onto the ground at my feet.

With a squeal, I float into the air on instinct, lifting my red strappy flats away from the mess. I rise above the crowd, arms outstretched toward a nearby wall. I press my back against the wall, then hike my feet up so they're flat against it. I set the pitcher on my knees and squint into the half-lit party in search of an alcohol vendor.

I do a double-take when I see a wolf in the crowd, moving along the wall on the opposite side of the street.

I suck in a breath—

This wolf is not like the others.

This one is handsome, with kohl around his eyes and gold studs in his ears. A black cloak hangs from his shoulders, blending with the shadows. Wolves shift around him, doing double-takes as they register the Kulapsifang's ala nearby.

Samson.

I found him.

And he seems to be alone.

The wolf scans the crowd, eyebrows pulled together with concentration.

I glance at our surroundings, double-checking that he's actually alone and that we're adjacent to an alley that I know well. Quickly, I pick out the narrow street that leads to Boonma's spa. Then I look back at the wolf as he searches the crowd.

I raise my hand to my lips to cast whispering magic into his ear. "Looking for someone?" Samson stops walking, head shifting as he scans those nearest to him. I tsk lightly. "Little birds like to sit up high, or have you forgotten?"

His features pinch with amusement, eyes roving toward the rooftops. Two and three-story buildings line the market district near the city center, penning in the wide avenue and its busy revelers.

Samson pivots toward me. Our eyes meet, sending a shock through my body. Then he's parting through the packed bodies with urgency, eyes fixed on me.

But I don't want this—

An awkward and half-real public greeting.

I've sat in those shale caves like a Host ought to for the past months, tending my demigod. And I sat in that tent like a good little witch throughout Imperatriz's meeting.

I've been trying to be a leader Samson would respect.

And even if I can't have the wolf how I'd like, I think I've earned a fucking hug.

Maybe some cuddles, too. And a lot of making fuck.

So I descend the wall, avoiding the warlockling's vomit, and beeline for the alley.

Boonmasent fortifies her spa with spellwork that clings to the massive wooden door and the stone vestibule it guards. But next door is a small library, and I don't fear the witch who runs it.

I battle the crowd, losing sight of the alley.

Given I'm shorter than most of the beings, I can't see Samson anymore—but I trust that he can follow my ala now that he's pinpointed it. My hair is down and strewn across my heavy robe; both are laden with my scent.

A little test, maybe.

In the alleyway, a gaggle of partiers loiter in a circle and pass around an herbal cigarette. Past them, the alley is dim and quiet. I study the line of doorways. It takes me a few minutes to find the library's door, taller and skinnier than I remember.

I flex my fingers, casting unlocking magic toward its metal handle. With a light click, the door opens into the dark library. I scurry toward it, glancing over my shoulder.

Still no Samson.

I reach the door and step inside. Hidden in the library's quiet shadows, I look around; like the spa, there's a square vestibule that precedes the main room. I snap my fingers to light any candles nearby. One simmers to life on a shelf near my elbow; a larger candle sits in a bowl on the ground.

Shelves line the vestibule; half are laden with books, massive chunks of selenite, and fresh incense in narrow holders. Others are empty, as though newly mounted.

I poke my head from the doorway.

My stomach clenches when I see Samson near the smoking group. Calmly, he scans the bodies nearby, then strains to lift his head farther above the crowd. I can't see his nose twitching, but I imagine it's working at full force.

He wanders further into the alley. He turns to the door and meets my eyes again.

I retreat into the room, then use magic to help me slide onto one of the shelves opposite the door. I push aside a shard of selenite and a spare book.

I hear footsteps, then the door creaks open further.

Samson pokes his head inside, then takes a step into the vestibule. It's large enough to fit both of us comfortably, sealing us into a vacuum of candlelight as soon as he shuts the door behind him. He leans back against it, setting his eyes on me.

I suddenly feel underdressed and childish.

My heart rushes to my throat, and a blush fills my cheeks—

My body fizzes with nervousness—

It's like being stuffed into a tiny room with a demigod. The kohl around his eyes makes his blue-black irises shimmer like shined obsidian. Coupled with the black cloak that hangs from his shoulders, he's like a man made from the heavy, somber winter.

I can't fucking remember if his shoulders were always this broad and if he was always so bulky. Maybe I've never been in such a small room with him before. Even his hands look suddenly mammoth, his fingers thick and his wrists sturdy and wide.

They wait at his sides.

I scan him again, tracing every part of his body.

I can feel my heart thump in my chest, can feel an oozing warmth fill my vulva. My hands clench the shelf near my thighs.

Oh, for fuck's sake, Helisent.

He's just a man.

In defiance of every physical response in my body, I lift my chin. "What the fuck are you looking at? I barely lost any weight. I don't look older, either. Esteban swears."

I'd go on, but my breath catches in my throat. It feels like I'm suffocating—

I hadn't thought it would feel this way.

It suddenly makes me angry. It suddenly brings tears to my eyes.

Two months—

I have needed him in these months, and I have ignored that needing.

I have even been ashamed of it.

I have been hoping our love would lessen its grip on me. I have been hoping my mortal wounds would heal, that one day I would wake up and wouldn't feel a golden dagger plunged into my heart. That I might see him in the streets and *not* lead him into a dark room.

Instead, I'm still dying, bleeding out in this library vestibule in front of him.

Samson closes the meager space between us. He reaches out and sets his fingertips against my chest, above my heart. I know he must be able to sense its rapid beating—possibly even hear it. I can feel its pump in my ears, in my throat right now.

Panicking.

Because I figured my love for Samson would survive these past months, but I'd never imagined it would grow so much stronger.

He's just a man—he's just a man—he's just a man—

He takes my wrist with his free hand and guides it to his chest. For a second, I'm confused, setting my fingertips over his peck. Then I realize he's placing my hand above his heart, and as soon as I press my palm to the fabric of his tunic, I can feel it thumping.

It's just as wild as mine.

When I look up at him, his eyes are glazed, too.

A thousand fruitless sentences pop into my head, desperate to name this uncontrolled feeling.

He swallows. "Helisent."

I move my hand from his chest to his cheek, taking his face between them. I open my mouth to ask for a kiss, but his hands are already wrapping around my wrists, holding my hands against his cheeks while he leans toward me.

His lips meet mine, gentle and soft.

I melt like honey with that kiss.

The dam in me breaks.

I arch toward him, straining off the shelf. His abdomen grazes my knees, and I swing my legs open. He doesn't release my wrists, deepening the kiss as he presses himself against me. My thumbs trace his cheeks, coarse with stubble, before I move my fingers into his hair. I push further off the shelf to press my abdomen against his.

One of his hands runs up my thigh toward my hips. The other fits around my cheek, fingers delving into my hair, too. With a groan, he leans toward me to flush our bodies together while he takes a handful of my butt and squeezes.

My fingers reach for his cloak's tie, desperate to pull off his layers and feel his skin. He does the same, his hands roaming across me. Disjointedly, he caresses my shoulder and kisses my neck, then tugs my dress's hem up toward my hips.

His elbow rams into a wall, then I knock the book off the shelf near my knee.

I flex my fingers to use undressing magic to slip off his heavy black cloak. I do the same with his tunic; it's much more efficient than my tiny fingers, and my body burns more with each second, desperate for his touch.

Samson reaches around to fumble with the back of my dress. I plant kisses across his face and his neck and his collar.

My dress's clasp falls loose at my back, then the fabric rips noisily down my spine.

Samson jolts back, eyes wide. "Oh, shit. Sorry—"

I interrupt him with a kiss. I lock my legs around his hips, tugging him toward me and grinding against him. He's fully hard, bursting against his harem pants. A whine starts in my throat, desperate for us to be closer.

The instinct pulses through my body, fiery and urgent. It blinds me—

Samson tugs my dress up to my hips, and I pull its cinched top down, exposing my breasts. With another growl and a long string of Velmic, the wolf looks down at me, jaw clenched and kohl smeared across one of his cheeks.

I whine again—I don't care what he does, just so long as he does *something*.

He makes another low noise, looking from my vulva to my eyes to my breasts.

I cackle with deviant joy when he kneels with another growl. I crane with a loud yelp as the wolf runs his tongue from my center to my clit in one go, then shifts to lick inside of me. I jerk on the shelf as he holds my hips in place.

But he doesn't linger, standing in the next second to kiss my face, my neck, my jaw. One of his hands cradles my lower back while the other tugs his pants down. I scoot the edge of the shelf, hiking my legs higher.

I've never been so desperate to be with someone.

Love isn't the right word; it's too feeble, too conditional for what I feel right now.

He nudges into me, his head angled near mine. His nose skims my neck, half-buried in my hair, while I raise my hips and he thrusts further and further. My chest wells as ecstasy whirls around my vulva, melting into my legs and taking my breath away. I realize I can smell him with each breath, a perfect blend of leather, musk, and cedar.

I can't remember if it always felt like this—

If I could feel each stroke like a golden bath of pleasure. Each Velmic word is like a spell that binds my soul. Like my body was made for his, and now that my flesh knows this, it will never let this go; will never cum so quickly, will never cum so hard.

I feel it for a fleeting second—

This isn't love.

This is hunger.

A hunger for Samson.

A hunger for life, for safety, for joy, for hope—

His body moves in tandem with mine, each of my moans perfectly timed to his groaning. Even the square vestibule seems to be the perfect shape now. I grip a shelf as he teases me with long and deep strokes. I watch his body move in the candlelight; the clench of his abs as he drives into me, the muscles of his arms as he caresses my breasts, my hips.

The burning of his eyes when he looks at me.

The light sheen of sweat along his chest.

The warmth and softness of his mouth when I put my finger into it, and he sucks on it.

His musky scent fills the room, along with mine. It drives me crazy, my entire body shivering and ready for orgasm when it starts in my feet. I clench my toes, one foot bobbing in the air and the other set on the shelf. It slowly ratchets up my legs, fizzling like a storm cloud waiting for lightning.

I grit my teeth together rather than cry out Samson's name. (Just in case I really am stupid for this.) Then he kisses me, coaxing my lips apart like he wants to swallow my moans.

"*Lo anata sevi-no,*" he growls.

Half-delirious with an orgasm, I whisper back, "Lo anata sevi-no."

"*Lo anata sevi-no,*" he repeats, slowly picking up his pace as my body unmelts.

I lean against the wall, my body thrumming with pleasure and aching for more. "Lo anata sevi-no."

CHAPTER 15

NEVER

SAMSON

Suin,
Does she lick you where you sweat, Samson? Those were the first words I ever
heard come out of her mouth. May Hetnazzar save your soul.
-Suin

In a tiny wooden vestibule, I sit with my witch.

The space is filled with our tangled alas; each breath is a reassurance. A relief. My tadmazzar fills the room's walls with a calming sound.

These last months without her were grueling—even more difficult than the months we spent apart after leaving Cadmium.

Now, everything is exactly how it should be.

I sit with my back propped against the door, naked aside from the black cloak hanging from my back and half-slung around Helisent. The witch sits at my side, draped against my chest. Her red robe is hanging from her shoulder, also half-slung around her. Luz is cool this time of year, but the vestibule is warm and humid from our lovemaking.

The witch yawns, adjusting slightly. Her white hair splays across my collar and shoulder, wrestled free from its tiny braids. Her jewelry is warm and heavy, scratching lightly while her finger traces a pattern on my skin.

Two small candles burn; one on the shelf and another on the ground near our discarded clothes.

Outside, the party slowly quiets. Dawn will come in the next hour, and I'll follow its light back to the Luzian Estate.

I'm determined not to speak. Our silence is too perfect, scented of us and layered with my tadmazzar. For the first time in months, my body relaxes. But that makes me wary; I don't want to waste a second of privacy with Helisent. Or miss my cue to go home. When I took off from the temple district with Hadadrimmon, we made plans to meet near the city processor before returning together.

Quietly, Helisent says, "I want to talk about Alita more. About what happened with the wand."

She lifts her head off my chest to meet my eyes. I'd forgotten how expressive and large her eyes are when moving in tandem with her white eyebrows. Even their red looks brighter than I remember, her vermillion irises filled with candlelight and almost aglow.

I gaze at her body, at the colorful necklaces hanging on her neck and across her chest.

On the three oval-shaped bruises below a golden band she wears on her upper arm.

I reach out and graze one of the marks with my thumb. "If we're talking now, I'd like to start here. Why do you have bruises on you? I saw them in Alita, too."

Helisent adjusts her arm to squint at the marks. "Oh? These? Zeu is training me and Esteban. These are probably from her. They swore no more sneak attacks, but... liars. Both of them."

My stomach drops with each of her words, tadmazzar swiftly quieting.

There is a horizon of rage in me; lightning streaks across it when I try to imagine Zeu training my witch. And her dainty mentee.

I'd hoped that was a temporary arrangement when I heard about it in Alita.

"Training?" I manage. "Sneak attacks? *Why?*"

"Zeu says it will help the next time a vampire attacks me. Or another larger being. That's what I've been doing all this time, by the way. Me, Esteban, and Zeu have been in Tet. We have a little homestead. It's not nearly as nice as Hella, but someday it'll get there.

Halcyon and Butter should've been there training with us, but... You know. They're super in love. Acting like teenagers."

'Zeu says.'

'A little homestead.'

Part of me agrees that Helisent and Esclamonde could use a bit of physical discipline and knowledge. The rest of me will spend tonight and possibly the coming weeks imagining the King of Night grappling with Helisent. I know what physical training meant for me, and it was not fucking pretty, and I can't imagine the vampire is overly gentle with her, and that idea MAKES ME WANT TO—

I take a deep breath, exhaling noisily.

I fucking told you.

Not now.

Just be cool, Samson. Be cool.

Helisent clears her throat. "Right. That's probably a lot to take in." Excitedly, she sits up and takes my forearm between her hands. "Here, I can show you—"

"No." It comes out harsher than I mean, but I'm struggling to keep the mood light.

She pouts, voice lowering, "I was going to do an arm bar."

"Can I... can *we*..." I take another large breath, striving for clarity. The witch blinks at me, holding my arm absentmindedly. "I know I brought it up, but what if we didn't talk about this? Just for now?" I clear my throat, setting my hand on her hip. "I get jealous of Zeu, and worried that... I don't know if it's hard for you, but it's hard for me..." *Lekeli Kelnazzar.* The witch tilts her head, eyebrows tugging together. "I take Vieira very seriously. Maybe too seriously. Maybe sometimes, it feels too real, and that, if you're with Zeu, then Vieira will disappear. I don't know why I feel that way about him specifically. But I do. I worry."

I stare at my hands and brace myself for a rude, if not soul-crushing, retort.

I'm here with my wife, after all.

The last months have taught me the complexity of having multiple partners. I have loved Brutatalika since our honeymoon in Rouz, and that love is becoming more complex, more meaningful, and more lasting now that we're wading through civil upheaval.

I have no doubt who I'd choose.

But... it isn't my choice, and I'm learning to live with that.

Or I thought I was.

"I already told you in Coil that I'd never leave," she murmurs, expression somber.

"I know." I try to swallow my insecurities. It feels silly that they'd come out now—when we're finally together and alone after months of uncertainty and exhaustion.

But it's becoming more obvious that this is all Helisent and I will have: fleeting moments hidden away.

And it's becoming painfully clear that this isn't enough for me.

"So... the wand," she goes on. "We only had a few minutes to catch up after I shadowed you to Mort. I didn't get to ask half of what I wanted to know."

I nod, happy to change the subject. "Ask away."

"What did it feel like? Have you noticed any changes since then? Just to make sure I didn't... do anything stupid."

"Stupid?" I ask. "Stupid how?"

She shrugs a shoulder. "The wand is very powerful. And it responded to you in the jungle. From the outside looking in, that looks a lot like wielding, Samson."

Part of me wishes that were possible.

That I'd held the wand in Alita and pointed it at the shadow and said, *Bring Imperatriz to me here in the jungle.*

But that's not really how it went.

I adjust, pulling Helisent back into my lap and against my chest again. I stroke her hair with a sigh, admitting, "It's hard to tell what has changed since I had the wand and Imperatriz returned. I feel like I've been running on adrenaline for months. The only difference that stands out to me now is the seething dreams.

"Most of the dreams are the same. I'm an adult or a child climbing through a yew tree. Maybe just standing below it. You're there, too— sometimes as a witchling, sometimes as an adult. We talk about nothing."

Dreamily, the witch sighs. "That sounds so lovely, Samson."

I smile faintly; at least I have my dreams of her. "It is, Helisent."

"And the changes?"

"Do you remember in Zarzynn, when I first dreamed of a faceless witch? I'm not sure if I told you about her. She doesn't show up often.

When I see her, she's sitting on the ground near the yew tree. She faces away from me—I don't know what she looks like. Just that she has something in her arms, and that I'm covered in red string anytime I see her.

"I used to wonder if it was Andromeda. But I saw your mother in Hella when Parsifal spoke with her in the mirror—I don't think they're the same."

Helisent rises, pushing off my chest to search my eyes. "A stranger? Is she red?"

I shake my head. "No, she's not in her form. But she has the white hair of a wielder. She wears a robe that looks older—not the robe itself, but the style. Like it's from another time. She scares me. You know how it is in dreams... some things you know not to wake or touch. That's how it is with the faceless witch."

Helisent makes a low noise. "But she doesn't hurt you?"

I shake my head again. "No."

A memory drifts up to me from a faraway place.

I hear my father's voice.

'It wasn't a normal string...'

'I buried it deep in the ground near a yew tree...'

For a second, it adds up. The red strings in the seething dreams; the yew tree; my father.

But that's another trail of crumbs I don't have the time or energy to follow. Not now, at least.

"I see." Helisent strokes the scar bundled over my heart. "And you haven't felt a second body since Alita, right?"

"No. And even then, I only felt it in the mornings. I haven't felt it since you took the wand back."

She strokes my hair next, setting it back in order. I watch the candlelight trace her soft brown skin, half-shrouded beneath the velvet robe. "And you haven't noticed any new abilities since we had sex with the wand?"

I raise my eyebrows, shocked by the question. "*Abilities?* Should I? I thought sex magic was to... introduce me to Vex."

"It was. Still, sympathetic magic usually involves a trade-off between magical twins. I gave Onesimos magical power, and he gave me fire magic. I gave Halcyon Mieiran language, and he gave me Zarzyd."

My stomach drops. I'm less jealous of Onesimos and Halcyon because I don't worry they're a physical threat to the witch. Still, it's a little embarrassing to admit, "I'm a wolf, Helisent. We don't have magical twins. At least, not like nymphs and wielders."

"You're the Kulapsifang."

I huff, ready to disagree.

But Helisent goes on, "I can sense your power, you know. It's gotten more potent since Imperatriz came back. You remind me of owls now. I realized that after we had sex. It's a quiet power, and it comes at night, and it's visionary and wise and lethal in equal measures."

I huff again. "*Owls?* We're wolves—"

"You know what I mean." She falls against my chest, this time more brusquely and possibly to shut me up. "It almost reminds me of Tet. Of Skull."

I wrap my arms around her, sighing before I bury my nose in her hair and inhale the full force of her ala.

A while later, she says, "I feel like we should talk about the march to Bellator. I'm a little wary of Night. I have a feeling it's going to be cold."

I can't tell if she's being sarcastic. "Helisent, it's going to be covered in snow. Some piles will be taller than you. I hope you and the Bloodies considered this."

Helisent strains upward to kiss my neck, her lips soft. "You know I can cast warming magic, right?"

"The cold is only half the battle. I think you might struggle more with the asceticism. Wolves live even more simply when we're travel-ing, especially during times of hardship. You need to pack your own brandy. Our supply line will only carry *houm*, which is a medicinal liquor. Tastes like fennel. You won't like it."

She tsks. "Fine. And what about vegetables?"

"Assuming the greenhouses aren't all destroyed, we should find some winter vegetables. Cabbage, kale, sprouts, and leeks. All the nice green stuff."

"My goodness—four different veggies to choose from?"

For a long moment, we sit peacefully; I stroke her hair while her head rises and falls with my breathing.

With a sigh, I tell her, "I figured you would agree to Imperatriz's request when we set up the meeting and you sent word that you'd come. But I want to make things clear... I don't expect this from you. You've given enough to Velm, Helisent. More than enough."

Her voice is quiet; I can't tell if she's sleepy or pensive. "I already told you, I will never leave."

'I will never leave.'

It clicks suddenly—a wolf or a nymph would say, *'I will stay forever.'*

But witches prefer to avoid the type of vulnerability that comes from obvious statements.

'I will never leave.'

She says *never*... but I think she means *forever*.

A smile wells on my lips, in my soul.

Before I find a response, she peels herself off me to stare at me, her eyebrows bunched. "Also, tell me what *lo anata sevi-sim* means. I'm tired of playing coy about it."

I love how her lips look when she says it. The tone of her voice, the slight mispronunciation of the words.

I trace them with my thumb. "It means, 'you are mine'."

She tilts her head when I pull my finger away. Her features go still, devoid of any concrete emotion. "Don't say things like that to me." Like her expression, her tone is hard to read. It's gentle, fragile like freshly fallen snow, and yet burning with something.

Don't say things like that?

What the fuck is she talking about?

I don't know; it makes me freeze, makes me rethink everything I've said in the last five minutes.

"It's... Samsonfang," I explain.

He's stayed close, lingering from the power of the recent triple-moon. He presses to the forefront of my mind, just like he did in Luz when Helisent put the wand around my neck.

Tell her I am hers. Tell her she is mine. Tell her—tell her—tell her—

I bite my tongue, unable to read Helisent's tense features.

She says, "Didn't we already cover this? I can't be yours. That's why we have Vieira. There, I'm yours. There, you're mine."

Then make Vieira.

I shake my head at the idiocy of that thought, at the abject passion with which Samsonfang sends the concept through my mind and body.

Quietly, Helisent goes on, "Your people need you, Samson. You, your mother, and Brutatalika. Together. As a pack."

I know she's right, but my gut clenches when she says those words.

Samsonfang fights them bitterly. ***You are the Kulapsifang; she is the Vexen. You can make many worlds***.

"What?" Helisent asks.

I sigh, torn between her logic and Samsonfang's insistence.

I trace her lips again with my finger. I try for another appeal, one that comforts me. "But you'll never leave?"

She takes my chin, telling me, "Never."

It's as close to forever as we'll get, and I'm happy for that promise in any form it takes.

I stare into her eyes. "I will also never leave."

She smiles, then leans forward for another kiss. "Good."

The celebrations have died down outside.

Fragile light fills the window beside the door at my back.

I know it in my gut now.

Helisent was right.

Dawn is pain.

Ten days later, I stand with my mother and wife.

Huddled groups and their mounds of supplies stretch across the hilly plains before us. Shadows blanket the valleys between them, deepening with dusk.

Hundreds of wolves sling their packs across their bodies and over their shoulders. They shift into position, preparing to set out once the sun sinks into the horizon.

Under Imperatriz's guidance, Brutatalika and I have spent the last days organizing our five-hundred-strong caravan. The planning hasn't been without its hiccups, even with the benefit of rest and nourishment in Luz. Now, it's time to see whether our first joint operation as married Alphas pans out.

The slowest in the pack will lead the caravan to set the pace; the Alphas will take up the rear. We'll sleep through the days to accommodate Zeu's den, then hike through the nights. It works well given the daylight hours are short this time of year.

But even with plenty of dove and magical power at our disposal, it's a finely tuned process. Most of the caravan is modular, able to readjust quickly thanks to its independent and specialized packs. At least, theoretically.

Like me, Brutatalika studies the groups of twenty like a hawk.

Imperatriz sets her hand on my shoulder and squeezes. "Feeling tired, my Alphas? Don't worry—you'll get used to the stress. It won't keep you up at night after a few years." With a long sigh, she pulls a cigarette from behind her ear, eyes roving over the troops of wolves. "Where's the witch? I take it you two decided to manage the Bloodies and Zeu's den similarly? I hope the den isn't late. I'd like to leave as soon as possible."

"There," I say, gesturing to the north.

I've been stealing glances at the Bloodies who wait in a valley nearby. Helisent keeps adjusting her robe, pacing as though nervous. Halcyon, Vulcan, Vega, and Butter sit nearby, playing a game that involves slapping one another's hands. Esclamonde hasn't left Helisent's side since they arrived. Now, the witches are focused on the dirt path from Luz.

"Zeu's den should be here shortly," I go on. "The vampires have a large yurt to share. We found plenty of dark fabric, but Vulcan agreed to light-seal its walls when the den rests. We have another yurt for the Bloodies. They'll set it up themselves."

"Ask the laborers to set up both groups' tents." Imperatriz toys with the cigarette, deep in thought. "The Bloodies will insist on doing it themselves, which is fine. But Zeu will appreciate the offer. He'll take us up on it."

I don't say anything, watching Helisent set her hands on her hips, and then toss one into the air. It looks like she's arguing with the mentee.

Brutatalika nods. "I'll have Exultet speak with—"

"No, Samson will fulfill the den's needs." Imperatriz squeezes my shoulder again, turning her gaze toward me. "I understand that you don't trust the King of Night, and it's clear Zeu doesn't trust you. I'd like that resolved sooner rather than later.

"Zeu was born in the House of Argot. He was sent to the House of

Serac as a young man. Serac is the cruelest of Velm's Houses. Hyd never told me what made Serac so evil—only that they were vile enough that her den concentrated their raids on its neighborhoods. Almost exclusively."

I shift onto my back foot, redirecting my gaze away from the women.

I know what makes the House of Serac so mindlessly cruel.

A Host named Suleiman.

But I'll happily keep the details of my torture from my mother and wife. As far as I know, neither has discovered the full extent of that Thing that happened in Bellator, and I'd like to keep it that way.

"During one raid, Hyd was wounded; she sent the den on. They had freed many, and she wouldn't let them be retaken on her account. Zeu, recently freed himself, rallied the vampires to help Hyd. But escaping Ezit is almost impossible—even for those in full health. The vampires refused to wait. Hyd didn't judge them. She knew that any opportunity for freedom was overwhelming. We are all selfish in our panic.

"But Zeu didn't go. He stayed. He hid in the sewers for ten days with her. When Hyd was well enough, they limped to freedom—and that took many more days. Almost a month." Imperatriz sighs, then lifts her hand from my shoulder. "Had the same happened to me on Pit, and I had the chance to either flee or save Hyd... I don't know what I would do. I really don't, and I judge myself for it often.

"It's easy to question Zeu based on his crassness and ego, but I don't fear his ability to endure and make the right decisions in difficult times. The latter is far more important to Velm right now. Especially if there are degivampires in my capital."

As though on cue, a mob of vampires skulks through a path in the oak trees where Hetnazzar left Hadadrimmon and me last autumn, moving toward the Bloodies. In the middle of winter, the grove's yellow ribbons have been swapped out for bundles of possumhaw berries, most of which have browned from their red coloring. The den leaves the oaks to greet the Bloodies, feathers dangling from their necklaces, braids, and belts.

Esclamonde rushes past Helisent to hug Zeu. He wraps his arms around her, then turns back to usher the rest of his group forward.

The Bloodies mingle with the vampires, standing through what looks like a formal reintroduction between the den and wielders.

"And you, Brutatalika," Imperatriz continues, eyes locked on the meeting groups, "will deliver maca root to the witches and female vampires."

I slide my eyes toward Brutatalika, eager to see how she takes the news. Maca root is a super-herb for men and women, but it's often rationed for women during winter. It's said to keep young wolves fertile while helping the elders through perimenopause and menopause.

Brutatalika gulps as she watches the Bloodies. "Of course."

"You'll also show them how to grind the root and steep it in tea."

Lightly, my wife clears her throat. "I didn't realize Mieirans used maca root."

"It's clear you hadn't thought about it at all, my dear Alpha." Imperatriz sets her hand on Brutatalika's shoulder next. Rather than squeeze, she strokes my wife's back. "We need to keep the den in good humor. But, for the love of Hetnazzar, my dear Brutatalika, we need the Bloodies. The Queen Bloody, too, if you please."

Sharply, Imperatriz exhales. She lifts her hand from Brutatalika's shoulder, then purses her lips to whistle. The sound cuts through the air like a knife, causing everyone in the vicinity to flinch and turn toward us.

"Cousin Hadadrimmon," she calls toward the wolf. "Bring my flint, please."

Cousin Hadadrimmon.

It's still hard to gauge how my mother feels about the wolf's presence—as the sole member of my pack and his existence in general. The term 'cousin Hadadrimmon' seems to be a delightfully cloaked insult each time she says it.

With a sigh that lifts his shoulders, Hadadrimmon drags his feet away from where Brutatalika's pack rests in a loose circle. He stops before us, a pessimistic smile on his face, then helps my mother light her cigarette with his flint. "Aunty Imperatriz. Hello."

She gives him the once-over, taking a long drag. "If I call you cousin, why do you call me aunty?"

He bows his head with an impudent flourish. "It's because of the age gap. I'd hate for anyone to think we were contemporaries."

"You spoil me. Thank you." Imperatriz watches my packmate return to his seat, a vibrant grimace on her face. She takes a long drag, then turns to focus on my wife. "Brutatalika, go greet Zeu's den and the Bloodies. Make sure they understand how the caravan functions. We're leaving soon."

My wife slips away without another word, leaving me on the hilltop with Imperatriz.

When she's out of earshot, she quietly tells me, "Verita's messengers haven't intercepted any letters moving in or out of Bellator. It's been two weeks. The city has gone silent."

I hadn't noticed the lack of messages, more focused on reaching Luz and finding a certain red witch. I turn toward my mother, chagrined at my ignorance.

She goes on, "Magic and degivampires in Bellator... and now, silence."

I speak steadily, hoping to reassure her, "We'll know what the Houses want from Velm soon. All we need to do is retake Bellator."

She looks into the sky, jaw clenching. "Can you feel it, my dear Kulapsifang? Something has changed."

I study her features, stepping closer. I can't feel it at all, whatever she's talking about—but I can see stress and uncertainty on her features.

Then I feel it—a pang in my gut. A wave of intuition.

Is Clearbold dead?

That thought sends a fresh wave of fear through my mind.

The implications are terrifyingly bleak.

If the city is silent, my father hasn't just lost control of Ezit's Hosts.

He's cold as snow.

But I don't say that, desperate to be wrong.

So I stand at her side, shoulder brushing against hers as the wolves spread out over the low hills and amble into formation. Like an arrow pointed south into the deepening night, the caravan starts inching toward Bellator.

The first week of travel is numbing but comfortable.

The Bloodies and Zeu's den fall into step quickly. Our offers to set up the den's yurt and provide maca for the women set a precedent of mindful sharing.

Every other day, we organize communal meals. All those working in the caravan are welcome to join; this garners respect from the Bloodies and Zeu, which relieves me. (Along with wielders and vampires, we have three Pletens to impress.)

The plans Brutatalika and I drew up seem to work well, too. The caravan is divided into three separate parts, allowing the crews responsible for carrying supplies and cooking to rest and then catch up.

With groups revolving around one another, we continue to push forward—slowly, steadily.

In the third week, we near the village of Halfleet.

The caravan stops in preparation; we need to take the village, and then divest it of as many supplies as possible. As one of the largest settlements in central Velm, there should be food stores available.

Rather than waltz in unannounced, I gather a small group to do reconnaissance. At the last second, I turn back and request Helisent's presence; magic is much more efficient than eyes and a nose when it comes to spying. Eager to be useful, the witch trails me away from the caravan with a group of seven. We creep toward Halfleet at dawn, while the others rest for the day.

We pass through a leafless, sparse patch of woods.

We crest a small hill, hunching down in case news has spread of our arrival.

Halfleet sits in the distance, its outer streets silent. The large village is obscured in the early morning, half-hidden by winter mist. The lampposts are still lit with warm firelight, though the wooden, single-story homes all look unlit. In the center of the village, a few two-story marble buildings stand out like pale beacons.

I don't see any white flags, to my relief.

I also see no black flags.

A breeze passes through the dry grass, cold and hopeless and scented of death.

Another gust of wind spreads the alarming scent.

I look over my shoulder. "Stay here," I tell the group.

I descend the hill, fixing my gaze on the wide dirt road that leads to the city. Again, I don't see anything worth noting. The barns encircling the village are quiet, their doors shut.

But the scent of death grows stronger as I approach the city. It condenses into one space, telling me that there's a corpse nearby.

My nose twitches as I look from side to side, desperate to find the body's location.

With each step, its ala comes into greater focus.

The corpse is female—and nearby, there's something that smells like her, and I can't tell if it's alive or dead. Mud, ash, dry grass, a female's ala, and...

A pup.

I pick up my pace, inhaling full breaths while I scan the area.

It's coming from the roadside.

I rush into the grass, nose working to gather every detail.

I start to make sense of what I'm smelling—

The corpse is female; her child is nearby. The child is a toddler. Male. His ala is curdling from life to death right now.

I find her body first, naked and pale where she's hidden amid the brown stalks of dry grass. Her eyes are open, her face spotted with heavy bruising.

I suck in a depth breath, twisting my body in search of the pup. He couldn't have gone far. Packs don't separate; the younger the pup, the longer they'll wait. Especially if they're too young to understand death.

"Where are you?" I call out. "I'm your Kulapsifang—make a noise, *atali*, you're safe."

I rip at the grass in hopes of seeing his pale skin. I move slowly, worried about stepping on the hidden toddler. Every breath feels like ten, every second a lifetime.

"Atali?" I say louder, body fizzing with desperation. I turn and call over my shoulder, "Helisent!"

"I'm here." The witch must have followed; she's only ten feet behind. She rushes toward me, holding her arms up as she enters the tallgrass. "What is it?"

She gasps, finding the corpse first.

"She has a pup—he's hanging on—we need to find him—quickly."

I keep searching the grass, moving farther from the corpse. Helisent raises her hands, preparing her magic.

I see a tiny foot before she casts a spell. It's almost gray where it pokes from the underbrush. The boy, aged no more than four years, is bundled in what smells like his mother's clothes. I rush forward, scooping him up. He doesn't make a sound as I do, his body cold and limp. I press my nose to his neck; his ala hints that he's alive, but my hands are shaking too much for me to feel for a pulse.

I squat immediately, pulling my shirt's hem out. I shove the child into the gap between my bare skin and my tunic. I start to tug off his layers, which are also freezing.

Helisent rushes over, eyes wide as she hovers over me.

I toss away the spare layers, then circle my arms around the toddler. "Can you heal him? Is it too late?"

The witch reaches into my shirt's collar, feeling for the child. She stares into the distance, features taut with concentration, as she spreads her palm over his scalp.

Now that he's warming against my chest, sheltered by my arms and cloak, I feel a faint heartbeat.

"Okay." A thrum of magic starts in Helisent's hand, its bass easing my fear immediately. The child exhales quickly, then one of his feet shoots out, kicking me in the ribs. "Good pupling." Her red eyes flash to mine. "Hypothermia. Give me a few minutes to work on his organs. I need to warm him slowly."

I nod, turning my gaze to the corpse. I can't see his mother between the tallgrass, and I'm thankful.

A naked woman on a roadside just minutes from a city?

Her hypothermic child in the grass nearby?

I glance at Helisent, suddenly nervous.

That doesn't sound like loyalists or Leolites. That doesn't sound like any type of agenda aside from chaos. And Velm... descended into chaos...

I'd rather face the Leolites and their allies from Ezit.

She looks at me, eyes still wide. "It's okay."

She repeats it every few minutes, but I'm not sure if she's saying it for my sake or her own.

CHAPTER 16

SHARPER EDGES

HELISENT

Honey Baby,
Mama hated Grandmama. She said she couldn't be trusted. Mama said that
when an emotion grows large enough, it begins to wield our magic. That's why
she kept a journal. Words can't wield.
The Boys

Halfway to Bellator, the silence filling the Bloodies' yurt no longer feels oppressive.

With dawn only an hour away, we shuffle into the dwelling and pull our bedding from our bottomless bags. Our duvets are thick and colorful, the pillows stuffed with feathers.

Esclamonde drags our bedding into place while I light the magical cylinders hanging from the angled beams overhead.

With a few yawns, Halcyon and Butter pair off for sleep. Near the yurt's entrance, Vega and Vulcan do the same.

Not even the most hopeless days in Hella were this tiring and numbing. Waking in darkness, sleeping through the daylight, constantly hugged by a frigid, unrelenting grip of cold. Even the ground is frozen. Even the stars looked brushed with frost.

As has become a habit, I pull out a large flask of brandy. The liquor sloshes in the glass as I tilt my head back to drink, then pass it on to Esclamonde.

The rest of the Bloodies watch tiredly, waiting for the brandy to make its rounds.

As the mentee sips and smacks her lips, someone rushes to the yurt's opening flap.

The six of us turn as someone hurriedly undoes the ties.

Frantic guests aren't a surprise anymore; we field desperate requests at least every other day.

What began with finding a frozen toddler outside of Halfleet has turned into a never-ending series of similar emergencies. Not all wolves have been as lucky as the toddler who, within a few days, had fully recovered from his injuries.

With a long groan, I scoot toward the entrance just in time for Zeu to storm into the yurt.

Now that we're exposed to the full force of Night, the King of Night has taken to wearing a fox fur cloak. The ostentatious piece is far more eye-catching than any of my robes. The stark white fur is fluffy and spotless, covering Zeu from his wrists to his calves. He battles the garment as he lowers himself through the yurt's square entrance. It blocks my view, bunching up around my face and chest.

I swat at the fabric as Zeu hustles in. "For fuck's sake. Shouldn't you be hiding from the light?"

With a frustrated sigh, the King of Night peels off the cloak and scoots into a cross-legged position. "What? No. There's no light on the horizon yet. I have time for a little brandy."

I scoot back to my place beside Esclamonde.

The witchling immediately hands the brandy to the vampire, who then throws his head back to drink. He shivers as he sets it back down. "I've been... trying to be optimistic... but it's becoming more and more difficult."

Once again, no one in the circle is alarmed.

Halcyon takes the bottle from Zeu. "We heard they found a vampire wandering last night. Did you interrogate her?"

"Him. And yes, I did." Zeu sets his hands on his knees, looking blankly at the bedding pooled between us. "It was not fun. I learned nothing remotely hopeful. And now the vampire is dead." With another shake of his head, he takes the bottle back from Halcyon and guzzles more. "I know you six sit in here commiserating. You can't really do that when you're in charge of a den. Dens are not like warrens, let me tell you."

Esclamonde pats his leg. "Tell us what happened."

Zeu slides his eyes around the group. "I think I've spared enough details. No one wants the rest. But I will say this... I imagine Bellator is being bathed in blood."

Halcyon snorts. "Bathed in blood? And what the fuck are we saying happened in Halfleet? I was there when Samson and the wolves started castrating the men. You want to talk *Bellator* being bathed in blood..."

A shiver runs up my spine. The dead mother we found on the roadside was one of many victims of a violent pack takeover—neither driven by Leolites nor allies of the Afadors, but an existing pack with a penchant for dominance. They were dealt with, then sent into the white night unhealed.

Zeu shrugs. "Castrating sexually violent men isn't unique to Velm. I was fine with the verdicts in Halfleet."

Vulcan reaches for the bottle next. "The teenage pack... that's what keeps me up at night. The bone pieces—"

"*Watch it*," Zeu snaps, turning a feral gaze toward Vulcan. "Bone jewelry is an ancient tradition. We tell stories with our—"

"I know," the warlock amends. "Your people have turned it into an art. And you take the bones from your kills—not because you saw an opening in an unruly time. The adolescents were... I mean, what was the point?"

"At the risk of sounding old school," Butter pipes up, taking the bottle from Vulcan, "I can't stand all the messages written in blood. I don't know what they say, but I can tell they're different in each village." She glances around the circle. "Has anyone asked what they say? The one we passed last week scared Imperatriz."

I sigh, staring at the magical cylinder overhead, reveling in its hopeful, golden light. "It said, '*Welcome home*'."

Like Imperatriz, I had stood and stared at the wall for a while, stunned and exhausted and morose. Samson and Brutatalika were taking care of the lone survivors we'd found in the village, so I'd stayed behind to look after the Kulapsifang.

Just in case...

Butter makes an unhappy noise. "The Leolites know we're coming? No one told me that."

I shrug a shoulder. "The caravan was never going to be a surprise, Butter. We're taking Bellator by force, not some clever trick."

Butter nods, turning her numb gaze toward the pile of blankets. "Right..."

"At least we're halfway there," I offer. "I know things aren't going *great*, but we haven't met any resistance so far. That's a plus, at least."

"Not from wolves, we haven't," Zeu huffs. "But the cold isn't helping a fucking thing."

A few more low noises, but that's it.

After Halfleet, we found a string of villages that were purposefully destroyed. Rather than raze the buildings, its raiders dumped water throughout the streets. They flooded the piles of firewood, the meager stores of herbs, the grains, and the jerky. All the village's supplies were frozen in clear blocks of ice.

The reconnaissance groups have also found several wells that reek of death. And I've stood beside Imperatriz 713 Afador to call the bodies up for proper cremations. The corpses must have been there for months, tossed down before the water froze.

I've managed to keep those adventures to myself, hoping to shield the Bloodies from the fouler details.

I pull the bottle from the vampire's grip and take a long drink.

Here's my concern (one that no other Bloody seems to see)—

Imperatriz returned from Pit less than six months ago. And even after eighteen years of absence, her demigod has yet to come to say hello. To check in on its chosen representative. To celebrate her return.

Nothing.

On top of that, this trip is chipping away at my faith in Velm, and I worry it will permanently change how the Bloodies see Samson's realm.

I worry that, even after Imperatriz returns to Bellator, these problems won't be easy to quash.

Things like a general suspicion of leadership, territory grabs, newly established blood feuds, and fragmented packs with a fresh taste for chaos.

These troubles might last for years; they might breed new problems. Or, like Halcyon quietly intimated last week, they might provide the perfect level of destabilization for Argot and Serac to launch full-on takeovers.

For a while longer, we sit and drink and chat. Zeu steers the conversation toward everything he plans on doing once he's back in Luz—predominantly, stay in Luz and never be pried from its loving grip.

He doesn't get far with his dream before another guest finds our yurt.

"Helisent West of Jaws," Brutatalika calls in quietly. "The women are bathing with birch logs and rosemary bundles. We're in the grayish tent near the back of the caravan. You'll see the smoke rising from it. We also have maca root tea. Plenty of it."

I glance at Butter; she eyes me with a shrug.

I'm not sure what to say. "Very good. Don't forget the armpits."

"Would you and the Bloodies like to join?" the Female Alpha asks awkwardly. "The women, I mean."

I freeze, staring at the yurt's closed flap. A bath sounds delightful after over a month of magical washing. But I'm not enthused by the idea of being naked and in immediate proximity to Brutatalika.

"We'd *love* a proper bath," Butter calls out, suddenly full of energy.

I lean over to thump the okeanid-witch-necromancer on the arm.

Brutatalika calls in, "Follow the smoke. We'll be inside."

"Cool," Butter responds. "We'll be right there."

The snow crunches beneath Brutatalika's boots as she turns to leave. In the next second, I hurl a pillow at Butter. "What the *fuck*," I hiss. "I was thinking of an excuse."

"I need a bath," she says, taking hold of the pillow and throwing it back at me.

"I'll stay here with you, Helisent," Esclamonde says. "Mother says I should never be naked around a wolf. They'll smell your... You know. And then they get obsessed. They can't help it. Something about the pheromones."

"Really?" Vega asks, eyes widening as she looks at Vulcan.

Vulcan turns his gaze to me. "Is that true?"

I roll my eyes like Samson didn't just verify that seethings aren't real. "How would Gautselin run Coil if all the wolves were seething for witches? I mean, not that it matters. We aren't going."

"It's a *bath*. With rosemary and birch. Did you hear that part?" With a huff, Butter starts to collect her things and head for the door flap. "I'm fine swimming in a tub with the wolves if it involves hot water." She turns back and blows Halcyon a kiss. "Sorry, my lover."

He offers a weak smile. "That's okay. I'll bathe again eventually. Hopefully."

Butter lunges and grabs Vega by the wrist. "You're coming, too. Think of it like a diplomatic meeting. The wolves are interested in the Pletens."

Vega follows with a whine. "I'm Luzian now."

Butter ignores the plea, snapping her fingers at Esclamonde next. "You, too. Bath time." She looks at me last. "Helisent. Let's go. Pick up your shit."

"I'm on my period." I toss my hair over my shoulder. "There will be blood everywhere."

"No, you aren't," Zeu counters. "Your cycle doesn't start—"

"Shut the fuck up," I hiss. "Why do you know that? Don't answer." I clear my throat and come up with another excuse. "I'm allergic to rosemary. I'll puff up if I walk in there."

"You're not allergic," Esclamonde says, head tilted. "You love when we eat—"

"I actually just bathed." I splay my hands for emphasis. "It was subtle. No one noticed."

"No, you didn't." Butter snorts, nearing the door. "You've had a smear of dirt on your neck for the last two days. *Now let's go.*"

I gasp, feeling for the spot of dirt.

With a vain sigh, I trail the rest of the women outside, cloaking myself with warming magic. We shuffle through the snow tiredly. In the east, the sky warms from navy to purple to orange. The stars shimmer brightly to the west in a blackened sky. The snow is bright, semi-illumed.

Velm's Night is like an in-between world, halfway descended into a peaceful, lightless death.

Quickly, we shuffle toward the only tent whose roof is split with a seam of gushing smoke.

Butter calls gleefully at the door. "*Yoo-hoo*, it's the Bloodies. Women only."

A wolf discreetly opens the flap toward the tent's inner wall. We slip through, then the wolf shuts the flap and seals it with a few buttons.

Inside, two fires sit at either end of the long, rectangular space. Sitting atop them are cauldrons with bubbling water. The firewood must be birch, while rosemary hangs from the tent's supporting beams in dried bundles.

I look around in wonder, immediately happy I came.

The air is heavy with fragrant steam. My shoulders relax as the warmth caresses my skin, its musky scent filling my lungs.

Between the cauldrons are five wolves wearing skimpy variations of the loincloths I've seen during waricons. The fabric hugs their wide hips, hiked between their butt cheeks. They squat between the fires and their cauldrons, a series of wooden bowls arranged on a raised wooden platform. Their long and thick hair falls around their shoulders, pasted to their backs and breasts, caught in their armpits.

Imperatriz sits farthest from the door, beside Brutatalika. Both seem focused on their bathing, unworried about the Bloodies. I must look at both of them a dozen times. Imperatriz looks more feminine than ever before. Her breasts are relaxed, her nipples dark and small. At her side, Brutatalika's are like literal peaches; round, firm, high.

Exultet, Leda, and Verita watch us hang our robes, then turn back to their bathing. They scoop water from the cauldrons with wide and short bowls. Nearby sit a few jugs of oil and bars of fatty soap.

Like me, Butter undresses and steps forward.

I turn back for the witchlings.

Vega stands frozen in place. A tight-fitting strap fits around her upper chest; fabric drapes from it, covering her breasts. Around her hips, she wears something similar to the wolves' meager loincloths, except it doesn't have long ties. It hugs her pubic bone, looking seamless.

I gasp when I realize what I'm seeing. "*Undergarments*. I've heard of these." I narrow my eyes, pinching the soft cotton. "I thought they'd look cooler."

"Speaking of undergarments..." Exultet picks up a bundle of dark fabric and leans to hand it to me. "Here. For you, Calypso, and Esclamonde."

I arch an eyebrow. "Witches don't wear undergarments."

"You might if you could smell really well." She smiles clumsily. "Not that you smell bad. It's just—a *lot* of pheromones."

Vega whines. "See? It's true."

Esclamonde snatches one of the pieces of fabric, bringing it to her hips. "I told you, Helisent."

I stare at the long and narrow strip, confused.

"Like this." Exultet stands to show me. She deftly loops the fabric around my hips, ties it loosely, flips it through my legs, and then pulls it back through.

I look down.

I'm wearing what is essentially a baby's nappy.

I try not to groan or curse out loud.

Hating how the loincloth feels with each step, I take my place at the end of the wooden planks. The Bloodies follow suit as the pack makes room for us. Brutatalika and the others dole out the supplies; first, a shampoo, then the fatty soap, then an exfoliator that scratches my skin raw. We watch the wolves, mirroring their application of each. Only Imperatriz remains silent, bathing herself as though in a trance in the corner.

Later, Leda reaches for a spiny birch branch near the soap. She squats behind Exultet, beating her bare back with the bundle. The Bloodies watch from the corners of our eyes, scooting closer to one another.

I lunge when Leda reaches behind me to set the branch down.

"A bit jumpy, aren't you?" The wolf laughs. "Relax, Helisent."

"Well? I'm all fucking..." I tug at the loincloth; it's all wet now, sagging and sopping. "This isn't good for me."

Butter looks at me with knowing eyes. She keeps shifting hers around, too, adjusting back and forth.

To my surprise, Imperatriz joins the conversation. "Your mother said the same thing. She destroyed hers and mine the first time we bathed together. It became a habit after that. She never tried one on." Quietly, she adds, "No matter how I pleaded."

What?

Bathing together?

I study the Kulapsifang as she wrings out her long hair.

My mother had mentioned Imperatriz 713 Afador during our brief conversation, but she didn't give any hint about the nature of their relationship.

Even when Imperatriz mentioned my mother when we met in Alita, she didn't have much to say. Only that the pair had been allies with hopes of encouraging the Northing.

"Did you two… bathe a lot?" I ask.

"She came to Bellator once." Imperatriz douses the ends of her long gray hair in oil, tress by tress. "We traveled to the city together and bathed in a tent like this along the way."

My head tilts. "She went to Bellator? I thought wielders weren't allowed in Bellator Palace." *Only our horns.* "That's what they tell us in the north."

And why didn't Andromeda mention this? It seems like a huge coup— becoming the *first* wielder to set foot in the palace.

Imperatriz twists her damp hair into a tight bun, then ties it into place. "As a rule, no. But rules aren't facts, are they? The Kulapsifang's ear is the most powerful weapon in our realm."

I purse my lips, nodding like I understand what that means.

Brutatalika catches my eye. Stoically, she adds, "Before Velm had organized law, it had Kulapsifangs. True order and rule come from Hetnazzar. The Afadors are the link between Velm and its demigod. Their words and experience become law. So, wielders don't go to Bellator—unless the Kulapsifang invites them."

I look between the wolves. "I see." I clear my throat, trying to keep my voice light and my questions casual. "And speaking of Hetnazzar… should we be expecting a visit from the demigod anytime soon? Maybe before we get to Bellator?"

The Kulapsifang fixes her gaze on me as soon as the question leaves my lips; the rest of the wolves look blankly elsewhere.

I meet Imperatriz's eyes, steeling myself before I go on. "Demigods aren't usually shy about saying hello to me. They sense my power. I thought Hetnazzar would have met us by now."

Nothing is more comforting or stabilizing than a demigod.

I need that reassurance; the Bloodies, too. Certainly the wolves.

Imperatriz raises her eyebrows. "Perhaps you should assume less.

Velm is far larger than any region the nymph demigods look after. Ours can't be everywhere at once."

I study her eyes, desperate to pick apart her words.

I comb through a few responses, but each is too pointed at the Female Alpha. Too tinged with unspoken questions and suspicions. Still, this is the moment I build a wall between the Bloodies and Imperatriz; while I stare into her eyes, clean and cradled by fragrant steam.

Not because I want to, but because trusting her feels suddenly dangerous.

I've grazed Samson's secrecy a few times over the last two years.

I know the feeling—

I sense the same in his mother now.

She knows something.

Imperatriz stares back.

Butter clears her throat, scooping up a handful of oil and bringing it to her hair. "Let's leave the demigod talk for later. I know the rest of us mortals would rather talk about men. Specifically, the gentleman in the scouting group. The one with the scar on his forehead. I don't mean to be crass, but I want to lick him where he sweats."

The women chortle again before silence falls.

They glance around, once again focusing on Imperatriz.

She glances across our ranks with a sigh. "Take it away, Leda. I know how you enjoy talking about our beloved scouting group."

Leda takes a large breath, turning toward Butter. "That's Wendel 453 Mastet. I was *obsessed* with him as a child. I grew up in Lampades —my mother is the pack leader there. Unfortunately, the incense gave me rashes, and the rashes gave me an awful temper. Most people hate my temper, but I have what most male wolves want—the *triple-b*. Boobs, belly, butt. This body survives Night and makes fat babies. *Fat.* They want them like that, and Wendel..."

It's the start of a ridiculously long bath.

And a tenuous friendship with Brutatalika's pack.

And a budding suspicion that something might be wrong with Imperatriz 713 Afador.

And a desperate desire to see or hear or otherwise sense her demigod amid this frozen wasteland.

A week later, I wake to another guest at the yurt.

Daylight fills the yurt's walls, causing me to flinch. I squint at the flap; a wolf looks to be hunched down, tapping on the taut fabric.

I glance around. The rest of the Bloodies are in a deep sleep.

Esclamonde curls toward me under our shared blanket, hands near her face. Not even Vulcan and Vega, who sleep near the entrance, have stirred. All I can see are frays of white hair poking near their pillow. A gentle rise and fall of their blankets.

With a curse, I use warming magic to seal myself off from the temperature. Even the yurt has started to freeze over the last few days. I pull my robe tight around me and tug the hood over my head before floating over the bedding and toward the door.

I unseal the flap, poking my head out.

I reel back a second later, eyes burning. I clench them shut with a curse.

Imperatriz whispers, "Put these on, then come outside. You may want to float. It snowed."

Something hits my leg, but it takes me a moment to regain my vision. I stare at what she handed me. "What the fuck is this?" It looks like a horizontal piece of wood with two slits cut into either side. A leather cord runs from one end to the other, leaving a good amount of slack.

"It's for your eyes." The Kulapsifang leans down toward the flap's opening, then pulls a similar-looking piece from her forehead down over her eyes; I'm not sure how she can see through the narrow slits. "Come."

With a grumble, I fix the piece into place. Then I follow the wolf as she turns from the yurt, using floating magic to dodge the snow piled on the ground.

Within a moment, I'm fully awake, rattled by the blinding whiteness of the world—even the sky looks lethally pale.

I'd never imagined snow would be like this. So heavy and so cold; so light and so quick to melt. Something that falls silently, that melts silently, that twinkles like a lethal jewel for its short life.

Hefty stacks of white snow blanket the land in every direction. The yurt is half-buried; if I were walking on the ground, the drifts would almost entirely cover me.

My neck bends as I stare around in wonder.

Like the yurt, most of the caravan is buried in white drifts. Amid the flat plains, our camp looks like a series of gentle white slopes, a few chimneys poking from them.

Only the blinding sun is tinged with a golden blush.

Imperatriz heads into the snow, pushing ahead with her hands joined in front of her. I float near her shoulder; it's awkward with the glasses. Though they prevent the snow from blinding me, they narrow my field of vision greatly.

"Where are we going?" I ask. "I can clear a path for you."

"We aren't going far—just to the head of the caravan." She keeps plowing into the snow, leading us away from the yurt and its neighbors. "I've been waiting for heavy snowfall like this. It should make it easier for you to use your sensing magic. Infrasound reacts uniquely to water and snow. That's what Andromeda told me."

I chew on her words as we hike into the abyss of snow.

Imperatriz must be talking about the fact that magic only takes a form when it meets matter. In this case, snow.

My head tilts while I consider her words.

For the first time, I realize I'm a much more advanced witch than my mother would have been. She never absorbed spells from the Hellastone. Never had a warlock like Halcyon to teach her about ejima.

Imperatriz stops with a huff, shoulders rising and falling as she pants. Though we've only gone twenty feet, it's clearly grueling work to walk through the drifts. Condensation fills the air with each of her exhalations. She lets her breath calm, glancing at the sky and then the path south.

Where Bellator waits far in the distant past Velm's dense forests.

"And what am I looking for with sensing magic?" I ask.

Imperatriz tells me, "We've wasted precious time saving the villages. Heading for each one has driven us slowly off track. We should be only a week or two from Bellator. I think we're more like a month away."

My stomach drops.

I've been consoling myself with the idea that we're closing in on the capital city.

Another fucking month of this?

Another month of this cold, this mounting doubt? This painful fucking nearness-but-farness from Samson?

I watch her carefully. "So, you want us to avoid the villages from here on out and beeline for Bellator?"

She sighs shakily. "No. I can't do that. We've found survivors in most."

"Well, I can understand that. So...?"

"When we bathed last week, you mentioned Hetnazzar."

"And?"

"That's what I want you to look for. My demigod. Try to find it using the snow. As far as your magic can go... Just look. Just for my peace of mind."

I clench my jaw, staring ahead and trying not to panic. *Look for her demigod?* The idea makes little sense. A nymph can sense their demigod wherever they wander. The same is true for me, given Vex's magic lives inside my veins and horns.

But Hetnazzar...

Can she really not feel her demigod?

Isn't she supposed to be her people's bridge to the demigod's power?

I was right to question her in the bathing tent.

Have I led the Bloodies astray? Very far astray?

This isn't good.

But I'll have that meltdown in private like a good leader.

For now, I go with, "I can try, but I've never called on a demigod like this. Searching magic would be the easiest method, but I need an object that belongs to the demigod for that to work. Sensing magic is another option. I don't need an object to cast a sensing spell—but I can't send a spell like that across your entire realm. Too broad. Too unfocused. And it would get everyone's attention.

"I could use speaking magic to send a verbal message from you to the demigod, just like whispering magic. But I'm not sure how that would help me in locating Hetnazzar. That's the problem here. Knowing where to find it. Let's see..."

I raise my hands toward the endless tundra.

I lick my lips as I prepare my searching magic. I don't have an item belonging to the demigod, but I do have a memory. It's the easiest place to start. "Cross your fingers. Here goes nothing."

I inhale a deep breath, focusing on the image of Hetnazzar that I remember from a dream in New Hypnos. The demigod had been lounging beneath a yew tree... gnawing on the Hellastone...

The wolf was larger than Samsonfang, its fur blacker and bluer, its eyes gleaming with what looked like constellations. I remember the fatal black of its claws, the cold white of its fangs...

I exhale as I cast searching magic, holding onto the image of Hetnazzar.

I take another deep breath.

For a long moment, nothing happens. I adjust my fingers, trying to think of another spell.

Then a low gurgle of infrasound catches my attention. It echoes from inside my layers where the wand rests against my solar plexus. Imperatriz turns toward me, fixing her gaze on my chest.

I clear my throat, trying not to let my shock show.

The demigod called back to us via the wand.

Which isn't just a wand; it's *my* demigod.

I reach into my sweater's collar, adjusting my warming magic to cradle myself from the chill while I fish out the wand. Like Samson once wore it in Alita, I've taken to wearing the piece like a necklace— so it stays within reach in case of emergency.

I tug it free, holding it in the air for Imperatriz to see.

It glows red with activated magic. Then it spews another gurgle of infrasound.

I stare at it, still in disbelief. It's not overtly surprising that my demigod would interact with Samson's—especially considering Hetnazzar may have bitten the wand free in a dream.

But I had no inkling that Hetnazzar could *reply* to the wand. Apparently, across a great distance.

Like our demigods are fucking conversing.

"What does that mean?" Imperatriz asks.

I clear my throat. "I'm not sure, but I think it's a response. I cast searching magic, and then the wand reacted."

"What kind of response? From Hetnazzar?"

"It's your demigod, Imperatriz. Your guess is better than mine."

I stare at her, desperate to pull apart her expression. But the Kulapsifang looks just as focused and unyielding as she has over the last weeks. Little emotion, only drive.

She tsks. "Well, a howl is more than enough to alert a wolf that you're in the vicinity. So if this is how Hetnazzar responded, my demigod must be out of range." She faces the south again. "Just like I thought."

I follow her gaze. All I see is a hopeless tundra, blurring the snow-filled fields with the horizon of white-gray clouds. "What does that mean?"

"Demigods stay where they are needed most. If there's a portal in my capital, I'd wager it's there." She turns back, retracing the canal she carved through the snow. "It means that whatever is happening near that portal is more urgent than the messes we've been cleaning up along the way. Let's hope the mountains have given shelter to my people." Her dark eyes flash to mine. "Thank you, my dear witch."

Her shoulders sag as she walks back through the snow. I float in her wake, my head cast downward and my belly full of anxiety.

I try to find the right words to give her comfort or confidence, but she continues onward, passing my yurt to push further into the camp without another word.

I watch her go.

The pit in my stomach deepens.

I head back into the yurt, relieved to see Butter is awake. She sits up, blankets bunched over her shoulders. Her white-turquoise curls are frayed and messy, her eyes barely open from sleep.

They fix on me when I shut the yurt flap and sigh. I pull my snow glasses off.

"What the fuck are those?" Butter asks, voice sleepy.

"They protect your eyes. It's blinding out there."

She grunts in response. "All good?"

I glance around the yurt, listening for the sounds of heavy sleepers. After six weeks of yurt-dwelling, I like to think I know the noises well: Esclamonde's heavy breathing, Vulcan and Halcyon's intermittent snorting, and Vega's steady snores.

When I'm confident they're all slumbering peacefully, I fix my gaze on Butter. "You're going to think I'm crazy."

She blinks her half-closed eyes. "I already think that."

I rub my face, striving for clarity. "You heard Imperatriz in the bathing tent—Andromeda has been to Bellator. We need to talk to her. She knows Imperatriz—maybe she's met Hetnazzar, too. We need advice about what the fuck we've gotten ourselves into."

"That's not a bad idea." Butter nods as she fumbles with her bag. "Get a space setup. I need a minute."

I head to the open space between my bedding and Butter's. It isn't much, but one of the support beams is perfectly placed for her to prop the mirror. While she arranges it, I bundle myself with a spare blanket, then cast a smothering spell around me and her.

Once Butter sets the mirror in place, we shuffle into position; her halfway behind the mirror, and me sitting in front of it.

I tell her, "I'll do the talking—but I think you should listen this time."

"Got it." Butter rolls her shoulders, then stretches her neck. "Ready?"

"Ready."

I fix my hair and robe one last time while Butter calls my mother into the magical looking-glass. I fish out the bottle of brandy from my bedding, then take a long swig.

When her image slowly comes into view, I'm struck again by how much the twins took after her. And how young she is. The latter is even more apparent now that I've spent the last six weeks in proximity to her contemporary, Imperatriz.

Andromeda glances around the yurt, eyes darting curiously. "Well, well... What's this lovely little shanty you're in? A bar? I've never been to a bar like this before. You must be someplace in Gamma or Jaws—"

"I'm in Velm."

She goes still, one of her eyebrows arching. "Velm? Why?"

Quickly, I cover our journey, along with a slew of other details about Mieira, Velm, and another world called Zarzynn. To avoid an hour-long deposition, I keep things as simple as possible and focus on our current goals. No direct mention of Anesot or Clearbold or Samson—just helping Velm through a magnificent upheaval.

"Anything you can tell me about the Kulapsifangs, Bellator, and Hetnazzar will help us in the coming weeks."

Andromeda stares at me for a long moment. Strangely, she says, "Well, you should be treading *very* lightly in Velm. Or you shouldn't be there at all, my daughter. I'm surprised you felt inspired to go in the first place."

I stare back, suddenly aware that I don't know how to read my mother's facial expressions. She could be highly unimpressed right now, or worried about me, or possibly even annoyed.

"Tread lightly?" I ask. "With Imperatriz, too?"

"With every wolf, and especially with the Kulapsifangs. I saw Imperatriz's brute. I can't remember his name—the next one. I met him when I spoke with Parsifal for the first time."

Imperatriz's brute?

Andromeda knows not what she says.

Don't freak out.

"His name is Samson 714 Afador." I glance at Butter, wondering if it was wise to ask her to listen in. "Why tread lightly? It sounds like you don't trust any wolf, Kulapsifang or not."

Andromeda snorts. "And why would I? I know that everyone in Mieira likes to pretend the War Years didn't happen, but they did, and every single wolf contributed to the end of the red line."

She says it lightly, but I can sense the glistening edge in her voice.

I sit up straight, eyes narrowing. "The red line continues with me."

She stares back, expression devoid of life. "So long as you bear daughters, and so long as they live to bear their own."

A beat of silence fills the tent.

This is not like our first conversation.

But I need answers.

"Let's focus on Velm for now. Tell me why the Kulapsifangs can't be trusted—and give me a better reason than a blood feud that's centuries old. I told you about Zarzynn. I share enemies with Velm. That's plenty of a reason to work together."

With a tsk, Andromeda looks down at her nails. "Because Imperatriz 713 Afador is a hollow fucking shell of power, and if you ask her what she thinks of me, she will tell you the same." She clears her throat and looks up at me. "But only one of us is right. And I was always much smarter than people gave me credit for."

Butter slides her eyes toward me. I glance back, realizing swiftly that I'm in over my head.

I have no idea where this conversation is heading, but I know it's not going where I'd hoped.

I pivot, glancing around the yurt to make sure no one has stirred; they haven't.

"A *hollow shell of power?*" I shrug. "I'm surprised to hear that.

Imperatriz hasn't made it seem like you two were enemies. A little antagonistic at first, maybe, but—"

"She betrayed me," Andromeda snaps, cold and passionate.

I look down at my hands.

I'd forgotten not to trust witches; I'd forgotten my mother is also a witch first, a mother second.

Amaro.

Papa always said she was bitter. Not refreshing like Milisent, not sweet like me.

And why the fuck had I hoped for something better? Because she swept the wool over my eyes during our first meeting, cajoling and gossiping?

I force my eyes back to Andromeda. She isn't my mother anymore; her face morphs into that of any other witch I've had the grave misfortune of underestimating.

I raise my eyebrows, trying to look unruffled. "Tell me what happened, then."

Andromeda straightens her hair, eyes wandering like she's deep in thought. "Once upon a time in Rhotidom, I stumbled upon a lone wolf only hours from the triplemoon. I'd never seen a wolf on the triplemoon...

"After she turned skin, I stayed and threw gooseberries at her all night. I shook the jacaranda and ilama trees so their pollen fell on her fur. It was spring. I stayed just out of reach.

"When she woke, I introduced myself. To my great surprise, it wasn't just any wolf I'd been harassing. It was the Kulapsifang. My generation's Kulapsifang, only a few years younger than me.

"We stayed together for days.

"I was curious about her.

"And Imperatriz was fascinated by me. She asked so many questions. Too many questions, without any respect. Like she'd been born to receive answers. Like I'd been born to give them to her."

Andromeda glances at me, an exasperated look in her red eyes. It takes me a second to realize she thinks I'm going to commiserate with her.

I could; I remember how brooding and reticent Samson was when we left Luz to find Oko long ago. It had grated on me in almost every way imaginable—emotionally, mentally, and even physically.

But I don't admit that.

Andromeda watches me, waiting for a response. When I stay quiet, she goes on, "So it went for a while. We would meet, and she would badger me, thinking we were bonding. She asked what color I was once—and I knew I had been right not to trust her. She wanted to see my horns, to learn about a witch's power, and where it comes from, and how it can be used. It felt like every question was a piece of me taken away.

"Like I was something to be picked apart and dissected.

"I had this feeling... that if she could, she would have kept me like a trinket on a shelf.

"Years passed. She married Clearbold, and that changed things. Compared to *him*, I found Imperatriz to be much more levelheaded. And... her marriage changed her. She'd been a girl before, with questions and stupid opinions, and then she was a woman, full of wisdom and quiet disappointment.

"She'd been hurt by him. I don't know how. Just that she was different after they married, and I liked her more with sharper edges.

"When she invited me to Bellator after ascending the throne, I went. It was the first time I felt she and I could be real allies. Imperatriz would lead me into the marble city, and I would be the first wielder ever allowed into Bellator Palace. We would commiserate on the misery of finding a husband and bearing children."

My stomach drops.

The other day, during our bath, Imperatriz didn't say she'd taken my mother into the palace—only the city.

The palace... and all its rooms...

Fuck, fuck, fuck.

"Prepare yourself, Helisent. It will bowl you over—how fucking massive the palace is, how the wolves managed to build such a thing without magic. It's a marvel, I'll admit. But I had made a grave mistake—not in coming to Bellator, but in coming to Bellator with trust in Imperatriz. Clearbold was my enemy; I thought that made Imperatriz a friend."

Andromeda shakes her head, jaw stiff. "But she betrayed me."

I stare into her eyes.

She thinks I don't know about the horns.

Butter squirms, as though uncomfortable. I can feel her urgently watching me, but I don't look away from Andromeda.

The witch goes on, "From the outside, you can see two rooms that are taller than the rest of the palace. The first is the throne room, where the Alphas sit in counsel. Behind the thrones is a little door... a little door that leads to the tallest room in Bellator Palace."

She shakes her head again, expression suddenly bereft. Her voice quivers, her lips tremble. "Pereline was sick. And Milisent wasn't born yet. I wasn't even positive that Parsifal was the warlock for me. Do you understand? I was... I was close to being the *last*... and that thought..."

I clench my jaw, staring at her.

The last.

My body shivers like my mother's.

An angry tear slips from Andromeda's eyes. "I don't know how you can do it—"

"Say it," I snap. "Just tell me what happened."

"She took me into the tallest room and I couldn't..." Feature by feature, her face twists into a mask of rage and sorrow. "I had never imagined..."

"The room is full of red horns," I grit out, desperate to move past this part. "I already know about it. Samson told me. Tell me what happened next."

"It doesn't matter, Helisent. Nothing will prepare you to see it."

I lift my chin. "I've survived far worse—"

"It wasn't just the horns. It was the fact that Imperatriz thought she was bonding us when she did that. She thought she was sharing a secret, and this secret would comfort me and lend to our trust. Evil had been waiting in me my whole life. And this was why." A few more tears fall down her cheeks. She growls, "I would not let it go."

My body shakes with anguish and dread.

The only question now is how viciously she responded—*a well-timed betrayal? A magical curse? A direct act of vengeance?*

Andromeda's voice rises. "This woman had befriended me after she had grown up sitting in that room. And she expected me to *thank her*. To help her pave the way for the Northing." She raises her chin, laughing without humor. "So, I gave her what she wanted."

I lean toward the mirror. "And what was that?"

Andromeda smiles venomously with tear-stained cheeks. "I tied us together. Just like she'd dreamed."

I shake my head, looking at Butter as I attempt to pull apart her statement. She looks back at me, eyes wide with alarm. The mirror shifts as she adjusts her legs, as though eager to stand.

I look back at Andromeda. "Tied you and her together? What does that mean?"

"Literally, Helisent—with a cursed red string. I called forth all that is owed to me and my descendants."

Ringing starts in the distance.

A cursed red string…

"I called in the debt incurred by the horns hung in that room. I cursed her."

No.

No.

No.

I jolt back like Butter, eager to stand—maybe to run, maybe to hide.

This is worse than I could have imagined.

This is the opposite of help.

This is…

My voice is a breathless whisper. "You cursed her?"

Her voice keeps shaking, her words fast and livid, "Not just Imperatriz—all of the Afadors. *All these fucking wolves who will sit in that room and meditate on our genocide—*"

"*You cursed Samson 714 Afador?*"

She huffs a terrible laugh. "All of them. There will be no peace for the Afadors until the debt is filled."

I slam my hands onto the soft bedding. I try to ignore my body, my mind, my heart—they're all roaring with separate thoughts and impulses.

Right now, all that matters is: "What were the exact terms of the curse?"

"Such things—"

"*Tell me.*"

"Helisent, you're—"

"I am greater than you could have ever dreamed, and if you don't tell me the truth," I rise onto my knees, prepared to bare my hands toward the mirror, "I will kill myself, find you in the afterlife, and then *kill you again.*"

Andromeda blinks at me, utterly still.

Butter does the same.

I can't tell who is more speechless.

In case they're not taking me seriously, I growl, "Do you doubt me?"

Andromeda finds her voice first. "I cast a blessed curse. It will compensate for the incredible losses our people suffered during the War Years. I left the terms open. The magic will call forth an offering. Maybe more than one. Whatever it needs to give survival and longevity back to our people. I tied the curse to a red string and gave it to Imperatriz. She thought it was a blessing."

I can't begin to process this.

I can't begin to forecast how this will change my future. How it will change Samson's.

Brutatalika's, even.

I shake my head. The hit keeps landing over and over. "Does Parsifal know that you did this?"

Andromeda stares at her nails again, flaring them out. "Not explicitly. He knows that I... did something... I should have thought twice about."

'*A blessed curse.*'

It's a polite name for a curse of forceful compensation. The only reason it's called *blessed* is that it can only be cast reliably when someone owes a substantial and objective debt. It will follow down generational lines; patient, unyielding, final.

The blessed curse is the only way to ensure a debt is paid.

Not an act of vengeance, but one of balance.

A debt for close to seven hundred sets of Vexen horns. For nearly ending the red line.

I try to quantify this—

Okay. She was angry—very angry—and Imperatriz clearly fucked up— but I'm not my mother—I'm not my mother—I'm not my mother—

Maybe it isn't so bad.

Then I see a red string in my mind's eye.

I have seen these before; so has Samson.

I sit back.

It's okay—they're just red strings—they're just dreams—they're just spells —and I am more powerful than my mother—

Then I see an unnumbered wolf in my mind, his body dotted with circles of light outside Coil's tower room.

Gautselin swears seethings aren't real.

What if...

What if this is what has bound me to Samson?

Not love, not a seething.

A curse.

What if this is why Imperatriz has been throwing me off over the last weeks?

Not only the absence of her demigod.

But a curse, too.

"The debt will be filled," Andromeda says, voice low. "It's out of your hands, Helisent."

"Fuck you."

I gesture toward Butter. She's sat at the ready, studying my face with wide eyes. She taps on the mirror's back; within seconds, Andromeda's face starts to fade from the glass. My mother says something and reaches out, but I stare at my hands, descended into a world of confusion and pain and shock.

When I look up again, I see only my face in the looking glass: reddened cheeks, wild and teary eyes, downturned lips.

I clear my throat, glancing at Butter. "Don't tell anyone." I wipe my cheeks as she calmly tilts the mirror's glass downward. "I mean it, Butter. Not even Halcyon. No one can know. Not until I figure out how to tell Samson."

She releases a long breath as she shrinks the mirror down to its portable size. Her hands shake lightly as she opens her bottomless bag and slides it back inside. "You don't have to ask me twice. No one will know."

"I didn't know," I whisper, voice shaking.

"I know you didn't." Butter scoots toward me, opening her arms. I fall into them, curled into a ball. "It doesn't change anything, okay?"

I shake my head where it rests against her shoulder.

How can she say that?

This news changes *everything*.

Worse, I don't feel any better about Imperatriz or Velm.

Instead, I have the same feeling I once did in an empty theatre in Alita when I learned that Anesot had manipulated Samson. In that instant, I'd questioned everything, including the wolf's love for me. I do the same now.

I question myself.

I've never trusted witches; I've also never clumped myself into the traditional witch category, but what would really make me so different?

I don't say anything.

Just buckle and weep against Butter. She strokes my back, calming me with gentle coos.

Eventually, she says, "You know, my mom's a bitch, too."

CHAPTER 17

SHE'S HIDING SOMETHING

SAMSON

Overhead, the sister mountains of Baladhari and Meledhari welcome me back to Bellator.

White snow clings to their purple-gray faces as they rise parallel into the sky.

Between them is a keyhole-like passage that leads from Velm's forested hills to its marble-plated capital.

Above, an archway of stark white marble connects Baladhari and Meledhari. Two brackets jut from it—

There's no longer a flag hanging in its place.

Instead, a heavy, narrow object dangles from a rope tied to the archway. Though we're close, I can't tell what it is from a distance. It swings back and forth, pasted with frozen snow like everything else in the dead of Night.

I stare ahead, vexed by my return to Bellator.

In the east, the sun rises, warming the gray sky. Stood near the towering treeline of Velm's thickest forests, the sun hasn't yet grazed us.

I'm eager for more light; eager for the chance to figure out what's hanging from the narrow pass that leads into Bellator. At my side, Imperatriz pops onto her toes, squinting.

We're a short walk from the stairs that lead overhead.

And yet, there's no hint that Bellator is occupied by Leolites and their Zarzynnian allies.

A spotless field of snow stands between us and the stairs.

No footsteps cut through the fresh powder. No spies seem to be watching from the mountains. No trails or hunting paths leading out of the capital or into it.

No signs of life at all.

Until this point, I've been squarely focused on keeping the caravan in order and moving; keeping the wolves in my orbit well-fed and well-rested; keeping my mother's spirits high.

It's gone well despite the hardships.

Now, staring at Baladhari and Meledhari, a great thrumming nothing sweeps through me.

I'm relieved, apprehensive, and uncertain all at once.

I'm numb, too.

Numb to this place. To what happened to my life the last time I walked through that mountain pass.

Helisent, Halcyon, and Vega stand nearby. A whir of infrasound surrounds them, sheltering the wielders from the bitter chill. They stand facing the mountain pass, chins lifted and eyes narrowed as they cast their investigatory spells.

With no signs of life visible, my mother asked the wielders to check on the city magically.

Halcyon's head twitches like he's hearing a far-off melody. Vega closes her eyes, lifting her hands and spreading her fingers as she concentrates.

Helisent chews her lip, head angled slightly away from me. Her velvet robe is pulled tight around her, its hood framing her face. She snaps out of it before Halcyon or Vega, looking at my mother. "Well, it's fucked, Imperatriz. The city is bleeding magic on the other side of the mountain pass."

Imperatriz nods without looking away from Baladhari and Meledhari. "I need specifics. How is it fucked? What sorts of spells have been cast?"

The red witch sighs. "I don't know. It's not my magic. It's from the Houses of Serac and Argyd. Halcyon or Vega might be able to sense specific spells."

Her words are patient, her tone soft.

It's uncharacteristic enough that I study her from the corner of my eye. She looks and smells healthy. Her brown skin is soft and supple despite the cold and its frosted gales. Even her nails look impeccably clean.

But I'm convinced there's something wrong.

Over the last weeks, Helisent's behavior has changed. Though we're physically near, we're emotionally distant. I don't know why she seems gloomy and short-tempered. Why she speaks to Imperatriz in such an appeasing tone all of a sudden. She's never been prone to bouts of sadness, which makes me wonder. (And stew.)

Halcyon turns to my mother next. "It's not just a spell or two. I can sense *layers* of Seracyd magic. Most of the spells are fixed, surrounding the city. They feel like a standard set of defensive spells. I'm not sure how complex they are from here. I can also sense a very dense cluster of magic. Seracyd magic, specifically. But I don't know where it is, exactly."

Vega stuffs her hands back into her pockets with a shiver. "The same for Argyd magic. I can tell that it's pooled around one specific area of the city, but I can't offer you anything more. Not from here. If I had to guess, I'd say we're sensing a portal." She pinches her lips together, glancing at Halcyon. "My power doubled after Ezit was destroyed. I wouldn't mind putting it to use. However you'd like, Imperatriz."

Imperatriz nods at the young witch. "That's good to hear. Thank you. Can any of you sense whether there are still wielders in the city? If the spells are fixed, maybe the wielders have moved on."

Halcyon and Vega glance at one another. The warlock explains, "We can't sense that—at least, not from here. But fixed spells still need a power source. It's unusual for a wielder to cast an extensive and complex spell, then leave the area—especially in a time of uncertainty like this."

Vega nods. "Wielders stay close to their active spells in case they need tending."

"And there's no way a Host would leave their portal unguarded," Halcyon adds.

"I see," Imperatriz turns away, setting her hands on her hips and staring down, deep in thought.

I study the seam of darkness between Baladhari and Meledhari, the pale and heavy object hanging from its marble archway.

I glance at Helisent and catch her watching me; she quickly looks at the ground, as though shy.

What the fuck is going on with the witch?

(I have a few theories. First, she did something she regrets. Second, she's nervous about being in Velm. Third, she recently slept with Zeu and is worried I'll find out. Fourth, nothing is going on with the witch, I'm just helplessly obsessed.)

Imperatriz looks back, focusing on Helisent. "I'd rather get eyes on the city sooner rather than later. Certainly, before we make a plan. Can you accompany Samson and me to the pass?"

The witch nods. "Sure."

My mother raises her eyebrows. "It's possible we'll run into trouble." She scans the witch. "Are you... prepared?"

Helisent glances down, as though confused. "Sure. I'm not shy."

Imperatriz turns to the other wielders. "Halcyon, please return to camp and let the others know we'll rest through the daylight like usual. Once the three of us have seen the city, we'll return and make a plan. Please look alive in the meantime. You and Butter will watch over the caravan while we're gone."

Without another glance, Imperatriz turns toward the sister mountains and takes off into the snow.

The drifts are hip-high this time of year. In the dead of Night, few wolves would choose to travel—and, unlike us, those who were forced to would have snowshoes. Over the last few weeks, we've taken to asking the wielders to clear our path. Without their leveling magic, we'd only be halfway here, still shoveling through fields of snow.

With a wave, Halcyon and Vega turn back to our camp. It's spread amid the trees, not nearly as compact as the plains. As far as I can see, tents and busy wolves fill the woodland.

Helisent watches them go, then turns to study the snow-covered slope leading toward the mountain pass. With a flick of her fingers, infrasound shivers ahead of us, clearing a narrow path that reveals the marble steps.

Imperatriz takes off.

We follow, the witch pulling her cloak tight around her shoulders. One step later, I tug on her cloak's sleeve.

I'm tempted to mouth the words, '*What the fuck happened?*'

Instead, "You may want your lilith. For the stairs, at least."

Surrounded by white snow, her red eyes have never looked more vibrant. It's hard to look away.

I wish she could read my mind; I wish she could answer my mounting questions.

(Are you no longer in love with me after what you've seen in Velm? Have I failed my people and failed you, too? Are you sleeping with Zeu?)

"Right." Helisent reaches into her bottomless bag to pull out her lilith. My mother keeps walking ahead of us, taking the steps two at a time.

Once the witch is comfortable, we take the stairs together.

I gulp, staring at the mountain pass overhead.

More memories, more anxiety, more uncertainty whirl through me as we ascend.

The last time I climbed these stairs, I had Rex on my right side and Berevald on my left.

I can feel their ghosts. I look around as though I might see them outlined with fragile snowflakes and wind.

The jingle of ornaments from Helisent's lilith gives me strength. I don't know why, but I like to think that the ghosts of Rex and Berevald can hear them.

That they'll know in the wake of those sounds arrives the witch, along with the wolf.

That their ghosts know their remains will be found, that their ashes will be sheltered inside urns, and then mourned deeply.

When we reach the landing, Helisent tucks her lilith away. Like Imperatriz, I study the area's untouched snow, searching for signs of spies or enemies. Wind soars through the narrow pass, kicking up the snow and carrying it all around.

When it settles, we tilt our heads back to study the object hanging from the archway overhead.

With a curse, I realize the object hanging overhead is yet another half-naked, frozen corpse. The wolf is strung up by a half-frozen rope, wrapped around the neck. The wolf's arms are stuck to their sides, a tangle of dark fabric bunched around their hips and thighs. Their legs are fused, bare toes clumped together like blueish nubs. I can't see their face at all; it might be wrapped in dark fabric or frozen hair.

The corpse swings lightly as wind batters against the purple-gray mountains again.

I step back when the scent hits me—a familiar ala curdled into a foul, frosted death.

Imperatriz hisses, low and angry.

My heart starts to ratchet.

I force down a breath, eyes locked on the pale toes overhead.

I was right. Clearbold didn't stand a chance against Ezit's Hosts.

Helisent glances from me to my mother. "Do you want me to... take them down?"

Imperatriz levels a wrathful, crazed look at the witch. "No. I think he looks nice like this. Watching over Velm. Clearbold was always such a vigilant Alpha."

Helisent groans, glancing overhead again. "Oh. I see."

For how much I've craved my father's death, I never considered what it would be like to smell his corpse.

It smells like me. Like danger. Like home. Like insecurity.

A legacy.

I glance at my mother. She paces, looking from the corpse to the mountain pass. My heart rate hasn't calmed since scenting Clearbold's corpse—and it's not for grief or surprise. It's from the shocking disappointment.

Had we found him alive, I would have had the chance to forsake Clearbold.

It's clear now.

I would have found him in Bellator. When my mother was satisfied with her vengeance, I would have imprisoned him.

Long enough for Clearbold to watch me succeed.

Long enough for Clearbold to see the Northing.

And that would have killed him. To see me thrive.

His death is yet another punishment.

I will never have this opportunity. Worse, after eighteen years,

Imperatriz won't have the chance to take her vengeance on Clearbold, or hurl an insult at him, or even make eye contact with him again. He died without confronting her ala or her will or her triumph.

She growls, "Fuck."

I glance at Helisent. She watches Imperatriz with a lowered chin. Almost like a nervous child.

With another growl, Imperatriz takes off through the mountain pass.

I follow the Kulapsifang, nervous about what waits on the other side. The wind blasts against us, forceful enough that the witch yelps and I grab her arm. We lower our heads to forge ahead; the wind dies down as soon as the narrow passage opens onto the opposite landing. There, we face another snowy scene.

The stairs descending below are covered in spotless snow, like those we just took. No guards, no spells, no footsteps in the white powder.

Bellator spills into the valley below; peaceful, undisturbed. Purple-gray mountains loom tall on all sides of the city, veiled with snow and gray mist that looks almost alive. The oaks, maples, and linden trees have all withered for Night. Like the two-story, marble-plated buildings, they're buried in snow. The square and rectangular parks are also smears of blinding white, layered with grayish footpaths.

The broad streets are clean and empty. The barns were repainted with a fresh coat of yellow before the coming of Night. The narrow chimneys chug heavy gray smoke.

I trace the streets that outline the city's distinct neighborhoods.

Safe, unharmed.

But there are no wolves visible—not in the windows, not walking or hustling along the streets, not loitering near entrances to taverns or schools, not driving their livestock in and out of the yellow-paneled barns.

Imperatriz says, "You and the Bloodies could sense fixed spell-work. Do you have any more clarity from here?"

Helisent's eyes roam across the city. "I sense bindings, illusions, and smothering spells in the outermost streets. They're not particularly potent, but they are complex. It feels like they've been in place for months."

She raises her hand to outline the city, explaining, "What we're seeing right now is a lie, Imperatriz. There are layers of spellwork designed to mislead us." Her finger straightens, pointing at Bellator Palace. "Then there's the palace. That's where most of the spellwork is concentrated. The spells are potent and violent. I'm not sure what's happening in the palace, but it feels like a stronghold."

"Whose stronghold?" she asks. "Seracyd and Argyd wielders?"

"I can't say who is in the palace, only that Seracyd and Argyd magic is protecting it."

Imperatriz hisses, eyes locked on the cubic palace. "Can you dismantle the spells?"

"My magic destroyed Ezit. Untangling a few fixed spells shouldn't be too dire. That won't be our greatest problem here." She gestures to Bellator Palace once again. "Samson, that's where you thought Clearbold would have let Suleiman build his portal? Inside the palace, right?"

I nod, glancing at the two tallest rooms that jut from the palace's rear. "Exactly."

The narrow, square rooms rise higher than the rest; the horn room is almost a floor taller than the throne room.

And I swear Helisent's finger is pointing straight at it.

She goes on, "I'll dismantle the spells that encase the city, but we need to take a more measured approach with the palace. I need to be close to the portal to dismantle it. It'll take time and effort to undo. There's also the question of my horns. I'd hate to damage them. They might still hold Vexen magic."

I glance from the witch to my mother.

At first, I'd wondered if the witch's strange behavior could be related to the horns in the palace—but Helisent doesn't seem vengeful or even annoyed by being in their proximity right now.

In fact, the witch has handled each of Imperatriz's requests with quaint acceptance, not with sass or a bribe or a bit of light extortion.

She hasn't referenced all that Imperatriz has asked of her during these past months.

Not even now that we're discussing the horns.

The witch is hiding something, after all.

My gut clenches, but Imperatriz doesn't react to her words. She keeps studying the city closely, as though moving street by street.

Without looking at the witch, she says, "Samson mentioned that you were... aware of the room."

"Yes." Helisent looks down at her nails. "Also, what kind of stone is marble? An oread once told me that there are three main categories of rock. Marble isn't sedimentary, is it?"

She knows something.

The thought grows in force, taking hold.

I watch the witch as she stares at the palace. Her red eyes stew.

"Neither," Imperatriz says. "I believe the Mieiran term is *metamorphic*. Marble is a metamorphic stone created from extreme heat. And why are you asking?"

"Because Vex is a demigod of stone and your palaces and homes are at least partly made of stone. Of *marble*. I can sense my horns from here, which means—if it had wanted to—my magic would have delved into your precious marble walls.

"Do you understand? The horns are full of latent magic. Your palace is full of stone. The real question is... why didn't my magic come *here* after I destroyed my Landmark in Zarzynn?

"This should have been the first stop... The horns are already here, and they're surrounded by marble. Unless..."

She gasps, setting a hand on her forehead, like a headache is coming on.

With a groan, Helisent says, "We're fucking idiots."

She knows something.

Like me, Imperatriz seems to toil over that sentence.

"Idiots?" my mother asks.

The witch looks into the valley, pointing nondescriptly around the mountains. "The Hosts didn't solely come here because Clearbold was keeping an eye on Anesot for them.

"Maybe that's how it started, but the Houses...

"The Houses rely on healthy Landmarks. And I doubt Zarzynn's Landmarks are thriving right now." She looks at me, concluding, "The House of Glaciers probably likes Velm's endless fucking cold. Are there a lot of geysers around here, by any chance?"

Imperatriz turns toward the witch. I do, too, consumed by those words.

Serac: House of Glaciers.

Argot: House of Geysers.

Velm's southwestern mountains are rich in both. Some regions are home to lakes fed by glaciers hidden in the valleys. Others are dotted with hot springs that spew boiling water year-round.

I haven't once put that together over the last months—not even when directly discussing what either House could be after in Velm.

It's too extreme to imagine Hosts in Velm—nonetheless, two demigods and their ecological Landmarks.

Here. In Velm.

The witch sighs, "That would also explain why the Houses of Col and Talos are in Septegeur. The sandstone pillars should be familiar enough to a demigod of cliffs. And some pillars have waterfalls woven through them—super beautiful. Also worthy of a demigod."

Like a two-legged selkie, the witch quietly prophesies, "It even answers why Hetnazzar hasn't come to our aid. It isn't watching the portal, but watching foreign demigods... delve." After a long sigh, she pivots toward Imperatriz. "Can I ask you something?"

For the first time since the pair met, Imperatriz slides her eyes toward me and, in their blue-black hue, I see the gleam of mistrust.

She looks back at the witch. "Of course."

"What did you think of Andromeda?"

Imperatriz glances at me again; no longer mistrust, but confusion. Distress. She shakes her head, surprised by the question. "Most of the time, I felt that she was the only being in the world who could understand me."

"Oh." Helisent clears her throat. "That's nice."

"Is it?" With a roll of her shoulders, Imperatriz steps in front of us to focus on the palace. "I'm happy enough to follow your lead into the palace—both in respect to the portal and protecting your horns.

"In the meantime, I'd like to see the real Bellator."

Helisent arches an eyebrow. "Of course. But we'll be giving our presence away—assuming the city isn't already aware."

Imperatriz looks at her, deadpan. "Are you frightened?"

"Only of the right things." Helisent turns to study the city. "Let's see what they've done, then..."

For at least thirty minutes, she huffs and paces, raising her hands and then lowering them. She talks to herself, saying things like, 'That won't work, ' 'Wow, who the fuck thought of this, ' and 'I should be writing this down'. Aside from two small gesticulations of her fingers, she doesn't do a thing.

Finally, she pauses, taking a deep breath.

She slings one hand back, then reaches forward as though tossing a rock as far as she can. A ripple of infrasound crackles from her fingertips and lashes through the air like a clap of thunder.

The skeletal trees shake, then the drifts of snow rise into the air and dissipate into fine powder as the bass shakes the ground, the valley, the mountains around us.

As the snow gently resettles, burying every surface with a white residue, a new Bellator comes into focus.

My stomach drops.

Debris litters the city. The remnants of buildings and their innards are strewn across the streets and wide avenues. I don't see a single yellow-paneled barn in the parks. The plaza stretching before Bellator Palace is piled with what look to be corpses. Their limbs are splayed like pale bones, their navy blue layers half-buried. A few fires gnaw at buildings throughout the city, clogging the sky with dark smoke.

Only two streets look to be in use.

One connects Bellator Palace to a few undisturbed square blocks. The other leads from Bellator Palace into the thick forest that hugs the city's eastern streets.

I squint at the first path, following it to the city's southwestern neighborhoods. Piles of wood and stone encircle the untouched streets. They tower like makeshift palisades around the clean buildings. I can't smell anything from this distance, but it's obvious that whatever wolves have managed to survive the siege of Bellator are within its walls.

I shake my head, more anxious by the second. The Hosts know we're here; they've likely known we're on the way for weeks.

Why not stop us?

I study the plaza before Bellator Palace with a long sigh.

I was meant to be the first corpse dumped onto the cold marble court.

Neither my mother nor the witch seems to register the latent danger; I will never be so foolish again.

Imperatriz points toward the area blocked with palisades. "Please fortify the barricades for the survivors. We'll return at night with a plan. By the next light, my capital will be free."

With another grand gesture, Helisent's infrasound fizzles into the air. This time, all I see is a few of the boards and barricades shift into new positions.

Imperatriz turns on her heels quickly enough that her black cloak flares behind her. Helisent takes off in her wake, as though afraid of being alone with me. With another sigh, I follow them back into the dark mountain pass. It leads into a tunnel of bitter, icy wind, then back into a world of blaring white snow and emerald, evergreen forest.

Neither spares a glance at my father's corpse hanging overhead.

But I pause for a moment.

I look up.

I don't think I've ever seen his feet before.

I don't know why—I can't get over that.

That this is the first moment I've seen his soles.

I pause to tell them, "I fucking told you."

We sit in counsel for the rest of the day, sealed into a light-tight tent as we devise a plan to retake the palace, then the city.

On one side of the tent sit the Bloodies. On the other are me, Brutatalika, and Imperatriz.

"Samson is right," Zeu reasons, staring down at a map of Bellator spread between us. He shakes his head, deep in thought. "The Hosts are aware we're here, which means they wanted us to make it to Bellator, which means we have something they want." The King of Night tsks, frustrated. "And what the *fuck* is that?"

"No, their focus is the portal," Helisent insists, pointing toward the palace. "Who gives a fuck what we're doing? They have the portal to bring over wielders and their Landmarks. They've had one for months. That's what they've been doing—bringing over their best and brightest."

"No," says the King of Night in a low, distracted voice. "They would have done that very quickly. Right at the start. Before anyone knew about the portal."

Imperatriz shifts her gaze to Halcyon. "Samson thinks Suleiman might have forged the portal. If that's the case, you'd be our best bet at dismantling it." She slides her eyes toward Vulcan, who sits behind Halcyon with his arms crossed and a pout on his face. "You or your son. Or both of you together."

"Vulcan will stay and defend the caravan with Vega, like you suggested," Halcyon says. He stares at the map, ignoring Vulcan's scoff and the way he nudges his father with his foot. "Calypso and I will enter the palace. I think being Seracyd will make it easy to dismantle the portal, but I'll still need her and Helisent's help."

"Wonderful, I'll be there every step of the way," the witch chirps. With a devious little smile, her eyes leap around the group. "And then I get Suleiman."

"Everyone is aware, Helisent," Imperatriz says. "No need to repeat yourself."

"So, what are we waiting for?" she goes on. "The sun is setting, everyone is suited up. Zeu's den has all their little daggers shone. Imperatriz, nice red axe. Love it. I think—"

"We haven't figured out what they're after," Zeu cuts in, glaring at the witch and then gesturing to my mother. "Also, Imperatriz is leading the charge this time."

"We have a powerful necromancer in our presence," Brutatalika offers. "If it's true that the portal in Bellator was simply a passageway for wielders and their demigods, then the city matters little. If the portal has served its purpose, then defending the city also matters little. But Ezit is empty of its necromancers, and a portal works two ways."

'A portal works two ways.'

I hadn't thought of that possibility yet—that Seracyd and Argyd wielders might be here to take pieces of my realm to Zarzynn.

Zeu nods, eyes darting across the map. "Good point. Then I suggest this—I'll enter the palace first with Helisent and Esteban. Suleiman and Kessrys will want to get rid of Helisent immediately—it makes sense for us to handle the most dangerous offensives first. Once we've gotten rid of the Hosts, or at least one of them, we'll call Halcyon and Butter in to work on the portal." He clears his throat, gesturing to Imperatriz. "If you like."

'Want to get rid of her immediately.'

I look at the witch, from her tiny hands to her smug expression, as nausea spreads through me.

This doesn't get any easier, does it?

I remember the weeks leading to our invasion of Ezit.

How afraid I'd been for Helisent's safety. For the outcome of that night.

I feel it again now, condensed into a single fleeting afternoon. Time is strange like that. Eighteen years of waiting for my mother; five months of marching across the continent; a single night to win Bellator back. Time moves in waves that gain and gain and gain before collapsing into themselves.

Imperatriz looks at Zeu, features stiff. "I'm satisfied with that." She takes a deep breath, turning to me. "Samson, you will enter the city with Hadadrimmon. Brutatalika will come with me.

"Once Helisent gives the signal, the four of us will raid the palace with Zeu's den. The rest of the wolves will offer support as needed.

"We don't need to spare anyone we find inside—but I'd like to speak with Malachai, Suleiman, or Kessrys. We need answers. Desperately."

She shifts her hands to her thighs, staring at the map one last time. Then she stands and heads for the tent's entrance, Brutatalika hot on her heels.

She pauses to look back, glancing over our ranks. "In case I fall, then Samson 714 Afador leads Velm. In case Samson 714 Afador also falls, then Bruatalika 567 Sigivald assumes control of Bellator. And if we all die, Bruatalika's pack will oversee the reformation of Velm with the help of the Fifty."

She tugs aside the tent's flap, checking that the sun has sunken past the horizon. Then she turns back, chin held high. "The sun has set. The world is dark. We are ready.

"Let it be known that I have been honored by your presence during this journey. Hetnazzar, too. Thank you for your bravery and strength. *De segen it tauma-kuro Kelnazzar*, my friends."

The women turn away without another word, leaving the tent's blackened flap swinging in her wake. Rather than sit in tangled silence, the rest of us follow.

Outside, the sun has slipped behind the mountains hugging Bellator. The distended light reflects off the glittering snow, filling the air with the peachy gold of dusk.

We follow Imperatriz and Brutatalika as they beeline toward the stairs that lead between the sister mountains.

Dozens more filter from their tents. The wolves hang back, gathering in columns behind Zeu's warmongers. Like they once did in Ezit, the vampires wear holsters across their bodies. The harnesses keep sheathed blades of all sizes tucked against their thick, skin-tight layers. The wolves are bundled, axes and knives strapped to their hips like the rest of our ranks.

Only Imperatriz carries a red axe.

It's stark against her black cloak, against the white snow as she leads us toward the stairs.

Hadadrimmon comes to my side, then we take our place following the female wolves.

My stomach is in knots.

I can't verify that my mother and my wife are ready. Both had seemed steady and confident when they turned away from me—but even a split second of hesitancy yields harsh repercussions.

Hadadrimmon says nothing, but I can hear his heart thump in his chest.

He certainly isn't ready for what comes next. Only two other wolves survived the mayhem of Ezit; neither managed to survive Bellator's cruelty.

I turn to double-check that Helisent and Zeu haven't lost their nerve. They're walking a few steps behind Hadadrimmon and me, the mentee squished between them. Behind them are Butter and Halcyon.

I hate that Zeu's presence comforts me.

I hate that I'm secretly relieved he'll protect the witch.

We reach the top of the stairs. Like most of the group, Hadadrimmon's neck tilts as he stares overhead and takes in Clearbold's corpse.

Imperatriz looks over her shoulder, eyes darting across the groups as they trail us up to the landing.

Zeu's denmates are separated into three troops of seven; hundreds of wolves have been organized into similarly small groups behind them. They'll spread throughout the city, looking for lone survivors and smaller groups that were separated from the main barricade.

Satisfied with our formation, Imperatriz leads us through the mountain pass onto the next landing.

Now that night has fallen, darkness blankets Bellator's streets.

Only the stark gleam of white snow and marble reflects light from the moons, hidden behind a spread of thin clouds.

Like Imperatriz, I don't stare at the city, but into the sky.

In it stretches a perfect silence—one that's full of the half-formed hopes of sleep, of winter, of all that must be achieved with waiting. It's a heavy and palpable sort of peace; not quite the ecstatic edge of desita from a nymph demigod nor the raw power of a wielder demigod.

Something slightly more refined and yet harder to define.

Hetnazzar.

Staring into the living hum of Night, I hear a howl echoing from far away.

It soars through the air, just as palpable as a bass-filled spell.

Hetnazzar's howl spans the sky like a battle cry.

The hairs on my arms and neck stand up in response.

The demigod is close by, at last.

We aren't too late. We aren't alone. We aren't forsaken.

Adrenaline courses through me as my gaze fixes on the palace.

Imperatriz starts down the stairs quickly, descending into Bellator.

CHAPTER 18

WHEN ARE YOU GONNA LEARN?

HELISENT

Honey Baby,
Don't choose Zeu. We don't care what his mother's name was.
The Boys

"Do we need to go over the plan again?"

Imperatriz looms over me, eyes darting from my face to the palace nearby.

She looks little like the woman I've known over the last months. Her jaw and brow are tense with concentration, her lips thin and pulled into a grimace. The blue is gone from her dark eyes.

Much like the fields of snow surrounding Bellator, the palace is like a wall of white—at least fifty feet tall, almost like a mountain.

A single gated entrance stands before us; the wooden barricade is locked and layered with complex defensive spells. Though I undid most of the city's latent spellwork, I saved the palace for last, preferring a more direct approach.

Time to concentrate, Helisent.

Our tiny army shifts into formation on the grand marble arena behind me.

Bodies are scattered around the ground, wrapped in the tattered remnants of clothes. Left here as an insult, maybe a threat.

I look from Imperatriz to the palace.

Though it's by far greater than any construction I've seen in Mieira, it doesn't quite add up to Ezit's mammoth scale. The walls almost look fragile, their marble glistening and dainty.

Zeu shifts around Imperatriz, lifting his eyebrows. Much like the Female Alpha, he's switched into warmonger mode; he's jumpy, his eyes roving from shadow to shadow like they did on the triplemoon in Ezit. The harnesses, the serious gaze, the tense stance.

"Helisent?" he asks. "Did you hear the question?"

The Female Alpha goes on, "As soon as you give the signal—a little voice magic will do—Halcyon and Calypso will follow you into the palace. The rest of us will follow shortly after."

I look from the wolf to the vampire. "Ready when you two are."

Samson stands nearby, gaze fixed on the palace. At his side, Hadadrimmon shifts from one foot to the next. Beside them are Halcyon and Butter; the pair lock their hands together in a white-knuckle grip.

Then there's Esclamonde. The mentee stands behind me, almost hugging my back like a shadow.

"Begin, then," Imperatriz commands, her voice low.

I walk ahead of the group, a smile on my face.

Unlike the invasion of Ezit, I'm not nervous about what comes next. My demigod is safe in Tet, and now I'm driven by wrath instead of fear. Only part of it is directed at Suleiman and what he did to Samson; the rest is reserved for Andromeda. (For the parts of her that linger in me, too.)

It's a decidedly different feeling.

Anesot didn't stand a chance against my anger.

Neither does Suleiman.

Red leeches from my eyes as my mind focuses on the task at hand. I manage to keep my form at bay, but probably not for long.

After months of stewing, Suleiman is within reach.

Zeu, Esclamonde, and I approach the wooden gate, little more than a grid of shadows.

I roll my shoulders, letting my body relax. I nudge Esclamonde with my elbow. "Alright, my dear mentee. No need to be nervous. All you have to do is listen to my magic. First, we cast sensing magic to gauge the spells and see which is weakest. Once we understand the spellwork, we destroy it however we want.

"Fire works great. Brute force is pretty fun, too, but it takes more work. Fire is expansive. It will do its thing all on its own. Just light a little ember and watch it go. Fun, right?"

I raise my hand and bear it ahead.

Esclamonde raises hers and wraps it around my wrist.

I move my fingers as I cast my sensing magic. Like I'd guessed from the mountain pass, the spells are defensive and potent, like a cord wrapped tightly around an object. It's hard to wheedle a finger between the strands, magically speaking.

I take steadying breaths as I methodically work through the fixed spells. They're certainly imaginative; shrouding magic, then shaking magic, then another disorienting sort of stabbing spell.

I remove each before it can harm me or the group behind me. Spell by spell, the palace's defense unravels.

Like she can sense each, Esclamonde breathes in time with my casting.

"It's... what's that thing?" she asks. "The big thing? The dense thing?"

It almost feels like a bundle of cords wrapped into a ball of lethal, coiled magic. Not spells made of strings, but thousands made from metallic strands.

"Probably the portal," I murmur.

(Unless it's the horn room. Worried about compromising the Bloodies conviction to aid Velm, I've kept the horn room a secret. Only Butter knows, and only because Andromeda revealed it.)

"Don't worry about that for now," I go on. "Focus half your mind on what's right in front of you. The other half should be prepared to leap into action."

Esclamonde leans closer to whisper, "I've never felt magic this powerful. This... condensed."

I keep smiling, delirious now that Suleiman is within grasp. "It is nothing to me, my tiny little bird."

"I'm not afraid."

"I know."

"Oh! I feel that—is that the main spell?"

"Yep. It feels like the outermost defense. After I dispel this one, we'll use fire magic to destroy the rest. Ready?"

As I flex my fingers to tug at the heftiest spell encircling the palace, a high-pitched clang sounds from inside.

It's like a spring-action weapon; as soon as I pull the outermost spell free, the rest explode outward.

The word *fuck* lodges in my throat as a leveling spell rushes outward like an avalanche. It sweeps us into its momentum, launching me, Esclamonde, and Zeu backward.

My shoulder hits something hard. Then my body twists and flies into the air—

Breathless and unsure which way is up, I throw out a hand and catch us with a hovering spell. I shift my other hand to blunt the force of the leveling spell, casting my magic quickly in the direction of Imperatriz's tiny army.

Just in time, my blunting spell deadens the leveling spell. Mostly.

Living bodies and frozen corpses fly backward, sliding across the plaza's cold marble. Wolves and vampires curse and shout as they're thrown back. Then they pick themselves up quickly, shifting back into formation.

I'm still hovering almost upside-down in the air. I grab Esclamonde where she's airbound below me, then Zeu, who grips the witchling's ankle. I set us back on the ground, then straighten my robe.

Under the force of the spells, a few marble panels fall loose from the palace's outer walls. They shatter when they hit the ground, almost as loud as the Seracyd magic.

Oopsie boopsie.

I turn back to the groaning troops, "So that was the magical barricade. We should be okay now. I can sense the portal. It's near the throne room, like we—"

A second explosion rushes outward and batters my back.

In a split second, I sense its pitch of magic; not from Serac, but from the higher-pitched Argot. Then I'm knocked onto the ground, sent skidding into a frozen corpse butt-first. Esclamonde falls over me, followed by Zeu, who squishes me against the freezing body.

I cast a blunting spell that prevents the others from being knocked off their feet again.

I was a little embarrassed by the first spell—

Now, I'm being made a fool of. And I'm about to gag from touching a fucking corpse.

I cast lifting magic to set the vampire and witchling back on their feet. With a growl, my form overtakes me—

Red light stains the white marble all around me.

I storm toward the wooden gate.

Fuck this.

Rampage time.

I bellow wordlessly, infrasound leeching into the air around me.

Esclamonde pants as she hustles to catch up. Zeu laughs, low and happy, as he plants himself on my far side.

I reach into my bottomless bag and call up the wand; it rushes into my hand like it's been waiting. Its glowing red hue is perfectly flushed against my luminescent skin.

I lift the wand toward the gate and cast a battering spell; its wooden slats explode into a dozen jagged splinters. They burst into the palace's interior plaza and skitter across another great stretch of marble flooring.

With the witchling and King of Night with me, I charge into its peaceful, loaded silence.

Unlike the exterior plaza, the inner courtyard has a glass-paneled rooftop. Like the Velmic Estates dotting Mieira, an arched colonnade encircles the vast area. It's lit only with the silvery light of the moons, dimmed by a thin cover of clouds and blurred by the glass ceiling.

I take a deep breath as I wander into the frail moonslight. My eyes leap around the shadows, primed for movement. "Do you smell anyone, Zeu?"

"No," he whispers. "They're further inside."

I focus on the next massive door that awaits us on the far side of the interior plaza. I keep my hands at the ready, trusting that Zeu will alert me to any physical threats while I focus on magical attacks.

I raise the wand to open the next door. Unlike the last, there's no spellwork waiting for us. The door swings open, creaking.

Silence ushers us further into the palace.

To my surprise, the foyer is relatively small. A low table sits with a tall vase, surrounded by a few shelves.

Our footsteps echo as we enter the unlit room.

Esclamonde presses closer to me, her breathing loud. Zeu shifts, keeping both of us to his right while a dagger waits in his left hand. From my periphery, I see his flat nose twitching.

We inch into the shadowy hush.

From one empty room to another.

I lose my nerve a bit more with each.

I'd expected an immediate brawl.

Not whatever the fuck this is.

Soon, the rooms branch out into a maze. Though we reviewed a thorough map of the palace, it took me years before I felt comfortable navigating the arts district in Luz.

After a few turns, I'm hopelessly turned around.

"Where are we?" Esclamonde whispers. "This should've been a library, according to the—"

"We're fucking lost," I whisper back.

"*Shh*," Zeu hisses.

Though we've lost the script already, I can still sense a potent source of magic deeper within the marble rooms. As we wander closer, I differentiate that source into two distinct channels.

One is layered with Seracyd magic, the other with Vexen infrasound.

The portal. The horns.

They must be close together, then.

I release a long breath, trying to let my instinct guide me.

But I have no idea where I'm going—each silent and dark room leads into another. They seem to grow smaller, too.

Zeu pauses in a sitting room. His head tilts, as though hearing something in the distance. "We aren't alone."

"Who is it?" I ask.

"Degis. They released the dens. I can't smell whether they're using rosfrost from this far away. Let's keep moving."

Esclamonde sucks in a breath, one of her hands clinging to my forearm.

I guide us into another sitting room, which empties into a long and narrow hall. Without a glass skylight overhead, the passage is almost pitched black. I squish Esclamonde against the wall, letting Zeu protect our exposed side.

The passage ends in a guest room with a neat bed in the center. Silver light pours in from the glass ceiling. I take a deep breath, relieved to have some visibility. I look around, trying to find the next doorway.

Zeu shifts as a sound echoes from the hallway.

Esclamonde and I also pivot—

I'm still raising my hands when an Argyd witch steps into the room from the hallway. All I see is a flush of a bright white cloak, white hands, and the abstract curve of large, glowing horns.

Ultrasound careens toward us from her raised hands.

My blunting spell is too slow to nullify the Argyd witch's casting. The spells glance off one another in the center of the room, ricocheting. I shift out of the way as Zeu launches himself toward the witch.

At the same time, Esclamonde grunts, then staggers backward.

I turn to see her eyes roll back into her head as her body falls across the foot of the bed.

Adrenaline soars throughout my limbs.

I turn toward the Argyd witch, face twisting with rage.

Her four massive horns glow like shards of living ice. Waves of unnatural ultrasound roll off her violently.

I know her—

Kessrys, Female Host of Argot.

Ultrasound crackles through the air as she prepares another spell.

My hand is still raised; I send an engulfing spell toward her.

It's easily the most unpleasant attack that I've learned—

A spell that pulls someone downward while piling them with magical weight from above.

A burial.

The engulfing spell shatters hers when they meet. Her body buckles toward the ground as my spellwork reaches her, then buries her. But with a flourish of her hands and a flash of light in her horns, Kessrys catches herself and races back into the hallway.

I lunge toward her, but she disappears into a shadow two steps later. Darkness shrouds her, shivering with ultrasound as it embraces the witch and transports her elsewhere.

I guess I'm not the only Host who can shadow.

I turn back once she's gone, eyes fixing on the unconscious mentee. Her skinny limbs are splayed across the bed, mouth and hands open.

Zeu twists to look up at me, where he hovers over her. "She's okay —it was just a graze. Her vitals are fine." With a grunt, he clutches her to his chest, then hauls her up. He hustles toward a nook between a wardrobe and the wall. He sets the witchling down and looks up at me. "Shelter her. We'll come back—"

"We can't leave her." Now that she's knocked out, she looks hopelessly childlike. "What if—"

"We need to get to Kessrys. Or Suleiman. We need to find at least one of them before they find the wolves. Or their degis."

I stare at Esclamonde, limbs now folded into herself like a dead spider. "*Fuck*."

Zeu stands, words quick and harsh. "Let's go. Shelter the witchling."

Against my better judgment, I take a tapestry from the wall to cover her. Then I cast a shielding spell around the witchling. Clutching the wand, I set aside a large portion of my magic; it might not be enough to stop an attacker who wants to hurt her, but I'll certainly feel them struggling to work past my spell.

Then I turn and take off toward the shadow Kessrys disappeared into.

Zeu clutches my arm as I rush forward—

I lunge into the shadow, willing Vex's magic to cradle me. In the first split second that the shadow engulfs me, I can sense a tendril of Argot's ultrasound.

If there's one truth I know that other Hosts don't, it's that the Houses are neither friends nor enemies.

Argot does not know that I'm hunting it.

That I will follow the sound of its magic through this shadow to its Female Host.

I rush out of the shadow, hands raised and at the ready, eyes wide and searching.

But we step into another dim and empty chamber.

I study the plain sitting room. Kessrys got a head start; three doorways branch out nearby, and I have no idea which she took.

I look at the King of Night.

His iridescent eyes lock on the central passage. He skulks forward silently. I follow, tip-toeing as my heart ratchets in my chest and my fingers fizzle with magic, the wand held tight.

I make out light footsteps as we head through the doorway. Then I hear the witch's heavy cloak dragging on the ground behind her.

We creep down the hallway, then turn into an adjacent passage.

As soon as I catch sight of Kessrys's white robe, I send another engulfing spell toward her.

Unaware that we've been stalking her, the witch doesn't have time to react. She sinks to the ground with a gargled shout, then turns. Her eyes widen at me and the vampire. Zeu rushes forward, unsheathing one of his daggers.

I prepare a smothering spell to prevent her from crying out and alerting others. But she jerks to the side, then nods upward—casting a spell that shatters the glass ceiling overhead. The panes crumble and crash toward us, every shard laced with a frosted and unforgiving gust of wind.

I raise my hands to shield Zeu and me from the onslaught of glass.

I lose track of the engulfing spell while I do, giving Kessrys the time to flee again. Her shoes slip on the marble as she runs, her breathing loud and uneven.

Zeu launches himself after her in hot pursuit. I follow, letting the glass fall once we've cleared the room. We round the corner to see the white glow of her horns as Kessrys disappears into another heavy shadow.

Zeu's hand clamps down on my arm to sling me in front of him. I leap into the shadow, his hand gripping as he follows. This time, only a few feet behind Kessrys, I easily trail her magic through the darkness.

It's like a twang of melody, a distant glow of white light that guides me through the shadow.

We emerge in another nondescript and small room. This time, shouting and mayhem filter in. Kessrys rushes ahead of us, almost in reach. The witch turns toward one of the doorways, then another, as though confused.

Her indecision gives me enough time to cast a breaking spell. Though non-specific and vague, it's quick. It unleashes from the wand as Zeu pursues the witch once more. She pivots, casting a defensive spell to keep the vampire at bay.

While she's focused on him, my breaking spell grazes her shoulder.

Kessrys cries out as she's knocked back. She clutches her shoulder with her free hand, eyes fixed on where Zeu stands frozen by an Argyd spell, within reaching distance. Her eyes flicker to mine next, wide and wild.

I raise the wand to double down on the spell, conjuring a great force from my horns, but Kessrys is a split second quicker.

She's more wicked than I am.

More practiced.

Rather than cast directly at me, Kessrys shifts her hand toward something behind me.

I should have learned this lesson from my very brief stint in the House of Lahar last year. When I'd shadowed into the stone clock tower on the triplemoon, the Male Host of Lahar didn't cast a spell directly at me—instead, he'd wielded an object straight into my gut.

Attacking wielders head-on is one way to fight.

It's a path preferred by the less experienced, like me.

Kessrys has been evil for many more years than I've been evil.

Zeu must have seen it coming; he moves just in time to grab my wrist and pull me out of the way as something soars toward me from behind. A heavy curtain sails through the air, one of its ends whipping my forearm with enough force that I'm left breathless as the pain lashes through my psyche.

I collapse against Zeu with a cry, sending us toppling toward the ground.

What the fuck?

A curtain?

War is so much stranger than I thought it would be. Everything gets turned into a weapon.

I stand, half-pulled by Zeu. By the time I'm back on my feet, Kessrys is scurrying into yet another dim hallway.

We rush after her, but an explosion of ultrasound from another room nearly knocks us off our feet. Then two bodies rush into the room, tangled in a brawl. I step out of the way, uncertain of which body to help.

Then I realize it's Brutatalika grappling with a vampire. I hear the snapping of a jaw, and I see a tangle of reddish and dark hair. I turn to help the Female Alpha, convinced the vampire is about to get the upper hand as they rise over her and cranks their fist back.

In the next second, she leans up and drives her fist into their solar plexus.

She takes the split second, driving her fist next to their throat.

Last is a right hook that knocks the vampire's head back.

All three hits land within two seconds; the vampire convulses for breath, slipping to the ground and curling up on their side.

Well, she has that covered.

We turn back to pursue Kessrys, but I have no idea which shadow she used as a portal.

I rush toward my best guess. But when we step into the darkness, there's no trace of Argyd magic to follow. In the gulf, my magic deposits us back where we first shadowed.

The guest room.

Zeu and I look around.

Esclamonde's body remains safe between the wardrobe and the wall, hidden beneath the tapestry.

"*Fuck,*" he hisses, sliding his dagger back into place.

I turn back toward the shadow, ready to retrace our steps and find Kessrys again. I shift my hand, feeling for the wand—

I gasp, splaying my hands and looking down.

They're empty.

I gasp again, a scream in my throat.

"The *wand*—the *wand*—the *wand*!" I search my robe, then my bottomless bag, hands shaking. "When did I lose it? We need to go back—the last room, the curtain. It must have slipped out of my hand when I was hit."

"Calm down."

My chest heaves in breaths. "*Calm down? It's my demigod. What if*—"

"Don't panic. Take deep breaths." Zeu glances around, taking a large breath himself. "Imperatriz didn't wait for us—the wolves and my den have stormed the palace. I can smell them—they're moving fast. It's going to be mayhem where we just were. We can't compromise the whole mission to get the wand."

"If Suleiman or Kessrys finds it, then—"

"It doesn't work like that." Zeu shakes his head, pacing. "You can't wield Halcyon's magic. He can't wield yours, even if he had the wand."

"You don't know that." Samson figured it out pretty fucking fast. "What if she already has it—"

"She doesn't. You saw her run—we almost had her." Zeu stops pacing to take my hands between his. They're cool and large, clamping down gently. "Look at me, Helisent West of Jaws." I stare into his iridescent, reddish pupils, desperate for a modicum of strength right now. My thoughts feel like they're leaking out of my head and ridding me of sense. "You've been training for months. You're ready for this. You don't need the wand. It's for raw magic—but you have skill now. You have finesse. You have experience."

My mind keeps up with his words easily; my confident spirit agrees. But my body is adamant that death is imminent without the wand.

My stomach rumbles, legs weak. "I think I'm going to throw up."

Zeu takes a step back, giving me space and glancing around. Once again, his eyes are darting, his nose twitching.

I set my hands on my knees, leaning forward. "Oh, fuck."

He moves from one passage to the next, glancing out of the guest room. "Just throw up so we can keep moving."

"That's not how this works." I gag a few times, but nothing comes out.

"Yes, it is. Put your finger down your throat. It happens to the best of us. Just yak it out so we can keep fighting. We're sitting ducks right now."

"I don't want to throw up in front of you." I dry heave, then straighten myself. My body shivers. Panic keeps shooting through my body like lightning. I can't think straight, torn between wanting the wand and wanting to die, and wanting to throw up. "There. I'm fine. I think. Can you look away for a minute?"

"The fucking *vanity* on you," Zeu growls, stepping past me. At a quick pace, he starts down the hall that leads further into the palace. "Let's go."

Afraid of being alone without the wand, I race after him, belly sloshing with doubt and bile. "Well, what now? We lost Kessrys."

"We'll find the portal instead. I can help—I can sense Seracyd magic. I can lead us to it. But it's not alone. Can you sense the other magic? It's not Argyd magic. It's lower-pitched. Either Lasan or Vexen —but I'm not sure why either would be here."

I scamper after him, surprised he can differentiate each House's magic. In the next second, I realize the implications of Zeu sensing my magic in these walls.

"It's Vexen. I'll explain later. Let's focus on the portal."

With an unhappy sigh, Zeu admits, "This place is a fucking maze.

The rooms don't match the map. The wielders must have changed the layout to confuse us."

It's not an issue for long.

With each step further into the palace, and without an enemy attempting to cut us down, I can sense my horns with greater ease.

In the same way I could once delineate Hella's place inside the House of Vex, I can feel my horns' magical presence. They're like pockets of power, nestled side by side. Maybe like seeds buried in the cold marble.

Hundreds upon hundreds.

Zeu stops when the hallway empties into another perpendicular passage. He whispers, "Three degis are close. I can smell them."

I nod. "Rosarium?"

He shakes his head. "They haven't taken it. They're probably too close to the Hosts—they wouldn't give the degis that chance."

"I'll handle them." I shift in front of him, but pause in the next second. I turn back, studying his face. "Imperatriz wants them dead."

He raises his eyebrows. "And?"

"They aren't her subjects. They didn't choose to be here. And you're the King of Night, aren't you? And it's nighttime, right?"

"I'd rather deal with them myself," he confirms.

"I'll knock them out. You can deal with them later."

He nods. "I'd prefer that—but don't risk my safety or yours. Understood?"

"Of course."

Then I round the corner with my hands raised. Three vampires whip their heads toward me, kneeling over a pile of supplies on the room's far end. Two have time to stand before my stunning spells knock them unconscious. The third makes it halfway to us, his eyes locked on Zeu, before my spell takes him down.

From there, I follow Zeu to a cubic storage room, then to a large laundry room with vast, circular pools.

Unlike our raid in Ezit, it's less certain how the battle is panning out based on sound. The shouts echoing into the laundry room could be from either side; the high pitches of ultrasound could come from Halcyon, Butter, or our enemies.

I take a deep breath.

I focus on my horns—

We're getting close.

This time, I guide Zeu from the laundry room. We skulk through more empty rooms, leaving the noisy fight behind us. The vampire stays close, hand grazing my arm now and then.

Certain we're nearly there, I lower my stance and keep my hands raised.

But Zeu pulls me to a halt. He clears his throat, his voice low. "Helisent... sometimes, in Ezit, the Houses kept the horns of their ancestors. They worshipped them. They borrowed their magic if they could."

I study his features.

It's easy to quantify mentally: he knows about the horns. He can sense them.

But my heart is in my throat again, my whole body fizzing.

Andromeda was right.

I'd considered what the horns would look like—but not what it would *feel* like.

It feels wrong. It almost feels like the demigods kept in Ezitlos; remnants whittled down into lank, powerless objects.

"Let's focus on the portal," I say.

Zeu's features pinch. His slitted pupils study me closely. "Did you know about this? Yes or no?"

"Yes. It happened a long time ago. I'll explain later. Okay?"

Zeu's nose curls, lips pulling back from his white teeth. "You are so fucking impossible to respect." He looks away with a hiss, shaking his head. "We're close. I can smell Suleiman and a few other degis. Your precious familiar is with them."

My gut clenches. "*Pel?* Is he here for me?"

I didn't see that coming.

For whatever reason, it sends me reeling a second time with terror. One that a few deep breaths don't help.

"Well, I doubt he's here for me," Zeu reasons, gaze leveled on the next room. "And what's the verdict on Pel? I don't particularly want him alive."

"I want him alive. And Suleiman." I'll figure out what to do with Pel later. "What about the rest of the degis with them?"

"I'll worry about the degis—you focus on Suleiman. Nothing else."

I straighten my hair and my robe. "Fine. Ready when you are."

Zeu turns and takes off rather than waiting for me. I can't tell if he's in a homicidal rage or if he's sick of waiting. Possibly both. I race after him toward a vast room with walls that go up and up and up.

Magical cylinders dot the room, though most of the light comes from above. Moonslight pours in from the glass ceiling, casting off the white marble walls to fill the air with glittering light.

In the center of the room sit two cubic thrones built of the same white marble. Between them stands an indigo warlock, his white robe spotless and perfectly draped around him; no opaque veil to hide his face and body.

Suleiman.

As it once went with Halcyon's brothers, I notice an immediate similarity. Their jaws, their eyes, the way they tilt their chin. Even their gait is similar, Suleiman rocking back onto a foot just like his youngest.

At the Host's back are three degis; each is larger than Zeu, and each has dead eyes and bruised hands and bloody mouths like they've already been fighting for hours.

No Pel, though.

Past the thrones, behind Suleiman and his cronies, are two bags. They almost look like they're filled with sand, heavy and bulging where they sit ten feet apart. The air between them crackles with ultrasound; it sparks with indigo color, too, spewing an ice-cold draft.

The portal.

Suleiman fixes his eyes on the King of Night first. "Kos. Look at you—haven't you come a long way? I knew you would. I knew you'd be impressive. From the moment I pulled you from Sos, I knew it."

I slide my eyes across the room, searching for some sign of Pel. Then I tally the massive degis, wary of how they've started to inch toward us.

The Host turns his attention to me. "And where is your little project? I realized I'd underestimated you when I found him in this room—alone. Who invests so much of their magic... just to let one go? Or have you not learned the rules yet, Helisent?"

My little project? He must be talking about Samson, but I have no idea what he's talking about.

Learned the rules?

I almost ask him—I almost take the bait—just to know—just to be sure—

Then Suleiman raises his hand toward me. In the same second, the degivampires launch themselves at me and Zeu. The King of Night lunges in front of me—

I recognize the movement.

We've practiced this before.

He takes my place to meet the vampires, and I take his to direct my magic toward Suleiman, making sure not to graze the King of Night with my spellwork.

Suleiman's ultrasound meets my infrasound with an explosive boom. The palace walls shiver and shake. As with the façade, a few panels of marble fall to the ground and shatter.

The vampires meet and grapple, twisting into a pile of violence in my periphery.

The second my spell disintegrates, another soars from my free hand.

I slowly exhale using my stomach, baring every ounce of magical strength into the engulfing spell aimed at Suleiman.

Concentrate.

Finesse, not power.

Intelligence, not rage.

Suleiman's magical power shivers; I wonder if my engulfing spell will get the better of him. In that split second, I look to my left. I raise my free hand toward where Zeu struggles.

I growl as I cast two new spells at the same time.

One eviscerates the largest degi who pins Zeu's legs.

The other, aimed at Suleiman, is a wild rush of unfocused fire.

It lashes around the room like a dying phoenix, searing everything it touches—me and Zeu included. Everyone in the room staggers while the air boils for a split second.

The vampires re-engage with vicious sounds.

I use a more focused version of the burning spell, happy with the results. Once again, Suleiman meets my magic with a vicious response. It's some type of icy void; the opposite of wind, a dangerous stillness.

Then I see the portal's indigo sparks trace the outline of a man. The figure walks through the shivering ultrasound, taking his place behind Suleiman. A vampire.

I recognize the vampire; a plain set of features, a rounded nose, a set of lover's lips that once fooled me in Cadmium.

Pel.

I raise my free hand and send stunning magic toward both targets: Host and familiar. I funnel greater magic into them, desperate to eliminate one of my targets.

The stunning spell sends Suleiman scrambling back toward the portal, but Pel doesn't react at all. The vampire sets his gaze on me, blinking slowly.

Can I not wield against a familiar?

I glance at him; he's holding something brown and slack.

I can't remember what Accra said about vampires and their familiars in Vex last year. I never asked Zeu to clarify, either, thinking Pel was long gone.

Fuck.

Using both hands, I send another pronged set of spells toward the Host. The first batter into him from the right; the next descends from above, a whirlwind of air. With a grunt, he's knocked to the ground and sent skidding across the marble floor, away from the portal.

My hand follows him, a killing spell pulling into focus.

"Now!" Suleiman calls as he struggles to rise.

Then something lashes toward me. It takes hold of my wrist, locking tight and jerking me toward the portal.

A thick brown rope.

With a gasp, I plant my feet on the ground and sit on my butt; thanks to Zeu's training, I know to rely on my dead weight more than my muscles.

Once I'm rooted in place, I raise my free hand—

I cast toward Pel as the vampire pulls on the rope, which is looped tightly around his hands. My spell does nothing; my wrist jerks forward, tugging me toward the vampire and the portal at his back.

Ultrasound flutters around the rope, as though it's been magically altered. It tightens around me like a snake with prey.

Oh, shit.

Pel loops the rope around his elbow, tugging forcefully with a grunt.

I shift my untethered hand toward Suleiman rather than attempt to fall Pel again. I at least manage to knock Suleiman back off his feet.

Tangled in his white robe, he slides toward the room's far corner once more.

It does little to help. I scream as Pel pulls again, this time hauling me over my planted feet. I land on my belly, knocking my temple against the hard ground.

I lay dazed, wrist outstretched as Pel pulls me toward him.

The portal—

With a gasp, I realize what he's doing—

Trying to drag me through the portal, back to Zarzynn.

They want me alive?

They want me alive.

Fuuuuuuuuck.

Something clamps down on my ankle. "*Helisent!*" It's Zeu, his strained words almost indiscernible with panic. "*Think!*"

My wrist screams with a pain that's mirrored in my ankle.

The vampires play tug of war with my body.

"*Ahhhhhhh,*" is all I manage.

I squint across the room, trying to think of something as Suleiman backtracks to the portal. He takes the rope's end from Pel; they readjust so that Suleiman holds its end, and Pel keeps the rope's middle length tied around his wrist.

Suleiman waltzes to the portal's edge with the end of the rope looped around his hand. It runs from him to Pel to me.

Suleiman looks at me, a crazed look in his eyes as he shouts, "This can go one of two ways, Helisent West of Jaws. Stop fighting now, and your future will be infinitely easier than it could be. You think you'd choose Velm, but Serac will be kinder—trust me, witch."

I'm too focused on fighting to think of a cruel retort.

To wonder what the fuck he's talking about.

Pel backs toward the portal, and Suleiman disappears into it.

They won't take me alive—they won't take me alive—they won't take me alive—

Get ahold of yourself, bitch.

Think.

I raise my hand and turn toward Zeu. Rather than waste another spell on Pel (which won't work) or Suleiman (who clearly doesn't want me dead), I turn to the vampires. The degis have Zeu pinned, grunting as they batter him with their fists. The King of Night curls into himself, hand gripping my ankle with all his might. One degi pries at his hand, features bent with a grimace.

I knock the remaining degis out, but Zeu doesn't move even after the vampires fall to the ground. His chest rises and falls as he pants.

"Zeu," I grit out desperately. "Get Pel."

A gargled groan is all I hear, his hand still clamped around my ankle.

I turn back to the portal, crying out as Pel yanks on the rope as hard as he can.

The rope grows taut.

I can't wield against Pel—but I realize suddenly that I don't need to.

Not directly, at least.

I raise my hand and cast bracing magic against the wall of the throne room, behind the portal.

Pel struggles as my magic pushes against the wall, preventing the vampire from pulling me closer. My bracing spell shakes the marble walls and splinters the glass ceiling overhead. The glass breaks with an ear-splitting crack.

Spent and occupied, all I can do is hide my face as the broken glass rains down in a slurry of tiny shards.

I barely notice the nicks and blood that come next.

My ankle and wrist and head scream for relief, my mind frantic with alarm.

"Zeu! Get Pel! Hurry!"

The portal's invisible pane flecks with light as Pel grits his teeth and pulls with all his might—

I grit mine, too, sucking in measured breaths and concentrating.

Zeu's vice grip shifts from my ankle to my calf. Then another on the back of my knee.

Cursing, Zeu takes hold of my body with both hands as infrasound and ultrasound whirl through the room. I can't tell what he's doing— too concentrated on my bracing spell, on preventing my wrist from being broken, on figuring out how to the fuck to get out of this.

The King of Night pulls himself from my legs to my hips, from my hips to my waist. With one last grunt, he shifts over me to lunge and wrap his hands around the rope. In quick order, Zeu rips the rope toward him, taking hold with both hands.

I cry out with relief, my hand and wrist going slack as the pressure lifts. Then I scramble onto my knees. I plant myself as best I can, free hand splayed wide as I double down on my bracing spell.

I take a deep breath to regain control of my thoughts.

I can sense the red horns nearby. I can feel magical power thrumming in each, as though activated by my presence and spellwork.

Their latent power almost reminds me of Vex's limestone mantle.

I take a deep breath as I take hold of the power.

With each second, I gain more control and clarity.

I take hold of the end of the rope that Zeu now clings to. My fingers close around its coarse fibers.

The rope…

Suleiman and Pel want to drag me back to Zarzynn.

They're using a rope infused with magic to do so.

A magical rope designed to drag me into the portal…

It's holding strong. They've done a fantastic job with the rope's spellwork.

Which means it should hold—

If I pull on it, too.

I shift and take hold of the rope with both hands. My bracing magic lifts, which causes me and Zeu to jolt forward again.

I cast gripping magic next, clinging to the rope.

Then I pull back with all my might.

Pel gasps as he's tugged forward, eyes widening on me. My magic doesn't work on him, but the rope is looped around his arm tightly.

The portal behind him shivers and shakes with frosty, indigo light.

Zeu senses the shifting tide. He grunts as he shifts into a more stable position, then leans back, putting his full weight into pulling the rope. Like me, he's covered in blood from tiny nicks of glass.

A breathless, maniacal laugh escapes me.

It's a battle of wills and magical stores, not wit and cunning.

Which bodes extremely well for me.

All I have to do is pull Suleiman back through the portal.

Then he's mine.

As loudly as I can, hoping to pierce the portal's veil where Suleiman stands with a rope wrapped around his wrist, I bellow, *"When are you gonna learn?"*

CHAPTER 19

IT DIDN'T START WITH ME (THE TAPESTRY)

SAMSON

Suin,
You've always been under the impression that you had to impress Velm. I think
it's the opposite. And, if I were you, I'd be very disappointed in us.
-Suin

I sprint through an unfamiliar palace.

The rooms are mismatched and rearranged. I have no idea how or when this happened, just that the palace's forty or so rooms are now entirely foreign.

Debris and corpses lay piled at odd angles throughout. The marble slats lining the walls have fallen loose, splayed across the ground in white shards. The same for half the glass ceilings. Cold wind whirls through the dark rooms.

I rush through them as infrasound rattles the palace floor and walls. My boots slip on the glass and marble, my cloak half-slung off my shoulder.

I pant, my body aching as I search for the portal.

I don't know what I expected of this night, but I'm not surprised it's ending with another world-ending bout of magic.

I'd be convinced Helisent was winning the battle if it weren't for the ongoing shaking.

It feels like a battle of wills is playing out somewhere deep inside the palace. Deep bass pounds through the air, interlaced with ear-splitting ultrasound.

I'd be happy to leave the Vexen to her vengeful rage, but I need Halcyon and Butter. I haven't seen either wielder for over an hour—

And a troop of wolves just witnessed Kessrys fleeing the palace for the mountain pass.

She wants the high ground.

Where she can brew a powerful spell to end this battle.

And I can't find my witch—

Again.

Hurry, Samson.

I skid to a halt in a relatively intact sitting room. My nose twitches; with the floor and walls shaking, with blood and sweat and glass spread all over the place, I'm running on instinct.

With a quick breath, I smell a lone and weak ala.

I study the debris in front of me: broken shelves, a vampire's corpse, toppled books. I clamber over the mess toward the room's corner, then kneel between the wall and a wardrobe.

I'm certain I smell Esclamonde beneath a bundled tapestry.

I feel for her shoulder, then pull her toward me. The fabric slips away, exposing her narrow face. Her eyes are closed, her body slack—but I don't see or smell any of the witchling's blood.

I feel for her pulse; it's strong. I bend to inhale her ala; she's healthy. Just unconscious and fatigued.

With a curse, I pick up the witchling and haul her against my chest.

Panicked, I rush back toward the exterior plaza.

The witch would not have left her mentee. This isn't good.

I rush through the rooms, back aching and legs burning. It's been hours of bare-knuckle fighting. What began with a few skirmishes in the exterior plaza turned into an all-out brawl between the Leolites and our ranks.

As it once went in Ezit, the sun will soon rise, and the vampires must find shelter.

Halfway to the plaza, I catch another off-putting scent. I stop in my tracks, attention fixed on what I smell.

The wand.

What the fuck is Helisent doing without the wand?

I follow my instinct to a small enclave; it leads me to yet another bundle of fabric.

Hurry, Samson.

I grunt as I kneel again, trying to manage Esclamonde's weight and avoid slipping into glass shards. I tug at the fabric with my free hand, unrolling it messily.

I jolt back when the wand slips free and clatters to the ground.

It's glowing with pure red radiance, just like it did in Vex.

It spews the bitter scent of Helisent's magic.

"Fuck."

Where are you, Helisent?

I pick up the wand, adjusting the witchling so it doesn't graze her. With another shuffle, I stand and head back toward the palace entrance.

How did she lose the wand?

And the mentee?

Fuck, fuck, fuck.

My lungs sear with each breath, my shoulders and neck barking with protest.

Though we were lucky not to face too many magical offensives in the palace, the sheer number of bloodthirsty degis overwhelmed us multiple times.

But that luck ends now.

With Kessrys in the mountain pass.

Hurry, Samson.

I skid to a halt when I see bright red fabric in an adjacent room. Halcyon races toward a hallway, cloak flaring at his heels. I bellow his name, rushing over rubble to meet him.

Halcyon turns to me. His eyes lock on Esclamonde. "What happened?"

"You tell me," I say, body sagging with exhaustion. "Where the fuck is Helisent? The portal—"

"I can't find it. I've gone through every single room twice."

My eyes widen. "You haven't found them?"

It's been Helisent and Zeu alone? This whole time?

"This place is a fucking maze! Butter and I got separated, and..." Halcyon's eyes widen on the wand. "Why doesn't Helisent have the wand?"

"Why the fuck haven't you found the portal?" I look around, desperate for clarity. "I don't know why Helisent doesn't have the wand. I found it on the ground. The same with the mentee. It's not good—"

"I'm going, I'm going," he says, turning as though to keep searching for the portal.

"No, I need you outside. I'll find the witch. Kessrys is going to the mountain pass—she's going to finish off the rest of us, and—"

"I'm not leaving Helisent and Butter." Halcyon shakes his head, backing away from me. Once again, his eyes lock on the wand. "Take Esteban outside, then use the wand to defend—"

A clang of ultrasound cuts us off. It rushes through the palace like a clash of metallic blades.

Terror spreads through my body.

Bellator is going to be destroyed.

Every single wolf in the vicinity; gone.

Rex's ashes, wherever they are; Berevald's and Colsep's, too.

"Let's go." I nod in the direction of the palace's entrance. I can't see it from here, but we're close, and we need to defend the helpless groups in the exterior plaza.

"The portal works both ways, like Brutatalika said," Halcyon shouts, jaw tense. "How they wielded in Ezit—do you remember? Yes or no? The spells—they would have come from above."

I sink to my knees and set the mentee down, exhausted and disoriented. I clutch the wand, desperate to find my witch and set it in her hand.

'How they wielded in Ezit...'

I couldn't forget those spells if I tried. Each had felt powerful enough to end the world. As Samsonfang, none had harmed me. But the notion of dealing with one of them right now, as a mere man, is incomprehensible.

With a wild craze in his eyes, Halcyon says, "Defend the city, Samson. *Your* city. I have to go."

I look at the wand in my hand, throat locking. I shove it toward him. "I can't—I don't know how—"

Halcyon takes a step back, eyes fixed on the wand like he fears it. And I actually step toward him, leaving the mentee to offer it again, hand outstretched.

He counters, "You know how. You already did it."

My voice rises, hysterical, "I *can't wield*—it was a fucking one-off—and only because I was dying—and my mother—"

"I cannot wield Vexen magic." Purposefully, pronouncing each word carefully, he says, "I cannot do what you want me to do."

I stare at him, thoughts wild.

Can't do what I want him to do?

He bears his eyes into mine.

I shake my head, trying to understand.

Can he really not wield Vexen magic—even with a wand?

"She gave you the wand. No one else has ever touched it. I'm not going to change that right now." He backs away a few more steps, and I keep following, the red wand glowing in my hand. "I need to find the portal. The Bloodies need me."

I take hold of his forearm with my free hand, desperate. "I do not know magic. I do not know a single spell. We will all die."

Halcyon stares at me with great and unmoving understanding. "Then it's a good thing you are holding the most potent magical aid in the world."

My heart thumps in my chest.

'She gave you the wand.'

Hurry, Samson.

"You told Vex what to do in Rhotidom, and it listened, didn't it?" the warlock goes on.

I stare at the wand, at the red hue it casts against my pale hand, my dark layers, the white marble shards piled around us.

I prepare one last argument, but the warlock turns into the palace as a massive crash echoes from within.

I look at the wand, then the mentee.

Fuck.

Moving purely on instinct and adrenaline and fear, I pick Esclam-onde up and rush out of the palace. Hundreds of corpses fill the corri-dors, along with the interior courtyard. I'm not sure which are friends and which are foes.

By the time I reach the entrance, my body is close to giving out. I stoop near the gate to set the witchling on the ground.

I sag toward my knees, panting to catch my breath.

I straighten, staring across the plaza where hundreds wait in tightly packed groups. Some are survivors who gathered here after escaping their holdout on the far side of Bellator. Others are slumping with exhaustion after surviving run-ins with degis and wolves loyal to the Leolites.

Snow drifts across the frigid marble, a fine powder that the wind carries high. They huddle around small fires, bodies bent as they tend the wounded. Once again, I don't recognize anyone. The night hides faces; alas muddle and blend mindlessly with my exhaustion.

I look across their ranks, uncertain whether to feel proud. Maybe we'll all die now, defenseless against the Argot wielder in the mountain pass.

But at least it's together, and with honor.

I wander between the fires, the seated wolves and vampires.

My breathing is ragged, my body burning with fatigue and twinged with cold. I grip the wand in my hand; it thrums lightly, gently. It reminds me of tadmazzar, comforting and familiar.

I glance over my shoulder at the palace. It shakes with the onslaught of Vexen infrasound and Seracyd ultrasound.

'She gave you the wand.'

Hurry, Samson.

I look up into the night. The mountains loom around us like the faceless shadows of demigods. Above is the gray-white of heavy clouds, the promising twinkle of the moons past their filament. Like a keyhole in a lock, I see the passage between the purple-gray mountains of Baladhari and Meledhari.

A flash of white light fizzles there like toxic lightning.

A hand wraps around my arm. I turn to see my mother, her features taught and her jaw clenched. "Atali—we need to hurry. If we go now, we can reach the pass before she casts. Brutatalika will find Helisent, and we'll pray that Hetnazzar reaches us in time."

I shake my head.

I stare down at the wand.

It's starting to make sense—

Halcyon knows something and, whatever it is, he's suspected it since Rhotidom. Butter, too. And Helisent has been acting cagey for the last month.

She knows something. They all know something.

I'm close to knowing, too.

'You told Vex what to do in Rhotidom, and it listened, didn't it?'

He's right. Even though I grew up meditating in that room of horns, Vex has saved my life on multiple occasions. My mother's, too.

For now, that's all I need to trust.

Hurry, Samson.

I set my hand on Imperatriz's. It's cold and knicked, just like mine. "No, mama."

I glance over her shoulder. Brutatalika approaches us, body slumped and eyes burning.

Both are just as exhausted as me. Imperatriz knows we'd never make it to the pass in time.

I'm close to knowing...

"Hetnazzar didn't come," I say.

"Hetnazzar will come. Until then," Imperatriz grits out, "we need to hurry, Kessrys is preparing a spell—"

"It's too late for that. Take the others to safety." I look away from the wand, toward my mother. Its red light falls across her pale features, her stricken eyes. "It's okay."

I'm close to understanding...

She steps closer, eyes fixed on me. "What are you—"

"I'm saying that we don't need our demigod. Go to safety. Take the others with you. Okay?" I search her face, hoping to find some semblance of trust. Right now, all I see is panic. "In Rhotidom, it wasn't the cylinder of dove that brought you back."

Her eyes flit across my features. "What are you *saying?*"

"I'm saying that something is happening, and I'm close to understanding." I hold up the wand; close enough that she can study it and far enough that she knows not to touch it. "This is a wand. Helisent's wand. It's... her demigod. And it... likes me. Hetnazzar... gave it to... to... to us. In a dream."

That's when it clicks.

Not in my cognizant mind, because my cognizant mind is focused on survival. My cognizant mind is panicking as it senses the adrenaline and cortisol leeching off my mother and wife; as it tallies the hundreds sitting in this plaza and facing death; as it watches the mountain pass overhead.

In my subconscious mind, things are pulling into order...

My hand tightens around the wand.

Imperatriz says, "*Atali*, this—"

We stagger backward as a piercing ringing descends from above. Though I still can't see Kessrys between the sister mountains, her magic collects the powdery snow into dizzying, terrifying shapes.

I turn to Imperatriz. "Get back. *Now*."

Begrudgingly, she drags Brutatalika with her. The women look from my face to the glowing wand, then they turn and start commanding the others to take shelter.

The shapes in my periphery scramble, abandoning their fires until I'm alone in the plaza again, surrounded by hundreds of watching eyes.

I push them out of my mind as I square up toward the mountain pass.

I am here.

I adjust my hand around the wand.

My cognizant mind fixes on the threat of Kessrys's incoming magic.

The rest of me is thinking about a conversation I had with Halcyon in Rhotidom months ago.

His musings on the wand drift around me, half-real in my memory. *'It isn't Helisent—it isn't a witch. It's a demigod. It wants things, and you'd be the dumbest fucking being on this planet to assume you can fathom what a demigod wants.'*

I am here.

Adrenaline courses through me and, for the first time since waking in that jungle, I feel my second body. I take a deep breath as it hovers around me; phantasmagoric, fizzing with energy.

Like something that's been lost since Rhotidom—

Like something that has suddenly found me again—

My second body settles back into place with a graze of infrasound. It sinks into my skin, causing my body hair to stand up.

It fits into my head, into my hands, into my core and hips and knees and feet.

Wave after wave of adrenaline courses through me. It's just as potent as the terror of a sudden scare, jolting me again and again and again.

I feel it pool in my body, then funnel into my right hand.

The wand vibrates; faster and faster and faster.

More adrenaline, more infrasound.

It leeches into the air, forming a sphere of violent red lightning around me.

I widen my stance and point the glowing wand at the mountain pass far overhead.

I am here.

My breath lodges in my chest as the snowy ultrasound rises high into the sky. Argyd magic screeches and surges, like sharp metal instruments clanging together. The spell rises taller than Baladhari and Meledhari, framed in gusts of snow.

My mind empties with abject fear.

Holy fucking shit.

We're all going to die.

Then comes infrasound, rattling through my body. Its magical lightning grows redder, wilder.

It sends the powdery snow jumping along the ground.

In an avalanche of keening and flares of white, Kessrys's spell tilts toward us and pours downward, gaining momentum with each second.

The second it descends, I almost turn and run.

I'm still a wolf, wired to fear spellwork and its sounds.

I steel myself in the next, hoping Vex hears me as the words rush from my lips. *"Please defend Bellator."*

The lightning around me disappears. The infrasound pumping through my body cuts out, too, along with the tides of adrenaline.

I feel it funnel in my right hand where my fingers cradle the wand.

A tendril of bass-riddled power shoots from the wand's tip and crackles into the air with a vicious growl.

I cling to the wand with all my might, eyes locked overhead.

I have no idea what I wielded; magic doesn't take a form of its own until it meets matter. I see pocks of red light, bunched and soaring in thousands of separate bodies. But they disappear as quickly as they animate.

For a split second, there are two forces in the sky; invisible and yet entirely palpable.

Something high-keening and unnatural. Something growling deep and vicious.

Vex's spell meets the Argyd magic above the city, infrasound and ultrasound meeting and tangling in a powerful deluge. Gusts of wind descend on us, laced with steaming gusts of air and earth-rattling bass.

I hear Kessrys's magic hiss with livid steam.

I hear Helisent's magic growl; it almost sounds like Hetnazzar.

After that comes a forlorn croon of ultrasound; it fades after a few seconds, followed by yet another triumphant growl of infrasound.

One final gale sweeps through the plaza, snuffing out the last of the fires with a loud *whoosh*.

Then there's silence in the cloudy sky.

No more ultrasound, no more signs of Argyd magic at all.

I stagger backward, head tilted up.

I look all around; the sky is empty, and my city is safe.

In a single breath, the energy leaves my body.

I have never known such sudden and total fatigue.

I sink onto my butt, then onto my back on the cold marble.

I hold the glowing wand up and study it.

Red light falls across my face.

I smile.

I get it now.

Hetnazzar bit this wand free in a dream almost a year ago.

Velm would have been falling by then; I wouldn't have known that in Zarzynn.

That's why Hetnazzar didn't come.

I almost laugh.

I'm so fucking dumb—*have I always been this dumb?*

The witch knows something.

I know it, too.

Axerxa's wives crafted the wand long ago so he could wield against Ezit.

It was lost until my demigod bit it free from the Hellastone.

First, so Helisent could wield the wand in Ezit.

Then, so I could wield it here in Bellator.

Two demigods in collusion.

I see it very clearly now.

There is only one reason Vex would keep me alive and keep me well.

There is only one thing in the entire world that Vex lacks.

A Male Host.

She is mine.

Once, Parsifal told me that life was like a tapestry. We weave thin threads into beautiful patterns, slowly composing a dense, heavy fabric. He said that, throughout life, I would feel the strings between my fingers. That I would weave them into place, thread by thread, with my own hands. It would give me the feeling that I was the master of the tapestry or, at least, my portion.

Her papa says that the only moment anyone sees its design in its full glory is at death.

I'm not dying in this plaza tonight.

But I swear I see a tapestry.

I can feel the threads in my hand.

I glimpse it.

A handful of beings.

All with dark horns.

I'm asleep.

Mostly.

I fever.

My lips are dry and cracked, my throat locked and aching. Beads of sweat roll off me; chills come in their wake. A soft sheet lies over me. Cool rags wipe my face.

There is a red warlock at my side.

We're surrounded by candles in my bedroom in Bellator Palace.

The warlock is tending me, wiping my face and murmuring kind words.

I've seen him before. I recognize his wide features, his large eyes.

"Axerxa?" The word barely sounds on my lips. "Axerxa, is that you?"

The warlock smiles roguishly, like he once did in a mirror in Ezitlos.

He's speaking Zarzyd again; I still can't understand him.

"What did you say to her?" I ask. "Last year—in Ezitlos—what did you say to the Vexen?"

He laughs loudly, slamming a hand onto my thigh. I lurch forward; hands calm me again. Another cool rag, more soft and reassuring words.

There are others here; I focus on Axerxa.

He responds, but I can't understand him.

I prompt him again, delirious and stubborn.

This time, he responds by shoving his hand between my legs and taking a handful of my groin. I jolt upward, taking his hand by the wrist—

I sit back in the next second.

Brutatalika's face is nearby. Her features are contorted with worry. "You're sick, Samson. Relax." I hold her wrist near my chest; in her other hand, she holds a damp rag. "Shhhhh," she coos.

I slump back with a groan.

What the fuck is happening?

I keep dreaming, but it doesn't feel like I'm asleep.

I try to stay calm. I watch Brutatalika tend to me, running damp rags over me and fixing my hair. She lifts my head and helps me sip a bitter tonic.

I close my eyes; when I open them again, I see another Vexen.

The witch resembles Axerxa, though her face is thinner. She stares at me with four large horns jutting from her head. Blood lines her lips, darker than her red flesh.

She presses her small hand against my chest. She tugs down the sheet to stare at the scar above my heart; it's just as red as her fingers.

She smiles at me, tilting her head as though shy. She says something in Zarzyd. I think I hear the word *Bathsheba*; it's a name I've heard Zeu mention before.

She prods the scar, and I take her wrist again.

I don't want her to break the spell.

Axerxa seems like a friend; this witch might be a foe.

We're near the room of horns, after all.

Vex knows.

I pull her hand away from me, shifting my aching body. I need to sit up and figure out how to translate a conversation between me and the Vexen ghosts.

The hand keeps me in place. "Atali," my mother says. "Relax. You have a fever."

I squint; this woman now has dark gray hair and broad, pale features.

I hold my mother's wrist, resting near my chest.

The sheet is wet and tangled over my body. My chest is exposed, the scar above my heart bloodred.

"Don't," I gasp.

She pats me again. "I'm not hurting you. I... I just wanted to see. Did you know about this, atali?"

I hold onto her wrist, too weak to pull up the sheet and hide the scar.

Axerxa and Bathsheba sit at my other side. They're watching her, and watching her hand, and watching my chest; they understand.

This is dangerous.

My mind rages with a fever, my body shivers with ongoing pain.

It's best not to respond.

I try to stay aware a bit longer.

Brutatalika must be here, too—she's whispering, "I haven't seen it turn red before."

"We'll tell no one."

"Hundreds saw what he did in the plaza. Everyone knows."

"It will be okay. We have Bellator. The city is safe. Rouz, too. Word came this morning. It's panning out, Brutatalika."

"Word will spread about what happened here. And then what?"

"There are many rumors and mysteries surrounding my son and his legacy. Dozens, even. This will be added to the list. Nothing more. Nothing less."

"What if... what if... what if..."

"Shh, let's get his fever down first."

"We need to speak to the witch."

"First, the fever."

"But, what if..."

I wake up groggy.

For a long time, I stare at the ceiling, half-asleep.

Slowly, I pull my senses into order.

I'm still lying in my bed in Bellator Palace, surrounded by the glow of dozens of candles. It is night, the glass ceiling overhead perfectly intact. I'm not sweaty, but the sheets cradling me are damp and cool. To my left, my mother sits at my bedside. Her head rests on her arms, folded atop the soft bedding. The nightstand is littered with cups, vials of tonics, cedar oil, mint oil, and piles of clean and soiled compresses.

My mother sleeps peacefully, her back rising and falling with deep breaths.

We won, then.

And where is Helisent West of Jaws?

Where?

I sit up and stifle a groan, hoping not to wake Imperatriz.

I look around, verifying that Axerxa and Bathsheba aren't here. I look for imprints in the bedding next to me; no deviations or impressions mark the blanket.

I look at my hands next. I flip them over, looking for evidence that I wielded. Nothing.

Like it once was in Rhotidom, the wand seemed to do all the work. I was just the breathing thing clinging to it, hoping to protect my city.

Still...

My body is sore, as though every single one of my limbs was treated to a thorough beating. My eyelids ache as I blink, my tongue as I lick my dry lips. I stretch my arms and neck next.

I glance around the room one more time, looking for any hint that the fever dream was more than a hallucination. Again, nothing. I take another moment to verify that this is my bedroom; someone must have magically righted the palace's layout since the battle. My bed sits in the middle of the room. On the far side is a wardrobe and a washing bin, then more piles of medical supplies. A narrow corridor branches off near the wardrobe, leading to the washroom and a large sitting room.

"Pssst."

Helisent leans into view from the dim passage. Her red eyes dart from me to my sleeping mother. "Hi," she whispers.

I lock eyes with her, relief washing through me.

She's safe.

Even better, she's still in Bellator.

She leans further into view, gesturing me toward her with a hand. I don't hear the sound of her feet as she disappears back into the passage, nor does her ala waft into my room.

Gently, I shift toward the bed's empty half. Imperatriz's fingers clench, but her head and arms stay heavy against the bedding.

I inch off the mattress carefully. It's not difficult—my body is too sore to move faster.

With a ginger step, I shift off the bed and turn toward the passage. I pause, pulling in large breaths to gauge where Brutatalika is. Her ala lingers in the air, but its potency tells me she hasn't visited in a while. I wait a moment longer, either for the sound of someone approaching or an incoming ala.

After hearing and smelling nothing, I grab a hefty cloak hanging near my wardrobe.

I pass the washroom first, then find Helisent in the square sitting room. It has a low glass roof, which slopes down from the ceiling to form one of the walls. During the warm months, the glass panels slide open and offer a stunning view of Bellator. In the dead of winter, they're sealed, arched over a plain beige rug, sitting cushions, and a bowl of cedar incense.

The red witch stands near one of the glass partitions, opened slightly at her back. I glance over her multiple times, searching for any hint of injury. I have no idea how long I lay fevering or how the battle panned out. Based on Helisent's prim, velvet robe and layers of twinkling jewelry, all is well.

Except for her darting eyes.

She scans me again and again, her mouth pinched. She clears her throat. "Hi," she repeats.

I still feel half-tangled in a fever dream. "Hi."

She leans back against the window, as though eager to keep space between us. "You know, if you're going to keep wielding, you could at least do it in front of me."

I wander to the center of the room, my heart thumping with each of her words. "Do you think there will be more times?"

Please say yes.

Please tell me you've been doing this on purpose.

"I don't know."

"But you know *something*."

Helisent's red eyes dart back to mine. "I know many things. I'm not half as dumb as people think."

I approach her slowly.

I know why the witch is acting strangely.

Or, at least, I can start to fathom why.

Still, the words don't form. Each conclusion is...

Too much.

So I start with, "How are you?"

She raises her eyebrows, as though surprised by the question. "Oh, well... good. All the Bloodies are safe. We're staying close to here. We've been putting the city back in order. Butter and Halcyon finished healing the sickest wolves yesterday. It's going well. There were a lot of wolves hiding in the mountains. They're filtering back in.

"Someone gave me a cow. A highland cow. She's beautiful—I can't tell if it was an offering or an insult. You know, because of her horns. And her stench. I call her Gracey.

"Kessrys took off—we don't know where she is. But the portal is destroyed. I have Suleiman... and Pel. Surprise, surprise. I shadowed Zeu and his den back to Luz. He... wasn't very happy with Imepratriz after he found out about the horns. And you. But that's not very surprising." She gives me the once-over. "How are you? It's been almost a week. I have the wand, but... they didn't let me... they said I shouldn't see you. Are you okay?"

"I feel better now. I had a fever... and I saw strange things. I saw Vexen ghosts. Two of them." I shift closer to her, desperate to hold her hand. But she leans back against the window, eager to keep a distance between us. I can't tell if she's scared, nervous, sheepish—maybe all three.

Enough dancing around this, then.

I clear my throat. "Axerxa... Axerxa has been watching me for a long time, Helisent."

She nods, looking down. "You said he gave you the axe in Zarzynn."

"Exactly. In Ezitlos last year, it looked like he said something to me. To you, maybe—but he'd been looking at me when he said it. Did he say anything about me?"

She looks at her hands, wrung together. "I don't want to have this conversation."

"You know something. I'd like to know, too. Right now, all I have are guesses. I don't want to guess when it comes to you and me."

Her voice lowers further. "He said that you were a good choice.

That our littlelings would be strong. He... wanted to know if you liked the axe. He wanted to offer you more gifts."

Each statement is like a stab to the chest.

Each statement greatly rewrites the course of my life.

I remind myself to breathe; one breath in, another out.

I don't know where to begin.

Our littlelings would *be strong, Helisent.*

It's not enough.

I will give you shelter; I will give you rich foods; I will give you bitter brandy; I will build your fires throughout Night; I will give all that your tender flesh needs.

A testament to wolves, not to witches.

How could you say this to me? I will never let this go.

Too true.

Too real.

Whatever the opposite of hopelessness is—that's what overcomes me right now.

A hope that's *too* great.

Too possible. *Too* close. *Too* meaningful to ever relinquish.

"I know it doesn't change anything," she whispers, voice trembling. "I won't interfere with your marriage, like I promised. He doesn't understand. Axerxa doesn't know that our children would be pith. That wolves and witches don't make wielders."

I close the distance between us.

Rage kindles in my gut, sudden and biting.

I take her chin, guiding her to look at me. "What about a wolf with a wand? I'm not nearly as impressive as my ancestors, but I am an heir of Hetnazzar." Tears fill her large eyes. She shakes her head, pulling away from my hand, but I go on before she can interrupt. "I am strong. I have some magic—or, at least, yours doesn't kill me. And Hetnazzar bit the wand free—doesn't that mean something, or—"

"I have to tell you something else first." Her voice keeps shaking, her breath rattling in her chest. "The *whole* story..."

"Then *tell me.*"

She blinks, setting a few tears loose. "You'll hate me."

I shake my head. "No. Never." My temper mounts; *does she not want a potential future with me? Does Vieira mean nothing to her?* "Say it, Helisent. Whatever fucked up thing you've been hiding from me for the past month. You think that I don't know you. You think that I'm just a man. Or secretly like every other wolf... I really don't know what you think, but I know you're wrong if you think I'll go. Try to scare me away, little bird."

I wipe her cheeks with shaking hands.

She clears her throat. "My papa told me that everyone called my mother Amaro. She was very bitter. Not like me and Milisent. Not like the twins. And... and..."

I turn when I hear footsteps.

Helisent jolts, hand tugging open the windowpane.

I step away from her just in time for Imperatriz to find us in the sitting room. Dark circles rim my mother's eyes. Her hair is tangled to her waist and half-hardened with oil. Her cloak hangs around her, wrinkled and lank.

The window pane creaks as the witch pries it open further. One of her legs hikes as she steps onto the sill, as though planning to float into the air—

And flee.

Imperatriz looks from me to the witch with a glint in her eye that sets my senses on fire.

She's not angry; she's livid.

I shift my position to pit myself between them.

I woke five minutes ago; I haven't had the time to wonder how Imperatriz has been handling the fact that I used the wand to wield. I haven't had time to think of how to frame what she saw.

I haven't even had time to consider the ramifications for myself.

She lowers her chin, eyes fixed on the witch. "I told you not to come here, Helisent West of Jaws."

Isn't this the Kulapsifang who dreamed of the Northing?

Helisent raises her other foot onto the sill. She inches away from me, hunching down to duck through the opening.

"But since you're here and speaking now..." Imperatriz moves closer with the slow intention of a predator. "I think I'd like to start the conversation."

In a split second, the feeling in the room goes from tense to oppressive.

Imperatriz stops a few feet away. I shift further, blocking her view of Helisent.

She cranes her neck past me to tell Helisent, "You have made a grave mistake with my Kulapsifang, witch. Whatever it is you're planning, think again." She inches closer, tone lashing. "I don't care that you've been handing out resources to my people. I don't care that you helped retake my capital. My goodwill ends here and now if you think I will let this stand."

I take a step forward to meet Imperatriz. I can't see Helisent behind me, but I can hear the window creaking as she stays primed on its ledge.

Multiple arguments come to mind.

Watch your mouth when you speak to Helisent West of Jaws.

Too threatening.

I will not choose you right now, Imperatriz—so don't force me.

Way too painful to admit.

You were the only wolf in the world who I'd hoped would understand my relationship with Helisent.

But did I really?

The words disintegrate in my mind, syllable by syllable, as Imperatriz and I watch one another.

I shake my head. "There's a lot you don't know," is all that comes out.

It's a poor sentiment to convey all that has happened between me and the witch and Vex over the last two years. It's especially useless considering there's still something the witch knows that I don't, and whatever that is, it seems to matter a lot right now.

Helisent says, "It didn't start with me."

Imperatriz throws a hand up. "What the fuck does that mean? Helisent, I'd like answers. Real answers. Not riddles. *Now.*"

Helisent falters. "My magic—and Samson—it's..."

"I'll explain," I say, setting my hands on my hips. "The House of Vex—"

"You are being used as a pawn," Imperatriz hisses.

Her tone is fierce enough that I fall still.

"Fuck off, Imperatriz," Helisent growls from behind me. "I told you—it didn't start with me. Or did you forget what you did? Did you really think there would be no consequences? That Andromeda North of Skull would waltz out of Bellator and give you a fucking gift for what you did?"

My mother scoffs, features bunched with confusion and exasperation.

Helisent goes on, "Ask your son if he's ever seen a red string before. Tell him where they came from, Imperatriz. Because it didn't *fucking start with me.*"

My mother's mouth falls open, eyes locked on the witch.

For a second, I balk, as shock, confusion, and distress wash through me. I turn, glancing at Helisent, where she sits with a morose expression.

Clearbold knew about a red string, one that came from Andromeda.

Which is a subject I haven't broached with my mother.

I turn back to see my mother reel, setting her hand on her chest. As though deep in thought, she looks at the ground, shaking her head slightly. When she looks up, she wears a mask of disbelief.

"No—no—no—no." She sinks to her haunches. "It can't be. She wouldn't have... we were *friends.*" Her breaths come ragged and fast. "*Lekeli Kelnazzar.*"

I almost go to her, concerned. It's a stronger reaction than when she announced her presence to the wolves in Mort, when she slit the throats of the criminals in Perpetua, when she found Clearbold's corpse between the mountain pass.

My mother rubs her face.

She doesn't say anything, gaze locked ahead.

I turn to Helisent to ask her for an explanation instead.

The witch watches my mother, her features heavy with sorrow. "What did you do with the string she gave you, Imperatriz?"

My mother smiles humorlessly as she rises to her feet. "What did I do with a blessing from the most powerful witch in Mieira? Well, I tied it around my wrist. And when my son was born, I took the red string and tied it around his ankle—to *protect* him—to *help us...*"

The scents of testosterone and cortisol fill the sitting room rapidly. Most comes from Imperatriz, but not all.

"A red string?" I ask Helisent. "Clearbold knew about it."

He said my mother tied it around my ankle after my birth. It incensed Clearbold; he removed it and buried it beneath a yew tree.

It was soaked with Vexen magic, and he didn't trust it.

"Oh, yes. Clearbold had forbidden me from trusting Andromeda."

Imperatriz looks at me, exasperated and nervous. "Can you imagine, atali? Can you imagine how fucking *evil* you have to be for *Clearbold* to see it coming?"

I watch her pace, my heart in my throat.

I start to piece it together—

A red string that Imperatriz tied around my ankle after my birth...

A gift from Andromeda that may not have been a gift...

"You want to talk about *evil*, Imperatriz—you took her into that room and you didn't even *warn* her," Helisent hisses. "You let her believe you were *friends* and then you *fucking took her into that room—* and then you had the *gall to ask for a boon*—how *dare* you? How dare you do that after evangelizing how all beings want love, safety, and possibility."

I see now.

The horn room.

My mother must have taken Andromeda into the room; Andromeda must not have realized what she was about to see. My mother must have thought it would bring them closer; Andromeda must have let her think that. Instead of offering a boon, she cursed her.

Holy shit.

My mind races; *what type of curse? And how powerful? And what are the terms?* All I know about curses is that they're incredibly powerful, incredibly varied.

I study Helisent's livid features. Her eyes are now lit with red light and glittering with tears. Her chest shakes like she's on the verge of weeping.

Her mother cursed mine?

Instead of saying that, I settle for, "A curse?"

Helisent nods. "A big one." She sniffles, turning her attention back to my mother. "For the debt."

"*Debt?*" Imperatriz cries. "The horns are from the *War Years.*"

The scent of testosterone and cortisol doubles, then triples in quick succession.

Now, most of it leeches from my body.

I take a deep breath, trying to focus my thoughts as they wheel through my brain. The images keep piling up.

I see my mother and Andromeda walk into the horn room; I see a red string looped around an infant's ankle; I see Clearbold stab a spade into the dirt beneath a yew tree; I see Andromeda North of Skull draw in her last breath, a tiny red witchling in her arms.

I remember dying with a copper ornament piercing my chest.

I remember the whir of magic that saved my life, the frantic pain on Helisent's blood-spattered face.

She is calling my name.

I see it clearly: Imperatriz thinks this was done against my will. She thinks that a curse binds me to Helisent, not love.

I turn my back to the witch, standing close enough that my butt grazes her knees. I follow my mother's movements as she paces, blocking her view of Helisent.

My temper snaps.

I'll deal with the curse in a minute.

In Velmic, I ask Imperatriz, "How could you do that?"

Imperatriz stops in her tracks. Her eyes fix on me, stunned. "Do what?"

"Take her mother into that room. Did you really do that? Without warning her about what she would see?"

All beings want safety, love, and possibility.

Imperatriz snorts, then starts pacing again, eyes wild. "There is no good way to do that. I had to sneak her into the palace, and then—"

"There's a good way to do everything—or, at least, a reasonable way." My voice rises as I stare at my Kulapsifang. Quickly, I wonder if I trust her. I wonder if she is more like Clearbold than I thought. If I've been sorely misled once more. "And now look at how you speak to Helisent West of Jaws. After *everything* we've been through in the last months—even after all of that, you have no fucking idea what the horn room means to—"

"They're from a time of *war*," she shouts. "A very violent *war* in which we also lost *thousands*—"

"It is a *genocide* when there is only one left," I say, voice rising to a shout, as well. "And there is *no respect* when you hang their horns like that. Why would we ever—"

"The red line refused to stop fighting, Samson. Did your father not have you read the—"

"I have read dozens of books about the War Years. I know all about the campaign to use magic to win the war. That's how we defeated the red line—by abducting one of their own. And even then, only an infant witchling because she was too young to fight."

How dare they?

I lose my mind with each word.

I have never yelled like this—but right now, in my mind, I can't separate them—

The infant Andromeda holds in her arms is Betty; the infant Aloysius holds in his arms is Helisent. They meld together into the same being: Betty, Helisent, even Milisent.

Every Vexen that has ever lived...

Every Vexen yet to come...

For a split second, Vieira is real.

And in Vieira, those are *my* red pups.

Mine.

And what threatens them threatens me.

"I know all about what Ilona and Aloysius did to Bloody Betty," Imperatriz counters in a lashing tone. "I know exactly how we almost ended the red line."

"Then you should thank Hetnazzar that we failed." I clear my throat, trying to control my voice. "If not, we would have lost our capital to foreign invaders. The scar on my heart is red because Vexen magic keeps me alive. Without Vexen magic, I die. And without Vexen magic, *you* would still be on Pit."

Imperatriz sets her hands on her hips. Slowly, purposefully, she says, "Unless a curse from Andromeda produced both of those outcomes—me being stranded on Pit and you being close enough to death that her magic could... wheedle into you like that..." She clenches her jaw, shaking her head. "You have *red skin* above your heart. I saw you *wield*. You want to talk about Bloody Betty—maybe you're right. Maybe that's what you are to Vex and Helisent. Her own Bloody Betty."

The words land like a blow. I almost turn to make sure that Helisent didn't piece together that sentence. We're speaking in Velmic, but I can't imagine it's hard to understand her name and Bloody Betty's side by side.

With measured steps, I leave the witch to close the distance between me and Imperatriz.

I'm exhausted and confused. But there's always a sliver of clarity awaiting me in life's most fucked up moments. Right now, I'm thankful for that.

I lower my voice and try to speak with strength and conviction. I study my mother's eyes and tell her, "I am not anyone's Bloody Betty. And I would appreciate it if you never insinuated that again. My ability to wield Vex's wand is the result of many decisions—every single one of which I made myself. Please understand me, Imperatriz… if I am wielding Vexen magic, then it *honors* me. I won't see it any other way, and you will *never* change that."

Her breath catches in her throat. She shakes her head like she might argue more.

When she doesn't, I go on, "And if you blame Helisent for what Andromeda did, then kill me, too. I am Clearbold's son, after all."

Her eyes narrow slightly as she stares at me.

More silence.

I take the opening, hopeful that Imperatriz might only need time and space to adjust to Helisent's announcement; I wouldn't judge her if that's the case.

"I need more rest, but before that, I'd like to take Helisent to the horn room." I take Imperatriz's hand between mine, desperate for her to stop and consider what we've discovered, and all I've argued. "Please stay here. I smelled masina and tobacco in my bedroom. Have a drink and a cigarette. Maybe a few. Just…" I lower my voice to a whisper, nervous. "I love you. I'm sorry that I'm not who you thought I'd be. I still love you, though. I want you to love me. And… they called Andromeda Amaro, but they call Helisent Honey. Because she's sweet. Okay?"

I back away, letting go of her hand.

It falls to her side as she stares blankly at the glass windows.

I wait another moment, wondering what sort of response I'm in for—maybe some type of punishment, maybe a lasting disappointment, maybe more arguing.

With a deep breath, Imperatriz raises her head.

She reaches out and sets her hand against my cheek. I don't flinch, but my body freezes. I can't tell if she notices; she runs her hand down my cheek once more. "Go, then. And bring more masina when you come back. Alone, please."

I nod, then turn back to Helisent. The witch remains perched on the windowsill, leaning against the pane and prepared to float to freedom. Her eyes dart from me to my mother as I help her down.

She steps down, eyes wide with shock. She scurries to follow me, hiding on my far side as we pass Imperatriz. The Kulapsifang turns to watch us go.

I look back once.

Imperatriz watches me like she's never seen me before.

Then I turn away, hurrying just in case Brutatalika heard our shouting and decided to investigate. I guide Helisent through my bedroom, then into the hall.

The palace looks so seamlessly reconstructed that it's hard not to pause and stare in wonder.

I lead us toward the throne room at the palace's rear. The revelations in the sitting room have left me with enough adrenaline that I'm spared from the depths of exhaustion. Still, my pace is slow.

"You yelled," Helisent whispers. "Also, am I allowed to be in here? That didn't seem like it went well."

"Everyone yells from time to time. I'd like to take you to the horn room. Now, if that's okay."

Her eyebrows raise. "Is that what you were yelling about? The horn room?"

"Something like that." I clear my throat. "Do you feel... ready to see it?"

"You yelled at your *mother*. Does this mean you're not angry with me about the curse?"

This time, my eyebrows raise. I almost laugh; *mad about the curse?* Here's how I feel about the curse: euphoric, haughty, and convicted.

Were it just love that bound me and the witch, we might never have a future.

But a *curse*... a curse is something Velm will have to respect. To contend with. To weigh.

"What the fuck are you smiling about?" she goes on. "I can't tell if you're mad about the curse. Say *yes* or *no*."

With each step, I'm more thrilled by the possibilities of what comes next.

A curse—a wolf who wields—

It's all pulling into focus.

All that's left is this one last part—

Then I'll figure the rest out.

"Wait until you see the horns," I tell her. "Maybe you'll curse me yourself. We'd just have this conversation all over again."

She tsks. "I'm not going to curse anyone."

"Well, if you curse anyone, curse me. Okay?"

She tsks again. "This is incredibly offensive. I've met Andromeda twice. I'm infinitely kinder than her. Trust me."

I slow when we reach the throne room. I take Helisent's hand as I stare at the place on the ground where Suleiman locked my calves and hands. I look up at the glass ceiling overhead, but that also gets my blood pumping. My strongest memories of the torture involve looking at the glass panes and waiting for the end; their image is lodged in my mind, detailed enough that I can see it when I close my eyes.

With a deep breath, I focus on the small door placed behind the cubic thrones.

Helisent's hand tightens on mine as we approach.

I stoop and crank open the door, then turn back. I block her view into the room and release her hand. "Do you want to go in first?" I study her nervous expression; she chews on her lip, then pulls her cloak tight. "I understand if you get emotional. I know it's not right, but I'm here for you."

"Fine." She clears her throat. "Let's go. You first."

I turn inside, surprised when the witch's hand takes mine again.

She keeps her eyes clamped shut as we enter. "I can feel them. I don't like this."

I nod, then force my eyes away from her.

It's been a long time since I sat in this room. At least once a year as an adolescent, Clearbold would drag me into it and sit me down on the floor. Now, there's no sign of cushions for meditation, nor the chunks of semi-aglow rosarium.

Just a trophy hall of cruelty.

From the floor to the ceiling overhead, sets of four bloodred horns cling to the marble walls. Moonslight traces them with silver, pink, and greenish hues, casting curved shadows below them. Though it's easy to pick out pairs along the bottom, they blend into an indistinguishable minefield of sharp edges near the ceiling.

They remind me of the fragile little thorns roses grow, tangled together below the moons.

For a split second, I regret this decision.

Even if the witch manages not to curse me, there's no way our love survives this...

And losing her right now, after all of this, and in this way...

"I don't like it either." Nausea rolls through me. "Take your time."

Her jaw clenches and unclenches. She takes a few deep breaths, but her eyes don't open. "Samson?"

"Yes, little bird?"

"I'm worried I'll react how Andromeda reacted. I know I just made a fuss that I wouldn't, but... I love you. I don't want that to change."

I take a deep breath, trying to calm my nerves. "I don't want that to change, either. But I want you to know the truth about me. No more secrets, remember?" I shift onto my knees to kneel in front of her. Once, the gesture would have grated on me; now, I shrink lower. And I shift closer, hugging her hips and setting my forehead against her soft belly. "If... there's a debt to be repaid... and if Vex is giving me magic... then..."

Then it's obvious, isn't it, little bird?

She shakes her head. "Then what?"

I've put it together since I learned about the curse in the sitting room.

It's straightforward enough—

"The only thing in the world your demigod lacks is a Male Host. And if Velm owes Vex a debt from the War Years, then... I doubt there's a better offering than a male Kulapsifang. Especially one who can wield your magic, Helisent."

The witch huffs, eyes shut. "You're still married, and I specifically remember promising not to fuck that up. And our children would be pith—that hasn't changed, as far as I'm concerned. And Velm is absolutely *not* going to offer up its Kulapsifang to the daughter of a witch who wielded a powerful curse against its realm. Should I keep going, my sweet wolf?"

I sigh, shifting my head lower. I fit my hands around her hips and kiss the fabric above her womb. "Open your eyes."

"*No.*"

"Do it."

"I said no."

"Open your eyes and you'll see the truth."

"I can *sense* the truth all around me. It's fucking awful."

I nuzzle into her warm layers. "If you opened your eyes, you wouldn't feel bad anymore. You wouldn't doubt what's owed to you."

She exhales through her mouth, then she opens her eyes. Her expression breaks as she takes in the horns, head tilting back. In a few seconds, her form unleashes; her brown skin transforms into a bloodred tone, her coarse horns exposed in their full glory. Her hands fit around mine, long and thick nails digging into my skin while her face bends with a grimace.

Her eyes are full of tears again when she looks down.

This time, she stares at me with conviction and pain and clarity.

She takes my chin with her hand, and I strain up toward her.

"You were right," she seethes, breathless. "I will never let this go, Samson. No matter how much I love you."

Tears sting my eyes. "Never?"

My witch is powerful; she will back this up.

And when she says 'never', I know she means 'forever'.

I told you.

The Female Alpha.

"*Never*. Now get me the fuck out of here before I level this palace again." She sighs angrily, then tears away from me and stomps toward the little door. With a frustrated shriek, she slams it shut, sealing me into the room of moonslight and red horns.

I lay back giddily.

She didn't say goodbye, but I can accept that.

This is only the beginning, after all.

CHAPTER 20

ESTEBAN & THE HOSTAGES
HELISENT

Honey Baby,
Here's the truth about Mama's death: nobody knew it was happening. She was
looking at you and smiling, and you looked back at her. The birth was over, and
you were both exhausted. You snorted a little snort, then you both closed your
eyes.
The Boys

I slide the heavy door shut behind me, panting, oblivious, numb.

One last gust of snow drifts in. It splays into the air like particles of dust.

I huff a laugh, reaching out.

I catch one with my bare fingers. Quickly, I bring it to my face and squint.

I count the fine details of the snowflake's ornate spokes. They're like rococo carvings, infinitely more complex than I would have imagined. Maybe snow is just piles of tiny jewels.

Samson was right.

The snowflake melts in the next second. I sigh, letting myself rest against the shut door. I press my fingers together, smearing the melted snow.

Rage stirs in my mind and body.

Love, too.

They are dual pendulums swinging within me.

I set my head against the door at my back.

It doesn't look like anyone notices a battle between love and rage playing out in my soul. I study the domestic scene before me, familiar enough after spending a week in Bellator.

The Bloodies' single-story dwelling has a large front room, a fireplace on one wall, and a series of inlaid shelves on the opposite.

Before the fire, Esclamonde and Butter stoop over neatly arranged vials. Vulcan takes a few from the women, then carries them to where Vega stacks the potions carefully on the shelves.

We finished healing the most dire cases in Bellator early yesterday morning. Since then, the Bloodies have split our time reconstructing buildings, sewers, and other necessities. We've also turned the city's limited number of winter herbs into enough potions and remedies to keep the surviving wolves healthy through Night's final stretch. The shelves are nearly full of our concoctions.

In the corner of the room, Halcyon sits guarding the largest of the three bedrooms that branch off from the main salon. Pel and Suleiman are both slumped and shackled inside. One herb Bellator isn't short on is timroot, which has made it easy to keep both men docile enough for imprisonment.

After Suleiman and Pel were captured, Zeu and his den took their time exacting revenge on the Host. Then came Halcyon and Vulcan; most of their efforts focused on getting the Male Host to reveal information about Serac's plans for Velm and any implanted indigo glaciers. Last were the wolves, who ferried Suleiman away and dumped him back at our doorstep the next morning, half-frost-bitten and knocked out.

No one managed to uncover helpful information from Suleiman.

I still don't know what the fuck the warlock was talking about when we fought near the portal—why Zarzynn would want me alive and what sort of project he thinks I'm undertaking with Samson.

What *rules* I still don't know.

Suleiman hasn't spoken a word, just stared ahead, half-dead and empty. Usually, with sweet Gracey the cow looming over him.

Thanks to Velm's massive doorways and dwellings, the cow has been sharing the room with the vampire and warlock at night.

The highland cow sticks her head from the doorway; she seems to be the only one in the room to notice my conflicted state.

Her pale tongue flaps over her wide, wet nose. To my great surprise, a second cow shuffles into view. Gracey has auburn hair, similar to a vampire's, but the second cow has jet-black hair.

Halcyon notices my double-take. He does one, too, squinting at me from across the small salon. "Someone dropped off another cow— it's for me. Also, why are your eyes glowing? Your eyes only glow when you're upset."

On cue, everyone turns to me. Vega pauses with her hand raised toward a shelf. Vulcan does the same, holding a tray full of clear concoctions in glass vials. On the other side of the room, Esclamonde and Butter watch me with wide eyes, hands frozen above the basins of herbal water set before them.

Nobody knows what just happened.

And I have no idea where to begin—

Samson yelled at his mother.

Also, he doesn't care that Andromeda cursed Imperatriz, or, at least, he doesn't seem to blame me for that.

He basically offered himself up as my Male Host.

Which he shouldn't have done.

Because I'm angry enough after seeing those horns to take him and never look back.

"Helisent...?" Halcyon asks, standing to approach me. "Say something."

I gulp down a breath, eyes wide. "I'm gonna kidnap him. I can feel it inside—"

"Woah, woah, woah." Butter stands up, nearly knocking into the basin, and rushes toward me. "No. Absolutely not."

Halcyon is close at her heels. "They gave me a *cow*. Apparently, it's a sign of thanks and honor—which is extraordinary considering every wolf can smell that I'm related to Suleiman. Let's not ruin that."

I shake my finger at the warlock, then the okeanid-witch-necromancer. "Velm owes you a lot more than a fucking cow. And what if the kidnapping is righteous and sexual and—"

"No," Butter snaps.

"No," Halcyon agrees, features contorting.

"No," Vulcan says without looking at me.

"Who are you going to kidnap?" Vega asks.

My chest wells with wrath and adoration. My fingers tingle with kidnapping magic—once, it would have been a pipe dream, but the Hellastone imparted many spells that will accomplish what I'm after.

I look at Vega, happy for the ally. "We're kidnapping—"

"Nobody," Butter shouts, planting herself in front of me.

Like a volcano bubbling over, I clench my fists and pull my shoulders back to scream as thoroughly and bestially as possible. Butter backs away, hands on her ears. Halcyon also covers his ears, bearing a livid expression at me. Esclamonde actually yelps, losing her grip on one of the glass vials, which shatters on the ground.

Gracey and the black cow huff unhappily from their room. Vulcan and Vega back toward them, craning their necks to check that all is well inside.

Then everyone looks at me angrily.

"I appear to be in a bit of a fucking *state* right now," is all I manage.

Butter looks at Esclamonde. "Get the brandy." Then she grabs my hands and guides me toward the fire.

I sit down on the fur rug beside the okeanid-witch-necromancer. Butter sets her robe into order and focuses her attention on me. Halcyon does the same, sitting on my far side as though prepared to detain me.

She says, "We agreed to stay here long enough for you to speak with Samson. If that's happened, and I'm assuming it has, then we're going back to Luz in the morning. Now isn't the time for an intervention with Velm." Quickly, she adds, "Though I hope he's doing well."

Halcyon speaks carefully, "If any part of my Landmark lives in Velm's glaciers, then I need to be in good standing with the wolves."

I study the warlock closely.

With Suleiman half-dead in the other room and his brothers long gone, I'm staring at the Male Host of Serac.

The pendulum of rage swings forward; the pendulum of love drifts out of sight.

"Goodness, aren't you a fit leader?" I ask. "Are you looking forward to your tail horn, Halcyon? Suleiman has a little sliver of bone. I looked. Once he's dead, I'm sure you'll have one nearly as large as mine. We can compare."

He blinks at me. "Don't do that."

"Don't do what—"

"Be mean because you're sad," he says quietly.

Before I can respond, Butter shoves a cold bottle against my arm. I take it from her, but start sniffling in the next second. I barely get down a healthy gulp before I curl toward the ground and cry.

I'm not even sure why.

Maybe it is the horns. Maybe my love for Samson makes it hard for me to...

To understand.

Halcyon scoots closer, draping his arm over me. Butter's warmth comes from my other side, her fingers taking mine. A third body presses against my back; Esclamonde.

"Also, Helisent, I don't think Samson wants to be kidnapped," the witchling offers.

"He wants a lot of things that would surprise you," I sob into my hands.

"I'm guessing you saw the horn room," Butter says, hand holding mine tightly. "That must have been fucked."

"We can talk about it, if you want," Halcyon goes on.

I whip my head toward him, baffled that he knows about the room of horns.

He clears his throat. "Butter told me."

Esclamonde adds, "And me."

I sit up, prepared to complain about the lack of secrecy—then I buckle with a fresh wave of sobbing. It feels like my body is lamenting the horns more than my mind or heart.

After all, I've known about the tallest room in Bellator Palace for months.

When I think back to the last hour in the palace, the first thing that comes to mind isn't the garish, unfathomable room with red horns jutting from the walls like hellish seedlings; isn't the way that Imperatriz sunk to the ground when she realized the red string was a curse instead of a boon; isn't the realization that Vexen magic truly and tangibly might be involved in Samson's life to serve him up as my Male Host.

It's the sound of his voice.

I remember how deeply my impression of him had changed after we almost drowned in Tet two years ago. I'd been hung up on how calmly he'd spoken to me as the flash flood began. Fearless, focused, and accepting compared to my mindless panic.

My impression of Samson is changing again—

I have survived some of life's most trying obstacles with the wolf at my side, but I have never heard him raise his voice with anger.

Until around an hour ago.

When not one but two Kulapsifangs decided to have a shouting match in my presence. I couldn't understand a word of Velmic, but it had been obvious that Imperatriz was leveling great accusations against me, and Samson was refuting each.

I'm also pretty sure he won the argument.

(*Ohhhhhhh...* he would be such a good Male Host.)

(*Ohhhhhhh...* the urge to kidnap my lover is strong.)

And then, just like that, the pendulum swings away from love back toward wrath.

I slump against the ground, still curled into myself. "Okay. Fine. You might be right. We might need to get out of here."

"That sounds good." Butter sighs, and then something hard nudges my elbow again. "Have another drink. We'll be gone before dawn."

I wake near a towering pile of offerings.

The hoard is nearly a foot tall and half a foot wide. As with the cows, we've woken up to find small treasures set on our doorstep. Cold, lonely, and left by unknown friends.

Warm light from the fireplace traces the piles where they're separated into bowls. Most are gold; chunks of unpolished gold, jewelry, brooches, buckles, ornaments, and just about every other luxury. The rest are hardy and leather: bags, satchels, straps, belts, harnesses, and more. Then there are piles of cedar resin and cedar incense, tightened into bundles. We also received brick after brick of peat, but refused these offerings. Same with the thick furs and pelts; though I'd happily don them, the wolves need these layers just as much as peat for survival.

We'll make the trip back to Luz easily—straight through a shadow.

But Bellator still has a month or two of Night on the horizon.

With a sigh, I toy with one of the golden pieces.

It's cold on one side, warm where it faces the firelight.

A hand comes to pull it from my fingers. "That one's mine."

I turn, startled. Dawn barely grazes the windowpanes near the door; I had assumed I was the only one awake.

Esclamonde, pasted against my backside where we lay near the fire, cranes to reach over me and take the golden piece.

"Do you feel better?" she whispers, sinking back onto our bedding.

"A bit." I feel like shit, but there's no use complaining anymore.

I'm leaving Bellator without Samson. Everything aside from that is a clear victory.

"Good enough to shadow us, right?" she asks.

"Yeah. I'll shadow us like I did with Zeu's den. We should end up in the same grove."

"The oak grove outside the city? Just to the south?"

"Yeah, that one. Where we joined the wolves' caravan."

"Do you think he's pissed at me, too?" she asks nervously. "Remember the big white fur coat Imperatriz gave him on the way here? He peed all over it and left it in front of the palace. I've never seen him so mad."

With a sigh, I tell her, "Zeu's angry because he thinks I don't respect myself." I clear my throat, admitting, "I should have told him about the horn room. I fucked that up. It was bad."

The words twist on my tongue. I feel a lot worse than bad. I feel like I betrayed him; I led him into that palace knowing that his mother's name was Heb and that the horn room might compromise his outlook on the Afadors and Velm as a whole.

"They aren't yours. The horns."

I go still. "What are you talking about? They're definitely mine."

"Sorry, I meant that you didn't put them there. They weren't yours to explain. That should have been something Imperatriz did, or maybe Samson. Imperatriz knew Hyd, so she must have known that the vampires revere Vex. She should have known to tell Zeu, Helisent. It was her responsibility first."

I stare into the fire for a long time, watching the warm flames consume the peat. "That's a surprisingly wise statement."

"I've been thinking a lot," Esclamonde says. "You know, since everything is going to change now."

I sit up, woken by her words. "What do you mean? What's going to change?"

"Well, we probably aren't going to see Zeu for a while. He *loved* that fur coat, Helisent. And Simmy is still in Jaws. And Draginine has been waiting in Luz for Butter. Meres, too. They're going to take her away and teach her GhostEating. Halcyon says he's taking Vulcan and Memphis on a trip. A *boys'* trip. So, lots of change. It always gives me stomach aches."

And Samson is staying here in Bellator, and I don't know when we'll see each other again, and I got so worked up I didn't even say goodbye to him.

She forgot to mention that.

"I've been thinking... do you think I could learn necromancy?" she goes on quietly.

"What? No. That's an okeanid thing. Why?" I shift toward where she's still curled on the bedding, turning the gold piece between her fingers and watching it catch the light. "Is that... what you want?"

"Maybe. I know I want to do something important. What are you going to do?" Her golden eyes scan me, lit with firelight. "Go back to Tet?"

I shrug, too sleepy for a solid answer. "Probably. I'll relax in Luz for a bit first. See if there's any new crisis from Antigone."

"What if we all go back to Tet together? Me and you and Butter and the GhostEater and the necromancer."

I turn to study her. Her tone is relaxed, her words slow and nonchalant, but her eyes stew and dart. "What's wrong? What happened?"

"Change makes my stomach hurt."

"Well, have a tonic. Nothing stays the same for long. Didn't Simmy always say life is like a river?"

"He says life is the river that cuts through stone. Gently, slowly, over centuries."

"Yeah, perfect. Chew on that for a while."

Concerned by the morose way she stares into the fire, I shift closer to her and run my hand down her back. Wordlessly, we cuddle near the fire until the others wake up.

In quick succession, Vulcan and Vega rise and then organize the wall of potions and tonics. They scribble a few labels and instructions for the wolves.

Halcyon and Butter focus on the prisoners instead. They re-up their doses of timroot, then drag the pair into the center of the salon.

Last are the cows, which Esclamonde leads out of the bedroom, through the salon, and into the street. They swing their heads, hooves clacking loudly on the hardwood floor.

With minimal chatter, we prepare for the journey, working swiftly before dawn can arrive in earnest. We gather in the center of the room, surrounding the slumped warlock and dazed vampire.

Outside, one of the cows huffs, and Halcyon heads to the door as though to retrieve them.

I use magic to shut it. "I'm not shadowing fucking bovine across the continent. We'll come back for them."

Everyone pauses.

With his hand on the door handle, Halcyons asks, "Isn't that offensive? Not accepting a gift?"

Vulcan goes on, "There's no way they'll survive out there."

Vega whines, "I was getting used to Gracey—she's a sweet—"

"You can shadow the cows when you learn how to do it yourself," I say, flicking my hair behind my shoulder.

I'd probably find it amusing if I weren't wondering where Samson is.

Whether he'd really be opposed to a kidnapping.

As though sensing the internal debate, Butter tosses her hands toward the windows. The fabric we've been using as curtains flattens noisily over the panes. "Fine. We'll return for the cows later. Let's focus on the prisoners for now."

She's right; I need them both semi-aware for what comes next.

Butter gestures toward the fireplace next; the flames extinguish with a loud hiss. Then darkness descends on the room.

With a sigh, I walk toward the group and find Butter's outstretched hand, then Esclamonde's.

"Is everyone linked together?" I ask.

They confirm.

"Aaaaaaaand, we're moving." I pull on Esclamonde's hand, dragging us forward. With the other, I cast toward the darkness, calling up a vision of the oak grove, the scent of dry dirt and wood in the winter, and the bundles of possumhaws that clank together like earthen windchimes.

The room fizzles with my magic's bass.

Then it reaches toward me, comforting and trembling.

I guide the group into it, driving us forward. Within two steps, we see a pale and faint blush in the distance, banked by shadows from a forested area. Sheltered on all sides by low hills, most of the grove is layered with thick shadows at this time. Past the tree line is a meager seam of light, the sun hiding behind the horizon.

I waltz through, then turn back to guide the group.

Unlike wolves, wielders can traverse shadows gracefully.

Butter and Esclamonde step forward first, followed by Vulcan. Vulcan turns back to tug Suleiman through, yanking him forward by his tunic. The half-unsconscious warlock stumbles forward onto the ground. He tugs his father through next, who pulls Pel in his wake. Last is Vega, who he guides forward gently by the waist.

We stand around the two prone hostages, who sit on the ground. As with Zeu's den, the group immediately reacts to the grove's warmth. No frigid gusts of wind, no piles of snow.

Just a mild wind. This early, it ruffles the mostly bare branches of the sturdy, towering oaks.

Halcyon clears his throat. "Helisent..." He nods at Suleiman and Pel. Both are slumped on the ground, hands tied behind their backs. Suleiman is barefoot, half of his toes darkened with frostbite. Comparatively, Pel is clean and healthy, a string of spittle roping from his mouth to his bare thigh. "You have around thirty minutes before the sun rises. I'd like to know what you plan on doing."

I raise my eyebrows. "I'm sure you do. But it'll just be me, Esteban, and the hostages from here on out."

"You're going to kill him, right?" Vulcan asks, eyes glued to his grandfather.

"Naturally." I smile at Vulcan, then Halcyon, hoping they'll take it as a cue to leave.

I'm much more practiced at shadowing now, but it still takes a toll.

I'm exhausted already, and the sun is rising.

"Anesot never told Halcyon his mother's name. My grandmother. He used to make up names just to be an asshole." Vulcan glances at his father, who slides an unhappy look his way. "We couldn't get any information out of Suleiman, but maybe you can. Just her name. If it's in there."

I huff. "Okay, goodbye now."

Halcyon levels a hard glare at me; he didn't make it far with his attempts to pull information from Suleiman, and I think it's mostly because he can't take the violence. He doesn't like the idea that I could.

I don't like it either, but Samson deserves vengeance.

And I want answers.

It's possible Suleiman was teasing me when he alluded to some kind of project with Samson, some set of rules to follow.

But it lines up too well with the curse. With the possibility of the Kulapsifang becoming my Host.

Halcyon heads to the north, where Luz waits a thirty-minute jaunt away. Vulcan and Vega step into line after him.

The warlock looks back once.

I offer him an optimistic wink.

Once the Pletens clear the tree line, I look at Butter. I raise my shoulders and chin, fighting my growing fatigue. "You get out of here, too. Draginine has been waiting for you in Luz for months."

The okeanid-witch-necromancer's eyes flit to the path where the Pletens file into the grass. "I'm not leaving Luz right away. I'll see you at home later, right?"

I nod. "This won't take long."

"Don't go back," she says quietly. "You swear?"

It takes me a moment to realize she's talking about Velm and Bellator and Samson and my urge to kidnap. I snort. "I know I've gotten a lot better at shadowing, but two trips in a day would knock me out."

Butter looks at the ground with a frustrated sigh. "Helisent..."

Before she can remind me that Samson will never be mine, I say, "You didn't see what happened. He *yelled*, Calypso."

Her eyes widen. "At you?"

"Fuck, I forgot how little you think of him." I roll my eyes. "*No*, not at me. At Imperatriz. When she... when I told her about the..."

Her golden-turquoise eyes widen further, like they'll burst from her head. "You told her about the curse?"

I nod. "She found me and Samson talking. I didn't have a choice. Believe me. She was *not* happy that he wielded... again."

She looks at the ground, as though trying to digest that news. "I'm relieved you told her the truth. The truth is always good. But... did we ... storm out of the capital after that revelation?"

My stomach clenches. "Well, *fuck,* Butter—it was either we leave or I kidnap—"

"Okay. Fine. Yeah. You're right." She gestures to where Suleiman and Pel lie slumped. "And... are we sure...?"

Her gaze drifts to Esclamonde.

The witchling looks like she's finally realized why Pel and Suleiman are alive.

Why she's the only one left here, assuming Butter leaves.

She shivers in her boots, lips pinched together and eyes teary.

Butter approaches her, setting a heavy hand on her shoulder. "Sweet little Esteban. You know what comes next, right?"

"Not really. Maybe. Is this because I got knocked out? I didn't see Kessrys—"

"This is because you marched to Velm, and you showed no fear, and you fought valiantly," Butter says, voice stern and deep. "This is because you are a Bloody, and a Bloody must do what must be done. A Bloody must be strong in case the other Bloodies aren't there with her."

Esclamonde watches the warlock and vampire with a frown. "Okay."

When the mentee looks at me, I offer a gentle smile. "My papa kept me very soft, Esclamonde. So did yours. But sometimes, we must be hard. Hard like diamonds."

"Like Zeu's diamonds?" she asks, voice shaking.

"Yeah. Like that. Are you ready?"

"I don't know." She lowers her chin, wringing her hands together.

"That's okay. Say goodbye to Calypso."

Esclamonde turns to Butter, who opens her arms to the skinny witchling. The embrace is quick, and then she takes off, her red silk robe flaring in her wake.

I don't wait until she's disappeared out of the grove. The shadows lighten with each passing minute; I'm still running out of time.

I take Esclamonde by the elbow and turn her toward our hostages. Suleiman lies on his side, shoulder rising and falling with deep breaths. Pel is semi-cognizant, scooting toward a tree on his butt.

With a deep breath, I use dragging magic to move Suleiman toward the nearest oak. I set his back against the trunk, legs spread in front of him. His head lolls downward.

Since Halcyon and Butter helped Zeu and me knock out Suleiman and Pel, then dismantle the portal, the Host of Serac has been heavily sedated. He wears the same tattered white cloak as that night, and a basic tunic and pants. Dried blood runs from his nostrils down his parched lips. His nails are cracked, his face swollen from multiple beatings.

I stand a few feet away from him.

I summon Esclamonde forward and raise my hand toward the warlock. "Pay attention." The witchling raises her hand and her fingers lace through mine, gently holding. "Can you feel what I'm doing? It's more subtle than the spellwork I used to storm the palace."

Psychological magic is much different than a physical spell—and given I only learned how to compel the body from my time meditating with the Hellastone, I'm not positive how to teach her.

This type of magic isn't nearly as direct. It's also not as easy to cast.

Only a truly incapacitated wielder would be susceptible to such an indirect and refined type of physiological spell.

Her skinny hand shakes atop mine. "I can feel it. It's like a whisper. Like a whisper sharpened into a dagger."

"Exactly. That's my magic surrounding his mind. The brain is where everything happens. That's where we decide what move to make—even before we realize we're deciding things. We aren't going to harm him in the traditional sense, okay? I'm going to look for information, like Halcyon and Vulcan did. He's not going to like it. Okay?"

Another sniffle. "Okay."

"Can you feel that?" My magic wheedles into Suleiman's ears; a dagger into the putty that is his subdued mind. "My magic will tell his brain to produce hormones, pheromones, and other chemicals. It will trick him. First into giving us information. Then into a painful illusion."

"You're going to hurt him?"

"Yes. He tortured Samson—and I think it was to get a reaction from me. Not just anger but... Suleiman knows something. Something that I'd like to know, too." I clear my throat, willing my voice to be steady, my stomach to be strong. "You don't have to watch, okay? And you don't have to listen. But don't move your hand, Esclamonde."

Her magic will remember what mine shows it; much like a mind or a soul, magic remembers tragic and foul and traumatic things in great detail.

That's enough for me—that the mentee's magical twin knows these things just in case.

Esclamonde angles her head away. I feel a light clang of Talosen magic as she casts a smothering spell around her ears.

I shift my hand as hers clings, wrapped tight.

I glance at her to make sure she's not watching or listening.

Then I turn back to Suleiman.

I inhale another deep breath; I exhale slowly.

"Suleiman. In the event you're too incapacitated to know what's happening, this is Helisent West of Jaws. Give me the information I want, and this will end quickly. Tell me what plans you think I have with Samson. Tell me what you meant by my future in Velm or Serac. Tell me why I'm worth anything alive."

Like a knife into butter, my magic pushes ahead.

I find a rush of terror and pain that catapults me into a labyrinth of cruelty. Emotions, fears, reactions—a windstorm of subconscious thoughts pours through the dark maze of his mind.

There are rushes—

Deposits of information like Suleiman's *desire* to pull me through the portal, the *need* to stabilize his House, and the *drive* for power.

But it's wildly overwhelming and evil, and I'm unable to separate information from instincts from nightmares.

I take a deep breath so as not to be overwhelmed.

Quickly, I pivot toward a more general spell—not one that searches his mind for information, but that tricks him into a sensation.

Fire.

The warlock's eyes open, and he lurches forward. His chest rises as he sucks in a full breath and then bellows, voice cracking and body shivering.

I close my eyes.

It's foul, unforgivable, boring. His panic magic activates, but it's nothing more than a series of listless and basic spells.

The sounds are so awful.

Awful enough that I swear the grove of oaks bristles and keens.

This warlock tortured Samson all night.

I don't think I make it longer than two minutes.

When I release the spell, the warlock is on his side again. He stares deliriously ahead, spittle lining his lips. His chest rises and falls, his frostbitten foot kicks out.

I prepare one last spell.

The Hellastone taught me to kill quickly—not via the heart or the throat, like I would have thought. Once again, the brain is where I focus. There's a node at the base of the neck where the spine meets the skull.

I shift my hand so Esclamonde knows to prepare for another spell. Once her hand resettles over mine, I send striking magic toward Suleiman.

With a minute spell, I shatter that little node.

Suleiman's body slumps dead against the dirt.

I watch him for a while.

It hasn't been nearly as gratifying as watching Anesot suffer and die. Worse, I learned nothing about Suleiman's plans.

I lower my hand. Esclamonde turns toward me, then slowly opens her eyes and looks at Suleiman. She gasps once, twice, and then beelines toward the open air past the grove. Her vomit hits the ground in the next second.

I turn to where Pel waits.

To my surprise, the vampire is awake now, eyes locked on Suleiman's corpse.

If he didn't look starved and exhausted, I'd swear he was smiling.

He looks up at me; the faint outline of the smile disappears. In its place comes cold acceptance. He tilts his head, nostrils flaring—

I take a step back.

He looks like Zeu for a split second; the shape of his lips, their fullness, the glow of his pale skin in the dim shadows, the way the light catches his iridescent eyes, the slump of his shoulders.

Fuck.

I raise my hand toward the vampire. But within a second, my appetite for vengeance has curdled into nausea and doubt. Suleiman deserved what he got—

And Pel bit my neck in Cadmium—

And he broke my hands in Mid City—

And he tried to drag me back to Zarzynn through Suleiman's portal—

But...

The mentee keeps hurling in the distance. Wind whistles through the bare oak branches and possumhaw bundles.

Sunlight grazes the horizon.

Fuck, fuck, fuck.

"What was your mother's name?" I ask quietly.

Pel clenches his jaw, staring up at me. I can't tell if he's overwhelmed or confused.

Maybe uninterested.

My stomach lurches.

I sink to my haunches. I stare at Pel, fighting the wave of compassion that builds in me.

I know, deep in my heart, that he didn't choose this. Even when physically free from Zarzynn, he wasn't psychologically free. Maybe he still isn't.

And evil... *what if his evil isn't something I can kill?*

Pel's evil would live on in me. I've already grazed Suleiman's, and that was bad enough.

Pel leans further away, looking past me. He watches Esclamonde. "Hurry." His voice is deep and calm. "Please don't let the sun have me. That's all I ask."

The vampire finally shifts his eyes toward me.

I stare at him and feel a flush of oxytocin warm my body.

Then I sense it, like a feather in a lake, floating and listless: Vexen magic. *My* magic. In Pel.

My familiar...

"Accra said you could sense where I am, along with my physical health." I set my chin on my hand, studying him from head to toe. Despite the last week of starvation and drugging, he looks largely unfazed. Just tired. "I feel like we need to expand that list a little. In Bellator, it looked like you could do a lot more than sense my location and vitals."

Pel watches me, expressionless. "Your magic can't be used to harm me. Only to help me." He looks at Esclamonde again. The mentee is now slumped onto her haunches, shoulders shaking as she weeps. "Not hers, though."

I study his slitted pupils. "You want to die."

"I want certain deaths, not others. That's all that's left for me. I do not want the sun to have me. Please."

Another wave of nausea swings through my stomach. His tone reminds me of Meres—of her subdued, listless voice when the House of Serac offered her up in Ezitlos long ago.

Pel looks from Suleiman's corpse to me.

He looks confused, annoyed, and defeated.

"Pel, my dear familiar... do you remember what Suleiman said to me in the throne room? It wasn't much. Something about Samson being a project. Something about... investing my magic in him."

The vampire studies my features feverishly, as though confused.

I suppose nobody bothered interrogating him.

I insist, "Whatever you know about Suleiman and his plans in Velm—this would be the time to share it."

Pel spares one last glance at Suleiman. Then, quickly and quietly, he says, "They brought over their Landmarks. Most of them, I think. Then the Hosts found something in the west. In Wren. A city called Wren. The city with the guilds. They found something, and it changed their plans. That is all I know."

In Wrenweary?

I look away, baffled about what the fuck a Host would want in Velm's misty, western plains.

I'll deal with that later.

With a curse, I reach forward.

Pel jolts backward, flattening his back against the dirt. I freeze, waiting for him to attack, but he lolls unsteadily to the side, hands tied behind his back.

I set my hand against his bare chest. His jaw clenches, lips pulling back from his teeth, but he doesn't shift as I gauge the markers of his physical health. The timroot is still active and, like I suspected, he needs nourishment.

I lift my hand and cast to untie Pel's bindings. His shoulders and hands relax immediately.

Pel falls still, looking at his hands as though confused.

I watch his hands and legs, waiting for signs of aggression. After months of training with Zeu, I'm not overly intimidated by Pel's size or strength. I glance at his body and tally several ways I could potentially best him in a grappling situation—at least, until Esclamonde could save me.

I stand and leave Pel on the ground. He shifts gingerly, first rubbing his wrists where the bindings left red marks, then scooting his legs in.

Past the grove's shadows and into the clearing, distended light fills the air. Though the sun hasn't peaked over the hilly horizon, we can't have more than a few minutes left of the golden hour.

I turn toward the mentee, shouting, "Esteban! Get over here!"

She approaches, sniffling and wiping her eyes. Wearily, she looks at the vampire. "Is he dead yet?"

"No."

I look at her, waiting for her to argue about how dumb this is.

Please tell me not to do this.

She watches me, sniffling again.

Pel steadies himself against the trunk, looking from the witchling to me.

Esclamonde narrows her eyes. "What are you doing, Helisent?"

"I'm having a fucking crisis of consciousness." With a sigh, I turn away from Esclamonde to refocus on Pel. "When I was in Zarzynn, I heard Vic say that every degi has a choice—they can lead a rebellion against their captors, take their life so they can't be exploited, or they can escape. Something like that. The point was—degis don't have to accept their position.

"I never liked that argument. Twisting someone's arm won't kill them, but it will coerce them. Zeu and Ret managed to escape, but not all are as bullheaded as they are. Or as lucky. I think softness is important, too.

"So, I'm going to take you with me back to Luz, and you're going to avoid Zeu's den at all costs. And you're also going to run for your fucking life if you ever smell Samson 714 Afador. I'm guessing you know his scent. Don't forget it—he's going to kill you if he gets a hold of you, and I can't change that.

"Until then... you're coming with me. Vex needs allies, not enemies. You're it's familiar now. Mine, too, I guess. And now that you have free will, maybe you'll start making better choices."

The vampire's only response is to slowly haul himself to his feet, grappling with the tree trunk for support. He looks from me to Escla-monde, baffled and afraid.

Esclamonde gasps, looking from me to the vampire.

"Prepare a shadow," I tell her, rolling my shoulders and then my neck.

I send my magic into action, taking deep breaths to manage my growing fatigue. Then I gesture Pel forward; he rushes toward the shadow as though entirely aligned with my goals.

Esclamonde clings to my arm as I take off to follow him.

She shrieks, "I'm telling Zeu!"

CHAPTER 21

TOO LATE

SAMSON

The weeks since we retook Bellator and Helisent shadowed the Bloodies back to Luz have been quiet and peaceful.

Night's bitter wind dwindles, and the piles of snow melt for a precious hour when the sun climbs halfway into the sky. I can't remember the last time spring's warmth, normally compacted into a few delectable weeks, started so early.

When the sun sets, my demigod howls from deep within the mountains.

I still haven't caught sight of Hetnazzar's blue-black fur or its twinkling eyes, but the sound of its dominion is welcome. It echoes through the reconstructed streets and the still-empty homes, offices, and shops.

Only one-third of Bellator's original population remains.

Another third lay in the columbariums outside the city, their bodies burned to ash and then stored in urns and categorized into clans. Thousands more dot northern Velm; many are likely to return, but not for another two months, when the snow has melted.

Until then, the husk of Bellator sits like a seedling tucked into the cold dirt.

Full of potential; waiting.

We make as many plans for the warm months as possible, spending half the days in meetings. Today, the palace's largest study is packed. Like in Mort, a vast and detailed map hangs from the wall. Notes and markers dot the Velmic and Mieiran portions, cataloging cities, villages, settlements, landmarks, rivers, and more.

The wooden tiles slotted into brackets have been updated.

Their flags, too.

Months ago, in Mort, half the map had been blanketed with white flags. Then came the yellow flags, which marked areas caught between the conflict.

Now, black flags populate most of the canvas map. A few even dot Mieira, marking where our most supportive allies can be found. The white flags are concentrated around Wrenweary in Velm's southwest, along with its southernmost mountains, where Hadadrimmon grew up.

Once more, Verita stands before the map, facing us.

In a semi-circle, I sit with Imperatriz, Brutatalika, Hadadrimmon, and two Members of the Fifty who recently returned to Bellator.

The first is Cartimandua 487 Ashurpanipol, head of the Order of Culture. She'd been forced out of the city a few months after I was ousted last summer, then led multiple revolts in the mountains surrounding the city. She also set up caravans to transport the wolves to safety in the north and east.

For how many times I heard her name growing up, I'm not sure I've ever seen her. She doesn't look like she's roughed it outdoors through Night's coldest stretch. Her hands are clean, her skin looks soft—not weathered.

I study her bold features, her thick eyebrows and the perfect spread of gray in her blue-black mane. Her cheekbones are high and broad, framing her almond eyes. She has a few dark freckles on them; a rare trait for wolves.

Verita has barely taken her eyes off the wolf since she entered the room and sat down twenty minutes ago. She looks from Cartimandua's hands to her chiseled face, as though honored or possibly surprised by her presence.

The second is Demre 511 Lengley, a member of the Order of Education and a prestigious scholar from Wrenweary. Though ousted from Wrenweary, he remains in contact with multiple scholars in the city. Like Cartimandua, he's provided critical intelligence over the last months, staying in close contact with Verita as we traveled from Mort to Luz.

The elder wolf is buried in his tunic and pants. He hasn't shaved in well over a week, though I doubt he's growing a beard. Like the crumbs on his sleeve, his unshaven face is more likely a sign of a genius mind enrapt in a mystery.

Since arriving in Bellator, Cartimandua and Demre have visited the study to deposit mountains of information. Their reports sit near the walls in tidy stacks: massive scrolls, tightly bundled letters, envelopes with paper and other odd pieces stuffed inside.

Now, both wolves study the map, comparing its details to the notes spread before them.

With a sigh, I turn to Hadadrimmon.

Like me, he doesn't have any papers or notes or note-taking supplies with him.

It makes me feel slightly better.

All I know is that we're meeting about Verita's latest communications with Antigone.

The wolf clears her throat to get the group's attention, her back straight and hands wrung together. "Thank you for coming—I know I was vague about the topic of this meeting, but I think it's worthwhile for Velm to stay... open-minded.

"Months ago, when Imperatriz led us to Luz, I spent an afternoon with Absalom Metamor. I've worked with Ethsevere and Cosisent for years. Based on what Samson told us, Absalom was to be my next ally in the Class.

"We met in Luz and spoke about many things. Most of the meeting was social—I'd never spent so much time with a warlock. Such an intriguing being."

I look at my hands.

I miss Helisent so much that I even miss Absalom. Anyone with a sliver of magic.

"Eventually, he told me about one of his latest interests. You can imagine my surprise when he said the word *Sennenwolf.*"

I look up, following Verita's skinny hand as she points to Tet. On the map, there are almost no details written about the region—not even a guess about where Skull might be, not even a note about the villages that border the misted stretch of swamp.

"He's been looking into the Sennenwolf on behalf of Helisent West of Jaws. Apparently, the red witch found notes that her sister had taken on Anesot and Oko. The pair were interested in Tet and, according to Milisent West of Jaws, the Sennenwolf.

"It piqued my interest—but I had many other pressing issues to focus on during this time. It faded from my mind shortly after we left the city."

My body goes still, hanging on every word.

Every mention of the Sennenwolf over the last years has led to nothing, if not more questions. From selkies, from GhostEaters, from dead sisters.

"Shortly after we retook Bellator, I received reports from Wrenweary. They detailed the Leolites' latest campaigns. Apparently, they've extended their reach to the west's far south—and to its far north, too. All the way to the border with Tet."

Verita clears her throat, heading back to the semi-circle where Brutatalika hands off a pile of notes. She rifles through a few pages as she heads back to the map. "I know little about Tet. As in, I know so little about Tet that any mention of the region is memorable. At least, to my energetic mind. A few days after I read the report on Wrenweary, I remembered Absalom's mention of the Sennenwolf. So I sent word to Antigone asking the warlock to send whatever he'd uncovered about the Sennenwolf on behalf of Helisent. Cartimandua, in the meantime, has been researching the Sennenwolf here in Bellator.

"A few days ago, I received quite a bundle of information from Absalom. Let's see..."

Verita squats on the ground to look through the unorganized pile of manuscripts, scrolls, and overstuffed envelopes. They reek of Antigone's wet metal.

She stands, holding one of the scrolls. "Absalom sent me excerpts taken from diaries, published books, unfinished manuscripts, and even interviews with the city's oldest residents.

"A few excerpts talk about Skull and the Sennenwolf as though they were the same entity. But the majority of the texts mention the Sennenwolf in direct relation to Bloody Betty."

My body locks, stomach clenching.

Bloody Betty?

Imperatriz also goes still where she sits at my side.

I hear her accusation float through my mind—

'You are her Bloody Betty.'

"According to Absalom's sources, Bloody Betty used the Sennenwolf on behalf of Velm to wage war against the wielders of Septegeur and Tet. It was a type of weapon. Something that had been carefully crafted and was impossible for just anyone to use."

A weapon...

That's what Kierkeline had told Helisent long ago.

"What type of weapon?" Imperatriz asks.

Verita licks her lips, opening three scrolls and rifling through them furiously. "Two sources say it was a whip. Three sources hint it was a type of rope—not a whip, but a... noose. Something like that. A fetter.

"Seventeen sources say it was a hammer. Absalom left notes where he found hammers mentioned. Some of the texts are outdated, so he wasn't sure how to translate a couple of terms. He thinks the descriptions of a hammer might actually be an axe—something wolves would have used."

An axe.

A Sennenwolf.

I glance at Imperatriz, but she doesn't lift her gaze from Verita.

Is the Sennenwolf... an ax?

"And what else did you find?" Imperatriz goes on. "Surely, there's more than a hint about an axe."

Verita clears her throat. "Unfortunately, not. I sent word back to Absalom asking him to seek out first-hand accounts written during the War Years. Those are our next best option for finding reliable information about the Sennenwolf—not rumors passed down by word of mouth."

Verita straightens her papers, waiting for another question.

"What does Absalom think the Sennenwolf is?" I ask.

Her eyes dart from me to Imperatriz to Cartimandua. "He doesn't know. But he agrees that it seems to be a weapon. I'd like to read the last few lines he wrote."

Verita glances at my mother, and Imperatriz nods in confirmation.

She recites, "'I hope my words will be plainly heard. I hope that Samson 714 Afador will vouch for my honor. When he came to me in Antigone in autumn, I welcomed him as a guest. I write this because my next statement will almost certainly be met with suspicion, if not offense. I mean neither—I only wish to speak plainly.

"If Bloody Betty ever wielded a weapon called the Sennenwolf, then Velm's wolves would have buried it after killing her. And if a weapon called the Sennenwolf was powerful enough to change the tide of the war, then it must be found again—this time, to fight the threats we face from Zarzynn.'"

Silence descends upon the study like an offense.

I look at my hands once again, thoughts reeling—

Did Velm really have possession of such a weapon?

Could it really be a hammer? Or a red axe?

And wolves wouldn't have buried Betty—so where is her urn?

The term Sennen could easily describe the red line, like it does the red moon—but how would a weapon created by a Vexen wielder fall into Velm's hands? And how could it be wielded by a non-magical being?

If that's the case, we already have one Sennenwolf: the red axe Imperatriz brought back from Pit. Clearbold took the other off of me and must have lost it to a powerful enemy.

As though eager to get back to her seat, Verita leaves the map. She gestures to Cartimandua. "As I mentioned, Imperatriz, Cartimandua has been looking into Velmic sources that discuss the Sennenwolf—"

"Well, I think we know why the Leolites want the west, then," Imperatriz says, eyes glued to Tet. "The geysers Argot would want are weeks south of Wrenweary. The glacial fields aren't far away. Why take control of the *whole* region of Wrot, then? Why bother taking any land near Tet?

"This is what they're after in the west. In Tet, too. Whatever the fuck the Sennenwolf is. That's why we barely encountered resistance when we marched south. Most of our enemies had already gone west." Imperatriz closes her eyes, pinching the bridge of her nose. When she opens them, she looks at Cartimandua. "Tell me you've found something useful. Anything."

Compared to the spread of notes around Verita, Cartimandua has only a few stubby piles. I recognize the Velmic parchment: a uniform size, uniform thickness, and a space at the top of the paper to list the moon cycles and seasons.

Cartimandua's long sigh gives her away. "Unfortunately not, Kulapsifang Draga. I haven't found any mention of the Sennenwolf. I've translated the word into dozens of Velmic phrases—but I can't find any documents that refer to a weapon, Sennen, or even a hammer or axe. Our language has not evolved nearly as much as Mieiran. I doubt I would have missed its mention."

She reaches for a lonely slip of parchment and holds it up. "But I did find mention of disturbances in Wrot, near Tet. They're dated around the start of the War Years. Dozens of farmers and shepherds were sending their grievances to Wrenweary, asking for help. I found descriptions of disappearing livestock, great storms, and seismic activity."

With another long sigh, Cartimandua sets the parchment down. "But the official reports would be in Wrenweary, not Bellator. All I have here are slips that recorded the reports had been filed—not the original copies."

Cartimandua glances at Verita; she looks back at the older wolf with a frown.

"Out with it," Imperatriz says.

Demre looks away from his piles of documents for the first time since the meeting began. He faces Imperatriz, blinking calmly. "They were burning libraries when I fled. It was the single most beautiful tragedy I had ever smelled. Velmic parchment is made partly with rosemary—you understand.

"There are many reasons to burn libraries. Sometimes, it's an act of purging. Impure ideas can be rooted out with fire—but what is an impure idea? And who decides what is impure? It's very subjective. So, the most pressing would be the strategic elimination of knowledge."

Imperatriz shakes her head. "Speak clearly, Demre. I hate scholars, and you speak like their king."

"Our enemies found information on the Sennenwolf in Wrenweary. Rather than risk it falling into our hands, they transcribed or stole the notes, then burned the libraries in case they held any more knowledge. They would have had plenty of time while you marched to Bellator. To simplify greatly: we're too late."

Imperatriz glowers at Demre.

Panic starts to whirl within me—

Helisent spends her time in Tet; she doesn't know about any of this, as far as I know.

Little bird...

Imperatriz covers her face with her hands, sighing angrily. "I see."

I can feel Hadadrimmon watching me. I glance at him, letting myself take comfort in his presence. Since Helisent left Bellator, we've become closer, solidifying his place in my pack and our status as more than allies desperate for survival.

I told him about the curse. About the yelling match with Imperatriz.

About the vague and haunting possibility of becoming Vex's Male Host.

And he's taken that information in stride. It's been a relief that Hadadrimmon hasn't had a bad word to breathe about Helisent. No judgment. No suspicions.

I've needed that type of acceptance. Though Imperatriz hasn't brought up the curse, it's left a palpable tension between us, just as thick and impenetrable as a wall. I know Brutatalika has picked up on it, which, in turn, has begun to drive a wedge between us.

She will choose Imperatriz; in public, in private.

It's caused me to shift my outlook.

I don't think I'll ever hand my trust and confidence over to another wolf again. That's a shame—until our blowout, I had been convinced Imperatriz was worthy of that. But it's also a blessing; my confidence has never been firmer.

I look at Cartimandua, then Verita. "I've heard the Sennenwolf mentioned twice over the last two years. The first time was when I met a selkie. I was with Helisent West of Jaws. The selkie mentioned a few things—including something about a Sennenwolf. I believe she mentioned it would reappear soon. That was at least a year and a half ago.

"I also read about the Sennenwolf from a note written by Helisent's sister, Milisent. Before she was killed by Oko, Milisent suspected they were after something in Tet. The Sennenwolf was a possibility, along with Skull, like Verita said."

"Does the witch know what it is?" Imperatriz asks. Her voice is neutral, but she knows Helisent's name.

I try to keep my voice neutral, too. "I don't think so, but she'd be interested to hear our thoughts on the subject."

Imperatriz watches me, a glint in her eye. "She doesn't know what the Sennenwolf is? Or that it's likely located in Tet? You're saying she just... ended up there? Randomly?"

"I don't speak for Helisent West of Jaws," I tell her. "But I feel confident she wouldn't put herself in a dangerous position. It's like I told you in Mort months ago—it's my understanding that she's in Tet on behalf of Vex. Helisent, being the very last of the Vexen, is focused on the well-being of her demigod more than anything else. She's there because Vex is there."

Imperatriz watches me, a grimace slowly forming on her lips.

I stare back as another series of arguments form in my head—things that Imperatriz said that I will not let go of.

She is wrong about Helisent.

No more backing down.

Never.

"What does her demigod want with Tet?" Imperatriz asks. "The last time I spoke with the witch, it seemed like her magic was overwhelmingly focused on Velm."

I raise my eyebrows. "Shale."

She balks. "Rocks? Is that why she asked me about marble?"

"Before she destroyed her Landmark to free Vex from Zarzynn, it dwelled in caves. Caves that must seem very familiar to those in Tet. And given that her magic is the equivalent of a demigod, I think it makes little sense to wonder what she's doing in Tet and whether it's moral.

"The same for the Seracyd and Argyd Landmarks.

"Absalom is following King Salem's lead in Antigone. He's doing that as a call back to the War Years. Thanks to the bounty of the demigods and their collusion in Luz, the War Years ended.

"What I'm saying is... if Seracyd and Argyd Landmarks are here, they're here. The same for Vex in Tet. Magic can be used as a threat, but it isn't inherently threatening. Our attention is better spent elsewhere."

Imperatriz watches me, eyes narrowing slowly. "I don't disagree—but we'd be naive to assume too much before we've seen these Landmarks for ourselves."

She turns, eyeing the group with a morose, unimpressed expression. After a long beat, she concludes, "As we retake the west, we will do so with great focus on Tet and the possibility of finding the Sennenwolf—here in Velm or there.

"We'll take a measured approach to the Landmarks. We certainly have Serac's latest Host, Halcyon, on our side. I'm happy enough with that for now.

"But first comes survival. Warmth is two months away. The snow won't melt for another cycle of Abdecalas, at least." Her dark eyes jump over the group again. "Until then, let's not lose focus on rebuilding Bellator and Rouz. Thank you for your work. Please leave your documents in the study."

Imperatriz turns and strides into the hallway, stepping over Demre's largest pile of stacked pages. We twist to watch her go, black cloak flaring in her wake.

From the hallway, she barks, "Atali. Come."

I offer a wilted smile to Brutatalika and the others before standing and following her. With each step, I try to calm the fear of there being a mega-weapon in Tet, of Malachai or Kessrys finding it before us, of Helisent unwittingly running into them first—

All while I'm stranded in Bellator.

Imperatriz leads us into a sitting room near the palace's residential wing. She's been using it as an informal office since we retook the capital. The soft blankets are soaked with her ala, along with the fluffy cushion sitting before the fireplace.

She walks past the desk and its messy shelves toward the small sofa where her blankets are strewn.

With a long sigh, she slumps onto the couch. She reaches over and picks up a small bottle of masina. It rests on her leg, upright, as she stares ahead.

She's been having trouble accepting the news about the curse.

I also think she's coping with eighteen years of trauma.

But I don't know how to comfort her. Not when I'm not sure whether to trust her, not when I'm preoccupied elsewhere, too.

She throws her head back to gulp down a drink, then she fixes her muddled eyes on me. Quietly, she says, "I have ruined this realm. Go on. Say it."

I take a seat on the couch and reach for the masina. I take a long drink. "Clearbold offered us up to Argot and Serac. Not you."

"You know what I'm talking about," she whispers, voice wavering.

I study her profile, backlit with flames from the small fire. I wonder what she really thinks about the curse. About Helisent. About seeing me wield with a wand.

"I mean it, Imperatriz." I offer her the bottle, bumping her arm.

"Clearbold didn't take Andromeda into that room, Samson. I did that. You were right." She takes the bottle with a heavy hand. "You were right about it all."

I blink, shocked to hear those words. *Right?* "Me?"

"I shouldn't have done that. I didn't think about it. You heard Draginine back in Lampades. I'm like my mother. Spewing words like diarrhea. And now it will fall on you, Samson. I can accept that I spent eighteen years on Pit for my misdeeds... but you..."

The GhostEater said, *Spewing words like vomit*, but I don't correct her.

I set my hand on her forearm. Since our fight weeks ago, I haven't imagined she felt this way. That she'd be stewing in so much self-doubt. I've been doing the same, toiling in a private world of second-guessing.

She doesn't turn to me, taking another long drink. "You are the one on whom the axe falls."

I lean toward her, pulled into a vortex by her words.

Is that why she's been so conflicted?

She thinks I'm afraid?

Part of me wants to remind her that the axe already fell and I already dodged it.

"You were terrified of magic as a pup," she goes on. "You should have seen how you clung to me when the wielders performed for us. You cried when they enchanted the puppets and made them dance.

You screamed when you saw them fill the cylinders with dove. And now... *cursed*... my Kulapsifang... You hate me. Admit it."

She finally turns to me. Silver tears line her eyes.

"No, I don't. Mama, I have real enemies. I save my hatred for them."

She turns toward the fire. "If I were you, I would hate me."

With a huffed laugh, I pull the masina from her grip and drink.

Publicly, she doesn't bat a lash, doesn't look uncertain even when facing a monumental puzzle. Privately...

Privately, I think we might be a lot alike.

She goes on, "We have Bellator and Rouz, but it's only the beginning. I'll stay here through the summer and split my time between the cities to rebuild the Fifty. Brutatalika has done a wonderful job as the Female Alpha—but she has a lot to learn. She needs to stay with me. She'll learn quickly, I have no doubt. But I can't teach her what must be gained with experience."

She sets her hand on top of mine, leaning away from the fire to face me. "Which means I would need to send you to Tet to look for the Sennenwolf. If I do that, I'm basically offering you up to Helisent. I can't put you in such proximity to her demigod. It could be dangerous for you. Especially if Vex has already... tried to... with you wielding..."

I can feel the truth bubbling inside me.

"I'll go to Tet." I nod, hoping to offer reassurance. "It's not a big deal."

Her eyes study mine. "I can't send you, Samson. I was thinking about Cousin Hadadrimmon. He's a little rough around the edges, but it seems like he thinks highly of the witch. If he went—"

"No." I don't feel my lips form the word, but I hear it clearly. "Not Hadadrimmon. Me."

"You are the Kulapsifang of Velm, Samson 714 Afador. I cannot risk our legacy, and *magic* risks—"

"It's too late for that."

"A curse isn't final. They can be assuaged and met in imaginative ways. Assuming Helisent won't hold a grudge forever, we can barter with her—"

"You are very much indebted to Helisent as it is. In terms of the curse and in terms of all she's done over the last six months. And you don't need to fear Vex. I know you think that Vexen magic created the circumstances that landed you on Pit, but Vexen magic brought you back. And it's still keeping me alive as we speak. Maybe the curse… maybe it isn't what you're assuming it is."

Imperatriz looks at me.

She shifts on the couch, sitting up to face me.

The longer she stares, the more her eyes narrow.

I stare back.

I don't remember what it was like to have a mother most days, but this feels familiar. I am her child; I attempted for years to hide little things from her. Treats, figurines, toys. She knew all my hiding places. She knew what my lies sounded like, what they looked like on my face.

She angles her head; I think she's figuring it out.

I clear my throat. I can't tell if I mean to tell her right now or if I'm just exhausted, enraptured, desperate.

She angles her head to the other side. "What?"

Like a nervous child, I start rambling, "We're stupid. Me and Helisent. I'm less transparently stupid, but still very stupid. She might actually be less stupid than me." I gesture at nothing. Half of me is painfully aware that I'm making little sense. The rest of me is untethered from reality. "We were both motherless. Kind of at the ends of our ropes. She had just gotten this mentee, and Rex had broken up with me—again—and then she got this stupid idea to go to Tet. She can't even fucking swim. Maybe it's the jewelry. Too heavy. Mama, if you ever see her get near a body of water, you need to—"

"Sh, sh, sh." Imperatriz bares her wide eyes at me. "I think I'm having a heart attack."

I fall still.

Within a breath, I realize her vitals are fine.

She's just being dramatic. That's fine.

It would be suspicious if she didn't react like this.

Totally normal.

But the silent minutes keep passing. Imperatriz stands up and paces, looking at me with a wild glint in her eyes. Then she sits back down and takes a long drink of masina. She slumps back on the couch and stares at me long and hard before standing and pacing again.

She polishes off the bottle of masina, then stares into my eyes. "So, the wielding... is... welcome?"

From the outside looking in, and from the perspective of wolves who understand nothing about magic and demigods, it must have looked like I was forced to sacrifice some part of my fangself to wield, hurled into an unknown of infrasound and wands.

I hold her gaze. "I want what is best for Helisent and Vex. For a lot of reasons."

She straightens quickly. "And... and the witch?"

I blink, uncertain about what she means by that. "Yes?"

"Well?" Imperatriz gestures around wildly. "Is this an... an unrequited situation or is the witch—is this why—oh, lekeli Kelnazzar." She bends at the waist, bracing her hands on her knees. "Is this why the red witch very happily toted me all across Mieira and Velm? And why she rebuilt my capital?"

Uncertain of how Imperatriz is taking this, I try for a reasonable response. "Well, I think it's mostly about stability in Velm and throughout Mieira. And I had also gone to find her when—"

"*You went Zarzynn for the witch?*" She lifts her head, eyes still wide.

"And to get you. Both."

"*You left Velm for a witch.*"

"And you, mama."

She straightens and stares at the wall, expression tense. After a while of mindless staring, she looks at me and announces, "I have no idea what you want me to do with this information." She laughs without humor. "And to think I spent years on Pit worrying that you were going to turn into Clearbold." She huffs, gesturing at nothing once more. "You know, Kulapsifangs should keep their affairs to themselves, Samson. I'd hate for you to sit and stew thinking about me nuzzling Cartimandua—"

"*What—*"

"—when you should be concerned about me leading a realm. I know you missed quite a few formative years of learning what is and isn't appropriate for Kulapsifangs, but let's not forget the obvious. You are married. And Helisent is a witch. And... and... well, that's it. There's nothing else to cover."

I groan. "Fine then. I guess we won't talk about Cartimandua anymore, either."

Nuzzling.

I make an involuntary sound of discomfort.

"Oh, I'm sorry. Samson, *have I overshared?*"

This time, when Imperatriz looks at me, I see disbelief in her eyes —and it's lined with mirth. I have little to no understanding of how Imperatriz is taking this news deep down, but that sign of laughter is my chance.

I take it, desperate for a sense of normalcy. I throw up my hands. "At least I didn't say anything about nuzzling." I look at the fire, frowning. "She seems too... old and serious for that."

Imperatriz falls back onto the couch. A faint smile traces her lips. "She's six years younger than me. And she tells jokes like a sailor."

I groan again. "That's great."

"You don't have any children I don't know about, do you?" she asks next.

"No. Definitely not."

"That's fine, then."

"...Do you?"

"Only you, atali." With a deep sigh, she sets her hand on my arm. "I always knew you would be special. Most mothers think that when their stomachs swell and they feel the baby kick. But I didn't think about it until after your birth. Few women experience birth as their fangselves. Sometimes, I wonder what it would have been like...

"You were born a few hours after I turned skin. It was a painful transformation, but I had felt it coming. Imperatrizfang knew. She'd known from the start of the pregnancy. I wasn't shocked, at least. You were born, and I cleaned you, and I could feel your warmth and your little drumbeat. But you didn't make a sound.

"I bit your grandmother that night. She kept nudging you when you didn't cry. She was worried. But I didn't like the nudging, so I bit her. And then it was just me and you. You fed, and I knew Sutnazzar had been wrong to worry. You had an appetite, and I kept you warm. We spent the night together, and at dawn, we turned skin.

"I'd been so worried to lose sight of you when I was shifting. I braced myself to hear your cries. But I woke up in my pale body and didn't hear a thing. I panicked—

"When I turned around, you were lying on your back. You had your little fists clenched, Samson, and your little eyes on me. You looked so different—hairless and not nearly as tiny as I thought you'd be. Still, you didn't cry."

Imperatriz turns to look at me. "The silence reminded me of Hetnazzar." She reaches over and strokes my cheek. "I knew, Samson. I knew something at that moment. I still don't know what I knew, but we're close to finding out."

A heavy silence falls over us, broken by the gentle crackling of the fire.

I know.

For a while now.

But it's too soon for that, so I go with, "I think you're drunk."

Imperatriz laughs, rubbing her face and leaning against me. "And hungry."

I lean back with a chuckle. "Me, too."

"Suin," I say, head hung. "You wouldn't believe everything that's happened since your death."

I study Rex's intricate urn. The marble piece is painstakingly carved with fine lines filled with liquid gold. Rex's urn sits beside his father's, Colsep's, and Berevald's. Someday, I'll take Berevald's remains to his village east of Rouz.

For now, the three urns sit side by side on a clean shelf in Bellator's oldest and most prestigious columbarium.

It's a relief to know where they are.

I set my hands on my thighs. A small blanket remains on the ground before the three urns; I return almost every night.

Tonight, I relight the cedar incense nearby, then arrange today's offerings. Masina for Berevald, bintsuke oil for Rex, and lingonberry sweets for Colsep.

As I do, I mention the possibility of becoming Helisent's Male Host.

I never pull my punches in this quiet columbarium. The dead cast no judgment.

So they hear every last detail about what's happened since their deaths. That I haven't found Riordon or Pietrangelo, but I will; that I never got the chance to punish Clearbold, but I figure Suleiman did; that I defended the city by wielding with a wand in the same place

Bellator's wolves tried to kill me last year; that I'm tied to Helisent West of Jaws by force of curse and love.

I conclude with, "You know, everyone always thought I would roll over on the witch at night and crush her. Her brothers, you guys. Even me, sometimes." I close my eyes and remember the sound of their laughter. "I never did, though. Not even a little bit."

I open my eyes and stare at their urns.

It's hard to quantify that this is how they exist now. Hard to admit that I'll never smell them again.

I know I'm not done mourning; maybe I haven't even started yet.

With a sigh, I bow to their urns and then say my goodbyes. I linger at the door, looking back at the shelf where they sit. It blends seamlessly with the rest of the columbarium.

With another sigh, I turn away and head back to the palace. This late at night, the roads are empty and peaceful. The frigid air fills my lungs; familiar, fresh, and invigorating.

I sneak into the palace, careful not to wake anyone as I pass the guest chambers. Then I pass the hallway that leads to my bedroom. I continue to the farthest chambers, to the throne room and the tiny door at its back.

I stand between the marble seats and stare at the door.

I haven't ventured into the room since Helisent stormed out of Bellator.

But I've been tempted many times—

I can feel Vexen magic in the horns. The longer I stand and sense their presence, full of magic that seems to crave animation, the more I wonder if I could cast without the help of the wand.

It's a potent enough drive that it overshadows the torture I faced in this room. Within a few weeks, those memories faded in lieu of brighter, more vivid possibilities.

I turn, flinching when I hear footsteps behind me.

Brutatalika approaches with her robe pulled tight around her. She looks from me to the little door as she walks to one of the thrones. She slides onto the cold marble, then adjusts to get comfortable.

Her eyes are like piercing coals, set on me and burning. She glances at the other throne; I sit, sensing that she'd like to speak.

I study her throne and the way she occupies it.

Only the reigning Alphas sit on them.

It's something we won't do until she...

Until *we*...

She sighs, long and forlorn. "You know, my mother and aunt wanted me to be cultured. They knew that I'd compete for a place on this throne someday.

"They saw Imperatriz fighting for the Northing, so they brought me books about life in Mieira to prepare me. There was one book—I think it was a series of folk tales from Eupheme. It was newly written. There was a story about a pregnant witch.

"Did you know there are mini-villages around Mieira designed for pregnant witches?"

She looks at me, waiting for an answer.

I'm not sure what's happening right now, but it's very calm and severe.

I clear my throat. "I didn't."

"The mini-camps are for the most powerful witches as they enter the final months of their pregnancy. As the fetus matures, it starts to wield. Did you know that Samson? That wielders start to cast before they've taken their first breath?"

My stomach lurches. I don't want to have this conversation.

I don't want to know why Brutatalika is bringing this up.

"I didn't."

"They don't understand what they're wielding. They're just... reacting to things they feel. If the mother is unstable, the fetus will wield in response to her whims. Even if the mother is stable, the fetus might wield when it dreams or senses something. Depending on the pup's inherited power, these spells could level entire buildings. That's why they send them to mini-camps."

I stare at her, chin lowered. "And why are you telling me this?"

"I first heard of Helisent West of Jaws when I was still a girl. My mother sat me down with the book of folktales and turned to a story about the pregnant witch. She said Andromeda North of Skull took her warlock to a homestead where she could be cloistered for her pregnancies. Far from civilization, her fetuses wouldn't hurt anyone. Because they were threats, Samson. Not because they were evil. Just because that's what they were."

Did Imperatriz tell her?

Did she figure it out herself?

My stomach lurches again.

"She wielded against her own mother. That was the first thing Helisent West of Jaws did. Took all the magic from her mother. And… and…" Brutatalika turns to look ahead. Her jaw works while she shakes her head. "I've known you for as long as I can remember, Samson. You are my first memory. Maybe not you, but… being walked into this palace. Hearing others speak your name. I can't… separate myself from you. From your existence."

She takes a deep breath. She stares at her hands.

When she looks at me, her burning coal eyes glisten with tears. "I will not be taken to one of those mini-camps. I don't care if they call it an Afador. I will not bear your pup if it wields."

I stare at her.

I feel the rift in my soul—the same that opened up in Luz when Helisent and I engaged in sex magic.

It tears open further, making way for a plummeting, silent, and hungry sort of sadness.

Brutatalika stares back. "You come here every other night. You think I don't notice."

I understand now.

Not a condemnation, but a question.

A thousand responses fly through my head.

I didn't mean for it to happen, Tali.

But I didn't stop it, either. I have begged Helisent for kisses multiple times, and I will continue to do so until someone clubs the virility out of me.

I remain loyal to Velm, to Hetnazzar, to Imperatriz, to you.

But I also remain loyal to Helisent.

I love both of you, but not equally.

So cruelly unfair. And I'm not positive Brutatalika would be swayed by love.

When she says that she can't separate herself from my existence, it's only partly about romance; it's also about honor, survival, and the fate of Velm.

She is my wife; she is my partner; she is one-half of the Kulapsifang's success and legacy; she is also one-half of the future Kulapsifang.

I stare straight ahead. "If you would like to listen, I would like to tell you the truth." I turn, hoping that she can sense the warning in that statement.

Imperatriz ordered me not to breathe a word about the curse—
Otherwise, I have free rein to speak my truth.
One that I'm increasingly interested in sharing.
She nods slowly, then says, "Don't make me ask."

CHAPTER 22

(SENT DISCREETLY
TO A BOY-WOLF)

HELISENT

To Hetnazzar's precious boy-wolf-

I figured I should write since I stormed out of Bellator without saying
goodbye. I've spent the last month thinking and stewing. It's been
good for me.

I've thought about many things. Mostly about how lonely I am. I've
pretty much skirted that reality for all of my life, but I keep seeing the
room of horns. I keep wondering what they were like, Samson. I
dream of one set often. I'm convinced they belonged to Vex's last
warlock.

It's very difficult to be alone. I don't think I've spoken to you about
that before. It hurts too much. It's like standing in the center of a vast
city that was once occupied. All of the stuff is still there. Wardrobes
full of clothes, fountains full of water, little gardens full of plants.
There are imprints in the sheets where the Vexen just rose from their
peaceful slumbers. There is condensation on the tiles where they just
finished bathing. But there's no one there, and I know there never will
be. And still, I wander every single room and street and store,
knowing that I won't find anyone but unable to rest. Like Hella, but
bigger and still lived-in.

It's taken me a long time to admit how deeply this experience of loneliness has shaped me. It feels like a deep part of myself. I think it makes me reckless. There's this part of me that wants to destroy myself, or maybe destroy the world, or maybe both at once. I'm not really in a position to destroy myself or destroy the world anymore. (I destroyed Ezit, and it didn't curb this feeling.)

So, after a month of stewing and rewriting this letter, it's come to my attention that I know what I want. And I feel that what I want is righteous.

When we were in the horn room, you said that Vex might be turning you into my Male Host. Is that really what you want, Kulapsifang? Are you fulfilled by a love that might be partly created and sustained by a curse? And what the fuck do you think will happen to Velm if you took on such a role?
I think I'd like answers now. The idea of not being alone in this vast city hurts me, Samson. It's too great a desire, and I'm terrified of what I will do for it. That's your problem now, too.

So this is how it will go.
This letter is sent on magical paper. Tucked inside is more magical paper—I'm sure you found it.
Write me a response and throw it into a shadow, asking Vex to deliver it to me. Remember last year when I said that your mind and Imperatriz's were like two ends of a string? Maybe ours are like that, too.
I'll be waiting to hear back. If you can't figure out even a very basic spell, then send a reply the old-fashioned way. It better come fast, regardless. This entire letter is very undignified.

-Your impudent little bird

CHAPTER 23

(SENT DISCREETLY
TO A LITTLE BIRD)

SAMSON

To the Vexen,

Assuming you receive this letter, the magical paper worked.
Thank you for writing. I've written and rewritten my words several
times, and I'm not getting any better at explaining myself. So I'll keep
this very simple.

You asked, *'Is that really what you want, Kulapsifang?'* I want to be your
lover, and your Host, and your friend, and your partner, and your
mate, and your confidante, and your ally. I want to start a pack
with you.
I have never once entertained the reality of seeing another man
become your Male Host. I know I said in Vex that I would stand
aside, but that was a zhuzh. The truth is that Samsonfang considers
you his Female Alpha, and so do I, and it's been that way for a while.
I've wasted enough time and energy feeling conflicted about this.

*'Are you fulfilled by a love that might be partly created and sustained by a
curse?'* If your magic scared me in any capacity, or our love, I would not
still adore you. The curse was at least partly justified. (Or righteous, to
use your words.)
Maybe, like Accra said in Vex, there are two fates. One of our fates is

love, the other a curse. I'm fine with the reality of that; wolves are suspicious of 'perfect' things.

'And what the fuck do you think will happen to Velm if you took on such a role?'
This is for me to figure out as Velm's Kulapsifang. It's a great honor, Helisent, to be considered worthy of this role by Vex. That's what matters here—Vex and Hetnazzar. (And me and you.)
Maybe this isn't bad for Velm, either. What if we think about our love like that, Helisent? Like it's good for the world? I like that.

That's how I feel. I think it's all fairly straightforward.

From your loving boy-wolf

(P.S. Please, don't let anyone read this note. I know how warrens work, but I'd like to keep this between us.)

(P.P.S. And please smell this letter. I rubbed my scent onto it for you. If you sleep with it under your pillow, our alas might start mixing.)

(P.P.P.S. Make sure you read the last letters from Bellator; they were sent to Luz's processor. Verita thinks the Leolites and their allies are looking for the Sennenwolf in Tet. Please be very careful if you go back. I'll explain more when I see you. Soon, hopefully.)

WANT TO KEEP READING?

Here's a little sneak peek at what's to come in the next book of the Sennenwolf Series, *Red Gold*.

(DON'T TALK LIKE THAT)

Brutatalika and I walk slowly down a residential street in Bellator.

The air is warm, the sunlight pale in the early morning.

Blooming linden and oak trees dot the wide lane, swaying in the breeze. A few lingonberry bushes cling to the single-story homes. Tiny birds dart amid their branches noisily.

This early, shutters cover the windows, the front doors sealed shut.

Only one wolf has woken in time to see us pass. An elderly wolf leans from her open front door, facing us. She pulls her shawl over her shoulders, narrowing her eyes toward where I walk with Brutatalika at my side.

Her wrinkled features bunch with a smile.

"Kulapsifang Laita," she calls to me in a croaking voice. She turns to Brutatalika. "Alpha Draga."

Laita; male. *Draga;* female.

My wife and I bow our heads and smile, small and fake, as we pass her.

Our shoulders are close, but they don't brush.

When we pass the elder female, Brutatalika readjusts her stuffed satchel on her shoulder, inching further away from me.

Since we left the palace twenty minutes ago, I've scripted a few gentle goodbyes. Half of me is relieved to have the next weeks to myself; the rest of me feels guilty. Nearby, my wife will meet her pack in a plaza. From there, she'll travel with Verita, Leda, and Exultet south to Rouz to stabilize the city council and re-establish communication between the cities. I'll wait behind in Bellator with Imperatriz.

Since I told Brutatalika about my relationship with Helisent two months ago, we've barely spoken.

She listened to my story—

About a desperate partnership to find Oko and Anesot; about a surprising love that followed; about a scramble to survive all that's come since.

We've spoken almost exclusively in public since then. She spares glances and words for me when I don't clean the sink well enough after shaving, when she wants me to pass her a plate during meals, when I get in her way and she doesn't feel like touching me.

The only coup is that she hasn't abandoned our shared room.

At night, before her breathing deepens with sleep, I apologize in incongruous ways.

"I hope you have sweet dreams."

"The cherry blossoms will bloom soon."

"Your new earrings are lovely."

Useless sentiments like that.

(Here's the truth: I've never broken anyone's heart before, and I'm not handling it well, and it's starting to break my heart, too.)

Brutatalika sighs as the plaza comes into view.

I hold back my own, hellbent on putting on a brave face.

The wide street leads to a square plaza neatly gridded with mature trees. In its center sits a marble water fountain with animals carved into its lip; mongooses, snakes, and swans all nipping at one another in a graceful circle.

Past the fountain on the far side of the plaza, my mother waits with Brutatalika's packmates. The women appear to be chatting happily, their voices low.

I fall still, shielding us behind a few bulky maple trees.

Brutatalika doesn't stop, heading straight for her packmates.

"Tali," I call quietly.

She turns around, but she doesn't retrace her steps to stand with me beneath the maples.

She lifts her eyebrows, waiting. Despite her poor mood, she hasn't let up on her personal care. Every blue-black hair is gelled into place on her scalp, and her bun is tight and round. Her new golden earrings twinkle, matching the perfectly shone torc hugging her neck.

All of my scripted words disintegrate in my head, syllable by syllable.

I take a step toward her. "I hope you're safe. And I hope you're happy with your pack. I hope all of you enjoy Rouz."

I hope I haven't destroyed that type of happiness, too.

Brutatalika watches me, totally still. "It will be a relief not to smell your ala, Samson 714 Afador."

She turns on her heels; I'm glad she turns away—my jaw actually drops.

I stay hidden amid the maples' shadows as she crosses the plaza. Her packmates turn when they smell her, faces alight with smiles. Imperatriz, too.

My mother greets her and then, after a few quick words, Brutatalika leads her pack toward the dirt road that leads to Rouz.

Imperatriz watches them go.

When they've cleared the plaza, she turns and locks her gaze on me. With a sigh, she wanders past the fountain toward where I stand under the trees.

"Atali." Imperatriz joins me, reaching out to smooth my hair. "She needs more time."

I barely spare my mother a glance, focused on Brutatalika's pack as they drift further and further out of view.

Imperatriz's words don't soothe me.

I felt a tear in my soul open after Helisent and I began a dalliance with her wand.

Now, it's deepening into a vacuous rift—one full of emotions that are writhing, insistent, previously unknown.

Who am I supposed to be?

"I mean it," Imperatriz goes on. "Brutatalika hasn't had long to process the news about you and... you and... the witch. Give her time. Give yourself time, too. It will get better."

I stare into her eyes, full of doubt. "Get better? Like they did for you and Clearbold?"

The more I consider the possibility of red pups, the more I think about the alternative.

Bearing the next Kulapsifang with Brutatalika.

Imperatriz balks at my words, leaning on her back foot. Quickly, her eyes scan me. "Me and Clearbold?"

"Sutnazzar doesn't live with her Male Alpha anymore, and she hasn't since they gave up the thrones and left Bellator," I go on. "She wasn't happy, either, was she?"

I wonder how far back it goes.

"Samson, don't talk like that," Imperatriz murmurs, her expression tense.

I look at her, overwhelmed with bitterness.

She bore me to be powerful.

She bore me to exist alone.

She bore me to carry a legacy.

She thinks I will do the same for my pups.

I look into her eyes, trying to find the right words.

She doesn't let me. She sets a heavy hand on my shoulder, turning me around. "Let's go home. Let's rest."

(IT'S STILL TOO SOON)

I slap Butter on the calf with a loud *smack*. "Do it. I'm not showing you mine until you've shown me yours."

I settle into place where I'm draped across the foot of the bed. On the other end, Halcyon and Butter watch me with dual expressions. The warlock looks patient and intrigued; the okeanid-witch-necromancer looks from her calf to my hand, visibly unhappy.

A few thin blankets are spread between us, half-covering her and Halcyon's legs. I'm covered up to the waist, my breasts freed of the fabric.

Since returning to Luz from Bellator, we've spent over a dozen nights together in my bedroom like this. Me as a pitiable third wheel in the pair's ongoing affair, usually with Halcyon encouraging me to feel proud of my horns.

I raise my eyebrows. "Well? You want to see my horns, Butter. And I want to see yours."

I'm desperate to establish a more positive relationship with my horns after gracing the tallest room in Bellator Palace two months ago.

Every time I manage to get into my form, my gut knots.

"Why do you need to see mine?" Butter asks. "Halcyon's are out all the time."

As usual, the warlock prefers his natural state at home. Four horns jut from his forehead and his hairline, smoothed and shone into indigo candy. They're slightly darker than his violet skin, which is almost as bright as my red hue. His cropped white hair is neat, not caught on fibrous horns like mine. They glow in a steady, indigo hue as he looks from me to Butter.

It's almost dawn, the light in the narrow window brightening slowly. At this hour, Halcyon looks like one of the last traces of night, like a dream smeared on the horizon.

With a long sigh, Butter looks at me. "If I get in my form, then I want to know what Samson wrote to you in the letter. You read it repeatedly for a week, and then suddenly decided you hated it. So? Do we have a deal?"

I take a deep breath.

I hate the letter talk even more than the horn talk.

The note is tucked away in my bottomless bag, the parchment soft after weeks of handling. "It's too early to talk about the letter."

Butter pushes off Halcyon's chest to sit up. With a demure tilt of her head, two dainty, golden horns appear on her forehead. They're unkept like mine—the golden husks rough and their ends semi-sharp. Butter's turquoise-white curls catch on them gracelessly as she pouts.

The okeanid-witch-necromancer looks at me, her eyebrows raised. "What was in the letter, Helisent?"

I tsk in response. With her hickory-brown skin overlaid with a golden hue, she almost looks aglow. She sits topless in the bed, the sheet wrapped around her lap. Even her mauve nipples are kissed with a warm sheen.

Halcyon sits up, angling his head to get a better vantage of his favorite lover.

I ignore them, staring at my bottomless bag on the other side of the room.

The letter...

With a frustrated sigh, I look at Butter and admit, "Basically, he's going to be my lover, my mate, my friend, my confidante, my partner, and *my Host*. That's what he wrote, at least. And... I can feel him, too. Sort of. It's hard to explain."

Butter's eyebrows lift, her lips pulling into a surprised smile.

And Halcyon even nods, as though unsurprised to hear that. Quietly, he asks, "Does it sort of feel... like a whisper? Like a whisper from far away?"

My eyes widen with shock—

I'd expected the pair to push back about the note—not for the warlock to lean in with a surprisingly accurate insight.

Since leaving Samson in Bellator, I've started to sense his presence in Velm's capital city. I wake in the mornings and hear his voice from far away, like he's whispering to me at the edges of dreams. Sometimes they wake me in the middle of the night, and they feel real, like he might be sleeping beside me—

All I know in these moments is that he's sleeping somewhere.

That his mind is whispering thoughts into mine.

That it's Vexen magic ferrying these gentle notions between us in the loving embrace of sleep and peace and silence.

Which I had thought was really fucking special.

I blink at Halcyon. "How do you know about the whispers?"

"Suleiman has been dead for over two months." Halcyon reaches up to graze his scalp above his ears. His fingers shift in his white hair, feeling for something. "My fifth and sixth horns are starting to grow in. I didn't notice the whispers until I noticed the new horns."

Butter reaches beneath the blankets, then pulls out the indigo, spade end of the warlock's tail. She taps it like a merchant with a cherished good. "And his seventh, too."

I crane toward them to examine his spade-shaped tail and the semi-rigid bone forming in its center. My mind drifts from the realization that Halcyon is going to look like me with all those horns to the fact that he can also sense a Host.

A *Female* Host.

"Holy shit," I manage.

"I can feel the Female Host—she's somewhere in Velm," he goes on. "In my dreams, I hear whispering in a voice I've never heard. It's unsettling. Do you feel the... the tugging, too?"

"No, what's that?"

"I think she must have the Landmark, or whatever piece of the glacier Suleiman and his allies took to Velm." Halcyon sighs, rubbing his arm and turning toward the half-lit window. "It almost feels like me and her are tied together by a rope, and she's pulling at her end. I only hear the whispers in the mornings, but the tugging happens at all hours. It's more jarring. Very attention-grabbing. I think it has to do with the Landmark—not our... our..."

He frowns as he stares at the window.

He doesn't look away when Butter strokes his cheek and says, "It's just a magical connection, Halcyon."

I nod, setting my hand on his calf. "It doesn't have to mean anything unless you let it."

Finally, he looks at me. He mopes, eyes burning when he asks, "Do you think Samson can feel it? The same things we're feeling?"

I consider the note, my gut knotting again. "I think so. At least, in his own way. He's been dreaming about me for years. It's called a seething. And he sent the letter back on magical paper—without the wand. It might not sound like much, but for a wolf, it's a big step."

I look up, expecting to defend Samson and our love and the painful possibility of getting everything we want.

That's why I hate the note—

It's like seeing a hoard of jewels delicately balanced on a ledge, prepared to be lost forever with so much as a slight wind.

But neither Butter nor Halcyon looks disgruntled.

Halcyon actually nods. "I suppose he's at least partly magical."

Butter lies back on his chest with a sigh. "Yeah. I mean, the scar turns red, right? The one on his chest."

"Yeah. Red like me." I relax with a sigh, closing my eyes. I swear I see a yew tree in my mind's eye, vast and bowed and ancient, where it sits on a mountainside.

GLOSSARY & WORLD

The * symbol marks terms that are newly introduced in Book 3, *White Night*.

- <u>Ala</u>: A wolf's scent. Alas are highly unique. They carry information on gender, health, generational count, family ties, and more. Only wolves can smell alas.
- *<u>*Atali</u>: (Velmic) Son
- <u>Bitterroot</u>: A bitter flavor preferred by wielders.
- <u>Centerheart</u>: A wielder who is unable to cast magic against those they love.
- <u>Demigod</u>: A very large and blue-glowing magical being that is tied to a specific geographic region in Mieira. Demigods are the source of elemental power that nymphs who are born in their domain can draw on. Demigods appoint kings and queens to help them with custodial duties related land-based resources. The only non-nymph demigod is Hetnazzar, who roams Velm.
- <u>Desita</u>: a state of ecstasy that the demigods and nymphs can energetically absorb. Wolves and wielders can feel desita, though it doesn't boost their physical and emotional health, as it does with nymphs.
- <u>Dextro</u>: Cocaine. Did anyone pick up on this? You guys, it's cocaine.

- <u>Driproot</u>: A sleep aid.
- <u>Dove</u>: A type of wild magic that wielders can store in order for other beings to use. Nymphs and wolves, though largely non-magical, can apply dove from a wielder for almost any purpose.
- <u>Ejima</u>: The intelligence and consciousness of a House and Landmark, which are enacted through magic. In other words, it's willpower.
- *<u>Exit</u>: The forceful removal of non-wolves from Velmic communities.
- <u>Fangself</u>: A wolf's form which is imbued with a secondary set of instincts and desires.
- *<u>The Fifty</u>: A group of 48 officials who represent Velm's geographic regions and infrastructural institutions; the final two members are the reigning Alphas.
- <u>Form</u>: A true physical appearance. A wolf will phase into their form, a giant wolf, on the triple- or doublemoon. A wielder will use magic to hide their form so others can't see their horns or tails.
- <u>Highmoons</u>: Midnight.
- <u>House</u>: A region in Zarzynn that is supported by the magic of a Landmark and its wielders. Zarzynn is home to six Houses, each of which draws its magic from a distinct Landmark.
- <u>Kulapsifang</u>: A title for the inborn Alpha of Velm, who is born from the previous generation's Male and Female Alphas. Sometimes abbreviated as "Kulapsi."
- <u>Landmark</u>: An ecological and magical core of a House, which generates and stores magic through natural phenomena.
- *<u>*Lanu lago*</u>: (Velmic) The gray winter sky that stays shrouded through Night.
- *<u>*Lekeli Kelnazzar*</u>: (Velmic) A curse that translates literally to 'a really bad Night' from 'lekeli' (fucked, cursed, bad) and 'Kelnazzar' (Night)
- <u>Lilith</u>: A cushion used by wielders for floating.
- *<u>Masina</u>: Velmic hooch; very potent.

- <u>Mixed</u>: A wolf couple whose alas merge to form a separate third ala, mixed from their original alas.
- <u>Northing</u>: To move North into Mieira from Velm.
- <u>Pith</u>: To be magically powerless. Nymphs born far from their homelands and demigods are pith by distance. Some beings, like the offspring of wolves and wielders, are born pith.
- <u>Pitroot</u>: A contraceptive for male wolves.
- <u>Seething</u>: To be compromised magically by a witch's sexual ala. This occurs only between male wolves and witches. Seethings cause a wolf to dream of the witch in question.
- *<u>Suin</u>: Velmic for 'twin', a term of endearment often used between close friends and lovers.
- <u>Rosarium</u>: A calcified stone that is mined from Zarzynn's dead Landmarks. Rosarium can be used to nullify magical power, including that of nymphs and wielders. It has no effect on vampires or gorgons.
- <u>Rosfrost</u>: A liquid potion made of water and powdered rosarium. It provides the drinker with magical immunity.
- <u>Stretch</u> (Plet, Pit, & Silt): A chain of islands that sit between mainland Zarzynn and northeastern Mieira. Plet is the largest and most populous. Silt and Pit are hidden amid clouds of fog; only a select few know how to find them.
- <u>Southing</u>: To move South into Velm from Mieira.
- *<u>Timroot</u>: A potent but rare sedative that can be used on any being.
- <u>Torc</u>: A piece of jewelry that wraps around the necks and upper arms of wolves.
- <u>Unnumbered</u>: To live as a wolf without a generational count or pack.
- <u>Vagueroot</u>: A contraceptive for witches.
- <u>Waricon</u>: A wrestling match common to wolves. Waricons are designed for friendly competition, entertainment, and to resolve disputes of leadership.
- <u>Zhuzh</u>: A way wolves finesse the truth without technically lying.

Words I Didn't Actually Make Up

- <u>Ala</u>: "Wing" in Spanish.
- <u>Saiga</u>: A species of antelope indigenous to the Eurasian Steppe; they are critically endangered.
- <u>Zhuzh</u>: This doesn't necessarily mean *to lie*, just to "fancy" something up. Some linguists think this word came from Yiddish. Others think it might be Romani.
- <u>Laline</u>: "Moon" in Haitian Creole.
- <u>Cap</u>: "Moon" in Mongolian.
- <u>Marama</u>: "Moon" in Maori.
- <u>Rosarium</u>: "Rose garden" in Latin.
- *The heartbeat as the first drum*: This is a concept Capes has only seen discussed in relation to Native American powwows and culture. If you want to do more research, look for Native sources.

CHARACTER GUIDE

The * symbol marks characters who are newly introduced in Book 3, *White Night.*

- <u>Absalom Metamor</u>: Member of the Class; Helisent's patsy.
- <u>Accra</u>: The eldest gorgon and matriarch of Dexerxes (Zarzynn), aged nearly 250 years.
- <u>The Accras</u>: A collective term used by the Mieirans for Accra and the three matriarchs who trail her at all times.
- <u>Accra-Four</u>: The youngest of The Accras of Dexerxes who invaded Ezit alongside the Mieirans.
- <u>Aura Hypnos</u>: A hypnotic okeanid with powerful water-based magic. She's one of the leaders of her warren, which is based in Mid City-Sunrise.
- <u>Boonmasent Luz</u>: Owner of Luz's finest witches-only spa.
- *<u>Cartimandua 487 Ashurpanipol</u>: The Head of Velm's Order of Culture; Imperatriz's super-secret lover.
- <u>Calypso 'Butter' Ultramarine</u>: Okeanid-witch-necromancer from Ultramarine who was taken captive by vampires alongside Helisent and Queen Otrera. Part of the Bloodies.
- <u>Ceyx Plet</u>: Halcyon's first wife. Vulcan's mother and Cleo's sister.
- <u>Chariovalda South Bend Gamma</u>: Hesperide, co-founder of Coil, and better half of Gautselin Mort.

- <u>Cleo Plet</u>: Halcyon's second wife. Memphis's mother and Ceyx's little sister.
- <u>Clearbold 554 Leofsige</u>: Samson's father and the Male Alpha of Velm by right of waricon and marriage to Imeperatriz 713 Afador.
- *<u>Clover Gamma</u>: Hesperide Queen who resides in central Gamma; a patron of Zeu's den and one of the King of Night's favorite lovers.
- <u>Cosisent Septegeur</u>: Senior member of Antigone's Class; ally.
- <u>Draginine West of Jaws</u>: Mother to Itzifone Bugs Alita and Mieira's only GhostEater. Manipulative, shrewd, covered in silver jewelry.
- *<u>Demre 511 Lengleye</u>: A member of Velm's Order of Education and ally to the Afadors.
- <u>Eos Hypnos</u>: A hypnotic okeanid with water-based magic and an interest in leading okeanids. She's one of the leaders of her warren, which is based in Mid City-Sunrise.
- <u>Elvira Ultramarine</u>: Unnumbered wolf who is Coil's most popular resident. A bit of a maneater. Hates Helisent.
- <u>Esclamonde Black Rock Antigone</u>: Witchling from Antigone and Helisent's mentee. Slowly becoming less of a burden.
- <u>Ethsevere Black Rock Antigone</u>: Head of Antigone's Class and uncle to Esclamonde; an ally.
- *<u>Exultet 514 Cecil</u>: Brutatalika's powerful right hand and pack member.
- *<u>Ferol</u>: Male pack leader of Luz, raider of Coil.
- <u>Gautselin Mort</u>: Unnumbered wolf and co-owner of Coil, Luz's sexiest pleasure house.
- *<u>Hadadrimmon 342 Aithesson</u>: Great-grandchild of Malasuntra 711 Afador; a 'semi' Afador from a bastard line and Samson's new packmate.
- <u>Halcyon Plet</u>: A four-horn wielder and one of Helisent's favorite friend-lovers. Part of the Bloodies.
- <u>Hemlock East of Alita</u>: A Rhotidic King who rules over parts of Mieira's Rhotidom Jungle. He's known for his jacaranda jewelry and lilac-colored cloak.

- Imperatriz 713 Afador: Reigning Kulapsifang of Velm. Disappeared eighteen years ago.
- Itzifone Bugs Alita: Bartender of Luz's seediest tavern, Solace/Soulless. Lazy in bed; lies about it.
- *Kessrys: The Female Host of Argot.
- *Leda 486 Kellybold: Member of Brutatalika's pack, known for her sass and love of gossip. The daughter of Lampades' female pack leader.
- Malachai 525 Leofsige: Clearbold's second heir to the throne. Not an Afador.
- Memphis Plet: Halcyon's teenage son; keeps sleeping in Esteban's bed and making her pillow smell weird.
- Onesimos Eupheme Jaws: Helisent's favorite lover and oread. Co-founder of her warren.
- otrera Hypnos: Hypnotic Queen who rules from Mid City-Sunrise. She was taken as a captive to Zarzynn alongside Helisent and Butter.
- Parsifal South of Jaws: Helisent's papa. Big gut, bigger heart.
- Pel: A degivampire held captive by House of Col. Pel is the drank Helisent's blood in Cadmium after biting her neck. This makes him Helisent's vampire familiar.
- *Ranavalna Red Tier: Sketchiest member of the Class; probably from Zarzynn and definitely a bird-killer.
- *Salem Septegeur: A Septegan King who rules over parts of Septegeur and Antigone; chosen by a dryad demigod. Keeper of the highly feared folviper.
- Suleiman: The Male Host of Serac and Halcyon's biological father.
- Vega Plet: Vulcan's girlfriend.
- *Verita 454 Melfrey: Former representative of Velm's Wrot region and part of Brutatalika's pack.
- Vic the Chosen, Queen of Night: Leader of Zarzynn's second-largest vampire den located in the former area of Vex.
- Vulcan Plet: Halcyon's adult son.
- Yngvi West of Jaws: Helisent's probably-oldest brother. Yves' twin.

- <u>Yves West of Jaws</u>: Helisent's second-oldest brother. Yngvi's twin. Insists he's the oldest.
- <u>Zeu the Chosen, King of Night</u>: Leader of Mieira's largest vampire den. His den was once responsible for aiding the escape of degis from Ezit through guerrilla warfare.

Ghosts

- *<u>Andromeda North of Skull</u>: Helisent's mother.
- <u>Dexa</u>: A male Vexen who helped found the gorgon village of Dexerxes centuries ago.
- <u>Bathsheba</u>: A female Vexen who joined forces with the vampires of Zarzynn to free their kind from Ezit.
- <u>Axerxa</u>: A male Vexen who died fighting the unified Houses of Ezit during their last campaign in Vex. He was the last Vexen to live inside Hella.
- <u>Berevald 522 Firstin</u>: Samson's third packmate, known for his long hair, open heart, and interest in vampires.
- <u>Kierkeline Ultramarine</u>: A powerful GhostEater.
- <u>Milisent West of Jaws</u>: Helisent's older sister.
- <u>Rex 507 Kaneling</u>: Right-hand, best friend, and former lover of Samson 714 Afador.
- <u>Tol, Princess of Night</u>: Now leading a den in death.

WIELDERS

Witches and warlocks descended from magical Landmarks in Zarzynn, also known as Houses.

Argot

Geysers | White

Serac
Glaciers
Indigo

Lahar
Volcanoes
Orange

Talos
Waterfalls
Golden

Col
Cliffsides
Jade

Vex

Caves | Red

HUNDREDS OF YEARS AGO...

As bloody conflicts worsened in Ezit, the Houses of Talos and Vex were forced toward the coasts by the armies of Serac, Argot, Col, and Lahar. Thousands of wielders fled from Zarzynn toward the islands of Stretch. Some even ventured onward to Mieira...

EVENTUALLY...

To save their people, the House of Talos capitulated to the will of Ezit. However, the House of Vex refused to admit defeat. The last Vexen sailed from the shores of Vex around five hundred years ago, coinciding with the War Years in Mieira.

WELCOME TO ZARZYNN

MAP

Nymphs

Mieirans born to demigods that rule unique ecologies.

Dryads
Born with forest-based magic, native to the jungle of Rhotidom and the forest of Septegeur.

Hesperides
Born with wind and seedling magic, native to the plains of Gamma.

Naiads
Born with freshwater magic, native to the rivers, lakes, and swamps of Mieira.

Okeanids
Born with tidal and moon magic, native to the shores of Hypnos and the Deltas.

Oreads
Born with fire and mineral magic, native to the volcanic cones of Jaws.

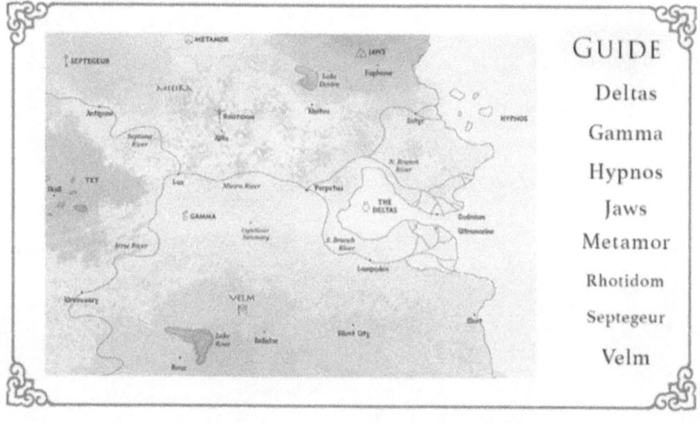

WOLVES

Shifters from Velm who are ruled by a wolf demigod, Hetnazzar.

Long ago, Hetnazzar selected the Afadors to rule and protect Velm. For 714 generations, the Afador line has continued unbroken. Mostly.

• THE WAR YEARS •

Though centuries have passed since the bloody War Years, its ghosts linger close in the wasteland of Tet. Some wolves still claim this region as part of Velm. Others fear the ghosts of Tet and the city of Skull.

THE AFADORS

(and the Aithessons, born from Malasuntra's affair with Aithe)

Malasuntra 711

Sutnazzar 712
Love 340 Aithesson

Imperatriz 713
Koli 341 Aithesson

Samson 714
Hadadrimmon 342 Aithesson

GREEN-GRAY

PINK-GRAY

RED

Abdecalas (V)
Laline (M)

Vicente (V)
Marama (M)

Sennen (V)
Cap (M)

OTHER BEINGS
Found in Zarzynn, Mieira, and Velm

Vampires

Night-dwellers from Zarzynn. They spend their days in hidden dens, then emerge at night to hunt. For centuries, Zarzynn's free dens have sought sanctuary from Ezit in the empty House of Vex.

Selkies

Pinkish fish-beings who reside in Mieira's freshwater channels. Selkie are known for prophesizing. Okeanids and other coastal inhabitants believe selkies turn into seals when they enter the ocean's saltwater.

Gorgons

Peaceful and long-lived beings from Zarzynn. Eye contact with a gorgon is deadly. Gorgons live in cloistered villages that are walled off from the outside world. Outside of their villages, gorgons wear blindfolds to protect others.

Ghosts(?)

Mostly-alive beings native to Tet. Many claim they appeared after the War Years. Others insist they're nothing but an illusion created by Tet's heavy fog and distended sunlight.

The LightEater

A mysterious being located in Gamma who attracts massive bolts of lightning. The LightEater does not move, speak, or act. Despite this, worshipping nymphs dote on the LightEater from a nearby temple.

ACKNOWLEDGMENTS

Yes, this book is also dedicated to my dead chihuahua, known lovingly as the Rat King. I hear his tiny ghost stomping across my apartment fairly often, which leads me to believe he knows I'm writing a fantasy-romance series in his honor and is intrigued by its progress. (It's not weird.)

Okay, anyway—

Thank you to E.V. and Cory Ryan. I don't know how you two keep signing up to help as beta readers when you're regularly served my hot-garbage drafts, but I love you for it.

Special appreciation for E.V. for reading my work when I know you regularly read well-known fantasy romances. Sparing time and effort and passion for my cheeky little fantasy worlds means a lot.

Special appreciation for Cory Ryan because you beta read my work regardless of what's going on in your life... which is sometimes a lot. Thank you for making time for me, my friend.

Another shout-out to Mr. Capes for supporting my wayward delusions. (Also, why do you like Zeu so much?)

Lastly, a big noisy-ass THANK YOU to the Tiny Dancers and my ARC readers. Please don't underestimate how much your presence means to me. None of this journey as Capes would be possible without you.

ABOUT THE AUTHOR

Capes is the pseudonym for author TL Adamms. She likes romance, fantasy, things with metaphysical ends, nature, the color red, and slow fashion. She writes to make sense of the world; she reads to forget it. She's very happy you've found her work. Please, indulge yourself!

Capes's stand-alone fantasy, *The Unburied Queen,* was shortlisted for the 2022 Foreword INDIES. *West of Jaws* was shortlisted for the 2024 Foreword INDIES.

Website:
WWW.CAPESCREATES.COM

Instagram:
CAPES.AUTHOR

Facebook:
AUTHOR.CAPES

Peace, Love, Unity, Respect... and Fantasy Fiction.